APPLETON'S LIBRARY OF HISTORICAL FICTION

Mistress Dorothy Marvin

By J. C. SNAITH

A Seventeenth Century Romance of England

WILDSIDE PRESS

INTRODUCTION.

ONE of the distinctive features of the trend of popular taste for the last two years has been the revival of interest in historical fiction. It is true that from some of the more exacting realists we have had vehement protests against "the school of the trapdoor and dagger," but the majority of readers show a readiness to stray from the paths of realism, tempted by the clash of swords. Crockett and Doyle, Hope with his "Count Antonio," Gilbert Parker, Yeats with "The Honour of Savelli," and Hotchkiss with "In Defiance of the King," are examples close at hand of this alert interest in the revival of the past, and with them we may now count Mr. Snaith. We are told often enough that coats of mail or velvet cloaks and plumes are but tarnished stage properties in the relentless light of modernity; but, without assuming to hold a brief for any school, there are wholesome reasons for preferring the romance of other days to the phases of *fin-de-siècle* fiction which deal only with the revolting daughter and the mismated wife, and the woman with a past and the man without a future. From the Troglodytes down to the problem-ridden readers of our day story-telling for story-telling's sake has kept its hold, and it exists now side by side with fiction which illuminates the life of which we form a part. For one mood there is Weyman or Doyle, for another Mrs. Ward, let us say, or Howells. The fiction which analyzes the motives of modern social units may enrich and strengthen us by its inferences, for the artist's vision is keener and truer than

the layman's, and yet "A Hazard of New Fortunes" or
"Silas Lapham" need not and does not close the door to
"Lorna Doone."

One may sometimes suspect that the majority of readers are less concerned with literary discussions than the
disputants like to believe, and it is quite possible that the
question, "Is it interesting?" sums up a popular literary
creed. If so, Mr. Snaith's salvation is secure. He has
written a romance of rare interest, with a hero whose
adventures fall thicker than Vallombrosa's leaves. Even
Alan Breck would pronounce him a very pretty fighting
man, and Monmouth's Rebellion, outlawry, and the coming
of William of Orange have afforded him every chance to
prove his quality. Sedgemoor Field, where the billhooks
and scythes of Monmouth's men went down before the
swords of the Horse Guards, the Bloody Assizes dominated
by Jeffreys's flaming face, adventures "on the road" and in
political intrigues, and the landing and triumph of William,
are among the scenes of the dual career pictured in this
moving tale. Innkeepers and kings, blacksmiths and princes,
were among those with whom he had to do at this time
or that, and the stern, silent Prince of Orange, the swarthy,
narrow-minded king, and politic Jack Churchill, the first
Duke of Marlborough, all play their parts in pages which
have the serious merit of picturing the conditions attending England's great revolution and of indicating with much
force the characters of the foremost figures. That Mr.
Snaith has done this, and that he has written a romance of
unfailing interest augurs well for his literary future.

R. H.

CONTENTS.

viii   *CONTENTS.*

MISTRESS DOROTHY MARVIN.

PROLOGUE.

New Year's Day in the West dawned cold and wet. A cheerless thaw succeeded a three weeks' frost, and changed a wintry landscape of glittering white into one of dripping woods and hedges, blent in sombre harmony with an expanse of uncomfortable mud. Accordingly, when the citizens of Exeter rubbed their eyes in the morning and saw this uninviting sight, much inquiry ensued concerning the changes of the moon; and forthwith the New Year was banned. For some were heard to remark "that if this was a thaw, they preferred a frost; that if this was the New Year, they preferred the Old; that '87 was bad enough, but '88 was worse, and that they knew mighty well there'd be no luck in the West so long as a Stuart sate king-crowned at Whitehall."

Yet towards the hour of noon these frost-bitten pessimists forgot their meteorological grumbles in a more absorbing matter, as they then saw a horseman riding through the narrow cleft of the rich Exe valley at a furious pace towards the city. At every yard he scattered mud in his track; whilst his horse, a brown sweat-steaming creature, with smoking flanks and blood-red nostrils, bore testimonials of a lightning journey. Ere long the horseman shot through the east gate. It was then seen that the mire of the western roads had ascended above the horse's withers, and had half covered the coat and hat of the rider,—a short, lithe, well knit, apparently youthful man, who kept the saddle with a singular mixture of ease and grace, and rode with a light hand, a loose rein, and a free tongue.

Every impediment to rider and horse called forth a curse of the fiercest; not an uncommon thing this,—indeed, politeness alone would have been so, because tacked on to every anathema was the tremendous announcement—"In the King's name!"

What could it mean? Had the nation again gone to war with those schnapps-swilling Dutchmen? Had His Majesty sickened and died? Or was it the Queen-mother?

In less than five minutes the news had spread half over the town that King's Messenger had ridden from London express, and that the bloody-minded papists (whom God confound!) had blown up Parliament House.

In the meantime, the courier swerved neither to right nor left, nor abated his reckless speed one whit, but rode straight to the heart of the city, and there drew rein before the door of the mayor's abode. In an instant the rider was out of the saddle, and had tethered the horse to the hook of his worship's shutter.

The fortunate few in the vicinity were now able to snatch a closer survey of the illustrious visitor; though their eagerness was balked in two particulars. What the curve of his nose was like, whether elegant or otherwise; or whether nature had given him two eyes like common folk, these they could not tell. For a large kerchief, tied under his cap at the back of his head, swathed half his face, and completely obscured one eye, and all save the tip of his nose.

The messenger executed a fierce tattoo on the most artistic knocker in the parish, which imperative summons was answered by a white-kirtled serving maid.

"Wench! conduct me straightway to your master. I may not sleep, sup, nor tarry till I have clapped eyes upon him. Service of the King!"

"Show the worthy gentleman into the parlor, Betsy," called a loud voice from within.

The rider followed the girl through the open door, to an apartment on the left side of the passage, and thereby escaped further stares from the vulgar.

The horseman having discovered blazing logs in the parlor, thankfully sat down on a settle beside them, and stretched his legs fireward. They were encased, as was the fashion of the time, in a strange length of riding boot that enveloped three-fourths of his thighs.

Presently the mayor himself entered to receive his visitor. The magistrate was a flourishing mercer of the city;

a pietist of more heart than brain, and of more self-esteem than either. He worshiped God with beautiful catholicity, adored his business, feared the King, and had a sublime conceit of civic distinction. In physical endowment, Dame Nature had been somewhat kind, for he claimed a pleasing, pot-bellied rotundity of person, and a floridly pacific countenance.

The horseman flashed a glance at the face of his worship, and inquired concisely—

"John Bunce, Mayor of Exeter?"

"Sir, I am he," was the reply, and the full-toned pomp of it made the messenger cough.

Without more ado the King's man began to fumble with one boot, then inserted a couple of fingers into the top thereof, and deliberately drew from between the leather and his hosen, a piece of parchment, tied with cord, and secured with wax.

"John Bunce," said he, "these presents in the name of his most gracious Majesty, King James the Second."

That breath-taking name much affected the mayor. His heart fluttered, his hands trembled, his chest tightened. With twitching fingers he broke the seals, and atop of the regal signature, decked by three unsightly dabs of red, beheld:—

"*We do hereby desire the presence, at our Palace at Whitehall, this day fortnight, of our leal subject, John Bunce, Mayor of our leal city of Exeter, touching matters appertaining to the well-being of our person, and the welfare of our state.*"

Five minutes went ere the mayor could focus his mind to the mandate; not that the courier disturbed the awestruck provincial wits. He laughingly peeped at the magisterial face, saw its verecund blank, and said nothing; but spread his hands to the warmth, and being a humorous man, grinned at the cat on the hearthstone.

When his worship lowered the missive he gazed at the man by the fire.

"Well, Jack Dunce——" began that gentleman, flippantly.

"Bunce, sir; John Bunce."

"Oh, well, Bunce or Dunce, it don't much matter! Thou'rt one or t'other, or both! Now, Jack, my man, what dost make of it?"

"It seems to me," replied his worship, with unspeakable dignity, "that his gracious majesty requests my presence at Whitehall."

"Quite so! That is a profound remark. Thou'rt certainly wanted at Whitehall. But why?"

"Sir, that I can not tell."

"Tut, John, on wi' the thinking-cap! Dost suppose he wants to ask whether thy health be sound, whether thy lady hath an angel's temper, and whether thy children are a credit to their parents?"

"H'm—er—no—not exactly—that is to say——"

"Out with it, man!"

"That is to say, it *might* be something *more* important."

" 'Pon my soul, John, thou hast more in that noddle than I thought! A man of gumption, I see."

The mayor bowed.

"Perhaps you know Tom Crofter, of Worcester?" King's man inquired.

"No, sir, I never had the pleasure of the gentleman's friendship."

"Friend, I once served a similar missive upon him. Of course, he obeyed the King's command and presented himself at Whitehall. That man came back *Sir Thomas*."

"Gadzooks!" and something jumped in the mayor's inside.

"Now, coz, set thine ear this way, and listen."

Master Bunce was blithe in his obedience. The way that dignitary forgot his self-respect, by placing with indecent eagerness his acoustic organ within three inches of the messenger's lips, was a sight to have tickled Ben Jonson, had he but lived to see it.

"When His Majesty handed me this document, he said——" The courier paused.

"Yes?" and the mayor grew hot and nervous.

"Said he to me——" King's man suddenly stopped. An Autolycusian twinkle leapt in his visible eye as he gave his worship a dig in the ribs, and added, his tone strangely melancholic, "Look here, John, it hath been 'spur and spare not' all the way hither; in fact, such hath been my haste, that I have ne'er tarried for a morsel of food this blessed day. And nature hath just whispered me that, till there's meat within eye-range, the tale must stand untold."

"But, surely, Master Apparitor, your plight cannot be quite so serious?"

"John, nature never lies." The messenger's voice tailed off to a husky wheeze.

"Yet, sir——"

His visitor turned his one black eye towards the ceiling, and laid his hand on his abdomen with a highly pathetic gesture. In desperation the mayor called for Betsy, the maid, bade her lay a repast for the gentleman, and irascibly added, "Be mighty smart about it."

Whilst she obeyed, the messenger assumed an air of sphinx-like gravity, but cold-bloodedly kept his eye on the fretful magistrate, who paced up and down the room, swearing softly to himself at such singular aggravation.

Presently Betsy arrived with some collops of red deer's meat, a mutton pasty, and a salmon cutlet. The recipient of these good things thanked her, took a seat at the table, and made a fine onslaught on the comestibles. He had thought for nothing but the pleasing business of knife and platter, and drove this thriving trade with diligence.

" 'Oons!" he gasped, his mouth full of venison, "this deer's meat tickles my palate so, I fain would have another serving."

"What, another? Come, my friend!" quoth his worship impatiently, excitement at last overcoming the politeness of compulsory hospitality.

"Nay, 'tis *go*, my friend," retorted he of the covered eye, and by way of adding example to precept, cut a huge slice from the pasty, and disposed of it in three bites.

Having ministered to the demands of nature, the man from London laid aside the implements of gluttony, and plucked poor Tantalus from the purgatory of hopes deferred.

"Jack Dunce, you patient man, methinks King Belly hath ta'en his fill, so shut the door and come you hither to hearken to my tidings."

His worship needed no second invitation. Within ten seconds he had resumed his former attitude of hope, whilst the narrator, having cleared his throat, began in a tone of surprising secrecy.

"Upon the day of my departure, His Blessed Majesty sent word for me to repair to his private apartment. 'Jeremiah,' said he to me (by the way, I should tell you he hath a noble affability towards all his servants), 'Jeremiah, I will thank you to make full use of your ears and eyes upon this journey. You must take particular notice of all matters that come within Master Bunce's jurisdiction, and report fully to me on your return. I may say much depends upon your affirmation. You, Master Harrison, are selected for this mission, because you are one whom I can rely upon not to let unworthy, dishonest, and ulterior motives influence your statement. Now, I am given to understand that the Mayor of Exeter is a person who might worthily bear three letters before his name; therefore I am despatching a responsible person to learn how he conducts the business of his city.' "

"And those were his words?" mused the mayor.

"Sooth! they were."

The sleek citizen rose, put his hands on his sides, threw out his chest, and cocked up his head an inch higher. Try as he might he could not conceal his pleasure, and the ridiculous picture of delight and dignity united in one and the same individual, set the King's man a-laughing at so brave a display of spontaneous humor.

His worship made a circuit of the room. Perchance, as he strutted round and round it, with eyes and chin aloft, deep in the raptures of imagination, he felt, as distinctly as possible, the light tap of King James's sword upon his shoulder, and heard the regal voice exclaim, "Arise, Sir John!"

Soon the prospective knight brought his mind back to more everyday matters, and asked his visitor, with a gush of generosity—

"Sir, what will you take to drink?"

"Let it be schnapps."

"I have liquids less homely in my cellar: Madeira, Oporto, and Languedoc; whilst we broached yestere'en as good a cask of cider as ever traveled from Somerset."

"Tut, tut, friend, schnapps is my panacea for all the ills of life, and I'll not desert it. Schnapps and hot water, say I, wi' a modicum o' sugar, a dash o' lemon, and a smack o' spice, will e'er bring comfort to a weary spirit."

The mayor again called the maid, and bade her bring forth a flask of his best Schiedam, together with the other accessories mentioned by his visitor.

Master Harrison sipped liquor in the pauses of conversation with an air of the connoisseur. It may have been by a strange coincidence, or by a latent principle of natural law, that the courier bubbled with genial talk, and embellished it by hot enthusiasm anent the beauties of a coat-of-arms; by mentioning the abode of the expertest emblazoner of heraldic devices in the kingdom; and by discoursing at length upon the correct method of kneeling before the King.

The man from London was a brave companion. He thawed the magistrate's dignity by his cheerful humor and his sparkling wit. His pungent jokes kindled a light in his worship's eye; the beneficence of his one uncovered orb set a mighty hope in his worship's heart. There was such a fine good-fellowship about the man, such a whole-souled joviality, that he raised the glass ten times to his lips, and pledged his host's health on each occasion; and insisted that the mayor should respond in draughts of cherry brandy.

Still one momentous question was for ever on the tip of his worship's tongue, one tremendous thought for ever uppermost in his mind. Soon the good man coughed short and dry, tried to subdue the twitching of his nervous fingers; tried to keep his anxious features fairly straight. But *veritas prevalebit;* so it must be recorded that Master Bunce blundered head-foremost into the fateful query.

"Master Apparitor, I—I trust you are satisfied with this city's affairs, and that your report will be favorable?" Here his heart failed him; so his tongue having run suddenly short of speech, he found nought better to do than to look red and ridiculous, and inwardly regret the weakness of his head and the strength of cherry brandy.

"John Bunce," said the other, in so cold a tone and in so marked a contrast to his former one that it filled his auditor with alarms, "I presume Heavy-Tree Gallows is within thy jurisdiction?"

"Y—e—s," he stuttered.

"Then 'tis good-bye to knighthood," and the courier hit the table, and set the crockery dancing, whilst a magnificent fire came into his visible eye.

"Say not so, sir; say not so!"

"But I do say so, sir! Dost think I wear this rag as an ornament?" and King's man placed a finger on his bandage.

"I—I don't quite understand, sir."

"Hark at that now! John, my man, if thy purse be as heavy as thy understanding, there is yet a chance for that coat-of-arms."

"But sir, I—I—I don't quite apprehend."

"Poor witling, must I tell the story? But I'll e'en plenish my glass ere I begin, for my throttle's as dry as a Godolphin oration. And, brother, you'll drain another dram wi'me, just for the sake o' company."

"I—I think not, sir."

"Psha, if I cannot have civility, not another word from me. I'll save it for King James, nor shall it be the sweeter for keep."

King's man rose and clapped on his hat. Now it was certain that the host's behavior much pained the gentleman from London, and when his worship's recantation came, as of course it did, so wounded were his feelings, that after due ponderation on the merits of the case, and on terms of the apology, he said, exquisite grief depicted in his face, "that being by nature a man, soft-hearted, long-suffering, and much prone to the folly of forgiveness, he'd overlook John Bunce's scurvy conduct, with the distinct proviso, that he (J. Harrison) should mix the liquor.

Mix it he did; but it should be observed the compound was concocted of two parts raw spirit to one part water. The tale in itself was short; yet, despite its brevity, it stuck Master Bunce on a cushion of thorns.

"It befell," began King's man impressively, "that this very day I was making all speed hither to deliver His Majesty's letter, when within ten yards of Heavy-Tree Gallows, I was accosted by a prick-eared Jack Presbyter (no true Catholic, I'll swear, would so insult the King's Majesty), who impertinently asked me the time. Being, as I have said, a singularly obliging man, I slackened speed, and pulled out my watch. ' 'Twill be eleven of the clock in two minutes,' said I. 'Pardon,' said he, bending his head nearer my mouth, 'I'm hard of hearing.' But, Holy Virgin! ere I could conceive the depths of his infamy, with one hand he grabbed the watch (purest gold, studded wi' diamonds, from Doubleday of the Crown and Sceptre, Westminster), and with the other hit me a gallows' blow in the left eye that knocked me heels over head from the saddle. Mayhap you'll not credit this, but sure as the sun's in the sky, before I might rise, pluck a pistol, or put up a prayer to the saints the peccant knave was upon me, with two ungodly knees squeezing my vitals. I was half through a yell when he cut it in two by cramming the butt of a barker slap down my throat as far as the voice-box. Quoth he, his laugh very impudent, 'Dear brother, speak not, or I use a little gentle persuasion,' and he cracked out three front teeth with the jar of the iron."

The narrator parted his lips: three teeth on the upper jaw were missing.

"This done," continued the victim, "he set his digits to work. In two minutes he had emptied every pocket on my person, and had relieved me of thirty guineas. In fact, he left me nought of value, save this precious missive, which he failed to discover, for ever since the outrage perpetrated upon me in Maidenhead Thicket, ten years agone, I always convey thief tempting articles in my boot.

"Now, all this had been performed ere I could gather my senses or lug the weapon from twixt my teeth; and when at last I was able to do so, the caitiff had wished me a very good morning, and was flying over hedge and ditch in full possession of my worldly wealth. May the devil annex him!"

"Oh, sir!" gasped the mayor, a weight of fear upon him, " 'tis terrible news!"

"Terrible news! Strike me purple, 'twill cost a knighthood!"

At this promised calamity the magistrate collapsed into a state of limp inertion, whereat the visitor was so kind as to proffer spirits with which to resuscitate his shattered nerves and intellect. In equity to them both, it should be said, this assisted to soothe his worship's nervous system, and to further befog his thinking faculties. Asked he, at last, his voice thick with brandy and emotion—

"Was your assailant a handsome man?"

"Handsome? Handsome ain't the word! Ods my life! twin-brother to Apollo."

'2

"I presume you mean Apollyon?" the magistrate corrected; then drew a sheriff's hand-bill from his doublet, smoothed its creases, and inquired judicially—

"Had he a chestnut horse? Was he very dark of countenance; black eyes, straight black hair, smart carriage, comely person, gentleman-like speech, stature five feet six, one inch scar on upper lip, and birth mark on right temple?"

"Jack Dunce, thou hast named the man!"

"Sir, you have met Black Ned, the arrantest knave in Europe!"

"What! he who robbed my lord Feversham, the King's Commander, in these parts last fall?"

"The same."

"The devil!" exclaimed King's Messenger, in loose-lipped astonishment. The injured man was seized with a spasm of anger, and spluttered a mouthful of epithets. "Pink my soul! trust a dunderheaded country justice to be cocking over his fire-grate, while every cut-throat unhung grins through his parlor window!"

Master Bunce groaned.

"That will not mend it, my friend! I tell 'ee, 'twill not mend it! You had best procure a warrant for his apprehension and a posse to execute it!"

Master Bunce groaned again, and added gloomily, "'Twill but be money and labor thrown away. Times without number he hath tricked the law, and made it the laughing-stock of three counties. He cares not a tinker's damn for justice, nor ever will while the commonalty favor him, shield him, and applaud his villainy. The West hath ne'er seen his match within living memory. He's as clever as Satan, and as artful as sin!"

"Methinks John Dunce, this is truly discreditable to thee and thy brother justices. By Heaven, I'll acquaint the King!"

"The King! Oh, don't, I conjure you!"

"Don't, quotha? Would ye seek to corrupt me, then? Dost forget His Gracious Majesty's words ere I set forth on this mission? Said he to me, 'Thou'rt one whom I can rely upon not to let unworthy, dishonest and ulterior motives influence thy statement.' And, John, you, in the face of those noble words, bid me perjure my soul. You arch-dissembler!"

He smartly slapped his knee, and fairly cowed the mayor with the flash of his baleful eye.

"But, please, sir, do not jeopardise my knighthood," pleaded Sir John that was to be.

Here the courier's demeanor underwent a startling metamorphosis. In lieu of high looks, a smile appeared as he playfully poked the citizen in the region of the ribs, and said, with a throb of laughter—

"Jack Dunce, dear man, I must tell thee that, under certain conditions, Jeremiah Harrison hath an excellent memory for forgetting."

The mercer stared amazed at the messenger, and though he strove to fathom the meaning of a hint so broad, he failed, because his brain was too befuddled to discover its full significance.

"Yes, that's a paradox," laughed the man from London, "and subtle enough for old Sam Butler. I see thy torpid provincial mind doth not fathom its meaning. But I have known a golden guinea to cast a spell ere now; in fact, I once knew one to be responsible for a lapse of memory." This sample of official rectitude gave a portentous wink; then fell to whistling a cheerful tune.

Precisely at this moment the bibacious citizen was favored with a glimmer of penetration. For an instant the cloud rolled back from his dram-befogged brain; his understanding jumped; he saw a light; he grasped a fact!

His worship did not pause to probe the depths of his visitor's moral obliquity; nor to analyze his double dealing.

"Master Messenger, would twenty guineas be of any service in this matter?"

"Pish! Dost think I'm a scald attorney, with a conscience like a weather-cock, who'd wipe his feet on his honor for the feel of a six-groat piece?"

"I'll make it thirty, sir."

"Thirty, quotha? 'Pon my soul, John, that magnificent sum for a knighthood! Why, thou man of generous mind, 'twould not pay for the loss of my self-respect!"

Thereupon they haggled and argued; twisted the controversy into all manner of shapes; examined the matter from every aspect; mutually conceded many minor points, and showed a charming generosity one towards another in regard to all side issues.   But on the main contention, neither budged an inch.   They debated man to man, and made a fair fight of it, with only one stoppage for refreshments.   Once, indeed, they tarried to drink.   They pledged each other's health, and clinked glasses with a punctilious politeness;   though, next minute, down came the flag of truce, and hostilities began again.   And whether it was that King's man's head was middling clear, and that the mayor's was undeniably fuddled;   or whether King's man's gift of rhetoric was finer than that of his worship, may never be known;   yet this much is on record: the courier gained the day, and, on this occasion, the value of a coat of arms was assessed at one hundred guineas.   For this sum, cash in advance, he undertook to speak a kind word in His Majesty's ear on his return to Town.   Having clasped hands on the bargain, Master Bunce went in quest of the money.   In a short time he returned with a bag of bulk, which he deposited on the table; and sighed as he did so.

"'Tis a hard bargain!"   The mayor's voice was regretful.

"Ay, *Sir* John," said the other softly, with something of an accent on the title, "it *is* a hard bargain.   Think of my perjured soul."

However, for his own part, he preferred to think of the fruits of it.   With quick fingers he untied the bag, and carefully turned its contents onto the table.   His visage inscrutable and his manner ostentatiously mild, he counted aloud each golden guinea as he dropped it back into the bag.   He had reached number ninety-six, when a rattle of hoofs sounded directly under the parlor window.   The messenger glanced sharply through it, hastily swept the four remaining coins into their receptacle, tied up the mouth of the bag, and slipped the fingers of his right hand round it.   Even as he did so the new arrival made powerful play with the door knocker.   Half a minute later the breathless visitor clanked into the parlor.   He was a small, shrimpy, pippin-faced man, red as a turkey and apparently as wrathful as that short-tempered bird.

"Which be John Bunce?" he shouted.

"I am he," murmured his worship blandly.   Be it understood, his mind was already tinged with a delicious foretaste of impending promotion.

The newcomer began with a brilliant fanfaronade of language; round, full-toned, symmetrical language; a credit to his lungs and his power of invective. Then he bounced about the room like a pea on a plate, and delivered himself, though every tenth word was trimmed with a hysterical interjection, as follows—

"My name is Joshua Pringle. I have ridden on King's business directly hither, wi'out stint of horseflesh and wi'out misadventure, to within five miles o' this city. All have respected the urgence and exceeding notability of my errand save one infernal child of hell, who accosted me this very morning. He greeted me with a wave of his hat, and cozened me into false security with sweet words and a glib tongue. He inquired the time with the air of a gentleman, and I, poor dolt! took out my watch to oblige him. At that, sir, as Heaven is my witness! he snatched it from mine hand, smote me out of my saddle, knelt on my chest, robbed me of every stiver upon my person, including the thrice-precious document the King hath entrusted to my keeping, set my horse a-galloping into an easterly direction, gave me 'good morning,' and left me to come hither as best I might."

The sense of his hard fortune completely overcame him. He danced and skipped about the room, swinging his arms in ill-regulated rhythm with his tongue, twisting his meagre body, and contorting his shrewish face into shapes, at once grotesque and fearful. Meantime, his language took a higher flight of violence, and while he invoked the powers of heaven one minute, with strict impartiality, he invoked those of hell the next. His volubility was truly wonderful; but there is a belief abroad that the little men try to atone for lack of stature by a superabundance of words.

While this was pending, his bewildered worship was stricken dumb. The civic hands grew clammy, the sweat came out on the civic brow.

Master Harrison took this new turn of events with egregious coolness; kept his seat, said never a word, and showed no sign of emotion beyond drumming his fingers on the table-cloth.

"Mark me," shrilled Master Pringle, "ere I quit the West, I'll see the scurvy villain hanged. If flesh and blood can compass it, his carcass shall adorn stout hemp! I demand justice, and justice I will have! I have been beset and robbed—most foully robbed—and I cry aloud for justice! And likewise ye may know, John Bunce, that upon our second meeting I'll prove to his reptile mind (aye, and to his reptile body also!) that the mouse's frame may hold the lion's heart!"

"I've heard an old proverb anent first catching your bear ere you barter his skin," cooed Master Harrison meekly.

"You sir! Who the devil may you be, sir?"

"I, sir? I'm a man of no consequence; a man of humble mind," was the sweet reply.

Hereupon the mayor found enough speech to interrupt this skirmish by asking victim Number Two what manner of a man his aggressor was.

"A black-eyed, smooth-spoken rogue; dark skinned, not uncomely in the features, and of somewhat shortish height."

"Was he riding a chestnut horse?"

Pringle gave an affirmative reply; whereat the mayor of Exeter subsided.

Seeing this victim Number One vented a great guffaw of laughter, and added, in a chirruping tone—

"Dear sir, didst happen to see whether thy opponent lacked three teeth in his upper jaw?"

"No, I didn't."

"Well, I will add, for thy information, for the sheriff's and for the furtherance of the ends of justice, that he doth."

Master Pringle was neatly puzzled.

"Sir," said he, "you speak in riddles."

Before an answer could be made, victim Number Two had discovered another enigma. His eye caught the red-sealed document on the table. He examined it eagerly, then vented a cry of astonishment.

"In the name of the Virgin, whence came this?"

The mayor made an inarticulate guttural noise, and pointed his finger towards Master Harrison. That gentleman rose to his feet with notable deliberation, saying gravely—

"Gentlemen, methinks ye would be aiding the law if ye supplemented the incomplete description at present given of that notorious malefactor, Black Ned, by stating that he lacks three teeth in the upper jaw." And once more he parted his lips and proved that three of his own were absent.

His hearers scratched their benighted polls, frowned, looked first at each other, then at the speaker, and internally wondered whether they were themselves bewitched, or whether the man of the covered eye had lost his mental balance.

"Gentlemen," he said again, his gravity exchanged for laughter, "own that ye are prettily mystified."

He enjoyed their perplexity for the space of half a minute, then with a quick movement twitched his hat from his head and ripped the bandage from his eye.

The effect was magical. The mayor gave back a step, changed color in quick transitions from red to green, and green to white; whilst Master Pringle's vaunted leonine demeanor seemed immediately to suffer a paralytic stroke. Cold terror chilled this pair, for the half-gay, half-sinister countenance of Black Ned mocked them. There was no mistaking his strange dark hair, the fine curve of his nose, and the black, evil, fascinating lustre of his eyes.

"Lord, what fools these mortals be!" he cried, clapping his hands to his sides, in a wild turbulence of laughter.

This impudent derision stung the mayor; he regained the power of words, to such an extent did honest wrath surmount the fumes of liquor.

"Base beast! Within a week ye shall taste Dame Tuckfield's Bounty."*

The highwayman still clasped his ribs.

"Curse thee, thou arch villain!" the mayor continued, his indignation superbly righteous. "Thou hast had the grace to make as hearty a meal as man could desire at my expense, and to accept one hundred guineas into the bargain——"

"And which, by a continuation of that grace, I will keep as a remembrance," interposed the trickster dryly, transferring the bag from his right hand to an inner pocket of his horseman's cloak. Next he turned on the empty Pringle.

* In the reign of King Edward VI., a charitable lady, the widow of Master Tuckfield, sometime Sheriff of Exeter, bequeathed shrouds and an interment place for the decent burial of malefactors executed on the gallows of Heavy Tree.

"Best keep a guard on that valorous tongue o' thine, my little bantam, or 'twill be a baneful thing for thee! Speak not so light of gentlemen in future."

To fully impress these remarks, he tugged their recipient by the ear.   That fire-eater pursed his lips for a howl, but happily, in the mean time, Master Bunce had bawled to his apprentices, who were working on hose and kersey stuff across the passage.

"Run, John! run, Tom! Haste hither, as thou lovest Our Lady, and seize this worker of iniquity!"

Black Ned loosed his grip of the real King's Messenger, and ran to the door; though in his progress he whipped up an untouched mutton pasty, and deposited this toothsome dainty into his pocket.   Hearing a clatter in the workshop, and other preliminaries of action, he retreated hotfoot along the passage, dashed through the street door, clipped the reins from the shutter-hook, bounded into the saddle, shot a word into his animal's ear, and was away to the east.

Scarce twenty yards had he made on his journey ere an eloquent congregation were at his worship's threshold.   The horseman turned half-around in his saddle; removed his hat with a flourish, and bowed with exaggerated politeness and lingering mockery.   By the time he had reached the first corner, volley upon volley of malediction sang in his ears; but for this he had no heed, for within the space of five minutes, Exeter city lay a mile in his rear.

The foregoing incident is without a place in the Armstrong manuscript, Sir Edward maintaining a reticence, at once praiseworthy and professional, upon matters pertaining to his public career.   Doubtless the advance of years blighted early vainglory, much in the same way that mature reflections deplored the follies of youth.

The editor has made so bold as to reclaim this exploit from the mass of second-hand tradition that for generations clothed the memory of Black Ned with a doubtful though none the less delectable halo of notoriety.   This one in particular is selected, because responsible authority can be found to back its authenticity; and also in the hope that readers may welcome an impartial portrait of the rogue in the prime of infamy.

From this point Sir Edward will tell his own story.

CHAPTER I.

KINSMEN ! the head of the House of Armstrong is about to drain the cup of humiliation ; I, your sire, am going to take shame unto myself in the winter of my days.

I have indited the above score empty words, yet cannot get beyond them ; and for the last hour I have been seated at my writing-table, gnawing quills to the stump in abject fatuity. I have near my elbow the warranty of Doctor Proudfoot, my physician, duly signed and attested to the effect that I am wholly sane of mind. I have before me a quire of foolscap and a horn of ink, yet am pulling my beard in lieu of a fretful duty. I tell myself to play the man, and so I will, if God be pleased to let me. A conscience rendered frail by years (in its prime 'twas never of the stoutest), hath asked me many times of late whether it really is my duty to tear the mask from the long-veiled face of truth ; to lay bear the chiefest secret of my soul, to degrade my gray hairs in your sight. Must I bequeath a legacy of scorn to a memory that had otherwise been cherished ? Must anathema be paid to him that held his head so high ? Is this my duty ? O God ! methinks the expiation obscures the crime !

I have had this purpose in my mind for years. This page would have been wrung from me a generation earlier, had not fortitude been warped by pitiless adversity. From day to day I have shirked the task, promising my soul to do it very shortly. But as now I know, the sands of life have nearly run, I dare delay no longer. Methinks this uneasy head will sit the kinder in its coffin, when its owner, having paid the debt he owes his kindred, comes in turn to pay the debt dark nature claimeth.

Accordingly I put all idle fears behind, and summon to my aid every ounce of tottering resolution. I pray that my Pegasus be endowed with strength sufficient to traverse a parlous path ; and upon hopes of this pen now meets paper.

The lines grow quick before mine eyes, but at every added word of this halt confession my cheek doth burn with pain.

I hope for no mercy from you, kinsmen ; I know your pride

of birth too well. There are some of you, my children, decked in your ruffles and your Mechlin lace, secure in the refinement of your tastes, in the ease of your consciences, and the consequence of your social states, who will upbraid me for a scatterbrain, or flout me with disbelieving jeers.

Why should I write so much for the disturbance of your minds, unless every word this goose-quill says be true? You may doubt my sanity, so I in forethought have provided the sworn testimony of my sage friend Doctor Proudfoot. It alone shall speak for the responsibility of my intellect. Nigh fifty years I have borne my head high amidst my fellows. I have been fawned upon and flattered; have reclined in silk and silver; have had a case of green sealed sack from London every month; have dispensed justice in the courthouse; and honest men wherever they have walked have breathed my name with reverence. But now of mine own free will I prostitute my honorable name.

Here have I lived this while, a skeleton in my closet; a viper in my breast. Unsuccessfully I have sought to erase from my recollection the awful stain that blots my youth with infamy. I take it, kinsmen, that ye have seen the head of your house, as he hath toasted his feet near the blaze on a winter's night, writhe in the throes of a quick convulsion. Ye have watched the livid terrors creep in his face in a season of mirth and sunshine. Or upon a clatter of hoofs on the courtyard flags, ye have beheld him start up shuddering with twitching limbs and the eyes of a hunted man. You have marvelled at these omens, but the best among you have found them dark, unwholesome mysteries ; and as a book that is closed to the comprehension. Now is the viper brought forth blinking to the light! So I conjure you all to read; but, should it please you when the end hath come, ye are free to curse your father.

*　　*　　*　　*　　*　　*　　*

There is a tradition in our parts, that the most notorious rogue ever bred in the West was plucked hence by the devil, an hour before his destined execution. Certain it is, the criminal was ne'er seen again in the flesh since that eventful morning ; and, to strengthen the theories of the vulgar, the only man in a position to throw light on the strange event, went out of his mind by virtue of such a dread phenomenon. Numberless accounts were written at the time, numberless exaggerations were made, and numberless songs were sung concerning " Black Ned and the Devil," so that to this hour the story is told in every family in these parts in a thousand different ways, with a superb divergence on all immaterial matters, but with fine unanimity that it was the *devil himself*, and none other who honored Black Ned and Taunton gaol on that chimerical occasion.

Black Ned the highwayman built up a mighty reputation fifty years agone, and to this hour it hath endurance. The extraordinary exploits the man performed thrilled the countryside, and made his name a household word in the West. And now, my cold, pride-bitten kinsmen, consult Doctor Proudfoot's statement, or stimulate your wits with wine, or burn my slow-wrought narrative; for that same Black Ned afterwards became Sir Edward Armstrong, of Copeland Hall—your father !

Prithee erase the inscription from my tomb in the church; by all means obliterate my name from the Armstrong tablets; then, if ye can, efface grim History ! Kinsmen, I mock ye with the bitter levity of a lifetime's gall.

In the following singular story I will show you in what manner my soul was lost, and how by God's mercy it was in a measure regained. Now and then, in the course of it, stirring events, landmarks of history, may be touched upon. Perchance the recounting of them may differ in minute particulars from what Mr. Oldmixon hath set down in his chronicles. I advise you to lay this to a failing memory, for I would not willingly lead you into bootless controversy with men of letters. I shall be perfectly honest throughout my statement. I shall neither offer palliation nor excuse, nor shall I crave your pity. Yet I would have you, the children of a noble land, remember she owes the world's part of her grandeur to the fidelity, the loyalty, the bright courage and manliness of her sons (your fathers) who have built up a freedom of thought and action for a supercilious posterity, by the mortal sweat of their brows, and the spilling of many drops of their life's blood. Upon this common ground alone do I look for the slender store of generosity I am like to get.

Dissertation is done, and I have merely proffered this preliminary that you may know what my purpose is for saying so much hereafter.

Two falchions gules, on a field argent, with the inscription "*Per crucem ad coronam,*" is the coat of arms that represents our house. So it hath stood for centuries, though I know not how many bars, quarterings, and transoms have been added thereto, throughout those past ages, by deeds glorious or otherwise. It is our boast that broad lands were ours long ere the covetous Norman came; indeed, we do affirm, that when King Alfred met the Danes in combat, the Armstrongs mustered by their liege lord. So be it; yet you learn more of this than I, for my head is too old to be concerned at all about chronology. It doth suffice to set me self-complacent, to know that should I hie across the stream, I may set eyes on crumbling tablets hewn from stone and marble, which recount how valiant forefathers bled at Poictiers and Crecy.

Well can I recollect how, years ago, half a dozen of you younkers came a-running to me with, " Do you come and see with us in the chûrchyard, father. We have surely found the tomb of one of the Armstrongs who perished at Senlac." Away I went with you, for were ye not my taskmasters in those days? But Nicholas, who has more knowledge in matters antiquarian than any three of the rest of you, hath since overruled that precious childish discovery.

Ah, well-a-day! we will say no more in regard to such musty memories. Copeland Hall ever harbored a warlike race. Much too prone to adventure and knightly feats with sword and buckler were its martial children.

Great deeds—deeds to thrill the heart with pride—were wrought in strange lands by its warlike sons, and on fierce fields of conflict in our own dear country too. Kinsmen, you who hold your heads so high, may guess quite well the Armstrong pride of race, 'tis fixt at a higher altitude than any in our county. And in face of you, and in face of this, I make bold to say that had we been more given to bowing our heads to our fellow-men, and our stubborn knees to God, methinks it had very often happened the better for your fathers. This defiance of spirit cost your sire dear, hence his doctrine of humility.

To travel down to later times, and to matters which concern you and me more nearly, my father was born in the reign of the first King James, on a May morning in the year 1630, fourteen months after his brother Peter had arrived in the world. He was twelve years old when the Royal Standard was raised at Nottingham; and by that deed our country was torn in twain. Her sons were at one another's throats in the cruelest inward strife that e'er hath wrought bloodshed in our fair land. Men could not stand aloof; there was no neutrality. Their neighbors dubbed them Cavalier or Roundhead, either one or t'other, for fight they must.

My grandfather, Sir Jasper Armstrong, having the family leaven fermenting high within him, needed no incentive to choose his side; but straightway struck for the Parliament,

and as heretofore our house was opposed to tyranny from any
man. At Roundway Down the baronet met with a grievous
scathe. A petard struck him in the left thigh, and ever afterwards he hobbled perforce, most painfully, until death claimed
him in the year of the Restoration.

He had been a shrewd and thrifty man, and mine uncle Peter,
who took the title, thus found the coffers full, and the estate
void of the least encumbrance. He, it should be said, had another thing that came part and parcel from Sir Jasper, for just
as he had his father's lands and wealth by hereditament, he
also had his careful little-spending mind by nature; so he in his
turn worthily carried this laudable chest-filling process forward.
Howbeit, I must observe, this trait, a mere pleasing idiosyn-
cracy in the sire, was, by the son, pushed beyond a virtue. I'
faith, I have heard men say, did he lay down a paltry groat, he
would have back a silver shilling for his recompense; and this
I do ascribe unworthy of our family.

Sir Jasper had been sepultured two years, when John, his
second son, bethought himself of braving the perils of wedlock.
Hence he took Jane Ashburton in matrimony.

My mother's father was the famous Colonel Ashburton, who
did such credit to the Puritan arms during the great Civil War.
He resided in Taunton, and though himself a staunch Independ-
ent, his daughter had little of the zealot's bigotry, but was
well endowed with sense.

My father also was a plain and godly man, untainted by
fanatic rant, high-thinking, speech-sparing, and wholly peaceful
in his creed.

Thus my parents gave small heed to the narrow sectaries
of their time, but worshipped God in the manner they held becoming; whereby true religion pervaded all our household. I,
Edward Armstrong, was the first pledge of their union. Two
other children were also the outcome of it; my brother John
and my sister Betty. It doth appear an odd contingency, seeing that the stock from which my father sprang was so hot-
blooded and adventurous, that he should be content to abide in
a little hamlet, shut off well-nigh altogether from men and the
outer world and the big affairs of life. He chose a farmstead
in Chilverley village, which nestles in the heart of the Quantock Hills, as the spot in which to pass his wedded life. And
such was the unambitious nature of the man that I verily believe he would have preferred to raise choice turnip crops than
to have become a great commander.

His piety had all the depths of silent waters : he had nought

to say anent it. He never would allow that God was glorified
by mere lip-labor, or that the tongue alone could prove a man a
Christian. No, that never was his way ; for if he gave much
thought to sacred things, he seldom mouthed a holy sentiment.
He read but one book, and that book was the Bible. Tighter
than wax did he stick to the Ten Commandments. Forsooth
they formed his choicest dogmas, and embodied all his Christian principles. His hatred of a lie was truly marvellous ; likewise of all hypocrisy, of blasphemy, and of double-dealing.
As for his faith, 'twas almost childlike in simplicity. Once, as
I remember, indeed it was the day I was eight years old, he
lifted me on his knee.

" Hearken, my pretty lad ! " he said ; " wouldst like to go to
heaven ? "

" Ay, that I should, daddy."

He placed in my hand a little brown-backed Bible, which
that same morning he had purchased from Taunton.

" This will take thee there, my pretty boy," he said, in his
slow, half-smiling way. " Cherish it, lad, and ye'll have no call
to be Churchman, Presbyterian, or Anabaptist."

For sobriety, only one man matched him in the place, and he
was the blacksmith, Master Hancock. 'Twas a fitting thing
that they should consort together. Oft-times have the twain
sate face to face beside our hearthstone of an evening, when
their carnal indulgence assumed the shape of three pipes apiece
of Trinidado tobacco, and a bowl of the richest rum punch between them. Seeing that it was mother's brew, I know 'twas
as good as I've declared. Trust a woman to look to creature
comforts ! And foremost in the sex for attention to the same
will I place my mother, Mistress Armstrong.

Her pride lay in her concoctions. Justly it became her boast,
that her press sent forth the choicest cider in the county. Not
that she thought overmuch as regards the liquids, because, as
father went so shy of them, they were but scantily requested.
Her greatest care was lavished on things eatable. She was
without a peer in the high piling of dish and platter with delicious meats, pies, conserves, pasties, and such-like stomach
ticklers. " Poor trencherman, poor servant," was her maxim.
Good nature and good temper ever held the sway of her, whilst
her liberality was truly noble, since she knew no stint in giving
whenever her purse allowed. Should any ill befall a villager,
he had but to apply to Dame Armstrong, and the remedy was
forthcoming. Did the crops fail, each sufferer was welcome to
her purse, her pantry, and her sympathy. Her bounty ne'er

was sought in vain, for this was her religion. No time did she spend in praising the Lord, when victuals lay in the pan, or when hosen had need of darning; whilst after her husband's manner, she accounted honesty the most cardinal of virtues.

Being thus reared midst sound precept and rigid moral rectitude, my upbringing should have equipped me more surely than a coat of mail for the stern battles of early manhood and maturity. But alack! the best armed may not be the boldest warriors.

From babyhood my chief delight was the fresh air and the fields. I was rarely happy unless rambling mid the hills and valleys, and kicking my heels among the rocks and heather. I could not abide inertion, but must be abroad on a new mischief, reckless of limb and skin, as behoved a youthful scion of those great spirited old Armstrongs.

It is on record that your hapless sire was picked out thrice in a single week—and on the point of drowning too—from his father's horse-pond, he having found that insalubrious spot by tumbling thence from an adjacent beech tree, that had enticed him by the hope of nuts.

Concerning education, I am afeared the sum of my book-learning doth muster a meek totality. I hated it, and there's the truth! though my master, a deep scholar of Cambridge, strove with monumental patience to knock, coax, or wheedle notions of Greek aorists and iambics into my empty noddle. Still the task was bootless. Scholarship and I did ne'er agree. Nest-seeking and tree-climbing were more to my mind than the rule of three; and if my knowledge was modest in algebraics and the classic lore, touching birds' eggs 'twas unlimited. I am aware this does not redound to my credit, yet am convinced that the minds of healthy boys are more prone to dwell thereon than on feats of learning.

My boyhood was uneventful, save that when I arrived at ten years of age I fell off a fence and broke my arm; also at Christmas time, in that same year, I came near ending my life altogether, as I chanced to slip into the stream in the bed of the ravine when it was topped with a coat of ice. School days over, I assisted father on the farm; being content to do this until I had passed my twenty-first birthday. Then befell the event which hath brought about this history.

As I remember, it occurred some time in hay-harvest. Our household ne'er seemed more full of harmony, nor the beauteous Quantock country more scented with kindly peace and quietude. There appeared no hint of coming trouble; no sign of the dread fatality that was to bathe the West in blood. 'Twas one evening, as the family sat at supper, when the first token of disturbance came. Just before the meal was done, our kitchen doorway was shadowed by the form of the huge Tobe Hancock. His face was livid with excitement, and his eyes were big and bright with a restless lustre.

"Vairmer Jan," he burst out, "hast heerd th' news? Tha Duke o' Moonmouth landed at Lyme yester mornin'! We mist go vaight vor 'im!"

Here was the prologue to the tragedy. The Duke had come and declared himself the champion of the Protestant religion, though the historians always said, and with a singular consensus of opinion, that he came not from the Hague on any matter of faith, but to wrest the crown from King James, his uncle, that it might ornament his own ambitious brow.

This Monmouth was the bastard son of Charles II., by Lucy Walters, one of his late Majesty's many mistresses; and, to support his claim to the Throne, contended that he was a legitimate child, declaring the King duly married his mother. Be this as it may, I never thought enough upon the theme to learn how just was his pretension. What I do know is, that father and Tobias sat a-talking these infectious tidings over until the small hours of the morning.

A thorough-going Puritan was the blacksmith, who stuck close by his tenets, and one of that uncompromising bull-dog breed that had consigned Charles I. to the block. The news of the Duke's arrival had ignited his fiery soul. Fondly he believed that His Grace had come for the sole purpose of restoring the Protestant faith; therefore he thought it became all men to strike for the true religion.

There was no sleep for me that night; and long before the first streaks of light stole out of the east, there was *my* mind at least made up, and my great determination taken. In the early morning, when father and Bill Kyte, the farm hand, came to the tool-shed, they found me there, burnishing the welded steel headpiece of my maternal grandfather.

No sooner had I swallowed breakfast than I ran round the corner by the church to the village forge. For once the jangling hammer lay unplied; the leathern apron was discarded. In the little parlor behind the workshop I found the blacksmith. A strange collection littered the table, and over it Tobe Hancock bent his eager body.

The first article to catch my eye was an old collar of bandoleers, with bullet-bag, cords, rings, and primer all affixed thereto,

though in sad need of adjustment. Hard by reclined a brace
of pistols, encumbered by a coat of rust ; and, to complete this
warlike collocation, were a snap-hance carbine, a half-pike, a
" hog's bristle," * a buff leather tunic, and a pikeman's pot-
helmet. The owner of these hostile implements was busily
renovating a corselet of rusty steel.

" Thease wan was mi vaither's, Ned," he said, holding it out
for my inspection. " Thease yer brit was dued at Naseby, lad,"
and he placed his finger in a deep dent of the metal.

A long talk had we that morning. The upshot was to arrange
to set out for Monmouth's camp in company next day. The
blacksmith was brimming with enthusiasm—in fact, he was a
zealot. Like good workmen, we labored as we talked. With a
grumbling wonderment did old Joan (Tobe's serving woman)
watch us rub away each speck of rust from cankered steel and
ordnance. She having nursed Tobias in his babyhood, 'twas
her privilege to draw good wages, and to grumble till her tongue
grew tired.

The tools of war had been taken from an ancient chest, whence
they had lain since the end of the Great Civil War ; the father
and uncle of the blacksmith having been numbered among Noll
Cromwell's host.

My head was whirling with many anxious matters as I hied
back to the farm, hugging the snap-hance and the tunic which
Tobe had given me. My heart rose at the mere thought of
what valorous deeds I should encompass in the fast-approach-
ing future. Our homestead seemed so sleepy to me now, that
methought it beyond endurance.

However, a great battle had to be fought. All day in silence
my father had heeded my demeanor. 'Twas in the evening
that I first spoke of my resolution. Mother, John, and Betty
were strangely startled ; they had not observed what was passing through my mind. Father showed no surprise, but simply
looked grave, then sighed.

" Ah, Ned," said he, " I was afeared of this. I marked you
when Tobias told the news last night. Methinks 'twere best
you stayed at home ; scant good can come of this affair. Mayhap the cause is a goodly one, yet a handful of men cannot
hope for aught better than a sore hide against an army."

" All the West will flock to the Duke," said I.

---

* A "hog's bristle," or Swedish feather, was a weapon introduced into
the English army in the reign of James I. It consisted of a single steel
blade of considerable length, and was for the protection of the musketeer
after he had discharged his piece.—EDITOR.

" No matter," was his answer, " 'twill be without avail.   Useless I trow to pit chawbacons against the trained soldiers of
the King."

" But Tobe says MacCullum More is to create a big rising in
Scotland."

" If so 'twill make no difference.   At least, lad, have a care
for your skin ; besides, if ye leave a peaceful domicile to shed
blood, it will go to my very heart.   Perchance I am too nice
i' th' stomach, for a true Armstrong, yet I speak as my feelings
direct.   Forbear, my lad, from this perilous action."

He talked long and earnestly to this effect.   Howbeit, I doggedly pressed the point, as I was one who, having once my
heart upon a thing, would waver not in quest thereof ; and so
by sheer persistence would get my will.

'Twas near midnight when Tobe Hancock came to bid good-
bye to father.   Thus our grave talking was disturbed, and well
pleased I was on that account—methought the blacksmith would
surely speak on my behalf.

When our conference dissolved it was close by two of the
clock in the morning.   And one was hurt and disappointed.
At the outset Tobias was all for me.   He called up every argument he could lay his tongue to, that he might win consent for
me to ride with him to Monmouth.   For long enough he urged
my cause ; tho' to small purpose did he lend his breath ; my
parent was firmer than a rock.   Then, having learned how inflexible his disapproval was, Tobe veered round altogether.

" Thee midden goa, lad.   Obey thy vaither, 'e knaw'th best,"
quoth he.

This doctrine of filial obedience hit me hard, although
naught else could he have counselled.   Out of righteousness
alone he would have been the tardiest of men to bid me defy
my parents.   Therefore the pair of them decreed that I must
bide at home.

That night I never slept.   I was young then, my spirit ran
high and bold, and blood was frisky in the veins.

Reverently I carried to my chamber those arms and equip-
ments which were to have done such noble service, and
deposited them at the bed foot, that my eyes might rest upon
their glory.   As a lump of lead was my blighted heart ; and,
alas, something like anger couched within it.   Every daydream
of honor and victory had fled—fled to gall and mockery.   I
rolled over every inch of my uneasy bed, spirit-chafed, balked,
and at war with all save my ill-used self, whom I greatly pitied.

Until the coming of the dawn the moonlight glinted on the

shimmering metal at my feet, which seemed to flout and tempt me, with its new unwonted beauty. Wickedness went crawling through my mind now and then, and it needed all my strength to fight it. No sooner did daylight reappear, than I dressed myself, and took my heavy head into the cold air. I wandered about with neither aim nor purpose. Naught could allay my vague disquietude, though I sluiced head and face with chill water, and afterwards set to work with such senseless vigor, that sweat dripped from my forehead. Cold and perspiration made no jot of difference, and having thus tried both, I perched on a stile for a weary hour, balanced myself on the topmost rung, and kicked my legs at space.

Thus was I occupied, when a clatter of hoofs came distinct from the road, which ran in my vicinity. I set my feet on the highest rail, that I might obtain a fuller view of horse and rider as the twain passed by. I beheld a mottled, raw-boned mare; and a large fellow, whose form I should have known the wide world over, was astride her. 'Twas Tobe Hancock, away to Monmouth.

Were I younger I might weep on what follows, as I write; kinsmen, my fingers tremble as I grasp the pen. Without a moment's tarrying I leapt down from my perch, and ran back to the house. None were astir, so I made straight for that seductive heap of leather and metal, lying upon my bed. At another time it must have been a great while ere I had accoutred myself, yet in some peculiar fashion I made the buff coat fit middling well, though it called for time and temper ever after to make it do so. With lively fingers I girded on the sword, and affixed my grandfather's headpiece on my mad-brained pate; emptied my slender store of money from its usual receptacle into my breeches' pocket; and finally pinned a paper on my pillow, with, "I am gone to the wars," upon it.

Below stairs I then returned; but not as I had ascended, since my equipment, being none of the lightest, forbade undue activity. Soon I had old Peggy saddled; double-quick her head was turned towards the town of Taunton; and away I went to the wars.

Would to God that on this woeful errand I ne'er had passed the peat rick at the corner. Here you have my first deep sin. Bitter, bitter, was the consequence of this first desertion from the cause of right! On the ill-fated campaign I will not dilate; of the things that happened ye know full well.

How the Duke came to Taunton amidst the joy of the people, with what high hopes all flocked to his standard; and how that flock was scattered to the four winds of heaven, and those hopes crushed forever, at Sedgemoor Field. To me, who was there that day, it seems but a vision now, of sturdy, stout-hearted fellows, standing up to be shot at, for Bussex Rhine lay betwixt us and the forces of the King. Shall I ever forget that thunder of hoofs, as the Horse Guards Blue came charging down upon us? What chance had bill-hooks and scythes against those flashing blades, the swish of whose every stroke dealt death. Still we fought till no strength was left. The Mendip miners, the Blackdown shepherds, and the simple husbandmen of the villages, budged not a foot, as that murderous horde of horse and men swept forth and slew them where they stood.

Tobe and I fought thigh by thigh; yet in the first wild onfall I found myself grovelling in the blood-wet grass. I struggled somehow to my feet, tho' every moment our comrades were cut down by the score. Tobias distributed lusty blows to all and sundry; his blade cleft deep where'er it struck. I saw him dealing out those fearsome knocks, till a cavalryman's sword spun and whistled above my head, next my shoulder went quite numbed and useless; a bloody mist swam before mine eyes, and for the rest I cannot say.

This was the glorious dream of war!

Propitious Providence saved me from the trampling hoofs, as they careered over the battlefield; and I was left with life enough to creep back home, beaten well-nigh unto death. Better far had my carcase rotted in Sedgemoor marshes, for now there comes an awful feature of my tale. Mother cried, out of both sorrow and gladness, that my life was spared, though so very little of it. Father chid me not, but was thankful for my return.

Forthwith I was put to bed, and a chirurgeon was called to dress the hurt. Still, despite his energy and vigilance, for a whole week I lingered by the verge of the Abyss. All that time no word came of Tobias Hancock, and he was mourned as a dead man in the village.

My injury, thanks to much maternal care, in the end assumed kind ways, and slowly took to healing. However, one day, as I was basking in the warmth of summer sunshine, there befell this grievous thing. I sate thus in an open field, my face white, much pinched, and woebegone, and my shoulder swathed in many bandages, when without portent or word of warning, an ugly, black-bearded wretch shot his unclean countenance over the privet hedge. Quite as quick he shot it back, and bawled in a tremendous key to some one down the road—

" Do you come here this minute, Dick ! As I live, here is another on 'em."

Straightway he bundled through the hedge, and came and stood beside me. As I beheld the man's appearance, a thrill of fear jumped thro' my brain. There was no mistaking the uniform he wore, though so ripped, and rent, and blacked with mud. 'Twas the King's.

" Lay me bleeding ! " he cried, grinning in my face ; " a damned rebel, as I hope for salvation. Oh, oh, my poppet, ye're as snivelled as a sucking calf ! If ye ain't a whelp o' Monmouth's, then I'm a sinner."

" Ay, we know ye're that, Old Wiggle," sang out another of the species, as he scrambled through the fence. " What hath that pig-sticking maw o' thine lit on now ? Some whining Jack Presbyter, I'll swear."

This animal was a variation of the breed, as granting his visage was equally ripe for Newgate, he bore himself with a swaggering gait, and waved his sword aloft, the point of which was stuck in a fine fat cheese !

" Strike me stiff ! " this rogue said, " this be a right goodly spot to hie to. A lack of rebels, but no stint o' bull beef, pork, and cider. Mighty poor stomachs have these 'ere clowns for fighting, but damnation good uns for Christian fare and victuals. Cap'n did right well to bring us hither, outlandish place an it be. Yon little farm's the snuggest as ivver I seed. An' all the boys boozy as lords ; Bodkin's i' the ditch, Cap'n's a rolling ; and Sile Bickersteth and his brother Bill are a-sluicing of one another wi' mulberry wine. Sich a flow of honest malt and throat-tickling liquor I never did see afore ; and s'elp me Holy Mary, hams and bacon flitches are thick as rats in a stack o' corn ! "

" That sooth, friend Dick ? Then methinks 'twere meet Old Wiggle should be among 'em. He hath a cultivated taste for sich like tuck. Do you mind the prisoner, Dickie darlin', while I'm gone, an ' I'll bring Cap'n back along wi' me to settle this 'ere job, as the lawyers, an 'heducated pussons like meself would say—*in toto !* "

The first comer took himself away to find this appetizing pro-vender. He having gotten out of earshot, the gentleman of the name of Dick produced a horn of cider from his coat pocket, and fell a-drinking, and at the same time bolted other booty, seeing that he gulped down the cheese in most tremen-dous slices.

" He, he ! " Dick growled to himself, betwixt the mouthfuls,

" best go seek for thyself, Old Wiggle, thy dirty claws shall have none o ' this. I would that rebels must be seized every day o ' the year i ' Somerset ! "

Presently a body of them came along, Old Wiggle foremost of any. A roystering ribald crew they were, fuddled for the most part. One half of them rolled from side to side like ships belated. Some waved their swords to the tune of a filthy chorus, whilst others trailed them through the roadway's muck and mire in sheer inanity. This licentious band formed a part of the most drunken and ferocious regiment in the whole of the British Army. Ye have heard tell, children, of "Kirke's Lambs " or " Tangiers Devils "—these being the names they went by —whose manifold wickednesses have been handed down to succeeding generations. " Kirke's Lambs," indeed ! Shakespeare may be dead, but the excellent art of irony hath not died with him, for here we have the living proof that it still doth rear its comely head amongst us. These devils in the guise of men, tho' they ne'er scrupled in wholesale committal of those twin monstrosities, murder and rapine, were actually let loose on the defenceless country folk. It hath been asserted that their ferocity was first occasioned during foreign service, by their intercourse with the barbarians at Tangiers. This day, however, their bellies were so overladen with the food they had gorged, and their heads so heavy with the liquor they had guzzled, for their owners to be much worse than imbecile.

The unchristian crew promptly came around me, and with them was the officer in command, who in bibulosity appeared by no means inferior to any among his company. By him I was freely plied with questions. As yet I had not learned to tell a lie, hence my treason against the King was at once discovered ; and upon the spot I was taken into custody.

Hereabouts mother chanced to come to see how her invalid was getting on. She was seized with a trembling horror when she learned what had occurred.

" Be not so afeared, good dame," implored Old Wiggle, grinning unctiously. " I've heard say that my Lord Jeffreys is a-coming from London. He will have him turned off decent, mistress, so do not fret, I prithee."

Dick then chucked her under the chin with malignant impudence, and a third insulted her most grossly. I, unhappy wretch I must have been, tried twice to rise and defend her, but was still too weak to do so.

Meantime, father was coming towards us, and he thus beheld the ruffian's act. My breath went quick and gasping, and my eyes grew strained in terror, for my father stroae towards the group, his chest heaving, and such a look on his face I had never before seen there. 'Twas white and drawn, his nostrils wide distended, his lips set tight together; and from his eyes there darted fury.

He stepped among this vile assemblage, and without a word turned on one therein. His fist shot out, and, ox-like, the rogue was felled. It was the only time I ever saw my father strike a man in anger. I had not recked that he, the mildest of men, could be thus transformed. At his angry act, a dozen weapons were uplifted. Howbeit, strangely enough, the officer spared him.

" Hold, ye bull-headed lack-brains ! " he cried, raising his hand to quell his officious followers. " I will have no bloodshed. Dammy ! 'twas a shrewd knock, indeed. 'Twere better on thy head, Jeremy, than on mine own. A curse on thee for an ill-starred wight. As for you, old gray hairs, this springald hath bided under your roof-tree, therefore you have wittingly harbored a rebel; thereby compassing a treason 'gainst the State. Dost follow my reasoning ? 'Pon my life, 'tis worthy of Westminster Hall. Proven, say I, so come ye along to Taunton. I'm thinking my Lord Jeffreys, the hangman, and the gallows—God bless 'em !—will soon be pretty busy."

Thereupon the diabolic villain set up a brutish howl of laughter. In mock respect, he flicked his queue in father's face, and made a leg at the wife who stood by weeping. No other word was spoken, but in sight of poor mother and her two remaining children, we were dragged away to Taunton jail.

CHAPTER II.

THE DEATH OF A SOUL.

WE lay three weeks under lock and key. I mended rapidly in body, yet as the days passed, my distress of mind grew terrible. My father heartened me as best he could, for he and I along with four others shared the same cell. Over a thousand prisoners were confined in Taunton by the first week in September. Awful rumors came to us day by day. My lord Chief Justice Jeffreys was leaving a trail of blood in the West ; at every rebel assize he held there was the same slaughter of the guilty with the innocent, the same horrible tale of butchery.

I began to have fears for my father's neck, as we learned that many, including the noble Lady Alice Lisle, had been executed for the offence of succoring rebels. I informed him of these fears, yet he was not distressed.

"If it be God's will," he said, "I am ready," and he pulled a little Bible out of his vest and kissed it.

He prayed with me in a corner many a night, and many a day did the same with our four rustic companions. The gaunt vision of death seemed to hover about us; and I say to my shame that the word of God appeared to me but cold comfort and a meagre consolation. What hopes could I have for the next world, when I had wrecked the peace of my own family, and had plunged it in the depths of grief and desolation?

On the second day of the assizes we were led forth to the courthouse. Ten of us were placed in the dock together, on trial for our lives. I cannot speak in cold blood of that chamber of solicitude, or of the unnatural monster we found therein; that godless arbiter of life and death, whose deeds and name to this hour stink in the nostrils of the nation.

The judges sate at the far end of the Court, and towering highest of the three was Jeffreys, resplendent in a flowing robe of scarlet, and a long white powdered periwig.

Kinsmen, ye have heard of the "Bloody Assizes" of 1685. Maybe you know every word of those awful traditions; how all the West was alive with gibbets, and how it was besoddened with the life-blood of her sons during those terrible weeks of the early autumn of '85. 'Tis but an old man's fearsome story now, raked out of the dying embers of the past; but hearken, children! ye may go down on your knees, and thank your God that 'tis but a time-worn tale.

To the right of the judges the members of the grand jury were arrayed, devoid of pity. They were there to hang the King's enemies. Close by were the Crown lawyers—fawning sycophants!—whilst behind them a body of his Majesty's troops had clustered. These were bloodthirsty wretches for the most part, who had come thither to be amused. Loudly did they guffaw at the sorry wit of Jeffreys. Below us was a little knot of friends—a sad-faced, anxious, trembling, weeping, congregation. Fathers, sons, husbands, brothers, must die that day.

The eyes of all rested on my lord Jeffreys. The other justices who sat one on either side of him were mere puppets, to nod at his every wink and to laugh at his every jest.

My old heart swells as I remember how we half-score, with firm lips and steady eyes, looked death in the face, and scorned the glance of the Lord Chief Justice. My father and I did not think ourselves belittled, as our high birth and family might have led us to do, at standing thus on a level with simple husbandmen. Truer hearts ne'er beat under woollen jerkins than did those of our eight companions.

We fixt our eyes on the vindictive monster before us, the most inhuman judge that ever disgraced an English bench. My God, he was a baleful object! Would that I might blot his vision for ever from my memory. But can I forget his malignant eyes, or his massive, brutal jowl? Can I forget his bestial countenance, his cursings, his ravings, his bellowings, or his sickening thirst for human blood? Can I forget his face—a flaming sea of red atop of a maleficent underjaw, unbroken in monotony save by close-drawn patches of black eyebrow, and by countless furrows that criss-crossed it with deep and livid lines? That awful countenance was never in repose. 'Twas ever alive with a smouldering and sometimes wholly kindled violence. Affixed above this twitching, quivering, hellish mass, was a huge white periwig, flaunting to and fro with the white powder flying out of it, whilst now and then two savage fists danced round it, and beat the cushions of his desk in devilish tattoos.

It is this unholy phantom of the past that I have had before me of a night time, and that hath scared me in the face of the morning sun.

For a minute or two ere the proceedings began the Lord Chief Justice snuffed, and cracked jokes with his brethren on the scarlet dais, then shot a glance at us prisoners, and, as he did so, the laughter left his face. A hush fell on the assembly, and the trial opened, or at least the outward form of it, for all the world doth know the thing itself was but a mockery.

" Colonel Kirke," cried my lord in a great voice, " I pray you let the guard be strong. Let all due precaution be taken, lest harm befall our person. Did ever mortal set eyes on such a mass of infamy! Mark their faces! See the Evil One stamped upon them! Avert your eyes, ye rogues. You, sirrah, with your brazen face, have ye not the decency to be abashed in the presence of justice? And you, with your red head in the corner. 'Tis not more fiery, I trow, than the place ye're bound for."

That was his opening address. The monster had begun his ravings; his bellowing filled the court. The soldiery grinned at his frenzy, and laughed outright at his wretched japes and pleasantries.

Grim and silent were the jury, and immovable, save for nodding acquiescence at all he thought fit to say. The witnesses stood up to give their evidence, only to be brow-beaten and insulted.

"What sayest thou?" he snorted; "thou canst give good reference as to character? Character, indeed! Thou liest most foully. A cut-throat villain who compasses a treason, and takes up arms against the King's Majesty with a character! Sink me, the conceit is sublime! We shall hear of an actress with one next. Stand down, you perjuring rascal! How dare you foist such a lie upon the court? By my soul, I'd commit you, were I not the most lenient judge alive. Stand down, I say; make way for the little wench in the blue frock."

A meek-eyed young woman, with chalky cheeks and fluttering bosom, stood forth. The wretch fixed her with his awful look. The frightened creature opened her lips to speak, yet scarce a word would come. She stammered a few confusedly, but these were not understood. She was fascinated and paralyzed by the being before her. 'Twas a case of the serpent and the helpless bird.

"Rend my soul!" roared the demon, "'tis well, my jade, that your mouth will not utter what your tongue would have it. 'Tis well you conscience hath warmed you of your crime. Pink me, another sublime conceit! A ranting Presbytery hussy with a conscience! Ho, ho, ho! 'Tis worthy of John Dryden. Be discreet, my girl; ye shall smart for a falsehood."

He leaned over in his justice seat, and shook his fat forefinger at her. As he did so, I caught the glint of his eyes: there was the devil in them. At that sight the fear-struck girl dropt senseless.

Close by I felt a violent quivering. I withdrew my gaze from Jeffreys and descried a sturdy lad beside my elbow. I remarked his bloodless brown cheek, the trembling of his frame, the clutching of his hands, the tight set of his teeth, and the evil in his eye. The girl was his sweetheart, who had come to plead for him.

"So her stomach be too nice for a court of justice," quoth Jeffreys, as they carried her out through the door. "Blister me! justice shames one among these treasonous dogs, and the gallows shall shame the rest; for I'll warrant their necks will soon be longer than ever nature made 'em. Any more witnesses? This shall be a fair trial. None may say that His Gracious Majesty, in the bountifulness of his mercy, hath not allowed a just and proper hearing, and a most humane and

righteous judge to conduct it. Any more witnesses, I ask?"
and he glared round with a wolfish smile.

" Ah! you little fellow of the tub belly?"

A small man with a red face and a squat figure came forward and took his stand. He, at least, was not sufficiently
abashed.

" Mark you, my little turkey cock," growled my lord, who
was but ill-pleased that any more witnesses should come betwixt him and his dinner, "ye had best be very, very careful!"

Scarce had the fellow begun to speak, when the judge roared
out—

" Stop, sirrah! A lie—I sniff it! Waste not the time of the
court with a pack of wicked falsehoods. Get you hence!"

" My lord——" interposed the man.

" ——Begone, I say!" cried the judge, shouting him down.

Here the witness showed his mettle.

" 'Tis no lie, my lord. 'Tis honest truth."

" Oh, oh! Master Jackanapes, the honest truth, is it? You
dare, sir, you dare to give the lie to the Lord Chief Justice
of England! By the Lord, you most peccant villain, I will
commit you."

The devil had gotten into the man once more; he shone in
his countenance more clearly than ever I wish to see him shine
in human face hereafter.

" Any more?" the judge demanded, as they led the late
witness away. "This most awful trial," he continued, "must
be conducted with all due form and ceremony. Not one of ye
that shall not have a hearing worthy of a peer of the realm."

Hereabouts his manner changed altogether. The fellow
could weep as easily as he could laugh, and sob as easily as he
could storm. Therefore the arch-hypocrite forgot his ravings
for the moment; his voice was caught up in many sobs, and
tears hopped down his cheeks as he exclaimed—

" Oh, most unrighteous children—most erring, wayward
children to lacerate the heart of the King, your father! It is,
indeed, a mercy the Lord above doth not send down His avenging angel and smite you where you stand."

The blasphemer cast his hands and eyes upwards to the roof,
as though to invoke the forgiveness of Heaven on our account.
Seeing that none dare face the wretch, one of the lawyers for
the Crown got up and informed the court that seven of the
prisoners pleaded guilty, and three not guilty.

The seven who avowed their crime were placed apart from
the remainder. I declared my fault, yet my father very rightly

protested innocence; for surely 'twas a monstrous thing to pronounce a man guilty of high treason, on the strength of a
simple act of humanity towards his own flesh and blood.
Jeffreys dealt with the guilty first, tho', for that matter, he drew
no distinction betwixt them and the innocent.

"So, ye monsters!" he cried, vengefully gloating over us,
"you avow your guilt? Have ye no sense of your wickedness?
Have ye no thought for the rottenness of your hearts?"

Having said this with grotesque solemnity, he took the hypocrite's cloak unto himself, and once more fell a-weeping. Soon
he mopped the tears from his bleared eyes by the aid of a large
red kerchief; also the sorrow at the time, for like a fiend he
turned on the other three, his face convulsed with anger. I
trembled for my father; he cared naught for a man so base.
I knew a fierce conflict was approaching, for, at my lord's first
words, I saw my parent draw up his body rigid, and fix his
stern, tight-set visage on the judge in a look of bold disgust.
He was once more true to his tenets; he ever set right before
might, and was a-feared of no living being. Furiously the
justice turned upon him and his two companions.

"What! not guilty! not guilty, ye abject hounds! How
dare you stand before me, and throw the lie in my teeth.
Would that the earth might open and swallow ye! I, your
judge——"

"You a judge? A devil, more likely," broke in my father in
a hard, quiet, contained voice, that pronounced every word distinct above the other's uproar.

Soldiers, lawyers, townsfolk, prisoners: all were startled at
this daring, and strained their eyes upon the twain. My knees
knocked one against the other, for the judge looked truly
awful at being thus bearded. I saw him beat the dust once
more from his purple cushion, I saw him writhe and wriggle in
his justice seat, I saw his eyes jump nearly from his head, and
watched the foam assemble on his lips. I covered my face in
terror, yet, though I might blot out the sight, the words tingled
in mine ears.

"What sayest thou, accursed one?" howled the wicked
creature in a transport. "Didst say a devil? A curse upon
your soul, you villain! you ruffian! you Presbyterian black-
guard! Curse you and your conventicles! A devil, quotha?
Ho, ho! you rascally Ranter, we shall see you at the end of
a piece of comely hemp ere long, dancing on space, to the
tune of your own cheerful piping. Who, then, will be the
devil, eh?"

In his satanic fury, he leant out of his seat so far that he came nigh toppling head foremost from it into the well of the court below. His ravings and maledictions filled the place most fearfully. Naught interrupted them, for the soldiers hushed their ribaldry, whilst the remainder of the audience were completely cowed and horrified.

My father paid no heed to the justice's ermine gown and flaunting periwig; he ne'er removed his cool, taunting gaze from that face, but kept his eyes, as heretofore, bent steadily upon it. Even in the midst of the paroxysm I saw disdain upon the prisoner's countenance, and this calm disgust was fuel to the judge's madness.

Now it so chanced that we criminals were unfettered, because so great was the number of rebels within the town, that rope and iron had run short, and neither commands nor money could procure them. Two soldiers, however, with shouldered pikes, stood at both ends of the row of us; and each of the lubberly wights had mouths agape, with never a thought for their charges. 'Twas as iron being driven into my soul to hear my father thus reviled; he so grand and lofty, too, and I the cause of his humiliation. I set my teeth with vice-like grip, and clenched my hands till the nails sank in the palms. My brain was a fiery furnace; the blood swept through my body in a scalding stream that boiled in every vein and artery. A whirling dizziness gripped me; yet despite it the vision of the being I most adored in all the world menaced me as he stood there in the felon's box. Oh, 'twas cruel, cruel!

Next my reason must have fled, as, for a time, I became a tearing madman. Verily the devil seized me, too, for of a sudden, with a crazy howl, I vaulted the high rail in front, and clattered down amidst the papers and the lawyers. I snatched up an inkhorn and hurled it full at the wretch in the scarlet. Then, like a flash, I turned about, and by a wild tigerish bound, made a dash for the door. He who guarded it had not collected his wits sufficiently to raise his weapon, ere I descended bodily upon him, my two knees to his stomach.

We were borne thudding to the floor, myself atop, and in an instant I was up, the breathless fellow's pike within my grasp. So marvellously rapid had been the act, that those who witnessed it were entirely petrified for the moment with stupefaction. Thus, not a hand was raised to arrest me till I had dashed through the door into the passage. Here, however, I was beset by numberless impediments; but I fought and struggled like ten men, with an unreasoning, madman's strength.

How I rushed through that crowded corridor I never could tell.   Men surged about me on every side, and did their best to stay my progress, yet the wondrous vigor that held my limbs enabled me to shower blows thick as hail, and, in the end, to shake off all opponents.

It was but a narrow place, and the aim of the assailants oft went awry.   Once I was conscious of a resounding knock, and next minute my head was singing, and a warm stream dripped down my shirt.   Howbeit, I dealt many broken pates in exchange for mine own misfortune.   Thence followed a vicious crack from behind, which glanced from my ill-fated scalp, and soon gave me knowledge of a fierce pain in the shoulder.   Yet, when a man hath desperation within him, he heeds such misadventures as trivial casualties.

I struggled to the broad patch of light that betokened the outlet from the loathsome place, and as I rushed into the outer air, blood soaked my garments.   No sooner did I feel the pure atmosphere upon my brow, than a desire to leave the courthouse far behind came into my crazy brain, and this at once gave birth to instant action.   Hitherto I had fought and struggled only to give vent to my overmastering passion ; and with no better reason.   But as I sucked in the fresh air and saw the sun so bright, and heard the twittering of the birds, I felt a wild longing to live ; and the hopes, the joys, the sweets of life came back.   'Twas a keen emotion that cut me in every fibre, one that set my heart a-leaping ; whereby 'twill be seen methought the world too good to be quit of so early.   This sharp sensation revived my strength, stimulated my power of thought, tempered my insanity, and succored failing limbs and jaded lungs.   Thus in despite of my predicament I set off at top speed down the street.

I made a strenuous bid for life ; fleeing hatless, bleeding, palpitating ; clothes half off my back, shirt and doublet tattered, and the soldier's pike brandished for the behoof of any meddler.   Not many yards had my quick feet covered when crack ! crack ! went the muskets behind, and the bullets came pinging by.   One whizzed past my cheek, others whistled round my ears and head, but never touched them.   Nigh a dozen sought the roadway just in front, beating sparks from the cobble stones ; and not one was billeted at its rightful destination.   Cunningly I turned into the footpath among the much-scared citizens, whereat rightly smart were they to scurry in all directions to escape the next discharge.   'Twas here my wits had stood me in good stead, for I knew full well the soldiery dare not fire again lest they did others an injury. Still, they gave full power to their tongues, while their feet pattered heavily in my wake. I was not molested, except that one valiant, half-tipsy servant of the King set himself determinedly in my path. Without a second's hesitation, I tightened the hold on my weapon and dealt him a wicked stroke, which knocked him spinning and reeling to the ground. After this I clenched my teeth in defiance of failing breath and faltering limbs, and away I went, unheedful of my heaving chest, for the sweat and blood I spent at every step; or without a glance behind.

Gradually the shouts grew feebler, the hedges and wheat fields hove in sight, and the pursuit became more and more remote. Soon the town was miles afar, and the hunters had tailed away from eye-range. The danger past, I became undone altogether; being barely able to totter over a stile ere my high-strung senses slackened; upon which I dropped my battered body in a field beside the road. I lay weary and weak for hours; being nearly dead owing to loss of blood, over-strain of energy, and tissue-consuming madness.

Very beautiful was this morning in September, with the second growth of grasses soft as velvet, and the noontide sun gold in an azure sky. Through the dust-speckled hedgerows peeped the gentle wheat, softly bowing to every breath of the autumn day.

Alas, it was all uncut! no reaper's hand had touched it. The bones of those reapers lay bleaching on the West countryside; their blood had bedewed the Sedgemoor marshes with its crimson flood; and more there was to flow. The grim reaper, Death, was in the West; but the birds gave voice to their dulcet melody. Their bright-hued throats dotted every branch and thicket, their music swelled through the meadows and re-echoed in the woodlands. What did they care for the tragedy?

* * * * * * *

At eventide the sun softly kissed the western horizon. Stealthily it dipped below the hills, over where the Mendips rose up gaunt against the sky-line. It garbed all around a radiant, glorious purple, till it was known to the earth no longer. Thick on the grass the dew fell. In a clinging mist it wrapped the silent landscape like some far-stretching spectre, that hath no movement, and clothed with an eerie garment the black blurred forms of the silent Quantocks. In the gathering darkness of the night there came no sound save the lowing of the cattle, the mournful wailing of the willow wren, or the noise of the dull-toned bittern.

A heartsore wanderer, without shelter for his stricken body, trampled the heather underfoot. Ye may have pity, my children, for he was your sire—the man who tells you this—the chief of the House of Armstrong. At that hour, he was a fugitive from justice, with the fiend despair in his soul; a broken creature, from whom, a cruel, shameful death had robbed one much beloved. An hour before sunset that same afternoon my father had been led forth to execution, along with his eight companions of the courthouse. He had been hanged like a common felon. Even now his limbs were dangling from a gibbet, his gray hairs bare to the night wind, his flesh the food of carrion. I, his first born, had set his body in that awful thing; my headstrong folly had blighted the home of my boyhood; it had carried death and desolation across its sacred threshold. The sickening misery of such thoughts! Why had I not died beside him; or on Sedgemoor plain? I felt as though I had lived my life, as though God had put forth His Hand; and as though that Hand had crushed me. There seemed no hope; no future. We have none among us who can portray that anguish of youth, that hath only the past to look to, when to-morrow is a thing of fear; when the harvest is in the spring-time.

Passionately despairing, I flung myself face foremost on the wet grass. The cold blades licked my fevered cheek, and caressed my burning forehead. How long I lay on that dewy undergrowth I do not know, but when I rose the light was gone, and the stars were in the firmament. Haunting wretchedness upon me, I turned my back to the hills; home was there no longer. With slow limbs I crawled to a place of terror, where four roads meet. A huge shadow loomed ahead, then the night wind crept across the fields, and stirred the iron thing before me. A dirge-like creaking came therefrom, when it swayed to and fro in the ghostly breeze, and as I stayed beside it, a bird came through its bars, and, with a ghoulish scream and a flap of its vampire's wings, flew into the gloom and blackness.

Close under the shadow of the hellish cage I crept. Down I sank on my knees and clasped my hands in agony. No sound struck the stillness save the creaking of the gibbet. There had been a time when those dangling knees over my head had supported me; the tongue within that rigid cheek had expounded chapter and verse of the Holy Writ, and those lifeless hands had encircled mine of a Sabbath morn; as to God's House we had wended our way together.

I thought of this even then, yet I cursed my God, and re-nounced Him. And then, the devil took courage and raised his head in my heart, for as I knelt there, I swore to hunt down and pursue to the death my father's murderers. My soul yearned for vengeance, my tongue cried for it, and there, under that loathly cage, I made the vow.

CHAPTER III.

CHILVERLEY FARM.

EMPTY bellies make full jails. I beseech you, kinsmen, re-member that. Hunger drove me to my first crime. I fought temptation for a time, yet in the end was beaten by the gnaw-ing of my stomach, so that one accursed day I became thief as well as outlaw, by stopping a Tory squire on a lonely track and robbing him.

From that time forward I flung virtue to the winds, and fell a victim to the devil. Day after day, week after week, I stripped honest men of their worldly goods, till my name became a ter-ror to the country side, and aroused the admiration of the vulgar. Very shortly I procured money enough to buy a horse, and as my reputation hourly grew, I began to take a pride in it, and to perform ambitious deeds of daring. Despair made me reckless of life and limb. I had no care for existence, knowing well, as matters went, it was simply a work of time ere I paid the penalty for my crimes.

My heart-wound never healed. Black thoughts of revenge against my father's murderers were ever uppermost in my mind, and these only spurred me on to further depredations. I have since come to think that Satan only was responsible for my existence hereabouts, for I certainly had no heed of God. The tragedy of that September day had been sufficient to set me against all the teaching and precept of my youth, and to fill my soul with gall. I had no hope, no future. I felt nothing but a dull sort of hatred against mankind ; yet in my old age I praise Heaven that even in my darkest moments I ne'er did aught more heinous than to steal my neighbors' goods. I always spared human life, always left the poor alone, and also the Whigs, if possible. 'Twas the staunch Tories who swore by the King and Jeffreys, and had helped to hang my father, who were the chief recipients of my vengeance.

Many things were in my favor. First was my utter recklessness, that ne'er valued life at all. Furthermore, my body was
lithe and agile, my eye keen, whilst necessity sharpened my
wits to a wonderful extent. Also I became redoubtable with
sword and pistol by constant practice and great celerity of
movement. Besides this, I had several qualities that told
vastly to my advantage in the common mind, and ensured me
popularity. I had a natural grace of manner and person, a
pert tongue, and could be generous on occasion. Therefore,
within a twelvemonth, I was beloved and feared in equal proportion by the common folk ; and so high ran my fame between
Exeter and Wiltshire, that it endures to this day. None guessed
my real identity, and I was known over the country-side by the
name " Black Ned." The prefix " Black " first arose through
the uncommon swarthiness of my skin, which partook more of
the Italian manner than the English. My greatest feat was
the robbing of the Earl of Feversham, the King's Commander ;
and so greatly did it run in men's minds at the time, that
ballads were writ concerning it, and these were sung in every
tavern in our shire. As for the countless times I outwitted the
sheriff and his posse, the feat became a veritable byword in
the West.

Kinsmen, again I have asserted the gruesome truth that I,
your sire, the head of your house, was Black Ned, the rogue,
the thief. My proud children, forget it not, and flout honest
men no longer. When these words first shall catch your eyes,
I have no doubt ye will pass your hands across your several
brows, and exercise your several minds as to whether you have
bibbed of late too freely. And when you find the tale is truly
writ in irreconcilable black and white, ye will call me madman
if ye dare ; yet I defy you with Dr. Proudfoot's testament.

Nigh on three years went by ere I set foot in the glen wherein my home lay. For months I was like one distraught when'er
some stray thought chanced to recall what my folly had cost.
Time, however, is a great physician. A multitude of wounds
he hath healed which the sufferer hath abandoned for incur-
able. Throughout many bitter days I could not even think of
the blighted home without biting pangs of torment. Howbeit
the months slipped by and the bitterness grew less, thereupon
a desire gradually crept within me to look again on my mother
and the homestead. Then came thoughts of my manifold sins,
and once more my heart did fail. How could I return to her
a thief, a traitor from the cause of truth and right ?

Another point here arose. Having become accustomed to

mine own misdeeds, I e'en began to twist facts to suit my case, until I persuaded my sinful self that, when all was said, my offences were by no means so enormous as I had at first conceived them. A man must live, I argued, and what more fitting than that he should take bread from those who had more than sufficient for themselves? Thus I cozened my better nature with specious logic, and for a while my scruples troubled me but rarely.

Hence my desire bore fruit one evening in the spring. Methought that, after all, no great harm could come of it; for never a word need I tell my mother of my occupation. 'Twas early in the season, when the shrubs and hedgerows had scarce begun to don their verdure. The shadows were lengthening fast as I reached the path I had traversed so often in happier days. Even though a misty dampness cloaked the hills, this sad pilgrimage recalled many kindly memories. Objects sweetly familiar beset my eyes each time I glanced around. Here was the grassy mound skirting the path, where for days together in the harvest-time I had rested at midday in the broiling sun to demolish, with no uncertain appetite, my meal of bread and cold boiled bacon. Afterwards, having dipped my face in the brook, I would lie lazily back, knees and elbows anyhow, watching the sunlight glint upon the hill-stream opposite, as it came trickling down from the heights, a glistening, glancing, dancing line of silver, which ceased not in its unending course, nor hushed its gladsome murmur. There, over the meadow, was the willow copse, and hard by the foot of it, reclining peacefully, was a circle of weeds and water, which grew or lessened as the seasons willed. Here the cows would love to bide, with knee-joints scarce showing above the surface of the pool. Often at sundown, in the old days, had I hied me thither to call them home ere the darkness came, only to find them passive. Large, listless eyes would be turned on me, until they were coaxed out of the stagnant water either by fair, caressing words, or, more likely still, by clods of earth thrown at their haunches. Further afield than this was the paddock close where the young colts kicked their heels at all the world, yet more particularly at their lawful masters. Another recollection came to me of this enclosure at the foot of the sheer hillside (now half-wreathed in the gathering gloom), and that was of one of the skittish animals, out of a mischievous spirit, galloping a tilt at me with open mouth, whereupon I was devoutly thankful to scramble through the hedge with naught worse to chronicle than a sorry rent in my second-best hosen. These trifles are the landmarks of our lives, which a failing memory will e'en cling to, though it hath no place for the events of yesterday.

Those were the happy days before the relentless world had begun its buffeting. Yet dost think they were accounted such? Man cannot recognize happiness until he hath lost it. He would sigh for the moon sooner than be content with what he has already in his keeping.

My way was taken in the dusk, with every stream and boulder keeping alive my recollection.

Soon the track took a bend to the left, and Chilverley village lay serene in the twilight. A little bridge of stone, with low parapets, spans the stream, as it comes swirling down from high up the valley and runs by the outskirts of the hamlet.

Thirty yards beyond it, on the village side, stands the blacksmith's forge, wherein Tobias Hancock had his workshop and abode. I have already made some mention of this man; yet I would like to tell you something of his appearance as I saw it in lusty manhood.

With him that evening the day's work was done, and his mind was given up to meditation, which he dearly loved. As I rode by he stood filling the doorway, his sleeves still rolled up just above the elbow, and a pensive, lack-lustre in his eyes.

In stature he was the grandest I ever beheld. Ox-felling thews and sinews were hidden in every limb. Two yards six inches was his height, and not one of these inches was lost in his carriage, as calves and thighs were massy, and brooked not the slightest semblance of a stoop. A noble expanse of shoulder he had too, the frame of Hercules and a mighty chest. He was a hairy-featured fellow, whose black, tangled beard could scarce conceal his firm set mouth and determined jaw. His cheekbones were high, and a scant covering of flesh upon them told tales of many an earnest vigil. Gray eyes had Nature given him, and strangely keen and bright they were, save when his thoughts went a-wandering, which was often in his leisure, though but seldom in his labor. Bristling thick, in a matted patch, his eyebrows clustered, a plenitude of lines and furrows was chiselled on his forehead, and surmounting it was a liberal bunch of hair harshly shot with gray, which aided the entire cast of countenance in its stern uninviting aspect.

At this time he was thirty-eight years of age, and his name stood high, not alone in the village, but for some miles around, for excellence of workmanship and for rigid honesty. He was something of a zealot and a sectary, belonging to the denomina-

tion of Independents—not that I know aught about them, except
that Noll Cromwell was once of their persuasion. The blacksmith was precise and blunt of speech ; and, furthermore, feared
not to speak his mind to any man, and bowed to none save
God. Born and bred of Puritanic stock, he ever upheld their
deep convictions. Mind, this hath no reference to those
impostors, who bring discredit upon every faith, and most of all
upon that of the Puritan, who, attired in sombre garb, are never
without Bible and Prayer-book, and are able to fire off whole
chapters of Holy Writ appropriate to any happening whatsoever, yet ever willing and just as capable to cheat their neighbors. Neither was he of that class (well-meaning doubtless)
who don their piety of a Sabbath morn with their Sunday
garments, and throughout that day carry their noses in the air
with a smug godliness; yet, alas, for their Christianity! the
next day being Monday, they sin with the ease of the devil himself, but nevertheless are hurt in mind if accounted Pharisaical.

Tobias had not the taint of any such mongrel Christians, and
if you beheld the man you beheld his faith, since the two were
never separate. There was a martial tone about him too, for
his father had drawn the sword at Naseby and Marston Moor.
Indeed, he had much of that spirit that led men to hold a Bible
in one hand and a sword in the other, there being always something combative and militant combined with his religion. His
pride was large in his own sobriety, therefore the alehouse
throve little by his custom, though at eventide a black jack of
October had some charms for him. Though his worth was so
wondrous high, he was more feared than loved in the village.
No matter, he was a power for good, and most sought to stand
well in his estimation. However, there were those who had a
reverence and an admiration for the inner workings of that
steadfast soul, and I was among the number. He was considered slow by many; yet once let a notion get into his head,
then neither prayer nor cudgel could drive it out.

Such was Tobias Hancock, the best blacksmith in the Quantocks, the man I had scarce hoped to see in the flesh again.
Yet here he stood, hard by his own doorpost, and my eyes
were gladdened by the sight.

I reined up my horse within two yards of the doorway.

"Zaikes alive!" Tobe exclaimed, his usual stolidity rudely
startled. "Be 'e man, or be 'e pixie? Whoy, 'tis Ned Armstrong, I dü declare!"

"Ay, Tobe, 'tis I."

"Thou hast coom back then arter many days, even as Moses

returned vroom oot o' tha land o' Midian, to Israel his birth·
place? My eyemers, lad, I be raight glad tü zee 'e ! "

He thrust forth his hand, and took mine, and so honest was
his grip that I grinned to avert an exclamation.

"Wull, an' weer hast been a zetting thyzell thease girt
time ? "

" Nay, friend," I said, "I fain would make inquiry first.
How comes it that you are now before me as lively as a morris
dancer, when methought you stark on Sedgemoor plain ? "

" 'Twas zo, Ned ; yet the Lord ordereth all things for tha
best. It zaved my neck did thickee cavalryman's zord, though
'er like tü ha' duëd vor me althegither."

He pushed the hair back from his forehead, and thereby
revealed a long deep scar.

" A weary journey home it was, I can tellee, and hence I
should ne'er ha' coom ef gude friends had not succored me
in my need."

" We had been taken ere you got back, Tobe."

" Ay, an' tha next week arter thy gwoing away, thickee Eras-
tian butcher, Kirke, himsell did coom. Tha zon o' Anti-christ
left poor Bill Marzon on yander zapling, an' Nat Biddle t'other
zide on it, wi' 'iz ole mother a zitting crazed at 'iz feet."

The blacksmith, as he spoke, pointed across to the field
opposite, where two slender trees were obscurely outlined
against the shadowy vapor of the sky ; and though the light
was nearly spent, I could plainly see the man's eyes blazing
from a face of wrath.

After a moment, however, his voice lowered, and the harshness left it. His visage softened also when he said—

" But tha Lord hath uz all in 'Iz keeping ; yea, we are 'Iz
chillern, and 'E mut needs chastise uz. Now, Ned, I ha' telled
'e on mine own adventures, zo et be toime thine weer heered."

If the choice had been entirely mine, a discreet silence would
have been preserved regarding them ; yet no backing out could
there be from the blacksmith's curiosity. Therefore I entered
into a full confession. My heart was not a good one for the
task, for I was fearful of offending his high integrity.

By this it had grown quite dark, thus I had no view of my
listener's face. Misgivings beset me at the outset, yet ere long
wrongs, to my mind, appeared to outweigh sins ; hence I
warmed to my task, and poured out everything for his behoof.
When my recital was at an end, stillness reigned betwixt us.
The only sound in the darkness was my restless horse pawing
the ground.

I awaited his answer, growing momently more uneasy at his delay in giving it. It came at last.

"Ned Armstrong, begone vroom oot o' mi zite! Thee art a cur!"

He turned his back on me, and without so much as a single glance behind he took himself inside.

I led my horse away towards the homestead with a strange coldness at the heart. Every false erection the devil had built to silence my conscience had been thrust down forever. My sins and my guilty soul were bared to the light of truth. The thunderous tones of the angry man loitered in mine ears, and burnt themselves into my brain.

"Ned Armstrong, begone vroom oot o' mi zite! Thee art a cur!"

This, from the man I loved best on earth, now that my father was no more; and he, too, had loved me dearly.

I came to the farm gate, but stood there a full ten minutes, having no spirit left to enter.

By and by, I summoned courage to lift the gate latch, and to lead my animal past where the pigs lay grunting, along the straw-yard. I duly fixed him in a vacant stall within the stable. Formerly Peggy had bided there; but the faithful gray had failed to bring back her bones from her first campaign.

The candles were alight in the kitchen window, and reflected whitely through the blind. Mother, John, and Betty sat round the fire—for the nights were still chilly—as I opened the door and strode in amongst them.

All three gave a quick glance towards me. Then mother jumped up, and ran forward with outstretched arms of welcome. She threw them around my neck in a quick embrace, crying out in joyous greeting—

"Oh, Ned, Ned, mine own bright boy! God be praised! Thou hast come back!"

Such is the way of mothers.

My brother and sister came towards me very glad, with an air half shy, half sprightly.

Some time went by ere these loving recognitions were complete. No sooner were they ended than dear mother, just the same as ever, set about with astonishing alacrity to prepare a steaming meal.

The four of us partook of it together, and smiling faces were freely borne. During these happy moments care was forgotten. 'Twas like the old days revivified—the beauteous old days ere the fell blow descended,—the thrice happy old days that passed heedlessly by, with never a care for the morrow, with never a thought for their fleeting delight ! To me, however, the joyousness of the evening was marred by a void there was no filling. The grave kindly face, which had always in my recollection adorned the table-head, was no longer there, to invoke God's blessing on the fare, or to smile benignantly at his children's early wit.

Supper having gone the way most of its kind do follow, I was snugly placed in the chimney corner-seat, wherein father ofttimes of an evening had sucked his pipe and drunk his beer. In this honorable position I emulated my sire's example by aid of the self-same pipe.

All three ministered to my comforts. John fetched a pair of slippers from the shelf, that my feet might be rested, for horsemen's boots were heavy. Howbeit, his manner of doing this was so monstrous stately, that mother and Betty had to gasp for breath, such was the vigor of their laughter. Betty, on her own part, gave a worthy exposition as to the proper mode of performing these kindly offices. In the twitch of an eyelid my churchwarden was charged from the tobacco-box over the mantel-shelf, and a smoking bowl of luscious rum punch was brewed ; and, as my lips shall surely testify, no other have I tasted since to beat it. Mark you ! all this was daintily done by a plump young maiden, who laughed the while, without any show of hurrying. Thereupon, so smitten was I with such amiable dexterity, that straightway I must needs jump up and kiss her, not twice, nor thrice, but six times over. This reprehensible proceeding set rosiness in her cheek.

" Fie, fie, brother Ned ! " she remonstrated. " I will brook no such unseemly levity."

" I' faith, mistress," I returned, " methinks thou wilt ere long ; for when pretty maidens learn to concoct rum punch, and to charge a pipe so very deftly, I'll warrant there is a cavalier at no great distance."

Alteration was apparent in them all. John had grown into a fine tall fellow, far outstripping me in point of stature. A soberminded one, too, who jogged along at his own pace, paying no heed to the world at large, but treading his own path in his own good time. He was three years younger than I, and certainly not ill-favored. A rare and comely lass Betty had become, she being born a year later than John. My gaze was pleasured by the sight of her ; and, I doubt not, so was many another's, seeing that she possessed a cheerful laugh and a healthful beauty. As for mother, she was changed the least of all. Save that a few silver hairs had stolen where aforetime there were not any, and, mayhap, that her spirits were not quite what they were of yore, she was still the same.

This blessed night hath lingered always in my memory. In a circle we were ranged around the fire; I in blissful comfort, with limbs at ease, and with downy cushions for my back. All eagerness were they for information of my adventures, as naught was known of them. Their impatience was soon manifest, seeing that Betty at once beset me with eager questions. Previously, I had determined that from no words of mine should they obtain the knowledge of my inquities. That this resolution had been too hastily made was quickly proven. At first I gave no answer, but thrust my head backwards against the chair, puffing gravely the while, and contemplating the rows of flitches overhead, as if meditatively indifferent.

This was very well to begin with; but soon their patience became exhausted, and I was sorely pressed to make reply. First one, and then another pestered me, tho' my intention was far from revealing the dark phases in my history. Therefore I sought refuge in evasion. Most concernedly did I inquire after the health of Parson Pridgin, our village pastor, and of that of the old ram, who once on a time had butted me with such severity in the region of the doublet, that no breath had been left behind it. However, my fencing mattered not, as ere long I was plied on every side; and at length my guard was fairly beaten down, when mother said straight out—

"What have you to conceal, Ned, that you thwart us so?"

"Hey, hey, I'm fairly pinked, mother mine. If ye must know, hast ever heard of Black Ned?"

"Of course we have!" exclaimed John with interest.

"'Tis said he is a desperate fellow, who hath fear for none."

"'Pon my word that's so," said John again. "Did he not beset and rob the King's Commander in these parts last year?"

"And did he not dandle the sheriff all over the county after him, and in the end did souse him in Shepton ditch?" put in Betty, for the deeds of this famous rogue filled the mouth of nearly every man and maiden in the shire.

"Hast ever seen him?" I queried.

"That I never have; would that I might; his name and fame are bandied everywhere," quoth John.

"Come, come, sir, have some respect for the truth, as behoves a member of our family."

'Twas plain this was one depth below his ability to fathom, for he scratched his head with a comical air of mystery.

" What meanest thou ? " he asked.

" Tut, man ! " said I, " my meaning is plain. Unless I am much mistaken, thou hast seen him often."

" Ned, I account this a weak jest," he answered, his temper ruffling.

" Ods niggers, boy ! I speak in good sooth. Did I not say you had seen him often ? Furthermore, you have held speech with him ; and, to be explicit, do so precisely at this moment. I am Black Ned."

The three auditors stared hard at me in blank astonishment. 'Twas my business then to startle folks, yet assuredly never did I see a trio more dumfounded.

" 'Tis a feeble jest," observed the unbelieving John.

" So you say, my master, but 'twixt ourselves 'twould be, me-thinks, something of a costly one for thee, should I chance to meet thee with a heavy purse some fine night a-coming from Kingston market."

At that they laughed outright, and refused in the most ab-solute manner to accept the truth. Here was the chance to play the coward ; and Tobe Hancock's rebuff being still hot in my memory, it undermined my new-found courage, and so worthy inclination broke and fled before the wiles of insidious temptation. Thus, between their scepticism and the black-smith's blow, I drifted into subterfuge, deceit, and a strange, new kind of trickery. Seeing that they could not on this occa-sion discriminate betwixt truth and untruth, I gave them an uncolored account of my exploits and mode of life, and hoped all the time that they would disbelieve it.

And this is exactly what they did. I laughed with them and joked with them, and kept my countenance (as best I might) continuously cheerful. My conscience gave me a twinge now and then, my honor, once or twice, a sharp reminder. Yet, somehow, I played the paltry game, and floundered through it with a craven's desperation. I was made to feel the sting of every jest, the bite of every smirk, the hollowness that lurked behind every gust of laughter. And to me their smiles were such an added source of torment that I presently dared not gaze upon their faces. Would bedtime never come ? I gave a vigilant eye to the clock ; but every five minutes appeared magnified to twenty. By and by I began to yawn, though I ne'er felt more sleepless in my life, and at last put an end to the bitter farce for the present time by rising, rubbing my eyes,

and calling for a candle. Not that I was allowed to say good-
night, until a hearty compliment had been paid to my powers
of romancing.

· I lay that night in my old chamber. I found everything unchanged therein, even to the pattern of the counterpane and
the color of the carpet. The window through which the sun
rays slanted over the hill-tops of a morning was just as wide
and just as high as heretofore. The old settle immediately
underneath it showed no more signs of wormwood and decay
than when I had last beheld it. All things were so unchanged,
so homelike, so swathed in precious, tender memories. The
very spirit of the old days seemed to haunt the place. For a
moment I breathed the air of childhood. Yet devilish mockery
lay behind this retrospection, for of a sudden I thought of the
bed the other side the wall, and of him who used to lie there.
I thought of a shimmering mass of metal that once reclined at
my bed-foot, and of a summer morning in the dread year '85.
Thereat fantastic images of Judge Jeffreys and the King leapt
before mine eyes, and that sight of them was as though
some fiend was trying to tear my heart out. Once I saw
the look of pride on my father's face, as he talked in
his quiet way of the antiquity of our house, and of the
unsullied honor of they who had borne its name. Then
my crimes came to me one by one ; they peeped round the
curtains of the bed ; they perched on my uneasy pillow ; they
lived with my ears and eyes. I jumped out of the sheets, relit
the candle, drew on my small hose, and sat on the bedside
shivering. But one solitary flickering flame cannot benumb
the power of morbid recollection. 'Twas Tobe Hancock's
awful face and the hypocrisy practised scarce three hours agone
that now menaced me.

After a while I redressed myself in all particulars, and left
that place of torment. I crept downstairs with infinity of caution,
but, as if to flout my vigilance, the third stair from the bottom
creaked loudly underfoot. I groped in the darkness to the
kitchen, and found a chair beside the feeble embers of the fire.
I sat there with my head in my hands, and did not look up till
a secret sound of rustling roused me from my lethargy. For
the moment I was startled—a white-robed, ghost-like figure was
coming stealthily towards me. 'Twas my mother.

Methought at first that this was some phantasy conjured up
by my disordered brain ; but 'twas no delusive apparition, for I
felt a light touch on my shoulder, and mother, clad in her nightdress, stooped and kissed my face.

"My poor boy," she whispered softly, "I heard you leave your room."

Her voice told me that sobs were fighting with her words. I made no reply, but felt a great dread of any questions.

"I, too, could not rest," she said again; then added, apprehensively, "Mine own good lad, please tell me the truth: you did but jest with us yestreen?"

By this my strength was spent; I could offer no resistance.

"Mother," I answered slowly, "I have told the truth already. 'Tis no jest; would to God it were!"

Coming at such a time, and in so cruel a manner, she had only one course, and that was to believe me.

"But you jested so," she gasped, clinging to the final straw, though hope was already dead. I could feel her bosom heaving pitifully, it being gently pressed against my shoulder.

"I played the coward last night. I lacked the courage to confess my hateful trade! O God, that I should confess it now!" I broke forth wildly.

Thereupon a silence fell between us, which at last was broken by poor mother's overmastering sorrow.

"Ned, my boy, my son," was her only reproach, her only exclamation; and three tears pattered on my hand. At each I winced, and afterwards drooped my head again, under my further weight of shame, of pain, of humiliation.

Mother left me as noiselessly as she had come. Silence held throughout the night, except when broken by the wind that wailed amid the chimney stacks, and screamed amid the half bare branches of the trees in the valleys, hills, and orchards, a mournful dirge-like note of desolation. Wretchedly I crouched across the hearthstone, and watched every ember fade to a residue of livid fluff and blackened charcoal.

When the east showed signs of growing lighter, I stretched my cramped limbs, unbarred the outer door, and stepped into the yard. I crossed it wearily and saddled Joe—my faithful friend and servant—in the half-light of the dawn. The willing creature took me hence, and for the rest I cared not whither the path might lead.

CHAPTER IV.

TREATS OF A WAYSIDE VENTURE.

THE morning accorded exactly with my thoughts. It was dull, damp, miserable. The lowering sky was an inky mass, that met the earth at no great distance from the eye, and enveloped the rocks, boulders, and wooded coombes of the hills in a shroud of mist. Worse than this, however, the rain pelted down with remorseless persistence, and drove hard at the dejected traveller. In this malicious office it was well assisted by the scurrying wind, which seemed to blow from every quarter. The light broadened slowly, yet the dripping landscape was not enhanced thereby; neither did the wind and rain abate. Before long my hat and cloak were sodden with the never-ending flow of water; and this added to my discomfort, for the dampness would creep into every crevice between my skin and garments. Not that I heeded the paltry matter of the elements on that unpropitious journey, as methinks, of all God's creatures I was the most sorrowful, forlorn, and desolate that morning.

Joe wandered where he listed, their being no guiding hand to check his course. However, with the instinct of his species, he pursued the road best known to him—namely, that leading to the King's Head Tavern, Bridgewater. I prayed that by some fortuitous whim he might carry me to Eternity—such was my despair. That prayer was vain, for he traversed the perilous byways among the hills without a falter, though often the path wound in and out, and frequently had naught else but name to boast of. At other times I must have dismounted and led him carefully over the rugged precipitous track; yet now, death would have been so merciful, he took singular care of my neck, unaided.

In the course of time, the Quantocks were left behind, Joe bearing me in safety to the king's highway, without false step or stumble. A heavy coat of mud lay on it pudding thick and sticky; and every rut—and they were plentiful, for road-making was an art unknown in Stuart times—was filled with dirty water; but in despite of this Master Joe picked his way with circumspection, and kept his pace distinctly sober and sedate.

For myself I had heed of no material things, being utterly bogged in the deadly muse that gripped me. As time went on and the terrors of reflection increased to their fullest power, my love of life, by an inverse ratio, waned and waned, and steadily diminished. I had dealt a hard blow on my nearest and dearest relative; had alienated the love of my fondest friend; had sent my father to a shameful death; had deceived my kindred; and had forfeited my honor, soul, and body to the devil. What was there to live for ? I had not one care or tie of life remaining.

I shudder for the natural end of this morbidity; methinks the upshot would have been perilously near a case of self-destruction. However, I was soon startled clean out of this melancholy state, and in a manner wholly singular.

I suddenly heard a sharp sound of hoofs behind me, and to learn the cause turned quickly in my saddle. At that precise moment a horse dashed by, betwixt my right hand and the hedge. I caught one glimpse of an enormous foam-flecked creature, with quivering nostrils, frothy mouth, and wild, dilated eyes, racing along at the utmost speed it could command ; and to this day I have not seen its velocity equalled.

Its awesome pace, and the way its head dipped towards the earth, proclaimed it to be a runaway—by no means the most thrilling matter, for there was a rider on its back ; and the rider was a girl. I saw at once that help was of the greatest urgence and necessity ; a tonic this for scattered wits, since it braced my blood for action.

" After 'em, my beauty ! " I growled in the ear of my dearest Joe, smartly shook his bridle, and touched him lightly with the spurs, whereat he darted after them, for I never begged his aid in vain. However, the runaway was yards in front, and though Joe was nothing of a wastrel, and of lighter build and make than he, 'twas as much as his willing limbs could do to keep the gap between us unincreased, without regard to its diminishment.

I may here confess that the sight of a maid in a plight so hapless afflicted me with fear, tho' ere long these qualms underwent some mitigation, for the mode in which the girl maintained a firm seat in the saddle, and fought the huge creature and endeavored to check its course by every means at her command, made me considerably more hopeful. In fact the way she brought every iota of skill and strength to bear on the bit, was a noble sight, and one to inspire a man with admiration. But in spite of the lady's coolness, courage, and dexterity, the

furious animal was her master. Meanwhile Joe was speeding
to her succor in his powerful deerlike stride, and flinging the
mud and stones of the miry road into an upstarting swirl beneath his hoofs.

I nerved my horse to put forth every inch of pace, yet nerve
him as I might, 'twas all in vain ; our quarry still maintained
its lead. That lolling-tongued Bucephalus, with every muscle
strained, and frothy lather flying from its mouth, ne'er halted
nor faltered in its mad career. At last I beheld its rider reel
back in the saddle, and terror fairly numbed me, for I knew
the reins had snapped and that her horse was entirely free.
Her final chance was gone, and methought naught less than a
kindly Providence could save her from death, or at least a
grievous injury. 'Twas a breathless time, kinsmen, the hedges
whirling by on either side, and the wind and rain beating into
eyes and teeth ; yet breast the elements as we might, we could
never get a foot nearer the insensate brute and its splendidly
courageous rider.

A minute later my heart bounced against my ribs, for of a
sudden, without the vestige of a warning, the maddened animal
stumbled, lurched, and crashed down on its side ; whilst it
thrilled me through with horror to see the brave, ill-starred
maiden pitched out of the saddle a full ten yards, like some
feather-headed shuttle-cock. Thereat I lost my nerve, groaned
aloud, and almost seemed to feel my heart go down. To me
the calamity was close akin to personal, for faith ! courage appeals to me like naught else I know of. I admire it in all
forms and shapes ; in all things animate and vertebrate ; in
dogs and horses, men and women, and even fighting-cocks !

Upon arriving on the scene of the disaster, I dismounted
swiftly, but found the attitude of horse and rider anything but
heartening. The thing that had occasioned all the mischief lay
on the track, dead beat, pumping breath out of its mouth and
nostrils, and its great ribs heaving and falling as though a
blacksmith's bellows was at work behind them.

My first care was for the lady. I found her stretched on a
fringe of grass beside the road, lying with body full extended, face down, and motionless. With her methought 'twas
a case of a broken neck, therefore was full of tremors when I
dropped on my knees beside her. At first I found no sign of
life ; and may I ne'er again set eyes on a woman in so dire a
plight. Her hat lay in the mire, her riding cloak was daubed
with dirt, and her left hand and wrist were dripping blood.
But 'twas a little simple thing that most of all did touch me ;

which was to see a very forest of rich brown hair, with a red ribbon tied round it daintily. To me it seemed so pretty, so insinuatingly coquettish, so emblematic of graceful girlish vanity, that for it now to be in such a dismal strait moved me strangely.

I picked her up carefully, tenderly took her in my arms, and placed her on a grass-grown mound of earth, then sought vainly to learn the beating of her heart or other harbingers of life. Filled with misgiving, again I knelt at her side. Supporting her with one arm, I fumbled frantically in my pockets with the other hand for a phial of *eau-de-vie.* This diligence was presently rewarded, for the elusive bottle was haled from a snug recess in my doublet. I parted her tight white lips with difficulty, and thrust some of the restorative down her throat. Howbeit this met with no success; her eyes remained still closed, nor did the color come; and in the interval of waiting I took upon myself a liberty—I plucked a handful of clotted mud from her fine dark hair.

Now I am aware this proceeding was the reverse of necessary, perchance to some it may even appear indelicate, nay, impertinent; yet so beauteous did that hair appear to my simple gaze, and so ill did the clinging dirt accord with it, that like a passionate sentimentalist, or (an you will?) an ill-conditioned Vandal, I increased its loveliness, and thereby fostered honest admiration.

After that I kept plying strong water, though at first the effect was discouragingly scanty. At last, inspired with the determination of despair, I assembled all my energies for one great final effort. Meantime I had placed the *eau-de-vie* on the grass beside me, one arm nipped the limp young creature's waist, a sympathetic paw tenderly encased her damaged wrist, anxious solicitude was writ large upon my countenance,—and this fair mistress quite unexpectedly opened her eyes; and lo! they lit on me!

Children, I am an old man now, but may God ne'er dim their lustre to my memory! No sooner did those drooping lids reveal the splendor hid behind them, than my addle pate became piteously disconcerted; and, boor-like, in answer to her look of wonderment, I opened my mouth, and disclosed the beauty of my teeth. Now do not for one moment think this was out of a spirit of rivalry or emulation with her eyes, 'twas just sheer inanition at the revelation of their glory. Doubtless the lady, in her secret heart, thought the staring dolt so close besetting her was neither more nor less than a

stupid country clown devoid of sense or manners; so the wider
your worthy parent parted his lips, the more expansive did those
eyes become, till at length the tardy blood burst forth, and
mantled crimson in her cheeks and forehead. Her senses quickly
mustered, and mayhap she had gotten a full complement ere I
gathered enow of mine to withdraw my idiotic gaze.   For my
life I could have found no words of speech at first, so much
had my situation daunted me.   And when I did avert my eyes,
'twas in a hang-dog style, with a tingling in the ears, and much
hot blood near the brain.

Hereabouts I manifested some desire to beat an ignominious
retreat, by jumping over the hedge and running away.   Who can
tell but what this might have developed into an actuality, had not
something seemed to tell me that to have let go my hold of the
lady in a fashion so precipitate, would have caused her, in her
weakly state, to topple backward into the ditch behind?   Having
overcome my clownish inclination for the sake of so sweet a
mistress, I made haste to wriggle out of a very compromising posture.   First I slipped my hand with the utmost
care off her injured wrist, then slipped, mark you, more carefully than ever, that arm from round her waist.   These feats
judiciously accomplished, I breathed with a trifle more of
freedom.

The maid was timid, blushing, coy at first, after the mannei
of her sex, when on strange ground, and in strange company.
'Tis wise procedure I trow, especially if this same company be
masculine, youthful, and warm-hearted.   For 'twill blush, too,
and be very miserable, whereat the lady hath undue advantage,
as she will undoubtedly be composed the soonest; for the sex
of womankind, as a general thing, is less easily abashed, and far
less lastingly than the other one.

Certes, 'twas very like this with me when the maiden opened
her eyes and beheld Ned Armstrong, in no very courteous position, at her side.   And this same Ned Armstrong, despite
grievous misfortune, being still youthful and warm-hearted,
and feeling wondrous guilty in his private mind, became a prey
to real scarlet-tinted confusion.   Verily I was a bold rogue then,
with the scantiest reverence for mankind; but let that other sex
come by, then I was an emblem of meekness and humility—a
gallant trait that once tempted a married friend, a meek-eyed
Benedick, to say that I was fitted choicely well by nature for the
stormy sea of matters matrimonial.

Presently the maiden glanced upon her hurt, looked at the
phial of *eau-de-vie*, and at the exhausted horses on the roadway.

5

Thereat she rose, and courtesying to me with a grace that we don't grow in England, said—"

"Sir, how can I thank you?"

From that moment I have ne'er seen a maid so beautiful. Despite the havoc of the accident, there was no mistaking the degree of this fearless brown-faced lady, whose noble air, gracious, yet lofty, sweet, yet commanding, told Ned Armstrong surer than the tongue that here was a gentlewoman.

Her breach of silence dispelled a goodly portion of my embarrassment. So I, seeing her so lovely and so finely bred, put on company manners, and bowed with a long-drawn-out politeness.

"I trust thou'rt not seriously hurt, mistress?" I asked, mighty solicitous.

"Not in the least, sir," she replied, in a swift, decisive fashion.

"But your wrist, mistress?"

"'Tis nothing. A mere scratch!"

"But it bleeds profusely. Please, let me bind it up."

"No, no, thank you, sir! It may bide with comfort till I get home. It hath only made acquaintance with a jagged stone."

However, I was obstinate, and pressed the point with diligence and such a power of pleading, that by and by she yielded laughingly to my importunity, and let me bandage it with her handkerchief. I was astonished to find how deep the wound was; it went almost to the bone; and while I handled it with the utmost gentleness and care, I could not help but marvel at the little thing she made of it, which appeared quite contrary to the custom of the delicately nurtured. Yet, upon a close observance, I found she was not wholly stoical, for her face blanched once more, and I could feel her little hand was trembling. Observing that I had detected these portents, she said, doubtless to palliate her weakness—

"'Tis a foolish thing, I know, sir; but I hate the sight of blood!" And she turned her head away confusedly, as though heartily ashamed.

Now this struck me as truly strange, but when I came to reflect, it seemed of a piece with her other characteristics. A young and beautiful lady who rode a war-charger, for without doubt that was the nature of the runaway, unattended, early on a rainy, windy morning, and who handled it with extraordinary courage and dexterity, must needs differ in many particulars from her sisters. In the course of my chirurgic duties, I took occasion to snatch a glance at my companion's face, and found it also very fine to look at. Still I was unable to drink in the

fulness of its beauty all at once, because if at any period I
gazed upon it more than ten seconds at a time, such was the
vivacity of her eyes, that she was bound to catch me staring.

"Sir," she said, when my task was done, "I fain would learn
the name of my kindly succorer; I could then thank him the
more explicitly."

"Prithee, mistress, do not set so high a value upon my services. It hath only been with me a case of gallop, instead of a
doleful walk."

This was, of course, a subterfuge. Her question had startled
and frightened me, for I felt myself to be in a corner that was
uncomfortably tight. Throughout those years of outlawry it had
ever been my desire to conceal my real name, that our high family
need not be dragged down with me, and not have their honored
and ancient patronymic bandied from mouth to mouth by virtue
of a rogue so vulgar. Accordingly, the familiar appellation of
Black Ned had been of such real service in cloaking my true
identity, that none knew the highwayman was John Armstrong's
son, save mother and Tobe Hancock. Yet how could I give
my professional name to this young lady? My blood chilled
at the thought. Howbeit she was not to be deterred by any
equivoque; therefore, upon the repetition of her question, I
replied—

"Edward Armstrong, your very good servant, mistress."

"Dost claim kinship with the Copeland Armstrong, might I
ask, sir?"

"I am mine uncle Sir Peter's nearest kinsman. And by
what token shall I remember you, mistress?"

"As the daughter of Sir Nicholas Marvin of Kelston Manor,
who will ne'er forget thy kindly services."

Even as I had pronounced my name I knew how deeply I
stood committed; yet in justice to myself I must advance an
extenuating plea, as just then I seemed the victim of a crazy
fascination, that somehow lulled my senses.

Together we paid heed to the horses. Old Joe, the best behaved of his species, stood watching us with indifference. Not
so the other animal. It still lay where it had fallen, and its
condition appeared woe-begone and pitiable. Ere I could guess
what her motive was, its mistress seized the bridle and raised
it on to its legs; and, as she did so, I felt mightily ashamed of
mine own backwardness, and also rare admiration for her skill
in the handling of horses.

"Master Armstrong," quoth she warmly, "if I only had a
man's arm, and a stout stick to assist it, I'd give this gentle-

man the biggest hiding he's had for many a year.   I'd either knock sense into him, or knock the nonsense out."

At that I could not conceal a smile.

"Nay, sir," she flashed indignantly, "tis no laughing matter. When Sir Nicholas sees him in this state there'll be an awful noise.   You see," she added, by way of explaining the cause of so dire an effect, "the bit wouldn't hold the brute; but I can promise him, the next time I require his services, I'll have a bit on him that I can break his jaw with, if I find such a measure needful."

Thereupon she turned on the delinquent fiercely, and gave his mouth a vicious tug.

"Thou great fool!" she exclaimed, hitting him across the nose; and proceeded to scold him with remarkable asperity. However, at the height of this abuse, she chanced to turn her head, and to see the woeful condition of one shoulder which had received a deep gash from whence the blood streamed freely.   For a moment sorrow and anger seemed to contend for mastery in her tone and countenance.   But, in the end, the softer emotion gained the day, for her fierce tones tailed off in the most comical manner possible, and she discarded anger for a sigh, and in a voice exquisitely sympathetic said, "Master Armstrong, I'm a brute!" stamped her foot to emphasize the fact; then caressingly slapped the late delinquent's neck.

Alas! that unappreciative beast shook himself, disdainfully accounting this cosseting no privilege.   Whereupon she turned to Joe, who had regarded the proceedings with a large-eyed interest.   Prettily pleased was he to receive her caresses, and having a much nicer perception of feminine beauty, licked her hand in response; so, having this proof of his kindly heart, she fondled his ears and kissed the white star on his forehead.   Next, she once more turned to her own steed, and leading him a few yards forward, said—

"I must give you good morning, Master Armstrong; I am keeping Sir Nicholas without his breakfast, and 'tis a very temerarious thing to do, sir; besides, poor Wallenstein must have his grievous hurt dressed as soon as possible."

Again she thanked me a good deal more than my services deserved, then turned her horse's head, and led him at a brisk pace homeward.   However, Master Armstrong, ætat twenty-four, marched after her double-quick.

"One moment, mistress!   It is more than a mile to the manor, I wot, and your horse will sadly encumber you.   Allow Joe to carry you thither.   I will bring poor Wallenstein."

"Thou'rt truly kind and good, Master Armstrong. But really, sir, I'm sure thou hast something better worth the compassing than aiding belated girls back to their homes again."

"May I never have a worse occupation, mistress."

At first she firmly refused my help ; but I, sorry for her misfortunes, and subtly charmed, persisted. Ultimately, with many thanks, and many more excuses, she assented to this proposal.

Oft-times in after days I have tried to square my behavior on this occasion with common-sense and reason. Why was it that on one of the most awful mornings of my life, when the gates of hell were open wide before me, that I should be so dogged in so trivial a matter? And yet 'twas by a chain of similar insignificant events, and by pandering to a wayward passion, that the greatest chapter in my life was writ; so that when all is said, the action of that spring morning may have been in strict accordance with the laws of human destiny.

Ere we started on the journey, I changed the saddles of the horses, though the lady would insist upon aiding me to do so ; and then, to my chagrin, she sprang upon Joe's back without tarrying for me to lend assistance. I said to myself, "Ned Armstrong, what an ungallant churl thou art. Assuredly, my friend, thou hast much to learn regarding conduct in the company of sweet ladies. Here you have been too forward once, and too backward twice already."

Our cavalcade of four did not set forth till Mistress Marvin had executed an office typically feminine. She took off her hat, all in the streaming rain, then patted and coiled her wayward wavy curls and ill-disciplined tresses into some uncouth semblance of order.

"There !" she exclaimed, smiling satisfaction ; and then she cocked her hat, a big, wide-brimmed one, adorned with a large white feather, a little to one side at the back of her head, in a jaunty and rakish manner.

We had a mile and a quarter to travel, yet for one of us twain, at least, our destination hove in sight too soon. My companion's spirit soared above her own misadventures, and over the gloom of the morning. Though the skies were lowering and severe, though her wrist was cut and painful, and her garments were soaked with water, she had never a care for such dreary mundane matters. The serious happenings of an hour agone were things of the past to her, brimming with life and fast-flowing generous blood.

Presently she thrust an ungloved hand from beneath her cloak, and held it out to gauge the fall of rain.

" 'Tis a splendid morning!" she exclaimed, fervidly sniffing the air.

" Indeed," said I. My tone was dubious, for I had yet to discover its delights.

" Sir, I said a splendid morning. Now the rain hath come the fields and verdure are green as can be. 'Tis three weeks to-morrow since the last drops fell. How cool and fresh the air doth seem. Methinks I would as lief be out this day, as on the finest one of summer. Oh, 'tis a healthy morning. 'Pon my word, my appetite is outrageously keen; and, I say, Master Armstrong, 'twill be a grand time for fishing this afternoon. And dost see the frogs, sir? Just look at the yellow-bellied monster yonder. Faith, the biggest I've seen this season! Friend, I'll have a closer view of you."

Kinsmen, she was off Joe's back in the batting of an eyelid, and like a cat pounces on a bird, she pounces on that unsuspecting reptile. She whipped him into one hand, and bore him captive to her saddle. I laughed to see the bewildered fellow's green eyes glint as she stroked his head, and tickled his scraggy throat. Having examined his limbs and general dimensions with a critical eye, she appealed to me to confirm her judgment.

" Isn't he a beauty, Master Armstrong?"

" No doubt of that," said I.

" Then, my Illustrious, there's the manor pond for you, sir! Gently, big King of Kelston—gently!"

And despite his reptilian majesty's squirms and struggles, she expertly slipped him into the pocket of her riding-coat.

" Mistress Marvin," I said, "I have a question to ask. I am puzzled for the reason that brings you abroad so early on such a dreary day, mounted on what appears to me to be a war-charger. From what you have already said, methinks I can divine the first cause, and, providing you do not think me impertinent, I would like to learn the second."

'Twas her turn to laugh, and ye may be sure she did not let the chance slip.

" Well, sir," she smilingly replied, "come hail, come shine, I ne'er fail to take a gallop before breakfast. But I was in a rare strait to-day, when Martin the groom declared my lovely sorrel filly, Boadicea, had caught cold, and that she must not on any account go out. That's nonsense, sir, preposterous nonsense! There was the mare fit as a fiddle; ne'er saw her looking better; but of course that Martin chuckled and said, ' I've spoken, mistress—take her by all means; but if you do,

I'll tell your father.' The ugly old villain—that's how I'm always pinned! You see, my old dad swears Martin's a man of experience, and that I'm only a chit of a wench, and that if I go against that experience, 'tis at my peril. Brutally hard on me, sir, I can tell you, as if I have any vanity it's because I know a bit about horseflesh. Then, to make matters worse, Tilly, the jennet, hath sprung a spavin. So what could I do, but take this booby Wallenstein, who hath naught near the pluck of his grandmother, who was shot dead under papa at Maestricht, when he fought with Turenne in Holland? Would she have been frighted at a covey of partridges whirring out of a hedge-bottom? Would she have broken away, and have done her best to break her rider's neck? Martin will live on this for a month, and papa will have just a word to say on the subject. Sir Nicholas is grand at the lingo; he swears brilliantly in six different languages; but methinks I can manage my worshipful sire."

'Twas delicious to see the roguish merriment that glowed in her eyes. Ah, kinsmen, such a sight would be all-sufficient to send any young man's brawling through his veins. She flashed the arch magnificence of those eyes on me. Thereat I grew confused, and felt my heart beat far quicker than the ordinary.

Be it understood I mean the heart of Master Edward Armstrong, aged twenty-four, nephew and next of kin to Sir Peter Armstrong, Bart., of Copeland Hall, in the county of Somerset. Regarding Black Ned, I cannot name the whereabouts of that notorious rogue with any degree of certainty, during that rainy morning in the spring. Perchance he might have been discovered in a baleful setting, deep down in your sire's hopeless soul; covered for the nonce by a foolish rapture. Perhaps he was lying dormant therein, assimilating fresh fuel of bitterness, wherewith to burst forth into new malignance; though, when all is said, this is only mere conjecture. Howbeit, from all of it we learn that even despair maketh not a young heart old; and, say I, let us be thankful that thus things are.

CHAPTER V.

SIR NICHOLAS MARVIN.

WE rode, the maid and I, side by side along the muddy high-way, till presently we turned into a small by-path leading from it, and five minutes later the abode of Sir Nicholas Marvin stood before us. It is known as Kelston Manor, and is with-in a couple of miles of Bridgwater. An avenue of tall trees leads up to the gates, and does its best to blot out the light of day, for its arched boughs meet overhead. The house itself is shut from the sight of all outside the gates, save for a doubt-ful glimpse of vane and chimney-stack, that peep above the trees. A heavy, close-grown patch of woodland forms an im-penetrable boundary to the manor lands, which, to the eye, doth appear naught better than a wilderness of tangled copse and flowering vine intermingled with a mass of roots and stems and unsymmetric herbage. Yet in despite of woeful lack of order, it looks quaintly picturesque, and when the birds hop from twig to twig, and the squirrels from bough to bough, it becomes a picture for the mind. Yet further afield than this disordered growth of briar, trim parterres and velvet sward may be found, set forth in exact manner as become habitations so pretentious. Behind it a meandering brook flows through a region of cool grottoes and shady branches, whilst higher up, nearer its source, grassy meadows skirt the banks, and 'tis said numberless fish lie in the depths of the stream, in a bed of yielding clay and moss-grown boulders.

Did time allow, I would speak at length concerning this favored spot, for 'tis one that hath recalled pleasant memories amid dreary days. To return to that gloomy morning of the spring, when I first beheld it, e'en though the sun never once came through the clouds that day, it stands out beautiful in my recollection.

Directly the manor gates (forbidding iron objects, with a wide mouthed stone dragon set either side of them), came into sight, I halted the injured Wallenstein, saying—

"I will leave you now, mistress, as you are so near home."

"I trust you will do nothing of the kind, sir," she replied

decisively. "You must share a meal with us. Besides you, who have **rendered** his only child such splendid service, must see Sir Nicholas, my father. He hath been a great soldier in his time."

This last was used as a clinching argument, and had I been unwilling to comply with the invitation (and I never could remember that I was), I doubt whether I should have found it in my heart to have refused her anything in reason.

Without more ado she led me through the gates, along a short broad path cut amongst the brushwood. The end of it was divided into two paths instead of one, the first leading to the front of the mansion, and the second to the back. Along the latter an oldish man, attired as a groom, and in his shirt sleeves, was approaching.

"Hi, Martin!" shouted his mistress, slipping off Joe's back and beckoning the fellow towards her.

He came up, and with a crabbed and sulky air listened to her full instructions anent the horses. When she pointed out Wallenstein's condition, he half smiled to himself. She ended by placing a piece of silver in his hand, saying—

"Be a good fellow, Martin, and say nothing about this to Sir Nicholas."

That caused him to smile again, but methought there was a world of meaning behind his affability. Having nodded his head, he chuckled, answered, "Very good, mum!" took charge of the horses, and led them briskly to the stables.

"Cantankerous old ass!" exclaimed his mistress, gazing after him. "I hope he'll have the sense to keep his mouth shut. And, Master Armstrong, I trust you will bear these desires of mine in mind, sir; for should papa hear of Wallenstein's condition, there'll be some hard words flying about, and perhaps some hard knocks too, for he hath promised them many a time."

To this request I laughingly assented. She left me for a moment to go and dispose of the frog, and upon her return we took that path which curved to the right, whereby we shortly arrived at the front of the house.

An old man was standing on the entrance steps, and he was the most grotesquely forbidding gentleman it was ever my lot to see. He was tall and spare of person, and had a harsh ascetic countenance. In height he was quite six feet, and carried every inch of it with ease and dignity, as a soldier should. His age seemed seventy or thereabouts, though what seemed to heighten it was the snowy whiteness of his hair. His face was surpassingly ugly, bloated by undue attention to the wine-pot, and adorned with one eye only. It was set deep in the socket, and was peculiarly fierce and restless, whilst the other was permanently closed. Two hideous scars intersected his visage, one running diagonally from his left temple in a livid seam across the bridge of his nose to his lower jaw, and the other, less maleficent, lay parallel with his hairless upper lip. For the rest, his mouth was large and thick-lipped, his chin square and unpleasingly determined, and to sum up in a word his whole demeanor, it gave one the idea of half-restrained ferocity. His face was destitute of hair, except for a two-days' down upon the jaw that sadly lacked a razor. His garb accorded with the singularity of his countenance. One foot boasted a handsome buckled shoe, yet the other had neither that, nor boot, nor slipper; 'twas simply encased very untidily in a capacious cloth. White silk stockings adorned his legs, and breeches of russet-brown plush, cut in the newest style, his thighs. Surmounting these was a vest, a flowery mass of silk brocade on a ground of purple; whilst a lavender coat, edged with silver, and with large bright buttons of the same to match, added further splendor to his rich attire. Strange to relate, his neck was innocent of any well-arranged adornment, his throat being covered by an unfrilled cambric shirt, neither clean nor prepossessing, which, in combination with his unshaved chin, his unwigged head, his swathed foot, and resplendent dress, gave him an appearance at once comic and remarkable.

I must have laughed aloud at an apparition so conspicuously whimsical, had not good manners come to my assistance, for this was Sir Nicholas Marvin. Accordingly, I suppressed my mirth to nothing more than furtive smiling.

At the first sight of us twain, he hopped gingerly off the steps and came towards us.

" How now, Dorothy! " he exclaimed in a loud grating tone to his daughter, and then continued in the language of our continental neighbors, which I at that time of day, being unlettered, and ill-found in knowledge, was at a loss to set a meaning to, " *Où as tu été ce temps ? Le déjeûner vous attends depuis une heure ou plus.*"

" Peste ! " exclaimed my companion petulantly, " a murrain on thy French jargon, father ! Do not remind me of that hateful country, as dismal as a De Profundis, with its eternal aves, paternosters, rosaries, and bead-countings. I am a-weary of France and convent walls."

" Art so, my wench ? " he replied in his mother tongue, " then

'twere best thou conquered thy aversion, for convent walls alone
fit the likes o' thee. Henker ! thither shalt thou return." Here
he broke into a flight of tremendous language, English and
foreign, that fairly bubbled with sprightly malediction.

"But, papa ! " interposed the erring maid, " I am very, very
sorry."

" Sorry, thou graceless hussy ! Pasques-Dieu ! thou hast
the very greatest need to be. Dost see the time ? " He pulled
out an elegant chronometer for her information. " One hour
and a quarter past the proper breakfast-hour, and I've had
never a morsel since nine o' the clock last night. And you
know full well, you limb of evil ! that to go so long without food
always gives me wind in the stomach. I have it at this moment."

Upon this his daughter coolly looked all round her at the
state of the elements, then said with a judicial air—

" Yes, dear papa, it is a very windy morning. Really, sir,
you should not open your mouth so wide."

She counterfeited innocent simplicity to such admirable per-
fection, that at first I was quite deceived and failed to mark
the satire. But the knight did: to him the shaft went home.

" Little bitch ! " he growled, and fairly gobbled in his rage.

Thereupon I glanced at the maiden, and beheld sly mischief
in her eyes ; and saw that the corners of her mouth were twitching. And ever after that occasion, whene'er it befell that I
was uncertain how to take her speeches, I always looked for
those secret signs of mirth.

At this juncture Sir Nicholas chanced to notice me. So
keenly had his grievances rankled hitherto that he had heeded
naught but them.

" Carramba ! " he exclaimed ; " who is this young man, you
wayward imp of wickedness ? "

The wayward one was prompt of answer.

" This gentleman is Master Armstrong, papa, my very true
friend, who did me the greatest service an hour agone."

" Humph ! I trust he did not hinder you from breaking
your neck. If so, I'm thinking he hath performed a very
doubtful service to myself and the world in general."

Peradventure having some conception of good manners, the
wrathful knight modified his tone to one more befitting a gentleman in his intercourse with a guest and stranger. He proffered
me his hand, saying—

" Glad to see you, sir ! infernally glad to see you ! But I
hope you'll be so good as to excuse my unkempt appearance.

'Tis all my daughter's fault; you'd best lay it to her account, sir.   Ah, my wench! mark my word, there'll be such a reckoning day yet you little wot of.   Here have I been all these hours waiting to be shaved and none to ply the razor; and my clean shirt I cannot find it high nor low, neither is there any who can dress my toe or arrange my neckerchief.   Devil take all froward daughters!"   He paused to thump his stout stick on the gravel walk.   'Twas laughable in the extreme how anger and politeness strove one against the other in his conversation.

" Howsoever," he continued, " I trust you will be so kind, sir, as to share a meal with us, though the capon is surely spoilt, and the *pâté* baked as hard as a musket-stock."

Hereupon he stopped and more closely observed the hapless Dorothy.   Something foreign hopped out monstrous quick, as he inquired—

" Why, my wench, what under heaven hath befell thee? Pink my soul! thou'rt worse than any baggage from Lewkner Lane.   You look a real credit to your sex.   Perhaps your ladyship will explain that smutty face, that confounded hair; and draggle-tailed attire?   And why dost keep one hand behind thy back, most elegant damosel?"

Before the maid could guess his motive, he grabbed her arm, and jerked the bandage into view.   "What is under that rag?"

" Nothing, sir, but the smallest scratch," she replied, trying to draw away from him.

" Then why advertise it to all the nation, and flaunt it in a great cloth as though a pound o' flesh were missing?   However, I'll have a look at it."

" It is nothing, sir; I assure you it is nothing," she said, apprehensively, and trying to avoid his violent handling.

However, without more parley, he ripped off the bandage; and a goodly sprinkling of blood was to be seen on the inside thereof.   Forthwith the hurt underwent close scrutiny.   He pulled apart the jagged edges of the wound, without the least regard to gentleness or mercy, probed the depth with his forefinger, pushed it calmly here and there within it; and all the while his daughter bore it patient as a lamb.

" Hum! a mere skin slit."

" That is all, sir," she answered faintly.   By this I could see her wincing under the brutal treatment.   Once more her face had blanched; whilst the blood, disturbed by such unkind usage, again flowed freely from her wrist.   I never felt a more earnest desire in all my life to insult a man as I did just then.

" Sir," said I, as calmly as I could, " I am afraid you are giving the lady unnecessary pain."

" Master Armstrong," returned the victim, her promptitude
remarkable, " my father hath great skill in the treatment of
wounds. Sir, you forget that he hath lived among them from
his childhood."

There was no mistaking the rebuke implied ; nor was I slow
to detect something significantly haughty in her tone and manner.
As for the callous old knight, he gazed at me with singular
deliberation, then asked—

" What was that you were pleased to observe, sir ? "

Being nettled at the demeanor of both father and daughter,
I boldly repeated what I had said.

" Pshaw ! " said he, " not much of the soldier about thee, mon
ami. Merely a damned civilian, I see."

" Sir," said I hotly, " your language is not that of a gentleman."

At that Mistress Marvin blushed a lovely red, and looked
beautifully angry.

Meantime her father curled his ugly lip and retorted—

" I repeat, sir, merely a damned civilian ! "

" And who may you be, sir knight ? " I sneered, for now
temper was mastering judgment and discretion.

" Who am I, my lad ? Wench, fetch my sword, and I'll teach
the callant who I am."

" Master Armstrong," said the lady, stepping forward, her eyes
magnificent, and every line of her imperious and queenlike,
" you ask who my father is. He is a great soldier, sir. I may
say he hath participated in eleven pitched battles, fourteen
sieges, fourteen ambuscades or bushments, five escalados, ten
intakings, eight camisados, twenty-three duellos, and divers
other engagements."

Methought it the finest sight in the world to see her so,
though 'twas plain I had unwittingly blundered into a hornet's
nest. Here were the oppressor and the sufferer both arrayed
against me ; for the one I sought to serve was taking up the
cudgels on the other side, and though I greatly admired her
staunchness to the knight, I was undoubtedly hurt at her in-
gratitude towards myself.

" Wench, do as ye're bidden, and fetch my sword," growled
the irate warrior.

" Dear father," she replied, " you know I'm always willing
that you should fight when the occasion demands and calls for a
passado. But this gentleman is our guest, he hath most kindly

succored me this day ; and 'twould be a cruelty to pit him, who hath not been bred to the profession, against one of thy proven calibre and experience."

"Madam," quoth I stiffly, for be it known by this I was pretty deeply galled, "I am entirely at your father's service."

"There, girl ! hear ye that ? " cried the knight with glee, "art going to fetch my sword ? "

"No, sir, I am not," she said with amazing boldness and determination.

For the moment I feared her enraged sire would belabor her with his stick. Apparently, however, he ultimately thought better of the matter, for after delivering himself of many lusty oaths, and presenting many ferocious grimaces to the pair of us, he exclaimed—

"By thunder, I'll fetch it myself ! " whereat he went hobbling towards the house as fast as his decrepit limbs would carry him. In an instant his daughter's manner changed.

"Oh, sir ! " she implored in a tone of eager entreaty, "for Heaven's sake forbear ; he would be a mere child beside one of thy youth, strength, and vigor. He is a fine-spirited old soldier, and hath a wondrous knowledge of swordsmanship, but alack ! he is seventy-two next birthday ; and see, he is that afflicted with the gout he can scarcely crawl. Master Armstrong, your readiness hath proved you a brave man, please prove yourself braver still by declining to unsheath your sword against him."

I was astounded at these changes of tactics. A minute agone she was his second, his aider and abettor, but now the extraordinary girl was endeavoring to avert the threatened conflict. In a measure she guessed my thoughts, for she added—

"I am begging you to withdraw, sir, because I know my father too well to attempt to persuade him to do so. When he feels himself affronted he is always willing to push the matter to the point of bloodshed. And he will ne'er make a single concession or recantation until his adversary hath made the first. Master Armstrong, I conjure you to grant me this favor ! "

I was utterly incapable of resisting so fervent an appeal.; besides, it would have been a paltry thing, no matter what the provocation, for a fellow of my age to have crossed swords with a man so old. Accordingly, accompanied by the lady, I hastened after him, and came up with him at the bottom of the entrance steps.

"Sir," said I, " I am willing to let the matter rest."

" No doubt, my man, no doubt. But, for mine own part, I am

not so far advanced in my dotage as to sit down by such talk from a mere civilian." And the fiery old war-dog commenced ascending the steps. However, his daughter came forward, and fearlessly seized the tail of his coat.

"Dorothy, ye she-devil, how dare you!"

"Hold, father! Dost not see this gentleman is very magnanimous? 'Twas you, sir, who began the quarrel."

"Mort-Dieu! then I'll finish it."

In the meantime the devoted Dorothy was energetically whispering to me—

"Conciliate, sir—conciliate! See what a mettle old game-cock it is! Smooth its feathers! Stroke its plumage! Retract, sir!—take back thy words, please do, sir!"

I was instantly obedient to her, whom, I may remark, cooler men than myself must have found irresistible.

"Dorothy, ye saucy slut," clamored the knight, "let go my coat! Unhand me this moment, or I'll——"

"Sir Nicholas Marvin," I interposed, to stifle more of his abuse, "in deference to your daughter, sir, I will withdraw all I have said that you may deem obnoxious towards yourself."

"In deference to my daughter, hey? In deference to my fiddlestick! Strike me purple! I like that; 'tis a jest that tickles my humor. In deference to your own precious skin, sir, ye should have said. But what can one expect from a puny commercial clown, from a thimble-rigging lawyer's clerk, or from a chuckle-headed chapman's 'prentice? Sooth, now I come to think, 'twould be daylight murder to draw on such as thou! I say again, y'are a mere mechanical peace-on-earth-and-good-will-toward-men civilian. Just that!" and this elderly Bobadil snapped his fingers in my face.

This was a terrible strain on a young man's pride and self-control. My hands itched, my fingers trembled, and the blood tingled in my veins.

"Sir!" I began furiously, when Mistress Marvin lightly touched my hand.

"Be merciful to *me*," she whispered; and somehow, strengthened by this new appeal, I managed with a struggle to overcome my very righteous anger.

"Dorothy, ye little beast, let go my coat!"

"Father," quoth the maid, dauntless as ever, and with sublime earnestness painted on her face, "you insult this gentleman."

"Silence, thou brazen chit."

"I say you insult him, sir! Dost know he is the kinsman

and next of kin to Sir Peter Armstrong of Copeland Hall? And you are aware that house is as famed for courage as our own. I never heard of a white-livered Armstrong yet."

At that the knight looked me keenly over, and declared—

"Why, to be sure, he is the image of his kinsman, mine old friend, Sir Peter. I wondered where I had seen that face."

At this revelation of my lineage and high connections his anger wonderfully evaporated.

"You will now understand, sir, that it is only at my express request that Master Armstrong declines to draw his sword," continued the indomitable Dorothy, who, like a skilful general, made haste to follow up her first advantage.

"Let no more be said," quoth Sir Nicholas in a fit of colossal generosity. "Since the lad hath avowed his fault, and eaten his words, we'll take it for granted that he hath the fighting spunk of the tough Armstrong stock. Yet, lad, hearken to an old soldier's advice: let not thy tongue wag so fast hereafter wi'out thou art minded to back it with sword as——"

"Bosh!" cried the maid, releasing his coat at last.

However, she at once showed she had by no means exhausted her designs upon his person, for she seized his right hand and placed it in mine.

At first we felt and looked very like a couple of snarling dogs, till I chanced to peep at the charming creature who had so cleverly patched up the truce between us, and I saw an expression of such lively gratitude on her face that I smiled at my enemy, whereupon he smiled too, and so the peace was consummated. The knight drew his delighted and triumphant daughter towards him.

"Master Armstrong," he declared, "a forward minx is this, sir! I have given Martin orders to procure a curb for her."

Afterwards the relentless barbarian betook himself to the original cause of the contention, as he further examined the bleeding wrist.

"Best go, my lass, and have some brine rubbed in, and then a drop or two of balsam."

"Ugh!" she exclaimed, even her bravery not proof against this. "Not that horrid balsam, papa—it hurts terribly, and salt is very keen."

"Hurt, be hanged, thou great milksop! How would ye be on the field o' battle, with half your face shorn away, as I have been? Ye might be permitted to speak a word then. But to make a wry lip over a paltry skin-breaking—bah!—I have no patience!"

"I am not a milksop, sir!" she said quickly, but for all that there was fear in her face. Yet without another word she darted up the steps, and left the knight and me to follow at our leisure.

CHAPTER VI.

A BALM FOR THE CARK OF CARE.

THE knight conducted me indoors to a bright and spacious room at the end of the entrance hall. It appeared particularly cheery and attractive by contrast with the gloomy weather, as the table was spread for breakfast, and a fire was glowing in the grate.

Sir Nicholas having recovered his equanimity, proffered me a seat beside the hearth, whilst he assumed one opposite. Only a few words of conversation passed ere the young lady joined us, her scathe bound up more exactly in a clean bandage.

"Ye don't find much amiss with it now, my lass?" inquired the knight, giving a sharp glance to the injured member.

"N-no, sir, n-not much," gasped the suffering maid, her mouth compressed, and her eyes full of pain.

"Master Armstrong," she said, turning to me and trying might and main to speak as though naught ailed her, "I must beg you to excuse my father and myself for ten minutes, that we may the more fittingly entertain you. This, sir, is Dr. Samuel Butler's 'Hudibras' to beguile the time; or stay"— and something of a smile played on a face so lately wan— "perhaps Dr. Joseph Alleine, pious man! more nearly befits your taste? Here is his 'Alarm to the Unconverted.' I'm proud to say 'tis bravely thumbed and dog's-eared—reflects real credit on me, you'll admit, sir."

Upon that they left the apartment. Still "Hudibras" remained unopened that morning, for mine eyes were busied with a careful contemplation of the room. 'Twas one truly beautiful; had a wide expanse of carpet, and was relieved of the faintest tinge of sombreness by low broad windows that admitted daylight in abundance. The most salient item was a big display of warlike implements that occupied the whole of the right-hand wall; and as the firelight radiated on them, they quivered brightly in their glittering profusion. I was examining them in open admiration when the knight re-entered.

6

"Ha, ha!" he exclaimed, well satisfied.   "Mon cher, I see
thou hast eyes for the right knick-knacks.   What think you o'
that sword?   Stamped Perillo, and the trustiest blade Julian
del Rey ever banged hammer to.   'Tis of wrought Mondragon
steel, and hath served our family for three generations.   I have
it in my memory how, when we lay before Nimeguen, it hewed
a bull-necked Dutchman's head clean off his body——"

"And how, at Naseby, it bit through the headpiece of a
captain in Ireton's musketeers," put in Mistress Dorothy, who
had slipped in unobserved behind us.

She had doffed her bespattered riding-dress in favor of a
more becoming garment, and had also disposed of the dirt that
so ill accorded with her skin.   If she had previously animated
me with admiration of her beauty, she charmed me now.   I
was completely bewitched by those melting mirthful eyes,
those mocking lips, and that mouth which was made for laughter.
Her form was tall and lissome as a willow; and each line of
it was grace.   Like her father, she bore every inch of height
very straight and easy, nor could she take ten steps but what
she must do so in a regal manner.   She carried her head
in a dainty way; there was archness in every feature of her
face; a furtive sauciness, a lingering tinge of flippancy; and
her general tone and bearing were a delicious mingling of
coquetry and pride.   Yet underlying this was a something
high-bred, a something queenly, a something imperious and
commanding, that at once forbade all liberties; whilst a black-
brown mass of wavy hair, and a jaunty cluster of precocious
curls, wayward as their owner, exalted the charms of her tantalizing countenance.

Razor and neckcloth had wrought material improvement in
the knight; yet far surpassing their beneficence was a gorgeous
periwig, superbly curled, and strongly charged with fluffy powder.
Without further delay the meal was given our best attention.   In
a short time the host was all good nature, and it occurs to me
that a man's temper differs according to the condition of his
stomach.

Sir Nicholas adorned the table-head, his daughter the table-
foot, whilst I was ensconced midway betwixt the two.

Unfortunately, peace was not allowed to long prevail.   The
soldier stuck a knife into an ill-cooked pie; then scowled, and
sought further refuge in his fine invective powers.

"This *pâté* hath far too much tint upon it.   It comes stiff
to the knife instead of yielding gently.   Faugh! it sets my
teeth on edge.   What has that jolterhead been about?"

The bell-rope received a vicious tug. A servant answered it.
"Send that dolt of a John hither!" roared the angry master.
A meek-visaged, placid fellow shortly appeared..

"John, thou nincompoop, dost see this *pâté de Perigord?* Art
not sore ashamed? Dost mark this uppercrust? Thou hast
had an hour o' the wooden-horse in thy campaigning days with
a shot bag round each ankle for a much smaller offence.
Would that I had one in the courtyard now!" He glared at
the mild cook, who answered not, but bowed his head in silent
humility.

"Thou art a graceless varlet, John. There, that is for thee,
John!" And to my amazement the irascible gentleman seized
an empty drinking-glass, and hurled it at the erring servant's
head. That personage caught it deftly in one hand, and
silently replaced it upon the table. He bowed, and left the
room, whilst the knight resumed the business of eating with a
very threatful countenance.

Presently a more important and more discomfiting incident
occurred. There was a knock at the door, and Martin the
groom entered. Instantly I perceived that he had a silver
coin in one hand. Mistress Dorothy was quick to see it, too,
whereupon she gave a hasty glance towards me, then settled
herself more firmly in her chair, and as she did so the look on
her face almost seemed to say, "I'm in for it now!" After
that she assumed an air of meekness by way of preparation for
the coming storm.

Martin stated his case concisely; and during the course of
the charge it alarmed me to see the knight working himself into
another tantrum. Finally, the triumphant Martin, who at every
word betrayed enmity towards his mistress, informed his master
of the bribe, and deposited that incriminating piece of silver by
the side of the lady's plate with a look of malicious glee.

"Wench, is this true?"

"Every word of it, sir," she said submissively, though methinks I saw that in her eye which proved her not quite so
humble as her tone implied.

The knight demanded an explanation. This the lady gave.
Upon receipt of it he commenced a torrent of abuse and im-
precation, which the recipient promptly cut short by rising and
giving him (bold as you please) a stately curtsey. She then
darted a look at the gleeful Martin, that might have withered
him had he possessed nerves or feelings, and with the air of a
haughty lady, bade him follow her from the room.

The pair of them having departed for the stables, Sir Nicholas
said to me in an ugly tone—

"What would you do, sir, with one so wilful? From men I
have commanded obedience throughout my life, yet I find it
easier to exact it from a troop of horse than from this young
chit. She flouts me at every twist and turn! She hath no
heed for chiding; if I threaten to beat her she vows she'll ne'er
touch a razor more, or will not dress my gouty foot. If I
threaten her with a return to that French convent she once was
so well acquainted with, the saucy minx declares I should
languish, or pine away for lack of kind attention. 'Tis sad,
very sad, Master Armstrong, to be afflicted with a kindly and
forbearing heart like mine; it makes one the butt of any
springald. But, by my soul, sir, ere I am a day older I'll have
an alteration! I'll teach that impudent hussy that I am no
longer to be played with."

I smiled at the arbitrary sentiments he indulged against his
beautiful tormentress. Quickly she returned. By this her
lofty disdain had fled, for laughter lit her eyes. She ran
blithely across the carpet, and halted by her father's elbow.

"I have set poor Wallenstein aright, old dad! I have applied a rare remedy to his scathe, and a warm feed lies at his
nose. He wants for nothing; neither do I, sweetest, but a kiss
from thee!"

Prettily she proffered her cheek for its reception, but her
angry sire vehemently denounced the wheedler, her delinquen-
cies, and her blandishments. Yet, mark you, kinsmen, never
for an instant did he allow his eye to stray whither the luring
bait awaited him. Much wisdom was to be found in this, for
I'll swear, had he once beheld it, 'twould have been farewell to
resolutions, for none save an anchorite could have been proof
against its loveliness.

Thwarted though she was, the maid concealed her defeat
under a smile, and as she resumed her seat, she favored me
with a glance of mischief. Our appetites being of the best
that morning she stacked our platters anew. These ministrations briskly performed, she looked at her father, and with a
face of exceeding gravity, said—

"Papa, touching our opinions of last week, I may say I still
maintain that naught can equal well-trained infantry on the
field of battle."

"Hey, what?" quoth the old soldier, bristling with attention. Even now I smile at the effect of her words. The old
gentleman forgot his wrongs in a moment, and was soon plunged
in a deep and, to my mind, incomprehensible argument. And
all the time I ne'er failed to observe his artful antagonist had

the same light in her eyes, and the same twitching at the corners of her mouth I have already mentioned.

"What sayest thou, Dorothy? I defy thee prove thy words!"

"Without any manner of doubt I can prove them, sir, and that right easily! The valiant and learned Montecuccoli lays it down to the effect that, '*Infanterie est comme la base et le soutien de l'armée, soit pour les batailles soit pour les siéges, et c'est avec elle que les Romains et les Suisse ont fait des choses si admirables. L'infanterie doit donc la principale force, et la grande partie de l'armée.*' There, sir! can you gainsay that?"

"Bah! ma petite, 'tis all nonsense! What doth that beggarly Italian know about the matter?"

"You do him a wrong, sir. I will not hear him miscalled. There is no man of this generation better versed in the theory of war. He was also named as a fine captain in the Thirty Years' War, and again bear in mind, sir, the great things he did against the Turks in Transylvania."

"Pish! a mere pack of heathen Mohammedans."

"Yet remember Trèves, remember Trèves, sir!"

"Donnerwetter! lass, shall I ever forget it? I was there myself that day, and saw the greatest captain of the age perish."

"And this same Montecuccoli? He drove the whole army across the Rhine like chaff before the wind," exclaimed this warlike mistress with a ring of triumph in her voice.

"So be it, wench; ye score one there. Yet out of mine own experience, what of Edgehill, Marston Moor, and Naseby? Didn't Rupert (God bless him!) sweep the Roundheads' left clean off the field? My girl, those were the times. We had the grandest cavalry in Europe, and, on my soul, the grandest commander too! 'Twas knee to knee then, and saddle-bows all of a row. 'Twas the sight of a lifetime to see us sweep over the field, a-laughing at Essex or old Noll Cromwell, and to see those psalm-singing Puritans chuck down their tucks and run. Don't talk to me of infantry! Did ever footmen do such deeds?"

I can ne'er forget the old warrior at that moment. Mayhap he felt himself bestride his charger again. Verily the breath of lusty manhood had returned to his time-worn frame. His voice was pitched to its utmost, his eye ablaze with a glowing fire, and the rapid movements of his body, and his wild gesticulations, one and all bespoke his intense excitement, and proclaimed the vividness of his recollection.

However, his daughter staunchly maintained her ground, in no wise daunted by this enthusiasm, though I must admit, under cover of it she took occasion to forward to me another eloquent glance of roguery.

"The famous Sir John Froissart," she continued, "avers that the footmen——"

"Confound Sir John Froissart!" interrupted the knight testily. "I will listen to none o' your musty chroniclers. I prefer the book of memory."

As it afterwards befell, it seemed the contest had scarce begun. For every episode the knight could recount demonstrating the superiority of cavalry, the lady had two at least to prove that infantry were better. The whole room rang with alarming talk of light horse, heavy horse, dragoons, musketeers, pikemen, escalados, camisados, onfalls, beleaguered garrisons, pallisados, estacados, mines, counter-mines, and a very Babel of amazing military jargon.

Of course I was a perfect ignoramus on such an abstruse subject. Swift as a falcon the girl divined this; and though her father was too wholly absorbed in the present topic to heed any alien matter, his quick-witted daughter mischievously appealed to me on a nice point, and to her own delight, and my discomfiture, I was compelled to exhibit ignorance.

For a considerable time the vantage fell to neither side, till at length Sir Nicholas mentioned some strange-sounding continental battle. Upon this his daughter pensively stroked her chin, and said with a fine show of reluctance—

"I am afraid this is a defeat, sir. 'Twill have to be a case of capitulation."

The knight, without a trace of his recent umbrage, rubbed his hands with gusto.

"But one moment, sir, I beg," cunningly said the lady, putting up one finger pertly. "This is to be a conditional surrender. You must allow the vanquished full honors of war."

"Quite right, ma chèrie; quite right."

Thereupon the vanquished rose and came to the victor's chair, and presented her cheek once more.

"The honors of war, papa," she said archly; and they were allowed forthwith.

Henceforward the elated warrior forgot recent resolutions, and displayed considerable good humor, which enhanced my amusement and his diplomatic daughter's satisfaction.

Breakfast disposed of, the knight would not hear of me taking my departure, until I had joined him in a game of piquet.

I, nothing loth, assented without demur, and soon the mysteries
of sword and musket were discarded for those, to my mind,
more alluring ones of piqueing, repiqueing, and capotting.

'Twas easy to see that my opponent had a keen love of gambling, and I being as crafty a rogue as God ever endowed with
breath, it must not surprise you to learn that Master Armstrong
was a loser that morning. Not a heavy one, certainly ; but his
losses were of sufficient amount for the knight to taste the sweets
of gain. At the conclusion of the game the blind fool said to me—

" Young man, we have very little company here, yet I shall
be willing to have as much of thine as thou'rt willing to bestow
upon us. Come as often as you like, and the more you come
the better I'll be pleased ; for I have already a liking for you,
and I have had a liking for piquet this fifty years."

And when this invitation was zestfully seconded by his
daughter, ye may judge my approbation. 'Twas plain I had
made a most favorable impression, and in my folly I vowed
that I would neglect no chance for its maintenance. The delight of that morning ! I, who had been in the depth of that
abyss, despair, had now my youthful passions kindled. I already felt myself a slave to that exquisite emotion I of all men
had least right to pander to. For was not the man who sat by
that enchanting maid, who marked her every bewitching movement, Black Ned, the thief, the proscribed, the outlaw ? He
was drunk with rapture. Drink ! drink ! weak wretch, drink
and be merry ! Away carking care ! give place to this ravish-
ment ! Let there be no thought for the morrow, no counting
of the cost !

Before I took my departure, Mistress Marvin importuned me
into going with her to a corner of the courtyard where her pets
were housed. Among this curious collection were to be found
a fox, a weasel, a couple of stoats, a couple of ferrets, and half
a dozen dogs, in which motley company she took considerable
pride, and, what is more, handled several of its vicious members
with exemplary skill. Upon leaving these animals she accompanied me to the stables, where Martin was discovered sulky
of aspect, and impotently grumbling under his breath. Joe
looked very handsome now the mire was brushed from his glossy
coat, and Mistress Dorothy's eyes glowed at sight of him.

" Master Armstrong," she said enthusiastically, " what a
splendid fellow he is ! How smart he looks ! and whoever saw
such fine legs and such a depth of chest ? And I say, sir, he
is the very shape of a jumper. Wouldst be so kind as to allow
me to put him at that fence ? "

I looked at the fence in question, and it was of such height that I should have been chary myself of asking him to leap it. Yet how could I say her nay? How could I resist the eager anticipation painted on her face?

"You are at liberty to try him at it, mistress," said I; "but I must admit I have some trepidation for your safety."

"Thank you, sir," she answered, delightedly commencing to adjust her saddle on him. "You need not have the slightest fear for either of us. I am quite sure he will clear it like a bird, though I have not yet got any of ours over it, and Tilly nearly broke my neck the other week. But I'm certain old Joe's the man for the job—aren't you, my splendid fellow?"

This may have been very reassuring, yet I had my doubts upon the point.

The rain had now ceased falling, and in a trice the daring girl was in the saddle. She cantered him gently to the far end of the yard to give him a good sweep for the spring. I felt more nervous than I'd like to own, and wished the matter safely finished. Just then Sir Nicholas joined me, and though an interested spectator he by no means shared my tremors.

Presently horse and rider came thudding by with a mighty clatter. Mistress Marvin rode as I had ne'er seen a woman ride before. She sate with extraordinary grace and ease, and never gave at all to the horse's motion, but remained firm as a rock in the saddle very like a cavalryman. However, the twain rose nobly at the critical moment, and the fence was cleared.

"Bravo!" I cried, much relieved in mind.

Directly afterward they sailed over from the other side, and clattered down and joined us.

"'Pon my soul, I call that uncommonly well done!" exclaimed the knight.

Mistress Dorothy reined Joe up sharp, slipped off his back with great agility, warmly caressed him, sent Martin to the house for sugar, then turned to us with a face of triumph.

"You have got to improve yet, ma petite," said her critical sire. "You inclined that left shoulder somewhat, and swerved a little as you took the spring. How many more times must you be told? Still, 'twas done very well; you may embrace me."

The maid, though flushed and breathless with exertion, was wonderous quick to seize this opportunity, and kissed him; and, what is more, unquestionably thought the act a luxury.

Host and hostess pressed me to stay to dinner, which invitation I declined. Yet so deeply had our game of piquet entered into the knight's mind, that he earnestly hoped I would pay another visit that same evening, which I readily promised to do.

'Twas within a few minutes of noon that I started for the King's Head, Bridgwater.

My spirit, lately so jaded, rose again, the herbage seemed greener, the air purer; and all nature more lovely to my gaze than it had appeared for many a month. And as I betook myself towards that goodly hostel, a neighboring squire passed me, and I knew his purse was heavy because it was market day. He was unarmed and unattended, yet he went his way unchallenged. Why was this? Surely, kinsmen, ye need no telling.

CHAPTER VII.

IN WHICH WE CONTINUE TO ENJOY THE SOCIETY OF EDWARD ARMSTRONG, GENTLEMAN.

THERE is a cheerful hostelry at Bridgwater, a house of genial entertainment, which hath the sign of the King's Head swinging above the doorpost. To this day it is a place where a man may be boarded and bedded with the best, but it can in nowise compare with its own beneficence in a bygone time, when Master Peter Whipple was host and landlord. During the period of my outlawry this hostelry was generally my abode, whence I would return each night, upon the transaction of the infamous business of the day.

In '88, which is the time I speak of, by sheer force of my genius for evil, my trade had become a flourishing concern; whilst I myself, to take a merely mercantile view of things, had become prosperous, opulent, and easy. I had attained the topmost pinnacle of my fame. It stretched the length and breadth of Somerset, whilst in a fair portion of Devon and Wiltshire my name and deeds blanched stout men's cheeks, and were the marvel of every household. Reputation standing thus so very high, folks dared not deny Black Ned, but surrendered their purses to him at the first demand. To be sure, the grace of the compliance was not always of the best; but argument was rarely used, whilst violence was ne'er so much as thought of. Therefore pistols (the delight of plebeian villains) were seldom exhibited.

Now I can only account for this docility in my shorn lambs

on the assumption that they one and all possessed an obliging disposition; also because (as it seems to me) that, as mankind hath it upon high authority that "discretion is the best part of valor," my conscientious victims felt it their bounden duty to act according to the text.

As for sheriff's men, so often had they been dodged, tricked, bamboozled, or led into an awkward pickle, that they became a laughing-stock for half the West, and thus were rightly glad, after a lapse of time, to relinquish a fruitless quest. 'Twill thus be seen I went unmolested, save when some exploit more impudent than the common run came to the ears of justice. Then half the magistrates in the shire would meet the sheriff at dinner, and suggest what should be done in the matter. Fine words would be uttered, good wine would be drunk, and the sheriff would issue a proclamation. And 'twixt the plenishing of the cups they'd all agree that Black Ned was a base, bad rogue, who must have his wings clipped, and that it was somebody's duty to set about and clip them. And they'd further agree that it was perfectly plain to the civilized world that they should have been clipped before, and that somebody was to blame (who they couldn't precisely say, but certainly nobody present), because the job was still undone. They would then wind up by drinking His Majesty's health—God bless him!—by going home tipsy, and by debiting His Majesty's Government ten guineas for justiciary expenses. For a brief while afterwards a brave effort would be made to arrest the rogue aforesaid, though in a fortnight, at farthest, this lukewarm energy would become quite cool, and Master Ned, utterly oblivious of the law's long arm, would continue to walk any way he listed. Accordingly, I might sit under a weatherproof thatch of an evening, and enjoy a supper, a black jack, and a pipe as comfortably as the smuggest go-to-meeting burgher. But at best it was a haphazard life; when all good instincts were rudely stifled; when life was accounted a little thing; when the devil was blindly served; and when the vague hereafter lacked any consideration whatsoever.

Mid-day had passed an hour, when Joe carried me into the inn yard of the King's Head. The faithful animal was quickly fixed in the stall which was always kept at his disposal, and then I betook myself to the snuggest little parlor ever conjured by the fancy of a weary man. I found a solitary individual within, ensconced in an armchair, busy upon the reckoning of a customer.

A queer fellow was this, not much above a yard in height,

with a couple of slits for eye-holes, through which peeped a pair of bead-like orbs. A stubbly chin and a fat person most folks would notice, yet more particularly the latter feature ; for if you took the girth and then the length of him, the difference would be scarce perceptible.

This was Peter Whipple, who had a larger brain than any three men of my acquaintance. Mine host peered upwards from the bill. Quoth he—

"Ods bodkins ! 'tis mine old friend, Ned, and with an empty belly, I ween." He puckered his ratty eyes till scarce aught was left of them, and indulged an ugly grin by way of kindly greeting. "What would accord with thy appetite, lad ?" he asked.

"Methinks I sniffed a hot venison pasty nigh at hand," said I ; "that and a jug of malt liquor would fit my palate nicely."

"Thou hast but to name the dish, and it shall be set before thee," was his cheerful answer. "Brains before brawn, say I ; so, Ned, lad, those heavy-limbed bumpkins i' the other room may wait awhile."

And wait they had to do ; nor was their meal relished the less by me because my stomach was comforted thereby instead of their own capacious paunches.

Master Whipple had flow of speech sufficient for a dozen men or half a dozen women. Thus I was extensively regaled with conversation, whilst I dined excellently well, yet only three-fourths of my meal had reached its rightful destination, when a raw-boned farmer strode into the room, and one look showed his brow was black and his dudgeon high.

"How now, landlord ! How much longer have friend Jobson and I to wait for our dinners ? If this is the way you treat your guests, methinks it is a crying shame, sir ; and I, for one, will not brook it !"

He was evidently a well-to-do fellow, with a liberal idea of his own importance, to judge by his tone and demeanor. Master Whipple let few things escape him, and once having learned a fact, he seldom failed to turn it to the best advantage.

"Just one moment, your worship, I beg," replied Pete, in a voice of obsequious humility. "Well knowing your honor's quality, I gave my rascally cook fully to understand that you would not abide ill-cooked victuals, and that it most certainly behoved him to give his very best attention to the venison pasty. But, sink me ! the careless jackanapes must needs let it burn, doubtless because he was told to be so careful. 'Pon my word, your worship, I'd sooner go to perdition than set such scurvy fare before one of your station. I' faith, one corner's nigh burnt to a cinder. However, the varlet is cooking another, and I do hope, good sir, you will this time forgive him. And if your honor be so pleasantly minded, ye shall not lack for compensation neither. Now, I am aware your cellar is of the best, yet I'll wager it hath no such wine betwixt its walls as I can put before you. Blister me, there is none to hold a candle to it throughout the county! 'Deed, I can truthfully say it stands unsurpassed over the length and breadth of England, save and except for that small, that very small, quantity His Gracious Majesty hath in his cellars at Whitehall. When the Bishop of Wells, t'other week, clapped his lips to the least drop of my glorious Tokay, so much was he smitten with its luscious, generous qualities, that he ordered a butt of it, forthwith, vowing that never since he was born had he tasted such heavenly grape-juice.

"Now, I am a godfearing man, as the world doth full well know, and the saints forefend that I should cast disparagement upon so pious a prelate ; yet, if the truth must be told, I laughed out loud, your worship—yea, I laughed out loud, when his reverence gave that order. Such is the beauty of this rarest of vints that, were the Pope of Rome to drop down on his knees for one bottle only, he'd go wanting. Yet, your honor having been so sadly neglected, I will e'en undertake that you and your friend shall each have a taste of it; nor shall the charge be excessive. Your delicate palates will ne'er forget the smack of it, I'll warrant."

Master Peter was the glibbest liar I ever heard. Besides, his untruths were so highly colored and so deftly clothed with verisimilitude, that it mostly needed a very keen discrimination to sort the fact from the figment. Now Pete's elaborate lie was palmed upon the unwary yeoman with such an attitude of studied deference, with such a deep politeness (acquired by long residence in London), and with such a circumstantial wealth of detail, that the honest man was quite staggered, and straightway forgot his wrongs, and even began to make excuses for his own uncivil behavior.

And all the time that self-same pasty stuck in my throat; and so immensely tickled was I at mine host's methods, that I nearly choked myself in trying to suppress my laughter. Touching another circumstance, whoever caused Master Whipple to modify his tone, as of late he had to do, would surely have to pay a pretty price for the same when it came to the settling of the bill. Humility had to be bought from him like more toothsome commodities.

"I hope you will not forget that wine, landlord," said the farmer, as he left us to rejoin his friend at the board.

"To be sure, the landlord will not forget," quoth Pete, as the door closed behind him.

"To charge it in the score," I added, laughing.

"To the devil with all country bumpkins," said he, flicking his thumb to his nose, as I have heard is the most approved mode of expressing contempt in Town. "They are as loose-tongued as dukes if aught goes amiss; yet do but flatter their dignity, and so blown out are they in their own conceit that they e'en forget on which side the grievance lies."

"Doubtless they will wax fat on that famous Tokay of thine?" said I mischievously; and I must observe, by way of explanation, that to me Master Whipple's methods were by no means new.

The innkeeper shook his head in a way that reminded me of that sagacious bird, the owl, and sighed the most comical sigh I ever listened to.

"My friend," said he, in his driest manner, "It will .be duly paid for in the bill. The pleasures of this life are in anticipation, and not in realization. The fee for this noble wine will be fetched from out their fobs, and having been paid for, who shall say they have not had it? D'ye see, it matters not to their great gullets (neither can they mark the difference) betwixt the truest Hainault vintage, and the washiest stuff that ever came from over the water. Enough of such senseless wights. Let us return to Long Bob Bickers. He was a man, if ever one walked on this earth. Such days will ne'er be seen again, as when he did these roads." And then, as his custom was when he dwelt upon this immortal though melancholy topic, his feelings overcame him, and tears sped quickly down his cheek.

"I recollect one shrewd trick of his," he resumed, striving like a man against this weakness. "He'd come in here of a market day, such as this is, and bold as you please would walk into the parlor. He'd find the squires and farmers there, a chatting about the price of bullocks, the prospect of the crops, and such like. And as they sate a-puffing at their pipes, and a pulling at their liquor, he'd make 'em his very best bow, whip out his barkers, and with his noted economy of words would say, 'Gentlemen, your purses.' Then they, stuck as their own porkers, would shut their mouths, open their fobs, and just cough up the bullion! 'Come, landlord,' he'd say, 'I show no favor.' So out would come mine as well. Yet, mark you •

this most carefully, mine old dogskin would find its way back to my breeches pocket the very next day, with five more guineas therein than ever it went away with. Here's peace to thy soul, Bob Bickers, may thy heart rest easy!"

Thereupon mine host raised his cup, pledged Long Bob's health, and drowned his woe in a draught of cider. Having swallowed his melancholy with his own toast, quoth he again, with a queer look—

"Ned, the front parlor is full of pursy yeomen. Now I hope thou hast not already forgotten what I have just told thee."

Seeing I had no mind to imitate the example of the illustrious Long Bob, Master Whipple looked grave, and forthwith imparted one of his favorite pieces of information; to wit, that Squire Pocock of Athelney had started on the homeward journey scarce an hour agone, with a goodly number of gold pieces upon his person. Neither did this rouse me to action, whereupon Master Peter made inquiry as to the cause of such inactivity.

"Young man," said he, "it appears to me thou art surely neglecting business. Why is this?"

"Can't I take a holiday, then, without asking your permission?" I answered in an injured tone, that he might quit the subject. To tell the truth (as in honor bound I must), the precise reason was, that for that day at least I had no stomach for my calling. Now you are to plainly understand, Black Ned was still an absentee. It was Master Edward Armstrong, the man who had met that self-same morning a young maiden, fair to the eye, and delicious to the recollection, bearing the name of Mistress Dorothy Marvin, who had just eaten his midday meal at the King's Head, and who thus confronted Peter Whipple. How could this gentleman of lineage think of any such rascally proceeding as highway robbery, especially as the events of that self-same day were still piping hot in his brain? Moreover, this worthy fellow did not by any means forget that evening, about the hour of sunset, to don his choicest suit and his silver-buckled shoon. Also, by the aid of fair words and a guinea, he borrowed, for one night only, Master Whipple's church-going tie-wig; though he had greatly preferred a periwig. But a decent one was not to be gotten at so short a notice, except of a very uncouth, provincial style; while his host (though a London man) declared in all his life he had ne'er paid a penny for such a pretentious article, because, as he said in his meekest manner, "he was too modest, and too deeply sensible of his own unworthiness to ever think of strutting to church in a peruke."

With the coming of darkness I stepped forth on foot to the manor, for I thought it unlikely that any one would recognize the highwayman in the darkness; neither was it probable that he would have been molested, had such a contingency arisen. The night was as sloppy as ever the day had been, and miserably cold withal. Yet naught was heeded in the elements, for being well and warmly cloaked, I set my best leg foremost, careless of wind and water.

The kindest of welcomes awaited me. Maybe it was over-pride of my smart habiliments, yet I most positively assured myself that father and daughter regarded me with pleased surprise. And, without boast, I appeared a very comely young man. The old knight and I zestfully played piquet (at least he did, and I made great show of interest); and Mistress Dorothy, instead of being busy with her needle, as I believe young girls should be in their leisure, worked hard and perseveringly at a fishing-net.

"Great sport this afternoon, Master Armstrong!" she cried, with the glow of the enthusiast. "I landed three eels, half a dozen perch and bream, also a pike, and that pike was nine pounds six, sir!"

"No lies," the knight inserted. "'Twas not an ounce beyond six pounds."

"Sir Nicholas Marvin," fired back his daughter, "you are no fisherman. Stick to the sword, sir—you can fight, but you can't fish."

Well, we played piquet, did the knight and I, and he was very happy during the course of it. He won, you must understand, and if a winning game gives no pleasure, then indeed it must be a singularly poor one. And was I also happy? To be sure I was; but mind, in a game of a wholly different nature. Part of my game consisted in glancing often (that is, as many times as delicacy would permit) towards nimble fingers, on a beauteous hand, on a lovely arm, on a delightful form!

By and by Sir Nicholas fell a-nodding, and no wonder, for the punch bowl demanded his attention many times. Had Master Edward Armstrong, aged twenty-four, been as well conducted as you and I had thought him, he must, without a shade of doubt, at once have bidden host and hostess a prompt goodnight; for, as we are all of us aware, he had been invited to play piquet, and for nought else whatsoever.

And why did he not act thus? Well, the rain beat hard on

the window-panes, the wind howled dismally, no moon was visible midst the wrack of rain-cloud, and verily the night was black as pitch.   And the fire emitted a welcome glow, all was cheerfulness and comfort within those four walls, and, furthermore, even the knight's slumbering resonance was in harmony. I warrant this is some excuse, if not quite sufficing for your prudishness.

Now, with his opponent asleep, what kinder occupation could this young man find than to talk sociably to the even younger maiden close beside him ?   Come ! high-principled people (for, children, you have long since grown tall enough to talk of " principle," " example," etcetera), your niceness cannot surely suggest anything very wrong in what I am now unfolding. Therefore Mistress Marvin and I held converse with one another—friendly, amiable converse; and the maid was young and very beautiful ; and I !—ah, what was I !—a fugitive, an outlaw, and a thief !

I learned many things that night, some of which lend a pertinent bearing towards this history.   The knight was a soldier to the backbone, one who had lustily struck for the ill-fated monarch Charles the First, and afterwards for his son,—the second Charles.   But after paralyzing his patrimony for their behoof, he was compelled to flee to foreign lands, where the fear of high-crowned hats and plaguy hymnals ceased to haunt him.

With good courage and a lean purse, what more likely than this unfortunate scion of noble family should look to the sword as a source of livelihood ?   Therefore he took service under the French king, Louis XIV., and participated in many actions on his behalf, and his valor and stainless honor won him advancement in the army of France.

Somewhat late in life he wedded a French lady of high birth, and a disciple of the Roman Church.   Their married life was not of long duration, for within a year she died in child-bed, and thus Dorothy ne'er knew a mother's love.

Until Sir Nicholas returned to his native land, with coffers well replenished (for his wife had left him goodly means), his only child passed some years in a convent.   The knight had now been four years at the manor, the home of his childhood, and his daughter had crossed the water with him.   This much I gleaned from Mistress Marvin's lips that night, and it amused me, when she came to tell me about the convent, to see her give a shudder of disgust.

The hour was late ere I crossed the outer threshold into the uninviting night. However, before I had wrapped my cloak around me, previous to departing, the sleepy knight awoke himself, thanks to an overplus of snoring, and bid me come the next evening to play him again, and to this invitation I made no demur, but accepted it readily.

It was an evening unfit for a dog to be abroad in, yet the journey to the King's Head seemed of the shortest, though at ordinary times it is a lengthy step. Once, by misadventure, I walked into a ditch beside the roadway, but swore not at this mishap, e'en though I felt the muddy water penetrate my stockings. The reason of this forbearance was not far to seek; it simply went unheeded, inasmuch that dancing before me in the gloom was the phantasy of a maid with wondrous eyes.

It was a wakeful time, was my sojourn in bed that night. Still it was a pleasing insomnolence. Nought could drive an entrancing vision from mine head.

According to promise, I paid another visit to Kelston Manor the following night, and the reception accorded me was equally as hearty as those I had at other times received. 'Twas evident I by no means abused my welcome, for Sir Nicholas proposed that I should come and play with him every week-day evening when it was possible for me to do so. And I in my folly had no more sense or foresight than to accede to this request. One night, during the first week, an incident befell that unsteadied my nerves, and for the instant seemed both dangerous and irksome. In the course of our usual game, Sir Nicholas gave me a shrewd look and said—

"Mon ami, if I did not know you to be an Armstrong, I should take you to be own brother to Black Ned the highwayman."

At that moment, by a singular mischance, a coin fell and rolled under the table, and without waiting to reply I dived below in quest of it. A very stubborn coin it was, and it took some little time to find. And where do you think it was discovered, kinsmen? Under Master Armstrong's foot!

Upon returning to my seat, a laugh greeted me from Mistress Dorothy.

"On my word!" she said gayly, "art not very proud, sir? Sir Nicholas doth flatter you by his comparison. My compliments to Master Armstrong on the achievement of his early fame. Black Ned shall be his name in future."

Fortunately I had the sense to laugh at her sally, and the matter passed away without assuming a more formidable shape than one of banter.

7

A week passed quickly. Every evening at sundown I failed not to appear at the manor to gamble with the knight, ánd afterwards to talk with that delightful maid, his daughter. These conversations commenced when the knight dropped off to sleep, and as a general rule he surrendered to seductive Morpheus somewhere about the eighth serving of brandy punch ; and I may also add, to accommodate the curious, that my losses at the card-table, during those first six days, amounted to the sum of thirty guineas.

CHAPTER VIII.

HIGH TREASON.

I now come to such a startling phase in my narrative, that it behoves me to set it forth with due particularity, because, as you are to learn, it made an abiding impression upon my mind, and at the same time swayed my fortunes in a highly remarkable manner.

However, it will previously be necessary to indicate the precise relations existing at the time betwixt Sir Nicholas Marvin, his daughter, and myself.

Another week quickly sped, and, faithful to my word, I visited the manor each evening, Sunday excepted, for the knight's edification and mine own. Nay, I even exceeded this arrangement, as on several occasions I found myself there in the middle of the day. The cause of this should be all too obvious, for just as I was always happy when within sight of Mistress Marvin, I was rarely contented when I lacked the solace of her company. Fortune aided me in many ways. Sir Nicholas ne'er mixed in society of any kind, and seldom received a visit from anybody, for he maintained a most uncompromising attitude towards the neighboring county families, and they, I suspect largely on account of his uncouth habits, were at daggers drawn with him. As for Dorothy, she had no friends or kinsfolk this side the water, and as her father's quarrel was always her quarrel also, this staunch daughter, as she herself once told me, would rather have forfeited her tongue than she would have made the least concession toward the county folk. This all reacted to my advantage. For one thing the knight and the maid ne'er had any one to enlighten them as to whom I really was; and again, the friendless Dorothy, to my inexpressible delight, from the outset evinced considerable pleasure in my company, which pleasure she showed in a thousand little ways. Her nature was as frank, free, and simple as her speech. She suspected nothing; on the contrary, she made no secret that she found me a companion much after her own heart, and in her open way treated me as such. In fact, so little was her warm, eager, affectionate nature smothered and degraded by the polite imbecilities that nowadays constitute half the outfit of aristocratic misses, that she looked on me as a sort of boon companion, and in confidential moments allowed me to share many secrets of her heart and mind.

Her father, the most terrible of tyrants in any matter touching personal comfort, like the rest of the brethren of the selfish tribe, had no such compunction for other people. Yet he was certainly not unaware of my constant companionship with his young daughter. But he placed no restriction on either of us. To him I was simply a country gentleman, well born, well mannered, and of abundant leisure; and he summed up his own sentiments on the subject far more pointedly than I can hope to do when he said, "My lad, y'are an Armstrong; that is enough for me!" And so he ne'er gave the matter another thought, but just sat in his chair gambling, swearing, and bibbing unlimited brandy punch.

Day by day the young lady proved a fuller source of delight to me. Methought her a fearless, high-spirited, passionate girl, tingling with life and laughter. Some might have said she was a trifle rompish and coquettish, perhaps she was, tho' I'll ne'er be made to say so. And once for all I counsel you, do not take my judgment as infallible, the bare remembrance of Mistress Marvin in the flesh hath much corrupted it, and 'twill be no surprise to me, should I, ere I've done, write her down *divinity.* What I will say is, she adored her unlovely father; and was always invested with the wild charm of being never in repose. One moment she was perhaps sad, then coy, then romantic, then playful, then gay, then satirical, then genuinely affectionate; yet, whichever mood she might be in, she ne'er retained it two whole minutes. And if ever I was tempted to think her incapable of depth of thought or feeling, I had only to notice the unwearied attentions, and the boundless respect and reverence she never ceased to pay her ungrateful parent, to give me the lie direct. 'Twas here the divining-rod of observation struck the first inexplicable problem in her character; and if this was not in itself enough to puzzle me, I had only to observe her

firm mouth, and the subtle prominence of her chin, to feel that
great unknown qualities lurked behind her blithe-hearted everyday demeanor.

With these preliminaries, I will now relate those passages
between this lady and myself that revealed some of these hidden
qualities, and which caused me to temper admiration with
respect, and at the same time gave me much disquietude, and
many sleepless nights. I have carefully searched my memo-
randa for the day I first heard of the singular business that
preyed on my mind for weeks and months and finally altered
the whole tenor of my life. Still, despite my efforts, they have
been in vain. I cannot fix the exact date with any degree of
accuracy, though to the best of my recollection 'twas towards
the latter end of March or the beginning of April, the year of
grace 1688.

The sitting-room clock had just chimed the half-hour after
ten one evening at the manor, and Sir Nicholas according to
established custom had once more exchanged the wiles of liquor
for the wiles of sleep, when his daughter said in that tone half-
serious, half raillery she could so readily assume—

" I believe, Master Ned, you are an admirer of nature ? "

"You surprise me, mistress," said I ; " I was not aware of
that. Though I will never deny," I added, with a significant
look toward my fair companion, " I have great admiration for
certain specimens of *human* nature."

" Tush ! I cannot pretend to understand you, sir. But 'tis
a full moon to-night, and the stream and woodland look just
lovely. You must come with me and see it ; " and without
waiting for my reply she rose immediately, donned her cloak and
hat, and half-playfully, half-commandingly, bade me follow her.
Though certainly not reluctant in my obedience, I was surprised
at this, because it was contrary to our habitude, and I had not
credited her with poetic instinct strong enough to entice her
from a cosy room into the keen night air at this time of the
evening.

The manor grounds were indeed a noble sight. The moon
was gliding through a mass of cloud, casting a spectral light on
fern and bracken, and on the winding snakelike waters of the
stream. The tree-tops in the spinney were gilded with a shift-
ing tinge of silver, whilst now and then out of the dark recesses
of the copse, a plaintive note issued from some wary night bird's
throat; and the quick play of the ghastly moonbeams on glade
and thicket in varying tints of light and shade, gave to the whole
scene an eerie aspect of mingled ghostliness and grandeur.

We took a path at right angles from the house. This led us across the grass by the borders of the woodland, and onwards to the stream. All the way I cogitated on this strange excursion, and turned the unwonted circumstance over pretty carefully in my mind. At first my mental animation was altogether foiled; I could sniff no vestige of a clue to the lady's singular procedure, or to the motives underlying it.

" Mistress," said I, my scepticism still unshaken, " you are strangely silent anent the beauties of the landscape, and I will make so bold to add, strangely unobservant."

" Hush, Master Armstrong, hush!" she exclaimed, one finger on her lips. " The air breathes the very spirit of romance. I'm thinking of Charlemagne, and good King Rènè of Provence; of ladies' bowers and tournaments; of belted knights and troubadours." Here she sighed softly to herself, and broke off suddenly, as so often was her way, into a new strain of thought and sentiment. However on this occasion it may have owed something of its origin to her little rhapsody.

" The Copeland Armstrongs are a fine race," she said; and then seeing me perhaps a trifle self-complacent, continued swift as lightning, a saucy inflection in her tone and gesture, " Ah, Lud! I'm in error there; I've stumbled in the matter of the tenses. Why didn't I use the past instead of the present? The Copeland Armstrongs *were* a fine race would methinks have been more accurate; so, dear sir, forget thy bows and smirks, and thy vain prideful fribbling."

" I am grieved for this emendation, mistress," said I with mock gravity.

" E'en so! yet men were wont to call your family ' The Fighting Armstrongs'; though I cannot hear that the name runs now on the countryside."

" True, mistress, I fear me that the title is somewhat blown upon of late years. Mine uncle, Sir Peter, prefers the pursuit of gold to that of glory, and I—well, I am a mere civilian."

" Very soothful too, sir, though, nevertheless, I thank you for your forbearance towards my father the other morning," and she laughed at the reminiscence.

Next minute the red was in her cheeks, the fire was in her eyes.

" But why don't you preserve the tradition of your race, sir? " she cried. " Have your ancestors bequeathed you no spark of their martial nature? "

The words fell from her lips with a deep and clear vibration. The wild, romantical girl was upbraiding me; she did not know that I had paid bitter penalties, and was paying them still because I had cherished the spirit of my fathers.

What follows may have been a vagary of chance, or as I had come to apprehend some subtle motive in the conduct of the maid, it may have been a bold design pushed to a skilful issue. Be this as it may, her voice and bearing acted like a spark dropped into the powder mine that nestled in my soul. Every word thrilled me, the fiery qualities of my fathers leapt up from slumber, and made reply ere prudence, sense, or rationality, could impose a check upon them.

"Have no fear, mistress; have no fear!" said I airily. "I am not so degenerate an Armstrong as you seem to think. If I do not fling away my scabbard and wear my weapon naked for the behoof of all men, do not set too harsh a name to my inactivity. I have an end in view—I am husbanding my strength. My matchlock is oiled, and my sword blade bright and speckless. I am waiting, mistress!"

"Waiting for what, sir?"

"For the chance of a heart-thrust at the accursed Stuart!"

There and then I knew my folly. My companion gave a smothered exclamation, and placed one hand upon my arm, yet instantly removed it, and drew herself some yards apart from me.

By this we had come to the rustic wooden bridge that spans the stream. We stood together on the fragile planks, and suspended as we were midway, first gazed at one another in irksome silence, then at the flowing waters. 'Twas a strange moment as I leant on the rail and watched the rivulet crisp and sparkle under the rays of moonlight; and saw the quick flow of the current illumined by numberless shafts of light, that leapt and quivered on the surface of the stream as it glided 'twixt the vapor-shrouded banks and wound its way down towards the sea.

"Sir," quoth the maiden in a voice that startled me, after a pause as long as it was embarrassing, "you have been imprudent."

Imprudent! Was that the name to set to my indiscretion? Here had I confessed treasonous and revolutionary sentiments to one born and bred a Roman Catholic, and whose father, her mentor and her darling, had spent his fortune and his blood in the service of the Stuarts.

"Imprudent," I answered, overwhelmed with shame and dread of the consequences. "I have spoken like a fool."

"That depends upon your hearers," she said, and then to my

bewilderment this extraordinary creature seized my hand and gripped it. I stole a glance at her face, and ne'er can I forget its animation or her eyes as the light played on them, and set them sparkling like lustrous gems.

"I do not understand you, mistress," quoth I astounded; "is not your father an old Stuart cavalier, and are you not a Roman Catholic?"

"I, sir? I am a Whig—a tremendous Whig!"

I could have cried aloud with glee, her ringing tones and high enthusiasm were so infectious.

"Master Ned," she said excitedly, "if one word, one single word could save the House of Stuart, and 'twas left to me to speak that word, dost know it should never come from lips of mine? And if a blow could crush them, as please God it some day shall, I would ask nought better than that my arm should be the one to strike it!"

"Mistress, those are heartsome words. They come kinder to mine ears than any since my father died."

"He is dead, then?"

"Yes; murdered by James Stuart and his servant Jeffreys."

"Tell me the story."

"No, no; that I cannot do. There are certain passages in my life's history that may never be told." Thereat I shuddered to think on what terrible ground our conversation had nearly led me.

"Methinks," said I, attempting to divert our talk from the dangerous channel it was like to run in, "these words of ours might sound to a listener uncommonly like high treason."

"Just so," returned my companion, "though if King James doth not hear something much more to his cost, and very much more treasonous ere long, I'm mistaken."

"You are a politician, Mistress Dorothy."

"Politician—rather! In fact, sir, to quote the words of my illustrious papa, 'I'm the very devil for politics!'"

CHAPTER IX.

A PERILOUS MISSION.

KINSMEN, you may be sure no word of Mistress Marvin's fell upon deaf ears; my mind was already worked upon to a pitch of disquieting curiosity.   Her hints, her innuendoes, her affectation of secret knowledge, the enthusiasm of her voice, and the singularity of her whole demeanor convinced me that she had either some startling information at her command, else that she was a facile and highly schooled dissembler.   Howbeit, not for a moment did I do her the injustice of allowing my mind to dwell upon this alternative.

"My friend," continued the lady gravely, "since tho 'rt so reticent in the matter of thine own grievances, I will tell thee why Sir Nicholas, my father, is a Stuart man no longer.   In the first Charles's time he spent his fortune and much good blood in that monarch's cause, and when the end of the miserable business came he went into exile with scarce a rag to his back, or a groat in his hosen.   By and by the second Charles was crowned, and the Stuarts were once more affluent.   Straightway Sir Nicholas hied back to his native land, counting upon a handsome recompense for the many sufferings endured in his and his father's cause.   Bitter was his fate!   Charles Stuart, the King, forgot the rich promises of Charles Stuart, the Exile. Many faithful friends of the days of his adversity were sent penniless and heart-broken from Whitehall gates.   The King had no longer any use for them, and no longer any care.   Ne'er a silver shilling did they receive from him, i' faith hardly bare civility; yet every day he lavished such sums upon certain of his female friends as would have satisfied the most expectant of the Cavaliers.   My father was one of these unfortunate men. He cursed the false monarch in the bottom of his heart, and set off back across the water.   There he need beg no man's bounty, but could earn a decent pittance with the sword. From that day to this he hath not forgiven the House of Stuart : my father never forgives an injury.   For years he hath fed the fire of his animosity, and that cold bigot James hath added fuel to it.   Monmouth's rebellion crushed any respect Sir Nicholas might have borne him on the score of his father's memory.   He is, as you know, a staunch son of the West, and the wholesale butchery of his fellows was more than he could abide ; so now he and many of the greatest men in the realm are engaged on an enterprise that hath for its object the *downfall of the Stuarts*."

I uttered a half-audible cry.   Instantly there shot into my mind the results of its success, and what they meant to me.   I beheld a vista of cherished hopes : freedom, the chance to earn an honest livelihood, the revocation of my outlawry, the avenging of my father's death ! Sure the lady looked so intent at me that she must have read every phase of my emotion.

" Suppose," quoth she insinuatingly, " a share was proffered Master Armstrong in this conspiracy ? "

" For Heaven's sake, madam, don't play with my suscepti- bilities ! Dost know I have sworn to avenge my father's murder ? "

" Aha ! there spoke a Copeland Armstrong." And she smiled a smile there was no interpreting.

Then an uneasy silence came between us. For myself I was digging my nails into my palms and endeavoring by every means extant to suppress the visible signs of my excitement. And I believe my most remarkable companion was trying to gauge the depths of my sincerity, and how far she would be justified in communicating great secrets to my bare word of honor. At least it struck me that this was her employ. Now this hesitancy and this prudence made me feel the least bit in the world like an injured person ; and such was the perversity of my pride, that e'en though my inside was burning to hear the whole gist of these weighty matters, I would sooner have jumped into the stream than have spoken one word for her en- couragement.

" Am I right in saying an Armstrong is always loyal to his word ? " she asked at last, her face a picture of admirable gravity.

" Perfectly," I replied stiffly and concisely.

She guessed that my pride was touched ; but next minute her woman's wit rescued her from a delicate situation.

" Begone, unworthy doubt; begone, unkind caution ! " she cried archly ; yet no sooner had her tone served its purpose (the usage being to stroke and soothe Master Armstrong's del- icate sensibility) than she relapsed into her former state of excessive staidness.

" Sir," she went on, " 'tis in my power to give you a com- mission in this enterprise. But I must tell you at once that the danger attending it is enough to strike fear to the boldest heart. Should you accept my offer, you will carry your life in your hand till the scheme hath seen fruition. One word in the King's ear would be your death warrant. Yet I must also tell you that success will be the biggest nail yet hammered into the Stuart coffin."

" Give me entire particulars, I prithee, mistress ? "

" Master Armstrong, I dare not until the formalities have been observed. Peers of the realm have had to submit to them."

This beautiful conspirator produced a small pocket Bible from the folds of her cloak, and in the face of the blue moonlight I swore the oath of secrecy. And to such a remarkable degree did this young girl enter into the solemnity of the thing that her hand trembled when I returned the book.

"Master Ned," she said, emboldened by this assurance, "a letter for the hand of my lord Churchill must be carried to London at the earliest possible moment."

"That should not be a very perilous matter," said I stoutly.

"Nevertheless," she replied, "'tis a bold man's task. You are not to think my lord belongs to our side. He is high in the service of the King. And the missive contains treasonous proposals to tempt him to adopt our cause and to renounce his master's. Therefore, should he be minded to take a hostile view of the matter, a nod from him will suffice to clap you in Newgate or the Tower. I may frankly say my lord's attitude hangs in the balance, and such is the jeopardy of the undertaking, that when the matter was mooted at the last meeting of our friends, one and all were so personally reluctant to forward the letter, that lots had to be drawn to decide who must do so. Fate decreed that my father should deliver it, but the gout hath since decreed that he shall do nothing of the kind. Of course, Fate is very dignified, but the gout is a stubborn, unreasonable, arbitrary creature, who hath gained his way as usual. Therefore, dear papa is confined to his chair, unable to move a yard, much less a matter of a hundred and fifty miles. For the last three days he hath been pulling his wig and abusing his luck by turns, and wondering what the Council will say at the next meeting, which is due very shortly. He says I shall earn his gratitude if I can get him out of the dilemma. I proposed that he should consult some of the other conspirators, but as they live in London, very little would be gained by that, for time presses. Next I proposed the servants. Them he dare not trust in such a secret and momentous affair, so I proposed myself. He brightened up at that, yet, in the end, declined my assistance, as he said the council had a pig-headed prejudice against women taking an active part in such a matter."

"One moment, I beg, mistress," I interrupted. "Were you quite serious in that proposal? Dare you have encountered the dangers of the road, and run the risk of the gallows?"

"And why not, sir? My father, old and enfeebled as he is, doth not shrink from the task. Why should I? I have four limbs quite sound, and if as yet I cannot wield a sword with any degree of skill, I can put a bullet through a rogue at forty yards."

"Hast no fear?" I inquired, aghast at these most unfeminine sentiments.

"Don't you dare to catechise me, sir," she replied, shaking her jaunty curls, whilst a laugh lingered about her eyes and mouth. "Didst say fear? Well, yes, I'm afraid of mice—and ghosts—and stupid questions—and—well, I think that's about all, sir. I am ne'er affrighted at human beings, not even at Master Edward Armstrong."

"Methinks you are a very strange young lady."

"Sir," she said, with feigned severity, "if you seek to keep in my good graces, you had better pluck the term 'young lady' from your vocabulary. I abhor it. I'm always thinking of those water-blooded creatures who hem tuckers, and stitch night-caps, and who weep tears of joy at births and marriages, and tears of sorrow at deaths and funerals!"

The wayward wilful girl fairly bubbled with laughter, and added saucily, "Master Armstrong is a good deal shocked, I'm thinking."

"I am, mistress," I felt constrained to admit; though 'twixt ourselves, kinsmen, I may confess he was much more bewitched and delighted. Hereupon the clock of a neighboring village chimed the hour of midnight. That was the signal for us to retrace our steps towards the house. After pledging my willingness to enlist in the mission, she promised to lay the matter before her sire, though she caused me to understand that he would thankfully accept my services.

By this we had come to the entrance steps. Accordingly, I said good-night, and set forth briskly for Bridgwater. From that hour till my next appearance at the manor, I had thought for nothing but the great conspiracy against the King. I weighed the chances of success, but, seeing the slender information I possessed, this was merely folly. I marvelled at the slice of luck that had enabled me to strike a blow at my enemies, yet never calculated at all the manifold dangers of my embassy. I was too excited, and too thoroughly regaled with the celestial hopes inspired by this new project, and too reckless of life, to have many fears for a matter so paltry as personal danger. Therefore, I passed the time till six of the clock the following evening in building air-castles, as youth alone can build them.

At that hour I once more passed the stone dragons on the manor gates. The first object I beheld in the swiftly fading light was Mistress Marvin coming at a clipping pace to meet me. One glance at her face was enough to learn that success had crowned her planning and intricacies.

"Holà, Master Armstrong," she cried exuberantly, "I have cheerful news. I whispered a word in papa's ear this morning. 'Suppose, sir,' says I, 'a young gentleman, whose grandfather bled for the Roundheads at Roundway Down, should consent to convey this missive to London, would that receive your approbation?' 'Wench,' says he, fierce as a buck rat, 'don't talk to me about grandfathers, and uncles, and cousins, and aunts, and the whole genealogical tree. They are no recommendation whatsoever.' 'But suppose, sir,' says I, 'he happens to bear the name of the Copeland Armstrongs?' Master Ned, that was too much for him. 'Dorothy, ye sly minx,' says he, 'get him to take the oath, d'ye hear? get him to take the oath! We shall then be right as ninepence. They're the sworn enemies of the Stuarts, and I'd quite as lief trust a member of that family as one of mine own flesh and blood!' 'Oh, father,' says I, ''tis a providential thing thou hast one of thine own flesh and blood to transact thy business.' 'Less o' your lip, you saucebox!' says he. 'Oh, well, papa, I was just going to tell you of an arrangement I came to with Master Armstrong last night.' 'Go on!' ne cries, mighty anxious. 'But I was to have less of my lip,' says I. Well, anyway, Master Ned, I had three kisses out of the man before I said another word. Then I told him how you and I took a walk, yestreen, to observe the beauties of a moonlit landscape, and what the nature of the compact was you entered into. My word, sir! after that I had a royal time. I have had more kisses from him this morning than ever I remember. He even called me 'a damned clever girl,' and declared that if I would pay more attention to his precept and tuition, I might live to be a credit to him yet."

Her high spirits were unbounded. All this time she had been conducting me triumphantly to her father. I discovered him in his chair, exhibiting quite a cheerful countenance. At my request he immediately apprised me farther concerning the conspiracy.

"In the first place," he began with immense consequence and emphasis, after moistening his lips by a pull at the brandy punch, "ever since James came to the throne he hath carried matters with far too high a hand. He is trying by every means in his power to foist Popery upon the nation. 'Twill not do. Neither rich nor poor will brook it. This is a Protestant land, and not all the monarchs in Christendom can make it aught else. It hath broken with the Romish Church full many a year; yet the blind fool cannot see that unless he desists he will get

such a bite from the old British bull-dog as will make him wish
he had ne'er put his ugly foot on its paws.

"Secondly, the King has mortally offended many of his
staunchest and strongest peers by his lack of honesty, justice,
and fair dealing. He hath no more honor than that cat yonder,
and those about him know it well. Young man, I have seen
something of the world, having grown gray in it, and speaking
to you as a friend, I set more store by honor than any gaudy
accomplishment. And, mark you, so doth any other man of
the sword. Corbleu! James hath not an atom of it anywhere
within his body. He will swear his very name away to win his
own lick-penny ends; hence his most powerful subjects are his
bitterest opponents.

"Thirdly, the kingdom is well aware that he is the cowardliest
tyrant breathing. His heart is as hard and pitiless as marble.
This land hath not forgiven the foul doings of his servant
Jeffreys in our own county of Somerset; and remember he was
but the tool. James Stuart employed it. The knave, the
brute, and the poltroon have peeped out many times in His
Majesty since he took the crown, and now he hath neither the
respect, the kind wishes, nor the confidence of the nation.

"Accordingly, there is a goodly number of us banded together
to wrest the throne from one so unworthy, and wrest it we will.
Day by day we multiply in strength and number. Men with
names that would make you stare have we gotten on our side
already. The leaders of the scheme meet one day in each
month, at some house in the country, to further our designs.
We dare not muster in Town, for this plot is the gravest of
secrets, and 'twould court publicity to assemble there. And if
by misadventure the King did get ear of the matter there'd be
another harvest for Jeffreys.

"I am reckoned amongst the leaders, and at our last meeting, at my lord Danby's place in Yorkshire, great news was
forthcoming. Nothing less than that my lord Sunderland,
Prime Minister of England, had espoused our cause. I can
tell thee, lad, it fired the pack of us, and that same day the
council decided to fly at game quite as high. It was resolved
to approach my lord Churchill, the best soldier His Majesty
doth possess, and to try to lure him over to our side. As you may
imagine, this is truly no light task, and one fraught with an
infinity of peril; for we are utterly ignorant of my lord's sentiments upon the subject. A paper was drawn up instanter
addressed to him, duly setting forth our scheme, together with
several notable inducements for him to lend us his assistance.

As every one seemed unwilling to take the responsibility of so grave a matter, we employed the arbitrament of chance to come to a decision. As luck ordained, it fell to my lot, and I may say it is signed by me alone on behalf of the rest, so that should any adversity befall it, I alone shall suffer. The cause will be unaffected, and there will still be plenty left to carry the great work forward."

Now, there was at least one person present who by no means shared the knight's unconcern. Suddenly a sigh stole forth from somewhere, and as Mistress Marvin and the Persian cat were the only other animate creatures in the room, I must certainly lay it to the account of the lady. Sure, a breath so plaintive and so heartfelt was never known to issue from the throat of the fluffiest cat that ever curled a tail. Besides, the girl was white as the window curtains.

I was unspeakably impressed by the icy nonchalance of the man as he made this statement; by the implacable resolution of his tone, the superb self-reliance it bespoke, and his never-swerving steadfastness to Cause. At first I held my peace, out of pure reverence, as it was a time when the child of a new generation himself beheld something of the grandeur, which hitherto he had only known as a tradition of an old one. This was a strong man; now decayed. But the seed was there; I recognized it, and was awed with admiring wonder.

Piquet was sadly neglected that night. My mission completely engrossed our tongues and thoughts. Ere long the letter was extracted from its receptacle—a large cabinet beside the fireplace—and handed into my custody. Upon that Sir Nicholas fully primed me with instructions and advice, dwelt with extreme particularity on the gravity of my errand, and recapitulated the paramount importance of secrecy and haste. Indeed, urgence was most necessary, for the next meeting was due a fortnight hence.

"My lad," quoth the knight, "I hope you will be back in ten days."

"Never fear, sir," said I, trying to imitate his strength; "without accidents I shall be back in less. I dine at Bruton at noon to-morrow."

"Had you not better take a couple of my servants to guard you against the dangers of the road?" he asked. It seemed even he could be thoughtful for others upon occasion.

"Pooh, not likely!" was my confident reply. "If a man cannot take care of the skin nature gave him, 'tis a pitiful thing indeed," a speech suited to the man's own heart.

"*Mon frère!*" he exclaimed, an unwonted lustre in his one gray eye. "If Churchill joins us, I'll warrant that sweet western blood so wantonly spilled shall be soon avenged."

"Bravely promised, sir knight," I said. "I am thine, heart and soul, in this enterprise; thou hast only to command me."

With that he bade me a propitious journey, and pressed a bag of money upon me to defray the expenses of my travels, which, after some demur, I accepted.

Mistress Dorothy accompanied me to the threshold of the outer door.

"Sir," she said, and 'twas music to hear her voice; 'twas so solemn and so fervent, "do not think me a female Machiavel, nor one who hath no care for brave men, other than how they execute mine own designs. Master Armstrong, I thank thee for my father, and I thank thee for myself. Please forgive this further reminder of thy responsibilities; but oh, sir! remember my father's life and honor are bound up in that packet!"

I could see her face was very white; I could see her hands were trembling. As for her voice, it had now subsided into a throbbing undertone of passionate vibration.

"God speed, dear friend! brave friend!" she said, scarce above a whisper, and timidly turned her right hand out towards me. I touched her fingers with my lips, and thrilling with joy, went hence, like princes in the fairy tales, with my hopes upon ethereal heights, to the King's Head, Bridgwater, prior to starting on my journey.

CHAPTER X.

TENDS TO PROVE THAT SAINTS AND SINNERS ARE NEAR AKIN.

MASTER WHIPPLE had passed many years of his life in London. Therefore, when I mentioned to him that night my approaching visit thither, he assumed superior airs, and proffered me words of admonition.

"Lucky dog!" he cried, "would that I might ride thence beside you. 'Tis a lively spot, my lad—I've had brave times 'neath the shadow of Holy Paul. If ye get Covent Garden way, step into the Piazza and keep your eye up for the sign of the Bullfinch. 'Tis the comeliest tavern in Town. I'd be driving my coach and six had I but stayed there till now."

"Then why did you desert so goodly a spot?"

"My delicate health," he replied with a chuckle, and tapped

his chest with unction. " Ye see it became a matter o' necessity that I should seek a change of air ; the London atmosphere threatened my constitution. 'Twas a most unfortunate thing, for I made a snug little income there. I served strong liquors all day, and kept the dice-box a clicking all night. The best men in Town would consort at my little shop, and lost or won many a guinea. But one day there cropped up a scandal, then there came a lawsuit and a lawyer ; after that a snuff-snouted Bow Street runner, with a warrant in his dirty paw for the apprehension of one Peter Whipple of the Bullfinch, Covent Garden. Not that he got his filthy fingers on Peter Whipple's sacred person—no, sir ! " and mine host smacked his fist upon the board in his grandest histrionic manner. " You ask where *was* Peter Whipple ? He'd bolted, sir, to the beautiful country, for the benefit of his health. Old birds don't wait for a salted tail, old thieves don't wait for a stiff cravat, nor men of intellect for Newgate."

Mine host prattled on in his usual windy way ; though it does not become me to set down all, or even half of his garrulity ; 'twould but weary you.

'Twas never my lot to know a man with such a perpetual flow of speech as was possessed by Peter Whipple. His tongue was seldom silent, and even then was only so on sufferance. Once let him become embarked on any subject, then no one else might introduce a word ; they had perforce to just sit still and listen.

The main outcome of his verbosity on this occasion was that I heard of a hostelry, where I might stay during my impending sojourn in the city. This was the house of one Jabez Fletcher, brother-in-law to Pete, and landlord and proprietor of the Three Crowns tavern in the Strand.

Just as Master Whipple was the greatest man I ever knew in the matter of the brain, in many other ways he excelled his fellows. His urbane and polite demeanor was a thing to talk about. He was a sleek and smiling animal, good-natured to the last degree, and full of worldly wise sagacity. He never so far forgot his rule of life as to let his serenity be ruffled by any of the disturbing minor incidents that are a bane to an ordinary man's existence. He never so far descended to the level of common mortals as to show anger at anything. If aught should call for it, he assumed instead an air of mild and sweet forgiveness. He had no rough edge to his tongue ; 'twas ever as smooth as his pomaded hair. Did a customer abuse him, Pete simply replied with an overpowering humility, yet experience taught me that this same humility made a portly figure in the score. The word "business" was the guiding star of his career, just as the three words "Long Bob Bickers" was that of his recollection.

Ere I retired for the night, he bade me heed another land-mark of the past. Said he—

"Friend Ned, perhaps you'll find yourself in the vicinity of Clerkenwell. There is a little green painted conventicle in Black Lion Place with 'Rest for weary saints' in neat black letters stuck over the door. My lad, I was pastor of that psalm-singing flock five years."

"You!" I exclaimed. "Why did you not say you kept a gaming-house in Covent Garden?"

"To be sure, my pretty innocent," he answered, his little eyes foxily eloquent, "to be sure I did. But, ye see, it is just as easy to be a saint as to be a sinner, and very near as profit-able. From six unto eight of the clock on week-day nights, and thrice on Sundays, I would hold discourse to my Puritan brethren, that my words might fructify within them. My con-gregation were a flourishing sect, with purse-strings long, hearts soft, heads softer, and brains a little this side fatuity. My text was ever '*It is more blessed to give than to receive.*' I would dwell on the fact that a man who had no charity, dispensed with it to the detriment of his soul. A hard heart, I would tell 'em, hath the devil for a foster-parent. And presently I'd tap the brine as I enlarged upon the miseries of their poorer brethren, so that when the trencher was passed round for the relief of the wants of the needy, it was always piled with gold and silver pieces, and I, being the most zealous of the chosen, took upon myself to dispense their bounty."

"Whew!" I whistled.

"Of course I did. And this select and large-hearted sect never interfered with business in the Piazza, as the 'bloods' did not assemble till Mrs. Polly Wilders could bewitch 'em no longer. Ah, lad, those were the times! They and Bob Bick-ers will never return."

"Pete," I asked, much struck with the methods of this man, which so far excelled mine own, "did no mishap ever mar the execution of your scheme?"

"Pish! not likely. Brains provide for mishaps and such-like, and oft turn 'em into disguised blessings. And now, young friend, I'll trouble you to hearken to the voice o' wisdom. In this wicked world, my boy, strict attention to business alone doth pay. You and I, were we ever so righteous, could not

8

reclaim it, and would probably die in a ditch for our pains. We all have our methods. I use my headpiece, you use your pistols, the parson his mouth, and the cut-purse his ten fingers. The mercer round the corner sells his wares at three times their proper value. The Westminster lawyers draw fees they never earn from crack-brained litigants who have no better sense than to squander their substance thus. By the way, beware of women and lawyers. They are the devil's creation. Again, the parson dons the cassock to fill his belly, and gives nought but words for good gold and silver. Every man to his trade, say I. You go your way, I go mine. We shall at least have a roof above our heads till the coffin or the gallows claims us. If then we don't get to heaven, methinks we shall find ourselves among friends at the other place."

I, having patiently heeded whilst he enunciated this outlandish dogma, bade him sweet dreams, seized a candle, and sensibly betook myself to bed. I rose early in the morning, and pushed on swiftly towards my destination. Indeed, only once did I slacken rein till I came to Bruton. Here I stayed three hours to dine, and to give Joe a rest. And then my peace of mind was hurt by a serious adventure. It occurred after I had ate my meal, just as I was on the point of re-departure.

I had sought the saddle, and was walking Joe out of the yard of the hostelry, when a man came towards me in a secret fashion, as if afraid of notice. Also, his dress accorded with his stealthy manner. A sad-colored cloak, long and capacious, covered him from head to heels, leaving only his spurred riding boots exposed, whilst a low-crowned, broad-brimmed hat, pulled low down over the eyes, and a face much muffled, did their best to baffle the public gaze. To my surprise this fellow approached my saddle, and laid a gloved hand on the bridle.

"Tarry a moment, good sir," he said, in an unnatural voice scarcely higher than a whisper; "wouldst like to earn a few guineas?"

"Certainly," said I, nowise averse. Forthwith a bag of tempting bulk was brought from underneath the strange man's cloak, and held up for my inspection.

"All these shall be thine," he said, still in his covert tone, "if you will hand me the letter you have upon you for my Lord John Churchill. Here is one hundred times its weight in gold, and the cunning villain shook the guineas.

The gold was held beneath my nose more temptingly than ever. That aroused Black Ned from his dormant state, for he it was who sniffed it. ⸜Without a word I shot out my hand, seized the bag, and grabbed it from its owner's grasp before he could apprehend my motive. Next I plucked a pistol from the holster, and thrust it in the coistril's face, at which he shrank back cowed.

"Peradventure this may teach you," I cried, "not to insult honest folk, you hangdog villain! Well may you hide your face from the light of day. Get you gone, or I'll break your bones, and for the future seek not to corrupt your fellows."

I might have struck the wretch with the butt end of my weapon, had he not been so much affrighted. As it was I contented myself with plenteous revilings, and in the end the coward sidled stealthily away. However, I may tell you much of my anger was merely simulation. It is a way with rogues to make parade of rectitude in their dealings with their equally dirty-minded brethren. Therefore this member of the tribe, being in my power, it pleased me to trade upon my surface virtue, which, as you know, was no nicer than his, though maybe not so grovelling and paltry.

This affair gave me grave concern, for it was patent that my mission was known, and it was more than likely other measures, not so gentle, might be used to obtain possession of the letter. I hugged the paper to my bosom, and swore Kelston Manor should ne'er see me again if any misfortune happened it. All my future was bound up in it. All my hopes were centred in it. Love and vengeance, the holiest and unholiest of passions, were, according to the bearer, encased betwixt its wrappers.

I rode briskly forward, seldom swerving from the direct road to London. The missive was jealously guarded, and for better precaution I stitched it into the lining of my doublet that night at my halting-place, and slept with it on my back, and thereby sacrificed physical comfort for ease of mind.

I may tell you a journey to Town in those days was not the pleasurable affair it is now, when comfortable and speedy stage-wagons traverse good roads thither. Also it was a serious matter then to travel unattended, for highwaymen and footpads abounded, though I had no fear of them until I passed the Wiltshire borders, as up to that point I was too well known to be molested. However, I pushed on without mishap, for I never travelled after sunset, and in the daytime my pistols always reclined, duly charged, close at hand in the holsters.

My head, by no means staid and sapient, as youthful ones are not supposed to be, was topsy-turvy with the events of the past

two weeks.   Briefly, Edward Armstrong, thief and outlaw, had
been buoyed from the bog of black despair, unto an altitude of
hope.   Two circumstances had combined to produce this change.
Foremost, the plainest and most visible, was Mistress Marvin's
narrative.   Here, indeed, was a wide vista of relentless longings
and angry passions, that embraced all my prospects for the
future.   My father's death could be visited on his murderers,
my sentence of outlawry removed, and my livelihood earned by
honest means, if only these designs should be compassed.   I
turned the matter over in my mind, examined carefully the pros
and cons, and pondered on the chances, only to decide that no
man could say what would be the fruits of the conspiracy, but
that they must be portioned out just as God determined.

Then another influence was at work, a stealthy, subtle influence, which was perhaps the *primum mobile.*   To this I was loth
and slow, in equal parts, to affix the proper name.   Throughout
my tedious journey, I could not eject the vision of a sprightly
maid with laughing eyes out of my maggoty pate.   I tried more
than once to do so, doubtless believing the effort was one to be
commended.   Still it was a thoroughly vain endeavor.   "What
business," I asked myself a dozen times, " has this lovely apparition in my head?"   The question was unanswerable.   To
speak plainly, it was God's business.   Man cannot say how his
heart, if he has one, may leave him, or to what address his affections may be consigned.

Now I was well aware that I had no logical right to love
Mistress Dorothy Marvin.   I, the base creature who had sunk
so low; but I could not help it.   I was well aware it was mor-
ally, ethically, casuistically wrong; but, again, *I could not help
it.*   I might fight with facts, I might grapple with common sense,
I might struggle with myself, but the fiat had gone forth, and
from that time onwards Ned Armstrong, highwayman, was a
slave to the pertinacious passion.

I suppose the chief deed of life is to fall in love, or else fall
out of it, though, of course, some there are who spend their days
without such high seasoning to their anæmic, cut and dried exist-
ences.   Then, I've heard talk of folks who go into this affair
of love in a careful, calculating manner; and contrive throughout the course of the palpitating business to keep their brains
alert, their faculties alive, and their eyes uncommonly wide open.
In fact, they're said to pay due regard to time and circumstance,
and to walk path-keepingly upon the intoxicating pilgrimage.
Now this is what I can't abide!   No doubt these cautious
wooers, at the mercurial time of declaration, will eat a full meal

ere they make it, and at the fateful moment, instead of parading warmth and divers kinds of soulful eloquence, will *not* go down upon their knees lest they crack their Sunday pumps, and so will actually perform the thing upon their feet with a disgusting phlegm that is a defiance to the Muses. Kinsmen, 'pon my soul! were I the ladylove of such a swain, I'd pack him off about his business. These unromantic methods seem to me nought less than insult to throbbing Dulcinea ; a sacrilege to Psyche! Anyway, I do hope these milk-fed creatures, who, because they know no raptures, lose the amplitude of love's delicious flavor, will be "completely bit," as the cant phrase goes, when they enter the courts of Hymen. For to take it as sedate as you would take your dinner, and with not so good a relish, is downright wickedness.

So I, a young man without discretion in matters of the heart, had suddenly made a profound discovery. I learned that the magician Cupid had waved his wand over Master Edward Armstrong, or Black Ned, or the pair of them, if it please you, whereat their collective wits had gone moon-raking, and they reduced to that direful state ycleped the high nonsensical. Children, be ye peers or peasants, honest men or felons, beware of maids with wondrous eyes !

Now when the full and clear result of my heaven-directed penetration was borne upon the remnant of my wits that was hid within the understanding, the same remnant said to the witless major portion, "Be no utter fool, Ned Armstrong." But sure Ned Armstrong was a fool, I make bold to say, the biggest fool alive when he let his mind run on the witcheries of Mistress Marvin. Thus what with one thing, then another, my headpiece fairly reeled under the burthen of so many things to think about. Certes, 'twas never made for so large a cargo.

Master Whipple had laid it down that all men were knaves and rogues to a high extent, though they varied in degree. He said their culpability was equal, and that they only differed in skill and method. I recollected one of his dicta (oft delivered), to wit, "that we might possibly be no worse than our neighbors, but then were certainly no better." "We lived," he said, "to best one another, and one mould fashioned the lot of us." "Though," said he again, "the wisest and the deepest of our brethren went through life in silk and broadcloth, and thereby did sometimes cheat the gallows." I thought on this till my brain refused its office. I ascribed it a queer yet pleasant subject. But what had Peter Whipple's dicta to do with love, my father's death, Mistress Dorothy Marvin, or my perilous mis-

sion ? Here is the solution to the riddle in a little compass—
Black Ned was a wicked rogue, cursed with a conscience, *and
he sought to bolster it.*

CHAPTER XI.

IN WHICH MY LORD CHURCHILL KNITS HIS BROW.

AT noon, on the third day of my journey, I found myself for
the first time in the city of London. I was amazed at it, as
every countryman must be. It was larger than Exeter, Taunton, and Bridgwater put together, tho' I considered it by
no means so kindly a place as any one of them. The shops
displayed much magnificence, with wares both rare and costly ;
the buildings filled the eye with wonderment ; houses abounded
on every side, jumbled close by one another, shutting out pure
air and the blissful sunshine ; whilst the atmosphere was stuffy,
and reeked with foul matters, that are not bred down in
the West. Yet the citizens make big pretence of attending to
the weather ; and, the day being bright, several declared to me
how welcome the sunshine was to them.

"Sunshine !" said I. "I see no sunshine in this murky
place—all walls and chimney stacks ! I account it a most miserable day ! "

They would shake their heads solemnly at this, and ask,
"Young man, what shall you account a rainy one ? "

I fervently hoped I might not be there to see it.

Also the people were neither so kind nor courteous as they
are in our parts. I found them perpetually on the hurry-
scurry, never tarrying to use politeness and civility. They
pushed and hustled kindred wayfarers, using knees and elbows
freely—for all the world as though the devil was treading
on their heels. The first time I went abroad on foot I marked
this lack of manners most particularly. The way they shoved
and thrust me from side to side, tripped me, kicked my heels, ran
me down and generally beset me, was truly shameful. And
Gothlike was their mode of doing this. They cursed me lustily
the while, and declared I incommoded the path, till, with body
and spirit very sore, I boldly bearded one rude fellow, who
cocked a bony knee into my poor ribs.

"Methinks you had best mend your manners, Master Jackanapes ! " angrily quoth I.

"Kennel puppy ! " was his insolent retort, as he sprawled a

leg behind my back, evidently desirous of tippling me into the filthy ditch which ran in the open street.

Few were cleverer than I in deft use of limb, or in alertness of body, as my pride was plenteously bestowed thereon.   Therefore I was too quick for his lumbering clumsiness, so brought two heels smartly down on his outstretched foot, and butted him atilt with my head to his stomach.   This doubled him up howling, thereupon I trickily kicked his heels from under him, and straightway the blusterer splashed on his back into the muddy water; and as I rejoiced to think the fellow was near a head my superior in stature, this adventure served as a salve to my injured feelings.

Master Fletcher had a royal welcome for me at his hostel in the Strand when I mentioned the name of his kinsman, Peter Whipple.   Still, the first meal I partook of under his roof occasioned much coaxing towards the stomach.   The sense of the delicate mission I had to accomplish afflicted my appetite and weighted my spirits, for now the crisis was so nigh, a fitting sense of its dangerous nature was too apparent to be agreeable. And every minute I lingered I more fully developed this whiteness of the liver.   However, I am not one of those persons, who, having a jorum of nauseous physic to take, begin by smelling it, remarking the color, and afterwards vainly wondering whether it is so queasy as reputation and the nose aver.   No; this is not my way at all.   I would toss it down without procrastination, glad to get it off the mind.   Thus it was, having ate so poor a meal, that Master Fletcher at once wished to board me at the rate of meals supplied, without heed to quantity partook of, I brushed my garments thoroughly, and removed all stains of travel, though even then, by contrast with the Londoners, I looked a trifle ungenteel.   Those folks dressed in the strict mode, if purse permitted, and if not, they would rather sacrifice the texture of the cloth than have clothes of homely cut.

By the knight's previous advice I set out for Whitehall straight away.   Methought 'twould be the surest means to learn my lord's whereabouts if I inquired at the King's palace, because he was often with His Majesty on business of the State.   I must confess that in all my life I ne'er felt more full of fear, since the Commander had only to oppose the plan, then Newgate and a stretched neck would undoubtedly be my lot.   Yet I gulped down these qualms and strode out bravely, though I was compelled to make more than one inquiry as to the direct way thither.

I came ere long to a large building, not near so handsome as others I saw in this city. A cavalier in gay attire was in conversation with the sergeant of the guard, beside the gateway. Resplendent he looked in purple coat of the brightest plush, and the great array of silk and silver lace strewn about his person; whilst a smart ostrich feather stuck in his cap enhanced the other finery. He gave me a curious look when I asked for my lord Churchill, as if he were not sure in his mind what so rustic a person could want with him; yet, when I spoke of the urgency of the errand, he stopped chewing his toothpick, and deigned to answer.

"If ye want my lard," he said in a curious mincing way, which I have heard since was much affected by the fops and courtiers of that time, though without improvement to their utterance, "he hath been closeted with the King for an hour or more, and is still with him. What is it to-day, Binkie, thinkest thou? Be it the quartering of troops among the Dissenters, or the advisability of active measures against the Dutch?"

"No idea," said the indifferent Binkie, taking a huge pinch of snuff from an elegant box, and conveying the same to his nostrils in a very artistic manner.

However, by dint of perseverance I was able to impress the courtier with the import of my message, which I declared was for his lordship's private ear. Accordingly, he had the consideration to put me in a position to obtain an audience. With this in view he led me across the courtyard, and up a broad flight of stone steps, into the palace itself. I followed him thence along a corridor, up another set of stairs, and therefrom, after several twists and turnings, into a small ante-chamber, surrounded by the richest Gobelin tapestry, and with a thick, warm-colored carpet for the floor.

I was destined to pass an anxious time, pending the arrival of his lordship; as this interval kept my hopes and fears upon the rack, and my mind upon the tenter-hooks of expectation. At last steps were heard outside the door; then pit-a-pat went my craven heart, and at once I wished the matter done with.

A tall man entered. His countenance was comely, his carriage beautifully erect, his attire scrupulous for elegance and grace, and his gait soldierlike and easy. He was certainly a person to look at twice, if only because he was my Lord John Churchill. He bowed to me with that high-bred air that comes to men by nature. Yet his courtesy had just that dash of condescension in it that I doubt not was intended to let me know that I spoke to a superior. Twenty years hence this

same John Churchill was to be famous the wide world over as
the victor of Blenheim, Ramillies, and Malplaquet, and as the
bane of the whole French nation. Yet how was I to know this?
Therefore do not blame me for not taking better stock of him
on this occasion. I grant you that 'tis an excellent thing to use
your eyes for the observation of your fellow-men, but throughout this awe-inspiring audience my heart was troublesome and
my head was nervous, so that, 'twixt the two, I was far too
anxious for the welfare of my neck to notice aught but his most
salient characteristics. So, kinsmen, at the risk of affording
you a disappointment, I'm sure I cannot say how his peruke
was curled, or what was the color of his snuff-box. Howbeit, I
somehow chanced to note, certainly without a pre-arranged
intention, that he had a row of silver buttons on his vest, had
a purple pimple on either cheek, another on his chin, and that
he blew his nose just like a common mortal. I can also refute
the scientific theory, that he owed his military success to being
cross-eyed, and could therefore see further than the French,
because he squinted.*

At first methought his lordship full to the brim with affability.
Yet I soon discovered this suave exterior was merely a gesture
garb, simply a superficial trick to hide the skilful politician.
The man was cautious. Every moment he peered slyly through
his eyelashes, and to vary this procedure, gave me keen, hawk-
like glances when he thought I was not looking. By this means,
ere we came to business, without the semblance of a stare, or
aught uncivil or unbecoming in a gentleman, he had secretly
fortified his mind with every outward fact appertaining to Master Edward Armstrong.

I handed him the missive. He examined it closely. It took
him some time to read it; indeed, I've heard say he was far apter
with the sword than with the quill. After possessing himself

---

* Kinsmen, I will maintain what is set down above, even though it runs
contrary to the received opinion. Of late many theories had been rife to
explain the triumphs of the Duke of Marlborough. I presume this is to
soothe the feelings of nonentities. 'Tis a favorite device of little men never
to admit that a kindred son of Mother Eve, begat of flesh and blood, can
do better than themselves. Therefore, when a neighbor does a brilliant
deed, and hath his praises sung, and doth achieve the crown of worldly
glory, rather than admit that he hath what is called a special genius, they
must set it down to a supernatural agent, or else call in " luck "—the fee-
blest word God ever put in the mouth of man—to help them. Yet, it seems
to me, the best way to deal with fools is to feed 'em on madhouse facts,
and let 'em batten on blunder muddle; so that, by and by, having gorged
overmuch of sophistry, they will sicken of the imbecile, and thus be sur-
feited with folly.

of the contents he stroked his chin, and knitted his brow, whilst I noted his demeanor with wholesome trepidation. Yes, my lord stroked his chin, and the wrinkles on his brow corrugated into ugly puckers. Presently he laid the letter down, stared at me with all his might, and finally drummed his fingers on the table.

As for me, I have always tried to pass as a man of courage, yet, frankly, beads of sweat sprang out upon my forehead. I sought to read the verdict in his eyes, but my gaze only quailed and dropped before his steadfast look, without having learned a hint of what was in his mind. Meantime his lordship's perturbation thickened. He set his lips as tight as wax, and shifted his eyes from me to a corner of the ceiling. Still in doubt, he seized the letter again, and carefully re-perused it. The upshot was for him to clench his fist, and to walk to the door and lock it. Methought I was surely lost, for he was a bigger man than I, and had a rapier at his side. Soon the room was filled for me with cold visions of Newgate and the gallows. Then Churchill fixed me with a lynx-eyed look, and asked—

"Young man, do you know what Sir Nicholas Marvin, your master, hath put into this missive?"

Here was a nice thing to ask! It was indeed an unkind question. Now, perhaps, I should never have scrupled to lie upon a meaner matter, yet by what I confess to be a peculiar mode of reasoning, I really felt that this was a pretty point of honor. And thus, though a falsehood would have so happily availed, not for a moment did I entertain the idea of any such proceeding. Therefore I was silent, being uncertain which course to pursue to creep out of the dilemma.

"No need to answer, my fine fellow," quoth my lord, still shrewdly gazing. "I can too well see thou hast knowledge of its contents. 'Tis the darkest treason."

The King's Minister laughed. That laugh jarred upon me. It sounded positively unchristian to my ears.

"Tush, friend!" said he again, observing my uneasy aspect, "ye needn't take on so." Thereat he sank his voice scarce above a whisper. "Palace walls have ears!" he added, his face still blank and meaningless. Shortly afterwards he continued in a brisker tone, "Now, sir, listen with every care to what I tell you. Inform Sir Nicholas Marvin that I accept the proposals here laid down. And you may tell him that, if I commit nought to paper, I am none the less prepared to fully support the enterprise. Yes, tell him, I'll embrace the cause heart

and soul, and will most certainly be present at the meeting
to-morrow week."

Then he scratched his wig, paused, maybe ten seconds, and
burst out sharply in a far higher key than heretofore—

"Ay, ay, Jack Churchill, J. S. is nought to you! Beshrew
the black old crow, and his bevy of sour, unlovely, wry-phiz'd
strumpets!" * Here he pulled himself up very short, and
blushed in unmistakable confusion.

"Rat me!" he exclaimed, half laughing, "I'm babbling like
a simpleton; but, young man, I hope you yourself are more
discreet."

"I should not be entrusted with this affair an I were not,"
was my retort, which was very well for one country bred,
because it implied reproof under the cover of assurance.

Now Churchill's words were sweetest music to my ears, and
by a phenomenon in physiological laws, they had the effect of
letting me breathe in comfort for the first time for half an hour.

After my lord unlocked the door (it had been so secured to
prevent intrusion), I followed on his heels along the passage,
until he disappeared through a curtained portal. Just as he
did so another personage, whose air and aspect seemed redo-
lent of latent thunder, issued at the same time out of it.

One gay-robed courtier whispered to a friend hard by, as
this gentleman passed them and went his way, "My lord of
Sunderland is not very amiable to-day."

So this was the great prime minister.

When I had safely left the outer gates of Whitehall, I may
tell you the putrid city air smote my inner organs less oppres-
sively, the people seemed less insolent, the rumbling vehicles
less noisy, the streets less filthy, and the whole place more fit
for Christians to abide in.

I gave half a crown to a needy man of letters, half a guinea
to a poor widow encumbered with nine children, to make no
mention of divers groats dispensed to beggars of the halt and

---

* It has often since occurred to me that this remark was wrung from
Churchill by years of irritation. All men about the court (being charitably
inclined, I'll not include their wives and daughters) felt it no inconsider-
able grievance that James II. should prefer uncomely mistresses. A man
can forgive a woman all things except her ugliness. Therefore people
came to look upon it as a standing abuse that the King, when he exercised
his *royal prerogative* of having a liberal share of females, should choose them
old and beautiless. Indeed, so much did this national nuisance rankle, that
folks, when they used a similitude for inelegance, instead of saying, "ugly
as sin," or "ugly as a toad," as was their wont, would change the formula
to "ugly as a concubine."

lame and blind persuasion.   I also bethought me of the home
folks at Chilverley.   Whereupon I bought a shell of pearl for
mother's hair, a necklet of virgin pearl for Betty, a gold watch
for John emblazoned with the hall-mark, to add to the owner's
pride thereof, and to beget the admiration of all who chanced
to see it.   Furthermore, I invested money in a book of the
classic poems of the good and great John Milton, knowing how
the eyes of Tobe Hancock would brighten when he beheld
them.   It was superbly bound in calfskin, and done exactly
into print by Richard Cooke at the sign of the Crown and
Anchor in Abchurch Lane.

Upon this I returned to the Three Crowns, and disposed of
such a meal that mine host rubbed his eyes in wonderment,
and cursed his luck for boarding me upon the terms he had
done.   And I chucked the serving-maids, which was not my
usual custom, and swilled beer into the ostler, the stable
boys, the drawers, and indeed all who would take my bounty.
Such was my joy at the success of the enterprise ; God grant
that it might end as it had begun !

I decided to pass the night at Master Fletcher's, for in regard
to time, I was well inside the limit.   Besides, this strange
London was far too wonderful a place to flee away from without gathering some further knowledge of its marvels and its
magnitude.

Accordingly I informed the landlord that I was about to visit a
playhouse in the evening ; from thence would hie to supper at
a coffee-house, and should then propose to put fortune to the
test at a gaming-house, as often enough I had heard Peter
Whipple say was the way young gentlemen of means spent
their nights in Town.   Now Master Fletcher agreed with me
that this plan was very fine, but to this opinion he added an
important reservation.   In fact, to my disgust, he shook his
head in superior wisdom, and even went far enough to hint that
I was young and foolish.

"Art mad?" he asked.   "Verily you know not the ways of
this London, you who have never been abroad in it before to-
day.   Why, man alive, it is a very Hades to those who don't
know aught about it.   Come, come, young sir, reflect, else I'm
thinking you'll repent."

However, in spite of this, I adhered to my determination,
whereat the only resource left mine host was to give his head
a portentous shake, and to prophesy the swift and sure
approach of evil.

Notwithstanding his prognostication, I went to the theatre in

Drury Lane. It was a famous one, too, wherein Mistress
Gwynne, whose intercourse with the late King had long been
common property, was wont to gain her histrionic triumphs.
On this night the piece was a lively one of Sir John Suckling's.
And though Mrs. Bracegirdle jauntily sustained the foremost
female character in it, I culled but scant enjoyment from the
play, for the noise was as a Babel, no heed being given to the
performance or the actors. The fops were incessantly busy
with their quizzing-glasses. They ogled the women, chiefly
court toasts and such-like painted hussies, who, I was surprised
to see, had no covering at all for arms, neck, and shoulders.
Sorry creatures I considered them. Their faces were painted,
powdered, and patched, and their bodies tricked out in gauds
and finery. Why the beaux should choose to pay them such
flattering attentions was a point beyond my comprehension.
Unless 'twas because these gallants knew full well that if they
peeped beneath the paint of the simpering dames and damsels,
they might find a weakness—or, as I am engaged upon so polite
a topic—if you please I should have said a foible, that goes by
another name than virtue.

CHAPTER XII.

THE SWORDSMAN IN HOMESPUN.

It is a popular weakness of youth to set greater store by its
own opinion than by that of persons with a wider and more
matured sagacity. Therefore, being flushed with success, if not
with wine, and unheedful of any man, much less of well-meant
counsel, I betook myself from the playhouse (which disappointed
me) to a coffee-house to partake of supper, instead of hieing
homewards as all peaceable and sensible citizens were wont to
do; for the streets of London were dangerous at this time of
the evening—a fact I was about to discover.

Thus it was I went abroad without a care for the perils of
the darkness, and with heart enough to fight all the town if
necessary. Supper disposed of, I set forth for Groom Porter's,
the most famous gaming-house in the city (*vide* Peter Whipple),
determined to test my fortune.

A choice company I found assembled, and very strange was
the place to my ears and eyes. The continuous rattle of coins
and the dice-box; the ceaseless clatter of tongues; the opulent

and varied stream of oaths ; the glitter of jewels, and the rich-
ness of the gamblers' attire, all tended to make the scene bewildering to a new beholder. Numberless small round-topped
marble tables were scattered here and there on nearly every
yard of flooring ; and the gamesters were ranged around them
in various nondescript postures. Some had eager, twitching vis-
ages breathlessly bent over the cards and cubes, others showed
all their sensibility in their restless gaze or in their chalky faces,
whilst now and then the player would lounge back in his seat
with a fine assumption of nonchalance, and would yawn when
he won, and laugh when he lost, and speak no word except
what was vital to the game ; and even though it was a matter of
a country house or the very last guinea of his patrimony, this
demeanor altered not, but he'd stake all his chattels and his
worldly wealth, until Dame Fortune coldly shook her head at
him for the last time, and so left him desolate and penniless.
Then the bankrupt would smile and curse her for a fickle jade,
and seek to forget her heartlessness in the mirthful pleasures
of the bowl. Yet the next morning this same audacious roy-
sterer would spit himself on his sword, and thus die as he had
lived—a bad example. Of course, his friends would proclaim
abroad the virtues of him departed, and attend the funeral
weeping. Not that the moral went home to *them.* No, that
was left for discreet men's children ; but their eyes were wet
because it was correct to have them so at funerals.

Well, I mingled with this careless, laughing, swearing, boozing,
brilliant company, and every man Jack of it had had more gold
than brains at some time of his existence. And I, unused to
such a profuse array of gorgeous clothes, marvelled at these fine
habiliments, and was minded to run away, being greatly disconcerted at the plainness of mine own. I vainly wished that I
had come to Town in my choicest suit, though, to be sure, 'twas
nought to brag upon, when compared with this magnificence.
However, nature conquered diffidence ; for, plainly speaking,
she had endowed me with a certain easy confidence of self that
rose to the demands of any company.

I threaded my way among the tables with fifty guineas clinking in my pocket and with my heart beating uncomfortably fast
behind my doublet. My progress gave me some prominence,
for my coat being long and the spaces narrow, it swept off one
table a mass of cards and coins, to the detriment of their
owners' play, yet not to. that of their tongues, however. In
fact, such a volley of robust abuse beset me that all in the room
gave a look towards my direction, and straightway saw my

coarse appearance. Nor was their surprise concealed by any of their own pains, for each asked the other what I did there. Accordingly I informed the room, in the calmest manner possible, "that being a gentleman myself, I sought to engage in play with gentlemen." This set them all a-tittering, which methought said little for their manners, their kindness, or their courtesy. However, by and by, one young man having so far condescended as to play with me, and I having grown more familiar to their gaze, I was forgotten in the moment of their own affairs.

My opponent was an overdressed coxcomb, both impudent and swaggering. His face had many tokens of a misspent youth—muddy complexion, furrowed forehead, fishy eyes, and a bloated skin. He was dressed in the height of fashion, and wore an ostentatious periwig, full bottomed, and carefully curled to agree with the current mode. A plum-colored velvet coat, a green vest of the same material, a frilled open-fronted cambric shirt, a silver-hilted rapier fantastically chased, shoes beribboned and silver buckled, and three glorious rings gemmed with precious stones flashing on his fingers, all combined to beautify his person, and to make him as pretty a clothes-pole as you'd wish to encounter.

Luck had certainly been against this dressy gallant, for under his supercilious guise there couched an angry petulance which clearly said he was not a graceful loser. The vicious way he threw the dice, and the harsh glitter of his eyes, put me at once upon my guard. Now, fortunately for myself, I was not quite the tyro I had been evidently suspected. The truth is, Master Whipple knew more of these midnight pastimes than the majority of those assembled. Therefore he had imparted to me a liberal allowance of his widespread knowledge. Nay, in confidential moments, he had actually whispered some naughty usages for thumb and finger, that rogues alone did practice. "Because," as he said, in that dry way of his, "to pass through a world so wicked, you cannot be too carefully equipped to combat the designs of your fellow-creatures."

Thus, at the beginning, my opponent reckoned without his host, for experienced as he doubtless was, I was aware of his every trick, and versed in his each manoeuvre. Besides, my breadth of information, as I soon discovered for myself, embraced a far wider sphere than his, or, in other words, to employ a pasteboard metaphor, "'twas like a court card up my sleeve."

Before long I had to call my fine gentleman's attention to sundry breaches of the rules, which he innocently enough (*sic*)

committed. Methinks this correction gave him umbrage, seeing that he received it with a scowl, but was sufficiently a man
to gruffly beg my pardon. I won steadily; and, be it known,
honorably, whilst my ill-tempered companion, quite to his credit,
after these two or three trifling lapses, adhered strictly to the
regulations. His breath became baited with oaths, as perseveringly enough I kept transferring golden guineas from his
pocket to mine own, deeming this a congenial occupation. Sure
the gallant was entirely destitute of fortune, wherefore ere long
his stock of cash became exhausted. So he staked one of his
rings, and I won it.

"Deuce take the luck!" he muttered. "There goes a bauble
that would fetch forty guineas from Dolman in Paul's Yard any
morning."

At this added stroke of victory, I had the sense to be content with my winnings. Therefore, instead of playing for another of the jewels, as I was pressed to do, like a prudent man,
I quietly gathered up my large quantity of gold and thrust it
deep into my breeches pocket, and also slipped the lately gotten
ring on to my middle finger. At this my opponent swore, and
his wrath burst out with meagre ceremony.

"How now, you bumpkin!" he shouted, getting swiftly from
his seat. "Don't you know 'tis the custom here for the loser
to cry enough?"

"Is that so, good sir?" I inquired with sweetest courtesy; I
assure you kinsmen it seemed then quite a natural thing to be
so polite.

He of the bloated countenance bubbled with indignation, and
consigned myself and luck to a place with a sultry climate.

"None o' your infernal innocence," quoth he. "Play on, I
say."

"Hum!" I murmured, sarcastically. His words had aroused
my spleen.

"Dost hear, chawbacon?" he loudly cried, wine and misfortune mastering him.

"Hum!" I grunted.

"Play on, I say," he screamed, nearly bereft at my cool demeanor.

This disturbance was not lost on the others, and they came
crowding round with apprehensive faces. Indeed, they appeared much more disturbed, methought, than the occasion
warranted.

Meantime my excited friend continued to rave at the top of
his bent, and I watched, with amused indifference, his face

turn a bluish purple. Verily hard drinking and hard luck had
maddened him. He was a big clean-built fellow, and the mode
he banged his fists about was not a pleasant sight.

"Art going to finish it?" he howled. "If not, by the Lord,
I'll finish thee!"

"Hum!" I reiterated, still feeding his exasperation.

All this while those around had gradually dropped their banter, and now strained their eyes towards the pair of us. I
began to wonder at their earnestness. Suddenly one of the
number, a man somewhat older and staider than the rest,
leaned over the back of my chair, and whispered quickly—

"Forbear, young man, for the love of heaven! You do not
know this gentleman. 'Tis Perry Wilmot."

"Hum!" I grunted, though 'twixt ourselves my manner
then was but idle braggadocio.

So this was the notorious Perry Wilmot, the most famous
and bloody of brawlers, and, rightly or wrongly, said to be the
best swordsman in England. His name had reached even as
far as our county. For the moment I was taken aback. But
'twas not a time for leisurely procedure. The fire-brained
gallant was so angered at his flouting, that no sooner had I discovered his identity, than he hit me across the jaw with the flat
of his hand.

"Perhaps ye'll fight, if ye will not play? Sink me, ye shall
do one or t'other, or I'll pin you as you sit!"

Instantly he threw off his velvet vest and doublet. Outwardly bold, I rose from my seat, determined now to play the
part I had already taken, e'en though it cost me my life. I may
say such was the height of my reputation in the West, that my
name was known there far and wide as a brilliant swordsman.
This I always strove to maintain; yet, as that matter goes, I
was not deserving of such celebrity, being, when all was said,
no master. Still I'll make bold to claim three high qualities.
Without boasting, which I do aver is a trait to be condemned
in any man, tho' it took me many years to appreciate that
sentiment, none possessed more agility of movement, keener
and nicer sight, or stauncher courage than myself. And
if I lacked any scientific schooling in the art, methinks these
characteristics stood me in better stead than a mere surface
show of fancy precept.

At this time I had yet to know my first defeat, therefore the
sudden flush of surprise allayed, my usual pluck and confidence
returned. Wilmot being so crapulous with wine, 'twas evident
he would be placed at a disadvantage. Thus I had no fear as

9

to the ultimate result, providing I was but sufficiently alert to avoid his early thrusts. Now, each and every onlooker was quite certain in his mind that it was not possible, such was the dire fame of my antagonist, for me to come out of the encounter scatheless. Accordingly the great man had a large and boisterous following. Having made up their minds that my time was nigh, the spectators, after breathing many hints of coming death, set about to expedite my leavetaking. The first step towards the grand finale was performed by piling up the chairs and tables, so as to make a decent fighting space in the middle of the room. Without a doubt I had to die, and derision beset me on every side, touching the climax of the contest.

One bold blasphemer went down on his knees, clasped his hands in the fervent piety of heartfelt prayer, and passionately pleaded for the better reception of my soul.

Alas for my chances in the next world! He had scarce poured forth a dozen words, when a ruthless neighbor, with no such kindly intention, dealt him a lusty kick on his nether part, whereupon a bout of fisticuffs ensued, which delayed my passing hence a full five minutes.

They crowded round the hero, the Honorable Peregrine Wilmot, and wrestled among themselves for the honor of holding his worship's doublet.

"Be not too hard on the oaf, Perry," said one. "I'll warrant he knows not the hilt from the point."

Thereat another took compassion on my hopeless plight and ran towards me, exclaiming—

"Oh, my poor young clodhopper, run back to thy mammy while there yet be time. This wicked man will slit that country skin o' thine as thou wouldst slit that of one of thine own lambkins. Why, my cherubim, he fairly pinked my Lord Graham and young Charlie Cook, the only son of Sir John his father, each within an hour of t'other in Lincoln Fields, last week!"

"One moment, gentlemen, I beg," I interposed, as my enemy was rolling up his sleeves, the cruelest glow in his eyes. "I would like to lay a wager. Will any gentleman among you lay odds at three to one that I do not beat my good friend Perry Wilmot by fair sword play, and without spilling a drop of his precious blood?"

"What!" clamored the bystanders with one accord; "thou art surely mad!"

Yet it was no big matter to show otherwise. Thereon many of them still possessed of a white groat piece eagerly beset me to stake the money. Thus it was I wagered with odds allowed at three to one that I beat the Hon. Peregrine Wilmot, the most capable swordsman in England, by the pure art of fence, without spilling a drop of his precious blood. I staked every silver shilling I had won, and a portion of mine own money besides; and 'twas only an afterthought of caution that prevented me risking the beauteous jewel that tickled my middle finger. And I made this wager because I knew my own head was, all things considered, tolerably clear, and that my adversary's was thick as a morning dew on Exmoor.

Neither did I doff my thick brown jacket to win it. Why was this? Maybe I was fastidious and over confident, but in sober verity, I was aware that my underlinen had known a fortnight's wear without heed to soap and water, and furthermore, that an unpatched rent was visible in the shoulder of my shirt.

Clash came our swords together, and the gay-dressed gallants fell back where the chairs and tables were piled, that our arms might swing with all due freedom.

Clash! clash! and my opponent's bewildering sword-steel was turned from my heart by a flash of the wrist and a twirl of the hilt. The song of metal filled the room with a deafening ring. Lunge upon lunge gave the far-famed Wilmot, furious, wicked lunges, that must have laid me stark upon the spot had one slipped my guard. I had nearly fallen into one of the most grievous errors a swordsman can, to wit, making too light of an adversary. His terrible onset may I never forget, and not since have I known it equalled. He sprang upon me with a fiendish fury. I felt his hot breath in my face, and was for the moment dazzled by the light that quivered on his thirsty blade. Inch by inch the fellow drove me back, and thrice his point came within an inch of my skin ere I could interpose a parry. Every nerve I strained to avert his steel, but soon the impetuosity of his onset lessened, tho' none too soon for Edward Armstrong.

Before long, I knew I was his master, for the wildness of his efforts told all too surely on his wine-clogged head; and the fire of his attack diminished as my defence became more certain. Then I fairly met each darting stroke without ever giving a riposte in return, because 'twas my game to let him vainly spend his strength until I had him completely at my mercy. Great was the chagrin of Mr. Wilmot's admirers, as they beheld their champion wax himself into perspiration and bad language, for never a whit did he get the nearer of ending the combat on his own account. For mine own part I had it in my power to finish it forthwith, had I been so minded, for my reckless opponent soon threw prudence to the winds, and attacked me so fruitlessly and so rashly, that more than one chance had I of pinking him. But I forbore, because of the wager.

Despite the force of his friends' appeals, the great swordsman failed altogether in beating down my guard and slipping past it. By and by the sweat steamed off him. The panting fellow ne'er sent home a thrust, and at length, in a frenzy of drunken desperation, he flung himself almost bodily upon me. I could have had his life then; yet, instead of a swift return, I stepped lightly to one side; flashed my blade beneath his own, and wrenched it from his grasp. It hurtled thence across the room, and met with the excellent good fortune of striking one of his loudest supporters on the nose.

The Hon. Peregrine Wilmot stood sheepish and wet with sweat in the middle of the floor, whilst the company gave vent to a hum of astonishment. Thereat I bowed, and began to stuff my pockets with the winnings, for one and all paid willingly.

"Gentlemen," said I, gravely saluting them with my uncovered weapon ere I departed, "I have two pieces of advice to offer. Never support the greatest swordsman in England when he be the worse for wine. Also take not every man who wears homespun for a country bumpkin."

Thus I paid them sweetly for their insolence.

Faith ! they looked a foolish crew as I left them, my person heavily weighted with their guineas ; yet a hubbub of loose-tongued wonderment arose as I passed out into the street.

I have since been told that "The Swordsman in Homespun " was discussed with bated breath, and together with his prowess (so cheaply revealed) formed a topic for many a day thereafter.

With great reputation left behind, I stepped homewards to the Three Crowns as jauntily as my pockets would permit. The chill night air bathed my hot temples refreshingly, whilst the moon had risen, and shed a soft light on the road. Before every tenth door a flickering oil-light was suspended, which I bethought an excellent practice. This was due to one of the very few wise decrees of the late king's reign. The folk abroad were nought seemingly but roystering swash-bucklers, who rolled, lurched, and staggered from side to side, and roared out many a scrap of ribald song in drunken merriment.

Midnight had passed an hour since, and I sought the shelter of the tavern with feet of the quickest. I went along as best I might through the vast labyrinth of ways and byways. With head aloft at my late success, I had no thought for the countless dangers of the place at this hour of the morning. My mind lay on the ring I had so lately become possessed of, when, without any warning, I bumped down all of a heap on the cobble stones, and had directly a couple of villains on my body. Also I felt unrighteous knees pressed hard into my stomach, whilst strong fingers came nigh choking the life out of me, such was the fierce grip on my windpipe. Ere I could utter a cry, the grasp was deftly loosed, and a rag thrust three parts down my throat. And all there was left to do that I might save my money was to vainly kick at the air whilst these parlous rogues rifled my pockets, and jammed their knees the harder on to my luckless body. But, to my relief, this wicked game was interrupted, for in a moment, a hoarse cry of "Bonaventors to the rescue!" was loudly raised but a few yards distant, and the clatter of many feet accompanied it. Forthwith my assailants loosed their hold, and made off mighty quick. Other hands were laid on me ere I could regain my feet, and I was dragged on to them limp and gasping.

Verily my deliverers formed an uncouth crew. All of them were young gentlemen, maybe two score in all, the worse for wine, with naked blades and cudgels freely brandished. I was soon informed that this was a band of the justly dreaded "scourers," the bane of all peaceable Londoners after nightfall. 'Twas they who beset honest men and rogues without discrimination. Also, when there was a lack of either, sooner than be idle, their time was employed to strip houses of their shutterhooks, and knockers, and ofttimes, when two separate bands of them came in contact, fierce fights ensued, till the city watch dispersed the combatants. My rude treatment had driven any knowledge I possessed of them clean out of my head. Therefore, with notable lack of courtesy, I gasped still breathless—

"Who the devil may you be, gentlemen?"

This query was ill-advised, and immediately a chorus of loud voices dispelled mine ignorance.

"Know ye not, then, most insolent and ungrateful knave, we are of the Worshipful Company of Bonaventors?" said a tall fellow, the foremost of them all, grinning and waving his sword about. Hereat the whole pack of them clamored among themselves to bring my lamentable lack of knowledge to boot forthwith.

"To the kennel with the scurvy fellow, that he may not forget us for the future!" called out another.

"Ay, to the kennel with him!" they acquiesced in chorus.

The "kennel," or filthy black ditch, lay stagnant with oozing

mud across the roadway. The prospect was not pleasant, and
already I began to shiver at the thought of my sousing. Rough
hands were laid upon me, and they began dragging me towards
it, my kicks and struggles notwithstanding.

I was hard by the brink, when once again my affairs, of late
so intricate, underwent another alteration. Just then more lusty
cries and ring of steel were borne upon the air, which further
saturnalian babel heralded the approach of a second company.

My persecutors halted, and the first speaker, whom I took to
be the leader, exclaimed excitedly, "Zounds, lads! 'tis Dicky
Bardswell and his boys. Holy mother! we'll serve 'em as we
did in Fleet Street last Monday but one."

The others came running up, mouthing all manner of warlike
sentiment. "Hooray for Dicky Bardswell, a bloody nose, and
a broken pate!" was their cry, and in one solid body they rushed
upon us.

Straightway I was released, yet there was no escape from the
impending battle. It was but a narrow pathway, and I found
myself in the front rank of the Bonaventors. The drunken
revellers met together with desperate valor, and the street was
alive with cries and blows. Lusty knocks were exchanged by
many a sword and cudgel. Scarce time had I to draw my
rapier, ere the foremost of the enemy were in our midst.

The Bonaventors were driven back before the mad onset of
the others. In a moment we recovered and set ourselves firm,
and a hand-to-hand struggle ensued, blows falling thick around,
thicker even than the curses.

At the first assault my light rapier was snapped by a stave
two inches below the hilt, and I, deeming the occasion warranted bold measures, flung the shattered weapon full at a little
fellow with a cudgel and bounded after it among the press,
whereat I, the little fellow, and the cudgel, came hurtling heavily
down atop of a recumbent combatant, where we writhed and
wrestled under the heels of the fighters. I got that cudgel, and
jumping to my feet, struck hard whither the fight was thickest.
The blood flowed freely, I may tell you, and soon the cobbles
were strewn with many forms, bleeding, half or wholly drunk,
but very valorous.

Our party was driven steadily backward, outnumbered by the
enemy, who indeed performed wondrous feats of daring. They
rallied round a bandy-legged, bull-necked fellow, the redoubted
Dicky Bardswell. This brawny Cyclops mowed down our
men one by one, and though, to say the least, his method was
truculent and terrific, 'twas not the less impartial. None could

withstand this foeman or the sweep of his mighty arm.   Before
long mine head fell a singing suddenly, and the blood came
pattering down my neck.   Our men were surely losing.   The
leader was felled by the arm of Dick, and a hoarse cheer went
up from his victorious warriors.   Yet the struggle ne'er abated.
With the thinning of numbers we clustered up the closer, and
broken pates were dealt with more precision.   And that bold
irresistible Dicky Bardswell pressed forever forward, and at
every stride our brave Bonaventors were knocked down like
bullocks before his strength of smiting.

Said I, under my breath, though a mist of blood swam in
front of me, "Here goes for that bull neck o' thine, Dicky
Bardswell!" and go I did right smartly for it.

Master Dick, mighty clever, dodged a skull-testing smack
from another quarter, then swirled his cudgel overhead, and
brought it down for my behoof.   Yet quick as thought was I to
slip in under it, and, locking my arms fast round his neck,
gripped a heel betwixt his own.   We swerved, though locked
so tight, and with a tremendous splash the puissant Dick and I
went toppling into the "kennel."   And I, alas, was underneath!

The combat ended suddenly, for when scarce a dozen were
left with legs to support 'em, the night watch came puffing and
panting in the conscientious execution of their duty.   They at
once took the wounded into custody, whilst the rest took to
their heels instead, being too far spent to give the men of law a
thrashing.

"Lie close," whispered the dauntless Dick, bobbing his head
below the bank, and at the same time jamming me deeper into
the slimy filth at the bottom of the ditch by lying full length
upon my saturated person.

"In the King's name," quoth the posse, as one by one the
prisoners were conveyed on shutters to the round-house.

"They only once came too early," whispered Dick again,
who was wondrous sociable; "that was many a year agone, in
the Brodribb days, when they were flung into the kennel every
man Jack of 'em, and after that we began again and finished
the discussion of our little differences."

The watch went at last, whereat Master Bardswell clambered
from the slough of muck, and very kindly gave a hand and
hauled me out of the caky plaster at the bottom.   Just then, I
have no doubt at all, I was the filthiest and dismallest animal
in creation.   The blood and mud clung upon me horribly, and
my skin was drenched with water.   We shook hands without

ill-will and went our several ways, did Master Dick and I, though, to be sure, time and circumstances would permit no superfluity of politeness.   But ere we did so, my genial companion, brimming with sociality, clapped his hand upon my bloodied scalp, and having fingered with an inquiring touch the damaged part, said with notable frankness and good fellowship—

"Old man, that crack didn't come from me.   I hold it a point of honor ne'er to hit a man upon the brain-box but what I smash his skull."

I reached the Three Crowns by and by, yet how I did so cannot be chronicled with exactitude.   Still I got there, more dead than alive, I trow.   My head was like a lump of clay, save for now and then a horrid throbbing to remind me that I had it still upon my shoulders, whilst my teeth chattered, my knees knocked, and I was too miserable altogether to do aught else but groan.

Master Fletcher left his warm bed, grumbling, to admit me. Presently he re-lit the candles, unbarred the door, stared at me, rubbed his eyes, stared again, and next minute lay back in a chair laughing till the tears rolled from his eyes, and he came nigh having a fit by virtue of his unseasonable merriment. Indeed, such was his plight, that naught availed against these symptoms, save and except a prodigious dose of the strongest brandy.

CHAPTER XIII.

THE MAN IN THE CLOAK.

MASTER FLETCHER recovered after a while, and in no time he rose considerably in my estimation.   Indeed, the expert manner he tended my hurts, and the vigorous way he swilled the coat of mud from my person inspired much gratitude within me.   A warm liquor revived my flagging spirits, and ere I retired to rest I had vowed eternal friendship for mine host since his handling was so deft, and felt myself to be the soul of amiability.   To be sure, half the gold I had had in my pockets had been left in the hands of rogues, else in the black ditch, yet this was accounted the lightest of misfortunes, for money was gotten easily in those days, and was valued in accordance.

Towards noon that same morning I set out on the homeward

journey. My heart was light, for success had warmed it, whilst a few hours' rest had wrought appreciable improvement in the condition of my injured head.

Having stowed away in my saddle-bags the presents and the money I had won, I bid adieu to mine host with kindliness. He, good man, setting store by future custom, bid me God speed, and furthermore begged that I would commend him to the love and prayers of his kinsman at Bridgwater.

To follow the king's highway 'tis a hundred and forty odd miles to London from that town. This is at all times a consequential journey, yet I returned thither without misadventure, a whole day inside the limit. Good news maketh men good couriers, therefore I did not tarry without sufficient reason, and on the evening of the seventh day following my departure, with steaming horse and mud-stained coat, I rode into the yard of the King's Head.

Ten minutes later Master Peter had a substantial supper set before me in the cosy parlor, and was listening eagerly to my adventures, and making such comment thereon as he thought befitted the occasion. Mine host strained his ears as I recounted my deeds in the gaming-house, and slapped my back to record his appreciation; tho' this was certainly ill-advised, seeing at that instant I was conveying a huge forkful of beef to my mouth; wherefore the consequences were painful.

"Ods bud, lad," exclaimed delighted Peter, "'pon my soul 'tis worthy of Bob Bickers! He, he! so ye fairly beat Perry Wilmot, and won nigh three hundred guineas? Well done, young un, say I, choicely well done, I swear. But, lad, I must take care on't for you, as ye will surely lose so large a pile if ye carry it about. Tell me who was there. Didst mark a little chap with a squint an' a pot belly? That's my lord of Tunbridge; the biggest rake unhung. One night at my little place he lost twelve thousand at Lansquenet, and 'pon honor he wagered his wife's jewels next night and lost 'em. Night following, when his town and country houses were gone, he staked his wife and lost her too. For a whole week she belonged to young Tommy Lunn, and then my lord borrowed money from me and won her back. And I fair bibbed, I tell thee, when my lady came back into his arms again, 'twas that affecting, ay, and so did the whole room full. After that his luck was wonderful, and he won back all his belongings, and a cheerful sum besides. 'God bless you for an honest man,' said he to me that night as he repaid me tenfold.

"Then did ye perceive a gent wi' a wry neck, in a blue coat

and drab breeches? He ne'er affects aught else. That's my lord Buthbungle, who doth possess many a fine cock. May I never clap eyes on better. I recall how one day he boasted that one of 'em was the best bird of its size in England. I' faith 'twas a lively pile game bantam, yet a quiet stranger chanced to be by and overhear his bragging. ' Pooh, pooh!' quo' he, ' call ye that the best bird in England. Tell thee what I'll do. I will e'en wager a hundred pounds I bring two to beat it in ten minutes.' ' Done!' gleefully cried my lord. Gadzooks! that stranger went and fetched a couple of birds of a similar size, then set 'em on my lord's. ' Here, I say, take one off, can't you, there's two against it,' called out my lord in the twinkling of a bedpost. ' Not likely,' answered t'other, ' I promised to bring two to beat it, and here I've brought 'em, and methinks my hundred ain't far off.' 'Twasn't neither, for the company adjudged the stranger had fairly won; and that stranger, let me tell you, was Long Bob Bickers, the greatest man that ever trod this earth."

Enough of Master Whipple. Howbeit he set forth his eternal reminiscences in so picturesque a manner that he scarce ever failed to raise a laugh for his reward. Should aught arise out of the common course of daily happenings, my very good friend was always able to patter forth examples by the score; and one and all had an immediate bearing on the case.

Eager to relate my success, I set out for the manor directly the meal was despatched. I had not seen Mistress Dorothy in the flesh for the whole week, though often enough in imagination. Therefore it would have been hard to find a more joyous fellow that night than Master Edward Armstrong, as he stepped out briskly through the darkness, flushed with pleasure at having done what he had done. He remembered quite well how the maid had bid him go and accomplish the great task. And now it was accomplished his heart beat high; he had his reward in mind. Albeit this cherished guerdon was but another glance from those peerless eyes.

To talk of love, and then to laugh at it; to think of love, and then to scoff at it, is grave lack of worldly wisdom, and far greater lack of understanding. 'Tis the very salt of life and the surest thing to flavor it! Maybe I oughtn't to speak thus to you children, but with far more decency might play the part of sedate preceptor, and shake my hoary head with gravity at your youthful amours, without heed to the days when the world and I were younger.

Kinsmen, in common honesty I cannot play it. So I prithee

do not curl your lips at one who is old enough to know, or hold
him guilty of mock heroics. Poets may lisp rapturous odes to
the goddess of beauty, and malicious philosophers may gibe
and remark that that self-same goddess had corns on her feet ;
yet, woe is me, nature hath given me the midsummer temper-
ament of the poet, though my hair is gray. My heart—no, to
be correct, the heart of Master Armstrong (for you must know
it was a joint affair, and belonged in part to Master Armstrong,
gentleman, and in part to Black Ned, thief)—was a chaos of
extravagant delight. It overcame the lowering shadows of the
night by virtue of its blissfulness, and caused the dark heavens
to seem a cheerful sight.

I dashed up the front steps of the manor three at a time,
and Mistress Dorothy came forward to meet me, and her eyes
were those of welcome.

" Here is Black Ned back again, papa," she called out gayly
to the knight.

Then I, the happiest man alive, stumbled backward as though
a man had struck me in the face. I recoiled, a chill of fear
upon my heart, from her eager hands of greeting. But she
laughed, as she alone could laugh, no sooner than the word
was spoke, and I heard the old man give a cry of satisfaction.
Fortunately I had the luck and the strength of mind to overcome my pangs. Thus I entered the sitting-room smiling. I
found the knight close by the fire, a bold array of bottles and
liquor bowls beside his elbow.

" Holà, mon ami ! " he cried, his solitary orb very large and
bright. " Back again already ; and, if I be not deceived, thou
hast good news."

" You've said a soothful thing, sir knight," said I. " My lord
is pleased to accept the terms laid down, and hath promised to
attend the council."

" Good lad," exclaimed Sir Nicholas, rising awkwardly to his
feet and hobbling towards me ; " I must have thy fist for that.
The work thou hast wrought for the cause will be undoubtedly
remembered. Mon Dieu ! we are hourly sapping the strength
of the King. He is all a soldier, is my lord ; I've been beside
him in Holland when he's led the storming party. He took the
eye of Turenne many a time, and is certainly the best of English captains."

" Sir," said his daughter, acquiescently nodding her pretty
head ; " there is no one else worthy to tie his shoe strings.
My lord Feversham is a mere baby by comparison, and as for
Kirke and Trelawney, bah ! "

Her demeanor was so assured, and her voice so utterly contemptuous, that without doubt she felt deeply upon the subject. "Ned, my lad," I soliloquized, "of a surety you must study every book of war your brains will let you. This young lady can tell more of such matters in one five minutes than you have ever heard of."

"There is ample time for a game of piquet, lad," said the knight, "and you can give all particulars whilst we play."

As a preliminary, he drank my health solemnly three times out of the smoking bowl, and bid his daughter do the same, avowing she had much to thank me for.

'Twas a sight to see her purse her dainty lips and just let the liquor touch them. Yet she made many grimaces as she did so.

"Ugh, poison!" she exclaimed. And, with a naughty eye on me, she allowed herself a little shiver, and hastily clapped down the crock.

"Poison, quotha! Dost know, impudence, that Prince Condé swore by this concoction? An' if he may bib it, 'tis not for the likes o' you to abuse it. Poison, indeed!"

The soldier, to prove the profundity of this, gulped down another bowlful, then settled to the game.

Two minutes later I had begun a faithful account of my adventures. One circumstance had puzzled and alarmed me sore. That was the appearance of the man at the inn-yard, Bruton. No sooner did I inform Sir Nicholas of the fellow's bribe, than his anxiety and mystification were deeper even than mine own.

"I do not like the sound o' that, mon frère," he remarked uneasily. "Sure the conspiracy is known; and there's rough times ahead, if that's the case. 'Pon my soul, the matter wears an ugly look."

The knight was much distressed anent it. He scratched his powdered wig till his coat became like a miller's; though more he pondered on the matter the more disturbed he grew in mind. Still, the nut was one beyond his strength of cracking.

"This is a serious affair, and must be laid before the council. Our chances are gravely imperilled. What was the fellow like? Cudgel thy recollection, friend. Was he tall or short; young or old? The thing must be bottomed," he cried excitedly.

I told all I could remember about the man. However, the sum total of my recollection was extremely meagre, for, wrapped up as he had been, I had obtained no glimpse of the fellow's features, and the tight envelopment of the cloak had much aided this concealment.

Now, I was setting forth every little point that could throw light upon it, when the room door opened noiselessly, and there walked stealthily, silently in, a man clad in a dark cloak. And his face was muffled and hid. At that sight I felt a curious tightness in the region of the chest. My heart began to beat much quicker than it had a right to do, for without doubt this was the covert fellow who had accosted me at Bruton. And here he was before us without a word of warning, in the identical hang-dog fashion, too. My eyes were rooted to this spectre (what else could it be?), and though the fire and candles emitted a clear, broad light, my knees knocked and trembled, such was the all-powerful effect of this man's apparition. The knight looked round, and saw it for the first time. "What the devil ——!" he exclaimed, yet, being so taken aback, he could get no further.

The pair of us, quite dumfounded, sat alternately regarding each other, then the spectre. By this it had stopped midway behind the table some yards distant. It halted silently, and turned towards us two. But never a feature of its face was visible. The knight and I had begun to doubt the veracity of our eyes and senses, when, with a desperate effort, I released my tongue from my roof mouth, whither it had cleft in the paralysis of profound astonishment, and gasped out some-how—

"'Tis he, 'tis he! Zounds, 'tis the man of Bruton!"

"Is it, by G—d! Then woe to his flesh!" And upon the spot the old gentleman, being vouchsafed new powers of speech and action, jumped from his chair, and sent card-table and contents rattling in the grate. His eye a blaze of wrath, he hopped gingerly yet wondrous rapid to the Perillo blade grandly gleaming on the wall hard by. But as he did so, a trill of laughter came from the dusky folds of the spectre's garb, and next moment the archest head and the sauciest eyes that ever man did see were thrust therefrom.

"What the devil!" exclaimed the knight again; and the sacred sword fell from his grasp and dropped a thud on the carpet.

Now, 'twixt ourselves, had not a wholesome conception of good manners still abided with me, I should not have let appeals to one devil suffice, but must have enjoined ten thousand. I felt a fool at that moment, and doubtless the knight shared this emotion. And the lady said never a word, but just stood quivering with mirth; whilst her row of white teeth flashed through her rippling lips, as they sent forth peal upon peal of laughter.

Once more her father sought the intervention of the Evil One, yet directly afterwards he shouted out—

"Good lack, Ned, do you come and see the hussy! She hath gotten on my riding-boots. Egad, she hath most certainly!"

I, being a reprehensible and equally impertinent young man, must needs come forward pretty prompt to get a view of a maid in riding-boots. This impudence of mine thoroughly disconcerted her. Forthwith her merriment was doffed for blushes and all manner of signals of modesty distressed. Thereupon, in an earnest endeavor to so coil the cloak about her person that our prying might be balked, she by misadventure let slip one corner of it, and, alack, plump before the unabashed and rudely staring eyes of man, a pair of long boots were revealed. And atop of them (if I dare tell it) there certainly was seen a pair of horseman's breeches!

Sir Nicholas and I clapped our hands and made the rafters ring with our guffaws, tho' presently the knight held surcease by virtue of a violent choking, whilst I forbore, out of a spirit of pure kindliness towards the lady.

Faith, by this time the tortured maid was ready to weep with shame. Yet run away she dared not, because such was her plight that, had she ventured to stir a step, the whole garment must have fallen from her altogether. 'Twas evident she had not expected us to peer behind her cloak.

Her father presently overcame his malady; then merciless was his persecution. The maid, scarlet-cheeked and tingling with shame, was obliged to stand passive and endure it.

"Ods wounds, lad, dost see her coat and collar? Heigh, heigh, pink me if ever I cocked eyes on aught so funny! Why, ma petite demoiselle, thy neck and shoulders doth not a quarter fill 'em!"

Hereupon the maid having, in the jealous hiding of nether limbs, by inadvertence left upper portions open to the public view, sought to cover her slender neck and sloping shoulders. But the hapless one by so doing exposed those tell-tale boots again, and straightway the relentless old curmudgeon beset her in a style that cut her far more keenly.

"Donnerwetter, what massy build, young man! What muscularity! What spread of chest and what firm strength of ankle! What a grand cavaliero it is! With such superb physique, thou art the model of a very horse guard. None o' your raw-boned pikemen. And oh, Dorothy, what thews thou hast, and what sinews! What arms, to be sure! Dost remark 'em, Master Armstrong? Great, ain't they? Ventre

Saint Gris, they'd give stauncher sword-sweeps than Abide-in-Me Jenkins himself! By my faith, lass, ye might cleave the skulls of all enemies of the State! Certes, we'll make you a soldier after this revelation. Bid the whole continent of Europe beware! Verily, here is a man at arms mightier than threescore rolled into one."

The young lady dared not look at either the one or the other of us, so she kept her gaze averted; and before the end arrived the most defiant of daughters was so far humbled as to plead—

"Don't, father; please don't."

Still the knight was pitiless, and as a climax, he went close to her and proffered his snuff-box.

"Here thou art, good master. Take one dip, and no more."

She refused this doubtful offering, but next moment the crafty knight cunningly and neatly grabbed the cloak completely from her form. But then, like lightning, the maiden, unencumbered, dodged under his arm, and bounded through the open door.

Ten minutes later she returned in the garb of respectability. Her sire greeted her with a sermon, and the text was "Decency." The beginning she suffered with lamblike meekness; but the knight, trading on her non-resistance, hammered his theme with such indelicate zest that I was stung to compunction for my own unkind behavior. So said I, to exonerate myself, and to divert the discourse of this purist—

"Mistress, I beg your pardon."

Despite my interruption the knight still pursued his homily, till at last his volubility received an unexpected check. Suddenly the erring one tossed up her head.

"Sir," she said, turning on her sermonizing sire, very fierce and haughty, "I'll come back when you're gone to sleep;" and the quick-spirited creature sprang from her chair, threw her astounded parent a sarcastic curtsey, and sailed from the room.

Now Sir Nicholas was far too pachydermatous to feel the full significance of this. He was not of a sufficiently fine mental fibre to be hurt by the tongue alone; a retort only appealed to him when driven homeward by the fist. But what he did feel was, that his authority was waning. This disturbed his peace of mind, for said he, after ladling a cargo of snuff to his nostrils—

"By God! she gets a nice young Jezebel! You saw her, Ned, my lad—you saw her! Fine thing this, at my time of life. But, by all the imps in Hades, sooner than I'll be served so by a chit of a girl, I'll pound her to a jelly!"

Then his worship took refuge in the useful word that bears
the name of "damn," and in a hundred others of a kindred
nature.

Fortunately the old knight's ire soon spent itself, whereupon
we resumed the game. Nevertheless he continued to imbibe
with freedom, and after winning ten guineas the leather-livered
warrior fell fast asleep—doubtless to accommodate his daughter. Strange to say, ere he had discharged his second snore,
the door was softly opened, and Mistress Dorothy crept in
silent as a mouse. Her face wore a look of comical humility.

"Master Armstrong," she whispered to me contritely, "what
a fiery-headed fool I am. One minute I insult my betters, and
the next I'm in sackcloth and ashes for my impudence. But
oh, sir, I've got *such* a temper! I expect my much-tried
father, patient man, will be half killing me one of these fine
mornings."

At that she stole up to her ugly parent's chair, and, laughingly, but as a matter of necessity, very lightly kissed the
slumberer. This daring feat successfully accomplished, she
came and sat beside me.

"Dost know, sir," she said gayly, "that these great men are
very difficult to live with? But I suppose it behoves common
mortals to put up with their eccentricities without complaint.
My old dad hath been so hard on me sometimes, that I've felt
a longing to drop a snail in his punch, or a black beetle down
his back. Sooth! I once did pin a worm in his wig, but,
Master Ned, I have ne'er been tempted to do so since."

Afterwards this madcap said nothing for a time, and did
nothing either, except to look provokingly pretty. But 'twas
plain she had something serious to say, because she began to
display anxiety, and several times glanced nervously at me.

"Master Armstrong," at last she said timidly, yet giving me
the reward from her eyes I had counted on, "I am filled with
gratitude for what thou hast done. I know not how to thank
thee, thou art so kind, and so very brave."

This little speech was softly given, and with a delicious embarrassment. It set me more at ease, and my tongue became
busy in protesting my unworthiness. After that I gathered
pluck enough to ask what I had so long desired, which was—

"Wouldst tell me, mistress, how thou wert so able to deceive
me by thy masquerading?"

She dropped her head, and spoke no word for a minute or
two, then answered doubtfully—

"Perhaps I ought to tell you, sir, or perhaps I ought not. I shall show myself an ingrate if I tell all, yet if I don't, you and papa will be much exercised in mind. What shall I do?"

She remained undecided till I besought her once more, whereupon she replied—

"I am bound, sir, to prove myself oblivious of benefits, and very suspicious of your honor; yet, if you must learn, listen. The night I persuaded Sir Nicholas to let you ride to London in his stead, and gave the letter into your keeping, within an hour of your going hence he became woefully uneasy in his mind. He began to think he had done wrong in confiding the letter out of his own charge, and declared his honor was grievously imperilled. And every minute he grew more scared, and imagined all manner of fearsome adventures befalling it, and thee. And, oh! forgive him, sir, and me for the recounting of it; he declared he had no proof you were a true man, and that you might betray your trust. He got cruelly excited, and worked himself into a fever of anxiety, and all the time became more convinced that he had compassed a wicked thing. He continued speculating as to whether you would stand by your word, till at last he declared he should ride after you on the morrow, and deliver it himself, otherwise he could not rest in peace.

"But, just then, Master Armstrong, his vexation of spirit brought on one of his worst attacks. He roared with pain, cursed everything, and reviled me for my share in the business. He hath ne'er sworn at me like he did that night; he said I'd ruined him, for now this attack had come, 'twas impossible for him to pursue you; and in his wildness he accounted this as one of the devil's machinations to thwart him in the prevention of his ruin. His pain increased, and as it did so he drank deeper, vainly hoping that liquor would relieve his agony. His ravings were cruel; I shudder for the words he hurled at me. And methought I had acted for the best. He went nearly mad, and the more he drank, the worse became his state, till at last I tugged the liquor from him, though twice he struck me with his fists."

Hereat methinks her eyes grew wet; yet she swiftly turned away her head, so that, even if they did, she hid her weakness.

"Next the foam came on his lips," she said. "But still he screamed that I alone had caused his downfall. Then I got frightened, and called the servants, and they carried him to bed, tho' all night long he lay moaning and coughing and swearing, and crying out he was undone. He would not have me approach his side, but thrust me away every time I neared

10

him. I never left him, though, till morning, and did my best,
poor man, to soothe his pain of mind and body. Yet, when I
applied cool bandages to his head, I had to slip behind the
curtain for fear he'd see me. He ne'er ceased to rave throughout the night, and I first did pray that God might spare him,
then tried remedies. Oh, I shall ne'er forget that awful time ! "
Her face went livid at the recollection.

" About the hour of dawn," she continued, " I had a sickening fear. Master Armstrong, I began to wonder what would
ensue should you play the traitor. Please forgive those
speculations ! "

She quickly turned towards me, and I saw in her eyes a
profound appeal, and that even her neck was crimson. I
made haste to grant this prayer, whereat she went on.

" Had you been one, I knew 'twould surely kill him; and
'twas I alone who had caused you to take the missive. This
horrid dread grew hourly greater. I could not get out of my
head that, after all, you might *not* be a true man, and I would
have given aught then to have recalled my evening's action.
Soon I felt a puissant desire to do something to save my father,
by averting any threatened staining of his honor; and I e'en
made up my mind to do it—ay, but what? There was nought
I could do. Sir Nicholas was far too ill to be left for any length
of time with only the servants to attend him. Besides, you
were fast speeding from my reach, whilst I had no notion of
your whereabouts. Verily the case was almost hopeless; but,
bad as it was, I did not give way to despair, which dear father
says is a word specially made for cowards. So I thought and
thought till I nigh split mine head with thinking. Never before
have I cudgelled my brains so sorely, because I decided, come
what might, to satisfy my terrors. I would learn for myself
whether you were an honorable man.

" I had but one fact to assist me. This arose through hearing you say you would not tarry to dine till you had arrived at
Bruton. Bit by bit my plan was pieced together. No time was
wasted neither, for 'twas very patent I must take prompt action.
I had not a minute to fritter; not even time for breakfast.
First, I rummaged out the smallest suit of clothes I could lay
my hands on. It was a very old one, which papa had worn
when a lad. Next, I took a dark riding-cloak of his also (miles
too big), which was quite easy to gather about my person so
as to nearly hide it altogether. Having thus attired myself, I
donned his riding-boots. These I had to stuff with wool to
keep them on my feet. Perhaps, Master Ned, you will now

understand I had disguise enough to deceive folks. Without leaving a word behind, I saddled Wallenstein, as none of the others were fit for service, and ne'er drew rein till I had discovered you at Bruton, whence I arrived twenty minutes ere you went forward on your way. I waited till you were ready to start, and then tempted you (as you know) with a bag of gold I had brought for the purpose. I found you not wanting, but true as steel, thank God! And, oh, sir, forgive me, I beseech thee ! "

When I heard these words, I felt for all the world like a man must feel when he sits, candle in hand, upon an uncovered keg of gunpowder. One stray spark, and his life is lost; one stray word, and so is my reputation. What had I done the afternoon she had accosted me? I had used savage threats, and worse, a thousand times, I had shown my true colors, and had half revealed to her my real vocation. Now it was my turn to do something, else I must for ever appear to her a rogue and trickster.

In supreme moments some of us may now and then display acute intelligence. Luckily, I kept cool. I knew promptitude was imperative, and therefore without delay I put my hand in my pocket. Oh, joy ! there reposed the bag unopened and un-touched. Instantly I whipped it out and laid it on the table, exclaiming airily—

" Mistress, you adjudged me a dirty rogue to steal your gold. But, 'pon my life, methought I was surely drawing the teeth of a wicked viper who went about tempting honest men. So, thinks I, you shall no longer have the means, you knave, to seduce, with such a tool, others from the path of virtue. Thus it came about that I snatched it from you, and have ever since desired to give it to the first deserving poor man I might chance to meet."

This was the biggest lie to which I ever lent my tongue. God forgive it! Upon uttering this atrocious falsehood, I went hot and cold (and well I might) at intervals. Still, next moment I was conscious of a throb of joy, for the maid no more perceived the depth of this duplicity, or the still greater depth of the man before her, than she divined my jocular laugh was the hollowest she had ever heard. And the knight still slept. Happily for me the danger was safely passed, whereupon I inquired how she came back again.

" Why, sir, as soon as you went your way, I went mine, know-ing well that I need not fear. Yet, mind you, sir, I was devoutly thankful to flee from you, as I was much frightened at your

anger. I reached home an hour after dark. I found dear
father mending somewhat; and tho' I strongly pooh-poohed his
fears, I concealed from him my errand."

"What!" said I. "You mean to say you touched no food
all day, and also rode along these lonesome lanes after nightfall, though so many robbers, highwaymen, and footpads are
abroad; and sat in the saddle during a fifty miles' journey, and
only once left it for half an hour?"

"That is so, Master Armstrong; and I could hardly move
for three days after, I was so stiff and sore. Also, I may tell
you, sir, I sometimes trembled at the rustling leaves; but my
heart was blither than a summer's day, because I knew that
father's fears and mine were groundless."

"Yet, why could you not stay the night, and get some food
and rest ere you made the homeward journey?" I asked, still
marvelling at her splendid courage and endurance.

"Poor father was so very ill," she answered simply.

CHAPTER XIV.

TOBE HANCOCK SPEAKS HIS MIND.

THE knight still slumbered with noisy resolution, therefore
we two conversed for a lengthy time.

"Master Armstrong," eagerly besought the great-hearted
maid, "please tell me of your adventures on the way, and how
my lord received the missive. I lost your narrative by slipping out of the room to play the part of the 'Man of Bruton.'"

In duty bound I was compelled to do so. 'Twas exhilarating
to see her ardor as I recalled the story of my strange adventures,
and to watch the rapture in her eyes as I told of my victory over
the redoubted Perry Wilmot, and recounted the lawless doings
of the Bonaventors.

"Master Ned," said she again, her face truly splendid in its
animation, "I wish I were a man, and as brave as thee."

And to see it so was a greater recompense than I had dared
to hope for.

It was within five minutes of midnight ere I walked into the
little parlor at the King's Head, and found my friend Pete, with
his pipe and black jack consoling him for the labor of the day.
He coolly eyed me as I entered, and half smiled to himself when

he heard my elastic step, and saw my cheeks flushed, my visage radiant, and my head cocked up in the air.

" Ods boots, young man," quoth he, " it runs in my mind that matters are coming to a woeful pass wi' you. Of late I have put two and two together upon the subject. What means this flying out o' nights, this sprightly demeanor, this sad neglect of business, this regular donning of Sunday garments? Shall I tell you? This noddle o' mine hath fathomed deeper mysteries. There is a woman at the bottom on't. You'll get no good by them—take my word for that. Oft have I told you they are the devil's creation. The very best woman I ever knew was a Charing vintner's daughter, and, man alive! she eventually came to be hanged as a common cutpurse."

Hereupon mine host removed his pipe-stem from between his teeth, waved it in my direction, and solemnly said, " Damn the women!"

With the delivery of this pious ejaculation he blinked in his owlish fashion, and proceeded to prove the fittingness of the malediction. He summoned scores of incidents out of his experience; but none the less I was disgusted, and debated the point staunchly. However, in despite of this, he still abided by his warning that I must entirely shun the sex.

Next morning I betook myself to Chilverley, to dispose of the presents; tho' I was beset by much misgiving, for my previous reception had not faded from my memory. At the busiest of times the village is sleepy, the villagers taking life serenely, and scarce ever moving faster than a jog-trot through it. The inhabitants numbered very few, and I trusted to them not recognizing me. Perhaps I was ill-advised to venture there in daylight; but, straightforwardly speaking, I was determined not to disappoint the knight of his piquet, as I must have done had I come at eventide.

As I arrived within sight and earshot of the blacksmith's forge, a series of howls and wailings disturbed the wonted stillness of the hamlet. The cause of this was not far to seek, for before the door I beheld Master Hancock, one hand holding the neckband of his youthful 'prentice, whilst the other was administering a cudgelling. Thus zealously occupied, he heeded not my presence, but continued to instil some belated Christian principle into the froward youth.

In time he ceased to ply the staff, yet, jerkin still in hand, he went on, without a trace of anger in his voice, to expound to the whimpering penitent the error of his courses. This admonishment bristled with Bible precept, intended for future conduct

and wellbeing; and bore more particularly upon the conveyance of false witness and the disregard of truth. The lad's
blubbering was not subdued till Tobe let go his hold, whereupon he was glad to run inside and resume the blowing of the
bellows. Then the blacksmith turned and noticed me.

"Thickee there bwoy's nuff tü drive me mazed!" said he.
"'E hath more thort, I rackon, vor a cudgel than pious exhortation; 'et tha well baying ov iz zoul shan't zuffer vor tha
laikes o' thickee matter. Du ee bide a minit, lad, an' I'll tellee
zummat."

These last words he spoke as though possessed of sudden
recollection. Ere I could reply, he disappeared through the
inlet, and returned with a bulky bag in his hand long before I
had ceased to wonder at his actions.

"Mebbee, Ned," he said earnestly, "I wor rayther hasty
loike t'other nite. I've thort 'bout 'ee mor'n wance. I knaw
'e nobbut nor a gert thief, 'et, lad, whoy cudden yü tarn honest
man agwaine? Now thease yer monies will 'elp 'ee tü goa tü
furren pairts an' start vresh. An' yü neddent rob volks theer,
lad. I've heerd zay ov bütivul lands acrass tha zee, wheer tha
zuggar and tha backy grow'th, an' tez zunny arl tha days ov
tha yeer. Bide not i' Zummerzet 'nother week. Twidden be
raight vor tü dü't. Tack et wi yü, an' goa an' get honest."

The well-meaning fellow pressed the gold eagerly upon me.
By the rapidity of his gestures, I guessed how much I had been
in his mind of late. My heart grew cold as my fingers closed
upon the bag, for then I felt the full import of this counsel.
How could I leave Somerset, even to become honest, with Mistress Dorothy Marvin still in it, and hopes of vengeance ex-
panding in my breast? A month ago I might have done so,
yet now I was no longer mine own master. I was like the fly
in the spider's web; only *my* fetters were formed by a web of
strange events. Therefore, at this gracious offer, I sighed and
shook my head.

"I cannot leave the county of my birth, Tobe," I said, uncomfortably tremorous.

"Whoy?" he asked sharply, his eyes fixed on my face.

"Circumstances have arisen which ere long will change the
affairs of the whole nation, and already I am deeply embroiled.
No, good friend, I must not take ship for foreign parts. My
duty lies in England—you forget my father's death."

Alack! I knew this was only half the truth, and for that
reason I could not have looked at the blacksmith squarely.
He never took his gaze from me, and the guilty and confused

way I answered him was enough for him to mistrust my utterance. His countenance was one of sorrow, as he replied with lowered voice—

" Now, dawnt 'ee zay zo. Thy veace tell'th me yü dezave a vrend. Tez vor tha welfare ov thy mother an' thyzel. She hath tüke on cruel awver thy knavery, I can tell 'ee. Thy vather wuz aveared ov God, an' zet gert store by righteousness. Yü midden stay, Ned, in the midst o' thy zin."

As in the days when war and its devilry had not come among us, so Tobe talked long and patiently, trying hard—very hard, by force of dissertation, to turn my mind towards virtue. The length and the breadth of the matter was, that I was truly ashamed of my livelihood, and would have gladly renounced it, had better prospects appeared. But it was impossible to live honestly now in my native shire. No Christian calling was open to an outlaw; and a man must live. Nor was Tobe's reasoning lost upon me. I sincerely wished to carry out his desires, yet how vain those wishes were, for there were pictures of a laughing maid with wondrous eyes, and the grim gibbet of the crossways in my brain. Thus the only thing left to do was to growl at Fate, like all weak creatures, who e'en spend more time and energy bewailing fortune than would serve to set their affairs to rights. Master Hancock persevered till he saw how fruitless his endeavors were like to be ; then steadily his anger rose. And as it came to the surface his tongue loosened, and burst forth in vituperation.

" Ah, Tobe," said I bitterly, " 'tis very pretty to prate about honesty and righteousness, you that have ever had a sound roof and a full cupboard ! Do but come to be hunted like a fox, with no place of refuge to run to for your life, and then see how you'll abide by the doctrines of prosperity."

'Twas an unkind and discreditable speech ; but, somehow, his words had stung, and I, being hurt in spirit, was, for the moment, unmindful for the feelings of the blacksmith. At my retort the smouldering anger of the man blazed out in sudden fury. 'Twas the fanatic peeping thro' his sober self, and I trembled at it. His visage went all thundery, his gray eyes stormy and foreboding as the tempest ; and a chill crept in my limbs as I saw this strong man's wrath.

" Zo, Ned," he snarled, his lips drawn stern and tight, " I zay thee'rt a cur, even as I zed avoretime."

I had dismounted, and now stood before him silent, with no words left to speak in self-defence, to stay the torrent of his anger.

"Ye are Jan Armstrong's zon," he continued; "oh, tha pity ov et! Weer be thy manliness an' courage? Yü zhame thy vather."

He thrust his big brown fist hard by my cheek, and I drew away from it affrighted. The passion of his features kept mounting higher. Quite suddenly, however, this harsh demeanor was forgotten, as a shrill scream of terror sounded close at hand.

The cause of it was soon apparent, for, as we turned our eyes to the bridge, we saw a small girl standing thereon, wringing her hands, and gazing horror-stricken into the rushing water. We ran straightway thither, and there beheld a child, being tossed on the surface of the stream. Ere I could move, Tobias had flung aside his leathern apron, and had plunged into the swirling current. He soon had the mute babe safe. 'Twas the third time it came to the top that the blacksmith seized it with one hand, and held it above the crest of the stream that air might find way to its puny half dead body. With the other he struck for the steep bank, and scrambled out of the brawling water, yet bore the child with tenderness. The wet running from him, and the little creature hugged to his breast, he set off at a trot down the road, the sister, with sobs now instead of screams, pattering after him.

I stood stock-still for a full minute after the three of them turned the corner. Thereupon I took Joe's bridle and led him to the farm. I had not the heart to tarry for Tobe's return, though the poems of John Milton were in my pocket. Again, as I neared the outer gate of the homestead, I halted, uncertain whether to go farther, for just then I felt baser and more sinful than ever I had done before. Albeit this backwardness was sufficiently overcome to let me cross the field and rickyard and put my horse up in the stable. The farm hands stared at me perplexed, and wondered much at the boldness of this stranger, who came with such assurance; although they recognized me not, neither did they ask questions, but merely scratched their country polls and ceased to puzzle them.

The family were seated at the midday meal as I entered. At sight of me, mother's face went strangely white. The first thing I did was to go and kiss her, and also at the time I bent over her took the chance to whisper, "Do they know all?"

She shook her head. Therefore I embraced my brother and sister less uneasily, now that I knew they were ignorant of my shame. I shared the meal with them, but John and Betty, though they received no aid from mother, questioned me again, as was only natural, concerning the nature of my calling. So it befell that they were first to learn my crimes from my own lips ; because in face of what mother knew, I dared not try to evade them in her presence.

" Have I not already told you I am Black Ned the highway-man ? " I answered, this time without any signs of mirth soever. And, in the absence of it, they turned to mother, and saw tears trickling down her face. At that they turned back their eyes to me, and saw mine glum and miserable. By this they were aware 'twas no jest, but unutterable truth. No more words passed between us. Both of them looked each towards the other, seem-ingly devoid of purpose, unless 'twas to divine the effect of this revelation. Shortly afterwards they stole glances at mother, who still wept in silence, and remarking this, Betty whose light-heartedness was fled, also began to cry noiselessly, and John, who was his father's son, had a look in his eyes more terrible than Tobe Hancock's. Not one of them gave a glance to me, but watched each other in an aimless way.

I was sitting in my dead father's chair, in his place at the table-head ; and God would not let me rest there. I jumped up out of it, took my hat off the peg, and crossed the threshold of my father's door in dull agony of spirit. I reeled sot-like across the yard to the stables and fetched Joe for further serv-ice. Through the open door of the house I caught a sight of John and Betty bending over mother.

Joe took me from the farm to the King's Head as fast as he could carry me. Arrived there I sought the chamber placed at my service by the landlord, locked myself inside, kindled a light with flint and steel, and set John Milton's book of poems blaz-ing. Next, I unstrung the necklet of crystal pearls, threw up the sash, and cast them out, one by one, in all directions ; and, lastly, stamped my foot on the shell, and John's costly hall-marked watch, smashed them beyond recognition, and flung the fragments out of window. This accomplished, I dipped my forehead into a bowl of water to allay the ferment in my temples. But to what purpose ? I threw my body across the bed in desperation, only to toss and moan upon it without allev-iation of my misery. And every time I shut mine eyes I saw my dear father in the courthouse, and the horrid demon reviling him, or the shimmering mass of metal and the moonlight still upon it. Yet even such phantasies as these, though they made me shudder and tremble as if I had got the ague ; even these, in course of time, gradually dwindled to that of a maid young and beautiful, with eyes big with gratitude. Here my moaning

ceased, and I got off my couch less wearily, and went downstairs into the private parlor.

"Why, Ned," said Master Whipple, "what hast been a-do-
ing? 'Oons, lad, I never set eyes on such a tozzled head of
hair. Hast been drawn thro' a thick-set hedge back'ards?"

I said no word to Pete, but started immediately for Kelston
Manor. That night I played and lost ten more guineas, whilst
Mistress Marvin concocted the punch and praised my courage,
and even the knight admitted it. I was also informed that he
set off for Wiltshire in the morning, hence there would be no
play for the next four days.

On coming back to Bridgwater, I lost no time in seeking
bed; whereupon my brain grew hot again, and things got
muddled, and churned one amongst another in my head. Before sleep came, mother's tearful face was near me. And looking over her shoulder, methought I saw Mistress Dorothy
Marvin. The last thing I was conscious of that night was that
the pair of them seemed struggling in a contest to be foremost
near me. But in the midst of it, they, too, mingled with the
other phantoms : notably John's cruel eyes, Tobe Hancock's
forbidding aspect, my dead father, and Judge Jeffreys—the
devil! Next morning I awoke, cheeks hectic and lips parched,
in a state of fever.

Peter Whipple shook his head with gravity, and being a
handy man and a shrewd one, bled me forthwith, avowing that
no physician must be sent for, else the sheriff's men would
soon have news of things, and would then come and arrest me
without hindrance.

CHAPTER XV.

THE DEATH'S HEAD AT THE FEAST.

In a week I was hale again. This circumstance was lucky
for me and unlucky for friend Peter.

One day during convalescence, mine host came to me in a
seemingly diffident manner, and delivered himself as follows—

"Young man, I'm uncommon glad to see thee on thy pins
again, but business is business."

Hereupon the worthy gentleman broke off short, drew his
brows together, twirled his thumbs with edifying solemnity;
pulled a very odd face, and coughed thrice in an apologetic
manner.

"Yes, friend, business is business, I'll remark again. Um, ah! have a drop o' cider, lad, it's good to keep the head cool." He poured me out a full tankard, did likewise for himself, pledged my health, and fell to twirling his thumbs a second time.

"What I was about to say," said he once more, "is that business is business."

"Why, confound you, Pete!" said I, very well knowing the drift of affairs by this, "you've made that brilliant observation nigh a score times already. What d'ye mean?"

"What do I mean?" Master Whipple refilled his tankard. "I mean business is business, an' friendship is friendship, an' a fee's a fee, and some folk are damned stupid, others damned blind, an', 'twixt you and me, there's none so blind as those that won't see."

"Very true," I answered, not daring to look at him, else I must have laughed. You see, I knew mine host of old.

"Ay, blind as bats in a belfry, ain't they? But, lad, business is the most beautiful thing extant, and friendship comes close after it. Combine 'em, and they are all-powerful. Now, hearkee, brother! I, your dearest friend, nursed you, and tended you, and bled you, and kept vigil wi' you, and plied cool cloths, and a thousand and one medicaments. Also, I kept mine own counsel all the while, mark you that! Therefore here ye are, sound in limb and body, thanks to pure friendship. Faith, I would have done the like for no other man that ever drew breath! And just think of the cost o' this attendance. There's the price o' the physics, the skilful treatment, the sleepless nights, and the dead losses in private business by inattention."

"Ah, yes; quite so!" said I, counting out ten guineas on the table, and pushing them towards him.

"What's that?" he asked, mighty solemn.

"That's the fee. Why in the world didn't you say what was required at first? I misunderstood you, friend, altogether. Of course, I perceive the force of your remarks now. I beg your pardon."

"No offence, no offence!" The gold dropped briskly, coin by coin, into his vest pocket. Then he commenced to cry.

"Forgive me, good friend!" he sobbed. "I am too ashamed to speak. I am your friend, and ye are mine, and I've done my duty by you, even as ye would do by me. God knows I would not touch a single groat as recompense, were it not for that cursed business. If I did not accept, I must perforce show a dead loss in the accounts, and that would never do for sure; just think of my poor family."

" Of course," and I nodded acquiescence.

From careful inquiry, both subsequent and previous, I was never able to gather aught concerning this reputed " family." He had none, for certain, in Bridgwater. The utmost of my gleaning was, in a moment of confidence, from Master Whipple himself—that is, when his breath was growing odoriferous. Then he hinted that this " family " was part of his business equipment and stock-in-trade.

Henceforth the days went briskly by. The springtime, the heartsome springtime, was gradually unfolded in its beauty. With it came longer days, mellow air, and cheerful sunshine. The tree boughs and the never-ending length of hedgerows donned their summer garment, the buds expanded, and all nature became verdant and inviting. I suppose 'twas by one of the perversities of human nature that at this time, when in all fittingness I should have been in black depths of despair, I was so very conscious of delight.

For a week after the proper power of thinking had been restored to me, I pondered much upon the prospect unfolded by Tobe Hancock. My duty to friends and self was very plain, but what avail is duty unless supported by the heart ? To be precise hereon, my heart was no longer obedient to my will; in fact, I could not now command it, seeing that it had deserted me and was in another's keeping.

And so the struggle was soon decided. Therefore I continued to lose money every night, and in the mean time endeavored might and main to win a heart in exchange for the one won from me.

April came and went all too quick, likewise May, yet early in June I learned a thing, which if it caused not the days to go the slower, certainly made me attend them more, because an event was pending which was fraught with import, both towards myself and towards the country.

I was at the manor one night as usual, and had just made the first replenishment of the coins upon the table, when the knight laid down his bowl, and stared fiercely in my face with that one eye of his which to me was far more impressive than a pair of other people's.

" Mon fils," he said, " I have news for thee ; you have right to know, as ye're one of us. A council is convened here at the manor on the eighth of July, when our course of action is to be carefully discussed. All the men of leading we can muster will come hither, and methinks 'twill have resolutions of rarest import for its outcome."

" That so ! " I exclaimed, taken aback at these momentous tidings.

" 'Tis so, Ned," quoth Mistress Dorothy, who was by.   " And you may bless your natal saint 'tis no house of yours these folk are coming to. Oh dear, what a place 'twill be ! For sure everywhere will be turned topsy-turvy all because of these dukes, and bishops, and knights, and peers.   Every room in the house will have to be put in fitness, mountains of bed linen to be aired, apartments to be furbished, overhauled, and hung with tapestry ; and Bibles placed in the bishops' bedrooms.   Also huge stores of provisions must be laid in, I can tell thee, for I've heard tell that e'en the Lord Privy Seal hath to eat and drink like a commoner.   And I say, Ned ! I am to be dislodged from my pretty chamber, which overlooks the copse and the stream, and receives the sun in the early morn.   But you know, daddy, I will not yield it up to any man amongst them, save my lord Churchill. He must sleep there. He will be a great captain yet (old Turenne said that), and I wish I had a score chambers for great captains to be bedded in ! So mind you, sir ! I will not be turned out for any beggarly speechifying Parliament man."

" Pax, pert one ! are you the master o' this place, or am I ? "

" You are, sir ; but I'm the mistress.   And, being the mistress, all domestic details must be left to me.   You'd no more be able to attend to them than you are to curl your wig."

The saucy set of her, and the bold roguishness of her demeanor, was a sight to warm the heart.   The knight was angered at this flippancy, and so allowed his six languages their exercise.   Though he swore so hard at her, she mixed his liquor meekly, and played the injured innocent naughtily yet prettily.   Still the irritated warrior would have none of her conciliating graces, but stormed much and lustily.   Not that this disconcerted her a whit, for she whispered slyly to me—

" Now I will play my master-card."   She did play it.

" Papa, you held dissertation this morning on the glorious victory of Edgehill.   I aver and am free to maintain that you are quite wrong. 'Twas a drawn battle, sir ; in fact, I am not so sure that the Roundheads, under Essex, did not beat you."

" Eh ? what ? Dost know what you say, wench ? "

" Know what I say, sir ? Of course I do.   Didn't Sir William Balfour make a flank movement and drive your centre before him ? Come, sir, I'm perfectly sure 'twas a drawn battle."   And she wagged her naughty head with an air of absolute conviction.

" It's a lie, it's a lie ! " shouted her excited sire, truculently thumping the table, but falling into the trap as usual. "Are you unaware that Rupert swept the Puritan left clean off the field? I ought to know, I was one of the men that helped him."

What useful purpose shall I serve in detailing this passado? 'Twas merely a repetition of many a one I listened to betwixt the twain; and to a man of peace their language might have been high Dutch instead of military jargon. On this occasion the disputants went to such a length that a plan of battle was mapped out between them. And, strange as it may seem, the lady was continually besting her father in the argument. All the while he grew more excited and loud-voiced. Methought the swinging of his arms was ominous, as he admitted first one false fact, then another. But at the conclusion he performed no more violent deed than the scratching of his bewildered head.

At this mistress Dorothy effervesced with laughter, made merry at the perplexed old gentleman's expense, and soundly rallied him on the score of his agitation.

"Mordioux!" cried Sir Nicholas, his high tones having declined to something perilously near dejection, "I'll be shot if ever I thought it so; but, strike me stiff! I'm damned if it don't seem right. Yet 'tis a queer thing that a bit of a girl, who can ne'er be a man-at-arms, should overcome a seasoned captain. Mon Dieu! I must summon my recollection."

To watch him twist his countenance into a mass of thoughtful wrinkles was better than a play. I'm sure his daughter thought it so. She soon showed that on occasion she could be every whit as merciless as her parent. First she clapped her hands, very victorious, but very impudent; then mocked his cogitating aspect, wickedly scratched her head, contorted her face, and corrugated her forehead. This done she flippantly cocked her thumb over her shoulder, according to the vulgar custom, then sang out loud enough to make her victim scowl, "Oh, Ned, do look at the seasoned captain!"

However, the next moment, her opponent, in all modesty, made an apparently unimportant observation. But it proved that this stray remark more than served his purpose. Instantly the maid discarded her triumphant demeanor in favor of a very puzzled one. Yet she gave me the tail of her eye; and I saw that in it which made me turn my head away to laugh.

"Dear papa," she said sedately, "I do believe I'm beaten. I cannot override that last contention. 'Tis a case of hauling down the colors."

She made the surrender very neatly; cunningly counterfeited perturbation, bit her lip, looked much annoyed, became elaborately contrite, began "to wish she had not had so much to say," declared "'twas all very fine to talk, but she knew when she was mastered," and so on, and so forth, till the old gentleman really persuaded himself that he had gained the day; therefore he plucked up courage, took patronizing airs, and reassumed bravado. I never saw a man more beautifully fooled, and certainly never one more self-complacent. He was in the highest of good humors for the remainder of the evening, and, victory being assured, he bade the sly vanquished go thither and be embraced.

There was no more play that night. Our minds were too full of the forthcoming great event to be occupied with trivial affairs. Sir Nicholas recapitulated the names of many of the guests expected, and a brave array they made.

"There is but one among them I do not hold in high respect," he said, "and that is my lord of Sunderland."

"Indeed," said I surprisedly, "why, sir, he is the King's prime minister. I recollect seeing him at Whitehall."

"Then you saw a scurvy rogue and villain, lad. Mayhap it is ungracious in me to so decry one of the greatest of men, and he of our side, too; but he hath no spark of honor. James hath been the very architect of his fortunes, yet now he is betraying and casting calumny on his master. The King hath made him his richest subject; but 'tis all money with this fellow. He will sell his soul and break his word ten times over for the gain of a silver shilling. Bah! Devil take such a paltry hound!"

The knight was wondrous hopeful that evening, being flushed with wine and his Edgehill victory.

"We are gaining strength every day, mon cher, and the King is getting weaker. This council we are about to hold will be the pivot on which the future of the State must turn. Mark me, lad, bold action will be the result of it."

This topic proved all-absorbing to the three of us during the days which elapsed between then and the chosen date. Nevertheless, other events befell in the interim that are set down at length in history. On the second or third day of July, I was coming from the manor at dark hour, when I saw the western sky illumined by a lurid glare. As I trudged towards Bridgwater it deepened as though fanned by the breeze of the night, whilst more strange than this omen in the sky, in the town itself, usually so quiet at this untimely hour, the townsfolk were astir discussing great news which had arrived from London.

These tidings were, that the Seven Bishops had been acquitted. Had ye lived in those days this would not seem so empty

sounding. From one end of the kingdom to the other the trial
of the Seven Bishops was a nine days' wonder. 'Twas felt to
be a test of strength betwixt the King and his subjects. That
you may the better understand this matter, here is the gist of it.

King James had made up his mind to force Popery upon his
people, whether they liked it well or ill. And, to make his purpose more fully known, he issued what he was pleased to call a
" Declaration of Indulgence," whereby his subjects were reminded of his determined character, and of the grievous mis-
chances which had befallen many a public officer who had
dared to oppose his will. Yet one and all were staunch
enough in their abhorrence of the Pope. Understand that,
children, or you will be surprised at many things I have to
tell. This land of ours, and the brave folk in it, detested the
Pope, his cardinals, and all his upholders. But, alas for the
English nation ! it was in the hands of an unscrupulous bigot,
who sooner than be thwarted in his aspirations, would shed
rivers of his people's blood, and would see his kingdom damned.
I do declare most solemnly James Stuart, king of Great Britain
and Ireland, to have been a bowelless wretch, whose aims were
self, and whose heart was stone. To oppose the tyrant, or his
red-handed ministers, was to hold life and property in direst
jeopardy, for the King and his servants had no scruples, as
the " Bloody Assizes " can amply testify.

Now this declaration was ordered to be read in every pulpit
in London on two successive Sundays, namely, those falling
on the 20th and 27th of May; while the same was to be done
in the country on the 3d and 10th of June.

This placed the English Church in an hurtful plight. It was
apparent to all, that should its bishops and clergy comply with
this order, they would assist at their own undoing. To read it
out meant driving terror into the hearts of the people, whereby
the King's designs would be forwarded. Should they refuse,
they were at once the King's enemies, and should they consent,
they were his tools to help pull down their own edifice, and
his minions to countenance his creed. To the everlasting
credit of the Protestant Church, its pillars showed themselves
brave men in the face of this dilemma.

Straightway the heads of it convened a meeting. The result
was to draw up a resolution, signed by seven of the highest
prelates in the land, refusing to obey the King's commands.
When His Majesty heard of this he lost his temper. He
promptly haled these men of courage before him ; and stormed,
and fumed, and threatened ; but to no purpose. The Seven

budged not an inch, and stuck tighter than wax to their resolution. So the King, in his might, had them clapped into the Tower, and determined to bring them to trial.

James Stuart was as blind as a noontide owl, and had no head for wisdom. He, stubborn fool, lacked the intuition to see that the country was entirely with the bishops, and that it hated the Roman faith from the bottom of its heart: neither had he the sense to know he was doing a thing every whit as perilous as the one which cost his father his head and his throne. No ; this man had the Seven arraigned before the Court of King's Bench on a charge of "seditious libel" (whatever that may mean), and tried all he knew to "pack" a jury for the hearing of the case. This "packing" process, as far as I understand it, means he selected men who were known to favor his cause to form the jury. Also my lord Jeffreys, the best hated and the worst-principled man in the State, who by this had risen uncommonly high in the council, exerted his devilish powers to corrupt the judges who were to preside at the trial. Thus, at the outset, it was obvious the bishops had little chance of an acquittal. Yet, in spite of everything, and to the joy of the nation, they were pronounced "Not Guilty."

England was delighted at this noble result. Bonfires were lighted, church bells set a-ringing, and effigies of the Pope and King were burnt in any number. Indeed, 'tis said one was set up and destroyed before the very gates of Whitehall itself. The glare I had seen in the sky was Dunkery Beacon blazing to proclaim the good news to the Cornishmen. And in Bridgwater, ere the light came in the morning, the bells rang out from every steeple. Also the alehouses, in a fervent spirit of religion, kept open all night, that pious souls might pronounce the healths of the prelates till their money was lost, and their wits had met with a like misfortune.

I discovered Master Whipple in the public room, dispensing liquor and retailing much information not known to the world at large. Remember, Pete was a London man, and if he could not enlighten the bucolic mind, who was to do, concerning things appertaining to the King, the Court, the State, and the Constitution ? Mine host was a Churchman for that night, at least ; and, to the admiration of his customers, he descanted with particularity about "Duty to the Nation," and rattled off the name, age, pedigree, manners, habits, and appearance of each member among the Seven ; whilst to hear him talk they must have been his bosom friends for certain. But when he came to relate how the Archbishop of Canterbury never preached a sermon in Town without he, Pete, chose the text for him, I had no more manners than to laugh aloud.   Not so his auditors. They took every word he uttered as unimpeachable truth, and set my behavior down to ignorance !   After the dispersal of the company, I tasked Master Whipple.

"Ye are a monstrous liar, Pete."

"Glad am I to hear it ; hearken to the voice o' Wisdom, friend ; never do a thing half-hearted.   Also go wi' the wind, it's so much easier to travel in that direction.   Besides, it's more profitable to go that way than to set your teeth against it.   If the wind blows for the Church, then be a Churchman, or if it blows for the King ye had better be the loyalest subject breathing. Yet, mark you this, *do nothing half-hearted.*   Churchman or King's man, Tantivy or Ranter, Papist or Anabaptist, no matter what your title for the nonce, be ever more zealous than your neighbors.   If ye pray, pray twice as long as your fellow Christians, or if ye lie, lie twice as large as your brethren in iniquity.   Half a lie is worse than no lie at all.   Do everything wi' all your might.   That is the first principle of business ; at least, Bob Bickers said so.   If he pinked a man, he pinked him through the heart ; or if he robbed a man, he left him nothing but his hosen.   He even stripped him of his sword and silver buckles ; and ne'er left him sense sufficient to tell the tale."

And now I will speak on a matter that deserves some mention.   'Twas a luscious thing to keep imbibing love day by day ; to get drunk with its geniality, and in the throes of its intoxication disregard the inward voice.   Now this inward voice, which tormented me after heavy bouts, was the death's head at the feast.   'Tis truly fine I trow to drink and be merry, and tilt the measure till the bottoms are gulped, and to laugh and forget cold care.   But drown it quite I never could.   No matter how little I heeded alien matters, this skeleton ne'er failed to appal me with its apparition.

'Twas delicious to play piquet with the knight, and lose other people's money; to see white hands concoct the punch; to watch red lips trill a rollicking lilt, and hear them whistle it. Or better still, to lie beside an eager form as 'ts owner fished under the boughs when the days were hot, for reluctant creatures in the stream ; or when they were wet to sit in a dripping cloak beside this self-same form, because the fish bit better then.   And to gaze at the maiden undisturbed as she put a finger up for silence when the line was tugged, and to behold the marble neck inclining and the face so keen, was reward for the best of men.   Sometimes we would discuss the art of quarte

and tierce, and even practise it ; when I'd thwart attacks from
maiden arms, and compliment my adversary on her strength of
thrusting.

At other times the two of us would seek to best each other
in the firing of pistols at a mark—in fact, I found the warlike
maid had greater knowledge of such weapons, and quite as firm
a hand and as steady an eye in their employ as ever I possessed.
Yet outstripping this in point of pleasurableness was a gallop
side by side with her, over hedge and ditch, hill and dale, along
the road or across the grass, ere the sun was fully risen in the
morning, and then have a mad race home to breakfast. The
delight of that! And, better still, to hear a soft voice call
"Ned;" and in return for this lack of title, to be enjoined to
call your companion by her simple name alone, without the
prefix "mistress."

Here, kinsmen, was the inebriating cup of happiness, that
was daily drained. And all the time your sire spent the money
of honest men, and averred to his inner self to kill biting pangs,
that this love was pure and sweet and holy. I could not muster
the courage to venture by the Farm, after what had befallen on
that last visit. Yet those heart-bursting incidents served to fan
stealthily into a flame the fire which so soon was destined to
consume my soul. Already, when I had the time to meditate,
I felt the portents of its agony. You have seen how I battened
on rapture; but in this stolen sweetness there was ever an after-
taste of gall. I might be eating of the lotus, but could not
abandon myself to its entire enjoyment, because I always had
a secret fear that it might turn to poison in my stomach. To
put this unharmonious sense in the smallest compass, being
naturally a creature prone to look ahead in times of solitude, I
was continually asking myself what would be the end of my
monstrous passion? What, indeed? Methinks this inner
questioning heralded the first struggle betwixt Black Ned and
Master Edward Armstrong.

CHAPTER XVI.

THE SWORD OF A TITAN.

KINSMEN, I see your scowls; I hear you cast contumely on
your father's name as I reveal the depths of my duplicity. I
can imagine you laying down for the behoof of one another, when

ye sip your wine and chew your walnuts, the path I should have trodden. Yes, 'tis easy to preach warlike doctrine in time of peace. 'Tis easier still to fight the devil when the devil sleeps. We can all preach charity when we sit in silk and broadcloth, and fling groats to our poorer brethren without hurt to our yearly incomes. Many's the time I have toasted my shins by the fire in after years, and have marvelled at my previous baseness. For, you are to understand, I was not wholly blind to honor throughout that time. I was not wholly lost in soul. I might be joyous for a day, but when reflection came in the silence of the night, a pang would convulse me, and I would remember who I was, what I was, and what I sought to do. I would recollect how my presence brought brightness to the maiden's eye, and how sometimes the knight looked at me in a way that was not unkindly. Yet I continued to play my cruel game, but rarely dared to speculate on its result. 'Twas like balancing one's self on the extreme edge of a precipice. The least breath of wind, the vaguest whisper of suspicion, and I should irrevocably be lost, even as a loose boulder or a loose word would send one hurtling to the gulf. I foresaw this as clearly as I write it now; so one day made a powerful resolve.

A week after hearing of the forthcoming council at the manor, I determined, come what might, to tell father and daughter all the terrible passages in my history, and risk the consequences. I knew I had some hold upon their affection and esteem. My successful visit to Churchill had smoothed my path, and had taken me nearer to their hearts. Again, I was a fellow-conspirator, and had not only shared their opinions, but had suffered for their sentiments. Then my family had to be considered,—then my trickery, my deception, and my thieving. And no matter how I compared each virtue and defect, 'twas palpable that in the eyes of honest men my sins eclipsed my nicer characteristics. I wrestled three days with cowardice. During that bitter struggle I ne'er set foot on the manor lands, though many times, to my eternal shame, I coveted my mistress.

On the fourth evening of this flesh-reducing conflict betwixt right and wrong, I sat opposite my friend and host in his little parlor. We smoked and drank together; yet whereas Pete was cheerful, I was gloomy, downcast, and perverse. He scanned me narrowly, then, in his dry way, raised one eyebrow.

" Young friend," he said, " thou hast gotten a dangerous and infectious malady. Thou hast caught it in its worst form, and I'm disturbed at the symptoms."

He drew down the corners of his mouth in a grim, unctuous fashion, with his pipe-stem described half a circle in the air, and continued—

" Some take the complaint with raving and divers kinds of madness. That is the mild form. They manage, as a general thing, to recover in a day or two; but when they catch it as you have caught it, and sit wi' words for none, and a face as jolly as the day o' judgment, I invariably notice they finish wi' an ounce o' lead; or maybe they do the thing in style—inscribe a last farewell to *her*, and are found at the top of a stream nine days hence with a glassy eye and a bursted gall."

" What d'ye mean ? "

" What do I mean ! Hark at that now ! Most excellent youth, hast never made the acquaintance of the best of her sex ? Hast never set eyes on the fairest flower on God's earth ? Hast never cast thoughts on one whose shoe-strings thou'rt unfit to tie, and for whom thou'rt willing to expend the last drop o' blood within thy body ? "

" Enough of this, Pete ! Go to ! " said I, annoyed at his sarcasm.

" Pshaw ! you vapid fool, you witless loon ! How many times have I warned you 'gainst the women ? Have I not prayed you, besought you, begged you to let 'em alone ? And here y' are, in sooth, a noble object. Two months agone you bid fair to approach Long Bob Bickers, but now ye bid fair to come by a bad and violent ending. Oh, man, I weep for you ! "

This caused me to swear fiercely at the innkeeper; whereat he clapped his hands, exclaiming—

" Bravo, Ned, my lad ! That's perceptibly better. Work it off like that ! Curse, swear, rave, declaim—do something, or, heavens, 'twill be another case of an ounce o' lead or a few fathoms o' water ! 'Tis more than flesh and blood can bear, for one afflicted with this love-sickness, to sit a-moping, a-grizzling, and a-thinking in a corner."

Truly Master Whipple was cold comfort. Still I could not help judging him correct in his observations; I felt the strain upon my mind beyond endurance. Methought the brain must collapse unless I got the matter settled.

Accordingly, towards dark hour on that fourth night, I put on my cloak, and went forward to the manor; but by the time the gates hove in sight, I felt my courage oozing, as the saying is, out at my finger ends. 'Twas like sweating blood to think of making a confession. Yet where was an alternative ? Certes, I might have kept aloof from my mistress altogether;

but instinct warned me that passion was stronger than conscience. I had not the power of will to abandon her without
a blow. I preferred to risk life itself sooner than tamely lose
her, so clutched this final chance as a drowning man clutches a
straw.

Upon my arrival at the knight's abode, I found the candles
lit, and Mistress Marvin in the sitting-room alone. Her occupation was truly a strange one for a gentlewoman. She was
polishing her father's sword by means of a rag and a bottle of
oil.

I had the rarest of receptions; her eyes sparkled when they
saw me. Meantime I perceived her face was wan, and her
eyelids heavy, whilst the expression of her beautiful countenance told me plainer than words that she was not by any
means her usual laughing self, but was bereft of her frolic
vivacity.

"Where is your father, mistress?" I inquired. He was seldom absent from that room.

"Alas, poor father!" she sighed, "he hath been very, very
ill, Ned; in fact, nigh unto death's door. Two learned phy-
sicians despaired of his life two days ago; yet now they tell
me he is mending fast, and is out of danger."

I gave a cry of surprise.

"And they tell me this noble news is entirely due to my
diligence of nursing. One of them said that when he fell sick
he'd send for me to nurse him—you can trust a man for impudence. I've just left poor old daddy's side for the first time
for fifty hours; but when I've finished this, I'm going to sleep
the clock round." She spoke in an easy tone, as though 'twere
quite an everyday occurrence.

"What a steadfast thing you've done!" cried I, moved to
honest admiration.

She was silent for a moment, being genuinely surprised at
this, then answered, with a thoughtful air—

"Well—yes—perhaps it was; but "—and she drew herself
up very straight—" I come of a steadfast stock, sir."

Perhaps she was very tired (no doubt she was); but for all
that a glow of color flew to her face, and a splendid light
flashed in her eyes.

"There! I'm boasting again." She laughed, then added,
with all the reverence due to such a sacred name—"but you
see, Ned, I'm *so* proud of my old father."

As if looks were not enough to prove that my visit had once
more made her alert and smiling, she continued briskly—

"I'm delighted to see you, lad. Now you've come, I don't feel tired any more. I'm afraid you have spoilt me, sir. Before I knew you, I could only talk on sufferance; to use my tongue was something of a luxury, and could only say what I had to say when Sir Nicholas allowed me. But I always say just as much as I like to you, sir; so talking, with me, hath now become an absolute necessity. It hath been truly hateful this last three days to have nought else to speak to but a bedpost. Upon my word, Ned "—and she looked as though she were saying something with a wicked flavor—"I do believe they must be all deaf mutes in purgatory. Anyhow, that's my idea of torment."

Then she fell a-talking in her delightful way; sometimes jestingly, sometimes earnestly; occasionally witty, and always frank and honest and outspoken. How she fascinated me with the melody of her voice, and the music of her frisky, saucy, skilful tongue! I say again, she may have been much wearied; but sure, upon my coming, her limp spirit was revivified. How she held me by her subtle witchery! No matter when I thought of her, or talked with her, I seemed to feel a rarer atmosphere around the heart.

"Dorothy," I asked her presently, "how comes it that you, who have not taken any rest all this long time, are doing a servant's work?"

She looked up swiftly, and gazed at me in unconcealed amaze.

"A servant's work!" Her voice was a comical mingling of horror and reverence. "This is my father's sword, sir!"

"Indeed!" And that word of mine had no room for any reverence whatsoever.

She was quick to note this disrespect. A wave of enthusiasm fired her and rebuked Ned Armstrong. Her face became suddenly brilliant, her eyes sparkled, and a warm flow of words echoed from a heart o'erflowing with pride and admiration.

"Look at it, sir! It hath done grand service to a great fighter. And it shall do more yet, if I can but get the gout out of its owner. See how beautifully the steel is wrought and the hilt is chased! Oh, 'tis a noble thing, a brave thing! 'Tis of proof, thrice-welded, Mondragon steel. Yet, after all, as father says, ''Tis not the weapon that makes the warrior——'"

"Scanderbeg's sword requires Scanderbeg's arm."

"Very true, and Sir Nicholas is one whom it makes my heart swell to call 'father.' 'Tis his boast that his name is known throughout Europe as a man of valor and of spotless honor. Dost see this dent on the edge of the steel? That was done at

Stamford Heath, when it shore through the headpiece of Sir Jasper Chaloner. It hath gained its owner renown on the counterscarp at Dunquerque, and on many a field in Germany and the Lowlands. Ay, and it caused the French King Louis to pin the Iron Cross on father's breast with his very own hand at his palace of Fontainebleau the same year that witnessed the birth of the good-for-nought Dorothy Marvin. 'Tis glorious to be a man like papa. See how high he holds his head in his old age, and has fear for nothing——"

"But the gout?"

"Do you know, Ned," she went on, after giving me a look of severe reproval, "that he hugs a grievance against nature for making me a girl instead of a boy?"

"Nay!"

"He certainly does, sir; and he reminds me of that same every day in the year. He says that Heaven hath sent him a baby-faced, kitten-hearted wench for his sins, instead of a fine lad to carry his name down to posterity. Alack, would I were a man!"

Her sigh was tremendous, and I have reason to believe it as heartfelt as it sounded. Anyway, I saw a strange wildness in her eyes, as she stroked the blade and pressed her dainty lips thereto and kissed it. Possibly I might have laughed loud at this proceeding, had not the maid been so intensely earnest.

"Wouldst like to be a soldier, Dorothy?" And I cleverly smothered a smile.

"If I were a man, I would worthily bear my name, and keep my father's fame lustrous. But you see, Ned, I am not built for fighting. Father says I'm not. He declares I'm only an ornament; a plaything, unfit for service. Methinks it is too true; for even you, that are not a fighting man, can disarm me whene'er you list. Again, did you remark that morning you succored me, that I was afeared of the salt and the balsam. And I am frightened of blood, though it grieves me to say it. Sir Nicholas detests these weaknesses. I know I shame my breed; yet, alas, I cannot overcome them! 'Tis hard; very hard! Ah, we miserable, puny, tucker-stitching women! Why was I made a woman?"

She propounded this question fiercely, and stamped her foot viciously at me with the fire I loved to see in her, as though I were personally to blame for that calamity.

"Ned, thou'rt a wondrous lucky mortal. Be thankful you aren't a woman. Oh, 'tis noble to be a man! They are so very, very different."

Her eyes sparkled as she said so. Yet I disagreed with her on at least one point, but had the sense to stifle my opinions. Now you must know that my vanity had been tickled by this enthusiasm. Besides, I had come hither for a purpose. Therefore, beset by acute misgivings, I seized my opportunity.

" Mistress, how d'ye know I am not a fighting man ? "

" I crave your pardon, Ned, 'twas you who beat the redoubtable Wilmot. I had forgotten that. I meant you were not a soldier."

" I fought for Monmouth at Sedgemoor, and for that reason am an outlaw at this moment."

At that she gave a cry, and repeated softly to herself the burden of my statement. As for me, I dared not look at her, for the word outlaw seemed to come out of my mouth so ugly. Besides, I tried desperately hard to finish the confession, yet failed to do so.

Meanwhile, the maid seized my hand, and her fingers trembled in their fervor, because (so inflexible are the laws of fate) my outlawry appeared a positive merit according to her way of thinking, for she declared her father would have fought in that same cause but for the gout seizing him at the time ; therefore I rose enormously in her esteem. She begged for a faithful account of the battle ; so I told everything I could remember concerning it. The heart-rending story was carefully recounted ; how we came upon Bussex Rhine in the foggy morning ; how we stood by helpless, and heard the orders shouted in the King's camp, and how we were butchered amid the marsh reeds by the hundred. Yes, all this was told, yet, try as I might, I failed when I came to the confession of my character. Heaven knows I tried my best, yet there stands the fact—the stern, cruel, biting fact—I failed abjectly.

My courage went at the critical moment. I glanced at my beautiful companion, who was absorbed in the tale of death. I knew she honored and admired me more than ever she had done hitherto. Even my outlawry seemed to glorify me in her eyes. But a thief ! How could I sit there and tell her that ? Ned Armstrong was a coward ; and of all beings a coward is most to be pitied and despised.

" 'Tis a story to make the blood dance and the pulses glow ! " she cried, when the tale was told ; and when I saw her face methought she was defining her own emotions.

" Mistress," said I, when her excitation permitted me to introduce a word, " I have to beg that you will speak of my condition to no other person save your father. Him I shall inform of it as early as may be convenient, providing he passes his word beforehand that my secret will be safely kept. I should tell you the name the world knows me by is a false one, so that none guess my identity. I have revealed my true state to you now because, having become so intimate with Sir Nicholas and yourself, methought it my duty to do so."

As I said this, I almost felt myself a liar, it seemed so lame and paltry. I had meant to say so much, and here had said so little. Yet now, having said what I had, it was essential to the interests of our family (which throughout my life I have been jealous of) not to let others know that I was Edward Armstrong. Verily, my position in the world was singular. The knight and his daughter knew me as Ned Armstrong, without guessing me to be Black Ned, whilst with other folks my titles were reversed.

The maid promptly granted my request, and knowing that I was anxious to speak with the knight, conducted me to his bed-chamber. We discovered him sitting in an armchair swathed in rugs, hard by the fire. On a small table to his right hand was a heap of bottles containing liquids and medicaments. He looked both fierce and maleficent; whilst his cadaverous cheeks, slim frame, and vacillating fingers caused me to institute a comparison, in my mind, betwixt his present figure and the one pictured by his daughter in her recent eulogy.

" So, daddy, you are awake again," remarked the maid at sight of him.

" Awake ? Of course I am," he answered, sharply querulous. " Where hast been, my wench, this time back ? 'Tis very plain I can go to the devil for you. What d'ye mean by it ? You dare not neglect me thus when I hold good health, and by my soul ! you shan't now, or I'll know the reason."

Now, if ever father was loved by daughter, assuredly the fortunate man, as I hope I have made plain, was Sir Nicholas Marvin, yet he had the brutality to swear at her. Methought him an abominable ingrate, and so angered was I at his churlishness, that I had more than half a mind to convey to him the information. Still, strange as it may seem, it was obvious Dorothy considered his complaint was proper, for she had paid him the most solicitous attentions. She smoothed his pillow, mixed his punch, arranged his rugs, asked his forgiveness many times, and finally whisked a kiss from his ugly visage. Her coaxing ways having reduced him to a plausible imitation of a Christian temper, I told him as much of my story as I had told his daughter, *and no more.*

Again my cowardice was my master. Fortunately or unfortunately, I know not which, Sir Nicholas heard the tidings in a propitious light, and readily passed his word not to divulge my name. Unhappily he asked for the one I went by—that was, Black Ned, highwayman. Thereupon I told him a premeditated lie. Said I, " Sir knight, they call me Master William Jackson."

Thus the only thing I accomplished that night was to forge another bond between the three of us. Their sympathies were entirely mine, and I was complimented many times upon having dared to strike against the monarch's tyranny.

It was near midnight before I left the manor ; and as Mistress Dorothy bid me good-night, she said—

" Ned, if it ever befalls that you are hard pressed by the law, and are in need of succor, come to us, and we will do the very best we can on your behalf."

I thanked her, kissed her hand, and went forth into the eerie moonlight. If I could but have unfolded all, and still have had that kindly promise extended towards me, what would I not have paid ? Oh, if I had kept honest ! If I had only spurned the devil ! The possibilities were so delightful, and the loss of them smote me so severely, that I might have cried out in pain of mind had I not sworn instead (owing to pain of body), for, being so engrossed in cerebration that I heeded not material things, I walked plump into the gates and bruised my head ; so trudged back to Bridgwater, with a great failure, a great baseness, and a damaged head, as the fruit of hours of internal discipline.

CHAPTER XVII.

THE COUNCIL AT KELSTON MANOR.

SANCROFT, Archbishop of Canterbury ; Lloyd, Bishop of St. Asaph ; Turner, of Ely ; Lake, of Chichester ; White, of Peterborough ; Trelawney, of Bristol, and our own good bishop Ken, were the brave seven who had struck a bold blow into the rotten hulks of Popery. From one end of the kingdom to the other their bravery was heralded, and their praises sung in many a ballad and yard of verse.

Sir Nicholas heard of this victory over the King with every sign of glee, and i' faith, it was a thing well calculated to raise the spirits of us conspirators.

Master Whipple still adhered by his admiration for the bishops, in accordance with the sentiment of the country, though he said " It mattered not a blind fiddler's wallet to him what was done by King or Nation, so long as his accounts showed a reasonable margin on the right side, of cent per centum."

It was due to me that this " reasonable margin" was increased in an unlooked-for fashion.

The manor was barely large enough to accommodate all the gentlemen who assembled there, and to allow them lodging and entertainment, to say nothing of the numerous servants who came with them; for persons of quality never travelled then without several outriders for protection against the dangers of the road.   Thus it was I, knowing Sir Nicholas had the billeting of this large company, mentioned with every mark of appreciation Master Whipple's name.   Therefore, upon this certificate, mine host had his house crammed full of them, and I, casually remarking to him that these fellows were all retainers of persons of quality, he at once charged double in the bill. But, as he said to me, " 'twas only the deep sense of his duty towards his family that called for this precaution."

'Twas a matter of emphatic import that the councillors under the knight's roof-tree should preserve secrecy as to their identities and the purpose for which they were assembled.   And this care was in itself successful, as very few had an inkling as to whom they really were.   These great men stayed only two nights at the manor, for many of them being prominent in Parliament, any prolonged absence was sure to be remarked.

At other times I had not failed to notice Sir Nicholas was dependent on his daughter for every minor office.   She it was who ordered the whole household, and did his smallest bidding, despite her frequent threats and her wayward, teasing outbursts.   Whether it chanced to be a matter of the arranging of his wig, the tying of his neckerchief, the tending of his foot, or the shaving of his chin, it ever befell that Mistress Dorothy was the one to do the needful.   But, as I afterwards learned from her, no sooner did the guests arrive than her father was another man.   Having quite recovered from his recent illness, he was up betimes of a morning, and so far forgot his habitudes as to completely dress himself ; took interest in all manner of household business, and managed, as his daughter said, " to play the part of master very well for a beginner."   Of course, as so many great folks were about, the manor knew me not for those two days.

On the second morning of their stay it happened that I was

abroad within easy distance of the knight's abode. 'Twas still early, being only an hour or so after sunrise. I was musing hard, quite lost for the time in the weight of mine own affairs, when a gentleman with a couple of servants behind him, turned the corner of the manor lane, and rode on just in front of me. Somehow my mind lingered on his appearance. Methought I had certainly seen him ere now, and loth indeed as I am to relate it, by dint of thinking, I carried my recollection back to my London visit. Thereupon I remembered my doings at Whitehall, and whom I saw there, not forgetting the man who had come out of the King's antechamber. Sure this was the self-same person—my lord Sunderland.

'Tis with shame that I tell what follows. Forsooth, I should not have touched upon this matter, had it not had afterwards a pregnant bearing on my fortunes ; and aware as I am that this miserable episode does the story little good, and me less credit, I must perforce recount it.

Now, being certain this man was the prime minister of England, an idea was born to my knavish brain. Of late I had been spending freely, and neglecting business ; and when a man acts thus his resources are bound to suffer. If I troubled to attend to the pursuit of purses, money, with me, was plentiful ; yet, being improvident, perhaps owing to the nature of my calling, I rarely had much laid by with which to take a holiday. Therefore, having none to augment it, the money I had brought from Town had by this dwindled into nothing. This discovery had been made that morning, and, to tell the truth, 'twas not the beauty or serenity of the country-side that had tempted me out so early. No, roused by my new-born knowledge, I sought to replenish the treasury.

Thus I was on the prowl for purses. In despite of all the tortures of the last few days I was willing to commit another crime. Recklessness had again dethroned repentance. Methought one theft the more or one theft the less would make no difference ; besides, stealing was the only source of livelihood for me in my native shire ; so the insipid argument once more came to the rescue of Black Ned of "a man must live." 'Twas with this specious platitude that he tried to salve his conscience ; yet only half succeeded. Thought I, my lord is a mean-spirited fellow. So says Sir Nicholas. If he be on our side, what matter that? 'Tis surely no excuse for stinginess. Why not combine business with morals, and visit his sins upon him ; pointing out at the same time the error of his courses ? This facetious bit of self-communing came from long contact with Master Whipple. I turned this notion over in my mind, and approving of it awaited my lord's reappearance, as I knew quite well this was the only road he might take to return to the manor.

In half an hour, the man came back unsuspecting. I moved to the corner of the lane, and as he drew near whipped a pistol from the holster. His lordship pulled up in a hurry, when I presented the uncharitable muzzle at his head. Had he been one of our county folk, 'twould have been unnecessary to have made this to do; but you must understand my reputation had not reached so far as London.

" My lord of Sunderland," said I concisely, as my gentleman drew rein, " I require your purse."

" Good lack ! you insolent rogue ! " he gasped, with an uneasy eye for the staring firearm. Then, recovering somewhat his scattered wits, called out to his servants, " Dick and Roger, come you forward and collar this foul scoundrel."

It happened that his pair of worthies had been jogging peaceably along half a score paces behind, until the occurrence of this stoppage. Now, when my lord halted, like the well-trained servitors they doubtless were, they halted too. And as Sunderland called to them, I coolly plucked another pistol, and gave them a goodly view of it.

It may never be known whether these fellows were stone deaf or otherwise, yet this much is put on record : they heeded not my lord's command, but remained stock still and silent. Yet I knew they were not blind ; else why should they each have had a fearful eye for the firearms ? Their master cried three lusty calls to them, and was half through a fourth, when I clapped the barrel to his head, which had the dire effect of nipping his voice off in his throat.

" Enough of this, my friend ; you need a little gentle persuasion. Your purse or your brains, supposing you wear such luxurious articles."

I am aware that this was impolite. Yet surely he that holds the pistols cannot be compelled to hold the tongue as well. My lord drew out two purses mighty quick, yet I have no doubt the secret of this precipitation lay in the fact that the unsympathetic iron touched his forehead. These received, I bade his followers approach under penalty of lead in their several hides. In mortal terror they came up, and were at once presented with Black Ned's admonition.

" Honest men, I am touched exceedingly by the courage and fidelity ye have displayed in your master's service. Therefore,

gentlemen, as a token of appreciation, I will e'en make no difference 'twixt yourselves and your betters. I will have your
money along with his lordship's, to show I favor not the great
alone. I love honesty and valor. And further, may it please
you to learn, Colman's Specific hath wonderful curative properties, and that five drops on cotton wool, administered with
regularity to the ears, is a certain cure for deafness."
To see their faces was truly droll. A dismal trio servants
and master made as they rode away mouthing maledictions.
I, being a boastful fool, and wishing to advertise my fame still
more, cried out as they left me—

"Your gratitude is due, gentlemen, to Black Ned, the best
man who hath ever worked these roads."

As you shall learn later, this piece of folly was to cost me
dear. The evening of the next day, my lords and gentlemen
having ridden hence to their own abodes, I, sprightly as you
please, presented myself at the manor, having done little else
but brood on love for two whole days. I had crushed my
pangs for the time ; cowardice had again made me reckless
of honor. In face of my late defeat I tried to choke my conscience by pandering to felicity. My mistress received me
radiant, and overflowed with news, as the women are but too
glad to do. Her father also had his share to tell.

"The saints be praised ! These great men have gone !"
cried the impetuous girl. "Ned, it hath been a truly dismal
place. Papa made me appear in my Sunday gown every day,
sit at the table foot, be as mum as a mouse, and act like a fine
lady. My orders were to hear all and say nothing, unless
called upon to answer questions. I was to be neither pert nor
flippant, and under pain of frightening the bishops was to wear
a becoming soberness and modesty. In the morning time I
showed the gentlemen round the gardens and the grottoes.
And I say, Ned, when we came to the pavilion beside the
runnel, one very fine lord begged for a kiss, and he was my
lord Churchill. I said he might have one if he would tell me
how he led the storming party before Nimeguen. And he told
me all about it."

The look that lighted her face just then, e'en though to this
hour it haunts my mind, defies me to interpret it on paper.
But for myself, had I tried, I could not have concealed my
anger and alarm. I had heard more than one waif word regarding the reputation of his lordship. Her father, too, seemed
in a similar case. I believe his fingers itched to strike her.
As 'twas, he used a speech I dare not set down, lest it should'
offend your sight, and looked unutterable things.

The girl said nothing. First she gazed at me, then at her sire ; but next instant the blood flew to her face, and in cold politeness she curtsied nearly to the ground.

"Gentlemen," she said, "you do me too much honor.   I am entirely overcome by the loftiness of your opinion of me."

The biting sarcasm of her tone cut me keener than a sword-thrust. This speech delivered, she deliberately turned her back on us, and walked to the door exceeding stately, her head erect, and her chin poised towards the ceiling.   But suddenly she stopped, and, to my amazement, once more turned about and faced us. Lo! her countenance was fiercely red, and 'twas evident her anger had not in the least abated.

"Gentlemen," the tempestuous maid continued cruelly, " I had merely meant to jest with you, to astonish you, and to laugh at you ; though had I for a moment guessed that the price of this diversion involved an insult to myself, I should have kept clear of so dangerous a topic.   But since you have so high a conception of my conduct, I will tell you the sequel to my story. When my lord claimed his reward, I proffered him my hand. 'Nay, nay, my pretty!' those were his own words, gentlemen, ' I must have something even lovelier than this. Sweet Daphne, I must have thy lips,' says he. ' My lord Churchill,' says I, ' I do but proffer you that which my lady Churchill would proffer you were she at your back just now.   Only, I'm thinking you might find her hand much heavier than mine, and it might even leave a sting behind it.' There, gentlemen, that was my reply, and ere he could retort I left him, and ne'er spoke one other word to him so long as he remained under my father's roof.   Now look foolish—sooth you do so to the very life ! "

Who would have dared to stand up thus, and have said all this to her father and her lover ?   None, I think, but one of sublime courage ; none, but one inspired by intensity of in-nocence. Kinsmen, I do believe that if only a woman be spurred sufficient, she can compass deeds that the boldest man would shrink from.   To his eternal credit, the knight forgot his punishment in mighty admiration of his daughter. Yet the man had no idea of delicacy.

" Par Dieu! mon ami," said he to me, though Dorothy still had her scornful eyes on us, "there's a streak o' the right stuff in that young wench. You can't buy breed, and you can't disguise it. That's a bit o' the Marvin pride. She gets it from her dad. It's not to be sneezed at neither. You Armstrongs have a pretty conceit of yours, but it can't compare with ours."

This panegyric completely killed the maiden's wrath. Beyond all beings I ever met, she had the fine trait of speaking her mind whenever her mind was hurt, and then of suddenly casting off her anger. She never sulked or nursed a petty grievance. I verily believe (kinsmen, I hope you appreciate my surprising honesty) that when she was fully roused she could say crueller things than any of her sex, but when she had said her say, the matter with her was dead. Of course this doth not apply to deep and lasting wrongs that might be inflicted on her, but merely to small vexations, because, being her father's daughter, she ne'er forgot abiding injuries. But on this occasion, the injury being on the surface only, she readily forgave. However, so deeply had her finest sensibilities been pricked, that for a full hour afterwards she very rightly treated us pair of arrant dunderpates and dullards with a tinge of condescension.

Presently another cloud dimmed the horizon. It came out in course of conversation that the maid had been obliged to suffer another hardship. During the stay of the visitors at the manor, every inch of sleeping-space being occupied, at the instigation of Sir Nicholas, who deemed his daughter the least important person then enjoying his hospitality, she had been compelled to make her bed on a bundle of straw in the hay-loft.

" And ye need not decry it," put in the knight with asperity; "you kitten-hearted creatures don't know when ye're well off. 'Pon my soul, many's the time I would have paid gold guineas to have had the loft wi'out the straw. When you come to have a limb or two broken, and are lying helpless on a battle-field, with nought but the sky to cover you, and a score degrees of frost creeping to your bones through the holes in your body, then's the time to pull a lip, and bethink yourself hard done to. Bah, wench, I'm ashamed o' thee ! "

I invariably noticed that when the callous old wretch was called upon to defend his conduct, he scarce ever failed to do so at the expense of this young lady, whom I certainly considered the most hapless and long-suffering of her sex. Verily, the knight was no more fit to have a daughter for his sole companion, than a lion is to have a lamb. I laugh now as I recall my youthful indignation at this new brutality thrust upon the maiden. Yet so much was the harsh warrior wrapped up in himself, and to such an extent had the reprehensible habit grown upon him of looking at all things from a personal aspect, that I am confident he did not scrutinize the matter in a rational light ; and am not sure either that the victim herself did not take her own squeamishness to task for being so nice upon the

12

matter; anyway, she usually embraced her parent's sentiments on all subjects, because, copying his method she consistently rated herself a good deal below her proper value.

"Much hath been done at this meeting," said the knight. "'Tis real business with us now. An invitation hath been drawn up to be forwarded to the Prince of Orange, for him to come over and take the throne. It hath been duly signed by several of the most influential men in the realm, including——"

"That good bishop who fuddled himself with Madeira. Mea culpa! what a woefully wicked suggestion." This was inserted by Mistress Dorothy, who broke off short, and, with an impudent merriment, crossed herself devoutly.

"Including," her father continued, setting aside the interruption with an angry glare, "my lords of Shrewsbury, Devonshire, Danby, and Lumley. Russell, Lord Admiral of England, Bishop Compton, and Master Henry Sidney, poor Algernon's brother. Yes, mon frère, the fat is fairly on the fire now, and we shall be all anxiety for the Prince's answer. Furthermore, we have discussed, at length, the best coast for him to land on, should he undertake this venture."

"And which have ye chosen?" I asked, full of interest.

"My lord Danby hath very urgently advocated the coast of Yorkshire. He hath great influence in that county, and could soon effect a rising there. He assures us the gentry in that part are favorably affected to the cause, and the roads are wondrous good to within fifty miles of London. We have debated this proposal, and seeing that in these parts folk seem quite overawed by what took place when Monmouth came, we feel justified in setting the West aside, and choosing Yorkshire. Again, my lord Shrewsbury declared that the Londoners loathe the Stuart, and that when the news of the bishops' acquittal was noised abroad, the troops on Hounslow Heath broke out cheering, even in the hearing of the King."

As the knight fittingly observed, there could be no drawing back now. The kingdom was moving on towards great events. For mine own part I cared not for the question of religion, nor even for that of the nation's welfare. A hideous wrong had been done one well-beloved; a crime had been committed on his defenceless body under the cloak of Justice, and with my dying breath I would have cursed his murderers, Judge Jeffreys and the King. I had sworn to execute vengeance upon them, and, cost what it might, was determined to bring my oath to fruition. Regarding my personal misfortunes, perhaps, according to law, they were deserved, as I had been guilty of high treason, so that on that score I had no grievance. Yet the horrid deed inflicted on my father festered enough to occasion insane delight when I heard of the bold, determined mien of the plotters. As affairs were going, all things seemed to prosper the enterprise, for it was widely averred that none, save papists and beggarly Irish, had any love for James.

That night love and vengeance held an orgy in my head. Vengeance is a dark unholy passion which I pray, my children, may ne'er be harbored in your hearts. 'Tis a gnawing beast-like passion which hath no bounds to girdle it. A man with that within him is a being whom I would bid you shun. To crave after it and live for it, to build high hopes and relentless delights upon it, and to cherish it more dearly than life itself, as I take shame to say your father did, is godless, vile, and horrible. And love ! To set one beside the other, and to ponder on the two of them, is to heed the greatest powers of earth. I cannot tell you, kinsmen, what it is when they run side by side in one man's brain. Although, as the world goes on to-day, it went on yesterday, so ye must perforce, in your pilgrimage through life, encounter torn creatures with both these passions intermingled. Let such have your pity, for they need it sorely. Beside vengeance, there were other hopes ; by driving the King away, and setting up another government, I should cease to be a proscribed outlaw. And, when I was that no longer, I had ideas for the future. Some of you may wish to hear the substance of these ideas ; sure you are not gifted with abundance of penetration.

Perchance, having poor memories, you have already forgotten Kelston Manor, the bower beside the stream, my lord Churchill, and the boon he sought there ? Not that you and I are at all concerned about him. But the token he had tried to win from Mistress Dorothy, I might win ere long more easily. All this, and one short day agone I had stained myself with another crime.

CHAPTER XVIII.

THE INCONVENIENCE OF A CONSCIENCE.

THE circumstance I now narrate occurred about a week after the meeting at the manor had dispersed. Peradventure, had it not been for this insignificant affair, I should ne'er have summoned the temerity to write one word of this history.

As I recollect, it was a glorious day of midsummer, when the air was soft and fragrant, the sun warm and generous in the heavens, the bees droning lazily, and all nature sleepy, except the busy flies atop of the shimmering stream.   Dorothy and I sate side by side on the brink of the glistening water, under overhanging branches, which were adequate shelter from the fierce rays of sunlight that streamed from a cloudless sky. She smiled at me with an insinuating playfulness.

"Tell me, Ned," she asked, methought a trifle saucily, "how it is you come here so very often now?"

"Fie, mistress, that is a needless question!" said I, smiling too.   "You know the reason far better than I can tell you."

"Aha, my master, I sniff an evasion there!   I tell thee frankly 'twill not serve, sir.   How should I know what brings thee hither?"

All the same, kinsmen, she did know.   Her half-veiled look of laughter told me that.   However, in her present mood, she would not avow the knowledge, so in the course of time I was driven to admit what called for my frequent presence.   .

"Dorothy, 'tis for thee I come."

"Indeed, Master Ned, and that's a beautiful compliment.   I had no idea of that now."

I can never quite forget that sight of her—the sway of her crisp brown curls as she shook her head at me, her eyes brimming half with fun, half with impudence; the sweet ripple of her brows in coquettish simulation of surprise, and her joyous ring of laughter.

"Mistress, thou hast wrung a confession out of me, so 'tis fitting thou shouldst pay for it!"   With a sudden movement I had her unawares, seized her hand, breathed my lips upon it, and thus straightway snatched the payment.

At this she jumped up quick as any squirrel, saying—

"Ned Armstrong, how easily you forget yourself!   That, sir, is a liberty I will not brook."

But, kinsmen, truth to tell, her voice belied her words.

Her face I did not see, neither did I dare to glance at it; for as I made that sudden movement, my hand brushed against a hard substance in the pocket of my doublet, and in an instant the truth flew in my mind—*the hard substance was the rim of my lord Sunderland's purse.*

The laughter was struck out of my voice; I felt my limbs grow palsied, and my brain grow cold and numb.   In very shame I turned my face from my companion.   How could I— how dare I jest and talk with her on terms approaching a suspicion of equality? Was I not a thief, a dishonorable man, a low trickster, a deceitful villain?

The girl had already noted my change of countenance.

"What ails thee, Ned?" Her query was soft and anxious.

I tried to laugh and scout my illness as a little thing, but must chronicle a failure. Thus, in face of it, I answered feebly—

"I believe the sun hath caught me, Dorothy." From which will be seen I was still able to use my tongue sufficiently to lie with.

She ne'er doubted that what I averred was true, though, had she paused, she might have done; for it was indeed scant sunshine that was able to penetrate the thick tree boughs which clustered in a green canopy above us. But it did not enter her head to question the source of this sudden malady. So away she ran to a place where the bank sloped downwards to the river's brim, and caught as much water as her hat and mine would carry. She plied this to my forehead with exquisite tenderness, and ne'er ceased her anxieties or her careful task of restoration till I was on my legs again, and till she had satisfied herself that my recovery was effected.

Soon I left the manor and returned to the King's Head miserable, heart-torn, and quite tired of life. For days and weeks events had been slowly drifting towards one supreme crisis. It had now arrived; this instinct told me more thoroughly than tome upon tome of clergy. A very little thing had sufficed to set my conscience and my sins one against the other in open warfare; and they had now to fight the matter out between them. Thus I went back to Bridgwater with my mind already on the rack.

During that short journey it had a bitter foretaste of impending tortures. 'Twas evident that until some resolution was arrived at I could not pay another visit to the manor, and though I often pined for a sight of my darling, I kept four miles between her and myself till I had determined on my course of action.

You are to plainly understand, ere I go further, that I had been fashion'd weak in the moral nature. Perhaps ye are already aware of this; and whether this is or is not the case, in the interests of the narrative I must impress the fact.

Upon arriving at the King's Head, I betook myself straight to my chamber, locked the door, sat down on the edge of the bed and tried to think. On that day, at least, the result was melancholy, for I ended by abusing fate. My brain seemed fire; my head a whirlpool of torment. An absurdly simple circumstance had washed down the barrier of self-deceit, and the long-pent stream of remorse and fear came rushing through the bursted flood-gates. Methought I saw the Hand of God in the horrid business. Hence arose my terror, for to the guilty it is an awful sight.

You have observed how a short time agone my better parts had triumphed sufficiently over infamy to let me make an honest resolve. Also you have seen how cowardice overcame me at the last moment, and how the knowledge of that cowardice caused me to become more reckless and desperate than ever. Now the fruits of it had struck a crushing blow. My duty was plain, too plain! Honor, conscience, and self-respect bade me go at once and reveal my secret. In my weakness, I was unable to muster a sufficiency of courage. Even had I the desire, I knew I ne'er could play the same cold-blooded game again. The stroke had been too sudden and too severe for its lesson to pass unheeded. I must either make a confession of my calling, and so run appalling risks, else relinquish all hope of my mistress without seeking her forgiveness. Either alternative required strength and fortitude. In the first case the danger was fearful, whilst the second was almost a torment to think of. How could I, Ned Armstrong, forego forever the sight of Dorothy's eyes, the sound of her voice, the thoughts of her love, and the delights of her society? No, no; I must make one effort, one wild attempt!

Day after day fled, still my heart never rose higher than my boots. Heaven knows, I grappled hard with cowardice, and also fought the devil. Often enough he whispered, "Why this to do? Keep to the old game till William comes; you will not be an outlaw then." I thank God I paid no heed to this atrocious counsel of Black Ned, for verily it was his, and not Ned Armstrong's advocacy. Hereabouts I knew not peace at any time; but lay awake with throbbing head through the maddening watches of the night, all kinds of fretful phantasies besetting him who longed for a tentative peep of dawn in the morning. Not that daylight was any benefit when it came, only 'twas less dreadful than the ghostly night.

One evening I sate listless and limp in the small parlor, when mine host Whipple was sucking his pipe and sipping his black jack of October, as per long-established custom at this hour of the day. Now, this gentleman, ever since that dire afternoon, had marvelled much in his secret way at what strange power had held me; but being a discreet fellow, and wondrous sagacious withal, had ne'er pressed for an answer to the

riddle. Howbeit, this particular night, my friend, in a seemingly casual fashion, sought enlightenment on the subject. I
was musing deep and pensive, thus when the question was propounded, I groaned, unthinkingly—

"Conscience!"

"Conscience, quotha!" cried he, upon the instant. "Didst
say conscience? Faith, lad, thy case is indeed a sorry one."

This interest of his aroused me somewhat.

"I feel for thee indeed, brother," Pete went on. "Of a
surety, thou wilt ne'er rise in thy profession. Alack! I too am
cursed with one. I am a kindred spirit o' thine, d'ye see? A
conscience is the most damnable encumbrance that belongs to
man. Long Bob Bickers had the rare good fortune to be without one; an' for downright greatness o' mind, that man I will
commend to anybody. Often enough he would say to me,
'Friend Whipple, thou'rt a mighty piece too conscientious.
'Tis a grievous error—correct it! Dig a hole in your back
garden, and bury it deep, then that will be the most truly
blessed day thou hast ever known.' Now, if ye seek to rise in
the profession, follow that true advice, and go straightway and
hide it somewhere, whither it may ne'er again exhibit its ugly
mug to trouble thee."

"Then how comes it, Pete, that you have failed to follow
this shrewd counsel?"

"Alas! there's the rub. Methinks old Dame Nature built
me for the Church; for 'oons, man, my conscience is like an
evil spirit. 'Twill not bide in its grave. Many a time have I
put it under the sod, but, zounds! the accursed thing will
always rise again to haunt me. Maybe it hath been snugly
planted 'neath the ground for a week, and I may fittingly be
rubbing mine hands over a sweet cargo of the rarest liquors
which hath just been safely thralled in the cellar, when, burn
me! a pathetic voice will whisper into mine ear, 'Good friend,
art aware this cargo hath not burthened His Majesty's Revenue one farthing?' Beastly uncomfortable, I can tell you, to
be thus reminded, for, 'twixt ourselves, I would fain have forgotten the fact. Ah me! if it be a case of conscience, thy
plight is evil, and I feel for thee. Bury it, lad; bury it deep
from the light o' day."

"Pete," said I, laughing, in spite of myself, and this was the
first laugh I had known for a week, "I'm afeared I'm like you,
and that Dame Nature meant me for the Church as well. This
beast o' mine ne'er fails to rise from the dead. It, too, will not
rest in its grave."

Peter Whipple sighed lamentably at this avowal, declaring my case to be extremely pitiful. And after that, being companions in misfortune, we drank each other's health in the October, though all the while mine host, with scarce a pause, went on to relate the manifold advantages the illustrious Long Bob Bickers did enjoy by being mercifully released from the toils of conscience. For the behoof of the ignorant, I here set it down that Long Bob Bickers was hanged before Taunton jail in the year 1684, and was afterwards drawn and quartered.

The struggle that was tearing me asunder lasted ten days, and I believe there did not exist a more distracted creature in any shire of the kingdom. As time went by, this consuming indecision steadily began to make its presence felt upon body as well as mind. Once or twice I grimly smiled as I looked in the mirror and saw the transformation taking place in my countenance. Instead of a healthy, keen-faced fellow meeting my gaze, I beheld a leaden wretch, hollow-eyed and white. However, on the afternoon of the tenth day of torture, I overheard a piece of news, and though it had no precise bearing upon my case, it served to accomplish what weary hours of self-reviling and self-communion had failed in. It befell that I was in the little parlor, and was unconsciously listening to Peter regaling his customers with the latest gossip in the common room. The door was open, therefore every word was audible.

"Death hath been truly busy among us," I heard the landlord say. "Joe Barton the baker hath lost his old woman. She gave up the ghost yestere'en. And Moll Wardell fell downstairs and broke her neck this morning; tho' they do say she was the worse for liquor, else 'twould ne'er have happened."

"Ay, gossips; but the man wi' the scythe calls away the mighty as well as the lowly," quoth a listener, his sentiment cheap, but his delivery uncommonly consequential. "Tom Carson the chandler hath just told me that Sir Peter Armstrong, of Copeland Hall, was found stiff in his bed this morning."

"Oh, indeed!" exclaimed three or four; for my uncle's name stood high in the county.

"I would I were his heir," said another.

But when the rightful heir of the deceased Sir Peter heard this recounted, he did not think it entirely a blessing. Not because he was bowed with grief for the loss of his miserly kinsman, but because it added another pang to his position; for, being an outlaw, he would be unable to touch a groat from his fat coffers.

CHAPTER XIX.

ALAS !

By the time I had fully grasped this news, an indisputable truth was clearly presented to my mind. By the death of my uncle, it was highly probable that inquiries would be set on foot regarding the heir, and it was equally as probable that his connection with Black Ned the highwayman would be revealed. Should events so happen, the truth would indubitably be learned by Sir Nicholas and his daughter from other lips than mine. And should this occur, my name and memory would in their sight be branded with tenfold blacker infamy. Therefore immediate action became imperative.

This was the truth I had gathered. The knowledge served as a spur to my courage. Methought I must be unworthy of the name of man to forfeit my one hope by dallying longer. A week's delay, and my confession might come to them as a necessary, instead of a voluntary, act. So plain was this contingency to my understanding that in ten minutes I had managed, incited thereby, to screw up my courage to its highest level, and to form the long-needed resolution. One final spasm of doubt, one final struggle between right and wrong, and honor triumphed for the moment in my soul—I made up my mind, come what might, to set out for Kelston Manor forthwith, and acknowledge my cruelty and deceit.

I spoke to none, but straightway betook myself to my bedroom and dressed myself in my choicest suit. If I must be hanged, methought I would grace the scaffold in my Sunday garments. Never did criminal attire himself on his execution morning with more pain and suspense than I did then. As I donned my plush breeches and cambric shirt, I remembered the precision with which so many times I had put them on to enjoy the maid's society. As I adjusted and powdered my wig, I remembered how I had studied the mode of displaying it to the best advantage ; the object had been the same. And now I was going to pay the score. I had tossed off my draughts of happiness ; had drunk so deep of it that Nemesis had laid a commanding hand upon my shoulder, and had sternly called on me to pay the reckoning. And I was going to pay it ! O God !

I was going to pay it! Well might my strength ooze from my limbs as I walked Joe out of the inn yard, and my heart turn cold with terror.

Suspense is a double-edged sword that cuts two ways; it attacks both mind and body. Thus, as I rode to the manor that summer evening, my brain seemed paralyzed midway between hope and fear, my spirit withered and sapless, and my body, now fevered, now frozen, by reason of the same emotions. I knew I had made my mistress love me; but was her love hot enough and sufficiently magnanimous to forgive my baseness?

By the time I had traversed half the distance, the devil once more whispered, "Why jeopardize your chances thus? 'Tis not necessary. You have played the game so long, that one day more or one day less can make no difference." I tightened Joe's rein, halted, and considered its plausibility. Yes; why scruple now? Could present conscientiousness avail for the past, or assure forgiveness for the future? Why not play the game to the finish? Was not atonement coming too late? What did it matter if the confession was made now or a month hence, would there not be still the same blot on my honor, the same irremediable stain on my name, which no repentance could purge away? An instant's hesitation, and the wiles of Satan were overcome. Instinctively I felt the rim of Sunderland's purse touch my finger tips, and there was no disregarding that cold reminder, for as I have already said, I saw in it the Hand of God.

Now and then a hare darted across the path a few yards ahead, or a covey of partridges flew up with a startled whirr from a clump of grass or a wayside thicket. I could see the mist rising far across the fields, and swathing the extremities of the landscape in a floating whiteness. Yet I had no thoughts for such sights and sounds as these. Could Sir Nicholas forgive me? Could Dorothy forgive me? At every step those questions sang in my ears till they turned to a delirious dirge. If I were not a thief, not a liar, not a cheat, not a trickster! I would cheerfully have given my right hand or ten years of my life to have wiped those titles from my name. My heart sank as I approached my journey's end. Was I once more to play the craven? I braced myself for the ordeal, because when the manor gates hove in sight, 'twas like steel to my vitals; however, I sent Joe forward, whilst the man who rode him fought his unseen foe.

At this moment a blackbird piped out cheerily from among the brushwood. It seemed to mock me with its jubilation.

Nature seemed to mock me too in the sweetness of her quietude ; the dew on the grass and the hedgerows' bloom menaced
my sight with their beauty and repose. Defeating Satan for
the second time, I dismissed my qualms, and for good or evil
shook Joe's bridle, whereat he moved smartly to the entrance.
To the end of life I shall ever associate this task with going
forth to have a stout grinder drawn from my head. Yet I doubt
not, had I been allowed to choose between having all the teeth
pulled out of my mouth and the pursuance of this business, I
should have chosen to forfeit the teeth.

As we went through the manor gates the sun was dipping
below the horizon, leaving a patch of purple in its track ; the
summer air was cooling after the heat of the day ; the cattle
lowed in the meadows and sucked in the cool sweetness of the
evening ; and over hill and dale all was peace and exceeding
calm. More qualms came to the coward when the vane and
chimney-stacks grew visible among the trees.

I dismounted and tethered Joe in front of the house, not
taking the trouble to put him in the stable, as I felt I should
not remain inside for long. I went up the steps, and walked
through the front door without the ceremony of a knock, this
being my wont, so much at home was I at that house. I discovered the knight and his daughter in the large apartment we
had passed so many cheerful hours in. The knight was in his
usual posture beside the grate, his concoctions hard by his
elbow, whilst opposite him Dorothy was seated, a ponderous
volume on her knee, bearing the inscription on the outer cover,
" An honest and faithful account of His most Christian Majesty's late Campaign against the Dutch, for the Publick weal."

She no sooner lifted her eyes—her glorious eyes !—and beheld me in the arch of the doorway, than she slapped the book
with a thud on to the carpet, and her face was lit with glee, as
she said—

" Father, here is the deserter ! "

This welcome hit me hard.

Sir Nicholas also was well pleased to see me, his solitary eye
yielding as much beneficence as it could.

" Oh, Ned," asked the girl, and her tone was wistful, " what
have we done to you that you should shun us so? 'Tis ten
days since last I saw you."

At first I did not give an answer, not being able to find a
word. In the midst of this pause she gave a keener look at
me, and saw my tell-tale looks.

" Ah, poor lad ! I see thou hast indeed been ailing. Methought that day 'twas but a passing malady, but methinks thou must have suffered by thy face.   Art better now, Ned?"

She spoke these last four words so tenderly, and with such an accent of womanly pity, that 'twas as much as I could bear to hear her.

"I am better now, Dorothy," I mumbled, for to distinctly frame and utter words was a sheer impossibility.

"I greatly fear thou art still unwell," she said again, her tone being still impregnated with anxiety.

'Twas in sooth a terrible malady that held me in its claws ; the dark fiend, self-reproach, froze my blood, and turned my heart to ice.   My errand was never absent from my mind.   It would not leave it for an instant.   When I replied to her eager queries it was only by exercise of fortitude that any words would come.   Perceiving this difficulty of speech, as well as the other matters, she withheld questions for a while, and superintended the drawing of the curtains and the shutters and the lighting of the candles.

The knight, caring nought for the ailments of any save himself, bid me as heretofore, play him at piquet.   I did so, hoping thereby to compose myself for the coming ordeal.   This proceeding was most unkind towards Joe, who was still tethered in the open.   Such was my woeful state of mind, that I dared scarcely look at Dorothy, although the maid looked much at me, and was greatly distressed on my account.   She brought cushions for my back, and sought to enliven me by brewing some mysterious French concoction, which she set much store by ; and whatever it might be it was choicely good.

These ministrations had but the scantiest effect.   In spite of myself my spirits were still gloomy and my demeanor downcast ; though I tried hard enough to banish the devouring demon that embraced me, if only to please my darling.   But the brave maid was nowise daunted by this ill-assortment of my humor.   Never had I known her preserve gravity for very long, and thus, this fatal night, seeing that sedateness was unavailing, she assumed sprightliness once more, and this made me somewhat easier, though foreboding still sate like a pall upon my heart.   Despite the chill within, I had perforce to laugh at various whimsical incidents which had occurred at the manor during the great conclave.   Yet the last of these I did not even smile at.

"Ned, you ought to have been here, sir, on the last morning of their stay," she gayly said, then paused to laugh at the recollection.   "My lord Sunderland went forth on the road, a couple of servitors behind him, to procure an appetite for breakfast. I heard him tell daddy the night before that nought was so agreeable to his taste as a quiet rural ride ere he broke his fast of a morning. However, in about an hour after he set out, my lord came back in a dreadful fume, vowing vengeance on that wicked namesake o' thine, Black Ned, the highwayman. Faith he is a bold rogue! He actually robbed my lord and his servants of every stiver they had upon them—a goodly sum, I'm thinking, for my lord swore that the knave had taken every groat he had brought from London, and that he had no money with which to return to Town. Sure methought the fellow would ne'er cease to prate about his losses. I'm sure he's a lickpenny; and, also, I'm equally as certain that a bad time is in store for his two attendants. Very loud he was in reviling their cowardly conduct. Furthermore, he hath sworn to interest the King in the matter, and seeks to have the villain arrested at any cost."

No, I never smiled at this; nor even looked at the narrator. I continued to play piquet, a hot stream of blood in my head, and my breath coming short and painful. All things seemed to conduce towards the rememoration of my guilt; here was one more reminder. I now felt that the crisis was at hand, yet still I sat and played. How to say what I had got to say, how to make some amends by word of mouth, how to preserve my calm and so do justice to my case were matters beyond my comprehension.

The knight was playing with his usual vivacity, and Mistress Marvin was laughing at me one minute and pitying me the next, when I began again to calculate the prospect. Could they forget? Could they forgive? At this renewal of suspense I commenced the sorry business.

'Twas during a pause in the game. Sir Nicholas was seated opposite at the card-table, whilst Dorothy was behind me, so I was midway between the two.

"Sir Knight, some weeks agone you swore an oath not to reveal my true name to any one because of my outlawry." I had hoped to speak quite clearly, yet as the first words issued from my lips, something jumped in my throat, and made my utterance harsh and indistinct.

"That's so," he said.

"Now, sir, I would like you to swear to me again that same, for, in face of what I am about to say, you may be tempted to forget it."

"I have ne'er forgotten one yet," he said sharply, nay, angrily.

I had offended him at the outset. Methought it an evil beginning. Dorothy, usually so quick of wit, failed to discover any omen of what was pending, for she laughed outright at my request and my unwonted tone of seriousness. Her father, however, exhibited a face of perplexity.

" I have something to divulge," said I, my voice getting huskier at every word. " I am Black Ned, the highwayman.".

The knight said nothing, but raised his head slowly from the table and peered straight into my eyes. A trill of laughter came from behind me. I turned my face to Dorothy, and in an instant she grasped its import. The laugh died on her lips, and terror superseded mirth.

" Ned, why d'ye look at me like that?" she gasped, horrified and tremulous.

Meantime her father had planted his elbows on the table, and was still gazing at my visage, as though to read my very soul.

" What d'ye mean?" he asked. " Art not John Armstrong's son?"

" Yes," I said simply; " 'tis on that account I gave you a reminder of your oath. 'Twould do the family much injury, should the truth leak out concerning me. Terrible misfortune hath dogged me since Monmouth's rebellion. It hath brought me to this."

The speech fell cold and barren from the lips like words from a dead man's throat. I heard half a sob and half a sigh against my shoulder. At that my heart sank down, down, down! fortitude deserted me, and despair enslaved my very soul. I covered my face with my hands. Next moment I looked at Sir Nicholas again, and found him staring still.

By this an icy smile had come on his lips, and his eye stupefied me with its silent cruelty.

" So thou art Black Ned, the dirtiest rogue unhung."

His voice was horrible. 'Twas not stormy nor passionate. 'Twas measured, relentless, cold-blooded; it made me shudder.

I said nothing.

" The dirtiest rogue unhung," he repeated, his one eye destitute of pity. " And so, Black Ned, I have been winning stolen monies day by day from *you.* And why have ye let me win them? Dost think I am blind? Dost think I cannot see with one eye only? Dost think I am too old to watch you and my poor lass very often? You have come hither, week in and week out, with a smile on your lips and a lie on your tongue. you

smooth villain! You plausible villain! You have duped that
girl, have you? I've only one eye, have I? I'm easily blinded,
hey? But I've two hands, Sir Thief; ye shall have early proof
o' that."

That was the end of his awful calm.

" Oh, oh! my God!" he screeched, and jammed his hands
upon his wig as if to save his head from bursting. He looked
at his daughter then, his face inhuman in its eagerness. 'Twas
as though his life depended on what he saw. At once I guessed
his meaning, and there came a confirmation presently.

For a full score seconds he glared at her with such an unearthly
gaze that methinks, had it alone held the truth, he would have
torn her heart out to obtain it.

" Praise God!" he cried at last, and crossed himself for the
only time in all my dealings with him. Afterwards he fell a-
babbling to himself, in a tone that was scarcely audible. " No,
no; she's my child—her mother's child! The viper's balked!
God be praised!"

I heard him. 'Twas a bitter stab; bitter enough to drive a
man to desperation. Dorothy also heard him. The words
wrung a moan from her proud pure lips.

I had had one secret pride, perhaps a frail one. It was that
I had cherished a spotless passion. Kinsmen, do not dare to
doubt me! But the knight did more; he condemned me. 'Twas
the last straw; from that minute I cared for nought.

His face distorted with rage, the knight sprang up from the
table. I rose, too, whilst Dorothy, who had been on her feet
some time, stood beside me white and terrified.

" Girl," the man said brutally, pushing her towards the door,
"get you gone, leave this cur to me." Thereat he ran to the
wall and grabbed the Perillo blade.

Ofttimes, in after years, we cannot account for our actions at
such crises; and now I come to think of mine in this extremity,
I cannot give an explanation. I can only say that as the man
turned round I whipped out my sword, snapped it across my
knee, and flung the broken steel clinking on the hearth among
the fire-irons.

Sir Nicholas ran forward; yet I was prepared to die without
a blow. I felt utterly incapable of striking one against this
man—the man I had so deeply wronged. My arms fell numbed
and useless. Inert and apathetic, I hung them limply by my
sides, without a thought for life, for my undefended breast, or
the thirsty steel. The man crashed aside the card-table, and
it, the cards and money, went rattling on the hearthrug. How-

ever, as he came towards me, his daughter slipped between us. She clung by both hands to his neck and shoulders, and tried with all her strength to hold him from me.

"Do not kill him, sir! do not kill him!" she passionately pleaded.

The fiendish fellow had no need for her, nor had he any mercy. He said no word, but shook himself free, grasped her slender wrists in his left hand, crushed them till she screamed with pain, then slung her yards away, and she only stopped when she bumped against the mantelpiece.

I knew my time was come. The man was mad; the lust of blood was in his face. I was half blinded by his gleaming steel as he shot forth his arm to deal the blow. Instinctively I drew back a step before it, whereat a streak of white jumped 'twixt my breast and the darting blade, and, strange to say, the knight recoiled, and with a fearful word dropped his sword upon the carpet. Yet I felt no pain : no twinge of agony. Between us stood my mistress dazed and quivering, blood soaking through and dripping from her white dress sleeve. Soon I understood the presence of that gory arm ; 'twas this that had saved me from the steel.

"Father!" she cried wildly, "he is unarmed. Do not kill him; 'twould be murder. Do you not see he is unarmed?"

"Fight, you villain!" he howled beside himself; "fight, you hound, and I will spit you! Dost hear me?"

My tongue being dumb, I found no word of answer. He fell into a paroxysm of rage, and heaped curse after curse upon me. Still I could not fight him; and though he itched to strike me dead, he refrained, mainly, I believe, because he found me passive.

"Ye refuse? Malefactor, do but set foot on my land once more, and ye shall be dipped head foremost in the midden till you die. Ye've escaped justice so far, but 'tis not for long. I will move heaven and earth to hang you. Begone, child of hell! A curse go with thee!"

Overcome with anger, he clenched his fist and hit me in the face, and for the only time in all my life I took a blow in silence. I quailed before his dread malignity; it recalled that of the arch-fiend Jeffreys.

I found Dorothy already in the hall. She opened the outer door, and stood beside it awaiting my departure. I stopped involuntarily as I neared the threshold. I was chilled by the darkness of the night, and the wind shrieking in the copse. Could I leave her thus without a word, without a plea, without a mitigation of her anger? But the mere sight of her sufficed to daunt me,

Standing there hard and rigid, she drew herself to her fullest height, and gazed at me with unutterable loathing. She was the cruelest creature I ever saw. Her bearing was truly brutal in its studied scorn, and her face had never a spark of pity in it. As I approached and stood beside her, she drew her skirts together as though fearful I should touch them. She did this ostentatiously, and hurt me with her cruel eyes—'tis a woman's way of bullying. At first she gave no speech, but maintained the torture with her look.

" Get you hence, you dog ! " she said at last, and waved one arm towards the door.

'Twas her wounded arm, and as she shook it warm drops of blood plashed upon my face, and even touched my lips—the blood she had spilled for me ! The thought nerved my courage and quickened me with life ; therefore I disobeyed, and still remained gazing at the blood, her own blood, dripping from her sleeve. How could I accept vituperation for farewell? So I vainly stayed for a sign of hope, one grain of mercy. I craved for these, quite wild with desperation.

" Dorothy ! "

" You Armstrong ! " she whispered softly—so softly that her lips seemed to caress the words as they stole slowly from her throat. Coming at that time, this unearthly softness numbed me ; 'twas a thing fathomless, a thing outside nature. 'Twas then I had a terror of the girl ; her voice set a fear-blight on the heart But I could not, dare not leave her so. I stammered " Mercy ! " and bent my head, whereat she bent hers also, peered up in my face, and her eyes they scorched my brain. Ere I could think of what was toward, she sprang like a tiger at the wall, and twitched therefrom her father's great black riding-whip. She swung it round her head ; I saw the snake-like lash glide quivering through the air ; heard a hissing " whish," and thought my face was cut in two.

I turned and fled like rain before the wind. I stumbled into Joe's saddle, untethered him, and, nearly blind, pulled his head and set him on his course. As I did so, the door was closed against me, and this re-echoed in my soul, for 'twas the closing of the door of Hope.

I rode from that house of torture, heart and face each torn and bleeding. I dug the spurs in my horse's flanks, and he, poor brute, leapt through the darkness, faithful and uncomplaining. The night was inky black, the atmosphere heavy and

13

muddled, and charged with a coming tempest. I galloped Joe over hedge and ditch, hill and dale, through wood and thicket, crop and pasturage, but never on the straight highway. Soon the dull thunder rumbled overhead, the lightning leapt along the sky, and the heavens spat upon the earth. The rain poured down in a soaking sheet, wetting me to the skin, and snatching what breath was left in my miserable body; yet I did but bury the wicked spurs the deeper, and the animal, faltering not, dashed through it all, and for a time defied its rider and the elements. Presently the water streamed off the pair of us, though that was no care of mine. My only cares were the knight, his daughter, the bang of the manor door, and the blow that seamed my face.

Thrice I pitched out of the saddle; but, being stark mad, it did not affect my neck, so I remounted only to ply the spurs afresh. Shortly I felt the brave fellow's limbs were flagging; and still he did his best. Alas, poor Joe! horses have better hearts than men. I knew his strides were not now so strong or certain, tho' like a fiend I urged him on, the brunt of the storm in our teeth, and the gloom an expanse of ink.

It may have been hours, for aught I know, when horse and man came crawling into the yard of the King's Head, Bridgwater, the animal clothed with mud and frothy foam, the rider a prey to madness. His eyes were bloodshot, his gait unsteady, and his soul sickened and despairing.

I called hoarsely to the ostler, who came running to do my services, just as Joe sank down, with torn and bloody flanks, through sheer exhaustion. I reeled into the little parlor somehow, and flung myself in a chair, and lay there panting and streaming with water. I was conscious of nothing but the throbbing of my flesh where the lash had bitten it.

By and by Peter Whipple opened the door softly and put his head in. He gave a glance at me, and muttered just three words—" Damn the women ! "—then cleared out quick and closed the door behind him.

Following that, I was not again disturbed; mine host was the wisest man I ever knew. I lay there, bereft of wits. I tried to think, but my brain was dull; to talk, but my tongue was dumb; to move, but my limbs refused to do my bidding. Once I tried to weep, but even that pleasure was denied. At length, quite suddenly, I burst out laughing. I jumped up, vivified by some strange power, and set up peal after peal of laughter. After that I danced and sung, bit my hands and gnawed my finger-nails ; then flung myself full length on the floor with heaving chest, useless legs, and with only the power to groan.

In time, daylight crept through the chinks in the shutters, and I got up only to fall down, but tried again and was more successful. Step by step I crawled into the yard. The serving-men, who chanced to be up already, hung back apprehensively from me, upon seeing my strange appearance.

The first thing I perceived in the yard was a dark mass lying impotent on the cobble-stones. I approached unsuspectingly, and saw it was a horse stretched lifeless. 'Twas Joe lying dead. He lay with glassy eyeballs staring wide, his limbs stiff and full extended, and his visible flank smeared with blood and torn and jagged. I uttered a cry of horror. This brought the ostler from the stable.

" Ye've düed vor un, I rackon," he said, shaking his head.

" Nay, friend," I said, e'en though I knew the truth.

I went down on my knees beside his head, stroked his cold muzzle, and called him twice by name.

The ostler shook his head again, and slowly growled—

" 'E wor a fery vine 'oss, 'e wor. I rackon I nivver knawed wan wi' zich a hairt as thickee ; noa, nor nivver wan zo mild an' vree froom vice, an' zo purty i' th' making."

" Peace, fool ! " I shouted hotly ; then rose and seized him by the jerkin, crying, " Not another word, you clod ! "

'Twas more than I could bear.

CHAPTER XX.

THE COUNTING OF THE COST.

I WALKED unsteadily back to the parlor. There I sought to draw my rapier from its scabbard, but found it empty. The blade lay in the grate at the manor. I hunted for a weapon ; and sure enough the devil, in his forethought, had caused a dagger in a case to be hung up as furniture on the wall. I laid eager hands upon it, ran one finger along the edge, and felt quite cheerful to find it keen. Placing it upon the table, I gloated over it with an hysterical kind of rapture.

I wondered what death was like, and was filled with qualms for the vague hereafter. It is certain I should have made an end of life upon the spot, had not a vision of that autumn night of '85 rushed upon me. And here we have a paradox—'twas only the dream of vengeance, the nonfulfilment of the devil's compact that snatched me from the jaws of hell. So with reluctant fingers I replaced the weapon on the wall, then opened the window and let in the morning air. I stood and gazed upon the street, and saw the housewives busy with mop and bucket, scrubbing the steps and cobble-stones, as each chatted to her next-door neighbor. Also I watched the plough-boys go singing and whistling past the door, and the farm hands close after them, laughing and joking, as they called for an early draught at Peter Whipple's hostel. In the darkness of my soul I cursed them. Why were such hinds as these light-hearted, when I, Sir Edward Armstrong, baronet, rightful heir to lands and revenues and rich estates, was the most miserable man on the surface of the earth?

If ever Peter Whipple showed discretion, it was during the week that followed these events. Some men have an instinct of what to do and how to do it under all varieties of circumstances. Such folks are never at a loss, no matter what tricks the world may play themselves or their fellow-creatures. Their mental faculties are elastic, they expand according to the demands of the occasion. Thus it was mine host had nought at all to say anent my strange return that night—the fate of Joe, and the weal that stretched in a blue-white streak from my forehead to my jaw. Herein lay great kindliness and wisdom. Furthermore, he performed many well-meant offices, which left me much impressed by his friendly disposition.

'Twill serve no purpose to dilate on my hopeless frame of mind. Those were dark bitter days of vain revilings against God and Fate, of futile regrets, and of black despair. Doubtless you who read have already foreseen a similar disaster.

During that week I slunk about disconsolate, trying to decide on my future course of action. To visit the manor again, in face of the treatment I had received, would be nothing short of folly; tho', in spite of this, an idiotic whim took possession of my senses. It seemed an utter impossibility to my disordered mind that I could live without seeing Dorothy again. I brought common sense to bear upon the question, but, beyond clearly demonstrating that Ned Armstrong was a fool, it gave him no other sort of recompense. 'Tis a bootless thing to reason with love, for 'tis a most unreasonable passion. It matters not a papist's malediction whether Amaryllis loves you, so long as you love Amaryllis. Next I thought of the blow that had sealed the tragedy of the fatal night. I still bore its impress

on my cheek, and its pain was branded in my heart for all
time. Yet I no sooner recollected this than it was more than
counterbalanced ; Mistress Marvin had shed her own life-blood
to save me. My pulses throbbed ; 'twas a glow of hope.
Could she by any unsuspected chance forgive me? Yet the
hopelessness of the thing was always there. How could a gentlewoman forgive a common thief? Again, even if she felt
disposed to overlook my crimes, I knew enough of her father
to be aware that he would not. And his daughter, who loved
him so steadfastly and so exquisitely, was not the one to set
him at defiance, or to act contrary to his sentiments. It has
since occurred to me that the only commendable plan available
at this time was to accept Tobe Hancock's offer, and quit the
country till happier times arrived ; but between the ecstatic
throes of imbecile love and the appetite for revenge against my
father's murderers, I never heeded it at all. " If I could but
see her I should be more content ! " was my mental cry for
days. It took the form of unquenchable desire. And though
this maid was dead to me, I craved for her like one who
craves for a friend who is in the grave. The utter madness
of the longing was a secondary matter ; so I set my wits
to work to get another sight of her ; and hoped that such indulgence of my passion might satiate it for a time.

When in a strait, a man of imagination, as a general thing,
will find ways and means to aid him. And I cogitated so
patiently on this hard problem, that ere long I met with due
reward, for I discovered a way of furthering my yearnings. I
knew the manor flower-beds were situated at the bottom of the
garden, which bordered on the copse ; and hither Mistress
Marvin came each morning to tend the flowers and pluck them.
No sooner did I recollect this than it struck me I could with
ease conceal myself among the brushwood, and thus, unseen,
could watch my darling—I still presumed to call her that, in
spite of everything. I wasted no time in the execution of this
scheme ; therefore, the following morning I set out to put the
plan in operation.

The sight of the manor gates once more made me wince ;
I remembered two dear friends who were wholly dead to me—
faithful Joe, who was dead to me in body, and Dorothy, who
was dead to me in soul. And 'twas I who had killed them
both. 'Twould be idle to state what I would have sacrificed to
be able to undo what I had already done. Were we but permitted to cancel the terrible past, instead of having to bury it,
this world would be a happier place than it is at present. In

a little while I banished these reflections, and made my way into the heavy growth of brushwood.

This stretch of it is of wide extent. It begins a good way north of the house itself, and runs along to southward till the stream, at the bottom of the manor grounds, is passed for nearly half a mile. The part of it which forms the avenue, close by the gates, is not nearly so thick as it is in other places; and the branches being twined together, it becomes a trackless patch of bough and bramble, with thick bracken underfoot and a leafy canopy above.

I plunged into this impenetrable wilderness, and my clothes suffered sorely in the passage, because the least trodden parts of this pathless thicket appeared a very wall of briars. By dint of perseverance, I worked my way to the spot for my purpose, which was on the outskirts of the copse, a few yards hither side the water. Here I could command a full view of the flower-plot, and of all who came to meddle with it; whilst, better still, did I but use reasonable precaution in keeping close amid the tangled growth, none might get a glimpse of me. To further this concealment I lay full length on the grass and waited. I was quite at my ease herein, though the sun was getting powerful, for I reclined well in the shade.

Presently my ingenuity met with due reward. Perhaps I had been lying half an hour in the thicket, when I heard a light quick step on the gravel footpath. I knew that step; I had heard it many times. Directly afterwards Mistress Dorothy Marvin came down the garden walk, a basket in her hand. The first thing I noted was that one sleeve had been rolled back to the elbow, and in lieu of it was a big white bandage bound firmly round her arm. This was a sight to banish coolness. It sent the blood tingling in a warm wave through me. Then I noted another thing, and I must confess it pleased me greatly. I know it was a mean and selfish pleasure, yet why conceal it? She was not singing and whistling French melodies as usual. There was a sort of wistful pensiveness in her face, and a sad pellucid softness in her eyes. I watched her pluck a rose. For a full minute she gazed at its petals, then kissed it and fastened it in the bosom of her dress. A month agone she had given me a rose. I had kissed it and had pinned it in my coat. Could it be that——?

A spasm, half thought, half emotion, thrilled me. I was both frightened and enraptured at this boyish folly. I had not the courage to look at her just then; my mind held a maddening thought. Kinsmen, I was *very* young. But the next in-

stant brought its quietus. What of the blow? 'Twas the hand .
that held the rose that struck it. 'Twas those eyes that had
had a tiger's fury in them. 'Twas that willowy form that had
menaced me with its abhorrence.

Ere long she filled the basket, and was on the point of
returning to the house, when the knight came limping down
the path with some papers in his hand. At sight of him she
disguised her melancholy, and her face flushed with greeting.
How she loved that ugly wretch with his scarred face, his one
eye, his intemperance, and his filthy tongue!

And I, who was so young, so nicely mannered, so well born,
and so fairly favored! I will not prejudice your minds unduly
with my pettiness; but the thought was hard.

"How now, papa?" she demanded cheerily; "what brings
you here, sir?"

"These," and the knight held up the documents. "I want
your help, ma petite. I never was very apt at scholarship. A
courier hath just delivered me this letter. He hath ridden
express from my lord of Shrewsbury."

"Ah, to be sure," she laughed lightly, "that hath a weighty
smack with it. Business of the State I'll be bound, or stay,
more likely of the State that is to be."

"I do not doubt it very nearly touches his Highness the
Prince," he said.

She took the letter from him, and read the contents aloud for
his behoof. Perchance it was wrong in me, yet the fact remains, I strained mine ears and listened to every word that
passed. Communing inwardly, I argued that I had good right
to hear these matters, seeing I was a party to the scheme. Her
interpretation of it was something like the following:—

"To Sir Nicholas Marvin, my very good friend: these—

"His Highness the Prince of Orange hath accepted our invitation of June 30. It is his purpose, however, to neglect no
opportunity. To guard against any miscarriage of the scheme,
he proposes to bring a larger army with him than we did suggest. He is pushing on arrangements with all despatch, and
trusts we are doing likewise.

"'Tis, however, on a serious danger which doth threaten us
that I seek to speak with particularity. Of late the King hath
become gravely suspicious, notwithstanding our great care and
discretion. His Majesty wears an evil look—I am afeared
some of our names are known to him. Perforce our meetings
must end. My friend, I regret to have to counsel you to leave

this country, and that right speedily; the Stuart certainly contemplates ill towards us.

"Edward Sidney Russell, and myself, set out for the Hague next week, and I am sure it is your best course to follow us. My Lord Danby remains in London to direct our affairs, although his situation grows perilous. You know his residence, and he will offer you counsel on any matter concerning this affair. For your information I may say that the barque *Aurora*, Captain Coxwell, hath been chartered to sail on the first Monday of every month from Harwich, for Holland. Adieu, my friend, may God preserve you.

"SHREWSBURY."

I heard every word of this, and also all that passed between the knight and his daughter.

"Mon Dieu!" exclaimed Sir Nicholas, "this hath an ugly sound, ma cherie. Methinks 'twill be a case o' flight instead o' fight, ere long; yet that irks me much."

"Hope for the best, sir; should the worst happen, then will be the time to fly."

"No use tarrying till you are rotting under lock and key before ye seek to quit the country; the matter that will give me the sorest trouble is what is to become of you, my lass. We are without friends this side the Channel, and you cannot stay here at the manor, seeing what troublous times are so close at hand. What can I do wi' you, wench?"

"Oh, if things come to the worst," she replied on the point of laughter, "I must turn soldier along with you, father, and push a pike for the confusion of the tyrant. How say you, sir?"

"You laugh, but methinks that will be your only chance. You can handle a pistol pretty tolerable, and might with some little tuition wield a light sword; and, besides, you are well acquainted with horses. By my troth thou hast really solved a problem."

She looked at him, flushed a lovely scarlet, became much confused, and said dolefully—

"You are not in earnest, father, surely? I did but jest just now. I am afraid I should make but a sorry soldier, and peradventure, in the face of the enemy, I might show the white feather."

"What!" and methought the old warrior was about to eat her, "you are no child o' mine then! Confound that pluck o' thine! Methinks there is something radically amiss with it.

Show the white feather, say you? Old as I am I do but wish there was an enemy now to whom I might have the chance to show it. By God, I'd show him a sweet steel blade instead, and deftly handled, mark you! 'Pon my soul, wench, your spirit is a degradation to him that bred you."

"You do me a wrong there, sir," she answered swiftly.

"Nay, nay, craven heart, I'm too lenient."

"I'm no craven heart, father, indeed I'm not! 'Twas but the blood I was thinking of. It turns me sick."

"Bah! ye shame me for sure. Why, even that black thieving scoundrel of an Armstrong could sing a better tune than you can. Bad as he is, he would have made no to-do whatsoever about a matter o' this sort; yet you, my own flesh and blood, shrink from it."

"Master Armstrong was very brave. Do not forget how he carried that missive to my lord in face of many dangers, and how——"

"Hold! not so damned much of Master Armstrong, if you please. That low devil is in your head again. But, alack! it grieves me to know his courage puts thine to shame. Besides, as ye've told me often yourself, many a Dutch burgher's vrouw defended her homestead lustily in the days of William the Silent, 'gainst the tyranny of Spain. And I'll swear that their stock was nowise equal to thine own. Oh, woe is me! to have a child like this. A lily-liver, say I, is the greatest curse that may fall on anybody."

She looked at him in silence, her face troubled; but not reproachful. As usual she adjudged the fire-eater in the right, and doubtless deemed herself a puny creature. Soon she cried out warmly—

"Father, I will do as you wish. I will cross the water with you and join the army."

"That so," he said with some complacence; "faith, that is more to thy credit. Ma petite, I will have thee hard by my saddle-bow, and I'll show thee how to ride into battle, and how to sweep infantry to perdition, as Rupert was wont to do. Hoity-toity, I can sniff a brave time coming! 'Twill be better then, methinks, than brooding over glib-tongued highwaymen. It need not be known in camp y'are a wench, for mayhap 'twould go against you, though I fail to discern the reason. Why should not a maid be a man's equal with proper training? Perhaps 'tis because many of 'em have a notable flaw in the pluck."

"Yes, sir," the girl said staunchly. "Methinks it will be for the best. You are everything to me; and while you are away I should be always moping and wondering whether any hurt had stricken you. Verily, this is a brave idea of yours. I can be your body-servant, whereby the pair of us will be saved anxiety. I am ready to start to-morrow, if need be."

"Shoo! you're too fast, sweetheart. We cannot hope to reach Harwich for this month's sailing. Yet we must not fail to be in time for that six weeks hence, providing James lets us bide till then. In the mean time we'll rely on fortune."

These were the last words I heard pass between them, for then they walked out of earshot towards the house. To me, who had overheard it all, the matter appeared wondrous strange. To think of this beautous gentlewoman becoming a man-at-arms, and fighting in the forthcoming war, was a thing much too weighty for my limited understanding. Yet, without doubt, both the knight and his daughter were fully bent on bringing the scheme to fruition.

Three days later I was watching in the copse again, for the weather still held fine, when I overheard another conversation between them, which, if of a different nature, was of equally great importance. This time they came down the path together.

"I prefer the soldiering," the maid was saying.

"As you will, lass," said the knight, with a show of resignation; "but methought the opportunity a good one. I like the lad, he hath honor and good courage, is well favored, and is of the best family (as, indeed, he must be, seeing how near a kinsman he is of your mother's) and hath a good estate. Also his heart doth lean towards you, and I half promised you to him when he was over here last year. 'Tis a rare chance for you, I wot; for I wish to see you safely cared for. I'm an old bird now, and may not be with you long, but am unwilling to leave you alone in the world. You had better consider this matter carefully. That lad thinks very kindly of you, and I tell you he is honest and true, and I like him altogether."

Master Edward Armstrong, hidden ten yards away, hereabouts grew nervous. And he strained his eyes and body not to miss any word or token that was forthcoming.

The maid shook her head.

"Don't be a fool!"

"Sir, I would not like to marry him."

'Twas a heartsome speech for Ned Armstrong's ears.

"Young wench," replied the knight with asperity, "listen to me. Don't be a fool. Ye have here a fair prospect of being

settled for life. The youth is in all ways desirable, and I am
sure he loves you."

" But I don't love him."

"You don't love the count," snarled the soldier, his anger
breaking bounds at last. " No, I'll tell you whom you love.
'Tis that vile Black Ned, a common highwayman. Yet, mark
you this very well, I will know no rest till that rogue hath had
justice executed upon his dirty, deceitful, thieving body. Mark
you that ! And how dare you show airs and graces to me,
madam ? I say you had better marry M. le Comte, and, sink
me, you shall ! "

" Father," Mistress Dorothy answered warmly, " three days
agone you bid me turn soldier, and I was squeamish and liked
not the task. Yet I promised to obey you ; and if it please you,
sir, I will. Now you alter your commands, and bid me marry
a miserable Frenchman, and of men I last would choose assuredly he'd be a Frenchman. I do not care for the lad. He
may be a very excellent fellow, no doubt he is ; but I pay no
heed to him. No, Sir Nicholas Marvin, I will go campaigning
with you, sir." And she shook her curls and stamped her foot,
and looked so bold, imperious, and defiant, that the old knight
paused ere he made answer. However, when speech came to
him, it did so in no uncertain manner. From experience of his
ways, I was aware that the thing beyond all others that was
most irksome to him was to be thwarted in his projects.

The six languages were called into requisition ; but, as
usual, this torrent of abuse was very coolly taken, though I
trembled lest the desire to do her father's will should lead her
to alter her determination. To my infinite delight, she showed
no sign just then of any such proceeding. In the end he bade
her stay there, and he would send her cousin, the count, to
join her, that he might press his suit in person. From this I
gathered that the young man was in the house, that these two
had come out into the garden to confer upon the matter. The
maiden lingered among the flowers awaiting his arrival, and all
the while I lay watching—watching !

Presently the gravel of the walk was scrunched underfoot,
and as handsome a cavaliero as one might wish to see came
along it and saluted her. His features were high, delicate, and
clean cut, his apparel of the finest, plentifully interlarded with
velvet and silver, lace ruffles at his wrists, and a rapier by his
side. He spoke long and rapidly in the French tongue. This
was to my intense annoyance ; for, having neglected early
scholastic opportunities, I was at that time ignorant of the

language. And what is the good of being eavesdropper—an unclean occupation—if you cannot understand a word of the conversation?

Now, Mistress Marvin was well acquainted with the foreign jargon, and though aught French was so much against her taste, out of courtesy she answered in the same mode of speech. Thus, between the two, I was completely balked.

M. le Comte grew impassioned; the maid grew arch and saucy. The young man placed his hand on his heart, whilst the fair one clasped hers behind her back, and shook her coquettish curls at him with a most amazing air of impudence. At that the gallant went down on his knees before her—kinsmen, you will understand he was a Frenchman.

"Ah ma belle cousine! je vous aime!" he cried eagerly. He was not content to say this once, but several times emphatically repeated it. That phrase stuck in my head. But 'twas quite too much for the lady's gravity. Still I can excuse that Frenchman, because she never was so irritatingly lovely as when she had mischief in her eyes. And she had it in them then.

"Raoul," she asked, in the goodly Anglo-Saxon—doubtless she was too warm to employ the less familiar vehicle—"what is the French for a clodpoll, a lumpish fellow?"

"Lourdaud, my lovely cousin, lourdaud," replied that innocent young Frenchman, in extremely creditable English.

"Then, Monsieur Lourdaud," said Mistress Cruelty, "on to your feet at once, sir! You are surely fraying that beautiful plush at the knees! Besides, I am not in the least edified when I see a kinsman of mine look like a scarecrow in a potato patch. Come, up you get, sir! or, 'pon my word, I'll laugh at you." And faith, kinsmen, she did laugh at him, and in the most tantalizing manner.

My fine gentleman rose from his lowly posture; but he blushed as he did so, and looked more than a trifle sheepish. Then the maid gave him a sound talking to; but to Ned Armstrong's disgust this harangue was in the confounded foreign tongue. Yet he had the satisfaction of seeing his rival blush again, and far more deeply, and to watch him grow still more sheepish in his bearing. Ultimately the pair of them went away together, the lady very voluble, the gentleman very silent —the lady laughing, the gentleman glum and crestfallen.

I felt almost sorry for the Frenchman. He seemed a simple lad enough, withal honest, and desperately enamored of the maid. He prosecuted the matter in a manly, straightforward way, and I could not help but think had been very severely dealt with. My own feelings, you may guess, were inexplicable. Being young myself, and filled with heroic notions, I could have found it in my heart to hate Dorothy Marvin for her flippancy. She did not seem to be honored in the least, and did not even condescend to be dignified upon the subject. She appeared to have toyed with his affections in much the same way that a cat does with a mouse, with similar feline sort of claws, that leave galling wounds behind them.

Presently I left my hiding-place, and returned to Bridgwater, lost in profoundest meditation. I had ample mental food on which to meditate, seeing that I felt myself to be seriously perturbed by this new development. It thrust the prize farther from my grasp than ever. True, the girl had obviously refused the count, yet I rightly felt this would avail me little in the end. Two men had set their minds upon this marriage. And one of them was the implacable Sir Nicholas Marvin. I felt that this fact alone would settle the question; for even if the girl proved obstinate, I had little doubt reverence for her father, if nought else, would prevent her flying in the face of his authority. Even if she did prove intractable, being so lonely, unprotected, and entirely at his mercy, she would not stand the slightest chance against him. He was one who would have his way at any cost. Verily the case, so far as I was concerned, was hopeless. Besides, when all was said, Dorothy had spurned me. Others might dash in willy-nilly and win the prize or lose it; but I was bound, and very rightly, by the bonds which some call Fate. Kinsmen, you may very properly inquire by what right I had indulged in this soliloquy? By what right had I entertained these doubts, these fears, these impertinent forebodings? By none at all. But, please remember, I loved Mistress Marvin, and love, as ye know, rarely jumps with common sense.

CHAPTER XXI.

THE GATHERING OF THE STORM.

THE evening of the following day, on returning to the King's Head to pass the night, I was confronted by terrible news, and by the first of a peculiar sequence of life-and-death adventures. Upon arriving at the tavern, I walked through the back entrance into the private parlor. The moment I was ensconced therein, Peter Whipple came noiselessly and joined me. He put his

fingers on his lips, whispered " Hush ! " silently locked the
door ; then seated himself close beside me, and in an undertone conjured—

" For the love of Heaven, make no noise, Ned ; neither raise
thy voice beyond a whisper ! The common room is full of
King's men newly come from London."

" What of that ? " I asked.

" By the Mass, you will learn all too soon ! 'Tis on your
account alone they have journeyed hither. They bear a warrant,
with the King's signature displayed thereon, for the apprehension and proper conveyance to jail of a notorious malefactor,
one Black Ned, and this same warrant is issued on the recommendation and complaint of my lord Sunderland, backed by
that of my lord Feversham. Also the document goes on to say
that under penalty of the King's weighty displeasure, it behoves
every justice of the peace not only in Somersetshire, but throughout the kingdom to furnish men and money for its execution,
should they be called upon to do so. Furthermore, it gives on
another paper a full and accurate description of you, along with
a hundred pounds reward to any person who shall deliver you
up to justice."

" Is that solemn truth ? 'Tis no jest, Pete ? " I asked fearfully.

" Would to God it were ! Every word on't is gospel, I swear.
Why, lad, I have e'en seen the sheepskin, and a mighty precise
and circumstantial bit o' scribbling too."

I groaned. This was no matter of pettifogging sheriff's men.

" No use to sit sighing and groaning, my lad," Peter went
on sharply. " If ever ye had need to show yourself a man of
action 'tis at this moment. I would Long Bob were here. He
was the man ! though, by my troth, he ne'er had a job so ticklish
to navigate. 'Tis a very bad business altogether, and it behoves
me to speak to the purpose. I would not give a week's purchase
for your life and liberty. On their way up they have spread
out their arrangements in Wiltshire, and to venture that way
would be madness. 'Tis plain you must not bide under this
roof another night, else they're bound to take you."

I groaned again, bereft of the power of thinking to any
remunerative end. To add to my sore predicament, I had poor
Joe no longer for my servant. Just then there issued from an
adjacent room a chorus of carousing voices. They were trolling
a lusty snatch of song, and this rang throughout the hostel.

" There they are," said Pete in a whisper. " Let 'em sing,
'twill keep 'em from doing mischief at present. Besides, my

lad Tom knows how to manage 'em. He's a smart youth, let
me tell you; the smartest in the parish. 'Train up a child in
the way he shall go,' saith the Scriptures, an' 'oons I've surely
followed 'em."

Neither of us spoke for several minutes, and the silence was
only broken by the hilarity in the common room. Master
Whipple was wondrous serious that night; far more so than
ever I'd known him previously; but he spoke first, and I could
have kissed him for his words.

"Ned," he said, thrusting his hand out, "thy paw, lad. For
two years we two have been staunch friends; and the weather
hath been sunshine. Dost think I'm going to desert thee now
the clouds are coming? No; 'taint my way. Thy hand, lad, I
say, and by the shade o' Long Bob, I'll surely pull thee
through."

"Thank you, Pete," said I. Here was a true friend.

"Now, my gossip," quoth Peter briskly, "I'll waste no time.
I've got a few brains o' mine own, and I'm going to use 'em.
Recollect I'm the skipper o' this craft at present. Now listen
to me. You have no horse?"

He scored this fact off on one finger.

"And no money, I wot?"

I nodded acquiescence, and up went another finger.

"And you are a fugitive with retreat cut off, and a hungry
pack of bandogs o' the law at your heels? Now, 'young un,
say not a word till I bid you. Old Dame Nature has given
me a head-piece, and it isn't a fancy ornament neither. 'Twas
made to be used, and, sink my soul, it shall be."

First he took his black jack out of the cupboard, and his churchwarden off the mantelshelf; set them in working order, and bade
me get mine and do the same. After that, for half an hour he
sate puffing and swigging, puffing and swigging, and staring into
vacancy. As for me, I also sate staring into vacancy, yet when
I tried the Trinidado it turned me sick, and when I ventured
on the October it choked me. At the end of a long half-hour,
Master Whipple emptied the contents of the jack, hung up his
pipe, and proceeded to make known the result of his deliberations.

"Ned, 'tis forcible to my mind that you must leave this hostel
to-night. I will not answer for your neck, should you bide here
another day. Now the question is, whither shall you flee. To
go eastward into Wiltshire would be but running into danger,
because their plans are in apple-pie order in that direction.
Also you are much known in the north o' the county, and would

surely be taken ere you could get any distance away. Southward the sea would soon cut you off, yet that might avail you better than aught else, if we did but know of a craft to take you over the water. But, as luck will have it, friend Billy Hardisty only sailed yesterday to fetch a cargo of French brandy. Now, lad, you are well acquainted with the Quantocks, as I've oft heard you say. Sure you can discover some snug fastness or retreat to seek refuge in till the pursuit becomes less keen. That is undoubtedly your best chance, and you must trust to your wits for food, as there are several homesteads in the neighborhood. Yes, this is positively your best outlook. You have no horse to encumber you, and with reasonable precaution, you should be able to breathe in comfort for a long time yet. Also ye lack money—a real misfortune that. A bit o' th' ready will overcome many difficulties. Y'are a thriftless youth, yet, sink me! so was Long Bob Bickers. But bullion you want, and I'll show you how to get it."

Master Whipple was a man of rare brain-power and invention, and in sudden emergencies of this nature his mother-wit bordered on the marvellous. At such moments he seldom failed to show his boundless superiority over his fellow-creatures. On this occasion he soon had an idea, and when he did happen to obtain one, as a general rule, it proved a thing of value. 'Twas necessary for me to procure money, and for a quarter of an hour mine host impressed most explicitly upon me the best mode of securing the same. Having made my course of action clear, and fully instructed me in the part I was to play, he unlocked the door and went out to assist his lad Tom in the dispensing of liquors to the soldiers in the common room.

As soon as he was gone, I muffled myself up thickly and covertly in the folds of a horseman's cloak. That I took from a cupboard, placed at my service by the landlord, four pistols, all of which I loaded and put carefully in a handy pocket under the folds of the cloak; pulled my hat low down over my eyes, and stole stealthily out of the parlor into the yard. No sooner had I arrived there than I suddenly smartened my carriage; briskly wheeled about, and strode straight into the apartment where the King's men were sitting.

"Haw, landlord," I cried, in a loud overbearing voice as though I were the greatest man in the realm, "a flask of claret, if you please; and if you set any of your washy stuff before me, it is at your peril."

"Quite so, my lord. Just so, my lord. I will bear that in mind, my lord," cried Pete, bowing with deference and solicitude. "My lord," he continued, "I will not forget to set before you a vintage which you shall surely smack your lips at, for in good sooth your own cousin, His Grace of Grafton, was even so kind as to take more than he could properly hold, though maybe I'm over bold to say so."

"Tush, landlord, I trust he took no more than decently befits a gentleman. If he did, I'll wager 'tis prime stuff, for Cousin Graffy hath the nicest tongue for a dram, and the shrewdest eye for a woman in the three kingdoms. Now trip it featly wi' those dainty feet, sir, and oscillate those shapely limbs, and generally outdo La Favorita at Old Drury in swiftness and grace of motion. Come, trip it, landlord; come, trip it, sir! My gullet is as dry as my old dad's coffers."

This I rattled off in the approved London fashion, chewing a tooth-pick the while, and infusing as much magniloquent vapor into my manner as I could command.

Master Whipple did as he was bidden, yet not ere he had bowed once more to this person of quality.

A dozen soldiers in the King's uniform sat round a table near the doorway, with a goodly quantity of liquor and beer ready for their throats, and were occupied in either playing cards or watching their companions do so.

No sooner did I make my appearance and begin to speak, such was the skill of my counterfeiting, that one and all ceased paying attenion to pot and pasteboard, and inclined their ears towards me. To hear mine host belord me as he had done, together with the assumption of my demeanor, straightway produced an extravagant impression upon their minds, which I vow were none too clear. And to crown all this, 'twas a comic sight to see these worthies exchange glances when cunning Peter made mention of the Duke of Grafton. As he went in quest of the wine, he shot a solitary glance at me, which, though seemingly insignificant in itself, was deeply charged with eloquence. Hereabouts I made believe to see the redcoats for the first time. I singled out by his dress a little fellow (whom methought I had surely encountered on a previous occasion) as the captain of the company. First of all I eyed him in an apparently critical fashion, and then said, still preserving my assurance—

"Good evening, captain."

"Same to your lordship," he replied, bobbing stiffly. As I inspected his waspish red face, shrewish lower jaw, puckered beady eyes, and round, fat, and stunted little body, my conviction grew firmer that I had indeed made his acquaintance under

14

different circumstances. And tacked close on it, there came into my mind the recollection of some transaction with this same individual and the Mayor of Exeter in a business capacity, some months previous. Yet, seeing how little the affair redounds to my credit, 'twill serve no useful purpose to retail it, though at that time the captain, who bore the name of Joshua Pringle, was only an apparitor of King's Bench.* But, as I subsequently learned, this man, thanks to a varied knowledge of the West country, and force of ability, had been chosen to lead the expedition against Black Ned.

"You have some brawny ones here, captain," I said, pointing to a couple of lusty fellows at his elbow. "By the Mass, I'll wager they could give shrewd knocks in His Majesty's service. But I've heard it said brains and brawn ne'er accord with one another. Now tell me, friend, is it not the case that, though you are scarce half the size of one of these lads, you could, in the matter of head-work, put them to the blush?"

"Quite so, my lord."

"And methinks 'tis not improbable that even in the matter of more manual exercises, though you do lack stature, you would not be altogether out of it. By the look of you I should say you could doubtless twirl a sword or handle a musket with any man."

"Quite so, my lord; quite so."

The little officer was certainly overcome by this insinuating flattery; which was clearly proved by the expansion of his chest, and the rapid exalting of his head. In very truth at that moment he appeared as patronizing and self-satisfied as an archbishop.

"And are all your company as deft and skilful in the handling of firearms as yourself?" I asked.

"They are a credit to me, your lordship. Of course they do not possess that neatness, that deftness of fingering, and that general elegance of mode I am proud to lay some claim to. 'Tis the head, there, my lord, the head. Nature doth not endow us all alike."

"Of course not, captain. I' faith all the world knows, men of brains blossom by themselves, and do not go about in companies. There is a great dearth of such, I trow. Yet do I understand you aright when I say these men, every one of them, though lacking your daintiness of manner, are capable of hitting a given target at ten paces with some degree of accuracy?"

* See Prologue.—Editor.

" Most certainly, my lord," he replied, fussy as a cat that is having its back stroked.

" Then, captain, luck hath certainly favored me in this matter. I will promise your men a guinea to drink my health with, if they do but consent to manage a small service on my behalf."

" They will be happy to do that, sir."

" You must understand, captain, 'tis a wager of a hundred guineas I have laid with my lord Feversham, the commander of the King's forces. He was airing his opinion t'other day that very few persons were proficient in the exercise of firearms, and were able to use them with accuracy. Yet I wagered, there and then, that I could walk into any country inn and choose half a dozen fellows who would put a bullet through a mug ten paces distant at the first time of asking. Ods fish ! 'twill be a rare joke ! My lord will be fairly hoist with his own petard. Here hath he been having your men trained in the perfect use of musket and pistol, and it to cost him a hundred guineas. See the joke, captain ? Methinks it will be mightily relished in Town."

The King's men grinned.

At this moment the landlord returned with the wine I had ordered. I bade him place it on one side for a while, and also commanded him to move the other table, at which none were seated, a distance of ten paces away, and place a mug thereon.

With an air of the greatest astonishment Master Whipple obeyed. Captain Pringle was the first to essay the task. Easily enough he shattered the mug, and certes the task was ridiculously simple. Another crock was set up, and the next man performed the feat ; and thus they continued until every man had emptied his pistol in putting lead through the earthenware.

These fellows had had wine sufficient not to make any awkward inquiries, as in sooth they might have done, for to men wholly sober it must of necessity appear a strangely vague proceeding. But they had bibbed enough to want more, and were all eagerness to get it.

Mine host expeditiously set the room to rights when the job had been properly performed. Having cleared away the mass of broken crockery, he set the table facing those of the soldiers a convenient distance off, and laid my wine thereon. Also he fetched a goodly serving of sweet wine for them at my order, whereupon I was belorded by all more freely than ever ; the payer very fittingly commanding respect.

I assumed a seat opposite these gentlemen, and had a perfect view of them as they stowed away their drink, whilst I sipped mine in a genteel manner.

This may have gone on ten minutes ; at any rate, long enough for them to recommence chattering, playing cards and casting dice, without further heed to me, when Master Whipple winked at me, outwardly without aim or purpose, and in a moment I slipped my four pistols stealthily on to the table. Laying three carefully down I took the remaining one in my hand and cocked it up in the eyes of the company.

" Gentlemen," said I, in a voice so unlike my previous one, that all of them started in astonishment, " I require your purses."

Each man in turn gave a witless stare, opened his mouth ; then closed it with an exclamation.

The captain was the first to find his tongue.

" Good God ! Black Ned himself."

" Ay, friend, that's true," I said cheerfully. " Now, I will have things done orderly. That you gallant gentlemen may play me no scurvy trick, I must beg the loan of your weapons first, and that of your purses afterwards. I beseech you un-buckle your swords, withdraw your pistols, and present them to me at this table one at a time, not forgetting every stiver ye may have about your persons. And, mark you this, should I see any one of you make a movement ere the correct season, I will most assuredly put a bullet into the carcase of him who is so unwise. D'ye see, I've got four loaded pistols, whilst all your own are empty, thanks to your exceeding kindness. There-fore it must be plain to you all that argument is useless. Now, Captain Pringle, you being the leader o' this enterprise, and the most intellectual man in the room, I require you first to come for-ward and deliver up what I have demanded."

They fell to swearing and shifted their eyes uneasily, first to-wards me, than towards one another.

Unquestionably their position was thankless. The deceit I had practised had left them with unloaded firearms, and ere they could have attempted to re-load I must have shot the one who dared to do it. Neither could a sudden rush have been at-tempted, without loss of several of their lives, and no matter how precarious the strait may be, life is ever accounted a momentous thing. 'Twas apparent to the entire crew that I was master of the situation, and no one was more alive to that unpalatable fact than diminutive Captain Pringle. I watched them narrowly, and as I did so beheld the captain fumbling slyly and care-fully under the table. In a moment he whipped this hand from underneath, and I saw the glint of a pistol-barrel.

Instantly there was a flash and a keen report, and the fellow sprang up with a howl, as the firearm dropped on to the floor.

"Oh, my arm! my arm!" he screamed; and the blood welled through his jacket.

"No tricks, captain," I said, with a calculated smile. I had been too quick for him. I reloaded my pistol with a sinister calmness, which made a visible impression on my victims. Next, I produced my watch, and laid it on the table, remarking sweetly, "Captain Pringle, if you fail to obey me in two minutes by this watch, I have a bit o' lead here that shall find your intelligent head; so bestir yourself for the sake of your abnormal wits."

There and then he came to me at the table, his bloody limb hanging limp, and his breath caught up in sobs of pain. I might have pitied him, could I have forgotten what his mission was. He reluctantly unbuckled his sword, laid down his pistol, and handed over a whole month's pay, or what remained of it, which was a good proportion, as it had not long been drawn. Every man Jack of them did likewise. Thereupon I marched them out into the street, where their horses were awaiting them, and away they rode to Taunton, being billeted at the Green Man hostelry in that town.

"Ye shall pay for this," muttered the bleeding and mind-hurt Master Pringle.

Yet I laughed and carelessly snapped my fingers. However, I had the good sense to know that this disdain was but the idlest of boasts. At that moment my prospects looked blacker than they had done for many a day. Master Whipple and I, as soon as they were gone, counted up the money (a comforting and worthy sum), and divided it equally between us. This was only common fairness, seeing this pretty trick we had played together had been conceived in that gentleman's head. We buried the weapons in a field at the back of the house, for their loss would be a sore inconvenience to their owners; a pleasurable thought, when I reflected how nearly they were my enemies. 'Twas deadly strife bewixt us—strife which meant my life and liberty. Already I had struck them a very unkind blow, though one that might be mended. Pete chuckled a hundred times that night, and praised me considerably for the skilful way I had executed his idea. He even went so far as to question whether the immortal Bob Bickers could have accomplished it much better. And this was an admission so singular in itself, that I took opportunity to record it on the almanac.

"There's one thing troubles me, Pete," I said; "do you not

think these fellows will come another day, and lay a charge against you of aiding and abetting me?"

"Tush, lad," he replied, with cheerful whistle, "hast never heard of ways and means? I *have got a tongue in my head, ain't I?*"

I was forced to admit this; whereat he set about whistling with greater vigor, and his owl-like countenance wore a look that nature does not give to a common person.

CHAPTER XXII.

THE FUGITIVE.

I CRAMMED my pockets with food; dressed myself in my stoutest suit, encased my legs in thick riding-boots, and had my cloak for an outer covering. I next stuck a brace of pistols in my belt, and filled my pouch with ball. Thus equipped, I bid adieu to Peter, and close on midnight set out for the hills, in no very cheerful frame of mind. Truly I had good reason to have this weight upon my spirits; as it might be days, weeks, months, or never that I should see my friend again. And if I have not already proved him to be so in your eyes, rest assured I will ere long.

I started for the hills a hunted man, which was a thing calculated in itself to fill one with a pessimist's reflections. I slept that night at least securely, as there was no likelihood of pursuit, in the open among the heather; and, as the air was warm and dry, I did not find my couch entirely void of comfort.

Next day, I roamed about to discover a sheltered hiding-place whither I might flee when hard beset, or in which to rest safely of a night-time. In the glare of the powerful sun I wandered, knowing no rest until such a retreat had been obtained. There were numberless little crags and hollows scattered here and there, mingled with thick clumps of furze and a wilderness of herbage. The surface of the Quantocks is much broken by little hills and glens, or "goyals" as they are called in our parts, cutting it up into meagre patches, and numberless brown-colored streams flow down into the valleys, whilst all manner of trees flourish close beside them. My quest went unrewarded during the first day, being unable to find a hiding-place to suit me. But I was determined not to abate my zeal till one had been procured, as then I should be better equipped against my enemies.

The next night I slept in a tree. I meant to throw no chance away; for life is the most esteemed when it is felt to be precarious. The day following I still pursued my object, though after a bright morning the sky grew clouded, and early in the afternoon the rain came dripping down. Yet e'en though it soaked my cloak, I persisted in my search. An hour before nightfall this perseverance was rewarded. Maybe, I had wandered five miles from Chilverley village, when I halted suddenly, for lying just below me was a deep valley possibly fifty feet beneath. It was as though a huge lump had been cut out of the earth, for there stood a sheer precipice of rock, steep as a house side, to form the near wall of the gully. I was now standing on the edge of this barren length, and peering into the depths of the recess. As I did so, I saw that the base of it was split up into little fissures, and methought it likely if I made my way to the bottom, I might find some nook among these clefts that would offer a place of refuge.

As I have said, 'twould have been impossible to have clambered down the rock, because 'twas like a huge house side, and every whit as precipitous. Yet I did not fail to perceive the high ground on which I stood sloped gradually downwards, till it came on a level with the " goyal." This deep glen was perhaps two hundred yards from the wall of the beetling cliff, to the narrow strip of bushes which formed the entrance, and the outlet also, for it was walled in by the rocks on three sides, and this short belt formed a small opening on the fourth. It crossed my mind that herein was my long-sought goal. To gain proof of this, I followed the sloping ground till I had gotten on a level with the " goyal," and, by climbing over a few scattered fragments of rock, and poking forward and breasting the bushes made my way into this gloomy enclosed space. I walked round the foot of its walls, hoping to find some sheltered nook at their base; for, to search higher up was useless, as the rock sides were entirely unbroken in their expanse.

To my joy, I presently discovered the object of my search, for exactly opposite the entrance, at the bottom of the hither side (above which I had stood), was a small archway among the fragments strewn about the floor of the glen, and this formed a little cave, which was bounded backwards by the cliff. This insignificant receptacle might hold a grown man with comfort; tho', to put another in beside him would have been an impossibility. 'Twas a sweetly sheltered nook, and my heart leapt up at sight of it. Here at least I might bide with scant fear of discovery, and with a weather-proof roof above me, as the rocks met together overhead. As I have said it was only a very little place, maybe a dozen feet from the cliff base to the tiny entrance, which was so narrow that only one person could get through, and then it was a squeeze. It exactly faced the mouth of the "goyal," and the mass of furze in its vicinity.

Forthwith I made this snug retreat my domicile. When the darkness stole like a thief upon the hills I drew my cloak about me, stretched my limbs at full length on the heathery floor, and being much wearied, without a thought to things past, present, or to come, I fell into a blissful sleep, and never dreamed at all. In the morning when I rubbed my eyes the sun was mounting in the heavens, and I ate my last crumb of food. 'Twas now a matter of much moment how to obtain a fresh supply. After some hard thinking on the subject, I determined to pay a visit to Chilverley as soon as night fell, being well enough acquainted with the hills to find my way back again in the dark. Throughout that day I brooded plentifully on my own affairs. Of a surety they had taken a turn for the worse of late. Whilst I lingered here in hiding, who might tell what was being encompassed at the manor?

My present position would have been perfectly tolerable, as among these hills I was not by any means affrighted at the law hounds, had not gloomy forebodings kept rising in my mind as to what might be happening to Dorothy. Now I am aware this was grave impropriety on the part of my mental faculties. Ye may well ask why they should be troubled about an innocent maid who had been my dupe, and who had execrated me over the threshold of her father's door. They had no business whatever to be concerned about her, yet that ne'er mattered a farthing rushlight to 'em. The images of a maiden with wondrous eyes, an old, gouty, vile-tempered warrior with a lacerated visage, and a passionate, handsome young French gallant, with "*Ah, ma belle cousine, je vous aime*" for ever issuing from his lips, jostled in my brain all the livelong day. If I had listened intent enough, I might have heard the clanging peal of wedding bells; yet I didn't. I only speculated, and amongst other things upon my future course of action. I hated the old knight and his designs; I hated the Frenchman more, and would have run him through with an unrepentant heart, and all this because—because I loved Mistress Dorothy Marvin in direct defiance to common sense and reason.

Yet, may I ask, what doth love know of common sense and reason? Why just as much as a sucking-calf does of wisdom, and no more. Accordingly, I hated Sir Nicholas and the Frenchman, because they sought to rob me of my unwilling prize. Placed as I was, I had no chance to hinder the threatened catastrophe, therefore wicked restlessness gnawed my heart-strings all that day; surely love is the foster-mother of hate.

Directly night had fallen, I descended to the valley wherein our homestead lies. I slipped through the village in the shadow of the hedegrows, till I found myself before the latch of our kitchen door. With a beating heart I pulled it, and walked in amongst the occupants.

John, now the day's work was done, had exchanged his heavy boots for slippers, and, in lazy repose, was smoking in the chimney corner. Mother and Betty were busy concocting a simple of herbs, such as was kept for minor hurts and ailments, and for dispensation to the neighbors.

One and all of them started back in surprise as they beheld their visitor. Mother kissed her son—i' faith, sons must be very far gone in infamy when mothers won't. Betty hung back, timid and distressed, whilst John scowled, and went on smoking.

"Mother," said I, "I have come for food. Victuals have run short with me."

That was sufficient for the moment. The two women, in the winking of an eye, had set out a huge supper for my delectation. Mother bade me eat and drink my fill ere I exchanged another word; whereat I took a chair, and sate at the head of the table close beside John's elbow.

With a darker scowl than ever my brother got up in an instant, and betook himself to the other end of the kitchen, so as to be far removed from me. I marked this keenly, and so did mother. Her eyes met mine, yet no word passed between us. It so chanced that a cushion lay on John's new seat, and mother bade him hand it her, and upon his doing so, she fixed it against my back, saying the while that I looked very jaded and weary. In a short time my brother retired to bed. Ere he did so, he kissed his mother and sister, and gave them good-night. I proffered my hand to him, yet he never heeded it, and, without a word or look for me, walked upstairs. It was not till mother and I were alone that I overcame the silence I had hitherto preserved.

"Mother," I said, "hast heard the latest news?"

"Alas, my poor boy, I have. 'Tis like a knife to my heart

to learn thou'rt hunted hourly like a fox. And all last night, after hearing what Tobe Hancock told us, I could not sleep for trembling and for thoughts of thee."

"I have gathered no tidings for the last three days, mother. What is this news? Nothing very dire, I trust?"

"Oh, 'tis terrible, cruel news! The King hath sent men down from London for thy capture, which, of course, thou'rt aware of. But worse than this, all the gentry in the neighborhood have taken the matter up, and one of them, by name Sir Nicholas Marvin, hath offered one hundred pounds to those who deliver your dead body up to justice, or two hundred should you be captured alive."

At this I uttered an involuntary cry. 'Twas a blow to stagger a stronger man than I.

"Also," she continued, "he is lending his own servants to join in the pursuit, and is paying men to assist, whilst other gentlemen, who pronounce you a public bane, have offered a round sum between them, and are furnishing men and money with which to hunt you. Tobe says that they have heard you are in hiding among the hills, and are about to search every place of habitation among them. They will look in every glen, and valley, and patch of brushwood in quest of you. They mean to cover every inch of ground, and, I hear, nigh a hundred men are afoot scouring the country side."

"'Tis cruel news!" I exclaimed. In those days I was a bold fellow, and one not easily abashed, yet this dreadful information seemed to strike me down.

Mother then proceeded to tell how the lawyers had come expressly from London for the purpose of telling her that her son's heirship had been forfeited to the King, on account of his outlawry. Ultimately she stuffed my pockets with food of all kinds, and promised to have a basket of it placed in a particular spot amongst the boulders on the hill-side every morning. After that, I left her to weep and pray for her eldest son, a thief, a fugitive, who was hunted by a hundred men, and who had a great price upon his head.

He, bereft wretch, went back to his place of succor in the bosom of the hills. The moon was up, and shed a blue resplendent glory over the dark masses of boulder, timber, stream, and brushwood. My heart felt cold in my breast, and my teeth chattered though the night air was warm and calm. The demon, Horror, seemed to clog my very soul as I thought of the hundred men who were seeking me night and day; and the reward for my apprehension.

The cruelest pang was the knowledge of Sir Nicholas Marvin's rampant hatred. 'Twas plain the man had neither forgotten nor forgiven. His vengeance was truly a thing of which to live in terror. And would he disregard the oath he had sworn to me? That was a new fear, for I ever sought to keep the traditions of our house unsoiled. Hitherto, I accounted myself safe from the law's clutches, for, with some show of reason, methought that a dozen King's men could ne'er be able to root me from my fastness. Yet now it was an entirely different matter.

As I learned afterwards, what mother had told me was, alas, too true. When it became known how anxious the King was for my arrest, the long-flouted gentry in the vicinity bethought themselves that the occasion presented a fair opportunity to make me pay for many tricks and indignities I had inflicted on them; and also to prove how much sympathy they had for the King in his quest, by aiding vigorously in the search. Certainly I had become most obnoxious to the County, and having laughed at the power of the Justices for so long a time, one and all of them combined to assist the King. Included amongst them was the High Sheriff, who called out his posse to join in the hue and cry. And so, between them, they raised many men, and offered a large reward for the criminal's body, dead or living. Also, every word was accurate concerning Sir Nicholas Marvin. In fact, he was the most anxious and most earnestly interested man in the business. Sooth, he was a terrible enemy. Sleep did not come to me so readily in my hiding-place that night; for many hours I lay awake with a weary restlessness, and with brain afire, pondering bitterly upon the great force of men and money arrayed against me. Verily, unless Providence was wondrous kind, I could not hope to escape.

About noon next day I left the remainder of the food brought overnight in my little abode, and went to seek the promised basket. To my exceeding thankfulness, it reposed at the spot mother had said it should. I emptied the contents into my pockets, and, leaving the basket where I had found it, returned to my sheltering-place, glad to seek a covering from the fierce rays of the sun. I crossed my legs tailor fashion, squatted down under the kindly awning, and ate my dinner.

I had not been thus engaged very long, when, without a warning, half a dozen men sprang through the bushes, two hundred yards away, at the mouth of the goyal. The distance that lay between us prevented them from espying me at once. There-

fore, I lay down flat that I might escape their observation. To
my horror, however, three went one way, and three the other,
and commenced walking round the base of the rocks, evidently
bent on neglecting no opportunity in their vigilant search.
Should they chance to come as far as where I lay, I could not
fail to be discovered. They neither swerved nor halted, but
kept following close by the bottom of the steep ascents; drew
nearer and nearer, and soon I knew my last hour of liberty
was come. But despite my desperate position, methought life
still worth a struggle. The three to my left hand had approached within ten yards of where I was stretched full length,
when I jumped up, my head coming within half a foot of the
roof of the cavern. Plucking two pistols out of my belt, I
cried out to them to tarry, holding a weapon in each hand that
the entire company might have a sight of them. They did
stop short, indeed, gravely startled by this apparition; but in a
moment Captain Pringle, who formed one of the number, gave
vent to a cry of delight, and waved his uninjured arm in
rapture.

"Found!" he exclaimed with malicious joy, and straightway began to dance.

They stood watching me with an apprehensive eye for the
pistols.

"Approach not a step nearer, or I put a bullet through the
foremost man," I shouted.

"Who will draw the badger?" asked the captain, his joy
cut short at this defiance.

None of them seemed willing to undertake this ticklish task,
least of all Master Pringle himself. They stood and took
counsel one with another as to the best means of laying hands
upon me.

"Shoot him," said one.

"Ay, ay," assented two or three.

"Nay, my lads," quoth the captain, "that will not do; 'twill
be a clear hundred out of our pockets. Did not Sir Nicholas
Marvin offer us one hundred pounds if we took him dead, and
two hundred should we take him alive, so that he might be
placed in the felon's box, and die a felon's death? No,
methinks it will ne'er do to shoot him; best take him alive."

"But how?" they asked.

The little captain knitted his brows and stared at me in deepest thought.

For my part, to stand there watching them decide my fate
was the reverse of cheerful. Still, I had already made up my

mind that, should they advance to take me, I would shoot down as many as I could. I was a desperate man brought to bay.

At length Master Pringle spoke, and he sent a chill through all my bones as the words issued from his lips.

"Tell you what, my lads," he grinned, "we will earn every groat of our guerdon. We will ne'er leave this place till he surrenders. We'll pitch a little tent across the opening against yonder bushes, then he can't escape ; and so will starve him out. One of you shall mount guard close by him in the night, and the moment he falls asleep he is ours. If three days doesn't settle him, I'll pay for a gallon o' sack."

"Bravo, captain ! "

"It's the head there, d'ye see ? You fellows would ne'er have thought o' that in a month. But, by my troth, 'twill be a sweet revenge. Master Black Ned, what say you ? A sweet revenge, you'll admit. I promised I would pay thee for that small affair the other night, and, so help me God ! I will. I'm reputed smart at repaying those kind of debts ; thou dost not play Joshua Pringle many such pranks. Good friend, how happy you will be to lie there foodless and sleepless. My eye, friend, you *will* enjoy yourself ! And then there'll be a lovely rope waiting to stretch that neck o' thine, and a beautiful gibbet for thy bones to rot in. And remember, we shall receive three hundred pounds for this little business—two hundred from Sir Nicholas Marvin, the best-hearted man in the county, and another hundred tacked on by the neighboring gentry. 'Pon honor, friend, we will drink thy health wi' it blithely, and wish thee a pleasant journey through the valley of the shadow."

The man's maleficence was disgusting as he danced before me, in heathenish glee. To cut short his foul exultation, I shouted—

"Hold, you little hound of hell, or I put a bullet through you ! "

I raised my pistol to get a sight of him as I spoke, and three parts made up my mind to shoot him dead. Mayhap in the end 'twould have saved me much anxiety had I done so, yet I can never be too thankful I had not his blood upon my soul. 'Tis vile enough to be a thief, yet how much worse to be a murderer ! My attitude silenced the creature, but forthwith they proceeded to take measures to starve me into surrender. They could with ease have shot me, but the thoughts of that other hundred pounds made them anxious to take me alive if possible. This was a further proof of the thirst for vengeance that possessed the knight. He was not satisfied that I should lose my life, but I must lose it in the direst shame and ignominy, at the hands of the common hangman.

One of the King's men was ordered to fetch a tent, and to call his remaining comrades hither, whilst the rest stayed to maintain a watchful guard upon me. Ere nightfall ? spacious canvas covering had been erected at the mouth of the "goyal," wherein the whole crew lay drinking, playing, and waiting.

CHAPTER XXIII.

THE STRANGE ADVENTURE OF THE "GOYAL."

To lie cooped up in that rocky crevice, and to know that when I came forth out of it into the world of men I must do so to a shameful death, was a revolting reflection. Escape was impossible ; my captors were in possession of the only exit. Even had I a rope, it would have availed nothing, as there was no means of securing it at the top of the rocks, whilst to climb up without such aid was quite beyond the range of possibility, since on the unbroken expanse of cliff there was nought to offer any foothold. The soldiers knew this, and therefore the whole crew made high holiday as they awaited my surrender. Not that this joviality offered the slightest hope of amendment in my fortunes. They were far too alert for me to steal a march upon them. Faith ! three hundred pounds had made them zealous servants of the King. They troubled their heads little about their prisoner, knowing thoroughly well that flesh and blood is no match for hunger, thirst, and lack of sleep.

Twice during my first night's vigil I saw a man's blurred shadow issue from the darkness. Evidently a soldier was listening for any sonorous sounds, so that he might seize me. However, I drove him away with threats on each occasion. This served to prove that I should be their prey the moment I yielded to the wiles of slumber. Herein lay my chief concern ; in the matter of food, I might have defied them for a week, because I was sufficiently supplied ; yet the mere thought of going without sleep for such a period was torture. Truly I must soon give in ; but, in despite of that, with a vain, pig-headed pertinacity, I was determined to hold out as long as I was able.

The King's men had brave times ; 'twas pleasant enough for them. They basked in the sun, or slept through the daytime, gambled and caroused all night, and made the silent hills re-echo with their songs, their oaths, and their Bacchanalian laughter. As for me, I declare that I had a very sober time indeed, and an intensely bitter one. Conscience is a coward ; 'twill not attack a man when he is hale and free in limb and mind, as at such a time it is likely to be worsted. No, that is not at all its method. Watchfully, stealthily, 'twill wait till its opponent lies weak and spent ; then like a demon it comes from a cobwebbed-corner in the brain, and sallies forth to tantalize its victim. And, oh ! the promises for future amendment it will extort at such triumphant times, for, like all cowards, it rides with a high hand in the hour of victory. Nevertheless these fair promises are forgotten when the penitent regains his rude, corporeal vigor.

Were I only to set down here a tenth part of what transpired in my mind during these moments of repentance, straightway ye would call me names, and account me the sorriest of storytellers. There is but one of these things I will mention, and that shall be the bitterest. I had been the dupe of love. Whether this contingency arose through the machinations of God or the devil 'twas more than I was capable of fathoming ; yet I never doubted its unpalatable truth. Here had I wasted months of time and energy on a hopeless thing, and was condemned to die spurned and cursed by the one for whom I might have sold my soul. Furthermore, but for this love which had so befooled me, I should have carried out Tobe Hancock's wishes, and have quitted the country. Oh, blind, blind fool ! thrice-duped idiot ! to clutch after a Will o' the Wisp till it leads you into a bog, only for it to dance away as you feel the black slough closing above your head, and as life is ebbing from you ! Oh, blind, insensate fool ! Yet, stay, why this to do ? Every fool doth advertise his name when he is called upon to pay for all his folly ; I suppose 'tis then for the first time that he realizes that " fool " should have been his natal title. This was the wearing of the mind and of the body, methinks something of the bitterness of death cankered it.

My plight was pitiable ; being compelled to lie hours in a narrow place, with limbs cramped, tongue parched, and eyes destitute of sleep. Times without number I made up my mind to leave this pestilential shelter and give myself up to the soldiers of the King. Aught was better than this cruel state. Yet no sooner did I get my limbs a trifle stretched by standing up prior to going out, than once more my heart failed, and I returned to voluntary captivity. Thus must I linger till the

time when nature would have her way, then perforce I should
pass into the hands of justice.

On the morning of the third day I had lain without sleep, a
new idea came into my head—and a welcome one. A bullet
through the brain methought would settle all things sublunary.
Thereupon I hugged the weapon to my breast, and blessed it
by the kindly name—Deliverer. By its aid I might escape the
gallows, and the gaping grinning crowd ; and thus balk the
knight, and so be saved ignominy. Verily this idea in itself
was heartsome. I set about reckoning the time I had left to
live. One more night, and this same day, methought I could
keep awake—perhaps twenty hours in all. Twenty hours to
make my peace with God! At once I knew I could not do it
in the time. Most folk do not trouble about the hereafter till
they meet it face to face ; and tho' I was one of that procras-
tinating tribe, and had to die a thief, and by my own hand, try
as I might I could not think of hell and heaven. God knows
I sought to do ; still it was in vain ; I even had no words to
form a prayer with.

I lay all through the day tossing on the bed of heather, lost
in a kind of stupor, thinking of nothing at all, with my eyes
fixed on the stern impassive rocks. The sun dipped gradually in its grandeur, till the purple flecked the sky; 'twas the
last sunset. I did not cry nor moan by this, nor roll and toss
about, having done with such emotions. I only lay with lips
cracked with thirst, heavy eyes, and the pistol soothing my hot
cheek with the stolid coldness of its iron.

As the evening came the sky clouded over, and a breeze
sprang up from the southwest. Once or twice I saw the
prowling shadows of the watchful soldiery close at hand; but
had the strength to cry out, and threaten them with my pistols,
whereupon they retired to their game. The rain began to
patter down, and this gave me a little vigor as I sucked the
raindrops, whilst they bathed my brow. Being thus revived I
felt more energy for a while, and commenced to think again,
not of eternity, but of my ride one morning in the spring, when
I sought to break my neck. Also of another ride a month
agone in the furious storm, when I rode my brave horse till he
died. There I had the beginning and the ending. Perchance,
after all, death did not seem so grim and terrible.

I and my kind companion, the pistol, lay there that last night
side by side. It, cold, callous, without feelings, without emotions, yet with the gentlest pity; I, calm, with neither joy nor
care ; waiting for my merciful servant to perform its office.

Soon Ned Armstrong, thief, with Death at his elbow, fell into a kind of half-unconsciousness. Once I gave a horrible start and shivered. 'Twas the face of Judge Jeffreys peering through the gloom. I saw his eyes, his glaring wolf-like countenance, his huge periwig, the white powder snowing out of it; and his square murderous jowl. I saw myself down on my knees before my father's gibbet tree; heard it creak in the wind, and heard the scream of the carrion bird, as it flew into the boding night. The raindrops mingled lovingly with the wind soughing in the valley, and murmured sweet harmonious music; a gentle soothing rhapsody; a surcease from sorrow; from hate and love.

Mine eyes kept closing as though pulled together by an unseen hand. There was no light in the sky, no object visible through the darkness; all things around were tragically silent, and the night fell like a terrifying pall of black. 'Twas a fitting night to die in. Suddenly I raised my arms and shivered; I could not keep my eyes open. The time had now arrived when the friendly pistol was to prove its worth. I stretched my hand out and got the iron thing within my grasp, stroked the loaded barrel; and my fingers touched the easy trigger. Here I closed my eyes, slowly raised the barrel to my forehead; but during the performance of this reluctant act I thought of her who had saved me from myself; who had lifted me out of utter depths of infamy. I thought of her who had inspired me to hate my fallen state, who had made me feel the happiness of living; of her who had made me more fit to behold my Maker. Then I felt the cruel stroke, and thought 'twas good to die; but directly saw her bleeding arm, and changed my mind. After that I grew maudlin, like the heroes in the fourth-rate tragedies of the playhouse. Would she be glad to know that I was dead? or would she weep? Would she hate me still? or would she hate herself? Or would——?

Here the wily demon sleep took hold of me, and for a time I had no care for earth, or hell or heaven. I became conscious again with a violent start. There was a hand on my sleeve. Oh joy! the pistol still nestled in my fingers.

"Who are you?"

"Hush, Ned," said a soft voice.

Hereupon methought my reason had surely gone. A hand was laid on the back of mine, and another "hush" was breathed within my ears.

"Dorothy, is it thee? or am I mad, or am I dreaming?"

"Poor lad! Here, drink this!"

15

Without any manner of doubt it was Mistress Dorothy Marvin down here in the " goyal," and on her knees at my side. To prove it was no phantasy of madness, I felt a phial as plain as ever mortal did, and also raised it to my lips, and gulped the spirit down.

"Whither hast thou come?" I asked in a sort of hopeful fear.

"I have come to save thee, Ned. For the love of Heaven, make no noise."

I was fully awake by this, tho' if ever a man was wideawake when he thought he wasn't, then without doubt that man was Edward Armstrong.

"Have you the strength to follow me?" she asked.

"That I have," said I, in a sudden thrill of vigor. "I will follow thee anywhere away from this accursed hole."

"Well, then, if thou hast the strength, and art noiseless and very speedy, thou art worth a many dead men yet."

"But how, mistress?" I whispered in amaze.

"A rope dangles from the cliff. If you climb that you are safe. Come, take another draught, and follow at my heels, and speak no word."

Carefully I took the charge out of the loaded pistol—my true friend—and stuck the weapon under my cloak. Then, afire with eagerness, I followed this good angel of deliverance. She led me to the wall of the rock, and slowly and cautiously made her way, feeling for the rope at every yard. 'Twas so dark that, though I was hard by her elbow all the while, her form was but a shadow. Suddenly she stopped and said "Hush!" into my ear again.

"The sentinel is lying here. Stride over him," she whispered.

I felt a strange sensation, yet just then, my guide took a wide step, and I beheld a dark mass lying at my feet. I did as I was bidden, so strode clear of it; and followed in the wake of my deliverer. Soon I found her standing still, a few yards distant; she had discovered the end of the rope. As I came up she gave the hempen strands into my hand.

"Up you get, sir!" she said shortly.

"What, and leave you till the last? Nay, nay, mistress, that cannot be. After you."

"Don't be a fool!"

Her tone was very low, but particularly fierce, and admitted of no controversy. It had more resolution and courage in it, than ever I've heard from the mouth of woman.

"Now, look alive, Ned, and get to the top. 'Twill be easy climbing, for there is a big knot for every four feet of rope."

'Twas as she had said, therefore the ascent was easy of accomplishment. In no time my feet touched the firm ground above, and a moment later, swifter than ever, Dorothy came up hand over hand and stood beside me.

"Quick, and help me unfasten this rope," she commanded.

Verily, she was like three men rolled into one just then; she had thought for everything. Her voice was a leader's voice, although so hushed, and her courage was truly marvellous. 'Twas a pity she was not a man, else she must have been a great one. The rope had been secured to a strong stake planted firmly in the ground; but in a minute it was untied, whereupon we drew the whole length out of the jaws of the goyal, and left it in a coil on the top of the precipice.

"There!" she exclaimed breathlessly, "we may tarry now. The King's men will have to walk round for a good half-mile to get on our track. Thou art saved, Ned."

'Twas too dark for us to make our way with certainty, as such was the blackness of the night, that we had to plant one foot carefully before the other, lest we tripped over some bush or boulder in our path.

"Best take our time," she remarked, still keeping sole command; "they have not yet discovered that the bird hath flown, and when they do, they will ne'er be able to follow in the dark."

"Mistress," said I, unconsciously leaning on this splendid creature, as the weak ever do on the strong, "whither must I flee? I know of no place of refuge. They will surely retake me ere long."

"Pish!" she cried contemptuously; "you talk like a man, and with only a man's wit. 'Tis lucky for you, sir, that I'm a woman, and with a woman's ingenuity," and she gave a little inward trill—even at so supreme a moment it seemed she had not forgotten the usages of laughter. "Now," she added, "I'll wager they never find thee. I have gotten the very best hiding-place for thee in the kingdom."

My heart leaped into my mouth at these noble words, for noble they truly were. A sense of awe of this girl was growing upon me. Could this be the light-hearted, laughing madcap? the slenderly wrought Mistress Marvin, with the maid's physique? 'Twas her voice that whispered thro' the gloom; but the spirit that burned, and glowed, and throbbed behind it would have honored indomitable Ulysses.

"We had best make slowly for the east, Ned, then we shall be following our course. 'Tis a rare piece of luck not having to cross their path to reach our place of succor."

After she had spoken thus we walked on in silence, side by side, yet very carefully. 'Twas still raining, and to prove this was no dream, several of the drops (with malice aforethought) found their way down my back and made me shiver. And so real was that shiver that I'll swear mortal ne'er had one so natural in sleep. We went forward for a quarter of an hour in silence. She did not say a word, whilst I felt strangely overcome by the sense of the noble thing she had done for me, of all men in the world, and also by the way in which she had done it. Truly she was her father's daughter. That night's splendid work proved to me at least, despite her feminine exterior, that she had more of the lion in her than the lamb. Yet stay, I run too fast.

We went on saying nothing for a quarter of an hour; but at the end of that time the voice of Mistress Dorothy Marvin of Kelston Manor (not her of the hills) quavered—

"Keep close by me, Ned. I feel unwell."

A moment later she cried out, gasping—

"Oh, Ned, I feel so strange. My knees are knocking. I believe I am about to fall. I—I—oh dear!"

I caught sight of her swaying in the darkness, so instantly put my arms around her, and supported her. She lay like lead in them. Tenderly I placed her on a hillock, and searched about her person for the spirits, and in doing so made another discovery, to wit, that she wore the garb she had done at Bruton. By force of patience I found the phial, and ere long brought her back to sensibility. Having quite recovered, we sat down together, side by side, on the wet hills, and waited for the first fleck of dawn that we might pursue the way.

"Ned," quoth Mistress Marvin of the manor, "I prithee do not laugh at me, but I feel a dreadful baby. Fancy to act like that. Why I simply might have beaten all the King's men myself, I felt so full of pluck, and then to make myself a fool now all is over. My word! old daddy would ne'er forget it did he but know I so demeaned myself; tho' I promise thee, Ned, he shall not know a word of this night's doings from any lips of mine."

"Mistress Dorothy," I said, though I know not whence came the strength or the courage to speak, "I am unworthy to talk to you."

"Oh, I'm a goddess, am I?"

"I have deceived you and the knight, your father," I continued lamely, "and yet you have risked your own life twice
to save my worthless one. I cannot thank you; I know not
how."

"Did I ask you to?" she asked pertinently; and then
enunciated "bah!" so bewitchingly that I felt a great regret—
and that was because I could not see the expression on her
face. "But I am sure," she said, "you are desperately curious
to learn what hath brought this night's doings about; so, to
while away the time, I'll tell you."

"Mistress, methinks I am in a dream. I cannot grasp what
hath just occurred. 'Twill be but another debt I owe should
you make matters more clear to me."

"Look here, Ned Armstrong, if I hear another word about
your debts, you shan't have a single word from me. However,"
she said, beginning the narrative, "you are quite aware of the
awful animosity papa bears against you. I love him dearly,
ay, more than I can really tell; yet I dread his hatred. When
he doth get a notion into his head that he hath been wronged,
then no earthly power will prevent him seeking vengeance.
And his vengeance is terrible; he frightens me when he gets
like he did on the night of your confession, and ever since he
hath sworn your death. He declared to me, morning, noon,
and night, he would ne'er rest till you had died on the gallows.
This he swore that night, and swears the same to this hour;
thus no sooner did the King's men arrive with the warrant for
your apprehension, than he jumped about like a youngster who
hath ne'er known the gout. Many a time had he cursed his
own soft-heartedness (as he called it), in not killing you when
he had the chance, and when these fellows from London came,
he straightway sent for them, and offered the terms all the
county wots of. He hath lent three of our serving-men to go
help and seek you, and, in fact, when his foot hath been well
enough, he has e'en gone abroad himself for that same purpose. Since their coming he hath had nought but you in his
head, and I tell you, Ned, I have spent more than one night
sleepless, thinking of his dreadful threats.

"Well, the most terrible thing happened this morning. That
wretched Captain Pringle came in high glee, and gave father a
full account of how they had got you like a 'badger in a hole.'
He told him how they were bound to starve you out ere long,
and the two of them seemed so delighted over it, that I could
not bear to be in the room and hear them. It made me desperate to think of you lying pent up there in that horrible hole,

and to know that you would ne'er come out of it only to death. And I thought, Ned, what a brute I had been to you the night you came and told us about yourself. I felt I could not rest without doing something to help you. Therefore, as the captain returned to his comrades, I followed him at a safe distance, marking my way carefully at every step, and when I came to the glen peeped over the edge of the cliff at you, and saw you lying there. And when I saw you, gaunt and pale, and like a rat in a trap, I knew my mind was quite made up. First I unrove a part of one of my stockings, tied a pebble to the end of the thread, lowered it down the mouth of the gulf, and so measured the height of the rocks ; and then went home, ne'er said a word to anybody about the matter, but got some rope about the proper length out of the hayloft, and by working hard made the knots in it, and thereby also made a sad mess of my gentle maiden's fingers. Feel, sir ! "

She laughingly brushed her open hands across my cheek, saying, " What think you of Dorothy Marvin, martyr ? " And truth to tell, in some degree she was a martyr, because her fingers were very rough and blistered.

" Methought," she added, returning to the narrative, " I might be perhaps a sorry climber, having had scant practice at the business. But, my word, sir ! you should have seen me this afternoon ! I climbed tree after tree, and swarmed the rope till I could go up like a monkey. Also I was afeared you might be weak and ill, therefore brought that phial with me. I came away before dark hour, that I could find my way to the spot with certainty. Upon arriving I fixed the stake, which I brought together with the rope, and waited till nightfall. But when darkness came, I am ashamed to tell you, my courage failed for long enough. Every time I looked down into that black abyss I shuddered, yet after a long struggle smothered my fears and descended. That done I felt equal to anything ; and verily should have been abashed at nought, I felt that bold and strong. Just then a sentinel came up, so I crouched down in the shadow of the rock, and as I did so my fingers lit on a piece of stone, whereat I happened to remember old daddy's maxim, ' that in war time 'tis your first duty to beat the enemy ; and that it is a commendable plan if the said enemy be in your power to kill him first, and beg his pardon afterwards.' Now, as that prowling sentry must certainly mar the scheme, I simply gave him a little tap behind the ear as papa hath often told of doing. Of course, I meant not to kill him, and God forgive me for laying hands upon him ! but methinks he surely will not die. 'Twas such a lady's tap, though wondrous neat of execution."

"Dorothy," said I, almost afraid of my mine own boldness, "would you like to hear the story of my downfall?"

"Ned, I have sought to divine your past these many days. I could wish for nought better than to hear the story from your lips."

With that I told her all in an honest manner. And the more I told her the easier the narrative became, for I felt the listener was sympathetic; and somehow it fell out that when the first streaks of day appeared, and the east grew gray, the hand of Black Ned lay in that of Mistress Dorothy Marvin.

As soon as there was light enough to proceed on our way, we set out for the promised place of refuge. I asked the maiden whither it lay, but she only laughed and bid me follow, and she would lead me to it. The rain had ceased falling now, and we stepped out briskly over the glistening heather.

Certes! she appeared a curious creature in her man's attire; but it did not ill-become her. Besides, her steps were so light and supple, her courage so bold, and her spirit so high and noble, that she might have donned it always, and without the least assumption. Once, however, she chanced to see me looking at her, and thereupon flushed up red as fire. This greatly disconcerted me, for I immediately remembered why she was wearing such habiliments; thus wished a hundred times I had not been caught a-staring. We trudged along straight to the manor gates, and these lay before us ere the sun had climbed over the ridge of the horizon.

I stopped at sight of them.

"Stay, mistress!" I cried, "methinks I am nearer the enemy than ever. I must go no farther if I am really to save my neck."

"Silence, sir; no questions, I beg. Am I not the leader of this enterprise? Therefore, obey your superior officer."

I did so, and then the meaning dawned upon my heavy understanding. She proceeded directly in among the undergrowth and brushwood into the thickest depths of the spinney; I ever at her heels. She took me among branches and brambles, stout thickets, close-grown clumps of timber and wild masses of herbage. Such sequestered spots among this little wood she led me to that I had ne'er visited before; and oftentimes we were so close beset with briers that our hands and cloaks were torn, and it was with difficulty that we saved our faces. At last we came to a spot more thickly entangled still. This appeared truly impassable, of such height, strength, and vastness was the intermingled density of verdure ; and so great was the power of its resistance, that it would have taken more than one man to have overcome it.

The maid, however, had a path at her disposal, as after a strict scrutiny of the landmarks, she parted a group of bushes some yards to her left hand; and thereby revealed a hidden opening. Thro' this we went and found a space splendidly fortified by impenetrable shrubs; and as I stood in the middle of this rare hiding-place I tossed up my hat for joy, because the prospect meant life to a hunted man.

It was very gloomy by reason of the leafy covering overhead, and the great strong blocks of brier and bramble on every side. There was, perhaps, twenty feet of clear grass, and to show yet another instance of my deliverer's forethought, there reposed two thick rugs on the ground, and upon raising them a basket of food and drink was disclosed to view. Without parley, I let loose my famished self and greedily attacked this blessed store, and Dorothy worthily seconded my efforts.

"Ned, methinks this is the finest hiding-place in the kingdom," she said between the mouthfuls. "One would think Sir Nicholas Marvin's estate to be the least likely spot in all the world to find Black Ned."

"Take back the foul blow, the coward's blow, I gave that hateful night," the sweet-blooded girl implored with peculiar timidity two hours after our arrival, as she left me alone, still a free man in body.

CHAPTER XXIV.

A LESSON IN THE LOST ART OF MANAGING WOMANKIND.

I MADE no answer to those last words of Mistress Marvin's ; any reply of mine would have been inadequate. She left me, promising to return ere the day was out to bring more food.

What with one thing and another my brain had been turned into a bewildered chaos. 'Twas hard indeed to realize that I was safe, that I had balked and evaded the King's men entirely, and still had my limbs unfettered. A fierce longing grew up within me to accomplish some great deed for the behoof of my rescuer. Just then I should not have accounted life too dear a price to have paid for such a blessed privilege. I was nearly mad with joy. After all the maid had dared and done for me, who could doubt that she returned my love? Yet that was

merely an argument of youth. A man more advanced in years
—one with a less supply of good blood and that far more
sluggish—might have known that the whole sex of womankind
is ne'er so strong in kindness nor so prone to noble deeds as
when pity hath entered into its heart.

And Dorothy Marvin pitied me, though I fail to discover any
good reason for her state of mind. With far better reason she
might have stuck to her revilings, for truth to tell, in my secret
heart (which kept rising uppermost as cork will in water), I
felt myself to be the most miserably weak and paltry creature
ever man did feel in a woman's presence. To me she seemed
to possess all the manliness. She was so strong, so indomitable, so fearless! And I, knowing this much of her, felt all
the smaller and meaner for the knowledge.

The maid was as good as her word, for that afternoon, as I
sat with my back against the tree, in the midst of my gloomy
retreat, I caught a glimpse of lustrous eyes glowing through the
bushes. Next moment Mistress Marvin stood beside me.

" Here I am," she said gayly ; " and oh, Ned, methinks thou
wilt bless me ten thousand times. See here, sir, what I have
for thee ! "

She had brought a full basket with her. Very deftly she
whisked away the cloth at the top and produced a rare roll of
tobacco, a pipe, and a dozen cigarros.

" There, sir, what do you say to that ? Are they not a brave
sight ? I stole them when Sir Nicholas went to sleep. Oh,
Ned, I am behaving very monstrous by my old father ! This
morning that rascally Captain Pringle came with the wriest face
I've seen for many a day, and told papa that you had escaped
them, and that he knew not how. And when he had told it
all, he burst out a-cursing, and then old dad went black in the
face. He seized hold of the little captain and howled at him,
' Sayest thou sooth, little rat ? ' The King's man answered that
'twas only too true, and swore louder than ever. And then,
Ned, you'd have laughed your ribs sore had you but seen it,
for my gouty old father cried, ' A kick for a curse, you fool ; '
and lifted him with his sound foot bang against the wall. But
poor daddy is in a terrible way. He hath done nought but rave
since he heard the news, and only to think his own daughter is
at the bottom of it, and you biding on his own estate. 'Twould
be a joke indeed, if he were not so genuinely angry. Oh, Ned,
I am a double-faced sinner ! I am behaving very wickedly, for
he is the very kindest of fathers. I do believe if he knew, he
would ne'er forgive me ! "

Her bright face clouded all at once, and there came a look of trouble on it. All the same, I held mine own opinion as to the kindliness and the fatherly qualities of Sir Nicholas Marvin. It ever passes my comprehension why this maid should have had no other feelings than the very deepest love and veneration for the callous old war-dog.

"Hast heard, mistress, what they purpose doing next?" I inquired.

"Alas," she replied, laughing again, "they are determined not to let the matter rest, and Sir Nicholas hath added another hundred pounds to what he hath already offered. Captain Pringle hath a very strong idea you are still lying in hiding in the hills; yet, Ned, I have a notion that you and I might be able to prove him wrong."

She was all gayety for the moment, and so arch and delightful was her demeanor, that I sighed to think what a rare prize she was, and how far she lay beyond my reach. Therein lay the gall which would forever dash the cup of delight with bitterness. Maybe that sigh of mine was infectious, for directly after, my companion fetched one just as heartfelt on her own account, and once more the laughter left her eyes.

"Ay, Ned, I too am sorrowful. Sometimes when I think of what threatens me, I feel as though, like King What's-his-name, I can ne'er smile again. Perchance it may grieve you too, Ned, for 'twill be my wedding-day, come a week to-morrow."

"What!" I exclaimed, sore taken aback. Just then I had forgotten that wretched Frenchman.

"You may well cry out, lad. At times I feel beside myself about it. Married in a week to a jabbering, shoulder-shrugging Frenchman. Ugh, horrible! Now, I might have abided a reasonable Englishman, but a Frenchman, never! I'm weary to death of that country, yet when I'm wedded to my cousin, M. de Crois, I shall have to return to France with him. Sir Nicholas hath declared I must marry him; he hath given my hand to him, and swears on oath he will make me. I've coaxed him, and defied him, and threatened him, and beseeched him, but he will list to nought at all."

All at once her face was lit with passion. She rose suddenly, and commenced walking round and round the little clearing like a caged animal.

"I love my father!" she exclaimed, half to me, half to herself. "I adore my father. I revere the very ground he treads. But I'll not be driven. No, I won't! I hate De Crois, I hate the man—I hate him!"

The poor, torn creature burst into frenzied sobs of anger, and forced her body through the gap in the brushwood, and went away and left me miserable. Forgetting danger, I went after her to try and proffer comfort, because 'twas more than I could endure to see her so. Yet, quick as I was, she was already yards away, and before I was able to get to her she had reached the border of the copse, where, to my terror, she came face to face upon her father. Instantly I flung myself face foremost in the thicket grass, and luckily the knight, being so much occupied with his young daughter, did not notice me.

"Hillo, Obstinate," he growled at sight of her, "what art doing here?"

"Nothing, sir."

"You look exceeding amiable, my pretty lady," said he sarcastically; "but ne'er mind, the dressmakers are coming to-morrow to start upon your wedding clothes."

The maid gave vent to a most unfeminine speech.

"Save your money, sir, save your money!" she replied fiercely. "I don't want new dresses. Finery will but mock me. A week to-morrow, I shall be nought better than a beggar at a feast. Why do you force me into this thing? I hate De Crois! I hate him!"

"So you still harp on the old string," he returned, an ugly rasp in his voice. "I tell you straight, wench, my patience hath nearly fled. I do all I can, and this is my thanks. I am far too lenient. In my young days, I should have given ye a sound thrashing for one half the tongue I have had from you. And 'twill come to it yet, mark my words, 'twill come to it yet! Years gone by strapping fellows six feet four in their stockings have had to obey my every word. Did they cavil and sulk? Did they say that they wanted to do this, and wanted to do that? Well, now I come to think, one of 'em did, and, by St. Louis, I had the skin flayed off his back within a quarter of an hour afterwards. Ods my life! 'twill come to it yet!"

He emphasized this by tapping his stick on the ground. The maid looked at him boldly; the threat cut her pride. Her eyes defied him as she answered—

"That's all very well, sir, but I am your daughter. You would never dare——"

"Dare? Don't you talk to me about daring. I tell you, you slim, pretty Good-for-naught, I have had about enough of your airs and graces. 'Tis quite plain I have pampered you till I've made you a fool, and now you are trying to make me one.

Nice thing, very! Who are you that presumes to bandy words with the man who hath led the finest cavalry in Europe?"

"Your daughter, sir," she said simply but defiantly.

Her courage touched me, for the knight was getting angrier every moment. This was evident by his liberal oaths, and the rapid workings of his face. Yet the maid drew herself up very rigid, and eyed him calmly, unflinchingly.

"Alack," he retorted, "you are my daughter, worse luck! And a pretty creature you are, are you not? A brave branch from a worthy tree? You who are sick at a drop of blood, you who are afeared of a grain of salt, you who faint over a sword-thrust in the arm, and weep over it afterwards. Alack, you are my daughter! I' faith, Heaven owes me a grudge to send me a poor, puny, white-livered, milk-and-water chit of a wench, that's only good to cry, and to show impudence towards her betters—men who have fought and bled for their Sovereign, and have carved their names in history."

The man knew that he had hit her hard. Grimly he watched her lower her eyes, and the blood glow in her cheeks.

"Father, did I not promise to ride to the wars with you? That doth not look as though I am afeared."

"I want deeds, not words."

"You shall have them, dear papa, if you will but give me the chance."

She was trying strategy now. 'Twas exquisite to hear the music of her caressing tones, and the wheedlingly graceful way she used them.

"Do favor me this once, sir. Let me accompany you to Holland, and I will be a credit to your name."

"Pish! You just marry the count, and be a credit to some one else's name. I'm not greedy. We will let the men of the family gain honor for the House so that its women can smirch it."

"Say not so, father. Please do not make me marry the count, or 'twill break my very heart."

She said this pleadingly, timidly, wistfully, and put her arms round his neck, kissed his cheek, and nestled her head closely against his face. Was there a man alive who could resist this coaxing appeal? Apparently there was, for the knight fiercely disengaged her arms from his throat, and thrust her roughly from him. He shook his finger in her face, and showed his stick significantly.

"Enough of this. The game is too old; the trick is too stale. This is how you have befooled me aforetime. Yet, not again;

my mind is quite made up, and my patience exhausted. Give
me another word, and I'll allow you a sore back for a wedding-
present."

This cruel speech hurt her severely. She threw up her head,
and stared straight at him without a spark of fear, for him or
his stick either. Her face and eyes seemed filled with fire.

"Then I will say another word, sir," she cried in a voice I
had ne'er heard her use to him before. "I'm not a puppet; I'm
not a doll stuffed with sawdust; I'm a living being. I've a
head and a brain and a heart like you, sir. I can think and
feel. I've said I don't want to marry the count; and I'll say
more—I won't marry the count!"

"Mille tonnerres!" shouted the knight at this defiance; and he
grasped his stick and struck her a horrid blow on the shoulders.

'Twas but the first of many. He seized her slim wrists in his
one hand's devilish grip, and with the other crashed blow after
blow on to her defenceless body. 'Twas a brutal beating. But
she took it without a cry, without one plea for mercy, almost
without a murmur, except a few dull moans of pain.

I, lying prone in the thicket, was stunned by the sight. My
brain was stupefied, my limbs paralyzed; and my entire body
went limp and numbed, and refused obedience to the will. And
though I would have forfeited my right hand to have felled the
wretch in his gray hairs, I could not move. This is a blot upon my manhood, at least I believe it so to be myself; lay it to
the door of nature, not to mine.

"There, my beauty!" snarled the knight when he had
finished plying the stick, "you have had it now. Perhaps——"

But he was interrupted. The girl turned on him in a fury.
I have ne'er seen a woman quite so beautiful. She was a tigress,
then, with her bosom quivering, her blood-lit face, and her
mercilessly cruel eyes.

"Perhaps you think I shall *now* marry the count. Sweet
Lord, will I?" And the fearless creature stood awaiting a renewal of the blows.

But the knight was a beaten man. He stared at her as
though not rightly sure whether he still enjoyed his natural
senses.

"You young devil!" he screeched betwixt his teeth; then
turned on his heel and limped away towards the house.

His daughter fell back against a tree; and though her nether
lip was twitching, she kept herself (God knows how!) from
weeping. Then I did the most selfish thing in all my life—I
got up and confronted her. At sight of me she looked as
though I'd stung her.

" Go away," she commanded.

" Dorothy——" I began.

" Go away, Ned!" she interjected fiercely; and brushed away the tears that glistened on her eyelashes.

" Why do you cry?" I asked, my method cruel; my motive subtle.

" I—I—f—feel unwell," she stammered.

" Because your father beat you?"

" Y—e—s, b—because he beat me—like a dog."

The words were wrung from her first reluctantly, then suddenly; she seemed to throw them in my teeth.

" He is a brute," I said.

" 'Tis a lie! He is the best, the noblest, kindest father in the world. He hath forborne till he can forbear no longer. Go away!"

" But I must speak."

" Oh, go away; I feel half dead. I'll come and see you soon."

For a second there was a hard struggle in this fragile maid; but all at once she dropped face downmost at my feet, and lay stretched full length upon the grass; then sobbed and sobbed as though her humiliated heart must break.

I stayed and watched the tempest of her angry pain; at first with a beastlike enmity towards one man; and it ran in my mind to beard him, and make him regret his deed. But reflection, the destroyer of heroic notions, stopped me; whereupon I tarried still at the poor maid's side, consumed by unutterable grief, with no courage in my heart to speak one word; till my blunted sensibilities discovered that my presence tortured her. Thereat I slunk away, and for many hours had no other thought than that of the brutality of men.

Do not think me unduly presumptuous, kinsmen, if I confess that after this time of brooding woe, hope was once more rekindled in me. Did I say presumptuous? O God, who was I that dared to exalt my thoughts towards her? An outlaw, a hunted criminal, a man who had to steal to obtain his bread! And yet she loved me; I knew she loved me. There was the hope, the pity, and the madness. But she loved her father also. The problem was truly purgatorial; I looked at it from every side; examined it from every point of view; tried to grasp it in the composite; then tried to analyze it, so reduced it to controversial fragments. I sought to deduce a result from bald facts, and failed. There was the cold-blooded conundrum, " If Ned Armstrong loves Dorothy Marvin, and Dorothy Marvin loves Ned Armstrong, and Sir Nicholas Marvin hates Ned

Armstrong, what are Ned Armstrong's prospects?" 'Twas as pretty a puzzle as any I've ever encountered ; but there was a sort of madness underlying it. A dainty problem truly, but one to send a man to Bedlam.

In the end I was thrust back upon the fundamental fact that the answer lay with Dorothy herself. Thus I waited for her coming. I felt that her arrival would solve it for all time. But the shadows crawled across the sky, yet I saw her not. Soon the darkness fell pitch black, yet still no Dorothy. The suspense was torture to me, burnt with a fever of the mind. Had aught befallen her? Had the knight inflicted more brutalities upon her? Or was she deciding on her course of action? And what would be her course of action? Would she cleave to me, or to her father? And if she clove to me, would she have the courage and the strength to successfully defy her father? Question succeeded question, thought succeeded thought, and by and by fear succeeded hope.

Kinsmen, what think you of this fool and his folly?

Hour after hour passed, and each hour seemed an epoch. Still I lay, love lapt, gazing wildly upon the darkness. I saw the starlight through the trees, yet never called on God. I was afraid of Him; yea, just then I hated Him. The more He exalted me above my fallen state, by the madness He had poured inside my veins, the more He tortured me.

At last the dawn broke, and with the first streaks of it there came Dorothy Marvin. I heard a rustle among the brushwood, and next instant she pushed her way through the aperture. She was white as death, but her mouth was firm and tight, and her eyes steadfast and lustrous. I rose at once. I knew by her demeanor that we had arrived at perhaps the supremest crisis in our lives.

" Ah, lad," she said, " thy face betrays thee."

Her voice startled me, 'twas so charged with great emotions. I tried to laugh, but could only tremble.

" Thou hast had never a wink of sleep this night," she said ; and her tone had depths I never yet had known ; " nor have I. Poor pair of storm-tossed imbeciles ! I have been struggling all night long to go with my duty and my conscience. It hath been as though my brain would burst through my head. I've known more of hell these last few hours than ever I hope I shall again. Ned," she cried, gripping my arm, and again I saw how deathly white her face was, " why did you come and cut my heart in two? 'Tis you that have acquainted me with sleepless nights. I've throbbed as I've heard your tread; tingled when I've heard your voice. You have enlarged my soul. You've given me a new life, new thoughts, strange raptures ! And you have crushed me like a worm ! You have set your heel upon my heart ; you have murdered me ! "

'Twas grimly spoken ; her tone was deep and terrible. 'Twas the travail of a profound abysmal nature.

" Had I ne'er seen you," she said, and her bitterness frightened me, " I could have obeyed my father, but I cannot now. You hold the key that unlocked my bosom. Ned Armstrong, you madden me ! You are cruel, merciless, murderous, to make me suffer so ! God, was ever maid so torn as I ! "

Here the half-wild tempestuous girl began pacing up and down once more in the throes of torture. Her face, bloodless, strained, and eager, looked unearthly to my sight. We were both in that ecstatic state of mind when ardent creatures live a lifetime in a moment. Each of us was packed with a multiplicity of passion. 'Twas a time when simple souls do deal in tragedies.

" Why did you trick me, cheat me, dupe me, fool me ? " she cried. " Why did you come with the air of an honorable man, with the mien of an honorable man ? "

" Because my love is honorable," I said with great violence.

" I know it, I know it ! I know your love is honorable. There lies your brutality. You say you are a thief, a fugitive from justice ! "

" And being that," I said, and my voice was bitterer than verjuice, " my soul is poisoned, my virtues are polluted. Because I steal a purse, I cannot earn an honest groat ; because I steal a purse, I cannot do a worthy deed ; because I steal a purse, I cannot cherish an honorable sentiment."

" You taunt me," she said haughtily brutal. " And I will not be taunted by Black Ned. You are as dirt beneath my feet."

Her eyes were very cruel.

" I may be dirt ; but I will not be trampled on," I flashed back savagely, then made towards the outlet.

But she was too alert for me. She ran forward quick as lightning, and set her back against it.

" You must not go ! you shall not go ! "

Knowing what I did of her, I was well aware I should have been obliged to kill her to have escaped just then. I stood chewing my lips ; and looked at her with unutterable scorn ; being almost convulsed with rage. I forgot all her nobleness, her magnanimity towards me, a thief ; I only remembered that

she had flung my crimes in my teeth when she had least right
to do so. She knew I was entirely at her mercy; she knew I
owed her more than life; yet had put her foot upon my neck,
and now sought to crush the life out of me. Had she delivered
me from death for this? I had a horrible desire to strangle
her. But quick as thought she read that devilish emotion.

" Ned Armstrong," she said simply, and though she did not
seem afeared, was humbler and sadder than ever before I had
seen her, " I've been a brute to thee, but a bigger one unto myself. I know that which Black Ned himself alone doth know.
Black Ned is a man of honor. Thou mayst tear my tongue out
an thou wilt."

She came softly from the outlet then, and left me a free
departure. Tear after tear dropped down her face—rebellious
tears. She wept for her own humility.

I gazed half-stunned at the proud, passionate girl, so powerful, so wild blooded and so courageous. She was utterly crushed
under the weight of her humiliation. Her anger had let her take
a cruel advantage, and now she felt what the deed involved.

" You'll forgive me, Ned?" she pleaded, and put one hand
upon my arm.

I said nothing; being something of an egoist, I felt myself
much injured. But next instant it struck me that I was acting
like a cur. How dare I stand so much upon my dignity?

" Mistress," I answered, " he that owes you his life twice
over, can ne'er have aught to forgive in *you.*"

" Then hear me, Ned," she said, wildly earnest. " I am a
girl, a young and undefended girl. And thou, Ned Armstrong,
art a hunted criminal, a thief, an outlaw, a man attainted of high
treason. Thou art hounded high and low, and thy life may be
forfeited any moment. Thou hast no friends, no resources,
and can barely evade the law. Yes, I know all this, and I know
I shall be condemned as mad or worse. Nor do I care. I will
go with thee. *Thou art a man of honor !*"

As she spoke these words, her voice grew more and more high
pitched, till at last it seemed to assume a ring of triumph.

Next moment she kissed me on the lips, and afterwards stood
before me rigid and dauntless, her mouth firm and unflinching,
and her eyes wild with sparkles. 'Twas as though she were
invoking all the world to witness what she had done.

When she spoke again she completely startled me.

" Ned," she asked softly, " dost thou believe in God? An'
thou dost, we will beg for the strength to fight our enemies."

In one hand she took a silver crucifix, which was suspended

16

from a ribbon round her neck (being bred a Romanist), clasped it in her fingers, and knelt on the ground and prayed.

I stood still and dully watched her do this. I was more a sheep than a man that minute. I did not like to look at her, yet did look by a sort of fascination. I was awed by this fine creature's faith—the faith which I had not. I was ashamed, unmanned, yet almost happy. 'Twas the newest proof that she could command my better nature; had I tried I should have been powerless, just then, to have fallen upon my knees, and so have played the hypocrite.

Soon the girl arose, and her face was such that it did a weakling good to see it.

"My lad," she said with a noble boldness, "you and I have got to fight, and shall have all the world against us. Art afraid?"

"Not unless thou art."

"Thy hand," she demanded, and upon receipt of it she squeezed it in a most unmaidish grip.

Kinsmen, she stood intrepidly upright, with the warlike eye of some heroic deity; waved one hand above her head, and snapped her fingers at the bushes. "We shall live to treat our enemies like that," she said.

It may have been bravado in her, yet I'll swear 'twas a true index to her feelings at that moment.

"You understand," she said imperiously, "you and I are not a pair of lovers, we are comrades. I am not your 'dear,' or your 'mistress,' or your 'lady,' but your brother-in-arms. A tremendous work lies before us. We must be staunch, whate'er betide, and fight together. And when we've gained the day, then, and not till then, can we spare time to talk of love and suchlike airy nonsense."

"Airy nonsense!" I reiterated, and, kinsmen, do you know, I felt somewhat hurt and disappointed.

"Yes, yes, yes!" she went on impatiently. "I did say 'airy nonsense.' We must work first, and play when the work is done. If we waste valuable hours cooing love-sick ditties, and babbling midsummer sentiment, some fine morning I shall be Madame la Comtesse de Crois, and you will be grinning in a tight cravat at Taunton jail."

And so in lieu of a better clinching of the compact, I had to be content with handshakes.

"Ned," she said, "'twill be no fault of mine, if my father and De Crois coerce me."

"But how can you hope to defeat them, and in what way can I

assist you?" I asked, feeling suddenly how hopeless it all was, and how helpless was Ned Armstrong.

"You can do but one thing for me at present, dear lad," she answered with rare simplicity—"that is, to nerve my courage always to its highest pitch. I shall have great need of every ounce that I possess."

"But how can you hope to thwart Sir Nicholas and the count?" I inquired, dubious though filled with admiration.

"By this," and she placed one hand upon her forehead.

"I presume that doth mean by strength of will?"

"Faith! thy wits are marvellously keen for so early in the morning."

Her tone was prettily satirical.

"Ned," she said—passion had somewhat subsided in her voice—"'tis a bitter thing to be in open enmity against him thou hast loved, admired, and reverenced from thy babyhood. 'Tis a cruel thing, but what can avail me?"

"There is one way," I insinuated. Kinsmen, I hope you sniff this subtlety. I was deliberately encouraging her present train of thought. Why? To learn if possible the precise strength of my position; in other words, to learn the magnitude of Ned Armstrong's advantage over Sir Nicholas Marvin.

"'Tis true," she answered sadly, not guessing aught of the subtlety in question. "I have merely to marry my cousin, then there would be a consummation of the peace at Kelston Manor. The fatted calf would be killed, my old dad would preach ten sermons on the 'young wench that went astray;' but he'd forgive, with a grunt, his rebellious daughter. And we should have the old gentleman drinking 'the health of the bride' so zestfully in brandy punch, that he'd have to be carried to bed by the servants, whilst his daughter would have the consolation of knowing that she had made him cheerfully drunk at the cost of her lifetime's happiness. It may be selfishness, but I dare not kill my soul to please my father for twenty minutes."

I was astonished at her bitterness. Yet she must have been above mere mortals if, in a case so cruel, she had been free of it.

"My lad," she continued, and her tone was bitterer still, whilst the smile about her lips was not one that gave me pleasure, "his worship's stick did not break his daughter's back, but 'twas the straw, though a somewhat weighty one, that broke the camel's. But that is not the worst. He was angry then, and was, methinks, quite within his right; the dreadful part is he hath told me since, when in his rational mind, with his blood cool and his temper normal, that he hath hated me from my birth. There have been times when I almost guessed this, yet could never spur myself to a full belief of it. Yet I know it now, I know it now! And I might have known it years ago, if I had but dared to think about it. I could ne'er bring a light to his eye, nor life to his cheek, nor a grip to his fingers. And I have loved him better than my life all these years, and I love him now; but we can ne'er be as we used to be!"

Her misery was unutterable. The old knight had already taken the most venomous vengeance possible. I had never credited him with much perception, yet that he must have had, because to have punished her so severely by that unpaternal speech could only have been by a deep and accurate reading of her sentiments. Meanwhile, it flashed upon me suddenly why this maid was willing to dare and to sacrifice so much for me. The reason may have been a mighty one, but 'twas not of a nature to make me at all vainglorious. Kinsmen, even the noblest women must have a supply of that gracious quality of which they give so much away; they must have sympathy. And to this hour 'tis my belief that I was the only person the forlorn girl knew in the world, from whom she could spontaneously seek it. I will not boast that I thoroughly understood the entire complexity of her character; yet what I did know of it I loved, admired, and reverenced; and this I consistently betrayed to her by looks and words and actions.

"Dorothy," I asked, "do you not fear your father? I must say I am desperately afraid of him, myself."

"Yes," she said, with the suspicion of shudder, "I do. I am a mere kitten in his hands. Every year I have lived with him I have known him to be my master; I might thwart him in little things, I might be disobedient for half an hour together, I might, when his gout was very good, be saucy to him, and so presume upon his kindly nature with my nuisance of a tongue. But when I arrived at what I knew to be my high-water mark of perversity, his High-mightiness would give me a look with a special eye, and would say in a special manner, 'Wench, let me have two more words from you, and I'll——' Ned, my lad, he'd clutch his stick; whereat the kitten would have to stand still and tremble, lest it had its puny little claws cut. But dost know, my lad, 'twas a most delicious feeling!"

Kinsmen, I confess I broke into a guffaw of laughter.

"I mean it," she replied, and she was laughing also. "'Tis a delight to know sometimes that there is such a thing upon the earth as your master. 'Tis a subtle, indescribable pleasure to feel the bit tugged occasionally. When you go for a week at a time with the gardener, the ostler, the steward, the butler, the cook, and the maids perpetually bobbing and doing your bidding; and with the dogs and horses forever obedient to your will—I never had one yet that wasn't—'tis, I repeat, delicious to hear his seventy-two-year-old worship thunder, 'Dorothy, you young devil, you do this,' and to feel, e'en if he hath bade you put your finger in the fire, that you dare not for your life relieve your itching tongue by replying, 'Sir, I'll see you hanged first!'"

"Then, dearest, you like to be obedient?"

"No, but I like to know sometimes that I have to be. My old father always says that it behoves all men to ride the women on the curb, and to keep the reins tight and well in hand. He says, if you give us women an ell, we take a yard; allow us a slack rein, and we mighty soon get superior notions. Had my father given me a taste of his stick once a month, whether I needed it or not, I had been all the better for it."

"What!" I cried, astounded. "Then thou hast no faith in the chivalry of man?"

"Chivalry!" and she curled her lip. "'Tis, very well for those who tilt at windmills. But with all due deference to you, my gallant, if I ever do allow myself a husband" (kinsmen, the naughty maid looked sly), "he must be a man, understand me, sir, *a real man*, not a pretty plaything, all sugar and sweet speeches, who daren't say 'be hanged!' to a lady. No, I must have one who can make me do things that I do not want to do —one who shall be my master. That's why I despise my cousin. I should be *his* master. Of course he is polite as a valet, and smooth as a pot of pomatum, but he's all polish, all tinsel, no true metal, all shell and no kernel. Ned, my lad, I should bully him, whereas I would like a man who could bully me sometimes. I should be tempted to be a tyrant and a brute to the pretty boy. Dost recollect what King Charles said of young Prince George? Said he, 'I've tried Prince George sober, and I've tried Prince George drunk, but, drunk or sober, there is nothing in him.' 'Tis the same with Raoul de Crois. I should be too strong for the lad. In a year he'd no longer be my husband—he'd be my lap-dog. And I don't want a lap-dog; I want a man, a real man, a man like my old dad, who could say, 'Dorothy, thus far shalt thou go, and no farther.'"

"Dorothy," said I nervously, "you forget your auditor."

"I don't," she said coolly. "I am talking to Ned Armstrong. I'll not deny that he hath his faults, but he's still a man, in spite of 'em."

She looked at me as solemn as a judge; and though her mode of thinking was so truly strange, certes 'twas none the less sincere. And for myself, I felt it one of the rarest moments in my life, because she had honored me with so much of her private mind.

Soon afterwards she left me. I had now the knowledge that the bravest maid in Somerset was mine. Yes, mine assuredly if I could but evade the King's men till William came and took the Crown, and if Dorothy could thwart the Frenchman and her father. Hers was the more immediate trial; and I must admit that when I thought of what she might have to undergo, I became woefully anxious. Her parent had no sense of mercy; yet, when all was said, methought that circumstance was certainly in my favor. Being so big a brute, 'twas plain that he would try to make the girl submissive to his wishes, not by persuasion, but by force; and this, I had the sense to know, was the most foolish course he could adopt. Whatever she might declare to the contrary; in extreme cases, that is, whene'er her pride was called in question, the only means of getting her to do a thing against her wishes was to coax her, not to drive her. It may have been her spirit, or a certain perversity in her nature, or the result of her rigid paternal education, I know not which, but I believe myself a little of the three, that accounted for this stubbornness. Anyway, I do know that this young maid, though forever at a tyrant's mercy, had a will there was precious little bending. 'Twas only susceptbile to fair words, and hardened into adamant when less kindly arguments were used. The knight had gravely erred when he had called personal violence to his assistance, for, besides losing his temper, he had lost his cause as well. Yet do not let me dilate too much on this condemnation of Sir Nicholas, because his stick and his temper were two very true friends of mine. Kinsmen, to your ears this statement may sound brutal, but I was just as sure of its reliability as I was that Dorothy, in the depths of her heart, would ne'er forgive her father's pair of injudicious satellites.

CHAPTER XXV.

BEATI PACIFICI!

THE afternoon of that same day she came again to see me. Soon she proved how kind and thoughtful she could be in little things, because, to my surprise, she brought two swords along with her.

"Here, lad," she said, "is kindness for you. I have smuggled these from the lumber-room—father keeps about a dozen there ; and as I know you are as miserable as a dog that hath lost its tail, to be cooped up here for hours with nought to do but count your fingers and brood on the way Dorothy Marvin does her hair, you'd better take hold of this, and I'll have a bout with you, so that you can keep your hand in."

I obeyed her with alacrity. 'Twas not the first time by many that we had encountered one another.

She promised me, in her wickedest way, three kisses if I could disarm her three times within ten minutes. I twice performed the feat in the first five, but try as I might (and I employed every wile and artifice at my command, and worked myself into a perspiration) I could not earn my guerdon. And I felt it somewhat hard when she flatly refused, and not without some sly hints and ridicule, to allow it me as she declared I had not earned it. The truth is, had she had a man's physique, she must have been one of the first fencers of the time. She could teach me much I did not know about the science of the art; could practically demonstrate her principles; and had remarkable courage, suppleness, judgment and dexterity with which to do so.

Presently we sate down side by side upon the grass, the pair of swords between us. Soon we fell to talking.

"How goes the war, dearest ? " I inquired, forebodingly anxious to hear how she had fared with her tyrant of a father.

"Badly," she answered dolefully ; "the belligerent hath been uncomfortably active."

"There has been no repetition of yesterday, I hope ? "

"No," and she began to laugh, "there's been no more assaults at present. But the besieger threatens to starve the garrison."

"Nay," said I, incredulous.

"He does, though ! There hath been a pronunciamento to that effect this morning. Sir Nicholas Marvin, owing to his

daughter's 'damnable obstinacy,' has postponed the wedding
till she surrenders. 'And,' says he, 'in the mean time he will
allow me one week to alter my mind and mend my manners
generally; but if in that time they are not changed to his liking,
he will clap me under lock and key in the garret, and keep me
on bread and water (like they do in the army) till I have found
my senses.'"

"Well, I'll be shot! And what said you to that?"

"I said that which Sir Richard Lovelace hath said for me
already—

> "'Stone walls do not a prison make,
> Nor iron bars a cage;
> Minds innocent and quiet, take
> That for an hermitage.'"

"And what said he?"

"He wanted to know whether 'minds innocent and quiet'
took as kindly to bread and water. For himself, he said he
had some doubts, because he'd tried bread and water in divers
Dutch dungeons, but after three days it grew mighty cold to the
stomach."

"But he'll ne'er do that," said I, aghast at such arbitrary
methods.

"Won't he? You don't know him, my lad. If he says a
thing he does it, unless Providence prevents him."

"What a brute he is!" I exclaimed fervently.

"Ned Armstrong, how dare you, sir!" she cried, her cheeks
aflame, her eyes fire, whilst she looked quite bewitchingly
angry. "If you live to the age of seventy-two, sir, and do in
that time one-half as much for your name and fame, and exhibit one-quarter his military genius, you'll be entitled to respect
from springalds, and to obedience from your children. My lad,
you forget yourself."

"Then you forgive him?" I asked humbly.

"Forgive him!" she echoed swiftly; "you said 'forgive
him?' 'Pon my word, that *is* magnificent! Dorothy Marvin
forgive her father! We shall hear of a candle next forgiving
the sun for melting it!"

"I don't understand the man at all," I said lamely, trying to
mend matters, but too crushed to do the thing becomingly.

"You don't," she answered coolly. "Look here, my lad,"
she demanded imperiously, "what dost think I am—a goddess?"

"Yes," said I; "to me you are a goddess."

She looked at me, keen as any hawk, to see if I were laughing at her; but beholding me exceeding grave and earnest, she calmly stroked the dimple of her chin, and said, with the most unctious deliberation, and impudent as possible—

"Well, yes, perhaps I am a goddess—a goddess with a temper."

"But, Dorothy, what does your father think you are?"

"A dog," she replied between tears and laughter—"a dog, to obey his whistle or else be beaten till it does. And I'd be only too blithe to obey it, because I know it to be my duty; but there's a contrary something in my heart that will not let me."

She had no laughter when she spoke those last words. Her face was full of pain, and her eyes of misery.

"Ned, 'tis cruel of thee to so oft recall my unhappiness, and make me dwell upon it as thou dost."

The reproach was thoroughly deserved, yet the cruelty was not intentional, but simply the outcome of human weakness, because, whenever we discussed her pitiable plight, the conversation, by vaguely recalling my fortunate position, always left a delicious after-taste of bliss which, in turn, distilled a sweet aroma of felicity.

"Hast thou seen thy cousin again, dearest?" I inquired, trying to deflect the light to the least terrible of our enemies.

"Yes, I saw him this morning. Full as usual of politeness and 'lovely maid, fairest flower of earth, I love thee' speeches. The idiot was abominably amorous. One uses the stick and t'other the tongue to batter me into submission. I know not which instrument be the worst. One stings and t'other irritates. He hath given me no less than seven opportunities of calling him a fool already. Ned, you that are a man of learning, just puzzle your brains, and find me a stronger word than fool. I want a word more expressive, a bolder word, a larger word, a word that's a bigger mouthful, but, at the same time, it must be one that shall sound decent from the lips of a maid."

"But I thought any word was good enough for Dorothy Marvin?"

"Not so, my master," she said, guessing my purpose, and nimbly defeating it. "I have to study Ned Armstrong now. You see, my mouth's so pretty, and that lad Ned admires it so, that I must not spoil the shape of it by the use of ugly words."

"Then I'll suggest jolterhead," I said, as gravely as I could.

"No, that's lame. It halts. I want a word that comes like a ball from a musket. A word that hits and makes one tingle."

"Then try coxcomb."

"No, I can't get my tongue properly round it. 'Tis cumbersome, awkward, clumsy; "'twould have no effect. 'Twould glance off him like water from a duck's back."

"Then try ass—fine word ass!" I cried with sudden inspiration.

"Pish! 'Twill not do at all, my lad. That would be flattery."

"Then, mistress, I'm afraid I cannot help you."

"I'm afraid so, too, you witless wight. But methinks the fellow is beyond all remedy. I've tried my best to hurt his feelings, but he hath the hide of a rhinoceros. And guess what he says. The cunning rogue declares that a girl of my spirit ought to take a soldier for a husband (my gentleman is himself a soldier). However, I told him I meant to do better than that, because if I had one at all I would have a great swordsman. That touched the boastful French soul of him. He began to brag in the most alarming manner. Swore he could give odds to the best man in England; declared again and again that he was the prettiest swordsman in France, and that he'd slit the skin of any man I'd a mind to bring forward."

There and then the fine-spirited maid looked at me in a way there was no mistaking. Instantly I was fired by that eloquent countenance.

"He said that, did he! Sooth! I'll show the frog-eater that we grow men this side the water that can tickle his heart! I'll prove that an English sword can cut him, if an English tongue cannot."

"Nay, nay, lad," interposed the owner of the latter weapon, quite as warm as ever I was, "thou'rt wrong about the tongue. 'Tis half French—more's the pity."

"I've a long score to settle with Monsieur Widemouth," said I, fairly thirsting for a fight, "and I'll settle it on his body."

In my youth, kinsmen, even my enemies ne'er accused me of false modesty.

"Then you mean to fight, sir?"

"Mean to fight? What a question. If thou wert Ned Armstrong, and a beggarly Frenchman talked to Dorothy Marvin like that, what wouldst thou do?"

"Faith!" she said, and her eyes were very big and bright and splendid, "I'd meet Monsieur Raoul some fine morning as he came from the manor, where he'd been pestering his cousin, who ne'er did him any harm, and I'd box Monsieur Raoul's

ears, and ask him what he meant by his words and his conduct.
And then, if he'd a mind to fight (Sir Nicholas tells me the
French are the willingest nation in Europe in the matter of
a duello), I'd off with my doublet, and ere he could make three
ripostes I'd allow him the benefit of that lovely little inner twist
of the wrist " (the trick of which Dorothy hath taught me so
often), "curl my blade past his, and pink him just here." She
indicated the centre of her breast. " If thou art very careful
of the lungs, Ned, 'tis not a fatal spot in a man."

" And that's precisely what I will do."

" There's mettle in the lad," she said, with that archly critical air of hers, then gazed at me in admiration ; "but there,"
she added coolly, " you needn't blush, sir, because I've said so.
Blushes don't sit well on a man ; besides, they look suspiciously like vanity."

" Will your cousin come again in the morning, dearest ? "

At that she discarded banter, and seriously asked—

" But you are not in earnest, Ned ? "

" You'll see," said I.

" 'Twas only my jesting," she said, uneasily.

" Then the Frenchman did not talk like that ? "

" Oh, yes, he did."

" Then we'll try to discover who's the better of the two."

Hereat she looked unmistakably apprehensive.

" Ned," she said nervously, "if you venture forth you will
court great danger."

" Not at all," said I doggedly. I had already made my mind
up on the matter, and felt genuinely disappointed at her altered
tone. "We shall meet in a secluded spot ; and I'll take due
precaution lest I be hurt." When that was said she grew visibly
paler. " But there is not the smallest ground for fear," I hastened to assure her. " You can depend on me to keep my
skin entire."

" But 'tis a foolhardy business."

" Not so ; there really is no danger. Besides, I'm sick of
being cooped up in this dreary hole. Now do be kind and let
me venture."

" Oh, if you put it that way——"

" And if I stop here and swallow the insult, I should show
myself unworthy of you, Dorothy," I added, to press the first
advantage.

" Chut ! " she shot back sharply, " that is what had better
not been said."

" 'Twill not matter," quoth I obstinately, because my purpose grew stronger than ever upon me. " I mean to transact the business with that Frenchman. It can easily be done."

Upon this, seeing how defiant was my demeanor, she began to coax me ; and *her* coaxing any man must have found nearly irresistible.

" My dearest lad," she said, " I dare not let you go."

" What ! " I exclaimed, " this from Sir Nicholas Marvin's daughter ? "

'Twas a telling stroke. She grew confused in speech and manner, and flushed exceeding red.

" Yes," she answered indistinctly, and I knew she hated herself for what she said, " I always did admit that I shamed my father. I'm not fit to be child of his. At bottom I'm a coward, a chicken-hearted coward. My lad, I cannot bear that you should risk your life when there is no reason for so doing."

" But there is little risk, and many reasons."

She shook her head, looked wistfully at me, and cried with a sudden burst of fervor, " Oh, my lad, I love you."

" Love ! " quoth I ; " did I hear that word ? " and I curled a scornful lip, and made myself a pretty hypocrite. " Mistress Marvin says love is airy nonsense." To my shame, be it known, I enjoyed that retort immensely.

" Did I say that, Ned ? "

" Ay, that you did," said I, and I'm afraid my visage was triumphant.

" Then I'm sorry I said it," she said, uncommonly penitent.

" At the time, dearest, I was equally as sorry myself, but I'll confess I feel quite glad now."

" Ned, thou hard villain, thou art teasing me ! Desist, or I hit thee ! "

I did desist, because she had a knack of keeping promises. Then she began again to coax me in deadly earnest. Her coaxing method I'll make bold to say was positively unsurpassable. She had the supreme gift of looking unconsciously innocent at a moment's notice ; and could also adopt a most admirable simplicity of voice, manner, and gesture, that lulled her unsuspecting opponent into a false security. So while she was conjuring me in most beseeching accents, and whilst I (as I thought very astutely) was attacking the weak spot in her armor, she was trying stratagem. The weak spot was her father. With quite remarkable address I took advantage of it. I kept reminding her that she was her father's daughter, and so much was she bound up in that old wretch, and so great was her admiration of his character, that because of it, she mortified her woman's tenderness, and disciplined the femininity of her nature. And to such an extent did I play upon this vulnerable spot, that to judge by her tone, her talk, and behavior, it certainly looked as though she was on the point of submitting to my wishes. But, I repeat, she was employing strategy.

Now, as I have said, the swords lay between us, and we two were in a sitting posture. And the diplomatic maid, seeing that her skilful tongue was of no avail, had recourse to her equally skilful fingers. Whilst she held me in earnest talk anent the danger to my precious skin, she stealthily, and wholly unperceived by me, got one hand round the swords, and her face the while was the very emblem of simplicity and innocence.

" Ned," she drawled softly, slowly, plaintively, and all the time did fix me with her eyes that were most pathetically wistful, " I am very, very grieved—and—very—very—hurt—to hear that thou hast decided upon this course without deigning to take heed of me—" and she raised her other hand (as I thought to whisk a sorrowful tear from her eyelid). But no, she did nothing of the kind. She gave me a vigorous push, which overbalanced me and sent me sprawling on my back.

I gathered myself up as quickly as I could, only to find that Mistress Dorothy and the swords were missing. I scrambled after them through the gap, but this precipitance only served to disprove a fallacy. We men always hold that girls cannot run, but, by my soul, kinsmen ! that rule did never apply to this one. With one hand clutching the swords, and t'other her skirts, she fled like a deer, and had gained the open ere I could overtake her.

I retired, angry, amused, crestfallen, and delighted. Once more she had shown me how meagre mine own wits were in comparison with hers ; and how impossible 'twas for me to hold her for long at a disadvantage. However, three hours later, she returned, imperious, but swordless.

" The lad is a grand runner," she began, in a kind of mocking song; " a grand talker, a grand fighter, and a grand boaster. But he's young—very young—and hath no more than his share of ingenuity. But, young man "—here her tone and demeanor became of a sudden singularly patronizing,—" I have considered your case, and have asked his worship's opinion of Perry Wilmot. No matter what the state of his temper may be, Sir Nicholas will always discuss one topic—that topic is swordsmanship. Here is what the old gentleman said, ' Peregrine Wilmot is the wickedest devil, and the skilfullest, pluckiest, hardiest, and fiercest fighter at the present moment in England,

and the man that can whip him, sober or drunk, may cock his hat in the eyes of Europe.' So cock it, friend Quickfoot ! "

Forthwith the saucy one made a grab at Ned Armstrong's hat, and rakishly cocked it over that gentleman's eye.

" Sooth," she exclaimed, mightily enjoying her own impudent handiwork, " if Mistress Dorothy Marvin, of Kelston Manor, in the county of Somerset will but condescend to take this lad in hand, and bestow a few pains on his education, she'll make a man of him yet ! Well, boy, as I've said, I have considered your case. I should like young Raoul to get a thrashing from *my man*—'twill do him good. Therefore I'll allow my man to fight him on four conditions."

" Bravo ! " cried I, dancing ten steps of a corranto.

" Firstly, as the parsons say," the madcap continued, " Ned Armstrong is to fully understand that he is only going to fight because Mistress Dorothy Marvin lends her countenance to the scheme, and because she is kind enough to *allow* him to do so. She hath heard a great deal lately from Ned Armstrong's lips about ' I'm going to do this ; I'm going to do that; I'm going to do just as I choose, whether Dorothy says I can or I can't.' Now, I want you to appreciate, my fine-feathered young bird, that 'tis only by Dorothy's express permission that you are going to do anything at all. See ? "

'Deed, kinsmen, I did see ! I saw that Mistress Impudence meant to exact a very high price for the privilege. Still, to this condition I assented humbly.

" Secondly, that you do not kill my cousin."

" Certainly," said I ; and added to myself, " come, that is better ! "

" Thirdly, that you do not boast should you happen to win."

" Boasting is not a habit of mine," said I stoutly.

At that she puckered her brows in imitation of an angry pedagogue, lifted her finger, and sternly said—

" Boy, be careful ! How dare you contradict me ? I say you do, sir. But you do it in a stealthy way. You have an atrocious trick of blushing when your ears are tickled with praise. As I've said, it doesn't look well in a man. It shows a susceptible heart, a heart that will batten on flattery."

" That I will try to amend," said I, still very meek. Be it known, kinsmen, I had not yet secured that sword.

" Fourthly, that you no longer treat me as though I were a goddess."

" But, dearest, to me you are a goddess. You are so much better than I."

"Wrong—quite wrong! How many more times must I tell
you that I am your comrade? There are no grades among comrades; all comrades are on an equality. I hate to see you so
confoundedly humble!"

"Dorothy, I owe you so much."

"Oh! so you think you can pay your debts with humility.
Cheap coin, my lad, cheap coin! Not for Dorothy Marvin,
thank you. You had better remember that. Besides, if I
could fight like you can, the woman's not made that I'd let say
the tenth part to me that I do to you, sir."

"But I must be polite to a lady."

"I'm a lady?"

"'Pon my soul! I shall ne'er see a finer!"

"Call me that once more, Ned Armstrong, and, on my life, I'll
betray you at once to King James. 'Ladies,' says Sir Nicholas
(and he hath been seventy-two years on the earth), 'have white
hands, white skins, and white livers; have so much water in
their heads that it doth ooze out at their eyes; have to powder
their faces to hide their follies; and have to squeeze their
bodies to keep their sins within a reasonable compass.'"

"Mistress, you are a traitress to your sex."

"Not I. The sex is a traitress to itself. Here am I, a
woman. I'd be very brave if I could, but I can't."

"Not brave? Then what, in the name of pluck! doth go by
the name of bravery?"

"Why, I would call bravery the splendid trait of being able
to do a fine deed as easily as eating your dinner, like my old
dad can. Whene'er I do aught above the common I have to fight
against my inner self till it is accomplished."

"But that is what I should call the very highest kind of
courage."

"Oh, is it?" And her tone betrayed that she was neither
convinced nor satisfied. "But where would I be in time of
war? Tell me that. Where would I be in a beleaguered city?
When besiegers put a garrison to the sword they spare the
women and children. And I should be spared scathless
among 'em, whilst my old father, nearly four times my age,
would, in the mean time, have spilt his last drop of blood, and
have died by the sword, rather than be spared by the foe.
Talk about betraying the sex! 'Tis already betrayed, when it is
classed with babes and sucklings as being too contemptible to
have good powder and shot and steel spent upon it!"

"Oh, well, well!" I exclaimed, laughingly, "I consent, most
lovely Amazon. Ne'er again will I treat you as a goddess, nor

insult you by the title ' lady.' You shall be my brother-in-arms, my comrade. Though, should you ever wish to be considered as a la— that is, I should have said, as a person that isn't a male, I shall be quite as willing to oblige you, mistress."

"Good lad ! " she said, though I would not like to be placed upon my oath to declare that I did not see mockery in her eyes, as she went and fetched the sword, which it appeared she had left just outside the enclosure. "Ned," she said, as she returned with the weapon, " I hope thou dost not think me over-bold ? "

" Over-bold for a maid in war, and over-modest for a maid in love," said I.

" And now, young man," quoth she, and her tone was very business-like, "thou art willing to be my cavaliero, my true knight, my faithful servant ? "

" Your very faithful servant, mistress ! "

" Then stand forth, in a soldierly manner, that I may see whether thou art worthy of my confidence."

I stood before her, rigid as an arrow, with head back and chest out. She looked me over in her prettiest fashion, with mock gravity and a critic's eye.

"Well set up and sturdy. A comely and a likely lad, with a stout heart under his jacket."

" Now for the sword," said I.

She gave me the one she held in her hand.

" 'Tis the very best in the whole collection, sir. You can rely on that—I have chosen it, myself, and I know a good sword when I see one."

" Many thanks, mistress. But I trust you will not deduct this loan from my wages."

" Your wages, sir ! What do they amount to ? "

" A smile and a kiss from thee ! "

" You rate your services very high, lad."

" Indeed ? And I must have the payment in advance."

" You will not get it. Earn it first, and claim it afterwards. I am told that is the law of commerce."

" But not of love and war."

"What know you of them ? You have been in the one but once, and never in the other."

" Your tongue is wondrous sly, Dorothy."

" And your chin is wondrous dirty, Ned. It sadly lacks a razor. And it shall surely have one, for no knight o' mine shall sally forth with a whole week's down upon his jaw."

Ere I could reply to this saucy threat, the audacious maid had left me for the night. She had left me alone, with my hopes, my schemes, and my happiness. This last emotion had been debarred for many months ; but now the stream of it had begun to flow suddenly and swiftly. You are at liberty to blame my folly, kinsmen, as much as ye feel it merits ; but 'twas delicious folly.

There may be folks who read their Bibles as night by night they sip their punch, and are ultimately lulled to sleep by a snow-white pillow and a snow-white conscience, who, on moral grounds, may set a hard name to my presumption. Yet a man, once down, must he ever be kept down ? He that hath erred, must he be calumniated tor all time ?

A pitying woman had solved this problem for herself ; and I was but too eager to accept her solution as a balm for many wounds. Perhaps we were both too young to answer it. Yet we had answered it in defiance of the world, and most likely in defiance of our inmost souls as well.

However, I am straying from the narrative to discuss the merits of a hearthstone theory. Let it suffice that we who had gone through the fire, and had seen each other suffer, had, rightly or wrongly, unriddled it according to our lights. And, that being so, I passed a sleepless night, not being accustomed to such happiness. I could not grasp my marvellous fortune all at once ; it seemed so airy and so dreamlike.

At daybreak in the morning I left my retreat and partook of a dip in the stream. Upon returning with clean hands and face, I found Dorothy already in my bower. She had brought more food, a razor, and a pot of lather ; and insisted on shaving me herself. Forsooth, she was very skilful in the art, by virtue of much practice with her father. Such was the deftness of her handling, that within ten minutes she had wrought a new creature of me altogether. But the way she twisted my poor jaw about; the way she admonished me to be particularly careful in not moving my face the hundredth of an inch, because, if I did, " the razor might slip, and cut those beautiful blue veins in the neck, and thereby save the men of law the trouble ; " the artistic way she pursed her lips as she delicately came round the chin-curve ; the way she stopped suddenly in the middle of the feat and vowed, as I had recklessly twitched one eyelid, " that sooner than run the risk of having a fellow-creature's death upon her conscience, she would take away the razor, and, by doing so, would leave me in the ridiculous posture of being one-half shaven and one-half bearded ; " and the way I had to coax her to complete the task, with my face half lathered as I did so, made me much regret her condescension.

17

The business was to be transacted that morning. Dorothy told me two things of greatest import, namely, that her cousin was expected at the manor during the forenoon, and also that he could speak and understand the English tongue with ease.

The maid showed me a place in the copse where I might overlook the gates, and could thus see when the count left the house. One moment she was afraid of what I was on the point of encompassing, and full of fears and regrets, and the other made jokes at the expense of the pair of us. And so long did we talk together, that in the end my companion forewent her usual ride before breakfast.

When at last she did leave me alone to carry out my designs upon the Frenchman's person, I made a hearty meal; then betook myself to the part of the spinney which commanded a sight of the entrance gates. For an hour I watched in vain; but after that the Frenchman came along and walked his horse up to the house. Having seen him move out of sight round the bend among the trees, I lay down in the thicket awaiting his return, and was blissfully content to do so. Without any possible doubt I should beat that Frenchman. I was not blessed with more than my share of wits at ordinary times; but now Cupid had got among them, the little god had made pitiable havoc.

All too soon M. de Crois came back; for he disturbed and scattered certain delicious day-dreams in which I took indulgence. As he was riding his horse at a foot-pace, I allowed him to get some few yards ahead, and then silently sprang out after him, that he might not see whence I came. My rival was pensive; I remarked his face was groundwards and that his horse's motion accorded well with a heavy mood. I followed behind at an easy distance, till we had arrived at a spot midway betwixt the gates and the highway; whereupon I strode up with boldness, and soon had my face hard by his saddle.

He stopped his animal altogether at sight of me, and, with a gesture of surprise, inquired my pleasure.

"You are the Count de Crois, I hear, sir," I began, and my tone bore a studied coldness. "And, sir, I also hear a whisper that you have some swordsmanship."

At that he bowed and twitched his shoulders in the continental fashion.

"Monsieur flatters me." He used sound English, though 'twas encumbered by the buzz of his foreign accent.

"I believe, sir," said I, colder than ever, "you have the acquaintance of Mistress Dorothy Marvin."

"I hold that honor."

In spite of myself, I was sensibly drawn towards him out of sheer sympathy, because at the first mention of that name his eyes lighted in the most wonderful manner.

"Sir, I share that honor with you."

"Ah!" he cried, and his face fell suddenly dark.

"Count," said I sardonically, "I have also heard a whisper that you mouthed some big words in the presence of that lady, regarding the way you would serve us English swordsmen."

Ostentatiously I laid a hand upon the sword-hilt that was at my side. That which the Frenchman did next will forever command my admiration. He simply hissed a nimble word, slipped off his horse, feverishly seized my hand, and cried at the same instant, "Monsieur, monsieur, we are choicely met!"

"Never a doubt," said I. "For the honor of our respective nations we must have a little passado—there's room here on the grass."

"One moment, monsieur! Hath my lovely, my angelic, my adorable cousin had an intimation of your enterprise?"

I smiled at him, not coldly either. The man would have thawed an iceberg.

"Par Dieu, she is divine!" And he shook his maggoty French head so lustily, and lingered so long on the "See ees deevine," that I was compelled to laugh at his comicality. At that moment I had but one regret; which was that our joint divinity was not there then to enjoy his words and actions.

"Sir Count, I can only venture to meet you on one condition —which is, that the victor shall deposit the vanquished in a place of safety. Somersetshire roads," I craftily added, to shift all signs of suspicion from myself, "are not the place for wounded men. There are enough cut-throats and thievish knaves at large in this county as would suffice to man His Majesty's Fleet. Therefore, should you disable me, I must beg that you will place my body in the custody of Master Peter Whipple, at the sign of the King's Head, Bridgwater."

"Willingly," he assented. "And on mine own part, the Green Man, at Taunton, is whither I bide at present."

This bargain struck, my opponent, who was fascinatingly rapid in his actions, dived a finger into the pocket of his vest, produced a gold piece (a Louis d'or, I think), saying, "There is an advantage in the sun"—which was very true—spun the coin in the air and called on me to cry. The cast fell against me; whereby my enemy had choice of ground. Albeit he deliberately chose to face the sun. This was a piece of the purest generosity.

I had made up my mind to hate the fellow, and also to punish him. Now, I think that all men will agree with me that he merited a punishment richly; yet here was I already feeling a grudging tenderness towards him.

The horse was tethered to the hedge. Then we took off our coats and hats, rolled up our sleeves, and unsheathed our swords. It was a scorching day, the sun was in the zenith of its glory; the insects flitted lazily by; and the yellow ears were motionless behind the hedges, with graceful heads bowed gently. The birds trilled sweet discourse in the heavens, and hard by, to my left hand, the hills rose up above the fields of wheat. The warm flood of sunlight revealed the wooded combes on the Quantock slopes; thick dark patches upon their surface; their clustered groves of beech and ash, telling of shade and shelter. Higher up the heights reared towards the sky, and were alive with a mass of furze and yellow gorze; whilst here and there the little hill-streams, both swift and sluggish, cut shimmering lines on the heathery slopes. Perhaps we were a pair of fools; but youth is prone to folly. Had we had more wisdom, we must have been less happy, for a wise man hath very rarely a spirit of content.

My opponent was truly a noble fellow, a good head taller than I, lithe and graceful of body, with a handsome, open, manly countenance. To see his wide bright eyes was to know that a brave heart lurked behind them, and from the first I never doubted that I must fight my hardest, if I was to claim the victory. Yet, be it understood, I never doubted my capacity to gain it.

We shook hands, crossed swords, and fell to. I gave back a step as I felt his blade for the first time; and gave back another as I felt it for the second. Ere long I feared that I could not hope to win; and that idea roused all the devil in me. But to what purpose? My rival was calm, unperturbed, and smiling. He drove me back with swift, firm, neat play of weapon, and 'twas only by great agility of body that a catastrophe was averted. This man was a master of the art of fence; there was poetry in the glance of his gliding blade; as swift as light, and dazzling as the sun. His play was delicate, serene, enchanting; and he had a wrist of steel and the Hundred Eyes of Argus.

As for me, poor fool! I was but a toy to him. I tried my rustic artifices, and the contemptuous way he turned them off made my heart drop like lead in my bosom. May I ne'er forget the smile which greeted them. A baby would have had as much chance against this inspired swordsman as Black Ned the undefeated. I knew I had no chance; and he knew it too, so simply laughed to himself as he measured my ability, and exhibited all his own splendid art. I grew sick as I bethought what this affair might cost me. Better a thousand times have kept out of it altogether.

With reckless fury I beset him, hoping by sheer vigor to beat down his guard; but without avail. He seemed to enjoy the thing as a jest. More than once a sharp thrust would have ended the matter, yet he preferred to frisk and fondle with me like a cat does with a mouse, and was content to give a deftly pretty riposte now and then in return. But love is a paradoxical power; frequently it will take brains away from one who hath them to lose, and, on occasion, may even bestow them on the brainless.

Certes, 'twas so in this case. Love gave me a bright idea. The disdainful Frenchman was toying with me, and was showing off his own great art. Methought I would toy with him. And this was the execution of the plan. I pretended to be quite exhausted (which I assuredly was not); my thrusts grew more feeble, and my parrying more half-hearted, yet all the while I took care to have my vigilance on hand, should a quick thrust be given me. Hereupon my opponent grew more and more careless, as he thought I was entirely spent, and might be despatched any minute. He expounded his accomplishments more fully than ever, whilst I, cunning rogue, gradually drew him from his defence. He was making vain show of some beautiful and ornamental trick with the wrist, when I saw my longed-for opportunity had come. I snapped my teeth of a sudden, tightened my grip of the hilt, and with a great gathering of every little bit of energy that was left me, made a powerful lunge, my blade dashed past his unsuspecting guard, and bit straight through his shoulder.

The poor lad groaned. The blood spurted on to his white shirt as he dropped his sword, and reeled and fell backwards like one dead. He lay prone and senseless on the grass, his white face bathed in sunlight, and his shirt soaked with blood. With many a misgiving, I went down on my knees beside him, and forced strong water betwixt his teeth.

CHAPTER XXVI.

A RACE FOR LIFE.

To my relief the count came somewhat to himself ere very long, yet so helpless was he that I pitied him. 'Tis easy to pity the vanquished when you are yourself the victor.

Now befell a most perilous and difficult part of the matter. According to the agreement between us, I must see him in a safe place ; and that place was the hostel of the Green Man, Taunton. Having in a measure revived him, and having staunched the bleeding to the best of my ability, I buttoned his coat loosely over his shoulders, and donned mine own. 'Twas no light task to place the lad on his horse's back, whilst to add to my difficulties I had to climb up behind so that I might support him with my arms about his waist. I deemed this the readiest mode of reaching a place of safety.

It was evident, from the outset, that my mission was fraught with the greatest danger ; not the least part of it being that the Green Man was the headquarters of the King's men. Without delay I set off, anxious to get the ticklish feat performed. The animal bore its double burthen in a highly creditable manner. In an hour Taunton came into sight ; the count by that time being weak, and very much spent through loss of blood, the pain of his wound, and the jogging of the horse. Fortunately the Green Man stood scarce two hundred yards within the town, yet, though we had only to traverse a single street, and had then to turn into a narrow lane, our passage thence drew the attention of the townsfolk towards us, and I confess my heart came in my mouth when I saw the stares and gestures of the onlookers, which plainly told me that they recognized their visitor.

Doubtless the mild folk were pretty considerably astonished to see Black Ned parading the streets in broad daylight, when so great a price had been set upon his head. Through excess of curiosity, a small crowd collected and began to follow at my heels, though 'twas not their purpose to offer molestation, for the commonalty were well affected towards me at this time. Seeing how precarious was my position, I hastened to dispose of the Frenchman, so that I might invoke the aid of my heels, and leave the town behind as speedily as possible. As soon as I drew rein before the door of the tavern I alighted, and calling to a lusty fellow close by to assist me, without more ado we bore the injured man head and heels into the hostelry. The landlord came bustling into the passage to meet us.

" Oho ! " said he, " what have you there ? "

" One of your customers hath had a sword thrust," I answered in a thick, disguised voice, my head bent low over the wounded man.

" Then bear him upstairs to bed."

We walked past him and up the staircase opposite. Just then a room door opened to one side of the passage, and a voice called out, " Hullo, Master Tonk, what hath now befell ? "

That voice sent cold blood thro' my veins, and set mine ears a-singing, for it belonged to Captain Joshua Pringle. Neither he nor the landlord had yet recognized me, therefore I kept straight on up the stairs, yet devoutly wished the while that I was well out of my predicament. We laid him on the bed of the first room we came to. Having done this, I immediately left the apartment to descend the stairs ; but, by the direst of misfortunes, the landlord, Captain Pringle, and half a dozen soldiers were leisurely ascending at that instant. The captain stared me full in the face.

" Thunder of God ! " he bawled.

There was no time for politeness and courtesy, so I bounded downstairs three steps at a stride, banged one fist into the bloated face of the little captain, the other into that of the bewildered landlord ; butted my head into the stomach of an inoffensive servant of the King, and thus made a passage through them. I rushed to the door, where the Frenchman's horse stood passive in the midst of an inquisitive multitude. In a trice I was in the saddle, and riding away for precarious life. And none too soon. Already my pursuers were giving their lungs rare exercise.

I could hear Master Pringle bellowing, " Stop him, in the King's name ! " " Saddle the horses, men, and be thundering smart ! " " A guinea for a loaded pistol ! " " Hi, you fellow there, down him !—down him, I say ! "

I never once looked back, but fled swiftly out of the town, and none sought to bar my progress. I galloped over the bridge, and directly the houses and the river were at my back, a white, rugged, dusty road confronted me, and a stiff eight miles burst to Bridgwater.

Presently I looked round to learn how I fared. To my exceeding perturbation I beheld a cloud of dust some distance down the roadway. I knew it was my pursuers, and that delay would mean my life. Their own animals were fresher than mine, but luckily I had a good start. I had no fixed plan of baffling them; yet had but two chances of escape. Either I must take to the hills and abandon the horse, as I was hard by them; or else trust to good fortune and Peter Whipple and make for Bridgwater. Mayhap I was ill-advised, but I chose the latter alternative; for Master Whipple was without peer in my eyes at that time, and methought if his wits could not help me, mine own would be assuredly of no avail. 'Twas a stern chase; the scorching sun knew no mercy for pursuers or pursued, the hedges danced by on either side, and the hoofs of my horse clicked harsh music on the flinty track.

The Frenchman's beast was well grown and powerful, and had a good heart withal, which is the chiefest thing with both men and horses. I gave the willing creature his head, and by voice and trick of body helped him forward. Perhaps we had traversed three miles of the way ere I looked back again. The distance between us had scarcely lessened. Another mile we went, still at the same mad pace, and then I turned again in the saddle. This time my survey was less to my satisfaction. One man, evidently with a splendid animal under him, was now yards ahead of the rest, and had decreased the distance betwixt himself and me by one half.

Presently, to my dismay, I could plainly hear the thudding of his horse's shoes and the urgency of his tone. I saw it was Captain Pringle, barely forty yards away, standing up in his stirrups. His animal, with head bent low and the foam all over its mouth, was flying onward nearer and nearer.

" Stop, in the King's name ! "

I protest that I had reasonable excuse for not doing as I was bidden on this occasion. Accordingly I lost no breath on words, but simply called on my horse more strenuously than ever.

" Stop ! " and I heard a trigger click.

I was too sore pressed to look round now; yet shortly afterwards did so, and with the bitterest of curses. A bullet sang by, and struck the road five yards ahead, just as the report hit my ears. Again the pistol cracked and my horse lurched and stumbled, and 'twas only by great firmness and quickness of hand that I prevented his downfall. My enemy shouted triumph.

I turned round as I felt the animal's faltering steps and perceived a track of blood-stains on the road. A bullet had buried itself in the fleshy part of the creature's thigh. The delighted captain had far outstripped his men by this, and was scarce twenty yards behind; and he was gaining rapidly now, for my brave horse was nearly spent, whilst his wound grievously retarded him. With an uncompromising hand I snatched a pistol from my belt (I ever carried one there at least) and eagerly rammed a charge home. Meantime the captain was howling at my horse's heels, and was also fumbling for powder and shot in his bandoleer.

Without a word, I turned of a sudden and fired full at his noble animal. Down it thumped with a crash, one white eye-ball glinting and its scarlet nostrils quivering. Its rider also fell with fearsome violence, and rolled over and over on the dusty highway. At the same moment my own horse had done its last yard. Rapidly it sank to earth, and I had to be alert to reach the ground ere it pitched me out of the saddle.

The main body of my pursuers still kept the track some distance away, so in a fever of fear I tore off my jacket and sword (Sir Nicholas Marvin's), discarded my hat, and kicked off my heavy riding-boots. Thus, divested of all encumbrances, save a pistol and a charge or two, I started to run to Bridgwater. I had a long start, but a good two miles in a sweltering sun had to be traversed. I kept on the margin of grass beside the road, because 'twas far less irksome to my stockinged feet than the hard middle would have been. Thus lightly clad, I raced along swiftly, with hands clenched and teeth set tight. All this had been remarked by the enemy, for I could hear their hoarse cries and shouts in the distance. Be a man the fleetest of his species, he cannot compare with a horse in point of speed; howbeit, I trusted to my advantage to bear me to the hostelry before my pursuers could overtake me, as in my youth I greatly excelled in running.

The King's men came galloping onward, whilst I, bathed in sweat, with throbbing temples and brain afire, ne'er faltered once in my wild career, but fled. for Bridgwater. As I neared the town the distance between us was greatly lessened; yet I still maintained a lead.

When I rushed in through the front door of the King's Head, the soldiers were lost to sight for a moment in a bend of the street. Peter Whipple was with me in an instant. In a glance he took in my panting chest, streaming face, and scant attire.

"Save me!" I gasped. "Pringle's at my heels."

Without a word he thrust me behind the door of an empty

room just as a clatter of hoofs arose without. Through the nick of it I could peer straight on to the doorstep and the cobble stones below the sign-board.

Master Whipple was a man of resource as well as of action, therefore he moved to the hostelry entrance to greet the King's men as they drew up their frothy horses.

"Landlord!" cried the little jackanapes Pringle, who had ridden along in full dignity of his office on the steed of one of his troopers, "have ye set eyes on that hell-hound of a Black Ned? We close beset his heels a minute agone. Answer truthfully as thou lovest life."

"Ay, to be sure, your honor," quoth Pete, in answer, and truth was stamped upon his countenance. "He hath passed this way a minute since. *He hath just gone up the street.*"

"Away then, lads, again!" cried the excited captain; and off they clattered, their breath heavy with curses.

Pete joined me, his face solemn as a judge's. "Lad," said he, "we have just time to breathe, and barely that. Unless I am mistaken, those fellows will be back again in the twinkling of a bedpost. Now, let us try to combat their designs. I am mighty pleased to see thee safe, for ugly rumors were afloat concerning thee. Yet this time is no time for congratulation. Now, submit thyself to me entirely, and by the Mass I'll expound the meaning of a master mind."

CHAPTER XXVII.

IN WHICH WE LIVE AND LEARN.

"FRIEND NED," said Master Whipple, "I have a snug retreat for thee."

He conducted me to the far side of the long room, and there showed me a cupboard hidden three parts from view by a table in front thereof. The room itself was of goodly size, with a door at either end of it, the one leading from the entrance passage, and the other at the far end, close by the cupboard, into the kitchen.

Mine host installed me in that cupboard. This made my position none too comfortable, as the air of it was stuffy, and if size be aught to judge by, 'twas ne'er intended to receive a full-grown man.

The long table and forms beside it were moved a convenient

distance away, so that a person might pass between them and the door of the receptacle.

" Young friend," said Pete, in his most impressive manner, " I am about to show you the true art of business. A cultured brain alone could conceive what I am going to show you, and I flatter myself 'tis a close observance of the methods of Long Bob Bickers, the greatest and skilfullest man in the three kingdoms in his day, which doth now enable me to imitate him in some little particulars, no matter how unworthily."

He spoke in the weightiest way imaginable ; though methought there was something unctuous in his speech, and something owlish in his countenance.

" Now pay strict heed to me in everything," the little man continued, " and I promise that you shall not go unrewarded. I was much pleased with your manner in that last affair, and mayhap you do not forget the guerdon that did accrue therefrom. Now do as y'are bidden. As Bob Bickers was wont to remark, ' obedience is a monstrous fine quality in *other* people.' "

Hereupon my worthy host placed me in the cupboard and securely fastened the door. After that he went and sought his lad Tom, and through the wall I could hear him issuing implicit instructions in the kitchen. What they were I could not tell. I know that before long savory odors found their way through the partition to my nose, whereupon I suddenly recollected that I was hungry. Other matters, however, soon arose to distract my attention. I had lain ten minutes in the cupboard, when once more a clatter of hoofs arose in the street, and shortly afterwards, Captain Joshua Pringle and his men clanked into the room. Mine host came bustling forth to greet them, smiling and obsequious. By good fortune it chanced that the keyhole was on a level with my eyes, thus I was able to see something of what passed outside. 'Twas evident His Majesty's servants were sorely perturbed in spirit, but mine host was all affability.

" Man," called out the captain, a mixture of sternness, dignity, and irritation, " methinks thou hast wantonly deceived us. It doth occur to me thou art in league against us together with that arch-villain, Black Ned. I accepted your excuses over that first business, yet I promise you I have my doubts, and, 'pon honor, ye shall swing, sir, as an aider and abettor, if I can but prove aught against you. Ye said the black rogue had gone up the street. Now I have questioned a score of folks, and they swear they have not seen him pass. Verily, landlord, ye shall swing if ye have deceived me."

" Dear, dear, how annoying ! " quoth Pete, in honeyed persuasiveness, and with the sweetest of humility. " Sink me !
your honor, these sleepy rustics have no eyes. 'Pon my soul,
where you and I come from, they would have clapped the fellow
into jail on their own accord. But, by my troth, captain, you
and your men look devilish thirsty. Hie, Tom, do you bring a
big stoup o' cider here this minute, and look damned lively, so
that the gentles may not wait. Come, sirs, be seated and take
a draught. Long Bob Bick—er—that is, I should have said,
my lord Buthbungle ever averred that good cider was a godsend
such days as these, and I promise you there is none better in
Europe."

Gradually, carefully, step by step, Master Peter Whipple
pacified them, and drove away by gentle benignity, and brave
show of kindly good nature, their disappointment and ill
humor. They sat down at the long table in front of me and
drank their cider. As a crowning beneficence, by which he
completely won them over, he set a smoking and choice smelling dinner before them. Instantly they fell to, with no lack of
appetite, their threats toward mine host smothered for the nonce
at this new proof of his worth.

" Gentlemen," said Pete, still monstrous polite, though quite
restored to their good graces, " I will look to it that you are not
disturbed. You shall have this room for your own use alone,
that you may discuss any private matters unmolested, as gentlemen are fond of doing. Yes, sir captain, I know exactly how
to treat persons of your quality."

No sooner did I hear those words of Master Whipple's,
than I guessed he had a set purpose in putting me where he
had.

Left to themselves, my enemies kept up a continuous din
with knife, fork, and platter. They talked noisily and loudly
among themselves for a length of time, vowing empty vengeance
against the cramped and cooped-up creature in the cupboard.
Towards the end of the meal their talk became more sober, and
in a short time Master Pringle directed attention to himself
whilst he gave them information on a matter of import.

" Pass the cider, Joe Walker, that I may wet my whistle, ere
I tell you fellows a secret, which only I and Tom Cox are aware
of. Is it not so, Tom ? "

" Ay, captain, that's infernally true."

" Now, list you, lads. I may not speak loud, or I may be
overheard, though 'tis my belief, when all is said, the landlord
is an honest fellow. I have told you nought before for fear of

your blabbing tongues. Still, pay good heed now, as the time
for action is nigh at hand."

The little officer spoke in a subdued tone, whereat I craned
one ear to the keyhole, and heard every word he uttered. And
long ere he had ceased his talk, my nails bit into my palms
with excitement, whilst every fibre of my body was a-quivering.

"What I have to tell is this, and do you guard it as your
lives," announced the captain. "The day ere we started for the
West on this wildgoose chase, His Majesty the King sent for
me, and we had a long and private talk together."

"Oh !" exclaimed half a dozen of them, actuated by this
illustrious name, and I beheld them as I peered through the
chink stretching their necks, and drawing their heads as close
to his own as they possibly could get them.

"King James," went on Master Pringle, " first required my
solemn oath not to divulge a word of what he might tell me until the time for action came ; and you fellows, being under my
command, were to be informed when the hour arrived. What
His Majesty said to me was that, 'twas upon the plaint of my
lords Feversham and Sunderland that this expedition had to all
outward appearance been organized to capture the highwayman.
However, the King said he had an object behind it all of much
deeper and further-reaching import than the arresting of this
scurvy rogue. This object was known only to himself, and he
now imparted it to me, that I might carry it out (which I faithfully promised to do) to the utmost of my capacity. James said
for a week or two past he had had black suspicions in his mind
anent a great conspiracy which he believed was afloat in the
land—a conspiracy that meant to oust him from the throne,
and one beside which that of Monmouth was the merest foolery.
He suspected a large number of his greatest ministers were at
the root of the matter. Mind ! 'twas only suspicion, for he was
without any direct proof whatsoever. Could he obtain it,
wealth and title should avail them not, but to the gallows they
should go, as prouder necks than theirs had ofttimes had to do.
'Twas plain to him, he said, that this smouldering fire of conspiracy must be stamped out with resolution, and could he
discover the prime movers, assuredly it should be. Further, he
declared the safety of his crown rested upon the matter. His
Majesty was sore perturbed in spirit, as I could plainly see,
and 'twill be woe betide all traitors that fall into his
hands.

" This is the duty he hath imposed on me. He hath a great
fact to work upon, and he trusts to my skill and fidelity in

making it a powerful instrument, in averting his threatened ruin. It hath come to his ears that several covert meetings have been held in various country houses by divers lords, both spiritual and temporal, and he can give a shrewd guess for what purpose. One of these gatherings hath been quite recently held at the house of Sir Nicholas Marvin, at Kelston Manor, here in Somersetshire. And, whilst everybody hugs the notion that we have come westward to solely effect Black Ned's capture, without creating any attention at all, I must set secretly to work, under the cloak of that enterprise, and find out for certain, by hook or by crook, whether this knight hath any treasonous designs. If so, I am to seize his body, and his papers, and convey him forthwith to London. Arrived there, he (James) will answer for it, that his favorite iron boot shall make him tell many things, and if the other birds have not already flown, one and all shall hang together. Above everything, I was to be mindful of strictest secrecy, and should Sir Nicholas Marvin show any disposition to make for Holland, which is a veritable hotbed of plotters, he must be taken at once. Furthermore, no stone must be left unturned to secure this conspirator, even to the shedding of blood. Anything I thought fit to do I was given the power to do it, yet, without fail, when I proved the man's guilt, I must bring him to London. To show what hath been vested in me, here is something that may make you rub your eyes."

He drew a short slip of parchment out of his inner doublet pocket, and read aloud the contents as follows :—

"' *It is by Our order and express desire that the bearer hath done what he hath done.*

(*Signed*)   "' JAMES REX.'

"There; what say you?" asked the captain proudly, "and in His Majesty's own handwriting too. That will bear me out in anything. Well, lads, I have not proved unworthy of the confidence reposed in me by my sovereign ; and while you fellows have sought this miserable, thieving villain, I have been engaged on State business, and weaved such a net of evidence about this Marvin that, by Jupiter, he'll swing! The blind old spitfire thought I was only concerned in this Black Ned business when I came to pay my frequent visits. He knoweth not Joshua Pringle ! Blind old adder ! Ay, I have gotten him like a stoat in a trap. I have bribed his major domo, and he hath given me the plan of the house and grounds. I have discovered

where the treasonous documents do lie. I have the most positive evidence of his guilt. All his male servants have at one
time or another been soldiers, and he is a rare old fighting man
himself ; still we shall have scarce any trouble if we come at
the right moment. Three of his fellows are away on this Black
Ned business, and I'll take care they keep on it. Our time
will be an hour after sunset on this Friday evening, when another of his servitors will be at Bridgwater, buying provisions.
That will leave but one male—the major domo, who is ours,
and will assist us in our designs. Mind ! not a word of this to
a living soul. We will ride up to the manor to-night after sundown, seize the treacherous old knight, and convey him post-
haste to London. Zounds, lads ! I smell preferment in this
matter. Still, I do not want you to overlook this Black Ned.
Have him we will at any cost. He hath played me more than
one trick, and it galls me, I can tell you. I'll show him I'm
not a man to be the butt of a rustic."

This was the most important part of what the fellow said. I
heard every word, and as I listened my breath came painfully
quick, and my brain staggered with this bewildering new-born
knowledge. I was fascinated by it for a time ; and when I had
the power to think in some kind of order, I felt as though I had
lived a year in half an hour.

So the implacable knight had been properly duped ! All the
while he thought he was bringing about my downfall he was
digging a pit for his own. And now, unless Providence intervened, he would perish by the arm of the law, even as my father
had done, for high treason—and much deeper treason than ever
he had compassed.

Throughout the little captain's narrative no man had put in
an appearance to disturb them ; but no sooner was it finished
than, strangely enough, Peter Whipple came bustling in to make
inquiry what the gentles drank. As usual he lauded his rare
and famous vintages till his auditors were thirsty by anticipation. The wine was duly laid before them in a large open
bowl, into which they dipped their cups and sipped it therefrom, and also enjoyed the seductive tobacco fumes the while.
Naught occurred to interrupt these proceedings for the space
of a few minutes ; then the far door of the room, which led into
the outer passage, opened, and a venerable white-bearded old
gentleman entered. His bowed body was supported by a staff.
With shuffling steps he walked along to the table where the
King's men were seated. He halted there, and leaned on it
for support close by the bowl of wine.

"Landlord," he piped in a thin voice, "I seek some little refreshment, for the day is hot, and I have not yet come to the end of a weary journey."

"Ah, yes, to be sure, sir," quoth Pete, grinning and winking at the soldiers, whilst they grinned back at the excellence of the joke. "Mayhap ye seek a flask of canary, or, better still, the Oporto vintage, or that of the Muscadine, or the prime Tokay, or the Bordeaux, or the Burgundy?"

"No, no, landlord, they are beyond my lean purse. A mug of cider and a bite of bread and cheese is all I ask."

"Ay, to be sure. Please to step across the passage, where you shall be duly served, for these gentlemen desire to have this apartment entirely private."

The feeble creature hobbled out of the room again as he was asked to do, and once more the dozen men at the table in front of me were left to themselves. Their conversation hereabouts began to flag. They had neither such a flow of speech nor such a zest for talking. Maybe 'twas the sweet lulling influence of the tobacco that affected them. Shortly one began to yawn, then another, and then another; but it should be observed that the day was drowsy and oppressive. Presently one of the dozen laid his head on the table, and two minutes later a sonorous snore told his friends and companions that the land of dreams had claimed him. Doubtless the excellence and substance of the dinner had caused this. But, to my astonishment, they all followed this example, so that in a quarter of an hour the whole pack of them lay about in twisted attitudes—asleep! Could I too, be asleep? It seemed an unheard-of phenomenon for all those men to pop off to slumber with such unparalleled suddenness; tho' this notwithstanding their snores and regular breathing ere long mingled each with the other in a somnolent chorus.

Then Master Whipple, who for the last twenty minutes had been out of the room, came in with noiseless tread ; and there was a solemn look upon his face. Strange to state, he was nowise surprised to find his customers asleep. After shooting a glance at the recumbent figures, mine host went and locked the door which led into the outer passage. That accomplished, he came to my cupboard and let me out. There was just margin wide enough for me to crawl therefrom without touching my enemies.

"Come on, lad, and stretch those limbs o' thine," he said briskly ; "I'll warrant they need it."

"But, Pete, these men ?"

"What of them ? They are safe for the present. A volley
of musketry would not wake them."

Of course mine host was the man to know, therefore I silently
accepted his extraordinary remark, and meanwhile fully enjoyed my liberty.

"What means this, Pete? What have you got in your
head?"

"Brains," was the laconic answer ; and I believed him.

For those twelve men to be slumbering thus, and that door to
be locked, and to see Peter Whipple standing there, solemn of
mien and self-assured in manner, to put the matter tersely, it
looked like business.

"Now, friend Armstrong, obey your leader. I bid you search
those gentlemen at the table, and take every shilling from their
pockets and put them into your own. Be light and gentle, deft
and nimble, and forget not a gray groat piece. Business is
business."

Forthwith I did as I was bidden. I began to empty the
pockets of mine enemies. And, when I had successfully emptied
two, the other ten were already empty, and they by the hand of
Master Peter Whipple. It chanced that one of my unpreten-
tious two was that of the captain himself, wherefore I took
particular care to secure the King's order from his pocket.

"D'ye see this, Pete?" I said, holding it up for his inspection, "we had best burn that, I trow?"

He seized it quickly, and muttered under his breath, "*'It is
by Our order and express desire that the bearer hath done what
he hath done. (Signed) James Rex.'*"

"What! burn this?" he cried; "oh, boy, I weep for you;
'Tis enough to make Rob Bickers uproot his tombstone. Twenty
golden guineas would not purchase it back from me. Thou
fool!"

He skipped away into the kitchen, and a moment later was
back again with scissors, needle, and thread. He flung off his
jacket, straightway ripped a hole in the lining, slipped the
precious parchment in, and sewed it up again.

"Burn it, lad?" he said; "I grieve to say you will never
rise in the world. You will be purse sneaking all your days,
instead of becoming churchwarden and justice of the peace for
the parish. But I've no time to play the dominie. By the
Mass! we have squeezed another goodly sum. Business is assuredly brisk. I reckon they have only just drawn more pay.
Now, Ned, you stuff every brass farthing into your pockets.
We will see to its proper disposal afterwards. And here also

18

is all I have about mine own person. Four shillings and ten-
pence. Take charge of that as well."

I put all the coins into my breeches pockets, marvelling much
the while at these strange proceedings.

"Pete," I said in lively wonderment, "they will assuredly
suspect you. You cannot hope to hoodwink them this time."

"Oh master mind! ye show most grievous lack of invention.
And a man wi'out invention, as Bob Bickers was wont to
declare, is like a ship wi'out a rudder."

"Pete," I insinuated, "bethink you, was it not my lord
Buthbungle who made that trite observe?"

He answered not, but twitched one eyelid; in itself an
acknowledgment that my shot had hit him.

"Did those fellows blab aught of import during their converse?" he asked; "methought 'twas not unlikely we might
earn an honest penny by what they chanced to let fall. You
cannot have too many ears, or too many eyes, in this world. Mayhap you caught something private. Is that so?"

I took pains to conceal the major part from mine host of what
I had heard, as I prudently thought he might be tempted to run
counter to my wishes. Besides, he had not enough of my confidence to know the whole of what had passed betwixt the
knight and me; neither had I an inclination to tell him then.

For the best part of an hour Master Whipple and I talked
together, unmindful of the sleeping dozen in our vicinity. At
least Pete was, and I, trusting him implicitly, regulated my
behavior in accordance with his own. And he having no fear
of their disturbing us by waking suddenly, we talked without
restraint. However, I could not help marvelling how my
worthy friend was to slip out of his present plight, for methought no amount of speechifying could be able this time to
soothe the injured men. But Pete made so light of the affair
that 'twas obvious he had a plan in his head. In the course of
time mine host glanced at the clock, and said—

"They will rouse themselves in another quarter of an hour,
lad, so we had best make some preparation."

Without more to do the innkeeper left me a moment, and
came bustling back from the kitchen with a coil of rope and a
long kerchief. I stared at these strange articles, though my
wits were not keen enough to appraise their value.

As a preliminary, mine host did another strange thing. At
the far end of the room a second cupboard was built into the wall,
and upon unlocking this it was found to contain a large assort-
ment of coins. In fact, Pete declared 'twas a month's till-

money. It consisted of copper and silver mostly. Mine host took every piece of the latter away ; after counting it, gave this also into my care; scattered the copper coins all over the cupboard, and leaving the door of it open proceeded to give me instructions how to act.

" You must now bind this kerchief tightly round my mouth," he said ; " but first stuff this other one into it. Then tie me down in that chair with the rope, and coil it so about my legs and arms that I cannot on any account get loose. When you have done that get back into your cupboard, lock the door of it on the inside and watch. If I cannot teach thee something this day, then either I'm a bigger fool else thou'rt a wiser youth than I have allowed for. Now, do all this quietly and quickly, and ask no questions."

" But, Pete——"

" Ask no questions, I said. Do as ye're bidden. Your instructions are sufficiently explicit."

Without further parleying, I carried out his orders to the letter. The result was, that when I lay in the cupboard again, with the inside locked, the key in my hand, and a huge mass of gold and silver in my pockets, as I peered through the keyhole, I beheld Master Whipple sitting helpless in the chair, gagged and secured hand and foot, the door of his money cupboard wide open, the outer door of the room still locked, and the twelve King's men still slumbering, despite their rummaged pockets. Thereupon the nature of the trick dawned upon me suddenly.

For a few minutes nought happened. Then one of the soldiers gave a sleepy grunt, rubbed his eyes, stretched himself, yawned, and gazed stupidly about him. This survey was insufficient for his bewildered senses, therefore once more he rubbed his eyes and stretched himself ; then with clearer brain, and clearer vision, he took in the silent room and Peter Whipple. Still he was not sure his sight was right, therefore sought in his pockets for his handkerchief; which act did ease his understanding.

" Mother of Jesus ! " he yelled, in a voice that shook the ceiling.

Instantly he wakened his companions, but not with any undue display of gentleness. Ere long they were very wideawake ; and sprang to their feet, a jabbering, excited, wrathful company. They used ornamental language, and accused one another of pocket-picking ; then saw Peter Whipple. They beheld him purple in the face, wriggling in his fetters.

"Who's that?" they inquired of no one in particular, pointing towards their host.

They ran to him, and soon cut the rope and ungagged him. Thereupon Master Whipple fell headlong out of his seat and rolled on the floor gasping and choking. They picked him up and managed after a while to restore him somewhat, and then asked him what the matter was.

In answer, Pete fell a-sobbing. The tears rolled down his cheeks in a never-ending stream, and he wrung his hands and wept aloud in the depths of his despondence.

"Oh, woe is me! woe is me!" he bellowed, in hysterical despair, with his utterance three parts choked. His victims forgot their own misfortunes for a moment, and inquired concernedly anent the trouble.

"What is the trouble?" he sobbed, "that is the trouble!" He led them to the rifled cupboard. "There, do ye see the trouble now? A whole year's earnings lost at one fell stroke. The kernel is gone, and only the husk is left. Oh, woe is me! The villain hath ta'en every gold and silver piece to the amount of several hundred guineas, and hath only left the coppers because they were too cumbersome to carry. What, in the name of heaven, shall I do? Great God! I am beside myself. Guineas—golden, bailiff-scouting guineas! 'Tis ruin! ruin! ruin!"

The injured man buried his head in his hands in a paroxysm of grief, and wept, and wept, and wept! till such was the copious outpouring of salt water that it was a mercy the ill-used creature did not dry up the blessed spring forthwith. His misery was cruel to behold. Even his victims tried to soothe him.

"No, no! there is nought for it but ruin, ruin!" he wailed. "Oh, what have I done to call down this awful judgment upon me and mine? 'Tis starvation that stares me and my poor family in the face, and I have striven so hard to keep a roof over the heads of my wife and children. And now they must starve. Oh, 'tis cruel! cruel! I shall surely die. Alas, my poor wife! alas, my poor family! 'Twill kill me quite!"

Nought could assuage his grief. He beat his head on the wooden table, and in after days (to his eternal pride) was able to show where he had knocked two splinters off of it, such was the vigor of his thwacks.

I will tell his story, as herein lay his greatest triumph, since his victims ne'er thought of questioning the truth of it. He made out that the old man who had come into the room for refreshment was none other than Black Ned himself disguised, and that while standing by the bowl of wine, he had taken occasion to slip a sleeping powder in it, thereby sending the King's men to sleep. No sooner had they fallen asleep than the old man came to Master Whipple, took him unawares by presenting a loaded pistol to his (Master Whipple's) forehead, threatening to blow out his brains should he speak a word, thereby forcing him to disclose where his money lay, and having been shown the place, he bound and gagged him, locked the door that none might disturb his own designs, then robbed the innkeeper and the King's men at his leisure.

"And there was my lad Tom," veracious Peter said, "dispensing liquors across the passage, whilst we folk were being robbed of every groat of our substance. Oh, 'tis bitter, unutterably bitter! And the rogue, when he had ta'en as much as he could comfortably carry, simply bowed to me, as his custom is, and went out, locking the door behind him—taking the key to boot, that we might not be discovered."

Not being Doctor Jonathan Swift, I have no pen to describe those soldiers as they heard the details of the disaster. Yet they believed every word the landlord uttered. I had ever given mine host credit for being a man of conspicuous abilities, natheless even he surpassed himself in the deceiving of his victims. His story had such a glamour of truth about it, and his tears were so salt that his auditors were ridiculously gulled. I had the key in my pocket, and, to lend color to the story, they broke open the door to get out of the room. I do assure you, kinsmen, they hurled maledictions and Antichristian threats enough at me to last the deepest-dyed rogue a lifetime. When at last, with further imprecations, they rode away, I unlocked the cupboard and rejoined veracious Peter in the middle of the room.

CHAPTER XXVIII.

THE COMING OF THE KING'S MEN.

MINE host apportioned out five guineas of the booty as my share. On the spot I refused this offer flatly, telling him 'twas I by rights who ought to pay, seeing how he had baffled my pursuers. Without any unnecessary show of words he admitted this obligation, pocketed the gold accordingly, and edified me

immensely by remarking that my sterling qualities, day by day,
appealed more nearly to his heart.

"Pete," said I a little later, "there is one point I am not altogether clear upon. Who was that old man in reality?"

"My lad Tom; rather smart youth, I reckon?" and Peter
Whipple assumed a pious aspect.

There still remained a serious matter to be transacted, ere I
might venture back to my hiding-place; namely, to purchase
a new outfit for my person. Therefore Master Whipple took
my measure, and went across the street to do my shopping.
He bought me a new suit of clothes, a new hat, and pair of
shoes; also was so kind as to make me a present of a tolerable
sword in lieu of the one I had thrown away.

I bid my succorer adieu with a thankful heart, and lost no
time in returning to the manor copse. I had no thought for
the journey, as my mind was completely immersed in the momentous tidings I had heard from the lips of Captain Pringle.

The utmost of my thinking could only show one way to render
aid to my old friend and recent enemy. So short was the time,
and so greatly was I handicapped by having to conceal my
identity, that one plan alone appeared feasible. 'Twas truly
desperate; tho' it was the only one to promise anything of
success. Accordingly I decided to act upon it, and to keep
mine own counsel till the time arrived for action. Upon reaching my retreat, the first thing I beheld was my love sitting
under the tree trunk, with a white and anxious face. As soon
as the rustle of the brushwood reached her ears, she turned
this pallid countenance towards me, and it flushed with
welcome.

She jumped up instantly, and came and seized my two hands
in both her own. Her eyes beaconed with joy and thankfulness, though I found her fingers cold and trembling.

"Mine own dear lad!" she said softly, and added in a whisper, "Thank God, thou art safe!"

Her tone surprised me, 'twas so very fervent. Also her manner was equally as strange, seeing that for a full minute she
said nothing, but looked rapturously at my face in a sort of ecstasy of happiness. 'Twas evident she had passed through a
time of severe anxiety. I cogitated much at this, because when
last I had seen her, she had appeared so confident of my success
and so free of apprehension.

"Dearest," I asked, "why this to-do?"

"Ah, lad!" she answered, "I have suffered. I have received
a bitter punishment for folly."

" Not from your father, I hope ? "

" Yes," she said.

I clenched my hands, and 'twas as much as I could do to restrain my anger.

" But not in the way you think," she added slyly. " He did not know himself what he was doing, though he hath made me live in an agony of dread since this morning."

" Tell me all about it, darling."

" Nay, not a word till I have had a precise account of thine own adventures. First, sir, let me have a look at thee."

Thereupon she gazed again upon me; this time her survey was universal. She looked me over from head to heels, and the pleased expression of her face announced that this scrutiny had resulted entirely to her liking.

" So thou hast returned with never a scathe or injury," she said ; " and dost know, my lad, that is what I'm proud and glad to see? Oh, Ned, I am so thankful ! "

Kinsmen, to say the least, she looked it.

" But my cousin ? " she continued breathlessly, in a sudden burst of recollection ; " is he badly hurt ? Is he dead ? Oh, Ned, thou hast not killed him ! " Her face was full of fear.

" Chut ! " I cried ; " he hath but suffered a flesh-wound in the shoulder."

" A flesh-wound only ? "

" Yes ; just enough for me to win with."

" You are quite sure of that ? " she asked nervously. " You know you fighting men hold such barbarous notions. My old dad for instance, ne'er calls a wound a wound until it shows signs of becoming mortal."

" But I'm not a fighting man," said I, remembering her somewhat light opinion of my prowess.

" Indeed you are, sir," she answered, with an inimitable brightness in her eyes. " I make bold to say a really great fighting man, and one I'm proud to speak to."

She said this quite free of her usual flippancy ; I had never heard her tone more earnest or more reverent.

" What is this, Sir Champion ? " she queried. Her quick eye had already noted the change in my apparel, and in a woman, as we know, Curiosity is a high grandee, who at all times doth exact the first and best attention. " New garments ! new shoon ! new hat ! new sword ! " she exclaimed in pretty wonderment. " My lad, I'll trouble you for an explanation."

Upon this command I entered into an account of all that had befallen me, withholding nought save the designs of the

King's men, the name of mine host of the King's Head, Bridgwater, and above all else—for which, kinsmen, to this hour I blush—the stroke of fortune that enabled me to beat the Frenchman. No, I treated my victory quite as a matter to be expected, and in a confident, light, and airy manner. Perhaps 'twas that my ears were greedy of praise in those days—I know there are young men who wax and grow fat upon it; or was it because Dorothy had evinced such singular admiration for my victory? Be this as it may, I am afeared young Ned Armstrong was far too big a coxcomb to ever think of denying ought to his vanity.

The girl sat down on a green hillock of turf opposite the narrator. She rested her chin on her hands, and her eyes, peeping above her finger-tips, seemed to glow and burn with excitement and with sympathy. Never a word she uttered in the course of the story, though the blood tingled in her cheeks when I came to tell of my victory over the count, and she whispered "what a man!" as I unfolded Master Whipple's scheme. And when at last she addressed a remark to me, I was startled by her voice: 'twas once more full of awe and reverence.

"Dost thou truly love me, Ned?"

I must confess I was taken aback by this question; it came so swift and unexpected. It was put not jestingly, nor to gain a compliment, but nervously—apprehensively. My only answer was to kiss her.

"And wilt stand by me, Ned, in spite of every change of fortune? Even when thou'rt Sir Edward Armstrong, the greatest man in this county, thou wilt hold to that? Promise me, lad!"

"I will e'en do more than promise, sweetest, I'll swear it. Having loved thee once, I must go on loving thee forever."

She rose and grasped my hand in hers.

"Oh, that I were worthy of you!" she exclaimed, in a kind of desperation, and blushed most beautifully. "I'm but a girl that's good for nought save to polish swords and cherish 'em after great fighting men have wielded them."

Sure her behavior was quite beyond the ordinary; 'twas so strange, so grave, so unfathomable. Methinks I must have laughed had her face not been so full of earnestness, or her eyes so much like embers of living fire.

"Ned," she said in a soft, solemn whisper, "thou art a great swordsman."

And then she set her head to one side, and scrutinized me more critically than ever. This was too much for gravity; accordingly I laughed.

" A very great swordsman," she reiterated with the same reverence, " and thou'rt scarce taller than myself. Wonderful ! But, oh, my lad ! what an eye thou hast, what a supple wrist, what muscularity of arm, and what agility of body ! Thou hast defeated the best swordsman in France this day. The Perry Wilmot victory is nought at all by comparison with this one. Wilmot was drunk when you defeated him ; and when I told you what my father said about the man, I told you far more than the truth. I was in wild spirits then—I do suffer with them sometimes. Besides, 'twould have grieved me to the heart to have disappointed you, as you had so set your mind on fighting. And I came to feel that you ran no danger, because the greater the swordsman the less will he say of his skill. My dear, dear lad ! I thought I had sent you forth to your death ! I have been bitterly punished for telling lies. Sir Nicholas told me scarce an hour after your departure this morning, all about young Raoul's splendid fighting qualities. My cousin and he had been having a little bout for pastime, and when M. de Crois left us, the old gentleman swore he'd wager a bin of his Lanquedoc that no man in England could match the lad in the art of fence. I' faith he went so far as to doubt whether he could have done so himself, even in his prime. He says the count possesses all the virtues of a master, and hath one weakness only."

" Over-confidence ? " I suggested.

" That's it, exactly. Never have I seen old daddy so enthusiastic as he was this morning. 'Twas as though twenty years had been lifted from his shoulders. He declared that to fight with that man would be almost an education in the art of fence. He said there was more backbone in this present generation than he had given it credit for, and it did his heart good to know it. He had not thought there was one who could maintain the traditions of the Forties, yet he had found De Crois worthy to rank with the best. So he just kept on pledging Raoul's health and sighing for his own lusty manhood back again, that he might have shown him what a Stuart cavaliero was capable of doing ; till at last he bethought himself of me. Thereupon he snapped his fingers in my face, and swore that if he had another word of demur from me about the forthcoming wedding, he would drag me to church himself, and so have the matter done by means of a special license. ' For,' said he, ' 'twas folly, nay, sheer criminal wickedness, to neglect so grand a chance of bringing a great man nearer to the family.' When I heard this, Ned, I thought that I had killed thee. Methought I had surely sent thee forth to thy destruction. Who'd have guessed that that silly, jabbering, Frenchified clodpoll had been such a master. When I heard of this, 'twas too late to alter things. So, for the last four hours, I have not known what it hath been to breathe in comfort. Methought you could have no possible chance against him. I am not ashamed to admit this to you now, for papa is not the man to bestow such praise without due reason. But, in spite of everything, here you are, safe and sound; and oh, lad——"

Here she broke off short, as though lost for words to express her admiration, and relied on looks alone to record the same. This unusual meed of praise set me protesting my unworthiness.

"No need, Dorothy, to hold me in such wondrous respect," said I, my vanity tickled immensely. Of course I used the boaster's favorite trick—false modesty. Therefore, you will understand that I vehemently protested against her eulogies, pronouncing myself unworthy of them. Still all the time I took great care that my voice should belie my words, so that no matter what I said my tone inferred, "Don't you believe me, Dorothy. 'Tis only my modesty—all great men are modest. I deserve all the praise I get from you, and, in fact, my dear, a good deal more than you can give me."

"Methinks I am the proudest and happiest woman in this county just now, Ned," she said, and *her* tones and looks did not belie her words.

"What hath brought you to that frame of mind, Dorothy?" I promptly inquired, sniffing further compliments.

"I have the honor to protect and succor the greatest man in England from the malice of his enemies."

"The greatest man in England, mistress?"

"Yes, my dear lad; you merit that title."

"Then you set swordsmanship and mere manual skill before book-learning?" Yet I knew full well she did. I only asked her to prolong the sweetness.

"I should rather think I do," she answered indignantly. "When I was very, very young I once asked my old dad a similar question. 'Hey, what? Book-learning, quotha?' said he. 'Did book-learning build up the Roman Empire? Did it drive the hated Spaniard from these shores? Did it enable William the Norman to conquer England? Did it make old Noll Cromwell Lord Protector? Book-learning, is it? Go to, thou fool!' And my gentleman tapped his sword, and told me I was not worthy of my breed."

"And you considered him quite right in this matter?"

"Right? Why, he is never wrong in matters military."

"And do you call it an honor to succor a man who owes you his life twice over?" I am happy to say that at this point my voice immediately discarded chicanery. I had arrived at topics that I never yet have trifled with.

"It doth not detract from your capacity," she answered. "And if you think you still lie under an obligation towards me, I will disabuse your mind, sir. This day's work hath wiped out all debts, and hath scored a heavy one up against myself."

"Thank you, dearest," I said, touched by her generosity; "but you surely forget 'tis no honor to protect a thief."

"Who says thou'rt a thief?"

"The King."

"The King is a tyrant and a murderer. He killed your father, and balked you of your bread."

"I am none the less a thief."

"Weil, if you are so very fond of that word! Still, I have it in my mind to prove you wrong."

"Try," said I bitterly, and with half a sigh at her enthusiasm.

"Hearken to me, young man. Pietro Negretti, in his celebrated work, 'The Usages of Modern Warfare,' says, 'It is a legitimate thing to seize an enemy's property when the occasion offers.' Have you gone beyond seizing the enemy's property to keep body and soul together? No, say I."

'Twas a delight to see her eyes sparkle in their triumph. Her reasoning was simply irresistible so far as it went; tho', like all woman's reasoning (that is, as much as I have encountered), one could not examine it very deep ere a flaw was found.

"This will not make me any honester in the sight of the world," I said.

"You are honest enough for the one that loves you, dear lad! Do I care for the world? Why should it come 'twixt you and me?"

There was such a glow in her face, and she spoke, oh, so tenderly! that forthwith I hauled down my colors.

"Thou art beaten, boy, quite beaten!" she exclaimed, midway between seriousness and laughter; "and I, being victor, must e'en dictate the terms of the armistice. Promise me that you will ne'er again use that ugly word in my presence."

"But, Dorothy——"

"Promise, lad, or the vanquisher of M. de Crois shall spend to-morrow fasting."

" But——"

" Promise, sir, or the finest swordsman in England shall be deprived of his cigarros."

" Oh, if it comes to that, I will promise, you young tyrant ! "

And we sealed this compact with—but, mayhap, good kinsmen, you can guess in what mode we did it.

Five minutes later she left me, promising to return as usual first thing in the morning. Alas ! how little she guessed what was pending ere another sun might rise. I had not said a word to her on that subject, because I felt that to do so would serve no useful purpose. I fell into a kind of fever of excitement. There was absolutely nought to do but wait for nightfall and the coming of the King's men. Upon looking at the setting sun, I judged there was scarce three hours of daylight left. I reviewed all the circumstances more exactly in the vain hope of finding a loophole of escape from so perilous a dilemma. The captain's plan was secret and skilful. The attack was to be made when the old knight would be able to offer the least resistance. 'Twould be quite easy to seize his person and his papers within the space of a few minutes—have a coach in waiting in the darkness, and hurry him to London without any being the wiser, save Dorothy, who would be powerless to save or to aid her ill-fated sire.

At last an idea struck me. If the coast was clear, there was still time for Sir Nicholas to slip his enemies. Thereupon I set out cautiously to reconnoitre. I made my way to the outskirts of the copse, and peered through the trees that skirted the carriage-track leading to the house. And the very first thing I noticed was a man on the fringe of grass, lying down immediately opposite me. I slipped hastily back into the shadow of the trees, for I recognized the King's uniform. Twenty yards further down another was concealed in an exactly similar fashion. Both these men overlooked the only road from the house. 'Twas patent none might pass along it without the alarm being given. And, even had the track been clear, it occurred to me that the old war-dog would not have fled, but would have fought the matter out ; I knew his heart was big enough.

This was how it would have to be. The shortness of the time had afforded me no opporunities for providing better. Therefore my plan was to lie in wait till the King's men rode up and had gone in to Sir Nicholas, who I was certain, when he learned their errand, would shed every drop of the blood in his veins sooner than yield up the incriminating documents. Thus I would seize the most favorable moment during the altercation, rush in sword in hand, and maim as many as I might ere they had gathered their wits sufficiently. This would reduce their numbers, and thereby mitigate the hopelessness of the struggle, as two desperate men, both accomplished in the art of fence, even when pitted against heavy odds, require dealing with by incompetent and unskilled swordsmen. Call this a wildgoose scheme if you will ; but "desperate cases, desperate remedies." And it was certainly the best that offered itself, for the more I considered the subject, the more certain I became that the knight would never fly, only as a final resource. Also there was a subtle thought forever rising in my mind. "Suppose, Ned," said an unbidden voice, "you make a brilliant effort this night, and save the knight and his papers; your cause cannot help being benefited by the circumstance. Sir Nicholas is bound to entertain much kinder sentiments towards you." In answer to this, the only thing left for me to do was to devoutly hope that matters would end so favorably, and to watch the sinking of the sun and the lengthening of the shadows.

As the time drew near I recollected that in this rush of great events one thing had been omitted. I had not warned the knight. This I had had ample chance of doing by the agency of his daughter. Then I asked the hard question of myself, "Why should I warn him? Is he not one of my fiercest enemies?" This should prove a key to my plan of action. I was not going to the knight's assistance out of any love for him. 'Twas because I loved his daughter. And to love her with impunity I must have her father's goodwill. The readiest way to obtain that goodwill was, to my thinking, by rendering him an important service. Here was the sought-for opportunity. Yet it must be one large enough to impress him with its magnitude. Now, a mere word of warning carries no glamour with it ; but a brilliant bit of fighting and half a dozen dead men heaped around you make a far deeper impression upon a soldier's mind than the most eloquent oration ever uttered, or than a million words of warning. From which, my children, it should be seen that, though your sire was at this time no older than yourselves, there was room in his head for other things as well as folly.

Ten times during the last hour I drew my sword from its scabbard, felt the edge with my thumb, and scanned the white blade to espy any speck of dirt or rust that might linger on it. I traversed every foot of my hiding-place. I could not keep quiet through longing feverishly for nightfall. The waiting I could not bear ; the business being one that must have unsettled any man. A torturing doubt seized me at the last moment as to whether I was really making the most of my chances. I went over all the previous ground again ; and knowing how high the game was for which I played, I rightly argued that the stakes also must perforce be high.

I left my bower as the shadows crept across the earth, and making my way carefully along, I reached a spot bordering on a trim lawn which overlooked the front entrance to the house. Here I hid myself as well as possible, with ears strained to catch a clatter of hoofs on the gravel, though the King's men were scarcely due yet.

Presently I saw the white blinds drawn of the room I had spent so many hours in, and the candles striking through them gave a feeble reflection for a yard or two without. The darkness came sneaking upon the world. God alone knows what is done in the darkness, the horrible darkness !

As I waited in my place of concealment, I could hear the strains of the spinet, accompanied by a familiar voice, which trilled a lively lilt. The sprightly sound was hard to hear ; it turned my heart cold.

The soldiers should be here by now. Then my heart ceased to beat almost ; I had caught the long-listened-for clatter at last.

Horsemen came thudding, with snorting horses, past where I lay. No lack of noise was with them ; riders being busy passing japes one among another, whilst their horses' hoof-irons scrunched the pathway. The King's men halted before the entrance steps, slipped off their animals, and fastened them together.

I crouched along in the shadow of the wall of the house to within a few yards of the soldiers, that I might hear all that passed. Ere they could enter the house, the front door was opened, and Dorothy came out on to the steps to greet them.

" We have news of great import for your father, mistress," said the captain.

" Anent Black Ned ? " she asked. " I do hope, Captain, you have caught the slippery villain." Whereat I knew she was tantalizing Master Joshua Pringle.

With that he followed her into the hall, his men trooping after him. No sooner had the last man passed out of sight through the hall door than I drew every pistol from the holsters of the saddles, and, gathering them in my arms, I ran and hid them among the brushwood, knowing that no sword can compare with a fire-arm ; and should any man during the forthcoming conflict bethink himself of using his pistol, there would soon be an end.to the business.

Here I noted a thing which stimulated my spirits in a high degree; I discovered that only six of Captain Pringle's command were with him; the ostensible reason being that his task was so simple he could afford to treat it lightly.

Afterwards I listened under the window of the big sitting-room, in which the candles were burning. I heard voices tolerably tranquil, then a little louder, then louder still. Following that I heard the knight's pitched high in anger; and the six languages plenteously used. Soon his rage was his master.

"No, you base-born hound," I heard him cry quite plain, " I will not give up the papers or my person either! Dost think James Stuart is to do as he lists in the matter? E'en though ye are seven to one, I will not surrender. We will have a little breather first."

"Don't be a fool!" put in Master Pringle.

"A fool, didst thou say, jackanapes? Thou shalt pay for that."

Thereupon methought I caught some muffled sounds of scuffling, and I heard the captain bellow—

"At him, lads, before he gets his sword. You, Bill and Tom, the papers are in the cabinet; seize them whilst we take his worship."

These instructions were not carried out aright, for directly afterwards there came the ring of steel.

In wild excitement to see how the land lay, I clambered to a precarious foothold on the window-sill, and thereby managed to gain a peep of the interior over the top of the blinds. I saw the knight, despite his gout and the infirmities of age, plying his sword, as a young man might have done with admirable deftness and vigor, dancing round the table the while to evade a couple of men; whilst the captain, with folded arms, along with the others, stood in one corner grinning in their relish of the joke.

Two more walked across the room to where Dorothy stood with her back to the cabinet containing the precious documents. They strode up to her boldly, and bade her make way for them to open it; but recoiled in a second, for the maid whipped a pair of pistols from behind her back, to their astonishment, and thrust the muzzles in their faces.

They halted, laughing; but the maid was not jesting. Her lips were tight, and her eyes terrible. Her fingers fairly seemed to twitch upon the triggers; whilst the look in her face had nought to do with that of a gentle maiden. Another step, and both of them would have had acquaintance with eternity. This was enough for me; I had seen those eyes ablaze, and those hands with two wicked weapons in them. I jumped off the window-sill at a bound, raced up the entrance steps, and sword in hand ran in among the company. Four men instead of two were now besetting Sir Nicholas, and one at least bore the marks of his weapon. Still the knight was quite outnumbered; another minute then all would have been over, for one of his assailants must have run him through. As I ran in and pinked the foremost of the four clean through the chest, cries of anger and surprise rang thro' the room, and then 'twas wildest chaos.

I can't tell what next occurred; I cannot set things down hereabouts as they befell in their due order. I know that in ten minutes or even less the beautiful room was a slaughter-house. The knight forgot his age, his stiffness, his infirmities —forgot everything but the lust of killing; and I—oh, I did too! We fought till we couldn't see; without cries, without words; but with the ferocious silence, the dumb blood-questing tenacity of bull-dogs. The sparks flew out of the steel. 'Twas sickening to feel the squelch of the blood at your sword point, to feel your adversaries' panting breath in your face; 'twas hand to hand all the time. Over the table, round the table, across the table, we fought and writhed and struggled, and truly that table was our guardian angel. It alone saved us from the press of the foe. We cut, hacked, and slashed, and ever at the men in red. Neither heeded his neighbor, nor had a thought beyond how to dodge the reeking steel.

Twice I was beaten to my knees, yet each time rose with little hurt, and fought again the harder, till at last my sword found the vitals of an enemy. With a moan he squirmed and fell in his death throe. I skipped away, yet still the devilish steel was at my body. The knight and I were side by side for a second, and I caught a glimpse of him as his Perillo pierced the throat of one poor devil, and then I saw his other hand was running blood. This was only a glance, for an instant later I was half blinded with my own, as it streamed from my brow. But I wallowed in it, and stabbed and thrust with a tiger's fury.

Again I was beaten to my knees, but hung by the hand to a murtherous blade about to descend. Suddenly it was left therein entirely; the knight had spitted its owner, and he, too, lay among the stricken. We two demons ne'er ceased till the conflict was decided, whereat we stayed our scarlet blades, looked round, and saw a slaughter-house.

Yea, we stopped and took survey when there was nought else to do. Faces and swords dripping blood, we stood side by side and beheld six men groaning and writhing, or stark dead upon the carpet. The seventh man, Captain Joshua Pringle, was nowhere to be seen. The butchery was horrible; the walls, the furniture, and the wainscot were all splashed with purple, whilst numberless articles were overturned, else smashed in fragments. 'Twas a hideous nightmare.

Dorothy still stood with her back to the cabinet, her face white with wordless terror. Her hands shook and her whole body seemed to shrink in mute horror from the sight. Albeit she grasped the pistols; and I knew by the magnificent determination which, in spite of all, still lurked in her frightened face, that, had either of her friends been in need of assistance, she would promptly enough have lent it.

As for the knight, he ne'er heeded the butchery nor the groans of the wounded; but simply seized my hand in his own bloody one, and sang out, "Man, y'are a beautiful fighter!" then wiped his sword on the tail of his doublet, mopped the blood from his face on the sleeve of it, and stuck his sword point in the carpet. His one eye burnt brighter than fire. Every fibre of his body quivered. He was a madman.

"A noble victory," he roared, "a noble victory! Seven to two, and there they are laid out for their coffin-cloths. Wench, we're a dazzling pair. This is life, my lass—we're back in the Forties now. Man, where did ye get that upper-guard?—I call it great—ay, y'are a beautiful fighter! Friend, I am young again; this night hath knocked forty years off my age-scroll. I've a score yet to settle wi' you, mon cher. That may keep for a minute, then we'll have another flutter—we'll make a night o' this. Let's have a drink ere we settle the game. Thirsty work, hey? Come, Dorothy, a couple of bottles of my Lanquedoc. Oh, oh! now what hath gotten the wench. A damned deal too nice i' th' stomach as usual."

The girl said nothing, but recoiled from his look. This, however, did not affect him. The unchristian creature, though wounded in at least half a score separate places, jumped across to the cupboard, and produced two bottles of wine. There was no cup about the place, therefore he simply knocked off the neck, and bade me do likewise. This much accomplished, he gulped down a great draught, and then holding the wine in a neckless bottle above his head in one hand, and, despite all injuries, his sword in the other, roared out in a wild, cracked voice, with scantiest melody—

19

> " Up wi' your cups to King Charlie,
> We pledge him in sparkling sack,
> To perdition we send wi'out parley
> Each ranting Presbyter Jack.
> A fig for the Huntingdon Brewer,
> A kick for old Ironside Joe,
> Stick 'em both on to this skewer,
> A curse for the prick-eared foe."

Thus he screeched the old Cavalier's drinking song, till he had finished his bottle and mine as well, and his voice failed him; whereupon he executed something of a hobbling dance, without the least thought for the blood that dripped from his person.

"Now, Ned, are ye ready? Y'are a rare fighting man, else I should not have shown you such courtesy. I am beholden to thee for what thou hast done, yet I do not forget old scores. Come, my lad, we have breathed; we'll now see who's the better man. If my luck abides, I shall have thee through the heart at the third pass."

I winced at this; the man was a horrible enemy. His bloody countenance relaxed into a gleeful grin. Just then one of the wounded men gave a more piteous groan than ever.

"Ventre Saint Gris!" exclaimed Sir Nicholas, "'tis evident I am not half the man I once was. Here am I forgetting the first of duties towards an enemy. I thank you, friend, for your kindly reminder."

He stepped across to where the wounded man lay helpless, raised his thirsty sword, and passed it straight through the soldier's heart. The blood squirted hideously on to the walls and wainscot.

"Any more?" inquired the monster. "Ah, to be sure, there are three yet."

He made a movement towards another wretch, and raised his sword again. Ere it could descend, Dorothy had rushed to his side, and hung with both hands to his sword arm.

"Stop, sir!" she cried.

"Stop! dost know what thou sayest, soft wench? 'Tis the fortune of war. Art mad?"

He tried to shake her off as he spoke, and there was murder in his eye as he glanced at his victim. Still the girl clung to him tighter than ever, entreating wildly—

"Spare them, sir; spare them! For God's sake, spare them! 'Tis murder, sheer murder! They are helpless."

And all the while the stricken wretches, who still lived, squirmed and writhed away as far as possible from the knight, in horrible fear of the uplifted sword, their eyes nearly bolting

from their heads in terror. Meantime the girl had let go her
hold on his arm, but had seized with both hands the hilt of his
sword. The fearless creature grappled with him, and struggled
might and main to wrest it from him. Twice he lifted his disengaged fist as if to strike her, then caught her by the throat
and hurled her half across the room.

CHAPTER XXIX.

THE DEATH-SONG OF MARS.

ONCE more he raised his sword to kill the stricken men ; yet
here the door opened of a sudden, and Captain Pringle thrust
half his stunted body into the room.

" One a-piece ! " said he.

In a moment the place was filled with smoke, and our ears
rang with two heavy reports. The first bullet passed my ear
and buried itself in the wall behind, and the second struck the
old knight full in the chest. I saw him tottering when the
smoke lifted. I ran to him, and straightway he fell back into
my arms, gasping. The wretch who wrought the murder,
having fired the shots, fled without waiting to remark the effect
of his deed. 'Twas grievous to see the old man as he lay in
my arms, coughing and spitting blood ; whilst I felt his atten-
uated body all of a quiver and tremble.

" Lay me down flat," he said in a choked, husky voice ; " I
shall rest easier. And now for the punch. Quick, wench,
and brew it! I haven't long to wait."

"Oh, father, you must not die ! " she exclaimed in almost
childish desperation, yet without weeping. Her eyes were dry.
I could not bear to look at her hard, unearthly, distracted face.

"Of course I shall die, wench ! " he said querulously. " 'Tis
the fortune of war. I remember old Major Leroux being struck
in the same place before Ruhrendorf, and he had growled his
last curse ten minutes afterwards. 'Tis grand to die sword in
hand, though 'tis scarce to my taste being potted like a fox in
a hole. But I can't have it all ways. I have gained a glorious
victory this night, and must be content with that. I would
have wished to cross swords wi' you, Ned, my lad, had I been
spared a bit longer. Y'are a damned black rogue, though a
beautiful fighter. Now, wench, bestir yourself over that punch,
else I must cock my toes with a thirsty throat."

The dying man said all this in a low peevish tone. His daughter did as she was bidden in a dazed way. She brought the steaming liquor and laid it down, and knelt beside him. His eyes lighted at the sight of it.

" Say you will not die, father !—oh, say you will not die !" she begged, with an impotence that was pitiful to hear.

" Not die ? Faith I've no say in the matter !" he answered, after sipping a modicum out of the bowl.

" Live sir ! Live for me ! I cannot part from you. I can't let you go; I love you so."

She flung her arms madly about his neck, and kissed in the wildest way his bleeding face.

" Now then, young fool, stop that !" he said. " I'm done for quite."

To prove it, with violent fingers he tore away the soaked garments from his wound, and laid bare his chest, a mass of gushing purple.

" Can you now understand the game is played? I've a couple of ounces o' solid lead in my inwards. It's giving me devil's delight. I can't abide it much longer."

He took a longer pull at the punch, and then trembled all over in a horrid spasm of pain.

" Here wench," he said slowly, and very composedly, " you can give me one kiss ; I'm almost done. You've been a good girl in your way. A trifle too soft i' th' heart maybe, and as stubborn as a mule, but I don't hold you accountable; 'twas an accident of birth. You were born a wench, d'ye see. You've been an eyesore to me. You've no pluck; but as you're a girl, you're hardly to blame. P'raps I've been a bit hard on you at times, but I'm not so young as I used to be. Maybe I have done things to you I ought not to have done to a wench, but the gout hath been mortal bad very often. I've ever meant well by thee; 'tis only my way. I say again thou hast been a good lass. Come, another kiss. How soft your lips are ! They soothe me, so kiss me once more for the last. If y'are so set against young Raoul de Crois, I will waive the matter. I would I might commit you to the care of some friend; I should then bide easier, for these are hard times for lonely gentlewomen. You have a sneaking likeness for that Black Ned. Come hither, sir ! Y'are a damned bad, deceitful, purse-snatching thief, and I curse you. But still y'are fine at the wielding o' the steel. It crosses my mind that ye have the impudence to cast an eye towards this wench. But you shan't have her ! Mark me !— you shan't have her ! We'll have no common cutpurses in this family. She may be a white-livered wench, but she's a daughter of mine and one Marvin, and she, a woman, is far too good for a million thieves. Dorothy, I'd like you to have De Crois; he's all a swordsman. As for Ned here, he knows how to fight. My lad, ye have courage and a notion of the art of fence, but do not leave your wrist so open, and give not undue prominence to the edge. 'Tis the point you should rely on. I'm sorry I didn't live to see you hang, and sorrier still that I've not had time to put a hole in your heart. Wench, more punch!"

Gradually as he spoke his voice became weaker and more feeble, till at last it died away in a whisper. After this strange farewell, he clutched with twitching fingers at the bowl, took a draught, and in a loud, unsteady tone he once more bade Dorothy kiss him. She did so, and then another spasm of agony seized him, and contorted his body. He lay there a hideous, writhing figure, and as the torment took a firmer hold upon him, he beat his fists about, and poured the punch down his throat without intermission. The fumes and the pain took effect on his head, and his reason went.

He screamed out hoarsely, "My lads, a slack rein and a bloody heel! After the crop-eared rogues! Slice 'em down; and no quarter! Now charge all together—saddle-bow to saddle-bow, and knee to knee! See, they're running! Your Highness, 'twere best to cut 'em off on the left, and take 'em by the river. Down wi' every Puritan dog among them. Hurrah for the King and Prince Rupert! 'Tis victory! victory!—a great and glorious victory, your Highness!"

Then the madman pitched his voice still higher and roared out—

> "Up wi' your cups to King Charlie!
> We pledge——"

'Twas his last word. A gush of blood sprang up in his throat and choked him. He shot out his limbs, and stared with his one glassy eyeball up at the ceiling—stone dead.

CHAPTER XXX.

THE FLIGHT OVER THE HILLS IN THE DARKNESS.

THE knight had scarce drawn his final breath when Martin, the groom, returned from Bridgwater to find his master dead. He had served with Sir Nicholas in more than one campaign, and the fellow blubbered miserably over the brave departed spirit. Between us we reverently covered up the lifeless body in a cloth, and bore it out into the grounds to its final resting-place. Dorothy followed behind us, carrying her dead sire's dripping sword. With dreadful calmness she pointed out the spot he was to lie in, and stood by white and listless whilst we dug the grave.

In half an hour we had it prepared ; tho' ere we could lower the corpse into it, the maid had knelt beside the body, had gently laid the sword on its owner's breast, and had kissed the cold lips silently and without a tear. Then she looked at me and whispered huskily—

" He would have liked it thus to lie with him, that none might sully its fair fame. "

As we filled in the first sods she turned her head away, as though the sight was beyond her strength to bear ; and when our task was done, she leaned her weight on me, almost incapable of standing.

Very slowly I led her back to the house, with Martin at my heels, and all the way she had neither words nor tears. Indeed nothing but a dry-eyed grief—a grief that had cut her down.

Upon returning to that slaughter-house of a room, the first things to meet our gaze were three dead men extended stark upon the carpet and three wounded lying in blotches of blood around them. Two of these latter were sitting up, limp, woe-be-gone, and weakly, and groaning so in their agony that it irked one's ears to hear them. Whether 'twas such sounds or the sight of me that touched her, sure I cannot tell ; yet quite suddenly something of the old brightness came into her eyes, and straightway she ceased her lethargy. Methought she gave a look at me as though fearful of my reproaches ; then hastily made for the kitchen below-stairs, where all the female servants were huddled trembling in a corner.

In a short time she came back staggering under the load of a large tray, which she set on the top of the cabinet. It contained a pitcher of warm water, bandages, cordials, some kind of balsam, and a jar of green usquebaugh. Luckily my wounds were scarce aught to speak of, though some havoc had been played with the flesh of my sword-arm by several imperfectly parried thrusts. So soaked with blood were my shirt and coat-sleeves, that to draw them away from the arm itself was an impossibility. Therefore my succorer took a knife and carefully cut the limp rag away therefrom, and revealed the bare limb, and 'twas not an agreeable sight. Indeed, had it been any one else's arm it would have given even me a qualm to have looked at it, for the half-clotted blood covered it in a horrible dark purple mass.

I watched the maid, and saw her go a shade the paler, whilst her fingers hung involuntarily aloof from the nasty mess of flesh and blood. Yet even as I saw this, something like a swift emotion shot across her face, and by the look of her eyes I knew it meant a resolution. She seized the injured member, quickly and almost roughly, as though afraid of her will being beaten by a natural instinct. Swiftly and tenderly, with soothing merciful hands, she bathed the wounds with warm water, and freed them from the blood, and stanched the bleeding. And though her sympathetic fingers were soiled and smeared with my unworthy gore, and though its aspect was so evidently repugnant, she performed her task with even more than woman's tenderness. My scathes being disturbed, they began to smart and ache, no doubt by contact with the water.

But I didn't wince; neither did I mean to do. And, in despite of pain and unwholesome sights, I had it in my heart to wish that my other arm was quite as badly injured. For such was the delicacy of her touch, the deftness, the skilfulness, and the caressing gentleness of her finger-tips, that they seemed to speak to me more plainly than aught else could have done. When the hurts had been thoroughly bathed and cleansed, and as she was about to fix the bandages, I asked quite boldy, " Where's the balsam, Dorothy ? "

She looked at me as if fearful of giving offence by disparaging my endurance. However, once more humanity was too much for woman's delicacy, and she answered with a world of meaning in her voice, " 'Twill hurt very much, Ned ; very much indeed, dear lad ! "

Still I was resolute, so she handed me the balsam that I might apply it, shrinking from the task herself, for 'twas not in

her nature to wantonly give pain in cold blood either to man or
animal.   Call me fool, call me charlatan ! either one or t'other,
if ye are so minded, kinsmen ; yet I most certainly rubbed that
balsam into the flesh, before her eyes, not carefully, nor tenderly, nor to the extent of a few drops only.   No, I gave my arm
a liberal quantity, smartly administered.   And when my love
began to wind the white cloths neatly round my injuries, she
whispered—

"Ned, I dare not have done that to myself, nor have let
others do it for me ; " and she shook her head, sighed "Ugh !"
and shivered.

The darling! of course she couldn't ;   I knew she couldn't,
and for that self-same reason I had applied it before her eyes
to duly impress certain things upon her recollection.   Howbeit,
very shortly, that right arm of mine began to smart, and then
to burn, then to sting, then to bite, and then to do these things
together.   I set my teeth, and tried to bear it, because Dorothy
every now and then peeped over her shoulder to look at me.   I
strove, Heaven knows how hard, to support the torture without
even winking.   Yet the horrid pains began shooting as far as
my armpit, and to execute wild vertigoes of torment, like devil's
dances all the way up the injured member ; till verily methought
I must faint with agony.   But I ground my teeth the harder
into my lower jaw, and gripped the palm of my other hand till
the nails cut the flesh.   Were those awful pangs ne'er going to
abate ?   Apparently not at present, for the sweat came out on
my forehead, and the convulsive spasms crept half-way up my
neck.   Thereupon a groan, half-subdued, but plainly audible,
sneaked out from somewhere, whereat the maid peeped round
again, and I blushed an eloquent scarlet.   Straightway my
torture began to lessen ; and, betwixt ourselves, if ever man
was properly punished for folly, presumption, and self-conceit,
that man was Edward Armstrong.

Meanwhile, the girl was for the time forgetting her position
in the world, and the tragedy of that terrible night.   She was
busy tending those of the fallen who still breathed, plying the
remedies and the water with unceasing vigor.   Though these
were her mortal enemies who had broken one great tie of her
life, she propped their backs, assuaged their thirst, stanched their
bleeding, bathed their wounds, and doctored them as well as
she was able.   They looked at her between the groans in
suffering yet grateful wonderment ; and one poor wretch with a
slashed face and a swordthrust through his ribs, took her velvet
hand in his own gory fist and kissed it.   Thereat I, Black Ned,

seeing this, turned mine head away, and for the first time since September, '85, had wet eyes.

Having accomplished so much for her foes, Dorothy took the precious documents from the cabinet, kindled a blaze with flint and steel, and burned them deliberately one by one. Shortly after, one of the three survivors (the least injured) set off for Bridgwater to bring help for his comrades, and for assistance to bear away the dead. 'Twas no time for tarrying now. In little more than an hour reinforcements would be at the manor, and 'twould be a particularly serious matter for us if we were discovered here.

" Dorothy," I said, and then stopped suddenly. The maid had re-assumed her listlessness and dry-eyed misery, while hard lines seemed to have gathered on her face, and to have shorn away her youthful beauty. All this went to my heart at once, and stopped my tongue ; though my wits, and I am proud to say they were indubitably keen in this crisis, told me that prompt action alone could save us. Thus, the urgency of the case bade me speak my mind without the least delay.

" Dorothy," I said again, this time in a tone of eager command, " we must be hence from this place, without one moment's bootless tarrying. Ere long we shall have the whole hornet's nest about our ears. Let us prepare for instant flight ! "

She gave no reply, and the misery deepened in her face.

" Darling," I said again, not daunted, but nerved to greater efforts by the pressing anxiety that beset me, " get away from this, if not for your own sake, for mine, else they will certainly arrest you and convey you to London, as an aider and abettor of treason. 'Twill be death to thee then."

Despite my tone and the appeal the words conveyed, she was still silent, passive, and lifeless. The blow had crushed her so that she had now no care for the world. And every minute we lingered we jeopardized our safety. Desperation set my brains to work, and enabled me to use wiles and cunning.

" Dorothy," I began once more, " you, who have gone through so much, and have faced so many dangers, are not going to play the coward now ? Come, be brave ; 'twould sorely grieve your father to know that you so soon forget his precepts."

It was an unkind speech, and I delivered it sharply, and without a spark of softness or any kind of sentiment. I even hated myself for my harshness, yet it did a thousand times more good than mere persuasion. She looked at me for few seconds as though she were dazed and half insensible.

" You say flee, Ned. But where am I to flee ? I have no

friend but thee this side the Channel, and thou'rt wanting a
home or place of refuge. I feel bereft and lonesome. The
world seems empty. I have none to look or lean to, but to one
that cannot help me."

It tore my heart to hear her voice so hopeless, and to see her
face so drawn and white. All the same her words were quite
true. Who was I to render aid at so dire a moment? I was
so hemmed in by circumstances, that I seemed really worse
than useless. But honor, love, and gratitude called loudly on
me to assist her now the time of her need had come. She had
nobly succored me in the hour of *my* adversity. Was I to fail
in this cruel hour of hers? Surely not. Therefore, it befell
that my mind, in some strange unaccountable way, suddenly hied
over the hills to a little hamlet, to a woman, a pitying woman,
and a mother. At this, I took my stricken love's hand, and
warmly said—

"Dorothy, we are comrades. I will take thee to a place of
refuge from the anger of the King, even as thou tookest me."

I spoke boldly, and though nine-tenths of this boldness I did
not feel, 'twas a very honorable deception; for I sought to give
her heart new life, new hope; and in a measure was successful.

"Thank you, lad," she replied, with just a spark of spirit.

"Dearest, follow me, and ere the dawn you shall be safe. We
must be expeditious. Collect your valuables, and let us set off
at once, for I doubt not when the King hath had his choice
there will be little left."

I threw as much cheerfulness and energy into my words and
gestures as I could, knowing well that it behoved me to act thus,
to inspire, if possible, my companion.

She asked me to follow her into another room in search of
the family heirlooms and jewels. She gave a little cry when the
room was lit, for there were the drawers burst open, with the
unimportant contents strewn about, and every article of value
gone. This was the full revelation of the villainy of Captain
Joshua Pringle.

As we afterwards learned, the knave had obtained, amongst
other information from the major domo, the place where the
plate and the jewels lay, and during the conflict he had slipped
out of the room and packed them all into a bag which he slung
over his horse's back, and in his rummaging had discovered two
old pistols of the knight's. On going to his horse outside he
found that his own weapon was missing, and hearing Sir
Nicholas' voice uplifted in the drinking song, he knew at once
that his men were beaten. Therefore he charged his new-found

firearms, and determined to put a bullet through the pair of us
that we might trouble him no more, whence he could ride
securely off with the booty, and, as hath been seen already, this
plan was put in practice.

Our discovery was still another blow to the unlucky creature,
tho' she bore it in silence. She sought for every piece of money
she could find, and having gathered it together, she wrapped
herself in a cloak, and leaving Martin in charge (he was an
honest man, though a cantankerous one), we set off for Chilverley farm.

I was perfectly easy in my mind as to how mother would
receive the fugitive. I never lacked faith in her bounty or her
largeness of heart. As for myself, the pursuit was bound to
slacken for some little time, seeing how sorely the night's work
had crippled the King's men. We were a pair of fugitives
together now, both fleeing from the King's justice ; although I
am sure the offences of one of us were not particularly heinous.
She had shared the conspirator's secret and had defended his
papers, but both of us were too well aware the King would not
now let the matter rest.

'Tis strange how the events of life sometimes befall. 'Twas
now my turn to play the part of friend and succorer. 'Twas I
who was leading her to the place of refuge this time. I knew
I had but to tell the maid's story to mother, and she would be
taken to her heart at once. My mother's charity towards her
fellow-creatures was boundless, if her heart was only touched
by their sufferings or misfortunes. All the way the maid was
dumb ; her spirits drooped ; the joys of life and hope with her
were dead. She asked no questions ; but simply followed, very
listless. I wished ten times to myself that she would weep.
'Twas this hard unyielding grief that made me so mistrustful ;
women should weep when the cup of sorrow is so full.

I walked with quick footsteps, hoping to rouse her somewhat
thereby and drive away her apathy. 'Twas a vain hope, however, though she kept pace with me in despite of everything.
The propitious moon lighted the track all the way, wherefore
we made fine progress among the hills, overcoming the dangers
of the broken paths, and fording the little streams at the shal-
low places by hopping from one boulder to another till we
gained the farther side. The night was mild and bright, with a
soft fragrant south wind astir which felt generous to our faces.
None knew the hills better than I ; therefore, under my guid-
ance, we ne'er swerved from the direct road. Yet it was a
rugged, broken, precipitous, and difficult track. One moment

we found ourselves deep down in a wooded combe, dark and close grown, with an eager runnel burrowing its course betwixt the oaks, and flowing with a soothing song over the stones in its bed; whilst as we made our way by the margin of the rising, falling water, with its gentle swish for company, rats scuttled away from our feet and rustled into the stream. On the other bank a gaunt heron stalked past with a silent lassitude instead of the water ousel which lingers here by day; and we heard the sweet soft pleading of the willow wren, harmonious with the summer wind whispering to the branches. Passing under the clustered oak-boughs, they casting their black shadows in the track, we crossed the red, flat river stones and rose toward the imperious heights gloomy and grand in the moonlight; deserting in our upward passage beeches and the mountain ash, till they looked blurred masses in the vale. Soon we felt the bending red-brown heather, heavy laden with the dew, mingling with our legs; and though we rose so high, and overlooked the misty valleys, our journey's end lay not there. We clambered down again and crossed another stream in close pursuance of the path, till we turned into a straighter road, and five minutes after were standing under the farmstead windows.

The dawn had not come yet, and showed no sign of its arrival; whilst the house was clothed in barren stillness. All were a-bed within those four walls. I could only think of one mode of obtaining admittance for the two of us, and of gaining mother's private ear; and surely both were very necessary.

"Dearest," I said, "we cannot stay here in the open till the doors are unbarred. Let me leave you here a few minutes, whilst I get matters amended."

She consented to await my return, not at all frightened to be left alone. I went round the house and stopped under the window of my old chamber. With a spring I alighted on the sill of the window underneath, and with another, begat of long practice aforetime, clambered on to that of the one above. In two minutes I had made a noiseless entrance through this upper one into my deserted room. From thence I betook myself to mother's apartment stealthily, being fearful of arousing the other inmates. To my joy I found the door unfastened and the blind drawn up. Thus the chamber was as light as day almost, by reason of the streaming moonlight.

"Mother," I said, laying a hand on the sleeper's shoulder, "waken, I pray you."

She started under my touch, opened her eyes, and shivered.

"Ned, Ned, is it you? Is it my poor boy? What do you here at this hour of the night? Whence have you come?"

She asked this apprehensively, and with the aid of the white moonbeams I saw her frightened face. I reassured her as well and as quickly as I could, for I was mindful of my waiting companion. Regarding Dorothy, I only told her in as many words what the maid had done for me; and what I now wished to do for her; that she had ne'er known a mother, and that very night she had lost her only protector. No sooner was this briefly narrated, than mother made me go down without further tarrying and let the hapless maid in; saying she herself would dress the while and come down to welcome her.

I descended into the kitchen, withdrew the bolts, turned the key, and stepped out to fetch the maiden.

"Here, darling," I said, with a laugh, though a deceitful one, "I have done well, as I have returned through the doorway instead of the window. Wilt follow me in? Mother will be downstairs to greet you in a minute."

"Thou art truly kind, Ned," she answered, giving me a cold hand, "and I thank thee for what thou hast done for me this night."

She came with me into the kitchen, and, placing her in a chair, I raised a light, just as mother came down the stairs. In a look she beheld her white wan face, and her eyes with the horror in them. Thereat she acted according to my presentiment. Though she had ne'er set eyes on the hapless maid before, she walked straight to where she sat, timid, miserable, silent; took both her hands in hers and kissed her.

"My poor girl!" she said. Dorothy gave an almost frightened glance at mother; she had not known such gentleness before, and did not expect it now. "Ay, but your hands are like ice, dear, and your face is whiter than a ghost's," quoth mother, in her true maternal manner.

Forthwith she set about remedying the maid's misfortunes. She bade me go and fetch the dryest logs I could find in the wood-shed; and when I came back with a huge armful, she had me down on my knees building a new fire in the grate whilst she prepared a cordial.

In a quarter of an hour a steaming basin of milk was prepared, and while the girl sipped it mother chafed her lifeless hands. Another quarter of an hour and she had seen her in a freshly ordered bed. Hereafter, she came downstairs and set out a rare repast for me. The occasion demanded that I should tell mother all the events which had brought about our nocturnal visit. 'Twas a long story, told truthfully, ay, so truthfully that I e'en touched on the feelings we bore toward one another. Mother's heart was moved by Dorothy's cruel misfortunes.

"Poor girl! poor girl! Ned, I am glad indeed you have brought her to me," she said, when I had told the story. "And I owe her more than I can ever repay! 'Tis her alone I must thank for having you still alive."

"I am sore afeared this blow hath crushed her, mother. She seems listless and broken. I have never seen her so before," I said.

This she would not have for a moment. 'Twas self-evident that the fugitive had gone direct to her heart, and, God knows, it was a large one and a warm one.

We talked for nearly an hour together. I even unfolded the plot for the downfall of King James, and as I spoke I realized myself what success in the matter meant. My whole life hinged on William's coming, and I made that clear to mother. The dethronement of the Stuart implied liberty, free citizenship, money, land, title, and revenge for me, and for the one I loved it embraced the same, save that I had yet to learn that she cherished aught so dark and unholy as revenge. Alas! *I* did, and with a grim, horrible intensity. The degrading passion smouldered in my soul, ate deep into it, and in a sense, thereby reduced me to a monomaniac.

We were still talking when John came downstairs to begin the day's labor. He stared stupidly as he discovered us sitting in the kitchen; yet, recovering at once from the first shock of surprise, he put on his boots, and without giving me one look or word, went forth to the fields. That hurt me more than a blow from his hammerlike fist would have done.

I was now able to breathe for a time with more freedom; knowing the bloody work of the previous night had sorely crippled my hunters; therefore, I rested undisturbed on a feather-bed for the first time for many days, and 'twas delicious.

After a few hours' sleep, and my wounds giving scarce any trouble, I rose, dressed myself, went downstairs, and found mother busy compounding a sovereign remedy; and the sight of her face stopped questions for the moment, for, in equal parts, it bespoke excessive care and excessive gravity.

CHAPTER XXXI.

THE VALLEY OF THE SHADOW.

WHEN I saw her countenance so full of unwelcome import, my heart leaped unbidden up into my throat, and then, as it were, just as suddenly dropped down below its normal depth.

" How's Dorothy, mother? " I asked.

Thereat she turned towards me, and I saw her eyes were wet.

" I do not like her looks at all, Ned. I—I'm almost afraid she is going to be very ill."

" Say not so," I said feebly, childishly, like one who fain would postpone a descending blow, though quite sure it must descend.

Just then my brother John came down the stairs on tiptoe, though—as if to flout his care—his boots squeaked and creaked at every step. He was dressed much above his week-day custom. Indeed, he was habited in his Sunday coat and hat, and carried a whipstock in his hand.

" Where's he bound for, mother? " I asked as he passed through the kitchen door into the yard. I did not dare to address this question to him in person, for he treated me, not as a fallen angel—as he might have done—but as a base creature, something meaner than the dirt he trampled underfoot.

" He hath gone to fetch the doctor," replied mother.

Gone to fetch the doctor! 'Tis a harsh plaintive sentence that hath struck deep into the hearts of many families.

" Is her malady so dangerous, then? " I asked, full of fear.

" It begins to frighten me, Ned. A delirium hath seized her, and it grows hour by hour, her heart beats faster and faster, and her eyes are becoming terrible to look at."

" Oh, mother! " I gasped, my heart fluttering in a most unreasonable manner. I asked to see her. Mother peremptorily refused this request; but I begged so hard and so persistently that, in the end, she was not proof against my importunity.

No sooner was the tardy permission granted, than she led me to her room. She opened the bedroom door and marched in before me, just the least little bit in the world officiously. The blinds were drawn, though 'twas midday and gloriously sunny. I came to the bedside, and, in the subdued light of the darkened room, I saw my darling lying prone and racked with fever. Her cheeks were hectic, her eyes full of horror, and unnaturally bright and restless; whilst the dark forest of her hair had become so dishevelled that it hung low down over her forehead, and, with these other things, made her appear so strange and wild that, at first, I did not like to look at her. Albeit she looked at me—stared straight at me with those eyes that were now filled with a vague terror; and that were perpetually roving. Still she gave me no glance of recognition, not a solitary feature moved by way of welcome, nor did she smile, nor speak a single coherent syllable, but muttered a host of words rapidly under her breath, so that none heard them.

"Dorothy," I said softly, to make her speak to me.

Again she stared straight at me, and then broke out suddenly in a high, quick voice—

"Their eyes, their eyes; see their eyes! Those are not men's eyes—they are devils' eyes. Ho, ho, ho! the blood! the blood! All on the walls—the blood on the walls! And their eyes; dear God, their eyes!"

Again she began to mutter incoherently, and stretched out her hand to Betty, who had been by her side for several hours. To me she gave not the slightest heed, whereupon the truth dawned on my slow understanding. She did not know me; my heart turned like ice in my inside to think that we had gone through so much together, and had endured and loved one another so continually. Verily, 'twas very hard; and this one stern act of nature cut me to the quick. Suddenly the sufferer sat up in bed, and thrust one finger towards me wildly. And though Betty had her hands upon her in an instant, and said, "There, dear!" soothingly, and endeavored to put her head back on the pillow, she failed, by virtue of Dorothy's stout resistance.

"That's Black Ned!" she cried; "he says his name is Master Jackson. He is not Master Jackson. He is a thief—a thief, I tell you. Dost hear? That's Black Ned. I have been deceived. He's not honest; not an honorable man—he says he is not. I've been tricked and cheated, tricked and cheated! He carried the letter to Lord Churchill. Master Armstrong carried it thither—no, Black Ned, the highwayman. I am deceived, duped, cheated! The man's a thief. I know he's a thief! Kill him, then, dear father, kill him! Curse the wretch, I loathe him!"

She fell into a state of frenzy, and wrestled with her nurses; and all the time her wild eyes ne'er left me. In my shame and horror, I was struck stupid at the outset, and clutched hold of the wooden bedpost for support.

My mother and sister each shot a furtive glance at my face, and saw that in it which made them avert their gaze. I could feel myself looking guilty. 'Twould have been a crowning mercy had the floor opened and swallowed me as I stood, for this awful advertisement of my infamy crushed me, felled me, stunned me !

Good God ! was she ne'er going to cease her terrible words ? Were her eyes ne'er to leave my face ? The blood in my veins was chilled, whilst shame burned itself upon my heart. In the end, I managed to stagger mechanically from the room. Would to Heaven I had not set foot therein ! The whole truth of the matter was that, for weeks, I had well-nigh forgotten that dark episode of the past; forgotten it, in my youthful bliss and rapture.

Man may make history, tho' he cannot unmake it afterwards. He may forget it for his own part, yet he may not wipe out the printed page, and blot it for ever from the sight of posterity as though it had ne'er been written. So with his sins. He may commit them in his youth, and forget them till old age, but, in the mean time, the world at large has them all by heart, and hands them down to future generations. 'Twas appalling to think that the revelation had been made to mine own flesh and blood ; and to conceive how they, kind souls, must view me— not as a mere thief by force of circumstances, but as a trickster, a liar, a cheat, and deceiver of an innocent maiden !

"Curse you, Ned Armstrong !" I growled to myself ; then walked up and down our deserted kitchen almost frantic. How must I seem to my mother and sister upstairs ? They who had borne so much, would they now abhor me ?

At the height of this inward disturbance, mother came downstairs to fetch a medicine. I seized her hand like one possessed, and said with a rush of words—

"Mother, all thou hast heard is true. And that maid loves me in spite of it. Canst thou love me, too, in spite of it ? "

Without a moment's hesitation she kissed me deliberately, and gently. What noble creatures women are ! A weight was lifted from my soul. I had suffered five minutes' torment, and this sweet forgiveness was as a balm to many wounds.

"Do not say a word of this to John," I implored, and she readily set my mind at ease. Kinsmen, he was not exactly a woman, but a cold-blooded, bowelless man, whose iron heel I had learnt to dread.

"Dost think, mother, thou canst bring her back to health ? " I inquired, misgiving much.

20

" It shall be no fault of mine if I fail, Ned. I have sent for Master Cooper, the best physician in these parts, to come and tend her. Mistress Dorothy hath done far more for my son than ever his mother can do for her."

Thus it will be seen my loved one had gone straight to mother's heart, not by means of her beauty, her bravery, or her many virtues; but simply because she had succored me, a thief, and trickster, in the times of my direst need. After this, I waited in a state of high impatience for the coming of the doctor. Of course, when he did come, I had to keep out of his sight, on account of my exceeding notoriety. I looked anxiously and fearfully for his departure. At last, perched as I was before my bedroom window, I saw him ride away on his cob, whereupon I lost not another second, but came down into the kitchen and sought for news. I found John therein, putting on his week-day boots, and I asked him what Master Cooper's verdict was.

" He says she is dangerously ill, and will be wondrous lucky to get over it."

I burst out thereat in desperation, " Is there nought I can do, bethink you, to assist mother and Betty? Must I continue to ramble aimlessly about, not a farthing's worth of service to Dorothy or her nurses ? "

" Nought you can do ? " said he comfortingly. " If you'll just be more of a man, and less of a calf, and take yourself off to the hills till bedtime, out of the way and sight of all, methinks that will be performing the truest service you're capable of."

I acted on this advice, and slipped stealthily out of sight of the farm hands to the hills. 'Twas hard to know that my love and prayers could not avail my darling in the least. The women folk, as usual, had full sway. 'Twas they who had to battle with life and death. What use were my vaunted, manly qualities, though her life hung in the balance? I wandered about the glen, and threw pebbles into the flowing streams to kill the time, till nightfall. Every minute thus wasted my brain brooded continuously on the chances. Would she live? Would she die ? Ultimately my mind was worked up to such a pitch that I was frightened to ponder on the future. All my hopes and cares for life were centred on that maid who lay grappling with death. When dark hour came, I went indoors, but with no appetite for supper. No welcome news awaited me. Mother sighed, and said she was afraid my mistress was no better, in fact, a trifle worse if anything. I passed a night of fitful dozing. Many times I awoke with a sense of great oppression around

the heart; and to wonder how the fight was going. And when
the early sun rose furtively out of the banks of mist that hung
over all the valley, I jumped out of bed, and dressed myself
for another day of cheerless waiting. I opened the window
and looked about, and saw, but did not admire, the beauty of
the prospect. For long enough I sat pensive, and filled with
gnawing fears, with scarcely any hopes to balance them. Thus
I began the day to the tune of the humming of the bees, the
lowing of the cattle, and the pangs of trouble in my breast. As
I went forth into the kitchen, that place of cold comfort, I beheld Betty kindling a light to burn something wrapped in paper.
'Twas a thick mass of black-brown tresses, and rapidly my
thoughts hied back to that dismal spring morning I had first
set eyes upon them.

"Pretty hair, pretty hair!" I murmured, and touched it
caressingly with my fingers, then very gently with my lips.

"Fool!" growled John's great voice behind me, "you know
'tis fever-ridden?"

Ay, I knew right well, but recked the less because of that
hateful knowledge. Meantime Betty gave him a reproving look,
and me a kindly one, for she had not guessed this softness in
my nature. All that day I sought further news of Dorothy's
condition at frequent intervals; tho' in no word was there any
comfort. As time wore on, her strength went lower and lower,
and the delirium slowly gave way to a kind of stupor. Hourly
the issue went steadily against the nurses, whilst gloom en-
thralled me. Every time mother or Betty came from the sick
chamber, I scanned their faces, yet never gathered one spark
of comfort, nor did their tongues provide it.

About midday I learned that she had fallen quite insensible,
and all through the afternoon this preyed on me, and gave me
a sort of cold despair. The doctor did not come till the approach
of evening, and I had to keep myself aloof for a weary while in
anxious waiting for his verdict, for he stayed in the sick-room
an hour or more; and when he went away he left no solace.
Of course, immediately he had gone I tried to learn what his
opinions were. Mother and John were in earnest converse as
I came and asked for news. Mother said softly—

"Her condition does not improve, Ned. I begin to have
misgivings."

"Dost think she will get better?" I asked dejectedly.

"Get better!" she replied, taking me up sharply; "of course
she will get better."

"With all respect to you, mother," said Master John, "the

doctor said he did not see how she could last through the night."

"Thou nincompoop!" exclaimed dear mother very angrily, "is not my word as good as any man o' medicine's? He hath only book-learning to go by, and ne'er sets a hand to preserve life, unless it is by blood-letting, whilst I assist with my limbs and wits. So 'tis for me to talk like that when the occasion demands it. Take notice of me only in this matter, Ned, and not of the witless doctors." However, at this point her spirit gave out suddenly, for she finished by saying, in a sinking voice, and with great reproach to John, "You should not have told him that, you cruel fellow," and fell to weeping.

"So ye call it cruel," quoth he, in his heavy way; "hath the man gone so long without truth, that it offends his ears to hear it? If it is cruelty to speak in an honest, straightforward way, these wonderful new-fangled notions are one too many for my wits. Methinks the world is no place for a plain man nowadays."

With the delivery of this long (for him) and wrathful speech, he strode away in a mighty huff.

Having now heard the worst, I tried to take the news with resignation.

"If she must leave me, mother," I said, "let me see her for the last time ere she goes."

She granted my request, but altogether declined to accept Master Cooper's word as final. But I knew she believed the man in her secret heart. Upon coming to the chamber where my mistress lay, methought my spirits rose a little. This admits of no explanation, unless 'twas the mere sight of her was always enough to make them do so. When I saw the white face on the white pillow in the darkened room, and came to think of all its owner's former zest of life, and sprightliness, and fire, I could not keep my thoughts from the inimitable smiles that had flitted across her face, and the way her bosom had throbbed with life aforetime. Perhaps it was the overpowering sense of these things, or the knowledge that she was surely going from me, that made this sight the bitterest one throughout all the days of my adversity. Tears are inadequate at such ineffable moments, therefore I bowed my head to my breast, as once before I had done in her presence, and hastened to reach the cool night air outside the farmstead. It seemed to me that God had willed this parting as a punishment for my sins. Wherefore I strove to bear it meekly, and to reconcile my heart to its tenderest chords being torn asunder.

CHAPTER XXXII.

THE KING'S MEN TAKE THE FIELD AGAIN.

I CANNOT write down in detail, kinsmen, a full account of this night of trial and sorrow. This inability arises from the fact that all minor things were swallowed up in one great catastrophe. I may only say that I marched up and down our fields and meadow-land from dark till the hour of dawn, sometimes with a savage hopelessness, at other times with a resigned hopelessness, or far more often with a hopelessness neither savage nor resigned, but simply stupid. Perhaps 'twas only just that I, Ned Armstrong, thief, should have the prize plucked from my grasp as I was cherishing hopes of reaching it. Doubtless it was a wise and beneficent ordination, that a man should be punished according to his iniquities. Still 'twas hard, God knows, very hard! Fate, however, had surely willed this as my penalty, for Master Cooper, in face of common opinion, could not do wrong, much less utter wrong in matters pharmaceutical. And so I tramped about all night on the verge of desperation, and always with an abiding sense of a stunning blow, the extent and power of which I could not rightly gauge.

The harvest was now thick upon us, bursting through the hedges, ripe and ready for the reapers. These thoughts of harvest time and reaping recalled the bitter year of '85, and I was fool enough to compare their several depths of bitterness. Not that I could work the problem out to any degree of nicety, but mainly dwelt thereon because melancholy likes morbidity to keep it company. Despite the fair harvest, I trod among it wantonly; and as I thought of the destruction I was causing, I even felt a devilish pleasure to know 'twas nature's handiwork destroyed. Sometimes I felt the yielding wheat against my legs, or at other times the stiffer barley bristles; and heard the gentle music of the wind in tender-cadenced harmonies as it softly swished amid the ears of corn, and passed away, to sigh along the valleys, and to join the murmur of ever-flowing waters. All this! and to think of the young life ebbing slowly behind the blinds of the bedroom window yonder.

In the midst of my biting pain, the moon sailed out of a bank of cloud and flecked it with tints of silver. A cloud with a

silver lining! Yes, *I* remembered that, and the old phrase
seemed to mock me. How bald, how barren, are mere inani-
mate words to the affairs of life, to the events of a flesh-and-
blood existence ! When the moon was fairly risen, it showed
me where the white flaked tops of the oats were lying, side by
side with those of the rich brown barley. Once a rabbit brushed
by my feet and startled me for a moment, whilst after that a
corncrake set up a discordant croaking, and gave me a longing
to wring its neck.

Still all these things lasted a minute only. They perforce
gave place to a white-faced maid, battling with life and death ;
one who had loved me dearly. I have said I had come to
accept this as a settled thing of Fate, and that God had willed
it so. I strove to the utmost of my fortitude to support the
calculated blow of the Creator; but 'twas more than I could
endure. And what mortal man could endure this sudden snap
in the pride of life, this sudden blighting of young blood ?
Surely not Ned Armstrong. Thus he trampled down the corn,
and felt himself abused.

Swiftly the darkness slipped away, yet I had a wholesome
terror of the morning. But when the first beams of sunshine
slanted over the hilltops and made the limpid streams to sparkle,
I became a whit more cheerful, because light must ever
triumph over darkness. However, this was but a momentary
thing, for as the east grew slowly lighter, the old heaviness
returned in such abundance, that by the time the dawn had
fairly come I was a thought more miserable if such a thing
could be. By this the birds had set up a mighty twittering
over in the ravine, whilst I could plainly see the poppies nodding their dainty heads among the wheat, and the foxgloves
blowing on the bank obedient to the south wind that gently
tickled them. Howbeit none of these sweet things of nature
pierced the gloom that clung around my heart, but only made me
brood again on my bright new hopes and their early downfall.

At last I managed to grapple sufficiently with terrors to enable me to put an end to my suspense. Therefore I marched
off with a firm step towards the farmstead, to hear the worst.
Doubtless the· terrible struggle between life and death had
terminated now, thus I inwardly braced my courage up to bear
the stroke of the final disaster. As I was turning the corner
that gives the first sight of our house windows, I sharply
stopped, and felt quite unable to approach a step the nearer,
because I knew I might tell at a glance whether my love still
breathed, as according to custom all the blinds would be drawn

down if she no longer lived. Hereupon I halted, willing to bear more wearing fears instead of the knowledge of dreadful truth. However, I soon overcame this qualm, strode a few steps farther, and took a hasty glance at the farmstead. Oh, joy! my love was still alive, for all the blinds were up, save in one window on the second floor, set in a frame of the twining tendrils of the vine, and of the clustering green clematis. I felt a thrill of strength run through me, and a new hope rise in my breast. This sight had proved Master Cooper wrong in one particular. But soon this kind emotion vanished, as I really could not tell whether the chance of life had at all in-creased. Accordingly I hastened to the kitchen to gather the precise state of the sufferer.

"Where have you been, my poor boy, this night?" asked mother with a grave and sorrowful countenance, and with a tearful glance at my dejected bearing.

I minded not her words, 'twas her sad face I alone paid heed to. Surely there could be no misinterpreting it. Thus I dared scarcely ask—

"How lies Dorothy this morning, mother?"

"Oh, to be sure, how is the maid?" quoth she so diffidently that I was stung at her unconcern.

"How is she?" I cried excitedly.

"Dear, dear, Ned, I had forgot that you loved her so. Well, she hath returned to consciousness, and hath woke quite sen-sible. The danger is now past. I declared all along that I knew more about the matter than Master——"

I cut her words short by involuntarily flinging myself upon her neck and weeping in an ecstasy of relief. Joy had burst down the floodgates built by brooding sorrow. As for mother, no sooner did she realize my state of mind, than she burst out weeping too, to keep me company. Not perhaps that the oc-casion especially demanded tears on her part, but because it is part of a woman's creed never to let the chance of a good crv slip by, when she can conveniently and decently get one.

Modesty whispers me to draw a curtain round my excessive happiness this heavenly day, and to dismiss in a single sentence extravagant things I said and did. John viewed it all in silence, and with a cynical coldness, Betty was wondrous pleased with it, whilst mother treated it with mild surprise. This last-named person I took to task later in the day by virtue of such cool behavior.

"I cannot fathom your calmness in this matter, mother," I said.

"Nay, my dear boy," she replied, "I am by no means calm about it. I am glad as glad can be, and well nigh overcome with thankfulness."

"Verily you astound me, dear mother," I answered ; "you have scarce a word about Dorothy's marvellous recovery."

"Oh, oh! Mistress Dorothy, is it? Well, who would have thought of it? I declare I had clean forgotten all about her."

"Then who in the world have you been thinking of this glorious day?"

"Just hearken to this son of mine! What care I for all the girls in Christendom now that you have come back safe. Methought you had surely gone forth last night to do yourself an injury in your despair."

So this was the real state of things. It humiliated me to know it. I could not comprehend why my dearest mother should cling to me in despite of everything. Another person also shared my perplexity, for John scowled in the corner. This day I have treasured up in my memory throughout all these years. The clinching proof of the fact is that I recollect the exact date at this moment without help of memorandum. It was the 22d of August, 1688.

For all this joy, I had another trial to undergo, though to be sure a most insignificant one in comparsion with my former sorrow. The brave and skilful nurses now tyrannized over me. I was all eagerness to hold speech with my darling now she was quite sensible, and so rapidly mending. But neither of them would hear of it. Mother laid down two distinct reasons why I should not see her yet awhile. First, I must wait till she could leave her bed and sit in her room, because it was not a proper and respectable thing that a man should visit a maid who was obliged to lie in bed to receive him, unless it was a case of dire necessity.

Now, I would not hear of this for a moment, and sought to over-ride it as paltry, and as extremely Puritanical. Mother met my arguments at first by saying that "it did not become a Christian family," and that "folks might be tempted to talk and say things." Nevertheless, for my life I could not tell how "folks" were to get to know, and what they might say even should they do so. Then she said my father and herself would ne'er have dreamt of such a thing before they were married, and that the younger generation was nothing near so modest as it ought to be, and finally wound up with the old saw "that wrong was wrong, and right was right, but wrong was no man's right," whereat I was fairly beaten by the irresistible force of this feminine logic. The other reason was that the maiden was barely well enough to see me. I was obliged to wait nine days for the privilege of a sight of her; though in the mean time I had abundant proofs that her old life and spirits were returning fast. Twice in one day her nurses discovered her out of bed clad in her nightdress only, gazing wistfully out of window. And as I learned from her own lips afterwards, the only inducement that kept her in bed was the threat that she should be debarred from sight of me a a whole day longer for every time she left it without permission. Again mother came to me shortly afterwards, saying—

"Ned, Mistress Marvin is very pretty, and very wayward, and I shall learn to love her thoroughly; but betwixt ourselves she hath some curious and most unmaidish notions. Methinks her education must have been a truly strange one."

"Why so?" I asked genially, for I guessed what was coming.

"Well, just now, for instance, she asked me whether we had such a thing about the house as a book with plenty of battles in it. I confess I was surprised at the question, but told her we had worthy Master Bunyan's 'Pilgrim's Progress,' and that there was plenty of fighting therein. 'Oh, that is only make believe. 'Tis like playing at war with toy warriors, to read of that milk-and-water campaign,' she said. 'My dear,' said I, ' 'tis a beautiful book, and is filled with the deeds of noble Christian soldiers.' 'Christian soldiers, indeed!' she replied with scorn. ' 'Tis no wonder the devil's host gains so many victories in this world, for these Christian soldiers are ignorant of all principles of war, and sing hymns and patter prayers when they might more fittingly be employing their sword-arms. I' faith it is quite true what my dear papa always averred, that religion was a spur to courage, but a detriment to swordsmanship.' Then directly afterwards she asked Betty whether she had any knowledge of the art of fence, and if not she would be most happy and willing to teach it her. Really, Ned, I cannot understand this maid of thine at all."

I simply laughed at this, and mightily enjoyed mother's perplexity.

In the end my patient waiting met with due reward, for one afternoon Betty came to me smilingly, and whispered—

"Ned, if thou'rt minded to climb the stairs, methinks I can bestow a guerdon upon thee for thy pains."

In the twinkling of an eye Edward Armstrong had jumped from his chair, trod on the cat's tail, and was half-way up the stairs, with his sister following. Soon the best bedroom door on the left-hand side of the landing had been thrust open, and me pushed through it, whilst Betty had called out laughingly, " An unwelcome visitor for Mistress Marvin ! " and had shut the door quickly, leaving me alone to face the invalid. This struck me as being both kind and considerate of my sister.

My love was sitting swathed in shawls in a chair beside the bed, gazing out of the window. Her face was wan, and a coif covered her head, and her eyes were half closed.

At the beginning she did not look at me, and I may say this made me nervous. 'Twas so long since I had last seen her, and now she appeared so sad and grave and pensive, that though for the first moment I felt a wild desire to rush forth and embrace her, her serious demeanor restrained me, and caused me to stand six yards away, timid and bashful, with all my speech dried up. She turned her matchless eyes languidly towards me, and said still more languidly, and with all the airs of an idle lady—

" Master Armstrong, is it ? And how is Master Armstrong this pleasant afternoon ? "

" My darling," quoth I, and then stopped. There was something in her tone and manner that chilled and frightened me. Certes ! this was not the old Dorothy.

Again she looked at me, this time with mild surprise, and with a bewilderment pretty to see, only that it hurt me so very sorely. I quailed before her steady gaze and its strange indifference. Many thoughts crowded into my mind ; all of them unpleasant ones. What could this mean ? Had she forgotten me already ?

" My darling," I said again, but this time hardly above a whisper. Something seemed to incommode my throat and stop all power of utterance.

Thereupon she put her hand to her forehead as though perplexed, whilst my misgivings changed to tangible certainty, and awful fears caused my heart to sink.

" Ah, Master Armstrong," she said measuredly, and with a feeble glimmer of a smile, but only the spurious imitation of her former one, " I remember now, oh yes, I remember now."

This did but add to my pain of mind, for all the old fire, the old spirit, the old vivacity had vanished, and in place thereof there was nought but cold lassitude.

" So thou hast forgotten—everything," I gasped, sweat springing to my brow.

She clasped her wasted hands, with the blue veins showing through the skin, and dropped them in her lap. She lowered her eyes and turned her face away from me, but never answered.

"You may have forgotten me, you may love me no longer !"
I broke out vehemently, "but ne'er can I forget you, or what
we have gone through together. I have heard before of folks
losing their memories and their former ties of life by reason of
great maladies. Yet I have not been ill myself, therefore my
heart and recollection are quite unchanged. I must——"

"Hush, hush, hush ! Master Armstrong, I am far too weak
to bear such loud talk. I must beg you to withdraw if you
cannot restrain your tone. My nerves will admit of not the
slightest noise."

"Dorothy, thou'rt surely not in earnest. This indifference
is cruelty."

"Cruelty it may be, but oh, I must be honest ! I must not
deceive you, by allowing you to cherish false hopes, and false
expectations. Master Armstrong, I no longer feel towards you
as I used to do. I—er, I—oh, I," she stopped and surveyed
her twitching fingers. My heart was like a lump of lead by
this. There was no hope for me in the marble face and the listless eyes. Little had I guessed that any ill, no matter how severe, could change a warm nature to a cold one, could change
passion to harsh indifference, could change kindly recollection
to stern forgetfulness !

"So, Dorothy, this is the end of all that hath passed between
us. Oh, my love, how can you ?" I cried wildly, and a sort of
madness came upon me.

Still her face was cold, calm, impassive ; whereat I swore
softly as I thought unto myself, kicked over a chair, strode past
her, turned my back towards her, and looked out of the window too.

"Ned, thou energetic gentleman, don't be so hard on the
furniture."

That was the voice of the old Dorothy. I turned again and
confronted her in an instant, and saw the face of the old Dorothy too. I saw the wonted fire in her countenance, the wonted
smile about her eyes and lips, and the warm blood glowing
'neath the soft skin of her cheeks.

"You once called me a goose, Ned, I believe."

"I may have done, perchance."

"I now call you a gander, sir, and with far better reason."

"But, my love, thou hast been very hard on me this day."

"Delighted to know it, young man. I meant to be. The
punishment hath been severe ; I hope 'twill be remembered."

"But what have I done to merit it ?"

"Just hark at that now ! Well, if you do not know, Master

Innocence, I will be at the pains to tell you. Here have I been sound in mind, and pining for a sight of you for nine whole days; whilst you, you coward, have been tyrannized over by a parcel of women, though in perfect health, and quite capable of resenting their behavior. Not so me, for I have been laid by the heels, my clothes taken away, the room door locked, and all manner of threats employed to keep me snug between the sheets. I have come to loathe these four walls, and to be bitterly angry for Ned Armstrong's neglect. But, I say, dear lad, I played my part very neatly, did I not? and have paid you according to your deserts. My word, sir! thou hast a fine knack of swearing soft and powerful, tho' 'tis not a gentlemanly habit. Very clever of me, I think."

"You young witch!"

"Now, lad," she said, in her sauciest way, "you may give me one kiss. Yes, methinks I have the strength to bear just one, providing it is proffered very nicely."

In the face of this encouragement, I gave her not one, but many more than the stipulation.

"Oh, Ned," she said, with girlish vanity, "is it not a pity that my pretty hair is gone?"

"Shows your snow-white neck to all the better advantage, love."

"And what of my thin cheeks, sir?"

"They allow of three extra dimples when you smile, dear."

"Very adroit, my lad; very adroit."

And then she fell to talking of her near escape from death, and for at least an hour filled mine ears with nought else but the praises of mother and Betty, who most certainly between them had saved her life. 'Twas fine to hear the warm-hearted young creature pour forth her words of gratitude, her cheeks flushed by their owner's earnestness. Yet the last words my loved one spoke to me that day touched on an entirely different subject.

"Ned, women are not expected to fight, are they?"

"Certainly not."

"I am pleased to hear thee say so. May God ne'er let me behold another fight. I have seen but one, and that I shall remember till my dying day. I must always shiver when I think of it. You and Sir Nicholas were like raving tigers who had smelt blood that night. Ne'er can I forget your eyes. Methinks they have seared themselves into my brain; and henceforth there is at least one woman who will be quite content to leave all fighting to mankind."

My mistress mended very rapidly now. Day by day her strength came back, and with it all her former gayety, playfulness and quick impetuosity. Albeit, there was one alteration in her sentiments. Her dead sire to her was glorified ; she did not once mention the circumstances of his murder ; and on one occasion when I chanced to embark upon the story for the enlightenment of the family, she rose hastily from her seat and left the room. And the next time she found me alone she besought me never again to allude to it in her presence ; adding, and her eyes were cruel—

" Ned, whene'er I think of the murder of that noble man, it seems a reproach to me, his child, that the wretch who wrought the deed still lives. Sometimes when I am alone it almost maddens me to think Pringle goes unpunished. Mayhap one day he will be in my power ; and then——"

Her face caught something of her dead sire's murderous look, and her mouth went hard and merciless. She looked noble, nay, magnificent, in her fierceness and her untamed passion. Once before had I seen her thus ; then she had been my enemy, but was now my friend and darling. This bare thought sufficed to keep me happy for hours afterwards.

Steadily the days slipped by, and each one seemed to give my love a greater glow of health, and a riper, fuller beauty. Never before had she known the meaning of feminine love, intercourse, and sympathy. Now all these good things were hers, and they gave her heart a warmer zest of life, and a larger share of joyfulness. But, strange to say ; her nature was not softened in the least. That word " softened " must not be ascribed to me, kinsmen. Should I live to be as old as Methuselah, I will ne'er admit that it needed any softening, as methought it quite soft enough already. Still, mother would maintain, in face of me and even my wilful mistress, that her spirit was far too high for a maid, and that (to use no stronger word) it needed softening or mellowing. She declared it did not become a girl to fence and play singlestick or quarterstaff with the male sex, to ride barebacked horses over five-barred gates, to beat the dogs into submission. and go badger-hunting with them afterwards, or to talk so much of war. However, despite these defects, mother was obliged to admit many times over that she loved Dorothy as a daughter of her own. And every time she said as much in my hearing, my cup of happiness seemed filled up to the brim.

I was truly happy throughout those sweet days. I was now waiting for Prince William's coming, and every morning I jumped out of bed it gave me joy to know that I had twenty-four hours the less to wait for his arrival. But one night, in the midst of all this happiness, John came home with heavy news hot on his tongue. 'Twas to the effect that Captain Pringle had received reinforcements from London, and that once more they were keenly questing me. Also a rumor had gone abroad that Black Ned was still in the county; and that a Nether Stowey yeoman had actually set eyes on him, scarce a week back, one morning among the Quantocks. It was evident from this that I must leave my present life of peace and comfort without delay; and that night when I retired to rest my slumbers were nothing near so pleasant as of late they had been.

CHAPTER XXXIII.

THE SUPERIORITY OF KING'S MEN.

'Twas no longer safe to bide under the sheltering roof-tree of home. I must be away if I sought to save my neck. Hiding-places were scarce, and the best of all methought was the one I had so lately occupied. There was but one drawback to it, and that was lack of food. Wherefore the three women, all eagerness for my preservation, undertook between them to keep me well supplied, promising to convey it secretly into the copse.

Two days they acted thus; yet ere the third had passed I had no further need of their bounty. In the early morning of that day, thinking that I might with safety venture forth into the open for a little while to ease my legs, as they were weary of being cooped up in so narrow a space, I was walking leisurely near the manor gates, when the hoofs of a horse sounded close by; and before I could spring into hiding, a voice cried, "Good morrow, my friend."

'Twas my vanquished rival the Frenchman. I tarried and held speech with him. Though neither of us bore any enmity towards the other, M. de Crois was not satisfied.

"Monsieur," he said, "you beat me. Being a stranger to defeat 'tis a thing to chafe my blood. Pray let me see your steel again—one more passado is the vanquished's privilege in France, and I think the same holds with gentlemen all Europe through."

I could not refuse him without greatly lowering myself in

his estimation, and it would have put me sorely about to be thus belittled. Accordingly, I acceded to his request, yet strictly premised that, should I fall before him, he was to place me under the care of Master Whipple, even as I had conveyed him to the Green Man at Taunton. My hope of success was of the scantiest, and, to add to my predicament, love did not urge me on this time ; 'twas simply a duty I owed to the vanquished. Granted that my claims to honor were peculiar, 'twas honor alone which prompted me now to engage.

We crossed swords within twenty yards of our former meeting-place, tho' now the sun had not reached any power, the dew lay on the grass, and the air was chilly and refreshing to the temples. The count made no vain display on this occasion, but went grimly to work, and ere I could retaliate he had set three sharp thrusts at my chest which needed great alertness and agility to escape. This man was a master of the art, as I have said. He fought me brilliantly, and there was no withstanding his skill and impetuosity. He drove me back from his restless blade, and do as I might, I could find no chance of averting the threatened catastrophe. My breath quickened, and the sweat crept on my forehead, still that merciless steel was quivering before my eyes, and seeking for its chance. And it duly came. I repulsed the vigorous onset more feebly every time, till at last the sword-point slipped my guard. I felt as though red-hot skewers were searing my flesh, my eyes swam, my head grew dizzy, and everything—the twittering birds, the lowing cattle, the dewy fields, and that maleficent rapier—settled into one universal blank.

* * * * * * *

When I opened my eyes, and could see and think and feel, I was not exactly sure whether I was wideawake, or had passed to the land of visions. I lay on a bed in a strange room, and it was filled with loud-voiced fellows, and close by my elbow knelt a chirurgeon looking me over keenly.

"He hath regained his senses, friends," he said, as he perceived my open eyes.

"Well said, sir ! Let's have a look at my admirable gentleman."

This was spoken by a voice which made me wish I was still unconscious. The little Pringle shoved his face between me and the red bed-curtains. He shook his fist in my face, and then, in excess of devilry, tweaked my nose viciously with his other paw.

"Oho, Master Thief!" he cried, showing two rows of teeth in an ungentlemanly grin. "Y'are mine at last. I ne'er forget my debts. You've escaped me once; yet 'tis the final time. A sweet length of hemp and a handsome gibbet-tree await you."

The others crowded round and looked at me in unmistakable delight. The generous captain called for wine and treated his men round. They danced and sung, such was their pleasure; and all the time I lay with a fearful pain in my right side, which forced a groan at intervals. 'Twas a refined torture to be lying helpless there, watching their joyfulness.

Having drunk plentifully, the little captain commenced strutting up and down the room, and declaiming very powerfully anent the immense, nay boundless, superiority of King's men over all other species of mankind.

"He, he!" sniggered the captain. "Trust King's men to carry a matter through when their minds are set upon it. We are not sheriff's officers and country dolts. We are differently fashioned; we say a thing and we do it, or else do know the reason."

To this day it hath ne'er struck me that 'twas any special display of ability on their part which brought about my arrest.

It appeared that when the count, according to the compact, was bearing me to Bridgwater on his horse, by a strange misadventure my enemies happened to accost him on the way. They beheld me insensible, and forthwith took custody of my body and bore it to the Green Man, Taunton, where they halted to partake of wine on the strength of their good fortune, and also, as I shrewdly suspected, to wait awhile to let the news of my capture get noised abroad, so that the townsfolk might assemble in force to see me borne with triumph to prison.

Having bibbed enough for the time being, my captors procured a shutter to bear me further on my way to jail, which, indeed, was not far distant. 'Twas an irksome passage down the stairs on the comfortless wood, carried on the shoulders of my captors, whilst their leader strode on jauntily in front, bidding the crowd, in his most aggressive and authoritative manner, make way for the upholders of justice and the public peace.

All the town seemed to have gathered and were surging in the path; but I was quite able to meet the eyes of the grinning, staring multitude. Mayhap 'tis one of the misfortunes of a great man to be trampled on when he doth chance to fall. Nought is too good or gracious for this same person when at the zenith of his glory; yet, when the downfall comes, the mob spits upon him with no better reason than they cheered him in prosperity. So 'twas now with me. Hundreds whom I had not harmed, and who had previously shown me favor, now howled and cursed with the loudest. 'Twas a mighty mob, a restless, glaring, threatening mob, and, moblike, seeing me quite incapable of resistance, threatened me repeatedly with divers kinds of violence. Natheless I laughed and scoffed at it, for I was always gifted with the rude surface courage that flourishes in wild animals and the lower types of man. This proceeding further incited them, and they became more aggressive in their abuse. One coward came forth and slapped my cheek to express contempt the better; but this laudable desire was fraught with infinite disaster, for a splendid fist shot out from the arm of a still more splendid fellow, and the coward dropped like a log 'midst the roar of the multitude. The smiter was my brother John.

CHAPTER XXXIV.

TAUNTON COURTHOUSE : TAUNTON JAIL.

My heart sank as the jail gates closed and thereby cut me off from the living world. The governor, a fat, heavy-witted fellow, came forward to meet us as we reached the prison yard, and, after expressing his great pleasure at the morning's work, led my five bearers and me along a dark corridor in the forbidding building itself, and from thence to a small, dark, bare room, with a stoutly barred window set up high in the wall, and a thick door of solid oak, grated at the top, to confine me securely. Seeing my condition so weak and unhappy, a mattress, a rug, and a blanket were allowed me in lieu of the wooden pallet usually allotted to prisoners.

When the door clanged to, and the jailer's key turned squeaking in the lock, I threw myself on my meagre couch and felt that my end was near. My wound gave me much agony, though the bleeding had been stanched. Every hour was fraught for me with grievous pain of mind and body, whilst my hurt ne'er seemed to mend a whit. The chirurgeon came to my cell once a day to tend it: and very zealous indeed was he for my well-being, that I might come to be decently hanged. 'Twas a wretched, fretful, exasperating time; and to lie prone and helpless awaiting the gibbet was not the slightest consolation. The assizes were close at hand; hence I had not long

21

to linger.   As the days passed my weakness of body increased, and my state of mind further aggravated it.

One morning, maybe a week after my arrest, the governor of the jail came to me and bade me rise and follow him; for the justices were down from London on their Western circuit, and they were now awaiting my appearance at the courthouse. Soap and water did their best to redeem my countenance somewhat; tho' even then I was but a woe-begone apology for a man.

'Twas a short journey to the courthouse, and it was made in a guarded vehicle.   The place of horror was packed as tight as it could be by a throng of pitiless spectators, who, with unanimity, bent their eyes on me as I was ushered into the dock. I failed to mark them then, as I almost thought I beheld the Lord Chief Justice in his scarlet robes, such was the power of imagination; yet 'twas not so, for three judges were installed on the dais who had less devilry than he.   And as I looked about, I thought to see my father at my side, and the other eight prisoners near him.   I thought to see the crowd of grinning soldiery, and to hear the japes and bellowings of Jeffreys. Then I suddenly recollected my present predicament, and I e'en wished that times had not changed since then.   Three years agone I could have faced God with name unsullied; but now I was sold to the devil, and was dishonored in His sight.

The multitude craned their necks and obtained a view of me, whereupon each wallower in curiosity looked questions at his neighbor.   Could this miserable, wan-faced creature be the man who had set three counties agog with amazement? who had tricked and flouted justice, and had made the sheriff and his men a laughing-stock?   A buzz of wonderment arose, whereat their lordships cleared their throats and reminded Master Usher of his duty.   Directly that same buzz was hushed, and the sombre-garbed lawyers fidgeted in their seats.

The men of law had come from London in considerable force to represent the King, and 'twas quite educational to see their mass of papers, and to mark the restlessness of their pens. Very generously His Majesty had allowed me a small gentleman (who was forever bobbing up and objecting) to plead for me.   And a monstrous fine pleader he was too.   He might have drawn tears out of a stone, yet never once out of the grand jury.   They were all blue-blooded Tory squires, from whom I had extorted the richest part of my booty, and when an unusually brilliant burst of eloquence arose from my small lawyer, somehow they always happened to be occupied in blowing their noses, or in helping themselves to Black Rappee.

The trial, like most of its species, was a mockery. I had to be hanged, and every one in the place was aware of the fact; and none better than myself. Perhaps 'twould not have been respectable for me to have been hanged without a lot of word bandying : 'twould mean taking bread out of the mouths of the attorneys. Their lordships were quite grief-stricken over my iniquities; the crown lawyers descanted at length upon the number and extreme wickedness of my crimes; whilst the witnesses came one after another to contemn and damn my frail character.

Captain Joshua Pringle stood forth in the witness-box, amidst a hum of admiration from those assembled. He spoke at length, and detailed with surprising imagination my hunting down and capture, and the desperation of my resistance. His veracity was properly rewarded, as he was publicly complimented by their lordships. The candles were lighted ere the end of the farce was played. At last the men of law ceased their babbling; whereat I waited dull and desperate for the end. The sentence was proclaimed aloud with its luxurious wealth of detail (even to the disembowelling), as so parlous a rogue entirely merited. I had ten days left to live—in which to make my peace with God. At daybreak, on the eleventh morning, the sentence was to be carried out. The judges were solemn as death itself; the lawyers, after their immense exertions, took advantage of the moment to snatch gulps at the liquor, which reposed in small bottles in their several pockets; the jury were gleeful; and the spectators clapped their hands in approbation. There was not a wet eye amongst them, which made me thankful, as it proved that none of the home folk were present. I preserved a reckless, defiant demeanor in face of them, and was grateful that I had still the strength to show so bold a front.

I was taken back to my dismal cell, with ten days to live. At first all emotion was frozen up. I lay stunned and devoid of care, yet 'twas but the calm before the storm. Neglected precepts will oft be rekindled, even though they have lain dead for many days. 'Tis not in our power to thrust aside early teaching and exhortation altogether. Kinsmen, we may trample upon it if we will, but its embers will indubitably smoulder, choosing a seasonable time to blaze again into a living fire. This resuscitation is greatly to be dreaded by strong men, tho' more especially by weak. And I was a weak man. I had turned my head away from God, and had served the devil faithfully; and had now ten days to live. Ten days to undo

all that had been done. As I have before averred, conscience
is a coward. It invariably waits till its victim is crushed by
adversity ere it makes the grand assault. When the mind and
body are alike attacked by some eating malady, and the gates
of hell are looming large within the brain, then down comes
conscience, grim and merciless. I had tried to cajole my mind
into believing that after all I had been too harsh in the judgment of myself. However, ere morning came, I had swept this
notion away forever. Ten days is a little time, and how to
employ it to the best advantage, I did not know. I sought to
make my peace with God, and once I tried to pray, but could
not do so with any inward sense of propriety. No, I could not
pray. I might frame the words, yet they did nought to mitigate my sins; there was no inspiration in them. In the morning I claimed a condemned man's privilege, and asked for a
clergyman. A Catholic priest was sent me, and he talked
about Confession, et cetera, and was particularly pat with the
Scriptures. He stayed two hours, and was doubtless a well-
meaning and holy man; but methinks he was a source of detriment to my temper, and no benefit to my soul. As I was
lying under sentence, my friends were allowed to see me, therefore that same afternoon my mother visited the jail to say farewell. She came paler than a ghost, and her white face hurt me
cruelly. She stood by my mattress and looked down at her
wasted son. I had nought to say to her at first, and she had
nought to say to me. She drooped her head, knelt down and
took my hot hand in her own.

"My poor boy!" she said at length.

I did not answer, and she stroked my head and wept bitterly.
By and by words came to my tongue, and I mumbled them with
rapidity; fearful of a failing voice.

"Mother," I said, "I have not much longer to live. Wilt
send Tobe Hancock to me? I must have speech with him,
'tis for my soul's well-being. I have been base and weak, but
have not dragged our name through the mire. None know that
I am your son; and I beseech you preserve the secrecy. Give
me your forgiveness and your blessing, and when Prince William comes, bid John go leave the plough and fight, remembering father, and tell Dorothy——"

I broke off short at my darling's name; my utterance was
choked. 'Twill be seen my last words were those of vengeance.
Even as I faced the grave 'twas rampant in my mind; a bitter
thing to harbor then, but one far bitterer to acknowledge afterwards. And then to leave my mistress, the one who had braved

so much for me, and whom I knew full well was longing for the Dutchman's coming, not for her own sake, but for mine—to leave her, added bitterness to a cup already overcharged with gall. 'Twas unseemly, I am aware, to countenance such thoughts as these at this awful season, yet I cannot alter truth.

Mother kissed me, and said good-bye; and when she walked away and left me, her steps they were unsteady. I, who guessed the tortures in her breast, stared at the chinks of the grating up in the wall, and watched the streaks of daylight glimmer through it. I watched them till there were none to see; till the darkness gathered, and there was no longer any light. I had asked mother to send Tobe Hancock to me, as methought he was a man who might prepare me better than any one else for what was about to follow. That night passed with more horror than the previous one. My wound pained me grievously; the hurt ne'er seemed to mend, and as the hours went, I felt the fever rising in my frame, whilst the torture of my brain continued. Nine days to make my peace with God.

Towards noon, next day, Tobias arrived. He came to me very grave, and with a dignified sorrow. He took my hand in his great brown one, and looked at me straight and simply, and somehow hope came into my mind at mere sight of him. I had half feared he would spurn and revile me, in fact, that he might e'en refuse to come and see me. However, I had misjudged him. In days gone by, I had flattered myself that I knew him and his character better than other people, yet 'twas plain even I did not realize his virtues in their full capacity. He gave me a look with his deep brooding eyes, and by some means I managed to tell him where my trouble lay. He said nothing for a while, but ultimately told me I was not so bad as he had at first supposed. Hereafter he talked to me earnestly, yet soothingly and gently; then read the Bible in his homely tongue, and explained the import of his reading with simplicity, but with acute knowledge of his subject. He ne'er grew tired; but meant to save me, if flesh and blood could do so in the time. He expounded and revealed to me many things connected with Holy Writ, of which I had hitherto been ignorant. He visited me morning, noon, and night, was ever the same; he had no fire of the zealot now; and was always calm, soothing, patient, unwearying. He avoided the past, but threw his whole soul into the work that lay before him. Albeit, the ten days that were left slipped by, one by one, and as each one fled my fever of mind and body grew.

In the day-time I could rest with tolerable ease of brain, yet when the stealthy horrible darkness came, the tortures of fear and remembrance seized me in a grip of iron and held me fast. The piety, the zeal, and the real friendship of Tobias lightened the misery of the day, but the black, haunted night, ah me! I cannot tell the horrors of it. The inflammation of the wound wrought horrid pain, and kept sleep from my eyes; therefore I did nought but groan and toss about and heap maledictions on my pitiable state. Despite the efforts of the blacksmith, I could not resign myself to death. I dared not think of the hereafter, though 'twas so fast approaching. And being so weak I surrendered to pitiful revilings. I cursed my friends, I cursed the King, I cursed myself; and directly I had thus delivered my puny soul, I grew terrified at my position. To die so infamous and unrepentant appalled me, yet what could avail? I might curse or I might pray. 'Twas all to no purpose; wherefore I became a victim to despair. If I could live a few weeks more I might make my peace. But no, 'twas not to be. I must die a thief and unforgiven. Was there no way out of that dread cell? Mine own understanding could think of none. What chance had a man so grievously stricken of escaping? Here another bitter thought came to me. The man who might be of the greatest service had made no sign. Peter Whipple had ne'er once appeared. If any mortal could assist me in my present pass, assuredly 'twas he. 'Twas a cruel reflection to think he had deserted the sinking ship. Why did not Peter Whipple, my friend and hero, come? He of all men might assist me, yet held aloof. He had renounced my cause, despite his many fair professions. Death had already a hand on my shoulder, but that did not prevent me giving mine host of the King's Head a malediction in the middle of the night. And having done that, I remembered the next night would be my last on earth.

Towards noon on the following day, another visitor was ushered into the condemned man's cell. One glance told me 'twas my darling. At that sight misery overpowered me for the moment. I had wished ne'er to set eyes on her again this side the grave, since all thoughts of her added one hundredfold to my tortures. What man could bear to be so vividly reminded of his loss?

I was alone, for Tobe Hancock was not yet come. Dorothy came towards me in her usual bold resolute fashion, yet no smile enhanced her lips, no joy shone in her eyes, for her face had a distracted look, and she shuddered when she saw me so haggard and strangely altered. She took both my wasted hands in hers, and pressed them so hard that in my feeble state I winced.

"Dear lad!" she said softly, and gazed at me with a power of wistful sympathy. Her face told me many things, yet not one was so plainly noticeable as the look of dull despair that had settled on it.

"Perhaps I ought not to have come," she said, still holding my hands; "but, oh, my lad, I could not keep away! I know it hurts thee to see me, and were I in thy place 'twould be the same with me." Again she looked at me, and I saw her eyes were heavy, and that her nether lip was quivering. "Methinks circumstances are too strong for us this time, Ned," she said, and her sad tone conveyed an after-taste of bitterness. "I have done all I can, but have failed in everthing, Yet I would not like you to leave me, thinking I had not struck and fought for your cause, and mine own."

I could not fathom her meaning, but she divined my perplexity.

"I have been to London," she continued. "I saw my lord Danby on your behalf, but he declared he could not help me, as he was in disfavor with His Majesty. Then I saw my lady Churchill, who hath much interest at Court. She declined to assist me, and as a last resource I pleaded for you before the King himself. Nay, I begged on my knees for your life. He was harder than the steps at Whitehall, for he laughed and said—— But I will not pain you causelessly by repeating his cruel answer."

No words can show how that simple story appealed to me. It told me that the world was not wholly bad, that men and women were not wholly pitiless. The staunch, indomitable spirit of the dead knight lived again in her who stood before me. She had done a thing that few would have dared to do. Her promptitude, her daring, her courage, and her steadfastness all touched my heart together. Yet now she had to acknowledge defeat, and she did so, brave as ever, though it called for noble fortitude to keep her eyes dry, and her sobs from breaking forth.

"Ned," she said simply, "we have fought much together; we have endured much for and from each other—this is our hardest fight. But we have had some happiness—my sweet love, I will remember always that rainy morning in the spring."

She fell upon her knees beside my mattress, threw her arms around my neck, and drew me like a mother to her breast. She kissed my hot lips, and I think did inhale the fever of my

soul, since she rose with a wailing sob, and in the wildness of
passionate despair cried out—

"O God, thou art unmerciful! Thou hast dealt cruelly with
me!"

I saw the young head droop; the noble lift of the neck was
no longer there, and I knew the proud spirit was at last subdued
and crushed. We parted here, and our farewell had such in-
effability that at first I felt a sweetness in it: love had brought
us very near to Heaven.

But as the cell door clanged to, and my love was lost to me
forever, the twilight seemed to gather round my heart, and I
began to long for death, as an antidote for present pain and
torment.

CHAPTER XXXV.

THE SIGNAL OF DEATH.

No sooner had the maid left me, than Tobe Hancock came
to pay his final visit. He said farewell an hour before sunset,
having done all that mortal man was able for the saving of my soul.
My kind friend had exhorted me to be of good courage, and
held out great hopes for the hereafter. As long as he remained
by my side I felt calm and hopeful; but as the sun waned and
the gray light dwindled into murky darkness, the fever rose
within me, and by the time the night had completely gathered I
lay moaning and tossing and thinking of the dawn. The dawn
was to mark my last hour of earth. To lie there wounded and
helpless, awaiting something keener than the sharpest pangs of
death; bereft of hope and reason; contemplating futurity as a
black ungodly horror, was in itself an appalling nightmare.

However, 'twas not the time for regrets; all such were useless.
But I felt I could not die with ease of mind. An hour agone I
had cherished the delusion that the blacksmith had equipped
me sufficiently for my end, but now I was only too well aware I
could not die. I clung to life. I clutched at it with every
fibre strained to grasp the fleeting thing. But it mocked me!
I could feel it ooze from my nerveless fingers. It laughed at
me. It was going from me. I prayed for it to stay, I implored
it, I begged it, yet it mocked me! As soon as daylight came it
would desert me. Every minute, every second it was fleeting
gradually away. I implored it to stay a while; only a little
time. I went down on my knees and besought it. I cried to

it, I wailed to it, yet it mocked me. My hands and brow grew cold, and my body shivered. Following that the fever rose and burnt me with a consuming fire. My wound was a live coal, in my side. I cried out in anguish, but the walls of the cell were unresponsive. Frenzy seized me ; I tore my hair and bit my hands, and beat my head on the walls and the mattress, and raved and raged and sobbed. The tempest of my madness grew, but my screams and cries were unavailing. The dawn must see the end.

A muffled noise came thro' the grating of the cell. 'Twas the dull blows of the carpenters' hammers. They were setting up the scaffold.

I snatched up the rug and blanket, and buried my head therein, but those devilish sounds still beset me. I thrust my fingers hard into mine ears, but to what purpose? The hammers never ceased. Then other noises forced themselves upon the ear. A murmur, a gentle creeping murmur like the sea, rose stealthily and mingled with the other dreadful sounds. It grew and grew, till it was hoarse and maleficent. It arose from thousands of throats, and their owners were gathered without in full view of the scaffold. They were there to witness a cheap entertainment.

The babbling multitude had come from north, south, east, and west to enjoy itself ; and included godless men and godly ones. And the godly ones : far better rob the Church than rob an honest man of an execution. Fancy the righteous creature not to be permitted to stand in front of the scaffold, and not to be allowed to howl at the criminal, and shake his fist at him, and spit upon, and fill the air with abhorrent malediction. Imagine this honest fellow not being allowed to shake his head, and sigh, and groan, and exclaim with pious fervor as that criminal dies before his eyes, "Oh, what an example!"

The execution over, the sainted gentleman will hie homeward to read a homily to his friends and family upon the enormity of sin, and the fruit it bears ; and proceed to dilate upon the glory of honesty and uprightness, and will sleep in peace o' nights, firm in the conviction that he hath discharged a duty due to himself and his fellow-men.

How excellent thou art to be sure, sir! Nevertheless, kinsmen, I would have you observe that some are born to wealth and affluence, and never know the feel of an empty belly. Their granaries and coffers are forever full. Then there are others who cry aloud for bread, who know not a roof on a winter's night. Well, what of them? Surely it is their function to provide an example for Master Honesty, the lord of the manor, and to furnish him with the sight of an execution, that he may borrow self-esteem therefrom, and have an example for his children, and a pretext to perambulate his piety.

The sounds of horror increased even as the crowd did. I could not lie down and listen. Half mad I staggered about the cell, and bruised myself on the brickwork. Yet the noise increased.

It was a heavy, close, dull night, with a storm evidently in the air. I could scarce see my hands before my face, so thick were the clouds that obscured the moon.

As the time of the dawn drew nearer, I grovelled on the cold stone floor. 'Twas the coolest spot I could find for my burning head. Verily, but a short time was left. And then my heart jumped into my throat as I heard footsteps along the corridor, and saw the glint of a light. I had just time enough to seek my couch ere the key grated in the lock. The heavy door opened, and two men entered. The foremost of the twain was the governor, bearing a bunch of keys and a lanthorn.

Surely my time had come, for methought his companion was the executioner. He was a very little fellow, darkly enveloped in a cloak. They approached my mattress.

" So this is the rogue," said the little man in a thick, husky voice.

" Yes, your honor," answered the governor.

Perchance some of you may disbelieve the facts I set down now. You are quite at liberty to do so; but I remind you, were they truthless I should not now be relating my adventures.

" Master Thompson," said the little man again, " what is that document I see just peeping out of the prisoner's breeches pocket ? Kindly seize it, and hand it over to my custody."

"Which, your honor ? What, your honor ? Where, your honor ? " inquired the flustered governor, bending down and rummaging my person.

Suddenly his eyes nearly bolted out of his head, and I confess my heart stood still, for the little man bent down too, and rammed the muzzle of a pistol to the governor's forehead.

"Not a murmur, or y'are a corpse." Thus spake the gentleman with the pistol.

Next he drew another hand from underneath the folds of the cloak, and in it I beheld a curious little phial. He pulled out the cork with his teeth, then said to his victim in a subdued tone—

" Drink this, Master Thompson, without speech or delay.

'Twill not kill you. 'Tis but a sleeping draught, and ye must sleep whilst I transact a little business. Time is scant, and I have much to do. Drink!"

The bewildered governor took it hesitatingly in his hand, but did not make any sign of swallowing the draught. Thereupon his assailant whispered a peremptory threat; whereat, with a frightened, dismal glance, the victim tossed off the drug whilst his enemy grunted satisfaction. The pistol-holder still kept that weapon hard by the governor's cranium, till in a little while the victim yawned and rubbed his eyes, and a minute later he dropped his head close by me in excess of drowsiness, and fell fast asleep.

Meanwhile I knelt on my couch half-petrified with amazement. What could it all mean? I was soon to learn. No sooner had the governor gone to sleep, thanks to the potion, than another and well-remembered voice came out of the folds of the cloak. It bade me rise, and make not the slightest noise. It was the voice of Peter Whipple. He had come to save me. Faith! neither mind nor body were in any condition for any exercise whatever; yet no sooner did I hear his voice and his words than my strength rushed back, and, dazed with wonderment, I sought to do his commands.

He impressed on me silence and expedition. First he produced a thick cloak similar to his own, ordered me to envelop my person therein, then proffered me a phial, but I promise you the contents of it were somewhat different to the other one.

With stealthy footsteps we went out of the cell together, leaving the unfortunate governor snoring with his head on the mattress. Having already secured the sleeping custodian's keys, Master Whipple locked the cell door after us. He then bade me follow close at his heels, and he would pilot me aright.

The great building itself seemed quite deserted by the turn-keys and the various officers of the jail. My true friend led me along a labyrinth of corridors, down steps, and up others, through several doorways, and out at last into the blessed air of heaven. We ne'er once encountered any person. Pete seemed endowed with the most marvellous knowledge of his whereabouts, and never halted in his course, but appeared to know every nook and corner of the prison.

When we reached the yard it was so dark that we had to grope our way along, yet Pete never swerved, but took me across it to a small wicket let into the outer wall of the jail. With the governor's keys he unlocked it; we stepped together into the world outside; and I was a free man once more. We were now at the back of the jail, whilst in front were thousands awaiting the dawn.

We went along several deserted by-streets, and thus left the town behind us, without being once accosted or molested. I could not then grasp the entire significance of this sudden metamorphosis. Arrived at the Bridgwater road, mine host of the King's Head asked me whither I intended to fly. He declared his own hostel, though quite at my service, would not be a safe place. However, when he told me the King's men had returned to London, and that they would have nobody to lead them in their search, I decided at once to return to the farm, for none knew who my parents were, and certainly the pursuit would not be nearly so hot now it was left to the sheriff only.

I promised to pay Pete a visit as soon as possible, that he might clear up many strange matters, and that I might bring him a reward in kind, if possible, for his magnificent services. With an honest hand-grip I left him, and that was all the thanks I could muster at the moment, my heart being too full for my tongue to be of any service.

I set out for the hills as briskly as possible, for despite the darkness, I was able from long practice to find my way. Yet, ere long, I became aware of my inflamed wound and my weakness. Cruel spasms of pain staggered my steps, and now the danger was past for the nonce, my feet grew heavy as lead. 'Twas a weary process this journey to the farm; tho' my mind was still much occupied with the most marvellous circumstances of that night. I could not fathom how Pete had managed the matter in so wonderful a manner.

'Twas a long while before I had traversed the hills. Gradually the east lightened; and I was dragging a pain-stricken body over the heather when the path became more and more distinct. Suddenly I stopped and turned; and looking long and fixedly at the eastern sky, beheld the dawn in its beauty and its kindliness. And this was the signal of death. Thereupon, for the first time after my renunciation of God in the shadow of my father's gibbet, I fell upon my knees and blessed Him.

CHAPTER XXXVI.

THE HOME-COMING.

I took the turn for Chilverley. My heart almost over-flowed with thankfulness at the extraordinary revelation of God's mercy. Nevertheless, I had an irksome journey home-ward, and the longer I kept the road the severer became my suffering. My teeth chattered under the nipping morning air, each limb had a palsy, and my body was racked with pain. But the nerving thought of freedom prevented my fainting by the wayside, though at every score paces I was compelled to halt and rest. Thus I dragged myself along, and it appeared hours hence ere I set foot in our rickyard.

As I slowly passed the sweet familiar scenes which I was spared to see again, the tears were in my eyes, though they were not unmingled with a tinge of gall, when I thought how such bounties had been vouchsafed to me, the weakest and most errant of God's creatures, who, at the first assault of mis-fortune, had turned from Him and had deserted to His arch-enemy—the devil. Ay, there were all the old landmarks—the duck-pond, the dove-cotes, the hayloft, the bean-stack, the old house itself, the kitchen window, and the kitchen door. And at sight of the kitchen door, I stopped to get breath, because a great ordeal was before me. Then I went forward with creeping steps, lifted the latch, and tottered inside. Mother, in speechless misery, sate upright in an armchair near the fireplace. The two girls sate a distance off, huddled together, Dorothy's head on Betty's shoulder. Both were staring hard and vacantly into the fire. The place seemed instinct with the very atmosphere of death ; its horror was reflected in the wordless terror of those three faces. Their cheeks were whiter than the breakfast table-cloth, yet their eyes were strained and dry. Mother, looking to-wards the door, was the first to see the spectre, and at sight of it she screamed, lurched, and fell forward on her face. What then happened I cannot rightly tell, because I was seized with dizzi-ness, and my brain turned to a kind of vertigo. But I have a distinct remembrance of my darling crying out, " Speak, Ned, speak ! Is it really thee ? " and of feeling her warm lips on my cheek.

After that, the room swirled faster and faster round me, my limbs tottered, though what was the next event I cannot say for certain. I know I found myself in bed without any effort on my own part, and that I lay for a weary while in a manner scarcely sensible, burned with inward fire. I remember tossing and writhing, head chaotic, and body consumed by fever. Yet throughout this purgatory there was one who ne'er left the side of my uneasy bed. 'Twas one who had wide brown eyes, and gentle soothing fingers. 'Twas one who assuaged my thirst when I cried for water, one who plied cold cloths about my brow, and with a cold light touch sometimes caressed my forehead. Once I recollect an awful agony convulsed my side as though red-hot irons seared it. And I called on God to be merciful to me, a sinner, for 'twas as though the last bond of life was breaking. But, in the course of time, the fever died down slowly, my pains grew less, and my brain came back to its normal state.

Then I heard from mother's lips how my darling, to the wonder of all the household—that a mere girl could do a thing so bold, so brave and skilful—had saved my life, by burning out the morbid flesh from my neglected wound, and had thus performed a cautery upon it, though during the operation my cries had rang through all the house, and though my noble mistress had fainted immediately after its performance. Not but what she stoutly disclaimed all knowledge of this latter feat, declaring 'twas a calumny invented by jealous-minded folk to set a blot upon her character. Be this as it may, 'twas quite a natural thing to do, for it was positively unheard of that any other than a chirurgeon should handle raw wounds with such determination.

In the matter of the nursing Dorothy tyrannized over mother and Betty. She took the entire responsibilities of the case upon herself, and by some means bore it through. As I learned at a later date, whene'er at this time she said a thing, she did it, in spite of the utmost opposition ; yet when others offereda suggestion, it was only carried out subject to her approval.

Now this is really singular, seeing that mother and Betty had a large faith in their own abilities. Yet the young maid, at the very outset, whilst the other two were still unnerved by the great shock of my return took sole command of me, and kept it throughout my illness. And when they came to tend me on their own account, they found my darling in full possession, and she said at once, without any disrespect for any persons, " that if her lad was left to her she would undertake to pull him through ;

yet if others had a finger in the pie [yes, she called it "pie!"]
she would not answer for the consequences."

This was taken in excellent good part, for they both saw my
love so bold, so ardent, and determined, that they knew it was
said in excess of earnestness, and without meaning offence to
anybody. Accordingly she sat by my bedside night and day,
refusing rest or offers of assistance, but just watched, and
worked and waited.

Thus there came a time when my speech was once more rational, and my head less afflicted; and presently a joyous day
when I was allowed below stairs for one hour only to begin
with. The women folk, without any such thing as parley, turned
Master John out of the chimney corner, and set me in it with
cushions for my back, rugs for my knees, and a hassock for
my feet. Yet what pleased me more than anything was to see
John sacrifice his chair with a tolerable good grace. And the
first words Dorothy said to me, after I was snugly installed
therein, were—

" Ned, Dutch Will hath put to sea!"

She spoke them softly, so that none but I might hear. Now,
this speech surprised me greatly for the time, seeing that it had
been uttered at such a joyful moment for us both. But no
sooner did I behold my darling's lustrous eyes and her eager
face, and the look of power that had come upon it suddenly,
than their full significance was borne upon my sluggish mind.

In the Dutchman's movements and the success of his mighty
enterprise lay our future. So long as the Stuart held the throne,
we must both remain outlaws, and be kept apart by stress of
circumstances; yet, if Prince William could by any means be
placed permanently on it, our troubles with the law would then
exist no longer. Thus every action of the Protestant champion was eagerly noted by the pair of us, and every effort he
made towards hastening the coming struggle we hailed with
joyful satisfaction. All men in England at this time cast their
thoughts across the water towards him who was to deliver the
kingdom from the papist and the bigot. And it was plain to
everybody that the throne could only be snatched from its present occupant by the arbitrament of blows. Thus the maid and
I waited with ill-concealed impatience for the day when I could
draw my sword and go fight for both our rights and liberties.

It may have happened, kinsmen, that some of you have been
tempted to do my mistress an injustice by virtue of my poor
powers of narrative, or—quite as likely—by virtue of the thickness of your heads. Perhaps you may wish to know how it

was that Dorothy, professing to love me so very much, should yet be so willing and so anxious for me to risk my life when I could easily bide at home and let others do the risking.

In the first place, she was so utterly fearless herself, that this quality was the one she cherished, cultivated, and admired the most in me ; and as she told me, just previous to my duello with the Frenchman, " to have a coward's fears for a true man's skin was only to insult him, and to fall in his estimation."

Now, by this term " true man," without any manner of doubt she meant a fighting man, for, thanks to her martial rearing by that fierce warrior, her father, she ever adjudged man's real vocation to be to fight for his hearth and honor ; or, in times of peace, when the trade was quiet, sooner than not fight at all, it behoved him to draw his sword for a little entertainment, and to keep his hand in. Well do I recollect her saying to me, on one occasion, " Ned, my lad, I do not know that your virtues are any nicer than your neighbors', neither am I aware that your intellect is greater than is barely decent for a gentleman ; but your sword-arm, dear lad, is the thing that puts silly notions in my head, and makes me admire you from a distance." Whereupon she sighed, a splendid light came in her eyes, and every feature seemed inspired with pride. And when I asked for the interpretation of that sigh, she answered, her voice full of awe and reverence, " I sigh because that noble arm o' thine sets you so far above me, and because it does not appear a thing in reason that a girl like I should ever gain you for mine own."

Thus, in face of this, I make bold to ask you, kinsmen, was it at all likely that one with so fine a spirit would seek to deter me from employing the gifts of which nature had given me such a liberal endowment ?

And I will add yet another reason, so that none of you shall have excuse to mistake my lifelong darling's high-strung, romantic nature, for cruelty and hardness. She had faith and fatalism. Her prodigious faith in my prowess shamed me at times, it was so deep and so unbending. As for her fatalism, it was greater than that of any woman I ever knew, and quite rivalled that of men who are soldiers born, who possess this strange quality in more abundance than plain civilians. She ever quoted her old father's tenet that God never left aught to occur as chance directed it, but that a man's term of life was determined at his birth, and that no amount of danger in the interim would cause him to quit the earth ere his appointed time, and no amount of care would let him live beyond it. But while I have been safeguarding a precious name from defamation, I have been forgetting myself, who am the chief, if even the most unworthy person in this story.

Day by day I mended slowly, yet always had a haunting fear upon me. Many a night the face of Captain Pringle afflicted my dreams. He had returned to town, tho' at any moment he might come back reinforced for the purpose of my recapture. And what added to my fears was the knowledge mother one day imparted. She declared that on the previous occasion the King's men had received sufficient information to make them suspect Chilverley of harboring me, and that for two days and nights the valley had been carefully watched by them. This thought gave me many qualms, and ever kept me on the tiptoe of anxiety regarding news of their reappearance.

That last night in Taunton jail dwelt often in my mind; and the thudding of the hammers and the murmurs of the multitude gave me many wakeful hours, and put cold beads of sweat upon my forehead. And what made this nightmare of sights and sounds all the more appalling was because I knew God had been so merciful, and that I deserved the punishment the law designed to give me. It will be seen from this that two great thoughts, one of hope and one of fear, ran side by side in my brain throughout every hour of my existence. Who would come first, Prince William of Orange or Captain Joshua Pringle? The hopes and fears begat by this hard problem seemed to churn in my brain till my head would throb with very weariness. And when I thought of the Dutchman's coming I would feel a thrill of joy, yet when I pondered on the law's strong arm and its tender mercies, I would lie awake for hours in the silent night, to weep softly to myself and to rise with red eyes in the morning.

Now I know quite well this is a pitiable thing for a man to do, and a still more pitiable thing to confess it afterwards. But this I will at once admit, and will at the same time unburthen my mind of a far bitterer and far more cruel secret. It is one that makes these lines come from my pen with pain—*I was no longer a strong man!* I was cut down in the pride of life; made old before my time. The old animal courage was there, the general outline of the body, and the old hopes and aspirations; tho' instinct told me that a great cord of life had snapped —the cord of fire and strength, the cord of buoyant spirit and firm endurance. At first I tried to laugh at it, then to thrust it aside, and then to disbelieve it. But all these attempts were vain. The ugly truth steadily impressed itself upon me. Then

22

I became frightened and oppressed with morbid terrors. Yet the hard fiat had gone forth, and I had to bend the head and bear it. From that day to this it hath abided with me. 'Twas as though my young brain had been blighted, and my young limbs bereft of stamina and vigor. Henceforward I was a creature without backbone, without resource, without reserve of strength. My spirit was broken, my soul was crushed, my tenacity was withered. I could feel the claws of suffering as if for all time they had been dug into my soul. This was the penalty exacted of the flesh for days and days of torture, for weeks of misery, of striving, of longing, of terror, of despair. Very rarely hath man to pass through such awful crises as I had had to do in one short epoch. And, kinsmen, whoever that man may be, he can rest assured nature will exact full payment for the undue strain upon her.

To all outward seeming I was still the same, and, knowing this, I carefully hid the dread secret from them all. The cruel fact added one more skeleton to my cupboard, for every hour since that discovery I have carried a young death in my heart, and a fear within my soul.

As time sped, and autumn continued its work of desolation, the nights closed in, the cold winds stripped tree and hedgerow, and nature changed from cheerful green to sombre brown. My wound took excellent ways, as in such hands it was bound to do; my health came back, and my limbs were knit into some semblance of their former firmness.

One day we heard that Dutch Will was expected, whilst the next rumors were rife that a big expedition was being organized in London to arrest Black Ned. Thus I was kept in a rotation of elation and solicitude. However, one night, ere any great event befell, a thing happened that fully deserves some mention. One evening, about the middle of October, when the rain was falling in torrents, and dripping monotonously on the dead leaves in the orchard, we were all ranged round the fire. John and I were smoking meditatively, and the women-kind were trying to play commerce, to talk, and to cheat each other at one and the same time. Presently a loud knock came to the kitchen door and startled the five of us. An evening visitor, except Tobe Hancock, was quite an event at Chilverley. 'Twas certainly not the blacksmith, for he ne'er stopped to knock, but always walked straight in.

"Make haste up the chimney, Ned; they have come for thee!" quoth Dorothy, laughing, whilst John made for the door and opened it.

"Does Ned Armstrong bide within?" asked a voice there was no mistaking, and the next instant a small personage hopped between the shadow of the door and John's big body.

'Twas Peter Whipple. For a moment he stood wiping his muddy boots on the mat, whilst the wet dripped from his cloak and formed quite a stream on the floor. However, no sooner did he behold the ladies than he whipped off his hat, and bowed to them with London courtesy.

Instantly I left my seat, shook his hand warmly, and said, by way of introduction, "This is the gentleman who delivered me from death."

This was all-sufficient. To be sure, at the announcement, John retired silently into his corner; but in a trice Dorothy was setting Peter's hat and cloak to dry before the scullery fire, mother was pouring forth her thanks, and Betty was preparing a meal for his delectation.

I may here state that on the night of my escape I had told Peter of my name and place of refuge, which methought was the least thing I could do to show my confidence in a friend so true. He expressed himself well satisfied with my restoration to health, but declared he should scarce have known me out of doors, and that I had aged at least ten years.

I shivered at this remark, and indulged in melancholy thoughts. Albeit supper drove them all away. 'Twas as happy a meal as any I remember. Betty was constantly stacking Peter's platter with the choicest the board could offer, and continually saying, "Have some of this, Master Whipple; I can recommend it," whilst mother was forever looking at him with shining eyes.

He bore all this without turning a hair, but simply went on eating. Howbeit Mistress Dorothy, in the end, made his face kindle with a look of admiration. For that vivacious maiden, by some means, filched mother's keys, took a candle, and tripped down into the cellar. And when she returned she carried a grimly cobwebbed bottle. 'Twas delightful to see her withdraw the dusty cork from the black neck of it very deftly, then to see her purse up her pretty lips, as she held a glass to the light, and with the utmost care pour very gently forth the rosy liquor. Then it was Pete became mightily interested, for in her practised fingers 'twas well-nigh a work of art the way she kept the ancient crust entire. Next she presented the brimming violet-scented wine to him, a smile rippling round her eyes and mouth.

"There, Master Whipple, this will drive the cold out. 'Tis

the Château Noir vintage of '41. I'll warrant three glasses of it would put an ordinary man under the table; but, sir, thou'rt by no means an ordinary man, that is if deeds are aught to go by."

Now this speech, delivered with all her high-bred gracefulness, and accompanied by her insinuating charm, completely knocked Peter Whipple from his vaunted cynical serenity. He bounced up like a shuttle-cock, took the wine from her, saying—

"Your health, my fair mistress," and drank it with indescribable politeness.

Henceforward his courteous and gallant behavior would have done credit to a Buckingham. This methought was very strange in Peter Whipple, and it tickled me very much. 'Twas the first occasion I had seen him in female society, and when one came to think of his harsh sentiments towards the sex, his demeanor was a thing to marvel at.

"Damn the women!" I whispered in his ear on the first occasion.

"Ay, damn 'em all but that one," he whispered back, looking across at Dorothy. "She warms the cockles of my old heart. 'Pon my soul, I'd have a—[here he wiped his old unlovely lips] were I—— "

Just then I pulled his ear, whereat he stopped, and saw much meaning in my countenance. At least, I opine he did, for he murmured, "Lucky dog! lucky dog! she's almost worthy of Long Bob Bickers," and subsided into silence.

Supper over, friend Pete was pestered into giving a full account of the things that had wrought my deliverance from death. He gave it with an excellent grace, though not before John had performed a most irregular act—indeed, nought less than to charge his richest colored clay. He handed it to the story-teller, that his thoughts might be thereby more readily composed.

Now all along I have fully recognized that, should I ever come to write my history (I have had the plan in my mind for years), 'twould be simply affectation in me to try to put in black and white, word for word, all that Master Whipple said, or to convey to paper his delightful way of saying it. Therefore I asked him at the time to write it down, which he very kindly did. But before you read what he hath written I will presume to say a word. Though, undoubtedly, his pen narration is very fine and accurate, it lacks that wealth of warmly colored detail that so embellished the efforts of his mouth. He was a born talker. Beyond an hour he held five people spell-bound, and

used every oratorical parliamentary trick in vogue to supple-
ment his story. Mayhap his second narrative may seem bald
and unnatural to you—it certainly does to me by comparison
with his first; yet I would have you remember that the whole
chronicles the feat of a man of a transcendent genius, and that,
were the gist of what he says inaccurate, Black Ned would not
be writing this.

———

CHAPTER XXXVII.

THE SINGULAR NARRATIVE OF PETER WHIPPLE : SET FORTH BY HIMSELF FOR THE INFORMATION OF POSTERITY.

To me it has occurred that, sooner than let a great deed die,
a man should be at pains to set it down for the behoof of others.
Moreover, when I gave the full narrative (I flatter myself, in
my best manner) to my juvenile friend Armstrong, he was so
impressed by my natural abilities that he begged me to put it
on paper in mine own style to give to his children, since he
said he might some day chance to sit at home and write his
life. Therefore being, as the late Robert Bickers always said,
very willing to oblige, I will proceed to commit it to paper,
though I know nothing about authorship ; nor do I want to.
'Tis a very idle trade ; a man who works with three fingers
only must be a lazy devil, unless he be a pickpocket. Not, of
course, that I shall fub you off with inferior matter. A man of
my capacity can turn his hand to anything, and pass muster
with the best. Anyhow, I promise that it shall be *better written*
than aught of Gentleman John's. A nephew of mine, by trade
a printer, once showed me a sheet of the fellow's manuscript.
'Twould have disgraced a pot-boy—letters ill-formed, words
crossed out and written over, and divers names that no simple
Christian uses !

I suppose the man, being paid to do what his betters do for
nothing, must think it detrimental to his dignity to use genteel
king's English, or to write a clerkly hand.* But look to yourself, John Dryden ! Many's the time I've filled a flagon for
you—'twas always small ale, and you'd wait for the farthing

* The Editor feels it only kind to mention that Master Whipple's handwriting was, for the seventeenth century, almost copperplate ; although his
sentences, if very ornate, were also friends to redundance, and were at
times involved, whilst his spelling was not so strong as his self-esteem.

out. Look to yourself, I say! I'll show the world what Peter Whipple can do when he dips the quill in the ink.

*   *   *   *   *   *   *

The countryside was ringing with great news: Black Ned, the boldest rogue (save one) ever known in the West had been condemned to death the previous day. He lay in Taunton jail. Three justices from London had tried his case, and twelve jurymen of the county of Somerset had sate and heard his crimes recounted, and between them had adjudged him guilty of them all, had declared his worthless body forfeit to the King, and his sinful soul forfeit to the devil.

There was a little man in Bridgwater town who was strangely exercised in mind over the news of this harsh decision. A very little man he was indeed; he stood but four feet eight inches in his shoon—though tradition is sure to tell you that his brain was out of all proportion to his size. It was a warm morning, and this stunted gentleman stood on the threshold of his own doorway, with a pipe in his mouth and his hands deep in his breeches pockets. Immediately over his head a sign-board hung motionless, and artistically displayed thereon was a man of high degree, a flowing periwig adorning his head, and a monstrous hook nose his countenance, whilst for the admiration of unlettered persons, and for the information of the passer-by, "Ye King's Head" was writ underneath in letters of gold.

The jacketless person in the hostel doorway was pensive and disconsolate. A scowl trimmed his visage and a bad word his tongue; as after staring straight and silently before him for twenty minutes by the clock of Bridgwater parish church, his lips parted of a sudden, and a deep "Damn!" tripped down the street to mingle with the sweet air of the countryside. He said to himself: "'Pon my soul it's hard, very hard, and such a nice open-handed, generous lad as well. He had the makings of a great man, but, hang it! he hath got to go like the rest of 'em. 'Twas a shortness o' breath and three yards of hemp that was such a mighty trouble to mine old friend Long Bob Bickers." Here these painful reflections were curtailed by the appearance of a handsome youth, attired exactly in the mode, who had a straight carriage and a polished manner. He inquired for Master Peter Whipple with the accent that comes from France.

"That's my unworthy self," promptly says the man of sorrow affably. "An' if my lord be blessed with a thirsty throttle, I'll make so bold as to set before him the neatest flagon o' Madeira that ever winked in the foggy land of England."

"Peste, landlord, bide awhile! I am come upon another matter, and one that touches my private peace. I must consult with you apart."

The man threw out his words in a breath, and in the comic manner of the foreigner; but what pleased Master Whipple was the nervous glitter in his eyes.

Immediately the gentleman was conducted to a nice little parlor at the far end of the passage. Arrived there, he delivered the following curious statement to a bewildered listener, who meanwhile redonned his jacket out of respect for his guest, twiddled his thumbs, and clustered his brows thicker than a Hampshire wood :—

"Master Innkeeper, I am in a hard strait, and come to beseech your help. Doubtless you have heard of the capture and sentence of one Black Ned, a notorious highwayman. I fought the man twice, and entered into a binding compact. I did not know his reputation, else I should not have touched his blade nor his body; but no matter, I found him strictly honorable in all particulars. On our sacred words, we swore on both occasions, that the victor should take the loser to a place of safety, providing the latter was sadly hurt, and the places agreed upon were—for mine own person, the hostel of the Green Man, Taunton, and for himself that of the King's Head, Bridgwater. The first time we met, he was the winner, and at serious risk to his neck he placed me, incapacitated as I was, in the place of succor named. Then we met again, and out of pure condescension to the vanquished, he fought me. On this occasion I defeated and disabled him, and I weep to tell you, as I was bringing him to your hostel his enemies met me on the way, and seeing his body, did take it from me, and now, by mine own default, he lies condemned to the scaffold. I have come for your aid, as I know of none other to render assistance. Help me save him, forgetful of cost; my honor is at stake! Money I will not stint; aught in reason shall reward you; I have great estates in France."

The Frenchman wrung his hands in despair, and his face spoke of shame and excitement. He talked much of his honor, his virgin honor, and continued to implore the assistance of the innkeeper.

As has been said, the proprietor of the King's Head had an uncommon share of brains; whereby his perspicacity was greater than that of mankind in the bulk. Besides, our landlord had a reasoning cast of mind; hence his intellect supplies what we exhibit hereunder :

"Here is a man with money, and money is the nucleus of business. He is young and a Frenchman. He thinks his honor is jeopardized, and from London experience I am aware a Frenchman's honor is tenderly made. He is willing to pay any sum in reason in return for a service. True, the service is difficult, but bank-notes strengthen the brain. Again, it is to save the life of a friend; and if friendship and business cannot stimulate the mental faculty, what can? I have excellent reasons for undertaking Black Ned's escape. I will procure it for a consideration, a pretty substantial consideration. Even should I fail, if I be wary, I need not suffer thereby, and shall at least have tried to save a friend. Certainly, I have not the remotest idea at this moment how the matter is to be performed; but men with my abilities need only a quiet ponderation and we have a plan. Now, Peter Whipple, I will at once put you on your highest mettle by accepting a respectable offer."

This soliloquy had taken place in three minutes. We hope the gist of it is understood.

Meanwhile the Frenchman opposite was not nearly so enlightened. Therefore, with babylike impatience, he drummed nervous fingers on the table, and spilt snuff as he conveyed it to his nose.

The three minutes having come to an end, as all time must, Master Whipple, calm in voice and manner, stared his applicant in the face, and answered—

"Good sir, I have considered your case. Black Ned is a friend o' mine, and for no other living soul would I wittingly jeopardize my neck. I am about to endanger mine own valuable life (and I have a wife and ten children) to save this man's. But, observe, sir, I must receive the sum of one hundred guineas down as an earnest of the bargain, and nine hundred more if I succeed in effecting the highwayman's liberty. And, mark you, 'tis pure friendship alone which prompts me to make this offer."

The count never thought at all, but seized the innkeeper's hand, wrung it, and offered him every groat of the money demanded should he bring matters to a successful issue. Be it remarked, this Frenchman was young, very young, with so many emotions that let us trust he will lose the majority of them ere he reaches maturity, else his magnificent patrimony will certainly have dwindled to a beggar's pittance.

No time was lost in making the bargain, and let there be not the slightest misunderstanding; Master Peter Whipple undertook for the sum of one thousand guineas due a fortnight from date, to deliver a notorious rogue, one Black Ned, from jail alive.

Item: the said Peter Whipple at this moment had no better idea how to accomplish the deed than the man in the moon.

The Frenchman left the King's Head with hope springing up in his heart. We presume he made allowance for genius. As for mine host, he whistled a dirge-like melody, and administered a severe reprimand to himself, as he muttered, "Burn my soul, an old fool is the worst o' fools! Had I asked two thousand instead o' one I must have got it." Admittedly this was avarice, yet stay, we are here as narrator and not as commentator. The worthy innkeeper next gave clear orders to his lad Tom, that he must not under any circumstances be disturbed for three hours. Then he locked the door of the parlor, took down his church-warden and his tobacco jar from the mantel-shelf, set forth a mug, and a jug of his October, measured a beaker, sat down beside the table with knitted brows, and thought in silence till his eyes grew dull. Bear it ever in mind, he had not the smallest idea how the deed was to be accomplished, observing the while with equal care, that a thousand guineas is never lightly lost by men of business.

The little man sat in his parlor, noonday sunshine illumining the room with a benevolent beauty. The bees hummed lazily outside, the cattle afar off on the sunny downs basked in the summer warmth, the crystal springs and waterbrooks shimmered and sparkled under the glorious rays, all nature was happy, peaceful, and serene, and an impertinent fly stood on a wart on the little man's nose—undisturbed. Ah, reader! mark you that, for this man of prime intelligence heeded not the brute creation, nor the soulless world of insects. He was thinking. And he thought, and thought, and thought, till he had consumed a gallon of October, and had smoked ten pipes of the best Trinidado.

Then, as the sun was waning in its beauty, as the busy insects lessened their activity, the impertinent fly aforementioned received a rude shock as the man of brains sprang up with an exclamation, and clapped his hands and danced about the apartment. "Pete, my friend!" he said in self-communion, "thou art a great man, a very great man indeed, sir. I see that thousand, ay, and I feel it too. Friendship and business man, friendship and business, they keep the world a-moving. This affair shall set a seal to thy triumphs. Better 'tis even than those London affairs, and a cool thousand, too. Whew! God bless thy soul and body!"

Master Whipple had had reward at last. *He had an idea.* He was not a man given to causeless ecstasies. He knew the meaning of business, and therefore was fully aware of the virtues of a thousand guineas. And for this idea. Keeping the door still locked, he produced a clean roll of parchment out of a cupboard, an ink horn, sealing-wax, a quill, and a knife. Again he divested himself of his jacket, inserted the knife in the lining thereof, and ripped it open. There fell out a strip of white sheep-skin, inscribed on which were these words—

> "*It is by Our order and express desire that the bearer hath done what he hath done.*
> "*Given this day under Our Hand and Seal.*
> "*(Signea)* JAMES REX."

Peter Whipple smoothed it out on the table, then chuckled. For the next hour no sound disturbed the stillness save the scratch, scratch of the quill. The words on the clean parchment were written in a bold, methodical, clerkly hand, yet towards the bottom corner of the document two words of five and three letters respectively were totally different from the others, and these two cost the writer more labor and screwing of the mouth than all the rest together; but when imprinted he sighed satisfaction and remarked, "Like as two peas, by Gad!"

Then followed a delicate and laborious process, in which a stick of red sealing wax bore a prominent part; however, an hour's steady work saw the task completed, whereupon more satisfaction followed. Peradventure we are over bold, still in pardonable curiosity we glance over the little man's shoulder and behold a sheet neatly writ as follows :—

> "*Order to admit the honorable John Peake to the jail of Our loyal town of Taunton, that he do superintend and carry out every arrangement he may deem fit to ensure the full execution of Our justice upon the person of one, Black Ned, a notorious malefactor, who hath sinned and plotted deeply against Our State and Person.*
> "*Given this twentieth day of September, under Our Hand and Seal.*
> "*(Signed)* JAMES REX."

A comparison of this and the lesser missive revealed the fact that His Majesty's seal and signature appeared duly set forth on both, yet how they came on the larger one we neither dare nor desire to tell.

Suffice to say Master Whipple chuckled again, concealed these missives in his breeches pocket, unlocked the parlor door at last, went upstairs to his bed-chamber, and donned the finest raiment he had. He carefully curled his wig, put a dainty pair of shoes with untarnished silver buckles on his feet, an elegant rapier against his thigh, Mechlin lace ruffles on his legs, and donned a white cambric shirt, a coat of gorgeous satin, and breeches of purple plush. Mayhap to a Londoner this apparel would have looked out of date, but what did country rustics know of current fashions? Having hunted up an equally elegant hat and cloak, he descended to the parlor, and took the two documents therefrom. Decently furnished with gold, he set out in the twilight for Taunton jail. He went forth rapidly, and never once slackened speed till the frowning prison gates forbade him farther progress. An authoritative rattle on those portals brought a man from the porter's lodge, who admitted Peter into the prison.

"My man," quoth the little gentleman in a tone which admitted of neither delay nor parley, "conduct me at once to the governor. I am on the King's service, and have ridden express."

"Yes, your honor," and the fellow bobbed a rustic obeisance.

Thereupon he led him to a well-lighted room in the jail itself, and this room was occupied by a man, middle-aged, fat and sleek, whose eyes and countenance had no more expression than the bottle of port at his elbow.

With an imperious gesture the little gentleman dismissed the man, and waiting till the door had clicked behind him, without a word, Master Pete handed the governor the larger of the two documents. That person perused it.

"The King!" gasps he in an awed whisper.

"Yes, and now read this," says Pete, giving him the second slip. Yet whilst he fumbled for it, the governor deftly but fearfully slid the bottle under the table.

The governor read, and Peter spoke, not in his usual way, but in the mincing tone of the London gallant.

"D'ye see those, my friend? They mean full power. I represent His Majesty."

Of course he represented the King; of course they meant

full power. Had not he, Joseph Thompson, seen that identical seal and signature on the death warrant which had arrived that morning? In the eyes of Joseph Thompson, the man he most respected, in that shire, at least, was the gentleman who stood before him. Fancy that small person to have full powers vested in him by the King; to have implicit confidence placed in him! Did not his credentials declare as much?

" Now hearkee, governor," says the Londoner. " I am come a-gallop from Whitehall on a matter of deepest import, and have but tarried to change my garments, for, ah, Lard! I ne'er did see the like o' these roads for dust. Now, this matter concerns the State, as ye shall learn. Are we quite alone and free from intrusion? Let a word escape, and the secret's advertised."

Having locked the door, the governor assured him such was the case. Then Master Whipple made him swear an oath of awful solemnity not to divulge a single hint of what he might tell him. The governor did as he was ordered, and the pseudo king's emissary, in a whispered tone, made the following statement; long ere he had ended the narration the governor's heart was beating his ribs in stress of excitement.

" D'ye list to me, man. 'Tis more than your office, or your neck, is worth should ye fail me in this matter. Bend your ear the closer. There is a daring and far-reaching conspiracy on foot to set this rogue at liberty. To the world at large he is known as a highwayman only. Mayhap it may surprise you to learn he is the vilest and most desperate political plotter of this century. That is the reason he hath been left in the country to be hanged, that less publicity may be drawn to him. He is really a man of the noblest birth, but is so mixed up in skilful and wicked plots to dethrone His Gracious Majesty, that so long as this arch villain is alive, the King cannot sit securely on his throne. But, by the mercy of God, these traitors are delivered into His Majesty's hands—he hath got wind of the plot. The conspirators' daring plan is as follows: The attempt is to be made an hour before the execution, which, I hear, is fixed for daybreak on the 10th. At that time the plotters, eight in number, are to climb along the roofs of the houses in Blue Boar Alley, which, you are aware, adjoins the north end of the prison yard. They are to drop from thence on to the top of the wall, and so gain admittance to the jail. Then, fully armed, they are to make a rush, overpower your unarmed assistants, and liberate the criminal. Desperate scheme, is it not? But here is our side to the question. We will catch them in the act; they shall be condemned by their own deeds. Every one of your jailers, including the executioner, must be armed to the teeth and lie in readiness under the shadow of the wall, and await their arrival, so that as they drop over they can be easily seized and bound. Now, again, I must impress upon you that on no account are you to breathe one word of this; the slightest indiscretion may set the conspirators on their guard. But, when the hour arrives, you are to give your men the necessary instructions, and you and I (the only officials left in the jail) will, to avoid the least miscarriage, attend the prisoner in his cell."

The governor, being a simple-minded man and a faithful servant, most implicitly carried out Master Whipple's behests, so that when the time arrived Fortune declared herself to be entirely on the side of intellect. No hitch occurred; and whilst the dupes were watching one side of the jail wall, like dogs over a rat-hole, the thick-witted governor was drugged by the false John Peake, and that notorious malefactor Black Ned was released, by means of the wicket-door in the southern side of the prison yard, forty-three minutes prior to his intended execution.

CHAPTER XXXVIII.

THE ARRIVAL OF WILLIAM OF ORANGE.

Now, when this tale of one man's nimble wits was ended, John rose solemnly and shook his hand with fervor; and afterwards mine host of the King's Head was exalted to one degree above a hero; and if ever man deserved mouth praise, ay, and purse praise too, assuredly that man was Peter Whipple. The story made a profound impression upon all who heard it, and to this day I can ne'er think of it without marvelling at the stroke of genius that gave me life, and himself a thousand guineas. I may remark, in passing, that since then I have been able to add another thousand to his honorarium; and also that I ne'er set eyes upon M. de Crois again; but he married into a noble Breton family within a year after these events, and subsequently gained soldierly renown under the French King Louis.

Pete took his honors meekly, as is seemly in true heroes, and fell a discussing with John and me the chances of the approaching struggle between the Dutchman and the Stuart.

In the mean time much rivalry was going on between the girls in the mixing of a cup of schnapps for friend Whipple's especial benefit. Now, Betty, getting the spirit first, clearly held the upper hand in this competition ; and Dorothy, though trying all her coaxing powers, and afterwards her trickery, to obtain possession, eventually failed to do so, and was obliged to execute the menial offices of adding the sugar and hot water, whilst Betty stirred the mixture, and set it by the recipient's elbow, and quite naturally counted on the praise. Albeit when Master Whipple took a sip at it, rolled it round his mouth to test its quality, and said—

"Blister me! this is the finest and most potent liquor ever made by the hand of woman. Never before hath my palate been suited to such a nicety."

At this, quick as lightning, ere the less nimble-tongued Betty could make a suitable reply, Dorothy courtesied her acknowledgments, and answered, methought somewhat saucily—

"'Tis a rule of mine, sir, on the rare occasions I have the honor to provide liquor for gentlemen of stupendous intellect, to mix it exactly twice as strong as I do for men who have no more than their share of brains to boast of."

Whereat Master Whipple smiled at her, and pledged her three times in the bowl; whilst Betty bit 'her lip and looked mighty vexed at the enterprising and triumphant Dorothy.

"Lucky dog!" called out Pete again across to me, so that all could hear him.

Now everybody showed signs of fully understanding his meaning except my very innocent mistress, who, having coolly regarded each smiling countenance, had the impudence to seek an interpretation of this remark from him who had uttered it. And so deft was she in the employment of that nimble tongue of hers, that Pete, despite his London cleverness, was promptly cornered, and had to use plain English to extricate himself, to the amusement of us all.

The hour was late ere this congenial gathering was dissolved by the departure of Master Whipple. He left a wondrous reputation behind him. Betty declared that his high, expansive forehead certainly betokened greatness; whilst mother said the shape of his head and the cast of his countenance showed it quite as clearly. And so deficient is every woman in logical conclusions that Dorothy, of course, was entirely of their way of thinking. But methinks hard-headed John somewhat put them out of countenance when he growled, with irritating sobriety—

"Humph! anybody can see Whipple's a very great man, what with the pomatum on his hair and the buckles on his shoon."

Whence Dorothy, who felt she had been bested, crept laughingly behind him, and cuffed his ear, exclaiming—.
" Thou solid nuisance ! "

Upon retiring to bed that night, and on reviewing the events of the evening over in my mind, there was one matter that called for some consideration. 'Twas the way that my love had managed in three short hours to captivate Peter Whipple so completely. His looks and bearing testified to that. Perhaps it is greatly to my discredit that I hesitated midway betwixt amusement and annoyance at her conduct. Yet the next moment I reviled myself for my unworthiness, and went to sleep.

However, it caused me to watch her behavior the closer. And the very next day I caught her practising her arts upon brother John. Very subtle ones they were, yet in three days she managed to command obedience from him by the mere raising of her finger. I did not know whether to take offence, or to laugh at her newest mischief, since the rogue displayed her command of the stolid lad with the very air of the showman as he exhibits the tricks of his performing elephant. She made the solemn, heavy fellow unbend, and took great pride in so doing. If she required him to talk, he did so, even in his most silent moments ; whilst in his serious moods he was made to laugh, and often was compelled to do her small services even to the detriment of business. And when he was in her presence when the day's work was done, I ne'er failed to notice how his eyes followed her willow form about, and how his face lighted up when she chanced to look at him, which she did now and then in a fashion so entirely captivating that methought these looks should have been reserved by rights for me. Perhaps this doth but show the pettiness of my nature ; but I certainly glowered at him very often with the sense of an inward grievance, though I was at pains to do so when neither of them were looking.

Soon England was agog with expectation. Dutch William's name was whispered everywhere, and his arrival was looked for at any moment. 'Twas thought his fleet would sail to Yorkshire, and there disembark the grand army it conveyed. Yet its appearance was much retarded by the fierce gales that blew from the westward. In the mean time the King's men made no sign, thus I was able to bide at Chilverley Farm in bodily comfort. Howbeit numberless emotions were alive in my heart. My shattered health and broken spirit gave me grave disquietude, and I was beset with fears as to whether in my enfeebled state I could bear the strain of a winter campaign. Still, come what might, I was fully determined to play my part in the forthcoming struggle.   Never for an instant did I forget my father's murder.   I had sworn to pursue with vengeance Judge Jeffreys and the King, and so long as body and soul kept together that oath held good.   Again, I had an inheritance to go in quest of, not for myself alone, but for the one I loved as well.   No, there could be no drawing back, and much as I might doubt my powers of endurance, I had all to gain, and nought but a half-spent life to lose.

Tobe Hancock and I conversed much together on the subject that filled the minds of all men.   The blacksmith, zealous as ever, was prepared to fight at a moment's notice.   He furbished his weapons and oiled his matchlock, and waited eager and couchant for the Dutchman's coming.   And come when he might Tobias would strike his hardest for the Protestant religion and the confusion of papists.   As for me, I was quite ready, save in one particular.   I lacked a horse, and had no money of mine own to buy one.   Neither dared I asked mother for one, because she was quite set against all fighting.   Indeed, I altogether avoided the subject as far as she was concerned, and knew quite well, ere I could set forth on my momentous errand, I should have the whole weight of her opposition to face.   And this constant thought of horses only added to my pain of mind, for I could not think of them without the death of faithful Joe being forever present in my memory.   Indeed to this hour I ne'er think of that brave creature being killed in my madness and brutality, but what I feel a sense of ignominy and shame.

While these events were pending, a far more trivial matter came to a sudden head.   Seeing that I had nought to occupy me, and that I was endeavoring to nurse my shattered health as much as possible, 'twas my custom to lie abed longer than the other members of the family of a morning.   It so happened on one occasion upon coming down to breakfast, that I found my mistress had had hers, and had set off, contrary to her wont, upon some excursion among the hills, without waiting for my company.

I felt somewhat aggrieved at this, and took it rather hard.   And what made it all the harder was that she did not return for several hours, and even then volunteered me no explanation of her unkind conduct.   However, on the first occasion we were alone together afterwards, I asked—

" Whither have you been all the morning, Dorothy ? "

" To Taunton with your brother Jack," she answered.

" Oh ! " said I shortly, shutting my teeth with a snap.

" Oh ! " she mimicked after me, with an exact copy of **my** tone and manner. And being quick to notice the exceeding gravity of my face, added with all her native impudence, "I'm not your property yet, young man, so don't you think it!"

"But, dearest, I wish you wouldn't lead John on like you are doing."

She looked at me with such a depth of cool satire that I began to feel uncomfortable, whilst her eyes seemed to dance with laughter.

"Oh, oh! I have found one flaw in a great man's character. Master Edward Armstrong, England's greatest swordsman, is jealous-minded. And now, your worship, read me a lesson, an' it please you. But really, sir, I cannot help the lustre of mine eyes. And you silly men are all alike. Even that fine commander, Lord Churchill, was smitten by them."

Pertly enough she said this, but then relapsed into a tone of penitential softness, and 'twas accompanied by any number of melting glances. Certes, she was exercising her powers on me, and in despite of all my efforts she more than half succeeded. Who could resist those looks, those smiles, that air of humility, and the half-veiled irony underneath it?

"'Tis not your airs and graces that I complain of, darling," quoth I, much mollified, "but methinks 'tis hard to prefer another's company to mine, and to leave me all the morning."

"Bo, thou goose!" was her only reply, and there and then she ran away.

I could not quite grasp her meaning then, but somehow felt that she had gotten the best of it, and that I was something very like a fool. Still, one thing pleased me mightily. 'Twas plain my remonstrance had appealed to her sense of right and justice. For that same night she charged my pipe for me, brewed me a bowl of punch, sat beside me, and talked earnestly of the coming conflict.

As I remember 'twas a cold wet November night, and half a gale of wind was blowing from the sea. It flicked the rain against the windows, went crooning down the valleys, and whining through the woods. It sobbed and wailed amid the naked branches, and the melancholy sound of it made me draw my knees nearer to the hearth, and set me gazing wistfully into the bright embers of the fire. I was in this posture when suddenly a dripping face was thrust through the outer door. 'Twas Tobe Hancock. His big gray eyes were filled with a weird vivacity.

"'E hath coom, lad!"

I jumped out of my chair excitedly.

23

"Where did he land, Tobe?"

"'E hath tricked the King's fleet, and hath put into Torbay."

Thus, after all, the Prince had come to our parts, for, as ye are aware, kinsmen, Torbay is a little haven on the coast of Devon.   Tobe was overflowing with the news, whilst I, brimming with questions, unceasingly plied them one by one, till he was pumped quite dry of information.   He enthusiastically descanted on the army that had come to restore England's freedom and religion. It had required a fleet of sixty sail to bring it from Holland, and an equal number of boats to land it. Mounted messengers were riding post haste to London with the news, and the Prince was expected at Exeter in a day or two. It was also averred that the famous Frederic Count von Schomberg had accompanied the Prince as his first lieutenant. At that great name Dorothy interposed in her swift, enthusiastic way—

" Didst say Count von Schomberg, Master Hancock?   Fine man that!   He hath more knowledge of the art of war, and hath greater military talent than any three men of his time. 'Twas he who gained the glorious field of Montes Claros, whilst his blood hath been spilled over all the map of Europe.   Dutch Will hath done right well to secure his services, though to be sure his years are beginning to sit heavy upon him.   But no matter, he's a splendid man, and there's life in the old dog yet ! "

Thus spake my mistress, and 'twas as good as one of Sir John Suckling's comedies, to see Tobias look at her as though not rightly sure whether it behoved him to believe a girl in such an unfeminine matter ; whilst, on the other hand, the excited maid was regaling John and me with anecdote upon anecdote of the great soldier.

'Twas now a time for prompt action, and both the blacksmith and I recognizing this fact, struck a bargain there and then.   I promised to be at his forge at daybreak in the morning; we would start for the wars together.

No sooner had Master Hancock left us, than I gazed at dear mother and beheld her face alive with keenest trouble.

" Ned, my boy, mine own son, you must not go to war," she whispered brokenly.

I had foreseen this cruel moment.   Therefore I braced myself up to keep my self-control, yet felt at the same time my determination was far too inflexible for a human agency to turn it from its purpose.   Kinsmen, do not think me ungrateful, do not think me cold-hearted !   You are to understand the hour had come for which I had been waiting, longing, and building hopes upon for months.

"Mother," said I, "the day father was murdered I swore an oath to punish his murderers. They are Judge Jeffreys and the King. The time hath come at last, and so long as my arm has the strength to grasp a sword, I will fight for that object."

"I am grieved to hear you talk thus, Ned. Do bide at home, if for no other sake than mine!"

"Dear mother," I replied with some uncertainty; for her pleading tones had touched me, "do not think I pain you wantonly, but my mind is made. I have suffered too long and too bitterly. Besides, I have all to gain and nought to lose."

"But think of what happened when Monmouth came," she said, not reproachfully, but fearfully, and terror sprang into her mild eyes.

"I shall ne'er return hither, mother, if our cause be defeated," I answered; "never again will I jeopardize the peace and safety of this homestead."

"My boy, you wrong me there. 'Tis not the safety of this roof, but your own for which I tremble. You are my firstborn, and hold the first place in my heart."

These simple words came near my undoing. 'Twas hard to think that I, who had caused her such pain in the past, could not spare her more when I had it in my power to do so. Nevertheless I found the courage to answer—

"Forgive me, mother; but please God I will go forth and do my best. More than that no man can do. I am like a ruined gamester, who stakes everything on a final cast. It hath been torture to me to sit moping in the chimney corner these last few days, unable to earn my bread, but solely dependent upon the generosity of others. Yes, go I must and will!"

She burst out crying then, and it was pitiable to hear her sobs, and to take home to one's self their reproachful meaning. Yet I bore them all in silence. Perhaps I was an ingrate, a cold-hearted ingrate, but arbitrary Fate seemed to draw me with its iron fingers towards the great struggle that held life and death in the balance!

CHAPTER XXXIX.

THE START FOR THE WARS.

In the midst of mother's distress I looked about me, and saw Dorothy gazing intently into the fire, whilst John's face appeared awful in its grimness.

At that moment poor mother chanced to look at my darling, and the girl seemed to inspire her.

"Ned," she said, "how can you go forth and leave the maid you love? Do you wish to break *her* heart as well as mine?"

That was very like a woman. She had discovered the tenderest emotion in my soul, and now her desperation led her to play upon it. I could make no answer to that, simply because I knew not how to frame one. A young man's love is not a thing to be tampered with, neither can it be discussed before an audience. I knew my position was an irksome and a perilous one, and mother knew it too. Therefore she pressed her advantage to the utmost.

"Ned, I do not see how any man, who really loves a maid, can go away for months, or perhaps years, or perhaps forever, to risk his life day by day, when he might just as easily bide at home. 'Tis not as though you are obliged to go. 'Tis but a mistaken sentiment that calls you. Oh, my boy, overcome your vain desires, and think of those you leave behind!"

This was a wondrous long speech for mother, and she delivered it with a power of pleading that would have touched a heart of stone. And my heart being tenderer than that, it appealed to it straightway. I felt that the tide was turning against me, and that my courage was ebbing slowly. But at the precise moment I was in the greatest need of help, Dorothy took her eyes from the fire and looked at mother timidly.

"Dear mother," she said, as if three parts afraid, but with a voice full and deep in its resolution, "please remember, that I am Sir Nicholas Marvin's daughter." Her warm fingers touched my hand, and their mute assistance buoyed my spirit somewhat.

"Then, thou hast no fear for him?" asked mother very reproachfully.

"A soldier's child should know no fear, dearest mother. And methinks when a brave man goes forth to spend his blood, and his life, if need be, in a noble cause, and in his mistress's cause as well, the very least we useless women, who are only fit to weep in war time, can do, is to preserve a bright eye and a cheerful countenance to keep his spirits up, and to save our weak tears and qualms till after his departure." She said this with face aglow with enthusiasm, yet mother was woefully disappointed, and having read her mind incorrectly, began to grow angry.

"Come, Dorothy," she replied severely, "I call that Cheap Jack talk, and not suited to grave occasions. It sounds very well in poems and in the playhouse, but I cannot think it befits a woman of flesh and blood, who hath a warm heart within her. Suppose your Ned was to be killed in this campaign, and that you were ne'er to see him more?"

"If God strikes him down," she answered, "He will give me the strength to bear the blow. Besides, no nobler death could be desired for any man, than that he should die sword in hand, fighting for himself, his country, and his darling. But why should we women, who do nought but stay at home and sigh, presume to raise our voices at great times like these? And perhaps, dear mother, you may set it down as mere boastfulness in me, but were I a man I would be under the Dutchman's Standard before another sunset."

The way that maid stood up before us all, with a noble intensity about her face, and a splendid light in her eyes, was a thing to be remembered. To hear the wild ardor of her voice was to know she was quite carried away by the words she spoke, and by the leaven which reposed within her of the dead knight of Kelston Manor, the man of war who had fought and bled, and had died sword in hand at last.

But mother at this was downright angry.

"You cruel, unfeeling girl!" she said; "'tis quite plain you do not care a jot for my poor lad, but have merely jested with him. No woman who really loves a man would be so willing for him to lose his life for the sake of such romantic balderdash and chicanery! Or, perhaps, you think men were only made for fighting?"

Those last words conveyed a sarcasm. Never before had I seen dear mother so thoroughly aroused. I could not have believed it possible that her placid nature could have let her be so cruel with her tongue. Yet even as she spoke she burst into a storm of passionate sobbing. Instantly my mistress replied, and in a way that was quite as hard and bitter.

"I am not certain as to what men were made for," she retorted fiercely; "but, methinks, women were only made for weeping!" There and then she sailed out of the kitchen, and away upstairs to her bedroom, from which she did not return that night.

Poor mother was utterly crushed at this, and rocked herself to and fro, still crying ceaselessly in her desolation. And Betty, seeing her so continuously tearful, came to her side to try and comfort her, and presently they clung to one another and wept together. As for me, a weight of sorrow lay on my heart. Here had I, a fallen, sinful, worthless fellow, gone and set angry passions in pure and loving hearts. This sad state of things oppressed me sore, and gave me many longings for daybreak in the morning. In the midst of my misery, John touched me on the shoulder.

" We'll get out o' this," he growled, and therewith we donned our hats and cloaks and set out for a walk in the darkness and the rain.

'Twas the first time for years I had received any such advance from him. Indeed, never since father's death had he sought my company, and, if the truth must be told, I marvelled at his condescension now, and felt very ill at ease in his society.

For an hour we walked side by side, whilst not a word passed between us. On my own part I was too abashed to speak ; whilst he did not utter a solitary syllable. But at last, as we came back again towards the farmstead, he halted near the stable-door, and told me to wait a moment outside, whilst he went within. I heard him grope about inside for a minute or two, and also heard a peculiar noise, as though one of the stones of the floor had been displaced. Directly afterwards he rejoined me, and I could dimly discern through the gloom that he held a large cloth bag in his left hand.

" Take hold," said he shortly, and gave it into my custody.

'Twas very heavy, and upon shaking it something clinked within, and the tinkling noise that came therefrom had, according to some men, no sound in the world to match it.

" Gold ! "

" Ay, gold," said he. " One hundred and forty-nine pounds, fifteen shillings and fourpence farthing."

" I—I don't understand, John," said I, completely taken aback.

" Ever since the week following father's murder," he replied, " I have ne'er failed to put one-third of my earning by for a day that I knew would come. It hath now arrived. It hath been a cherished wish of mine to use this money myself in the Great Cause, and that mine own thews and sinews, the fruit of

my father's loins, should strike a lusty blow, that his death be
not unpunished. However, methinks, 'twould kill our mother
for the two of us to go ; so I will bide at home. You are the
eldest, your father's firstborn. 'Tis more meet and seemly that
you should go. And, Edward, I can trust you to employ this
sum zealously in our own and the Prince's service."

Thereupon he gave my hand a mighty squeeze, and led the
way indoors.

Straightway I betook myself to bed. 'Twas the same room I
had bided in one night three years agone, when a similar errand
lay before me. Everything was the same therein. Yet three
years gone I had lain down with bright hopes, bright ambitions,
and a young, unbroken, high, and buoyant spirit. What was I
now ? Merely a wreck of a man, with a black history branded
in my soul, with my youthful vigor sapped, with my spirit
broken, with three years of shame and ignominy written in my
book of life, which nought could purge away.

A whole lifetime seemed to keep that bright day of '85 and
this dark one of '88 apart. Yet now, as then, I could not rest.
Hours that should have been utilized with slumber were passed
in fitful dozing. Perhaps the thing that gave me the greatest
pain of mind was the knowledge I was leaving those so dear to
my heart, and that maybe I should ne'er set eyes on them in
the flesh again. Also there came the hard fact that I had set
my two noblest friends at strife with one another on my account ;
and what made it all the harder, was because I could not
discover the way to an amendment. 'Twas plain to me neither
understood the other. Each of them loved my unworthy self
jealously, and in a fashion entirely opposite. But they were
blind to one fact. They could not see that, though their
methods and sentiments of love were so very different, they all
amounted to the same thing in the end. Indeed, this was a
galling grief to me on the eve of my leave-taking ; I could not
bear to think I must bid them both good-bye, and to know that
I had torn their two hearts apart ; for they had learned to love
one another dearly.

I rose and dressed myself very early, so that by daylight I
might be prepared to keep my tryst with Tobe. Judge of my
surprise, upon going down into the kitchen, to find it alight with
candles and a cheerful fire, and to find all the household stirring. By that I knew that others beside myself had been thinking, to some purpose, of my departure. Mother and Betty were
particularly busy among the victuals. Bacon was frizzling
before the fire, and every now and then spitting into it, the

kettle was singing on the hob, and a strong odor of mulled ale pervaded the fireplace. Dorothy had the sleeves of her morning dress rolled up above the elbow, and was furbishing with all her energy some huge article in her lap. At first I could not rightly see what it was; but upon approaching nearer, inspection told me it was a beautiful steel breastplate, that was polished as bright as any mirror. My love looked at me with a face flushed by reason of its owner's violent exertions.

"Off with your doublet, lad," she said, in a cheery, decisive way.

Without parley I obeyed her. Thereupon she deftly tried the breastplate on, and exclaimed—

"Beautiful! It fits you to a nicety. Methought it odd if I could not gauge that sturdy chest of thine with mine eyes, seeing that I have looked at it so often."

Yet this pretty speech gave me no elation, simply because the black, half-forgotten past rose unexpectedly before me. Her arms, half-bare, snow-white, and delicately rounded, had been in the vicinity of my eyes during this operation; and just above the wrist of one of them I saw the livid cicatrix of a wound. 'Twas the first time I had seen it, and instantly it flashed into my mind how it had come there. 'Twas a fearful scar, deep and wide, and quite three inches long. Then a movement of her arm showed me the underside of it; and a look at that revealed another scar in a similar place, which was not quite so extensive or so hideous. But it made me wince far more than the other did; since it told me plainer than any words that her father's sword had passed right through it. This harsh jogging of my memory completely unmanned me for the moment. However, directly afterwards, half-unconsciously, I pressed my lips to the cruel scar, and murmured, "How brave of thee, my darling!"

She did not reply to this, but paid remarkable attention to the breastplate; tho' one glance told me that her whole face had crimsoned, and that half a smile lingered upon her parted lips. Meanwhile her nimble fingers had duly affixed the corselet. Then she stood in front of me, and looked me over very critically.

"Now, then, my lad," she said sharply, her eyes twinkling like stars on a frosty night, "pull yourself together. Throw out your chest, sir; set up your head, exalt your chin and keep it smartly backward. Set your hands—so. That's it; excellently well done. Now straighten your carriage, as becomes a worthy man-at-arms, and as behoves a cavaliero of His Highness's. Bravo! I call that fine—just fine. Thou'rt every inch a soldier, dear lad, and the best swordsman in England,—and the noblest, truest, dearest gentleman in Christendom !"

And, in broad daylight, she jumped into my arms, clasped her hands firmly round my neck, and fairly hugged me, whilst her warm young breast was pressed against that emotionless breastplate, that resisted all the efforts of Ned Armstrong's foolish heart to leap through its lifeless steel.

Just then mother came and caught us in this very compromising attitude.

"Hypocrite !" she exclaimed indignantly.

At this my mistress let go her hold on me precious quick, and fairly defied dear mother with her eyes. For a brief space they stood silent and bitterly angry a yard or so apart, each gazing at the other with a contempt so lofty that mere words were quite powerless to convey it in its entirety.

To me 'twas an ugly moment. I owed well-nigh everything to these two women ; yet here they were, ready and willing to hurt one another on my account. I felt chilled and miserable to behold them thus ; but in the midst of my distress, kind Providence favored me with something approaching an inspiration. I seized Dorothy's injured arm, and held it firmly before mother's eyes. The maiden said, "How dare you, sir !"—that is, at least, as plain as looks could say so—then made an effort to get free, but discovered my grasp was not affected by any struggling.

"Mother," said I—and my tone enlisted her best attention—"I have already told you how some months agone your son duped, cheated, and played upon Sir Nicholas Marvin and his daughter. But I have not told you yet that, when Sir Nicholas discovered your son's infamy, he swore he would send him at once to the place to which he deserved to go. Accordingly, he seized his sword there and then, and thrust straight at your son's heart. And that would assuredly have been the end of him, had not Dorothy interposed her arm. She preserved his life by receiving her father's steel right through it. And to prove the truth of this, here is that arm ; here is where the sword entered it, and here is where it came out of the back. Therefore, dear mother, methinks ' hypocrite' is a very harsh word to use."

Mother seemed bewildered at this, whilst her younger adversary still faced her squarely, with fierce looks and lofty silence and a bold challenge in her eyes. However, no sooner had I said my say, than mother's eyes grew wet, and she exclaimed, midway betwixt a sob and a sigh—

"Forgive me, you noble girl, for wronging you in my heart! There is something in your nature, child, I don't quite understand."

"Dear mother," replied the maid softly, and in a voice that was all timidity, "please let me recall that unkind speech I used last night. I was angry then, and——"

I waited to hear no more; but, with a bosom alive with happiness, strode hastily to the door to look at the weather. And I came very near colliding with John on its threshold; whilst the sight of my gleaming breastplate nearly upset his mental equilibrium as well as his physical one. But very soon he recovered, and cast a glance at the two occupants of the kitchen, clapped me on the shoulder (quite a flippant proceeding this for one so solemn), and remarked, "Our Ned is a cleverer fellow than I thought," and then assisted me in my study of the precise condition of the English climate. Still we had only just managed to discover that it continued to rain, that the wind was in the west, and that the atmosphere was too warm for the time of year, when Betty called us in to breakfast.

When I had got out of bed half an hour since, I could not have dreamt that I was to be allowed to sit down so shortly to such a joyful meal. I have a recollection of pausing in the midst of a vigorous attack on the eggs and bacon, to ask mischievously, "Why have you pulled your sleeves down, Dorothy?" whereat mother's face shone with smiles, and pleasure glowed upon it.

"Because you rude men stare so hard at arms that are not brown and hairy, like your own ugly ones," she returned smartly, and tried unsuccessfully to hide her satisfaction at her own retort, by looking as unconcerned as possible.

By the time the meal was finished there was still over an hour of darkness left. Thus I had no need to hurry to the blacksmith's forge, which was within a stone's throw of our farmstead.

"Ned," whispered my mistress in my ear, "there is but one thing lacking for your complete equipment. Thou hast no horse."

"Yes, that is indeed a misfortune," I answered cheerfully, trying hard to emulate her courageous spirits ; "but I will make the best of an awkward matter, and do without one."

"I'm not so sure I shall allow you, sir ; it does not become a knight of mine to start for the wars ill-found. Now, if you will come with me, peradventure I may give you a little surprise."

She procured a lanthorn, and led me across our sloppy stack-yard to the stable. Arrived there, she took me past the heels of three of our farm horses, until we came to the end stall, where-upon she turned the light on a handsome, powerful animal that was tethered there.

"What think you of him, sir?" she asked triumphantly. "He's every inch a war-charger. Here," she added, in her imperious fashion, "just hold the lanthorn, my lad, and I'll introduce him to his new master."

And, to my exceeding wonderment, she gave the great fellow a slap on his flank, cried, "Come over, Gustavus!" slipped betwixt him and the wall, and proceeded to handle that animal as though she had lived amongst horses all her life. She laid hold of its head and pulled its jaws apart thereby displaying two rows of gleaming teeth, and exclaimed excitedly—

"See, my lad, he is scarcely six years old, so is well within his prime. Mark his lean head, and his bright, well-opened eye. There's breed for you!" Next she stooped and seized a big foreleg with one dainty hand, and ran the other over it. "'Pon my soul, 'tis a noble thing!" she cried more excitedly than ever; "set the light this way, sir, and look at your new property. Dost see the high withers, the fine breadth of knee, and the full six inches or even more of bone betwixt it and the fetlock? Oh, 'tis a noble thing!"

Thereupon she descanted for a full five minutes upon the manifold beauties of its limbs, whilst the way she handled the four of them, utterly destitute of fear, was something quite astonishing. Ultimately she returned again to its upper parts, dilated on the straightness and shortness of the back, and wound up by stroking its big white muzzle, and by declaring—

"Thou'rt indeed a wondrous lucky fellow, Ned, to have such a horse at thy service. His name must be Gustavus Adolphus, and I have not the least doubt he will emulate his immortal namesake, whilst I have but to ask that you will treat him as you did dear Joe, then he will have scant cause to grumble."

Those last words touched a very tender place. Yet the stab had been given quite unwittingly, for she had never learned the manner of that faithful creature's death. This was the second time already that morning that bitter things had been uncon-sciously recalled. Albeit, in the midst of my embarrassment, I had the sense to proffer many thanks for her generosity.

"No need to thank me, lad," she replied, "thy thanks are due to Master John. Some weeks agone I confided my plan to him of purchasing a horse and breastplate for the champion of my cause. Accordingly he kept his eyes about him, and the other morning we hied to Taunton together, and struck this notable bargain."

So this was the meaning of that neglect of me which had disturbed my piece of mind. And if I was made to feel a fool on that occasion, I was made to feel both a fool and an ingrate now. My mistress narrowly scrutinized my face, and methinks she guessed something of this humiliation, since she made haste to add—

" I have another gift for Master Armstrong, of course by no means so precious as steel and horseflesh, yet I would like him to cherish it now and then, that is, if I do not ask too high a favor."

She said this half saucily, half sadly, with something like an echo of lingering sorrow in her voice. Then she produced from her pocket a small box and handed it to me. I made haste to discover its contents. 'Twas a little portrait of Mistress Dorothy Marvin. My heart fairly jumped, for if ever a picture could have been said to speak, it was the one I held in my hand. There was the same glow of the eyes, the same eager beauty of the face, and the same lurking strength and subtlety about it, whilst it was surrounded by a rich mass of tangled black-brown hair. She looked over my shoulder as I gazed at it, and with all a woman's vanity commended that self-same hair to my notice by pointing it out with one finger, saying—

" 'Tis not so fine now as it was then, but, I may say, sir, that by the time Dutch William is King William the Third of England, and by the time Ned Armstrong is Sir Edward Armstrong, baronet, of Copeland Hall, Mistress Marvin's hair will be as profuse as ever it was aforetime, for it grows thicker day by day."

" Then, Dorothy, thou hast no fear for the result of the campaign ? " I asked, overjoyed to hear her hopefulness.

" None whatever, lad. Dutch Will hath a mighty army, and mighty men to lead it. Let me see! there'll be Schomberg, Churchill, and himself, not to mention Mackay and the lesser captains. Neither have I fear for thee, Ned. Something tells me you will return ere long with all your rights and liberties."

This courageous speech, and the inspiring way of saying it, set a longing in my heart that nearly overcame me.

" Prithee, sweetheart, I will take one of my rights forthwith," and I made an attempt to kiss her. Very prompt she was to frustrate this laudable endeavor, and answered with a mocking kind of gravity—

" Forward youth ! You call this a right, do you? Let me tell you, sir, I call it a liberty, and I'll not allow it ! "

" You have allowed it many times before," I pleaded.

" I'm thinking far too often, sir. My cheek will surely lose its market value, if you have access to it whene'er you feel inclined."

Thereupon, I was driven to do the next best thing, namely, to kiss the one in the portrait.

" Silly lad ! " she cried at that, with fun dancing in her eyes. "Oh, what would Sir Godfrey Kneller say, if he knew you used his handiwork so cavalierly ? What art thinking of ? Do you know you will fetch all the paint off ? "

" Perhaps that is why thou art so careful of the real one."

" Nay, nay ; you can ne'er take color from this cheek o' mine, though you may very often bring more to it. How many times have I had to blush for you, and your forward manners, sir ? But wit in a man must be rewarded, for one so seldom finds it. Here, you may try, sir ! "

And try I did my level best, but must chronicle a failure. For to prove that she was right and I was wrong, my efforts only added to its rosiness.

" Art satisfied, Master Impudence ? Then I may say, for your information, that next to a fighting man I place a witty man, but before them both I place one who knows himself in the presence of his lady."

Thus having got the last word, as woman will always have, she ventured on an entirely different subject.

" Now, when you return, young man," she said, " do not dare to come and tell me how brave you felt in your first battle. And if you do, I shall certainly not believe you ! "

" Why, mistress ? " I inquired, aggrieved at this disparagement of my courage.

" Because dear papa always declared only fools and liars boasted of their first engagement. Even he, in his first battle, kept ducking his head at every volley from the enemy, whilst he hath seen hundreds of recruits, as the bullets have whizzed by their ears, bowing as politely as the fops in Spring-Garden of a Sunday."

This started her on her warlike strain, and with sparkling eyes she gave me a wonderful store of military information. She told me how to ride into action, how to handle my horse and weapons when I got there ; how to deport myself, how to charge, how to retreat, and, in fact, instructed me in every duty of a horse soldier. Indeed she even gave me some idea of what was expected of the captain of a squadron, avowing that she had no doubt I should find it useful shortly. Verily 'twas an education in the theory of war to listen to this martial mistress. And to duly impress these things upon my unreceptive mind, she made me repeat them after her, as though I was some hulking schoolboy, till I had learnt them all by heart. After this she told me how to treat and dress those unpleasant adjuncts of a battle-field ; I mean the wounds that accrue from scenes of glory. Finally she said—

"If black blood flows from a cut, bind your kerchief below it, but if the blood is bright and pure, bind above it. Also, dear lad, I have placed a bottle of your beloved balsam in your saddle-bag; but please apply it when no one happens to be looking."

This was a terrible home-thrust, delivered very deftly, in a tone of the utmost gravity, as though she was begging an especial boon.

"Mistress, methinks it is a mercy I have gotten my breast-plate on, to shield me from thy tongue," said I, like a very gallant gentleman. I was determined to play my part, even as she was playing hers. She was concealing the pain of parting that gnawed her breast, to maintain her dignity in my sight, and to keep my spirits alert and cheerful, for she knew full well that I should need them all in the great task that lay before me.

She assisted me to saddle Gustavus, and then bade me go back to the house to bid the family good-bye, and to fetch all the articles I intended taking on my journey. Thither I returned, and habited myself in my riding-boots, hat, and cloak, strapped on my sword, and put two pistols in my pockets, with the bag of gold John had placed in my custody, together with a smaller one given me by mother. The leave-taking was a sad one, for poor mother broke down utterly, whilst Betty's case was nearly similar. But John, for his part, found neither words nor tears, till as I was crossing the threshold of the kitchen door, with my heart like a lump of lead, he squeezed my hand, and muttered in a short low voice, "Remember!" I glanced at him, and saw his great eyes glowing, and his face looking grim and terrible. As I came to the stable, I found Dorothy had led out my horse, and was holding his head, heedless of the dripping rain.

"My darling," said I, "you must be more careful, or you will surely catch your death of cold."

"What care I for that?" she replied, and then said slowly,

dwelling on every word, and looking hard into my face the while, "Thou art setting forth on a great mission, Ned, my brave lad. Go forth and win, and then come back to me. Thou hast four things to accomplish. Gain thine own heritage, then mine, avenge thy father's death, and, if possible, avenge mine. Is it too much to ask thee?"

"My darling!" I exclaimed, slipping my left arm round her.

"And promise me, dear," she whispered, so brokenly that she could scarce utter the words, "that whatever may befall, you will ne'er forget me. I could not bear to lose you now, Ned."

At that I thought of the wet morning in the spring, when the gates of hell were opened out before me; I thought of the night at Kelston Manor, of the night in the goyal amid the Quantocks, of that hour in Taunton Jail and the fever-haunted ones of a month ago. All these thoughts swept into my mind together, and coupled with the courageous maid's wistful tenderness, mastered me completely.

"How can I forget you, Dorothy?" I asked, and the tears were near my eyes.

"Don't, Ned," she said, drooping her lashes, because my face unnerved her, "else I must cry; and I would not like to cry!"

I mounted great Gustavus, and my mistress let go his head. She came to his left side, and I lowered my face to the level of my thigh whilst she put up her lips.

"Good-bye, brave heart."

"Good-bye, dear lad, good-bye."

I touched my horse, whereupon he began to sedately pick his way among the mire. Yet almost instantly an irresistible impulse made me look back o'er my shoulder. I saw the girl limp and listless against the stable door, with the first rays of daylight flecking her hair and forehead. Her face was white to the lips, her mouth was quivering and her eyes welled tears. I shook the bridle of great Gustavus, whereat he exalted his head, and set his big legs forward; and so in the gray of the morning I rode to the wars.

CHAPTER XL.

THE GREAT GATHERING AT EXETER.

TOBIAS HANCOCK was awaiting me close by the doorway of the forge.

" My eyemers, lad ! 'er be a booty, I rackan," said he, as he caught a glint of my fine corslet that peeped from under my cloak.

Next moment our horses were breasting bravely westward. His was a raw-boned gray, very high in the shoulders, and stiff on its legs, which might have come out of the ark with Noah for aught I could tell, such was its grave bearing, and ancient cast of countenance.

By this the east was flecked with stealthy gray, that came glancing slowly over the hill-tops. It rolled gradually away like a thick white curtain. Presently the wooded, leafless combes peeped out of it, and afterwards the autumn-tinted valley. Now, though the sky was streaming with a steady flow of water, and the clouds were murky, dark, and lowering, and though they dipped among the hedgerows and the stubble at every few yards distant, my spirits soared high above this gloom and sombreness. Whether 'twas the pride of love within my heart, the sweetness of my darling's kiss still hot upon my lips, the nobility of her courage, or the mighty enterprise that lay before me ; I cannot say, with any degree of certainty, which of them it was that heartened me so thoroughly. Perhaps each fact contributed a share of solace, nor must I omit to mention another cheerful circumstance.

I had no further fear of the King's men. Dutch Will had arrived before them, as I had prayed he would do. 'Tis this matter that hath given birth to the whimsical tradition concerning Black Ned and the devil.

Master Thompson ot Taunton Jail was never a perfectly sane man after the strange events of the night of my escape. He always averred (even on oath) that the little man in the cloak was the devil himself, who had done Black Ned the immense honor of delivering him from the scaffold in person, and that he had fetched me hence to abide with him ever after. What added color to this story, was the fact that Black Ned was never afterwards recognized. My illness left a permanent mark upon me, and this, combined with my exalted station, proved an ample disguise for Sir Edward Armstrong when I assumed that title.

We found Exeter in a state of turmoil and extraordinary excitement. The populace, with one voice, had already declared for the Invader, whilst the magistracy and clergy had declared for the King. Indeed, Lamplugh the bishop had deserted his diocese, and with his subordinate the dean, for company, was fleeing in haste to London. Wondrous stories were afloat concerning the might and magnificence of the Prince's army. Expectation was rife throughout the city, yet that day brought no definite news of His Highness's intentions.

Tobias and I had some difficulty in securing a lodging for ourselves and horses, for the town was thronged with yeomen from the surrounding districts, anxious to witness the Dutchman's coming. Eventually we had the good fortune to procure one at a hostel hard by the Cathedral Close, bearing the festive sign of the Pipe and Tabor.

On every hand treason was freely spoken against the King, and the utmost good will was manifested by the citizens towards the Prince of Orange. True, some surprise was expressed that he should have ventured to strike from the West, seeing how Monmouth had failed. Nevertheless 'twas plain to all this was to be no pettifogging business of a few hundred ploughmen and country yokels. Not that I seek to disparage them either, for no men ever fought tyranny and superior strength more gloriously than did those simple sons of the soil in '85. But, in this enterprise, all things had been carefully prepared. The sentiments of the nation had been sounded and the Prince had been invited over by a representative body of the people.

The day following our arrival an incident occurred that whetted the public appetite, more than all the hearsay had done. A company of horse appeared before the city with my lord Mordaunt at its head, and with Prince William's chaplain, Bishop Burnet riding by his side. At the report of their approach the mayor had ordered the gates to be closed, but at the first demand they were opened to admit them. The company rode to the market square, whereupon the chaplain, a thick-set, broad-shouldered, squat fellow, with a great bullet head, and bull neck, proclaimed aloud that His Highness would arrive next day ; whereupon the whole place went nearly wild with excitement and eagerness.

The Deanery was instantly prepared, and set in order for the Prince's reception. The citizens brought out flags and bunt-

24

ing, and decorated their houses, and an arch of triumph was set up close by the west gate, and inscribed in gold letters thereon was, " Welcome to the Champion of the Protestant Religion," on one side, whilst on the other was, " God Bless the Upholder of the Rights and Liberties of the English People." 'Twas an eager, tumultuous time, kinsmen, I can tell you, and even now, as my old head recalls it, I seem to feel the flush of expectation come back to my worn-out frame.

The great day arrived at last. 'Twas the ninth of November. Tobe and I took our stand betimes, hard by the west gate of the city, to have a goodly view of the spectacle. 'Twould but be presumption in me to dare try to fully describe the army as it marched in. Its greatness thrilled those who saw it with awe, and all men concurred that it was the grandest sight ever witnessed in our parts. That day all the city was in the streets. The display of bunting was really brave and gay, whilst flags and banners floated from well-nigh every bedroom window. As for the throng, it was everywhere. The footpaths were clogged with it; and the house windows were thick with a strangely expectant mass of humanity; nor was this all, as the house-tops were clustered with the same, whilst every signboard over shop or tavern, which offered the slightest vantage-ground, had at least two limbs dangling from it.

At length the distant blare of trumpets broke in on the murky November air, mingled with the huzzahs of the thousands who had gone forth for miles along the road to meet the army. Every eye was strained to catch the first glimpse of the Invaders. By and by the shouting came nearer and nearer, and the rolling of the drums struck out quite audible. Then came a broad line along the rich Exe valley, and through the mistiness of the morning it was seen to wind past Haldon Hill on its march from Chudleigh. The broad column came creeping up to the western gate, and when the head of it was in full view, a roar broke forth from the concourse within the city enclosures, and amidst this babel of voices the vanguard came prancing by.

My lord Macclesfield was the first man of the army of deliverance to come into the city, and he was unmolested. Close behind him followed two hundred gentlemen—of England for the most part. The sight of them alone called forth a hubbub of admiration, for every man was attired in glittering cuirass and helmet, with sword on shoulder, and mounted on a Flemish war-horse. By his side each had a black negro from the Guinea coast in attendance on his person. And to see their

grinning ebony faces, embellished by curious turbans, embroid-
ered sashes, and white feathers, set the crowd more agog than
ever. Next came a splendid company of Swedish cavalry.
Fine-grown men they were, attired in suits of black armor, and
with bearskin cloaks slung over their shoulders, the original
owners of which they themselves had slain. Their gleaming
broadswords and martial aspect called forth great admiration.
Yet this was nought at all compared to the wild enthusiasm
when, amidst a band of gentles and pages, a huge floating
banner appeared, having upon its waving folds the inscription,
" The Protestant Religion and the Liberties of England."

I talk of enthusiasm in this matter, but what of the shouting, and the frantic joy when the deliverer himself rode in?
Forty resplendent footmen ran beside him. On a picturesque
white charger there sate—to our eyes at least—the greatest man
in Christendom.

I have a vision of him before me at this hour; I see again
the white plume of his Montero hat, the glint of the armor on
his back and breast, the sombre velvet of his breeches, the
broad expanse of his brow, the lustre and keenness of his hawk-
ish eye, the rugged thoughtfulness of his features, the firm set
of his mouth, and the commanding and soldierlike aspect of his
whole deportment and demeanor. He rode by without heed to
the crowd, without a smile or relaxation of a single feature—a
carved statue for gravity and sedateness. I cried out till my
throat was sore, yet 'twas only as the sound of a drop of water
falling into the uproarious ocean. 'Twas whispered that the old
man, with the faintest stoop in his bearing, was the great Merechal
Schomberg. He rode beside the right-hand of His Highness.

Following these heroes came a long line of the famous Swiss
footmen, great alike in valor and discipline. They were men
of the ripest experience in warfare, being the mercenaries of
many a continental army. At their heels regiment after regiment of British troops poured in. And not from the camp at
Hounslow, either. They had undergone service in Holland,
Germany, and France, and had bled on the field of Seneff,
whilst others had fought the Mohammedan Turk in and around
Vienna. After them came a regiment of swarthy black-bearded,
six-foot Brandenburghers, armed with pike and musket, and
bringing up the rear was an immense crowd of English refugees,
who had now come to avenge their wrongs and regain their
liberties. Amid this motley crew was one who did not fail to
take back my recollections three years at a bound to the less
glorious and less majestic pageant of Monmouth.

This sudden flood of memory was brought about by a glimpse of a fanatic knave in a Geneva cloak and a pent-house hat. I beheld, for a moment, his face hideously marked with the scurvy, his restless eyes, and keen twitching physiognomy; and instantly I knew it for that of the Scotch doctor, Robert Ferguson, who was a cross betwixt a rogue and a madman. Many wild discourses had I heard from his lips during the few weeks which had elapsed between the Duke's landing and the final affair of Sedgemoor. It brought a smile to my face to see him now at the tail of the array, whereas he had formerly been at the head of it, for the company of great men, both military and ecclesiastical, was no place for this half-witted, canting creature.

. After the refugees came twenty heavy pieces of brass cannon, each drawn by sixteen cart horses. At sight of these, the awe and admiration of the populace was not anywise diminished, whilst a strange wooden contrivance, drawn on wheels, excited wonderment, till it became known that it was a movable smithy for repairing arms.

This was the close of a brilliant pageant; whereupon folks dispersed to discuss the scene and the prospect of their champion's success.

Tobias and I followed on the heels of the multitude back to our hostel, and as we walked thence I found him heavy of wit and unwilling to talk. 'Twas but a natural way of his, for the more he was impressed by any sight or circumstance, the less he sought to impress his friends of the same by word of mouth.

A rude surprise was awaiting us when we returned to the Pipe and Tabor. 'Twas a comfortable tavern, and the landlord a keen fellow; indeed, a thought too keen for friend Tobias's liking. We were enjoying a nicely cooked meal when this person came to our apartment.

" Gentlemen," said he, with a very becoming perturbation, " I am much distressed to say that you must quit this hostel to-night."

" Whoy ? " demanded the blacksmith.

" Your pardon, sirs; but it's this how. Two of the quality have just arrived, and as every hostel in the city is full, they have offered me treble the price I am receiving from you. Therefore, gentlemen, I have accepted their terms, and will beg of you again, to quit this night."

Master Hancock planted his two arms on the table, stared straight at the innkeeper, and said shortly—

" Rather peart, I rackon, this man, landlord. But here I be, and here I bide till the army moveth vorrard ! "

In the face of this mine host argued, mine host coaxed, mine host swore, and finally threatened my friend the blacksmith. Yet Master Hancock hugged a grievance; therefore, all these oaths, threats, and protestations only served to make him still more stubborn. In the end, the landlord left us, breathing hints of summary proceedings in the immediate future. Tobias had right on his side, for mine host had not consulted us at all in the matter, which he should have done, if only out of courtesy. Accordingly, here we were, and here we were going to stay, quite prepared, if need be, to vindicate our position by blows as well as words. Indeed, this appeared to be a very probable contingency when the noblemen came to claim their lodging, if they should chance to be as determined as Tobe and I.

I was somewhat despondent that evening; I had heard very discouraging news. 'Twas to the effect that His Highness had already avowed his intention of only admitting the lustiest and brawniest recruits to his regiments, as he was not wishful for an indifferent army. He had brought so fine a force with him, that he could afford to be nice in the selection of his men.

Now I not being blessed by nature with anything of a physique to boast of, my chance of becoming enrolled was of the slenderest. As for the blacksmith, he, too, was distressed to think of my ill-fortune. On his own part he had no qualms, for I gravely question whether there was a man in the whole army so liberally endowed with bone, muscle, and inches. This edict was undoubtedly hard towards me. And 'twas a cheerless reflection that I should be obliged to return to Chilverley without striking a blow for the cause. No, I could not do that. The maid had bid me go forth and win. Then, and not till then, would I return to her. Besides, I had determined, long ere the words had issued from her lips, that I would ne'er go back until I had regained her freedom and mine own.

I brooded on this new misfortune for some time. Presently my thoughts were disturbed quite rudely, as a clatter of tongues and a jingle of spurs came from the inn passage, and instantly our room door was flung violently open, and two brilliantly attired cavaliers stepped in, with the grinning landlord at their backs.

I must pause one moment to describe the foremost of these gentlemen, because 'tis a fitting thing to give ample allowance to a great man, though I knew not the might of his reputation then, or the illustrious name he carried. He was in the prime of life, halting in gait, and very narrow-chested, but his face was one to bear in mind. 'Twas perfectly livid, i' faith almost deathlike in its pallor. It bore a roving, restless, careworn look, that seemed to tell of both mental and bodily suffering, though whether this was so I cannot say. Otherwise his features were regular, cleanly chiselled, and handsome in themselves, bespeaking a goodly share of birth and intellect. There was also a bright strong glitter about the eyes that strangely belied his uniform haggardness and the general listlessness of his deportment. His body accorded well with his countenance. 'Twas of painful thinness, all bone and corner, whilst even the thickness of his suit failed to conceal the gaunt outline of his fleshless limbs. His dress well became a man of wealth and station, inasmuch that his cloak was of purple satin, edged with sables, and his breeches exactly matched it. A neat periwig was set well back from a high and bloodless forehead, and a broad-brimmed hat, with a large white feather, that added a touch of jauntiness, surmounted it.

"So these are the cuckoldy rogues, host?" said he in a decisive fashion, and with the air of a great gentleman.

"Those words in your teeth!" quoth I angrily, for his insolence was more than I could brook.

"Landlord," said he, betwixt a smile and a snarl, "I trust you have a horse-trough in the yard."

"Certainly, my lord."

"Then will you have the goodness to summon the drawers and stable-boys, so that these fellows may make its acquaintance?"

"Certainly, my lord," and the host grinned over the speaker's shoulder at Tobe and me, and skipped away to muster his forces.

Meantime the new-comers stood just inside our apartment chatting. As for me, I felt my anger rising steadily; whilst Tobias drained his mug of cider, and murmured something about "Zons o' Antichraist" under his breath.

Hereupon the landlord re-appeared, with half a dozen of the inn-servants at his heels. The person addressed as my lord instantly instructed this little company to kick us out of the place. This they promised to do, and forthwith set about its accomplishment. However, they did not make allowances for Tobias, seeing that in two minutes, with some assistance from me, he had distributed sundry broken pates, black eyes, and bloody noses. Neither did he stop here, since he seized each of the gallants unexpectedly by the nape of the neck, and cracked their heads smartly together. But this was quite too much for gentlemen to put up with, therefore they whipped out their rapiers with the fury of wild cats and sprang at us. For a moment there was a fierce scuffle, during which our opponents' steel flashed unpleasantly near our breasts. Still, we were able to draw our own weapons, and Tobe's superior physique and my superior skill enabled us to get the best of the argument. The blacksmith soon disarmed his man, but the haggard fellow whom I had engaged I speedily found to utterly belie his appearance. 'Twas evident he possessed considerable knowledge of fence, and it was only my youth and vigor that gave me the advantage. In the end I was victorious; and then it was that our assailants showed themselves true gentlemen. They accepted their defeat without any tinge of animosity; and so gracefully did they compliment the pair of us upon our prowess, that very shortly all the ill-will between us was dispelled. Yet when the elder of the twain announced himself as the Earl of Danby, I may say that I felt none too easy in mind, for that nobleman was one of the most influential of William's supporters. Peradventure he is better known to the younger generation as the Duke of Leeds, perhaps the most celebrated politician of his time. Howbeit Tobias certainly did not share my qualms, for in the face of this avowal the blacksmith remarked with stolid gravity—

"Thou hast a mighty thick 'ead, my lord—a mighty thick un."

The result of our bout and subsequent reconciliation was that a compromise was arrived at, and the four of us occupied the two rooms between us. The famous earl and his friend took to us in the most surprising manner, and I ne'er wish to meet with men more sociable and kindly disposed. Later in the evening I chanced to mention my difficulty in regard to the army, and whilst he accepted Tobe's services on behalf of the Prince forthwith, he promised to do what he could for me. And the following day he proved himself equal to his word, seeing that he brought good news.

CHAPTER XLI.

THE OPENING OF THE CAMPAIGN.

I say the earl brought good news. He also brought something more tangible, to wit, a permit from the Prince to admit us into a regiment of British foot. As a consequence, next morning we were duly installed in that of Ossory—at least, it still bore that nobleman's honored name.

That very afternoon began a time of tribulation. 'Twas shoulder musket, present musket, poise musket, draw sword, present sword, shoulder sword all the livelong day. We were among a band of forty new recruits, and were put through that infernal manual till our arms and legs ached nigh to dropping off our bodies, and our muscles were as sore and stiff as though they had been in receipt of a daily cudgelling. Neither of us groaned, nor complained, nor flinched, but went through the irksome duties day by day, and, being quite jaded, slept sound o' nights.

His Highness was a great soldier. He would not have his army a rabble, therefore he chose his recruits (who were not too numerous) with the utmost care, and only the best grown and healthiest of men could hope for enlistment. And once he had selected them, for hours they were rigorously drilled, that they might be a credit to the army when the time for action came. We were not permitted to enter a horse regiment— indeed, none of the new soldiers were. Therefore our horses were sent to the rear, to assist in bringing up the transports and artillery.

Exeter at this time was a veritable theatre of war. The city rang with warlike talk and sounds. The smith's hammer ne'er ceased morning, noon, nor night, neither did that of the armorer. On every open space of green, square, or common, the recruits were fashioned into soldiers throughout the day, whilst men of warlike mien and aspect were to be found in all quarters of the town.

The strictest discipline was maintained. 'Twas the best behaved host ever known. It neither caroused, nor swore, nor gambled. It did not steal or pillage; but was sober and marvellously well conducted. Mind, I do not mean to say this army was so admirable in its behavior of its own free will, but the long and the short of it was, it had a leader, a master, a giant of determination and strength of will and mind. The Prince embodied all this, which his soldiers knew. His word was law. There were times when English, Dutch, Swiss, and German felt disposed to swear, yet, no matter whom he might be, he swore under his breath. Otherwise there was the wooden horse to teach him that His Highness would be obeyed. Perhaps one man would quarrel with his ration of beer and might drink that of his comrade, but three turns of a drumstick round his scalp speedily made him regret the dryness of his throat. The

commander inspired no love, but immense respect. He had
the captain's eye, the captain's mind, and the captain's arm.
And the first was trusted, the second admired, and the latter
feared. Though I regretted the harshness of the discipline,
my heart was glad, for I had found a leader, a great leader, a
mighty man, and, I doubted not, a conqueror. This was no
Monmouth—a mass of fears, revilings, entreaties, and hesitancy.
No ; here was a man of strength and judgment, a rock on whom
every trooper might and did lean.

After ten days tarrying within the city, preparations were
made for a march forward. The King had assembled the main
strength of his army at Salisbury, in Wiltshire ; and perhaps
the man on whose military skill he most relied was my lord
John Churchill. My lord was playing a bold game ; tho' James,
his master, suspected nothing. He shared the King's entire
confidence, as forsooth he had far greater military talent than
any one else in the Stuart's army. However, there was a private soldier of Ossory's foot in Prince William's host who, if
so minded, could have told enough to have startled King James
out of his senses. But this simple trooper kept his own counsel, and imparted the extent of his knowledge to no one till two
days previous to marching out of Exeter. Then he took his
patron, the Earl of Danby, into his confidence.

Tobe and I, being plentifully supplied with money, still
shared our lodgings with my lord and his kinsman (the younger
gentleman being nephew to the earl), so long as the army
remained in the city ; as the common soldiers were billeted in
any hovel or cowhouse, the place sadly lacking the necessary
accommodation for so immense a gathering. Therefore Tobe
and I greatly preferred our present abode to the precarious one
offered by the regiment. And as any soldier was at liberty to
sleep where he was so minded, providing that he answered roll-
call in the morning, we remained at the Pipe and Tabor. Accordingly, after the labor of the day, we returned thither, and
indulged in a mug, a pipe, and a game of backgammon along
with our condescending friends. I' faith such times as these
made all men condescending. Great men perforce herded with
the lesser ones, the town being swollen out of all size with its
thousands of inmates ; and doubtless many a coronet lay down
beside a shilling-a-day trooper.

Now, the night but one before the break-up of the quarters
within the city, we four became engaged on the subject of the
leaders of the war. My lord was saying with exultation how
we had several fine captains and the enemy had none.

"Not so fast, my lord," said I, for the sake of argument. "What of my Lord Churchill? Do you not call him a man of rare talent in the profession?"

Hereupon the earl smiled a curious smile, and one strangely full of superior understanding. I was nettled to think my patron was pluming himself on knowledge of which I had greater store than he. He thought he was in possession of a profound secret, and I at once made up my mind to let him know I shared it with him. However, I did not divulge mine own knowledge there and then, for neither time nor place was fitting. Indeed, was not the information the deepest of secrets? Besides, I must have been very imprudent to have revealed it in the presence of even such men as Tobe and my lord's kinsman. Thus I concealed what I knew for the time being, and let the earl's smile pass seemingly unnoticed. I waited quietly till supper had been disposed of; then as we fell to talking again, the earl chanced to sit beside me, whilst Tobe and the young cavalier were seated away from us across the table.

"My lord," said I, "if you are disposed to step out into the yard with me, I will interpret your smile of an hour agone."

His eyes met mine for an instant, and they were full of bewilderment. After that he laughed softly, and, imitating my secrecy, whispered back—

"I'll wager ten guineas you don't."

"Done," I returned. We clinched the bet upon the spot.

Still surprised, but continuing to laugh in the same stealthy fashion, he left the room, and I followed immediately in his wake.

I was not likely to do harm by my confession, for you will remember the Earl of Shrewsbury, in his letter to Sir Nicholas Marvin, had stated that Danby had been appointed the representative of the conspirators in London. Therefore I told my lord all I knew and all I had done. Neither did I forget to detail my interview with Churchill at Whitehall, and afterwards to treat of the death of the baronet and the final disposal of the papers. The story took a good quarter of an hour in the telling, the pair of us strolling up and down the inn-yard as we talked.

"Gracious Heaven!" he gasped, when the recital was ended. "I believe every word. 'Tis so wondrous circumstantial. Thy hand, friend; thou art a spunky fellow!"

He seized it in a feverish grip as he spoke, and I felt his own thin one tremble. 'Twas as though I held a bundle of nerves in my grasp.

" ' Tis marvellous ! " he said. " You won Churchill over to
the cause, and do you know what you did for me ? You saved
my neck. If the King's men had captured those papers, there
would have been sufficient evidence to have brought me to the
scaffold. And I was in London at the time. 'Pon my soul,
what a fine fellow you are ! "

I felt flushed with pride at this repeated praise from one
of the highest men of the time. For that night, at least, I did
not get the feel of his trembling hand from out of mine. There
was silence between us for some minutes, and by the rays of the
moon I could see his livid, haggard face strained, and his brows
knitted in deepest thought. By-and-by he said abruptly—

" If you have a mind to risk your neck once more, my friend,
I will make your fortune."

" Or my grave," I answered lightly, for it occurred to me the
word " neck " admitted of such a possibility.

" Tush ! " he cried in haste, " a man like you doth not consider such mishaps. 'Pon honor you have rendered us a rare
service, and I know how to give you a chance of great advancement."

" My lord," I replied with eagerness, already fired by his
manner, " I am ripe for aught, if it shall only benefit the cause
one iota."

" I promise you, Master Armstrong, 'tis a mission that shall
stagger you. And if it be only carried out like the other one,
'twill end the campaign ere it hath begun."

" Then I am yours to command, sir."

" Well, friend, go spruce yourself up a bit. Get your cloak
and sword and I will do the same, for we must repair to the
Prince to-night."

" But why to-night ? " I asked, surprised at this precipitation. " Will not to-morrow do equally as well ? "

" Certainly not. Ere daylight in the morning I shall be
riding post-haste for Yorkshire."

" What ! and leave the army ? "

" Yes, for a time. There is a great blaze waiting to be kindled in the north, and I am the spark to light it."

I understood his meaning perfectly, but will unfold it by
and by. I confess I was about wild with excitement regarding
the course matters had taken. I had not bargained for such
unheard of fortune. I was about to be brought face to face
with His Highness, and I had been promised advancement by
one of the highest men in the state. All this for a little adventure !

Here was I, Ned Armstrong, thief and fugitive, and more lately private soldier in the Dutchman's army, about to be brought under the personal notice of the rising star of Europe. I trembled as I brushed my hair; I trembled as I gathered my cloak around me, and as I buckled on my sword. I trembled as I thought of the risk to my neck? Surely not. Nay, I thought of doing a mighty service, of which my lord had promised me the chance. And when I had done it, I thought of returning to my darling—celebrated! my name on all men's lips.

Had not Mistress Dorothy Marvin bid me go forth and win, and then come back to her? Here was I—— Bah! thou inane old fool! better blush and conceal thy youthful follies sooner than bare them before the eyes of thy children. But 'tis fine to be young, to have a sword, and an imagination! Still my featherhead was afire, and there was palsy in my frame as I girded on my sword to visit the Prince in company with the earl. At every step I took there was ringing in my ears, "Go forth and win, and then come back to me!" and Taunton courthouse and my father's gibbet before my eyes.

CHAPTER XLII.

THE AUDIENCE.

As we set out for Prince William's abode, my companion slipped his arm through mine. This was yet another mark of the esteem he bore me. The night was keen and frosty, but free from mist and fog. The sharpness of the air certainly braced me in body, if it failed to make my mind any clearer.

The Prince was quartered at the Deanery, a large house in proximity to the cathedral. We found it bathed with a blaze of light. Every room was brightly lit, whilst in addition the moon illuminated the exterior, and thereby greatly enhanced the boldness of its aspect. It appeared to me very like a palace on a small scale, for a company of soldiers was drawn up in a line before the front entrance, with their musket-butts resting on the pavement, and their forms rigid and motionless in the moonlight. Whilst to heighten the effect of the scene, half a score noblemen's coaches, with liveried servants in charge of them, stood one behind the other in the roadway opposite the Deanery windows.

The first we came to was a carriage of sombre shade, which attracted Danby's best attention. He gazed earnestly at the panel, and reading out the coat of arms therefrom exclaimed—

" 'Pon my soul, a Seymour ! Can it be the Duke himself ? Let me see."

He examined the armorial bearings still closer, and said—

" Ah, to be sure, 'tis Sir Edward. James, my man, thy days are numbered ! Thy throne is tottering. If such staunch Tories as old Ned Seymour will join us, 'twill be good-bye to the Stuart dynasty."

" The sooner the better," said I.

At this point a wave of enthusiasm swept over my lord. 'Twas not unnatural, for hour by hour the Dutchman's standard covered a larger throng, whilst James's host just as surely diminished. As we arrived at the entrance, the guard promptly barred the way with their muskets.

" The word, gentlemen ? " asked the sergeant.

" London and Luther," whispered the earl.

On the instant the muskets were drawn back, the whole company saluted, and one of its number ushered us across the hall to a large ante-room. 'Twas crowded with a brilliant assemblage of men of all ages, nine out of every ten of whom bore the unmistakable aspect of the soldier. Yet there was not the least trace of levity, gayety, or frivolity about it. It was split up into many little groups, each of which emitted a buzz of low-toned, animated conversation, and this, combined with the grave demeanor of all present, clearly showed that some big event had happened.

" Hast heard the news, my lord ? " cried half a dozen cavaliers excitedly, at the sight of my illustrious companion.

My lord shook his head.

" The King hath arrived at Salisbury this forenoon," was the information proffered.

" Excellent ! " replied Danby warmly ; " I trow, gentlemen, we shall soon have our swords out of the scabbards."

This warlike sentiment delivered, we lost no time in making our way to the far end of the apartment, where a solitary individual was discovered beside a curtained doorway. He was a small portly man, clad Dutch fashion, in Low Country knee-breeches, and with a broad white collar round his throat.

" Is His Highness engaged ? " queried my lord of this person.

" Yes."

" With whom ? "

" The merechal and the chaplain."

"Well, do you go and tell him, Van der Kempt, that I am here, concerning our conversation this morning."

The little man did as he was bidden. And now numberless qualms and tremors took hold of me. Sure I cannot say whether 'twas the mere prospect of going into the great man's presence, or the sense of his majesty, or the ice of his demeanor that was responsible for this unworthy feeling, but certain it is, I felt very miserable, wretched, unheroic, and dejected. In half a minute the Dutchman returned, and I could have wished that his alacrity had been less, for I was in no hurry to make my bow to the Prince of Orange.

"Please wait a minute, my lord, then I will announce you," he said.

Here the curtained door opened again, and two men, Burnet the chaplain, and Merechal Schomberg, came forth together. Directly afterwards Van der Kempt led the way through that same door, and as he did so, my lord, with a backward glance at the departing twain, whispered—

"One is too nice, and t'other too garrulous for our business."

Another curtained door was opened, and as we passed through, it appeared to me as though my heart was taking unwarrantable liberties with my ribs. The apartment was small and simply but tastefully draped and furnished.

The Prince, with two elbows on the table, was leaning over a chart and tracing a line thereon with his finger. He did not glance up when my lord and I were announced, but continued his occupation till Van der Kempt closed the door and retired. Thereupon His Highness interrogated my companion.

"Well," he asked, "and who is that gentleman ? "

He stared at me with such directness that I must have taken it for rudeness in another.

"Allow me, your highness, to introduce him. Then perchance you may the better understand our visit at an hour so untimely."

Thereupon he gave the Prince almost word for word the narrative I in turn had given him, nor did he forget to add my assurance that I was willing to do aught for the cause. The Dutchman nodded his head, and methought I caught a softened look in his taciturn countenance.

"Tell Van der Kempt," said he, "not to disturb us for half an hour."

I slipped out of the room and informed the attendant. When I came back, Danby and the Prince were talking together in whispers, one each side the table, their heads nearly touching in the middle of it. They spoke so low I could not gather a word they uttered. Neither had I any desire to do, but simply stood bolt upright twirling my hat in my fingers. After five minutes of this their heads parted, and the Prince shot a question at me.

"How is it, sir, you are willing to risk, and have risked so much for our cause? 'Tis not religion."

He looked at me with his keen eyes as though he would read every thought in my heart. How did he know 'twas not religion? Nevertheless he was indubitably right.

"I have suffered, your highness," I replied, marvelling at mine own hardihood, for my tone was a much stronger one than I thought possible to employ before him.

He raised his dark brows.

"How?"

At that question I banished unworthy qualms, and I told him every word of my downfall, but not of my sins. I suppressed them, yet I briefly sketched my early misfortunes of the year '85. Somehow though I scarce paused to collect my breath or to weigh and turn my speech, the words formed into proper order and fell from my mouth distinctly, whilst my two august auditors ne'er lost a word of the recital. Having finished, I took breath and stood regarding the Prince with anxiety. His brows relaxed ever so little, a line in his mouth appeared less harsh, and there was less sharpness about his tone as he turned to Danby, saying—

"You have done very well," and then turning to me remarked, "I believe you, Sir Edward."

I started to hear my title so suddenly applied, and from the lips of such a man.

He saw that start, ay, he saw it, and with coolness asked, "How does it feel, Sir Edward?" He inflated his voice ever so slightly on the "Sir," and there was a biting tinge of irony in his tone. This cut me deeply, so deeply that I flushed crimson. And he saw that, too, for he quietly stroked his chin, and without the ghost of a smile added, "Well, well!" and bid me come close up to the table.

"Sir Edward," quoth he, "you will be useful;" but I never replied. I was hurt by his mode of treating me. His veiled sarcasm set me on my mettle, and as my spirit rose I forgot my qualms and nervousness. Therefore my only answer was to keep my head erect, and to peer hard and straight into his discerning eyes. They met mine, and I am happy to say I neither quailed nor flinched. Thereat he stroked his chin, repeated the words "Well, well!" and continued to look very grim.

All this time Danby had been busy with his pen. However, no sooner had the Prince finished speaking to me, than the earl handed him a sheet of paper half covered with writing. His Highness read it carefully through, nodded his head approvingly, sealed it with his own hands, and gave it into my custody. At the same time he presented me with a second document (unsealed) and a purse of gold. Still he gave me no instructions, and though this continued to keep me anxious as ever as to what was required of me, I was mighty thankful to leave his presence. Truth to tell, I was awed by him, and was afraid of him into the bargain. He seemed so calm, so strong, and so emotionless. His icy demeanor froze my blood, and added a tinge of hatred to my fear. Yet I knew quite well that I had conversed that night with a leader of men and a maker of nations.

CHAPTER XLIII.

THE ENEMY'S CAMP.

FORTUNATELY for my peace of mind, my patron did not keep me long in doubt as to what my mission was. Upon emerging from the Deanery, at my lord's suggestion we walked leisurely round the town, so that we might talk undisturbed.

"Thou art a lucky fellow," my lord began, "thou'rt still very young, but art already on the highway to fortune. I was doubtful at first whether the Prince would trust you in this important matter, yet he hath seen fit to do so; and he is seldom deceived in any man. Verily, my friend, you have great opportunities, you are young and bold, and have a head and a sword, and William trusts you. And his confidence, let me tell you, is not to be the least esteemed. Now listen to your instructions, for this is the mission entrusted to you."

I strained my ears, and felt unduly excited as the earl began.

"My lord Churchill hath been appointed the King's Lieutenant-general, and is now quartered together with His Majesty and the Army at Salisbury. You are required to deliver this sealed missive into my lord's hands. Mind, it must be done secretly and carefully. And the risks you run are great, as you will be obliged to penetrate into the midst of the enemy's camp. This letter is signed by myself, and remember you have come from me only. His Highness must not be known in this affair. Recollect then not to mention his name. There is a matter contained in the letter which will require the co-operation of Churchill and yourself, and you are to carry the matter out as well as you can between you. My lord will give you full particulars of what is required, yet I do not exaggerate when I say success will assure your fortune, and the termination of the campaign."

" And what of this paper of the Prince's, my lord?" I asked, doubting the veracity of my hearing faculties.

" Friend, His Highness hath foreseen much, and hath therefore provided you with money. As for the document he hath given you, it is a blank order for a company of men as large as you may deem necessary, to assist you in the enterprise. It is imperative that you should see Churchill at nightfall to-morrow, therefore you must set out betimes in the morning. Personally, my friend, I would advise you to take a score of picked men along with you. You must have your company hidden away in one of the villages just beyond the outposts, while you go alone into Salisbury and confer with my lord. You cannot be too careful in the execution of every detail, and do not forget what I have said already—success means your fortune, and certain victory for our cause."

To expedite matters my companion, who was singularly eager over the whole affair, went round to the officers' apartments at a house behind the Deanery, and arranged with Colonel Mackay to have twenty picked men, well armed, well fed, and well mounted, to await me at daybreak in the morning beside the east gate of the city.

Danby did not fail to thoroughly impress again upon me the immense honor and confidence that had been placed in me, and begged, if only for his sake, that I might show myself not unworthy of it. Though the entirety of this enterprise was not revealed to me, I was continually reminded that it was one great enough to startle the three kingdoms. I longed for the morning, that I might go forth and prove myself. I craved for success, for you can well understand what it would mean to me. Albeit, despite the fevered workings of my brain, whenever my mind returned to the cold, calm, freezing Prince of Orange, I felt suddenly chilled. And as I thought of that man I made up my mind come what might, I would sooner lose my life than acknowledge defeat to him. Of course there was another I thought of too ; one who had said, " Go forth and win, and then come back to me."

25

Yes, I would go and win! I would set the kingdom on fire with my celebrity. I would extort a word of praise from the Prince, I would kindle a magnificent light in my darling's eyes!

I was too eager and excited to swallow much breakfast, and before the first streak of daylight had silvered the sky I stepped out into the inn yard. The first sight that confronted me was my lord Danby, ready to start with half a dozen outriders on his journey to the north. Still, he had not forgotten me. No, he certainly had not, for there was a beautiful and fleet sorrel mare ready saddled for my use; and 'twas due to my lord that the animal had been placed at my service, in lieu of great Gustavus, who was assisting the conveyance of the transports.

"Sir Edward," quoth Danby, as I was about to ride away after profusely thanking him, "I go north to light a beacon, do I not? but you go east to fire the kingdom. I trust you; the Prince trusts you; and I would I were younger and less known to my enemies, for then I would go along with you. You will ne'er leave my thoughts all the way to York. Thy hand, friend, and also put thine ear to my mouth. I did not tell thee the precise nature of thy mission last night, else thou wouldst not have slept. *It is to bring King James a prisoner to Prince William at Exeter.* Thy hand again, Sir Edward; then go, and God speed you!"

Next moment my mare's hoofs were clattering over the stones, bound for the east gate, and her rider was trembling in his saddle. I could still feel the hot grip of the earl's thin hands, I could still hear his voice, and that of the Prince, our master. And they had both addressed me as "Sir Edward."

The troopers were waiting as I rode up, and within two minutes of my arrival we were following the road to Salisbury to fetch the King. The white frost lay everywhere, and imparted a soothing chilliness to the air. The hills and bare hedgerows were bedecked in this raiment of winter, and the roads lay hard as flint at our feet. There was no sign of war in the land; everywhere was peace and serene beauty. By and by the red winter sun appeared, and for miles the hoar frost glistened and sparkled. Nature was glorious that day, and the cold breeze sent the blood of healthy creatures a-swirling through the veins, and set a keen glow in their cheeks. Yet two great armies were lying watching each other, less than a hundred miles apart, like foxhounds in a leash, straining and crouching, each ready for a spring.

The lovely west countryside was to be bathed in blood once more, and as I looked at the landscape my heart did ache to think of it. Then it flashed upon me what I was about to compass; and, surely, if I succeeded there would be an end of the matter. And it hath since occurred to me many a time that the most important man in all England that frosty morning, was neither King James nor Prince William, but Ned Armstrong, robber and outlaw.

But now was not the time for dreaming. A tremendous and terrible work lay before me, and it soon dawned upon my understanding that nature had never made me for such mighty enterprises. A man at such puissant moments as this should be keen-witted, cool and collected. Yet here was I, trembling all the way I went. Albeit, 'twas not fear, nor the risk to my neck, but the bare idea of the appalling task before me. However, one circumstance gave me hope, and a certain amount of confidence. My lord Churchill had many brains, and was sworn to the cause. Thus with an ally so powerful I might hope for the best. Howbeit, the demands for the present were caution and courage.

Every step took our little cavalcade nearer the enemy; and I was its sole leader. All the way I had my mind anchored to one thing. It was my beacon, my guiding star, my hope of life; and that was—success. Two things told much in my favor. I was thoroughly acquainted with the country I had to pass through; and also had concentrated every ounce of my intelligence on this supreme adventure. And when a man hath so summoned all his mental resources, they cannot be of much quality if something creditable doth not accrue for their efforts. I neglected no single opportunity so far as lay in my power. I was bent on success, and success I would have, though I spilt every drop of my blood to procure it.

Acting according to the earl's orders, it was imperative I should myself reach Salisbury that night; but eighty miles is a most arduous day's journey. We pushed on and on, always well-nigh at the top of our speed. My soldiers shook their heads at this rate of progress, and the oldest man of the company ventured to remonstrate with me, saying that if we had to travel far the horses would be spent in a very short time. However, I knew mine own business best, which I was not slow to prove to their satisfaction, for after a smart burst we came to Ilminster with tired horses. And then, whilst the troopers ate a mouthful of food, I sought the landlord of the inn at which we halted, and struck a bargain. I paid the man ten pounds to procure me twenty-one fresh, speedy horses (if so many were to be had in the place). As security for their proper return, I left our own jaded beasts, all excellent animals, in his keeping, and promised him more money when we came back and resumed their possession. I strictly enjoined him to look to them well, and to have them prepared for our use at a moment's notice. Herein lay wisdom, for methought it not unlikely that we might be hotly pursued on our backward course. In that event we should have a fresh relay awaiting us. 'Twill thus be seen this plan answered two purposes: it enabled us to advance and retreat with greater expedition.

When my small command came forth, after a quarter of an hour's halt, and discovered a fresh lot of animals ready saddled awaiting them, I went up at a bound in their esteem. For mine own part the only refreshment I partook of here was a crust and a mug of ale. I was too eager and anxious to do justice to any more substantial meal. 'Twas think and fast with me all that day. I neither spared my head nor my body in the service. I was playing for a huge stake, and, Heaven knows, I did all that flesh and blood could do to win it.

Upon pressing forward again after this short halt, we soon began to ride into real danger; and 'twas then that my wits were needed. We rapidly approached the King's army. As we neared the Wiltshire borders, I inquired rigorously at every little wayside hamlet as to the whereabouts of the enemy. Fortune certainly favored me in this matter, for I found the peasant folk heart and soul for the Prince, therefore they imparted all they knew.

Leaving Wincanton on the left, we crossed into Dorsetshire; a little later and we were traversing the Wiltshire roads. 'Twas in this county that King James and his host were lying, thus I felt that the crisis was at hand. The surrounding hills were now settling into gloom, the cold, November sun had already retired behind them, and the shadows were creeping along the valleys, whence I knew that night and the enemy would prevent much farther progress.

We tarried at a small inn at the village of Hindon to make new inquiries, whereupon we learned that an outpost lay at Warminster, a town eight miles distant, whither Kirke and Trelawney were posted with four regiments of Irish. No travellers were staying at this little hostel, so by means of a guinea mine host was prevailed upon to harbor our company for the night, and to hold a discreet tongue in his head. But for me the day's work was only beginning, and to carry it properly through I had recourse to sheer boldness, which more often succeeds than it fails.

I had had the forethought not to don the Prince's uniform upon starting from Exeter, therefore I was able to pass tolerably well as a Catholic gentleman who had hastened from his country home provided with a letter of introduction to my lord Churchill, Lieut.-general of the army, that he might receive an appointment therein to fight for his religion. Accordingly I gave my horse a short rest, took a pull at some strong water, to keep out the cold, and then set out in the darkness for the Stuart's headquarters.

At ordinary times 'twould have been a cold and weary journey in the cheerless night, yet now I snapped my teeth upon a determination to brave all weariness and danger; and Danby's missive in my pocket, I urged my horse briskly forward along the bleak and wintry roads under the winking stars. I evaded the enemy's outposts, and thereby escaped interrogation. Having some knowledge of the country hereabouts, I pursued my way along the by-paths till at last the lights of the city were twinkling ahead.

As I neared the town my heart began to beat quicker than its custom was, yet I still went forward, fully determined that only prison bars should prevent me seeing Churchill that night. I rode without hindrance into the city, for, as I was soon to discover, the military order was of the poorest. I entered with outward confidence the first inn I came to within the town. Having inquired of a roystering crew, half English and half Irish soldiers, I was directed to the Bishop's Palace (the King's headquarters) as being the most likely place to find my lord. Thereupon I wended my way thither, having first procured a lodging for my horse the while.

'Twas a large building, with a spacious interior, yet 'twas nought near so crowded as the Deanery at Exeter, and the cause of this required little seeking, seeing that the Stuart's popularity was waning day by day, and his deserters mostly found their way to the Prince.

Fortunately Churchill was still there, and to my near pleasure, upon preferring a request for a private interview on the ground of " important business," an attendant forthwith went in search of my lord. He came back in a moment, and conducted me to an empty apartment, which, though small, was warm and well lighted. Thus far matters had prospered far beyond hope or expectation ; indeed, the place seemed quite devoid of military order and precaution.

Presently my lord appeared. He was richly attired, and I have rarely seen a man with more beauty of countenance or carriage. He looked me over every whit as keenly as when I had encountered him in London; then showed he had a rare faculty for remembering faces by recalling mine with a start of surprise.

" You are over bold, young sir."

" These are bold times, my lord," I answered, handing the letter into his custody.

" Body o' me! the most daring letter-carrier I know.'

He broke the seals quickly, and read the missive. His eyes dilated as he scanned it; his handsome face flushed; and then he walked the room in uncontrollable excitement.

" By Heaven, it is a great scheme!" he exclaimed at last, banging his fist a tremendous thump on the little table.

Forthwith he scanned me again from head to heels with a strange glare in his eyes.

" Friend, I presume you know the contents of this letter?"

" I do, my lord," I replied, striving hard to make a show of calmness.

" And you know what you and I between us are to essay?"

" Certainly, my lord."

In great agitation of mind he quickly secured the door, and turned up the lamp to its fullest light; and all the while I could see his white hands trembling. First he told me he implicitly trusted me. He said he had every reason to do so, as he had already a knowledge of my daring and shrewdness. However, far above all personal observation, my Lord Danby had seen fit to confide so great a mission to me. Thus it was Churchill, with the scantiest parley, bid me assist him in devising a scheme —a scheme to kidnap the King! Were I a boastful man, I might enlarge at length on the strange hour I passed with the most brilliant military genius of his time. First he asked what assistance I could render him.

" My lord, I have a score stout fellows, well armed and well mounted, lying at Hindon, under my orders; also, I have a re-lay of horses in readiness at Ilminister for the return journey to Exeter."

" Good!"

Then he became pensive, stroked his lips and wig, and afterwards communed half aloud with himself.

" Let me see, there's Cartwright at Wilton. No, that's too near. There's Williams at Heytesbury, and he's too thick-headed. No, he'll not do. H'm! and there's Kirke at War-minster; yes, there's Kirke at Warminster. Zounds, that settles it!"

He sprang from his seat, and began pacing up and down once
more. With the growing of his excitement mine also increased.
Shortly afterwards he unfastened the door, and called out to a
soldier hard by—

"Go seek Colonel Kirke ; and if he is anywhere to be found,
tell him to come hither to me on the instant."

Meanwhile I had casually glanced at the open letter on the
table. Perchance this did not become me then, neither doth it
any more become me now to set forth one clause which caught
my eye, and every word of which I still remember. It ran,
"Should this affair be executed in a proper and fitting manner,
I have no doubt His Highness will wot of a dukedom ready for
disposal." Since that hour my respect and admiration for the
famed Duke of Marlborough hath ever been less than that
borne towards him by my fellow-men.

Presently the door opened, and a big, swart, fierce-looking
man, in an ostentatious uniform, entered.

"Good evening, Colonel Kirke," was my lord's greeting.
"You have not forgotten our converse of the other day?
Friend, the time to act hath now arrived."

The colonel started, and cast a look of inquiry towards me.
I was at this moment in the company of the "Tangiers
Butcher," one of the biggest of traitors and the hardest-hearted
of men that was ever endowed with life. Yet 'twas neither the
time nor the place to cherish private sentiments, nor have I the
inclination to air them now.

In a few words my lord informed the soldier what had to be
done. Upon recovering from the first shock of his surprise, he
and his superior laid their heads together to devise a plan,
whilst I waited with ill-concealed anxiety and impatience for
the result of their deliberations. They carried on a low-toned
conversation for the best part of half an hour ; and the outcome was that Churchill suddenly exclaimed—

"Verily, colonel, thou hast solved the riddle—that is, if thou
art quite sure of Trelawney. Come with me and impress the
King with the extreme urgency of the matter. And you, sir,
wait quietly here till we return, when we will lay a definite
proposal before you."

Thereafter the pair of conspirators went out together to seek
an interview with the King. I marvelled much at the audacity
of these two traitors ; had I been in their position I could not
have met the man I was betraying with the eye of innocence.

In the course of a quarter of an hour they returned to me,

and relocked the door after them.   My lord spoke, and I list.
ened eagerly to each word he uttered.

"D'ye know the little town of Warminster?"

"Yes, my lord."

"And Bugley village?"

"Yes, my lord."

"There is one hostel in the place called the Wheat Sheaf.
You and your men are to be there at noon to-morrow. His
Majesty is to review the troops at Warminster, and will then
proceed with myself and Colonels Kirke and Trelawney, and a
company of six chosen men to reconnoitre and examine the
country as far as Bugley, which is two miles away. We shall
call at the Wheat Sheaf for a drink of cider.   Have your horses
in good condition for a speedy flight, and keep them and your
men concealed from the roadway.   There will be a resistance
offered, so have your pistols primed, with which shoot down
the soldiers.   I and the two colonels will endeavor to drag His
Majesty outside to the horses, but of course we shall be outnumbered and overpowered.   Now do not fail to have your
men there before noon to-morrow.   You will be in no danger
of discovery, as it shall be looked to that you are not disturbed
by our troops.   You understand, I hope.   Be cautious and
speedy, and we shall have our man under lock and key this
time to-morrow."

I told my lord I understood perfectly.   The scheme was
wondrous simple, indeed, almost too simple it looked at first,
seeing how great the idea was, and what would be its outcome.
Yet its simplicity was easy of explanation.   The misguided
Stuart, cold wretch as he was, was the most unsuspicious of
men.   He had at this time the sublimest confidence in Churchill,
his right-hand man, and chief adviser.   His eyes had yet to be
opened concerning that arch traitor, and the cool-headed rogue
profited by the blindness of his master.   And though I knew
all this, I did not feel the least pity for my father's murderer,
neither had I regrets or scruples for the work I was myself
encompassing.   They tell us "all is fair in love and war,"
whilst with me vengeance was an even greater stimulant than
either of them.   Accordingly, my conscience was not sufficiently delicate to give me any twinge of compunction, and I now
say without shame, that even in my old age it has not taught
me to feel it anent this matter.

'Twas after nine of the clock ere I set out for Hindon.   I
returned thither without misadventure, never being once chal-
lenged within the city, for the army was far too busy wine-

guzzling and dicing to pay heed to a young man of four--
and-twenty, who held the future of the kingdom in the hollow
of his hand.

That return journey to Hindon seemed a wild dream. What
would William say, and how would he look when I rode in
with the King? What would Danby say? What would the
Nation say? What would Mistress Dorothy say? And be it
distinctly understood, she was of far greater account than the
Nation, Prince William, and the Earl of Danby united. I could
scarce realize my splendid fortune. The plan was so simple
and certain of success, that methought nought could balk it.

I reached Hindon in safety, and found my men had been undisturbed, since none of the enemy had appeared, as the outposts lay more to the north. I did not breathe a word of the
mission upon which we were engaged to the company. Still
they obeyed me in every particular, for the army had been
thoroughly taught that finest of military virtues—obedience to
superior officers. There is one thing I recollect doing that
night that stands boldly out in my memory. Perhaps it was
foolish in me to sit on the edge of my bed for an hour gazing
at the portrait of my darling; wondering what the morrow had
in store. Howbeit this veracious history bids me recount e'en
so slight a circumstance.

Next morning I looked to it that the horses were well fed,
and that the men made a hearty breakfast. Then at a steady
pace, and with extreme vigilance for lurking enemies, we left
the quiet hamlet of Hindon, and made our way northward in
the direction of Warminster. The frost still held, and travelling
was by no means irksome, despite the nipping morning air.
Avoiding the main highways (the enemy occupying much of
the countryside hereabouts), we skirted Great Ridge Wood and
Brixton Deverill, and within half an hour of the appointed
time were snugly ensconced in the parlor of the Wheat Sheaf
at Bugley. This is a point nearly twenty-five miles west of
Salisbury and two miles from Warminster. I stationed two of
my troopers to hold the horses in the inn yard; who were
made ready for immediate service, that there might be no delay
upon the arrival of the conspirators and their victim. Then I
enlightened my men in a measure in regard to the meditated
trepanning. Certainly I mentioned no names, but fully instructed each man as to the nature of his duties, and saw to it
that his firearm was properly loaded for instant use, if necessary.

As the appointed hour drew near, my eagerness and excitement became intensified. Twelve o'clock midday chimed at the

little church across the road; and every sound of the clock sent
a thrill through me. At any moment now they might arrive,
therefore I stationed a man on foot in the middle of the road
to keep a sharp look-out up the highway, and bade him instantly come and advise me when the ten horsemen hove in
sight. Half an hour went by, and though they were doubtless
approaching, I fervently hoped their coming would not long be
delayed, for 'twas a great strain on my nerves. One o'clock
struck at the rustic church, still the man in the road made no
sign. I hurried out to look for myself, tho' my anxiety went
for nought. The bare, white road, wound ahead without a
speck upon it as far as the eye might scan.

I returned indoors and tossed off a cup of mulled Hollands,
for now I felt my courage to be steadily drooping. Two o'clock
sounded, whereat I grew more uneasy. I went outside again,
and strained my eyes on the track, yet 'twas still one long streak
of white. I now ordered relief for the man in the roadway and
the men with the horses. I was growing strangely nervous.
Three o'clock sounded. By this an ugly foreboding had taken
the place of hope and triumph. The rogue on the look-out
could offer no consolation, and the minutes still continued
monotonously to flee. I walked up and down dolefully, and
even more anxiously than my lord had done the night before.
What did it all mean? And the stern countenance of Prince
William was beginning to rise in my brain.

Presently the sun began to sink, and my heart with it. What
could have happened? Churchill had certainly said noon at
the Wheat Sheaf, Bugley. I became frightened and more
restless; and my heart sank lower. Must I go back and tell
William I had failed? I dared not. How I feared that man!
I waited till my spirit was sore with vexation. Still the man
in the road could offer no consolation, and the wintry sun was
waning, ever waning, but no King, no Churchill, and no news!
I paced about the road in a fever of agitation, and clutched
miserably at my hair, for His Highness, icy and cold, was before me. Now I was beginning to hear his voice whispering in
my ears. This hallucination chilled my blood. Why did they
not come? Why should I be thus balked of my reward when
the plans had been laid so skilfully, and success had been so
certain? 'Twas maddening to tarry thus with the gray of the
twilight creeping on, shadowlike, ghostlike, with the night so
fast approaching, and with the frost-laden air getting keener
and more piercing as the moments passed.

In desperation I sought refuge in another mug of Hollands.

Yet still the shadows were closing in, and there was no cavalcade of ten, no Churchill, no King, and no glory! I stamped my feet impotently, worked myself into an unavailing rage, and let forth a stream of oaths. Then the night wind came rustling among the naked hedgerows and moaned sadly over the bare and silent plain, whilst the white length of road became gradually blurred and indistinct. The maid of the inn was just bringing lighted candles (for the dusk was growing deeper) when the watcher outside came running in, crying, "They're coming, captain!"

I ran outside, and peered eagerly into the gloom. The click of hoofs sounded clear to my ears, and I could plainly see a body of horsemen fast approaching.

———

CHAPTER XLIV.

THE AFFAIR AT THE WHEAT SHEAF, BUGLEY.

AT last the time had come. I rushed round to the yard; the men still held the horses. I gave a hasty glance at the animals, and saw they were all in readiness. Next I returned indoors, and as I did so could hear the coming cavalcade so plainly that their talk was distinctly audible above the harsh music of their horses' feet. Instantly my men were alive and eager.

A hubbub arose outside, in which stamping hoofs, champing bits, and many voices were intermingled. It struck me that this company of ten was showing a very small respect for its King, to judge by the noise it made. The outer door was pushed open, and a crowd of soldiers came scrambling in, treading on the heels of one another in their haste.

"Quick, my lass, a pint of ale for me! We ain't much time to tarry, and its mighty co——" "Hey, wench! a pint for me, and——" "Prithee, good mistress, a flagon o' sack——" "Quick wi' a black jack of October, wench!"

"Peace, gentlemen! I cannot serve ye altogether," quoth the girl with a pout.

This cold crew were not those I had expected; though 'twas evident they belonged to the King. Suddenly one of them took notice of us, and cried out at the pitch of his lungs—

"Holy Virgin! those are Dutch Bill's Hollanders!"

A mighty exclamation made the rafters echo, and the fellows came crowding round us. 'Twas a desperate situation; at such

moments a man may be pardoned many things.   They instantly
prepared to arrest us.   To judge by the babel 'twas a whole
regiment that had arrived.   Our pieces were loaded, so I gave
the word to fire, and then to charge.   Seventeen pistols cried
out together; the little room was choked with smoke, and the
doorway was hideously cleared.   The smoking weapons were
discarded, and, sword in hand, my band made for the door,
striding over and trampling on prostrate forms in our progress.
The press being very thick outside, a fierce struggle ensued,
and blows and cries were everywhere.   With our blades we
hewed vigorously, and in two minutes a dozen of us had sprang
into the saddle and were spurring for dear life out of the hostelry yard, down the road to westward over the Somersetshire
border.   We fled with a loose rein, yet soon our enemies were
in full cry after us.   However, we had a good start, and the
horses being fresh and the darkness rapidly advancing, we had
not many fears as to our ultimate escape.   We were now thir-
teen in all.   Thus it will be understood eight of our number
had failed to make their way to the yard, and had either been
struck down or captured.

Ere long the pursuit ceased, but the enemy being now apprised of our presence, there was nought else for us to do but
to return to William's camp.   By the aid of the moon we rode
all night, through Frome, and by way of Glastonbury and Somer-
ton to Ilminster.   Arrived there, we knocked up the grumbling
landlord.   Very soon we resumed the possession of our own
steeds, and they being fresh and well cared for, bore us towards
Exeter at a sprightly pace.

Oppressed, stricken, and defeated, I sate listlessly in the saddle, my thoughts of the bitterest.   Thus had ended all the
dreams of glory and success.   I sank my head on my breast in
despair.   God knows I had done everything within my power.
I had left no stone unturned ; I had striven to provide against
every possibility ; I had not spared myself or my command ; I
had pushed on without tarrying.   I had seen and arranged with
my lord, he had passed his word that every plan was complete,
and here I was flying beaten before the King with the mission
unfulfilled, and nearly half my men left in the hands of the
enemy.   'Twas bitter! bitter!   How to face the Prince after
such a woeful ending I knew not, nor did I dare to think.   How
I feared the man !   I grew ominous once more at the thoughts
of my forthcoming interview, and shuddered at what was in
store.   That icy countenance, that demanding eye; how I
dreaded them !   Yet, even in this hour of defeat and desolation,

I bethought myself of the portrait I bore in my breast-pocket, and, under cover of the darkness, I drew it forth and kissed the face it bore. I tried very hard to be as brave as my mistress was, but was wholly unsuccessful. Again that iceberg of a man, the Prince of Orange, came into my mind. And at his apparition the fear of him completely overwhelmed me. Then it was I knew my old fortitude, endurance, and courage had deserted me, and that God had set the seal of a broken man upon my spirit.

Half frozen with the severity of the weather, we came to Axminster towards eight of the clock in the morning. Here a surprise awaited us. We had only reached the outskirts of the town, when a body of our troops pulled us up curtly and demanded our business. From them we learned that the Prince had marched out of Exeter the previous day, and was now lying in and around Axminster, having left his headquarters strongly garrisoned, under the command of Sir Edward Seymour. Soon I was to hear something to disquiet me. 'Twas that His Highness had already inquired for me, and had given orders that I must repair to him as soon as I arrived. Therefore I had no alternative, other than to go and give an account of my dismal failure. Straightway I made for the Prince's headquarters. He was stationed at the principal inn in the town. I set out thither, without even stopping to souse my face, or to brush my coat, or to thaw my limbs; being desperately anxious to get the interview done with. It almost maddened me to brood on it, and to conjecture what the result would be. Van der Kempt was in attendance outside the door as usual.

"I am glad you have come," he said. "His Highness hath already inquired thrice for you."

This did not tend to reassure me. At that moment I bitterly repented having told so much to Danby. Then I should not have had this ill-fated enterprise entrusted to me, and the nauseous pill of defeat to swallow. Van der Kempt ushered me in. I strove hard to pluck up spirit and smarten my dejected bearing.

As I stepped into the apartment I caught a full view of myself in a large mirror opposite the door and I gave a start as I did so. My person was a mass of glistening hoar frost, my face was pale and worn and haggard, and a dark stain of blood ran from my forehead to my jaw, the presence of which I was now aware of for the first time. 'Twill thus be seen my appearance accorded very ill indeed with the presence of the Prince my master.

His Highness was seated at a table facing the doorway, and had a huge mass of papers and a map before him. He looked up as I entered, and presented me with a stony stare.

" Well ? "

" Your highness, er—I—I—I've—— "

" Failed ! " he inserted icily, then gave me another blood-chilling stare. Said he, " Sir Edward, I require a verbal account. And don't stammer. It jars on my nerves."

By some means I told him all, tho' I can never say how. Perchance it was because my finger-nails bit into the flesh, because my head was singing, or because I had the hot ache in my toes. Anyway, I told him everything—everything, even to Churchill's excitement and mine own, and how I had left eight troopers behind with the enemy. He listened immovable. When I had uttered the last word, I folded my arms over my fluttering heart, and prepared for the worst. What would it be ? How I feared that stoical wretch ! How I feared that ice-cold Dutchman, and how I hated him ! He said nothing. He did not even glance at me again. He simply turned to his documents, seized a pen, and began to write, his countenance inscrutable, but very acid. He did not dismiss me. He did not bid me tarry. He kept me standing there miserable, dejected, pale, bleeding, with a whirling head and frozen feet, yet still he wrote in silence. Once more I fell to twirling my hat. At last his pen ceased. He looked up quickly and regarded me. My teeth set with a snap.

" Come hither, Sir Edward," quoth he quietly.

I did as I was bidden, and as I approached him I felt the power of speech come back.

" Your highness," said I, in a low tone, " I have done my best. More than that no man can do. Methinks Providence hath been against me."

I looked at him doggedly, sullenly, and thought myself an ill-used man. As for the Prince, he returned my gaze, with a cynical turn of the lip ; then handed me the paper he had written, and commanded me to read it. I did so, and emotion nearly mastered me in the mean time ; 'twas a captain's commission and an appointment as one of his aides-de-camp.

" You are a brave man, and I like brave men," said the Prince softly.

" Your highness—— " I gasped, with notable lack of breath. I got no farther.

" Tut, Sir Edward, that will do. Go to bed and dream of your baronetcy. You are excused from duty to-day."

He smiled as he said these last words, and as I left him, tho' I was not precisely sure whether I employed my head or my heels to walk with, I felt exquisitely proud of myself, and took out again the portrait, and passed delightful moments in anticipating how my great-spirited mistress would thrill with the news.

After some hunting about I found a bed of warm straw in a farmer's hayloft. First I procured quills, ink, and paper; penned a tremendous epistle to Dorothy, then flung myself down amongst the straw, and slept for ten hours. Yet I disobeyed His Highness, for I dreamt of nothing at all; nay, not even of his smile.

CHAPTER XLV.

THE NIGHT RIDE TO LONDON.

THE Prince remained several days in his present quarters, and was well advised in so doing. King James was eager to fight for the excellent reason that every day his own supporters dwindled, and his opponent's increased. However, William would not risk a battle with matters going so favorably; hence waited, but with the shrewdest eye, for passing events.

Two days after my second interview with the Prince, a messenger came riding into the camp post-haste from the north, and brought the news that my lord Danby had succeeded much better than I had. He had lighted the beacon as he promised he would; he had surprised the garrison at York, had disarmed it, and was now in possession of the city. A rebellion had risen in the north, and was rapidly spreading to the Midlands. When this news became known in our camp, there was scarce aught else to be seen, but smiling faces; indeed, the cause was prospering beyond expectation. As for me, the soreness begotten by my late misfortune wore gradually away. His High ness had much astonished me by his behavior, and 'twas particularly congenial astonishment. Wherefore I admired him more, and hated him less; tho' I was sadly puzzled in mind as to why I had failed, I could not bring my mind to believe that Churchill had wittingly played me false.

Upon the morning of the twenty-fifth of November, all doubts were suddenly and unexpectedly dispelled. I was in the room next the Prince's apartment, which had been formed into a kind of ante-room for the use of the officers. Accordingly I, having already assumed my new dignities, was ensconced herein, when a gentleman in the King's uniform entered with hot haste, and inquired for His Highness. A hum of amazement ran through the crowded assembly, since the new-comer was none other than Churchill himself in riding-dress. He bowed with his usual charming grace to the company, and was then conducted to the Prince. Meanwhile all of us eagerly speculated on what had brought him hither. Mayhap I was not so surprised at his coming as some of my comrades were, for methinks no man in the kingdom was better able to gauge the dark depths of the man's heart than myself. My lord and the Prince were closeted together for half an hour in private, and then the faithful Van der Kempt threaded his way through the throng and touched my shoulder.

"His Highness wishes a moment's speech with you, captain."

I gave an exclamation of surprise, yet followed at his heels on the instant. I discovered the Prince and the soldier deep in conversation. Churchill, without any ado, smilingly offered me his hand. And I, being loth to accept it, he said—

"Confess, friend, thou art ruffled with me. You do me grievous injustice. 'Twas the hand of Providence that was the marplot; and, let me tell you, John Churchill is no match for Providence."

My heart went out to the fellow in spite of myself. He was so frank, and genial, and spoke with such easy grace, that I accepted his hand. It appeared another mission was waiting for me, and 'twas for that reason I had been summoned. William was as glum, silent, and icy as ever, though his latest friend was all smiles and affability. The Prince it was, however, who gave me the orders, in a pointed and precise manner.

"Captain Armstrong," he said. "You will not tarry another hour, but must ride post-haste to London. The Princess Anne, whom I am assured is very well affected towards our enterprise, must be conveyed from Whitehall at once. Her father, the King, is already in retreat, and may contemplate evil towards Her Highness if she be not put out of his reach. You will therefore start with all speed, and get her away before her father arrives, as he hath heard of the state of her mind, and is very wroth thereat. Here is another purse for your expenses by the way, and, also, I give you leave of absence till our army arrives in London. And, my friend, you will not have to wait long for its arrival."

Those last words he spoke with the clearest confidence. 'Twas not boastfulness. 'Twas merely the faith he possessed in his own ability and that of his command. I was in the presence of this great man several times, yet on no occasion was I so much impressed with his self-reliance as on this one. I made preparations to set off at once on my journey, tho', ere I started, I held a short conversation with two persons; and they were my lord Churchill and Tobe Hancock.

Ye have heard, kinsmen, of Providence, and similar vague matters. And, certainly, what my lord had to say in his own defence savored very strongly of its mysteries. However, it appeared that his statement, strange as it was, did not overstep the bounds of truth, and it hath since passed into history. It seemed that at the very moment King James was stepping into his coach to review his troops at Warminster (as Churchill had promised me he should), he was suddenly seized with a violent bleeding at the nose, which prevented him from setting forth. This hemorrhage lasted three days, and thus completely baffled the designs of Ned Armstrong, Danby, Prince William, and those arch-traitors, Kirke and lord Churchill. I was loth to believe this singular story at first, but ere long it was amply corroborated.

As for Tobe, I had seen little of him of late; therefore I snatched a moment with him before starting. I confided my horses to his care, for, as I was going to ride at such a pace to London, I should be obliged to change horses several times upon the way, and I was unwilling to trust my steeds to the tender mercies of roadside hostelries. The blacksmith at once fell foul of my new mission, as he had done of my former one. He declared that the cause would not in any wise be benfited by such "hole-and-corner work." He had come to fight for his religion, and that being so, no amount of argument could convince him that he would be doing his duty to the cause by trepanning kings, or placing princesses out of danger.

I rode to Town as though the devil pursued me. I stopped only to gulp food occasionally, and to obtain a fresh horse to speed me on the journey. I had failed already in one enterprise entrusted to me by His Highness, but please God, I would prove myself on this occasion. In my desperate anxiety to be of service to him in this latest affair, I ne'er thought of fatigue or the frailties of the human body. I rode all day, and all night, till my coat was flecked with horses' foam, and my legs were so stiff that I could scarce put them to the ground without an exclamation, though in former days I had spent hours in the saddle, and was a practised horseman. I set out at midday on the Twenty-Fifth, and twenty-six hours later was in the streets of London.

26

Alas, I had come too late to be of service ! The Princess
had fled (none knew whither), between midnight and dawn that
morning. 'Twas a bitter reflection when I heard this news, to
think what I had gone through, only to fail again. Verily the
fates were set against me, and once more my heart drooped
when thus confronted with my non-success. And 'twas all the
harder to bear, as I considered I did not deserve such harsh usage.

I say that none knew whither the Princess had fled. Nevertheless absurd rumors were rife. Some of the ignorant stoutly
maintained she had not fled at all, but had been decoyed
away, and murdered by the bloody papists. These wretches
were considered capable of every crime under the sun, and
were treated accordingly. Never in the whole history of our
land had the popular mind been so incensed against the
Romanists. Their lives and property were not worth a
moment's purchase. Men called down curses upon the hapless
creatures, spat upon them, threatened them, robbed them, beat
them, and generally maltreated them in the most inexcusable
manner.

However, before the day was out, it was known for certain
that Anne had gone of her own accord, at the earnest counsel
of Sarah, Lady Churchill, her trusted friend and adviser, and was
now fleeing northward, in high dread of her father's anger at
her treachery towards him. She was accompanied by my lord
Dorset, and, to the profound astonishment and scandal of all
zealous churchmen, by Bishop Compton who held the diocese of
London. And this spiritual lord, not content with lending the
episcopal presence to the affair, had actually sported riding-
boots and a buff coat, not to speak of pistols and a sword,
for the occasion ; a proceeding which for long afterwards
gave great offence to the sober-minded, and associated the most
calumnious of stories with the name of his reverence. I was
bitterly disappointed at this latest turn of events. So, disgusted with myself, the world, and my luck of life, I wended
my way to good Master Fletcher's at the Three Crowns, where
a rapturous welcome awaited me (or my guineas). In no time
a hearty meal was laid before me. This was done ample
justice to ; the unfortunate Ned Armstrong having tasted but
the smallest portion of food during his journey.

With my legs somewhat eased by the rest, I determined to
take a stroll in the streets before going to bed, as my head was
not calm enough to entertain sleep.

An unlucky chance led me to the vicinity of Whitehall Palace.
'Twas growing dusk, and a mob was assembling round the

gates. I inquired the reason of this, whereupon I was told the retreating, defeated monarch was expected, and, to judge by the lively epithets employed, those assembled had no sympathy for him or his misfortunes. Neither had I; yet I lingered anxiously awaiting his arrival—the arrival of my father's murderer! A cruel joy seized me to know that this man was coming from the seat of war crushed, and fleeing from his enemies. I had no mercy; but gloated over the misfortunes of the heartless wretch James Stuart. He had had no compassion for hundreds of his noble misguided subjects, and, now he was in need of theirs, 'twas very rightly denied him. Aye, the time was fast coming for which I had longed and prayed. I did not forget my hellish oath; I did not forget my father's death; I did not forget the hideous courthouse; I did not forget the first night of exile. I felt the devil rising in my heart; and one fierce triumphant throb as I waited for the stricken wretch—the great man who had fallen. And all the while the crowd increased till a mighty concourse surged about the palace gates.

CHAPTER XLVI.

THE HAND OF GOD.

SUDDENLY the crowd struck up Lillibullero.* A brawny rogue, with a villainous squint, who stood by my elbow, bellowed horridly in my ear—

> " O den, broder Teague, dost hear de decree,
>   Lilli bullero, bullen a lah !
> Dat we shall have a new deputie?
>   Lilli bullero, bullen a lah !
> Lero, lero, lilli bullero, lero, lero, bullen a lah !
> Lero, lero, lilli bullero, lero, lero, bullen a lah ! "

* The editor appends the following extract from Percy's " Reliques," vol. ii. p. 365 :—
" Lillibullero, slight and insignificant as it may now seem, had once a more powerful effect than either the Philippics of Demosthenes or Cicero : and contributed not a little towards the great Revolution of 1688."
Let us hear a contemporary writer—
" A foolish ballad was made at that time, treating the papists and chiefly the Irish, in a very ridiculous manner, which had a burden, said to be Irish words, ' Lero, lero, liliburlero,' that made an impression on the (King's) army that cannot be imagined by those that saw it not. The whole army, and at last the people, both in city and country, were singing it perpetually, and perhaps never had so slight a thing so great an effect."—(Burnet.)

Hundreds of voices caught up the strange, wild, idiotic—

"Lero, lero, lilli bullero, lero, lero, bullen a lah!"

Meantime, above the strains of this chorus—which boded the greatest ill to every papist—was plainly heard the rumbling of carriage wheels and the howlings of the mob down the roadway.

Who can forget those tumultuous moments in the gathering gloom? The hundreds chanting that baleful ditty; the oaths, the cries, the curses, the savage joy of the London multitude. Then this pandemonium swelled into one great roar as a coach and four horses, with postilions lashing furiously, hove into sight at the bend of the road.

"The King!" shouted the mob, and another howl broke forth from the midst of it. However, the horses burst through the press, but not before I had caught a glimpse of a white face, paler than death's, cowering away from remorseless men.

The sight of this mockery of majesty brought up the devil quicker than aught else could have done. 'Twas the first time I had set eyes on the infamous king. My head began to grow tempestuous. And that was the herald of coming madness. I know I was mad that night. Why disguise the fact? I had caught a glimpse of my arch-enemy—the man who had done what nought could undo. My limbs had ceased to ache, my head had ceased to think. My eyes lost sight of the crowd —of everything but a cowering wretch in one corner of a coach, whose ghastly countenance was whiter than the virgin snow, whose fearful eyes held no sign of life. And then I did a thing of which to this hour I am ashamed. Seized by a sudden gust of frenzy, I picked up a large stone from the footpath and hurled it through the carriage window. I do not think it struck the King, but 'twas no fault of mine that it did not do so. This act accorded with the brutal humor of the crowd, and it set up a hoarse cheer of approbation. After this, I paced the streets like an infuriated animal, and every whit as pitiless and savage. I could not rid my disordered senses of the vision of the stricken King cowering before his subjects. It must have been hours ere I returned to the Three Crowns in the Strand. I do not know what I looked like, yet am aware Master Fletcher recoiled from me as though I had been a wild beast. I went to bed by and by, though not till mine host had given me a soothing potion, else I should ne'er have obtained a wink of sleep.

Next morning I awoke sensible, but, alas, 'twas not an un-adulterated blessing. Gradually the incidents of the previous evening came back to my mind, and the pangs of remorse they occasioned I do not care to dwell upon at any length. I had entertained the devil aforetime, yet God had spared me; and now, in gratitude, I had entertained him again, just as I had begun to think the undermining monster had deserted me forever. Besides there was a maid down in Somersetshire who had said, "Go forth and win, and then come back to me!" Was I to go back to her devil-possessed, with a madman's heart and a vengeful soul? If I could have passed over that hideous dream of the previous night, I would have foregone my expected baronetcy! As I lay in bed that morning, I felt the most utterly weak and unworthy man on all the earth's surface. If I could but blot out last night's doings; if I could but undo that cowardly act! I knew my father would not bide better in his grave for what I had done.

I rose and dressed myself and remained indoors all day, and lay mentally snivelling and repentant for hours over the hearth-stone. I opine, children, ye are about heartily sick of your wretched sire. Contrition is cheap coin to exchange for folly, and more especially when it can be entertained without loss of appetite, for I grieve to say I disposed of three slices of deer's meat at dinner-time.

The candles had been alight an hour on the evening of that day of humiliation, when the parlor door opened and admitted a little man in a riding-coat and jack-boots. I felt a thrill of pleasure; the traveller was my friend Petter Whipple.

"Ods, bud!" he exclaimed with a lively grimace of recognition, "mine old friend! What do you here?"

An explanation followed, and when mine host of the King's Head had divested himself of his riding attire, and had before him his perennial churchwarden and black jack, a similar question was put on my part.

"Business, lad," he replied, as a blue puff of smoke curled up to the ceiling. "I move wi' the times, d'ye see. Bridgwater is too quiet just now. There is need for a man o' brains in this city. These are the times when men wi' headpieces make fortunes. I have work to do here. Before I go back, I doubt not my purse will be fatter by a whole year's profits."

It was a real pleasure to me to have my friend's company, as I was seldom depressed in his presence.

Those were awful times in London. For some weeks there was no real government or law in the city, whereby the place was a veritable inferno. The Stuart's power was broken, and in his palace at Whitehall he remained crushed, not knowing whom to trust. He could offer no protection whatsoever to his

papist friends. They were the common enemy, and victims of
the lawless, ay, and of the self-believing righteous, too. Their
property was seized, and its owners were threatened and generally maltreated ; their houses were burnt, and the law had
not sufficient power nor sufficient inclination to protect them.

Pete delivered his mind on many matters the night following
his arrival.

"Do you mark my words, my lad," he said, "that prince o'
thine will find himself in a corner yet, if he doth not be very
careful. Men are flocking to his standard every day, and such
men—Jack Presbyters, Anabaptists, Independents, Churchmen,
Tantivies, and the deuce knows who. 'Twould take a head
like mine or Bob Bickers's to manage all that crew. Then he
hath gotten an army of Dutchmen—and this country will ne'er
take kindly to Dutchmen. You say His Highness is a rare
strategist. We shall see that. I shall be able to judge him the
better in another fortnight."

"He will be on the Throne in another fortnight," said I.

"Will he? Then he'll be off it again in a year. If this
Dutchman knows his business (and methinks he doth), he will
not seize power greedily. Let him avoid bloodshed, and
calmly wait till James takes to his heels of his own accord, and
till the whole nation hath begged him to assume the crown. If
he does things in a hurry, and shows an undue eagerness, he is
a fool. His game now is to play *the disinterested benefactor to
the country*, and to wait awhile, till the throne is vacant, and till
he is invited thereto."

"But, Pete," I interrupted, "he is properly entitled to it."

"Psha! you argue like a woman. Where's the man who gets
his deserts? I'm properly entitled to a place in Heaven, but
I'm not there yet. Besides he hath a mighty many friends to-
day who are friends of the moment. They're like Bob Bickers
and my meritorious self, they go with the wind. Dutch Bill
must have no real fighting, else this nation will turn on him.
'Twill ne'er watch its own men whipped by a set o' schnapps-
sucking Dutchmen. No, sir; if the Prince wants a firm seat on
the Throne, let him coax James out of the country, and then be
decently and duly invited to it by the voice of the nation.
That is the only way to wear the crown securely."

Pete abided close by his opinions, and methought them sound
enough. 'Twas undoubtedly the course likely to be followed
by a shrewd tactician, for should the Prince make a greedy grab
for power, then most assuredly folks would set it down to his
ambition, and would mistrust him in accordance. 'Twas evident

patience, watchfulness, and careful diplomacy alone would be able to seat him firmly on the Throne. By that means he would gain the confidence and full trust of the country at large. Still, I was not at all pleased with this plan, as it meant much weary waiting ere the great hopes I cherished could be fulfilled.

CHAPTER XLVII.

THE FLIGHT OF JAMES STUART.

'Twas plain that the Prince had equally as clear a perception of the situation as mine host of the King's Head, Bridgwater.

The King still remained at Whitehall, tho' every day his case became more hopeless, his power weakened, and his friends left him in larger numbers, whilst the populace grew more clamorous for William to mount the throne.

However, he did not hurry his march to the capital; but avoided anything likely to cause a conflict between his army and the scattered bodies of King's troops. The days went slowly by; and the Prince marched over Salisbury plain, and reached Hungerford on the sixth of December.

There were several parleyings hereabouts betwixt James and William, and from them it was plainly seen, by the patient manner in which the Dutchman listened to his foe, that he was playing the part of "benefactor to the country." Nothing of much import was the outcome of their talk, but on the tenth of December London woke to discover that the Queen and her infant son had fled.

The next day I overslept myself; but was rudely aroused, however, by a slap on the back from my friend Pete.

"Now then, you sluggardly varlet!" I heard him say, "awake and hear the news. King James hath fled!"

"Hurrah!" I shouted, jumping out of bed at a single bound, and executing a dance barefoot in my nightshirt.

Albeit, that was a thoughtless dance, for now we were in the throes of a terrible crisis. London was at the mercy of the mob. The King had fled; the Prince was miles away; and there was none to preserve order. Also James had sent orders to my lord Feversham to disband the army. The night that followed was a truly horrible one, and hath still a large place in my memory. As soon as darkness fell, Master Whipple advised his kinsman to bar his doors.

" If I am not mistaken," said the omniscient Pete, " we are to have such a time this night as we shall ne'er forget."

He had read the signs correctly. In the busy thoroughfare called the Strand ere long the noise of an immense rabble was heard. An hour later Master Fletcher bid us come up into his top garret, and climb from thence through the skylight on to the tiled roof of the tavern. We did so, and I beheld the most awful and most awe-inspiring sight I ever set eyes on. All round was one lurid glare ; on every side flames leapt skywards. Chapels, monasteries, mansions, dwellings were on fire, at the instance of the mob, because these buildings belonged to the papists. A hideous throng was gathered in the streets ; and we could clearly see it as we looked down from our coign of vantage. A wicked company, the pestilential scum of a great town, jostled one another in the narrow way, bent on plunder and destruction. Thieves, cut-purses, ring-droppers, money-changers, house-breakers, and the like were mingled with hundreds of foolhardy 'prentices, as they paraded the streets with the booty. Some bore an ivory crucifix, others a piece of rich cloth, others a picture, others rare candelabra. Yet this was in one hand only, for the other held a stave or a sword ; and bloody brawls were rife.

As the night advanced the howls of the mob increased with the flames. Casks of beer and wine were seized from private dwellings and were broached in the street below. 'Twas a loathsome sight to see the wretches grovel on their knees in pursuit of the liquor, and gather it in their hats. They fought and screamed, plundered and sacked all night through ; whilst as the hours went by the flames shot up higher and higher. On every side sparks, smoke, and the leaping tongues of fire rose nearer the sky. The convent at Clerkenwell, and its rich furniture and treasury of books were reduced to ashes ; and nearly all Catholic meeting-houses had only four walls left standing by morning. When at last the mob had spent its fury on these places, it turned recklessly on the mansions of the foreign ambassadors. Foremost among these was that of the Spanish minister, Señor Ronquillo. His house, close by Lincoln's Inn Fields, was burnt to the ground, his rich plate, seized by the greedy hands of the multitude, and many works of art and valuables destroyed. Upon the appearance of daylight the thousands hied back again to their dens, with the city a wreck ; leaving in every street grim windowless walls blackened and gaunt as a testification of their handiwork.

The day following this terrible night must not be passed

lightly over, as an event happened in the course of it which, even now, sets the blood flowing the swifter through my veins when I chance to recall it. Pete and I were taking a walk in the vicinity of the Tower, when there slowly came towards us a frantic mob. Men were fighting and howling and striving one against another to reach an object in its midst. As it approached, we could see it was a coach they sought to attack, and that it was protected by a large company of pikemen. The soldiers marched around it, and presented a thick hedge of steel points to the crowd to keep it back; tho' such was the frenzy of the populace that the foremost of its members came near spitting themselves upon the steel.

"Poor devil!" remarked my companion. "Some other milk-livered papist, I'll bet."

'Twould have gone hard indeed with the man, whoever he might have been, had they got hands upon him, for the fighting throng would undoubtedly have torn him to pieces. As it came up Pete and I, curious to discover the cause of this strange commotion, mounted the highest steps of a house beside us, and from this point were able to overlook the struggling mass beneath. The coach, the pikemen, and the maniacs passed slowly by, and inside the vehicle I beheld a creature which made me a maniac too. I could plainly see a grotesque object, blackened and begrimed with coal-dust, in the garb of a sailor, whose eyes were starting, and whose face was smeared and bedaubed with blood. This creature was imploring the soldiers with clasped hands not to let the mob get at him. There was no mistaking the mouth and the jaw of the unhappy creature. It was Jeffreys; the man who had held life and death in the palm of his hand; the debauched, vile judge, the man whom all the nation had trembled at. Despite his disguise, despite his abject terror, he could not conceal that satanic countenance. Those black brows had been seen too often. The mob had recognized him, and the man beside Peter Whipple also. Taunton courthouse was rising in my brain again. I was fascinated for a moment; then whispered hoarsely to my friend—

"For the love of Heaven, Peter, lead me hence! Take me anywhere away from this."

I had not the strength to move of mine own accord.

The innkeeper did not reply; only gave me a contemptuous glance, and obtained a powerful hold on my sleeve.

Just then the crowd made one bold sweeping rush, and fought the pikemen hand to hand. I could hear the screams, the clash of arms, the oaths, and finally a cry of triumph. The coach was rocking, and far above the din, a voice, the arch-fiend's voice, was raised in supplication.

"For God's sake, gentlemen," it wailed, "don't let them come! Don't, don't! They're coming! Save me! save me!"

"Let me go, Pete!" I cried, attempting to drag my arms free.

The little man grinned, and tightened his grip.

"Unhand me, d'ye hear! It's Jeffreys. Hands off, I say! I must and will go and tear him limb from limb wi' the others."

Master Whipple got his two hands on my wrists like a vice; yet I struggled and besought and finally fought him in my madness. Still I could not free myself. Pete and I jostled desperately, but the crowd pressed on towards the rocking-coach, amidst the shrieks of vengeance. A terrific struggle ensued at the Tower gates. Albeit, in the end, the coach and the soldiers got through, and the yelling multitude was thrust back, and was thereby balked of its prey.

Whereupon Peter Whipple whispered, "You oaf!" into my ear, shifted his devil's grip from my wrists to my doublet collar, and bundled me back to the Three Crowns with the peremptory expedition of a Bow Street runner.

I felt faint and sick by the time we had returned to the inn. After a while I recovered somewhat, and thanked Pete for his kindly offices. That night I told him my strange story, whence he understood my violence of the few hours previous.

So this was the second of my foes humbled and brought low. I cannot tell whether 'twas God's judgment; yet from that day forward I have ever been inclined to regard it as a Divine manifestation.

A few weeks later my Lord Chief Justice died in the greatest agony of mind in the Tower. I will not dwell upon this episode; if you have carefully followed my fortunes thus far you may well understand how I was affected by it.

I doubt not, kinsmen, ye have heard the story in its entirety, as to how the monster was recognized in his foul disguise in a low alehouse at Wapping; how he was dragged forth by a vengeful mob, who would have beaten him to death had not some of the trainbands come to his rescue; how he was brought before the Lord Mayor; and how finally (as you have seen) he was conveyed to a prison from which he ne'er afterwards issued alive.

Another night of tumult and riot followed, and one accompanied by a fear of the lawlessness of the disbanded Irish

troops. A rumor was launched just after nightfall to the effect that a horde of them were marching on London, and were slaying every Protestant man, woman, and child in its progress. Of course this was a wicked lie. Some mischievous scoundrel had raised it to further disturb the mind of the populace.

All night long the citizens paced the streets in patrols. They were armed to the teeth, and were fully bent on thwarting the common foe. However, no enemy appeared.

In such times as these men live fast; events sufficient for an ordinary decade are crowded into a few weeks; and so much hath been said by the historians (though perhaps without any over-nice regard for the truth) that I will refer you to them for any fuller account. I do but simply lay before you those matters which most nearly affected myself in these turbulent times. Bishop Burnet and Mr. John Oldmixon will tell you all about the politics. I shall be quite content—nay, shall e'en consider my task worthily performed—if I do but faithfully recount all that came under my personal observation hereabouts, and for the accuracy of which I myself can vouch. So much was crammed into this short period that my old head is sadly confused thereby, and so great a lapse of time hath passed since then that, should any small particular differ from the printed accounts, then I will be content to have it set down to a failing memory sooner than be involved in any controversy with the chronicles; not, however, that I consider them any more infallible than myself.

CHAPTER XLVIII.

HIS PROTESTANT MAJESTY KING WILLIAM III.

As ye are aware, I have been lately discoursing at some length upon the hopes, aspirations, and fortunes of kings and princes, and have sadly neglected those of the humble Edward Armstrong. But my tale being conceived in a homely key, I shall from this point to the finish, which is happily not far distant, give Master Ned my best attention, and as far as practicable leave exalted folk to the historians.

Shortly after the downfall of Jeffreys, I had a serious conversation with Peter Whipple. I discovered him alone in the small chamber Master Fletcher had placed at our service. He was seated before the table counting golden guineas, and diffidently whistling. But when I came to his side, in immediate proximity to the money, he suddenly changed his tune, and with extraordinary haste gathered up the gold into his bag and safely deposited the same into a pocket of his coat.

" It is a wise man that knows his master," said he gravely.

"I would like you to withdraw your insinuations, Pete," said I, feeling hurt in my mind at his behavior.

" I insinuate nothing," he replied, with a little cough.

"Then why so insinuatingly cautious ? "

" I wasn't born yesterday," he returned sweetly ; " methinks I am rather old in the tooth."

" So you wish to infer that your money is not safe when I am near it ? "

" Ned, my friend, you do me a wrong in your heart. I am deeply grieved. Yet natheless I am mindful of a lesson I once learnt from Bob Bickers. One day I was sitting, just as I am now, counting guineas, when in he walks, and says he, clapping me on the shoulder in his hearty way, 'Well, old friend, and how is the old complaint ? ' Then he shook my hand as his cordial fashion was, and made himself generally very affable. But harkee, lad, when he was gone I found ten guineas minus. Thereupon I remembered that his coat-sleeves were wide, and that his reputation was just a trifle blown upon. When he came next time, I made the charge direct to his face. Quoth he serenely, ' Dear friend, experience hath to be bought and duly paid for ; so take my advice and buy it early. You pay the dancing-man to teach you how to foot the minuet, and to trip the sprightly corranto. You pay the musicianer to teach you how to finger the harpsichord and spinet, and to make harmonious music, as Will Shakespeare hath it. Then why in the world can't you pay the man who understands human nature, to lay bare the malpractices and unchaste devices employed by your fellow-creatures ? ' Yes, lad, those were his words. Fine, were they not ? Still, I have ne'er seen those guineas since, but have kept the lesson well in mind."

" Pete," quoth I warmly, and fully determined to set him forever right concerning a solemn resolution I had recently made, " I have done with thieving and dishonesty now. Never again will I stain my fingers with stolen property."

" Yes, that's highly correct," he assented with a smile. " But faith, I must weep ; 'tis most touching and pathetic ! Indeed, I am deeply moved. Where's my handkerchief? 'Tis the devil's own thing is an emotional nature ! "

He brought forth his rag, folded it carefully to fit his eyes with decorum, and wept with such vigor that all the while my hands did itch to knock him down as flat as his own ale.

"I'm not jesting," said I shortly.

"And who said thou wert?" he asked aggrievedly between his sobs.

Here my worthy friend brushed his eyes smartly with his coat-sleeve, gave one significant gulp, and looked up with a watery smile.

"So you're going to start in a safer line?" he said, then sank his voice to a confidential whisper, and affecting a cat-like countenance to match his purring tone, continued, "I presume, my gossip, you are going to embrace the religious business. I'm afeared 'tis not what it used to be; still, methinks there's room for an enterprising man. I've worked the trade wi' some small success myself in my early days, and am not above giving a friend a hint or two. First, your demeanor must undergo some alteration; it's far too hearty, too healthy, too bucolic, and too rustic. Ere you can commence in earnest, you've got to make it about the length of a Cremona fiddle; also yellowy gray, and meek and smug and humble. And when ye first open the shop, begin by making the responses in a loud voice, and give the 'amens' plenty o' lip, so that you'll be heard above your neighbor. And when it comes to a moan, or a groan, or a sigh, roll 'em out as though you meant 'em. And let your singing be lusty and out o' tune, and your general demeanor sinlessly pious, and you may take my word for it your chance will come. The chosen will begin to notice you after a time, and will see how the spirit doth fructify within you. Then you'll be promoted to passing round the collection plate, and if you will but keep your left arm stretched fairly over it, and exercise your thumb and middle finger as you ought to do, your fortune's made."

"Pete!" I broke in severely.

"'It's a cold heart that tries to hoodwink a proven friend,' said Long Bob, and, 'pon honor, I'm entirely of that way o' thinking myself," he went on, giving me no chance for righteous expostulation. "But touching the highwayman business. Thou hast been a creditable scholar. Not exactly a Bob Bickers of course. We only have one of his kidney in a century, but still pretty well for a yeoman's son. I have my doubts as to whether you would have risen very high in the profession, for candid, lad, betwixt man and man, your headpiece ain't of the best. It's right enough for a bit o' common purse-snatching, but, bless you, when it comes to the real tasty bits, the real *artistic* bits, then, say I, nature stinted you in the matter of natural genius. Still, lad, I wish you luck and success in your new undertaking."

" Thank you ! " sarcastically quoth I.

" No call to thank me," he returned, with noble pathos in his voice ; " I'm of a trusting and confiding turn by nature. And I stick to old friends and do my little best. Methinks I'm ever ready wi' kindly counsel, and with the blessed coin o' the realm at a pinch. But 'tain't my style at all to blow my own trumpet." So he blew his nose instead.

I took advantage of the pause thus offered, to commence a tremendous retort. But the first terrific sentence fell stillborn from my lips, since he withered it by the politest bow he could command, and continued with sweet dignity.

" Many thanks, friend, from I that am so unworthy of your kind remarks. Yet what I had to say was this. Methinks you will soon find a worthy successor in the West country. If my lad Tom doth but fulfil early promise, he'll make some stir be-twixt Bristol and Bruton. You take a word from one who knows. That boy hath more o' Long Bob Bickers' qualities than any youth I've known."

At this juncture I did a wise thing ; I submitted. Neither my tongue nor my intellect were sufficently nimble to cope with those possessed by Master Whipple, Therefore I swallowed my grievances and called for two flagons of sack. My companion pledged my good health, emptied the pot at one draught, and called for another at my expense. Hereupon I broached the subject that dwelt in mind.

" Pete, what hath brought you to Town ? " I asked as a preliminary.

" Private and confidential matters. In fact, it's a *family* reason."

And he chinked the gold in his pocket.

" Can you find time to transact a piece of important business for me ? "

" Might I inquire what it is ? "

" You know Captain Joshua Pringle, do you not ? "

" My friend, you are wasting words."

" I want you to deliver his rascally body into my custody."

" Terms ? "

" One hundred guineas. But mind, no violence must be used."

" You had better make it two hundred, then."

I remonstrated at the exorbitant demand, but he waxed **so** eloquent concerning "the duty to his family;" "the serious tax upon his time;" "and the bodily peril of the undertaking," that in the end a compromise was arrived at; and he accepted one hundred and fifty.

Perchance, kinsmen, you are tempted to look upon this bold offer of mine as a truly strange one. However, as a matter of fact, 'twas not my offer at all. Upon the morning of this trans- action, I had received a letter from Mistress Dorothy. It in- formed me that my darling had received a small legacy left by a member of her mother's family in France. She had at once decided to devote this sum to the capture of her father's mur- derer. Having heard of my lack of success in the matter, she had commanded me to employ an expert. And who could be more of an expert than Master Peter Whipple? Verily the case was hopeless if he could not manage it. None had more extensive knowledge of London than he, none had keener wits, and to no man was I under deeper obligations. Thus 'twill be seen I had every reason to place the matter in his hands. Ever since my sojourn in Town, I had been ceaseless in my exertions to lay hands on the despicable little villain, but, like all the other things I had undertaken in this unlucky enterprise, I had failed. As for the letter that had reached me from Chilverley; when I came to peruse it, I found warm affection for me to pervade almost every line. Accordingly, after I had read it six times through, I cannot say which touched me most : the fidelity the maiden showed towards her friends, or the hatred towards her enemies.

Conceive me, kinsmen, at this moment to be like a man with two mistresses ! My first mistress is Private Events, the other Public Events. And one is clearly becoming jealous of the other. I have been favoring the former lately, but now the latter, like a very ill-mannered, ill-bred person, pokes its nose in, and bids me show it more deference, by letting it sing for a few minutes in a major key. So, to keep harmonious to the end, I am obliged (much against my inclination) to humor it somewhat; therefore listen to the tenor of its song.

Thursday, the thirteenth of December, brought with it a curious rumor. 'Twas said, first suspiciously, then boldly, that the King had not escaped. By nightfall the report was fully confirmed that he had been captured by a body of fishermen in the vicinity of Sheppey Isle, and had been prevented from crossing the water. To the disgust and disappointment of the Dutchman's friends, James, being thus balked in his attempted flight, returned to Whitehall. Still this event provoked no spark of spirit amongst his slender, disheartened following. His prospects grew hourly worse, whereas, in proportion, the Prince's grew hourly better, and his friends became increasingly exultant.

The Prince was now at Windsor. On Monday, the seventeenth, he called a council of his principal supporters. The result of this was, that a message was drawn up, and sent to the King, requesting him to withdraw from his palace to a house in the country. There was nought for the stricken monarch but prompt compliance, as he was now entirely at the mercy of the Invader. Thus it befell, on the following morning, that His Majesty bade adieu to his capital. Few men had sympathy for this broken and despairing man. He had totally alienated his subjects by the mercilessness of his heart and the folly and bigotry of his actions.

Then came one of the finest scenes of the drama. That same day William and his troops took possession of the city. 'Twould be idle to attempt to describe his reception, and 'twould be equally so to speak at any length upon the enthusiasm that bade him welcome. The entire town seemed in a transport. Bells rang for hours from every Protestant steeple. Bonfires were burnt at night, and even the staidest and soberest citizens were reckless and extravagant regarding the number of window candles they used to celebrate the coming of their champion. As for me, I employed my vocal organs so zealously and so unwisely, that when I went to bed that night I had a goose-grease plaster on my chest. It was indeed a great day for England; 'twas once more free from a tryant's yoke; folk might live henceforth in peace, comfort, and prosperity, instead of being at the mercy of a malignant bigot. Monmouth had erred. He had come before the nation was ripe for this grand blow, that had shattered the power of despotism. But now the seeds sown by the brave West-country yokels three years agone had borne fruit.

This momentous affair hath been called "The Revolution," and is justly looked upon as one of the wonders of history. It appears an incredible thing that so great a stake as the Crown of Great Britain should be won and lost with such small expenditure of blood. Nevertheless, scarce a score lives were forfeited, and only a few score shots were fired. No battle had been fought, either by land or sea; yet the Stuart was flying with his birthright left behind.

Pete took this triumph with philosophical calmness. He didn't get maudlinly drunk, like the quality; or aggressively drunk, like the commonalty; or even decently drunk, like Jabez Fletcher and I. In fact, he didn't get drunk at all. No, he received it in his cold-blooded, critical way; and was blithe to lay down the law in the morning to the effect that the country was going to the devil.

I remonstrated with him for this harsh decision; whereupon I learned that a cheerful nation would be overrun with sour-faced Dutchmen, who drank nought better than schnapps and small beer. At that I sought to console mine host of the King's Head, Bridgwater, by ordering a butt of Malmsey to be delivered three months from date to Sir Edward Armstrong of Copeland Hall, in the county of Somerset.

Now Pete, not knowing overmuch of my affairs, scratched his wig thereat, and said, " Well, I'll be damned ! " as though he meant it. But he took the order; and, for mine own part, I took unction to my soul for having mystified a man of great qualities and intellect.

And now we fell upon the busiest part of this bustling time. The arrival of William in the city set everybody talking politics. What was to be done with the King ? Rational men, who had been staunchest to the cause, wisely held their peace, and hoped for the best. But those who had bided at home, with words for neither side during the struggle, having seen the way the cat had jumped, came forth like patriots, and gave out uneasy hints concerning the year '49, and what happened to the late King Charles, his gracious Majesty's father ! Of course this was child's talk, and folk of sense accounted it as such. Yet, in the midst of this high language, and whilst every one was telling his neighbor what ought to be done, and what ought not to be done, the King suddenly placed the matter beyond all controversy. News was brought to Town on Sunday the twenty-third that the monarch had embarked in a skiff on the shores of the Medway, and had sailed for France, relinquishing all claim to the Crown and the Kingdom.

William had now the game in his own hands : the Revolution had been consummated; the Throne of England was within his grasp. The Council of the Nation begged him to take it; but he was such a close man in himself, and kept his private mind so secret, that many had doubts at first as to whether he would accept the Crown. I was among the sceptics, and the suspense preyed upon me so that I could not bide content whilst the matter was in abeyance. However, in the end, as all the world knows, he took his uncle's place and held it honorably and wisely till the day he died.

27

While these final passages were pending there intervened a time of weariness; and throughout the whole of it I remained in London. Till the Government had been firmly established I had no chance of obtaining the patent for my freedom. And you will remember I had sworn not to return without it.

During the first fortnight I had the company of my faithful friends, Tobe Hancock and Peter Whipple. The latter gentleman was exceeding serious in his efforts to earn the reward offered by my mistress. Still, despite the vigilance of the pair of us, Joshua Pringle was more than our match. He seemed to have disappeared from the earth's surface. At last, however, we gathered his whereabouts. We had the information from a former comrade that his sins had overtaken him in the form of a fever, and that he had already gone to answer for them.

In my heart I was by no means sorry that the gallows had been cheated; though Pete was quite grief-stricken to hear of his timely end. However, mine host's efforts in the matter did not go entirely unrewarded, and this considerably mitigated his distress. Shortly afterwards he and Tobias returned to the West together, leaving me behind impatient, but not bereft of hope.

'Twas one day in February that the Dutchman became King, and had regal rights duly vested upon him. A week later I secured an audience with him. I was ushered into his private closet, where he was alone with a thoughtful brow and a great litter of papers.

He gave me no chance of speaking ere he glanced at me quickly, said, "Ah, Sir Edward!" with something like a smile, and extended his right hand towards me.

In an instant I was on one knee and had his fingers to my lips. As I rose, the sun peeped over the naked trees in the park, and glittered coldly on the steel buttons of His Majesty's vest; and its frosty light seemed to exactly match the King's inscrutable countenance. But this time I feared him not. 'Twas now I felt the dawn of hope, and for the first time for many months the joy of living. His Majesty remembered perfectly well my late adventures for the cause, and showed a marked acquaintance with my private history. When he had the full facts of it, he gave me no word of sympathy; but upon leaving his presence half an hour later, I carried with me an order for the restitution of my heritage, and that of Mistress Dorothy Marvin, another calling upon the Chancellor to pay me one year's revenues forthwith, and a third annulling the sentence of my outlawry.

CHAPTER XLIX.

THE RETURN TO THE WEST.

IT chanced that along my line of route betwixt Whitehall and the Three Crowns there was a goldsmith's shop. Thither I went, and made a purchase—not a costly one ; simply a slender band of precious metal.

Two days hence my London business had been transacted. Thus I said good-bye to Master Fletcher, and turned the head of great Gustavus towards the West. I rode at quite a sedate pace, tho' all the way thither I ne'er ceased to think of my tide of joy ; nor could I keep my mind from dwelling on it. I reflected on God's mercy, too, and marvelled at the fulness of its revelation.

I reached the Quantocks as night was closing in, on the third day of the journey. Knowing the ground, I determined to push on to the farmstead in the darkness. Accordingly, as the grim shadows stalked along the valleys and shrouded the black summits of the hills, I set my horse briskly over the frozen ground, along the hollows, through the silent ravines, and across the ice-coated water-courses.

Presently I arrived at the farmstead gate. Can I ever forget the crossing of the rickyard that night, and how the sight of the kitchen candles thrilled me? My feet seemed to linger lovingly at every step on the familiar paths, as if to draw out my joyfulness still longer. I put my horse up in the stable, and then walked into the kitchen, to the cheerful fire and the beautiful faces.

I trow 'tis not a seemly thing for any man to expatiate upon these supreme moments in his life. Therefore, instead of exalting my happiness before you, I will drop the veil of discretion over this joyful evening, and will only say that we did not retire to rest till three of the clock in the morning.

I awoke next day with the consciousness that an irksome duty was unfulfilled as yet. Being a plain man, and an inexperienced one, I had many qualms, which I believe were only natural. I had also a presentiment that I should make a fool of myself, unless I had some assistance from the lady, and that I could by no means depend upon.

At breakfast-time I ate a poor meal, and felt ridiculously nervous throughout the course of it. On the other hand, Dor-

othy, who sat opposite, made an excellent one, and kept innocently asking what had become of my appetite. Mother laughed
outright when the sly maid had propounded this question for
the tenth time. Natheless my mistress declared my attitude
towards the eatables was a direct reflection upon herself, as she
had made the pasties.

"Wilt have a ramble with me among the hills this lovely
morning, dearest?" I whispered into her ear when the meal was
done.

She ran to her room, and came forth presently attired in her
hat and gloves and walking-coat. I donned my headgear also,
and taking John's hazel stick, set forth with my love for company. But as we were crossing the threshold of the door, that
heavy-witted wight, John Armstrong, rose and put on his hat,
saying—

"Bide a minute, Ned, methinks I will walk out with you.
'Tis a rare day for walking; besides, the occasion is so joyful,
I will honor it by allowing myself a holiday."

"Nay, nay, John, not this morning," put in mother promptly.
"'Tis a very throng time this week. Best have an eye to the
hedging and ditching. You know the men are that idle, they
will do no work unless there is somebody by to keep them
to it."

John decided on this course, though not without demur.
Meanwhile dear mother's face betrayed such a wealth of superior understanding that Dorothy blushed; whilst I felt a foretaste of my expected foolishness, when Betty whispered to my
mistress—

"All men are fools, but I believe our Jack is the biggest and
most perfect of the breed."

I shared that sentiment. And I have no doubt Dorothy
(being a woman) in her private mind was just as severe towards
the clumsy interloper. However we set out by our two selves
along the pastures, crossed the fence where our farm land borders the ravine, and so reached the hills, which had the whiteness of winter upon them. In the beginning I found no conversation, although in my natural state I have that noble gift—
self-confidence.

Suddenly my mistress stopped, picked up a frozen clod of
turf, and threw it at a robin redbreast as it trotted over the rimy
heather, then fiercely turned on me.

"Oh, boy! why so tongue-tied? Art like a deaf mute at a
funeral!"

"Am I?" I returned abstractedly.

At that she tossed up her chin, and fell a-whistling " Lillibullero." The mad lilt jogged my memory.

" Dorothy," said I, " I have your freedom in my pocket."

" That you have not, Sir Edward. You gave it me last night,"
and she produced the papers with the King's seal thereon, and
brandished them before my eyes.

" Dear gentlemen, I can plainly see he is not used to this sort
of thing," she said, making capital out of my confusion.

" And if he were ? " quoth I, at last upon my mettle.

That question was more than she had bargained for. Yet
able tacticians are not routed by a side wind or a stray word.

" And if he were—well, he is a great swordsman."

" And if he were not a great swordsman ? "

" He would simply be mine own, dear lad ! " Her face
flushed with this sudden gust of fervor. " Ned," she continued
impertinently, " I would give ten guineas to tease you as I would
like to do. You are the very worst lover I have met. Dear
papa always averred that a good fighter was a good wooer, but
I take it thou'rt the exception that proves the rule. My Lord
Churchill said more pretty things to me in one five minutes than
you will have the wit to say in a lifetime."

" Damn Lord Churchill ! "

" 'Tis a very sedate young gentleman, I'm thinking ; " the old
ring of impudence was in her tone, and the old look of mockery in her eyes, " and I am charmed to see he hath learnt to
conduct himself before his lady. Yes, sir, now the great work
is done I am your lady. You may be Sir Edward, but I'm your
lady, and what is more, I'll exact from you all the courtesy that
is due to ladies."

Methought my position was getting peculiarly irksome, so I
hastened to relate a piece of news that was fraught with every
import.

" Captain Pringle is dead," said I.

" Did he die in his bed ? " she asked. 'Twas wonderful how
levity gave way to eager gravity in her voice, how wild her look
was, and how firmly she clutched my sleeve.

" Yes. A fever sent him hence."

A cruel light sprang into her eyes, her mouth was very merciless and swift emotions lighted her splendid face.

" He deserved the gallows if ever man did," she said. " I
would have watched him hang with a dry eye. But perhaps 'tis
best as it is. You said last night, Ned, that you had tasted the
cup of vengeance, and that you had found it truly vile and very
nauseous."

" 'Tis quite true, though it took me many months to learn it,"
I interposed with a sense of deep humiliation.

She made no answer, only murmured " Poor father ! " under
her breath, and turned her head away from me.

" Darling, how often hast thou thought of me during the last
four months ? " I asked.

" I have prayed for thee every night, and thought of thee
every hour of the day, dear lad."

" I shall never go forth to war again," I said. " I have done
with all fighting. From this day I will keep my sword sheathed.
My youthful spirit hath been sapped. I long for peace and
a quiet life, like one with a mortal wound longs for death. I
am a broken man. Art willing to take me on such terms,
mistress ? "

She gazed wistfully on my face, and beheld the hard lines
adversity had stamped upon it.

I took off my hat, saying, " I am old before my time. Dost
see my hair is gray ? "

" Hum ! 'twill match my complexion."

I bethought myself that minute the most injured man in the
universe. The exact truth of the matter was that I had traded
too much upon her tenderness. My dear maiden looked at me
with a smile broadening round her lips, till all at once she broke
forth with a great cry of laughter—

" The miserable, mumping man ! expected me to weep, did
he ? This day of all days I will not weep. Pish ! thou'rt
properly paid, my master."

No doubt of that ; I was properly paid. So I put on my hat
very shamefacedly when I thought she was not looking. I had
played too much upon her feelings ; and she, ever quick to find
a whimsicality, had observed me cross the delicate border-line
betwixt pathos and bathos, and it was this indiscretion that had
turned her sadness into mirth.

" Sir Edward——," she continued, when I struck in with—

" Why so long a title, mistress ? I prefer a shorter one."

" Oh, I must give your worship your honorable patronymic,
just to see how it feels. Really, Ned, it comes from my tongue
very fine and heroical."

" If you persist in this," quoth I severely, " I shall address
you as my lady."

" Yes, I shall be your lady."

" You shall be my queen," said I.

" Splendidly said, young man, splendidly said ! " she cried,
her face aglow with rippling smiles, though I have my doubts

as to whether her enthusiasm was not half a simulation.　" 'Pon my soul ! the lad hath brought back a London tongue."

At this I had to kiss her, she looked so saucy, and so *very* pretty, whereupon she was blithe to add, " And I notice he hath brought back London impudence to match it."

" And here is yet another thing from London," said I eagerly, slipping a ring into her hand.

She put up one white finger, and tried it on, to learn whether the fit was satisfactory.　And having discovered that I had gauged the girth of it with skill and nicety, she linked her arm through mine and we went together down the hill—even as we were to go down the hill of life—together.

THE END.